D1351332

WESTERN HEROES

WESTERN ★HEROES★

ZANE GREY

RIDERS OF THE PURPLE SAGE
THE LAST OF THE PLAINSMEN
LONE STAR RANGER

CHANCELLOR PRESS

Riders Of The Purple Sage was first published in 1912
The Last Of the Plainsmen was first published in 1908
Lone Star Ranger was first published in 1915

This collected volume first published in 1992 by Chancellor Press
an imprint of Reed Consumer Books Limited
Michelin House, 81 Fulham Road, London SW3 6RB
and Auckland, Melbourne, Singapore and Toronto

Design and arrangement copyright © 1992 by Reed International Books Limited

ISBN 1 85152 226 3

A CIP catalogue record for this book is available at the British Library

Typeset by DSC Corporation Limited, Cornwall, England
Printed in Great Britain by William Clowes, Beccles

CONTENTS

RIDERS OF THE PURPLE SAGE

CHAPTER ONE
Lassiter

A sharp clip-clop of iron-shod hoofs deadened and died away, and clouds of yellow dust drifted from under the cottonwoods out over the sage.

Jane Withersteen gazed down the wide purple slope with dreamy and troubled eyes. A rider had just left her and it was his message that held her thoughtful and almost sad, awaiting the churchmen who were coming to resent and attack her right to befriend a Gentile.

She wondered if the unrest and strife that had lately come to the little village of Cottonwoods was to involve her. And then she sighed, remembering that her father had founded this remotest border settlement of southern Utah and that he had left it to her. She owned all the ground and many of the cottages. Withersteen House was hers, and the great ranch, with its thousands of cattle, and the swiftest horses of the sage. To her belonged Amber Spring, the water which gave verdure and beauty to the village and made living possible on that wild purple upland waste. She could not escape being involved by whatever befell Cottonwoods.

That year, 1871, had marked a change which had been gradually coming in the lives of the peace-loving Mormons of the border. Glaze—Stone Bridge—Sterling, villages to the north, had risen against the invasion of Gentile settlers and the forays of rustlers. There had been opposition to the one and fighting with the other. And now Cottonwoods had begun to wake and bestir itself and grow hard.

Jane prayed that the tranquillity and sweetness of her life would not be permanently disrupted. She meant to do so much more for her people than she had done. She wanted the sleepy quiet pastoral days to last always. Trouble between the Mormons and the Gentiles of the community would make her unhappy. She was Mormon-born, and she was a friend to poor and unfortunate Gentiles. She wished only to go on doing good and being happy. And she thought of what that great ranch meant to her. She loved it all—the grove of cottonwoods, the old stone house, the amber-tinted water, and the droves of shaggy, dusty horses and mustangs, the sleek, clean-limbed, blooded racers, and the browsing herds of cattle and the lean, sun-browned riders of the sage.

While she waited there she forgot the prospect of untoward change. The bray of a lazy burro broke the afternoon quiet, and it was comfortingly suggestive of the drowsy farmyard, and the open corrals, and the green alfalfa fields. Her clear sight intensified the purple sage-slope as it rolled before her. Low swells of prairie-like ground sloped up to the west. Dark, lonely cedar-trees, few and far between, stood out strikingly, and at long distances ruins of red rocks. Farther on, up the gradual slope, rose a broken wall, a huge monument, looming dark purple and stretching its solitary, mystic way, a wavering line that faded in the north. Here to the westward was the light and color and beauty. Northward the slope descended to a dim line of cañons from which rose an up-flinging of the earth, not mountainous, but a vast heave of purple uplands, with ribbed and fan-shaped walls, castle-crowned cliffs, and gray escarpments. Over it all crept the lengthening, waning afternoon shadows.

The rapid beat of hoofs recalled Jane Withersteen to the question at hand. A group of riders cantered up the lane, dismounted, and threw their bridles. They were seven in number, and Tull, the leader, a tall, dark man, was an elder of Jane's church.

'Did you get my message?' he asked, curtly.

'Yes,' replied Jane.

'I sent word I'd give that rider Venters half an hour to come down to the village. He didn't come.'

'He knows nothing of it,' said Jane. 'I didn't tell him. I've been waiting here for you.'

'Where is Venters?'

'I left him in the courtyard.'

'Here, Jerry,' called Tull, turning to his men, 'take the gang and fetch Venters out here if you have to rope him.'

The dusty-booted and long-spurred riders clanked noisily into the grove of cottonwoods and disappeared in the shade.

'Elder Tull, what do you mean by this?' demanded Jane. 'If you must arrest Venters you might have the courtesy to wait till he leaves my home. And if you do arrest him it will be adding insult to injury. It's absurd to accuse Venters of being mixed up in that shooting fray in the village last night. He was with me at the time. Besides, he let me take charge of his guns. You're only using this as a pretext. What do you mean to do to Venters?'

'I'll tell you presently,' replied Tull. 'But first tell me why you defend this worthless rider.'

'Worthless!' exclaimed Jane, indignantly. 'He's nothing of the kind. He was the best rider I ever had. There's not a reason why I shouldn't champion him and every reason why I should. It's no little shame to me, Elder Tull, that through my friendship he has roused the enmity of my people and become an outcast. Besides,

I owe him eternal gratitude for saving the life of little Fay.'

'I've heard of your love for Fay Larkin and that you intend to adopt her. But—Jane Withersteen, the child is a Gentile!'

'Yes. But, Elder, I don't love the Mormon children any less because I love a Gentile child. I shall adopt Fay if her mother will give her to me.'

'I'm not so much against that. You can give the child Mormon teaching,' said Tull. 'But I'm sick of seeing this fellow Venters hang around you. I'm going to put a stop to it. You've so much love to throw away on these beggars of Gentiles that I've an idea you might love Venters.'

Tull spoke with the arrogance of a Mormon whose power could not be brooked and with the passion of a man in whom jealousy had kindled a consuming fire.

'Maybe I do love him,' said Jane. She felt both fear and anger stir her heart. 'I'd never thought of that. Poor fellow! He certainly needs some one to love him.'

'This'll be a bad day for Venters unless you deny that,' returned Tull, grimly.

Tull's men appeared under the cottonwoods and led a young man out into the lane. His ragged clothes were those of an outcast. But he stood tall and straight, his wide shoulders flung back, with the muscles of his bound arms rippling and a blue flame of defiance in the gaze he bent on Tull.

For the first time Jane Withersteen felt Venters's real spirit. She wondered if she would love this splendid youth. Then her emotion cooled to the sobering sense of the issue at stake.

'Venters, will you leave Cottonwoods at once and forever?' asked Tull, tensely.

'Why?' rejoined the rider.

'Because I order it.'

Venters laughed in cool disdain.

The red leaped to Tull's dark cheek.

'If you don't go it means your ruin,' he said, sharply.

'Ruin!' exclaimed Venters, passionately. 'Haven't you already ruined me? What do you call ruin? A year ago I was a rider. I had horses and cattle of my own. I had a good name in Cottonwoods. And now when I come into the village to see this woman you set your men on me. You hound me. You trail me as if I were a rustler. I've no more to lose—except my life.'

'Will you leave Utah?'

'Oh! I know,' went on Venters, tauntingly, 'it galls you, the idea of beautiful Jane Withersteen being friendly to a poor Gentile. You want her all yourself. You're a wiving Mormon. You have use for her—and Withersteen House and Amber Spring and seven thousand head of cattle!'

Tull's hard jaw protruded, and rioting blood corded the veins of his neck.

'Once more. Will you go?'

'*No!*'

'Then I'll have you whipped within an inch of your life,' replied Tull, harshly. 'I'll turn you out in the sage. And if you ever come back you'll get worse.'

Venters's agitated face grew coldly set and the bronze changed to gray.

Jane impulsively stepped forward. 'Oh! Elder Tull!' she cried. 'You won't do that!'

Tull lifted a shaking finger toward her.

'That'll do from you. Understand, you'll not be allowed to hold this boy to a friendship that's offensive to your Bishop. Jane Withersteen, your father left you wealth and power. It has turned your head. You haven't yet come to see the place of Mormon women. We've reasoned with you, borne with you. We've patiently waited. We've let you have your fling, which is more than I ever saw granted to a Mormon woman. But you haven't come to your senses. Now, once for all, you can't have any further friendship with Venters. He's going to be whipped, and he's got to leave Utah!'

'Oh! Don't whip him! It would be dastardly!' implored Jane, with slow certainty of her failing courage.

Tull always blunted her spirit, and she grew conscious that she had feigned a boldness which she did not possess. He loomed up now in different guise, not as a jealous suitor, but embodying the mysterious despotism she had known from childhood—the power of her creed.

'Venters, will you take your whipping here or would you rather go out in the sage?' asked Tull. He smiled a flinty smile that was more than inhuman, yet seemed to give out of its dark aloofness a gleam of righteousness.

'I'll take it here—if I must,' said Venters. 'But by God!—Tull, you'd better kill me outright. That'll be a dear whipping for you and your praying Mormons. You'll make me another Lassiter!'

The strange glow, the austere light which radiated from Tull's face, might have been a holy joy at the spiritual conception of exalted duty. But there was something more in him, barely hidden, a something personal and sinister, a deep of himself, an engulfing abyss. As his religious mood was fanatical and inexorable, so would his physical hate be merciless.

'Elder, I—I repent my words,' Jane faltered. The religion in her, the long habit or obedience, of humility, as well as agony of fear, spoke in her voice. 'Spare the boy!' she whispered.

'You can't save him now,' replied Tull, stridently.

Her head was bowing to the inevitable. She was grasping the truth, when suddenly there came, in inward construction, a hardening of gentle forces within her breast. Like a steel bar it was, stiffening all that had been soft and weak in her. She felt a birth in her of something new and unintelligible. Once more her strained gaze sought the sage-slopes. Jane Withersteen loved that wild and purple wilderness. In times of sorrow it had been her strength, in happiness its beauty was her continual delight. In her extremity she found herself murmuring, 'Whence cometh my help!' It was a prayer, as if forth from those lonely purple reaches and walls of red and clefts of blue might ride a fearless man, neither creed-bound nor creed-mad, who would hold up a restraining hand in the faces of her ruthless people.

The restless movements of Tull's men suddenly quieted down. Then followed a low whisper, a rustle, a sharp exclamation.

'Look!' said one, pointing to the west.

'A rider!'

Jane Withersteen wheeled and saw a horseman, silhouetted against the western sky, come riding out of the sage. He had ridden down from the left, in the golden glare of the sun, and had been unobserved till close at hand. An answer to her prayer!

'Do you know him? Does any one know him?' questioned Tull, hurriedly.

His men looked and looked, and one by one shook their heads.

'He's come from far,' said one.

'Thet's a fine hoss,' said another.

'A strange rider.'

'Huh! He wears black leather,' added a fourth.

With a wave of his hand, enjoining silence, Tull stepped forward in such a way that he concealed Venters.

The rider reined in his mount, and with a lithe forward slipping action appeared to reach the ground in one long step. It was a peculiar movement in its quickness and inasmuch that while performing it the rider did not swerve in the slightest from a square front to the group before him.

'Look!' hoarsely whispered one of Tull's companions. 'He packs two black-butted guns—low down—they're hard to see—black agin them black chaps.'

'A gun-man!' whispered another. 'Fellers, careful now about movin' your hands.'

The stranger's slow approach might have been a mere leisurely manner of gait or the cramped short steps of a rider unused to walking; yet, as well, it could have been the guarded advance of one who took no chances with men.

'Hello, stranger!' called Tull. No welcome was in this greeting, only a gruff curiosity.

The rider responded with a curt nod. The wide brim of a black sombrero cast a dark shade over his face. For a moment he closely regarded Tull and his comrades, and then, halting in his slow walk, he seemed to relax.

'Evenin', ma'am,' he said to Jane, and removed his sombrero with quaint grace.

Jane, greeting him, looked up into a face that she trusted instinctively and which riveted her attention. It had all the characteristics of the range rider's—the leanness, the red burn of the sun, and the set changelessness that came from years of silence and solitude. But it was not these which held her; rather the intensity of his gaze, a strained weariness, a piercing wistfulness of keen, gray sight, as if the man was forever looking for that which he never found. Jane's subtle woman's intuition, even in that brief instant, felt a sadness, a hungering, a secret.

'Jane Withersteen, ma'am?' he inquired.

'Yes,' she replied.

'The water here is yours?'

'Yes.'

'May I water my horse?'

'Certainly. There's the trough.'

'But mebbe if you knew who I was—' He hesitated, with his glance on the listening men. 'Mebbe you wouldn't let me water him—though I ain't askin' none for myself.'

'Stranger, it doesn't matter who you are. Water your horse. And if you are thirsty and hungry come into my house.'

'Thanks, ma'am. I can't accept for myself—but for my tired horse—'

Trampling of hoofs interrupted the rider. More restless movements on the part of Tull's men broke up the little circle, exposing the prisoner Venters.

'Mebbe I've kind of hindered somethin'—for a few moments, perhaps?' inquired the rider.

'Yes,' replied Jane Withersteen, with a throb in her voice.

She felt the drawing power of his eyes; and then she saw him look at the bound Venters, and at the men who held him, and their leader.

'In this here country all the rustlers an' thieves an' cut-throats an' gun-throwers an' all-round no-good men jest happen to be Gentiles. Ma'am, which of the no-good class does that young feller belong to?'

'He belongs to none of them. He's an honest boy.'

'You *know* that, ma'am?'

'Yes—yes.'

'Then what has he done to get tied up that way?'

His clear and distinct question, meant for Tull as well as for Jane Withersteen, stilled the restlessness and brought a momentary silence.

'Ask him,' replied Jane, her voice rising high.

The rider stepped away from her, moving out with the same slow, measured stride in which he had approached, and the fact that his action placed her wholly to one side, and him no nearer to Tull and his men, had a penetrating significance.

'Young feller, speak up,' he said to Venters.

'Here, stranger, this's none of your mix,' began Tull. 'Don't try any interference.

You've been asked to drink and eat. That's more than you'd have got in any other village on the Utah border. Water your horse and be on your way.'

'Easy—easy—I ain't interferin' yet,' replied the rider. The tone of his voice had undergone a change. A different man had spoken. Where, in addressing Jane, he had been mild and gentle, now, with his first speech to Tull, he was dry, cool, biting. 'I've jest stumbled onto a queer deal. Seven Mormons all packin' guns, an' a Gentile tied with a rope, an' a woman who swears by his honesty! Queer, ain't that?'

'Queer or not, it's none of your business,' retorted Tull.

'Where I was raised a woman's word was law. I ain't quite outgrowed that yet.'

Tull fumed between amaze and anger.

'Meddler, we have a law here something different from woman's whim—Mormon law! ... Take care you don't transgress it.'

'To hell with your Mormon law!'

The deliberate speech marked the rider's further change, this time from kindly interest to an awakening menace. It produced a transformation in Tull and his companions. The leader gasped and staggered backward at a blasphemous affront to an institution he held most sacred. The man Jerry, holding the horses, dropped the bridles and froze in his tracks. Like posts the other men stood, watchful-eyed, arms hanging rigid, all waiting.

'Speak up now, young man. What have you done to be roped that way?'

'It's a damned outrage!' burst out Venters. 'I've done no wrong. I've offended this Mormon Elder by being a friend to that woman.'

'Ma'am, is it true—what he says?' asked the rider of Jane; but his quiveringly alert eyes never left the little knot of quiet men.

'True? Yes, perfectly true,' she answered.

'Well, young man, it seems to me that bein' a friend to such a woman would be what you wouldn't want to help an' couldn't help. ... What's to be done to you for it?'

'They intend to whip me. You know what that means—in Utah!'

'I reckon,' replied the rider, slowly.

With his gray glance cold on the Mormons, with the restive bit-champing of the horses, with Jane failing to repress her mounting agitation, with Venters standing pale and still, the tension of the moment tightened. Tull broke the spell with a laugh, a laugh without mirth, a laugh that was only a sound betraying fear.

'Come on, men!' he called.

Jane Withersteen turned again to the rider.

'Stranger, can you do nothing to save Venters?'

'Ma'am, you ask me to save him—from your own people?'

'Ask you? I beg of you!'

'But you don't dream who you're askin'?'

'Oh, sir, I pray you—save him!'

'These are Mormons, an' I ...'

'At—at any cost—save him. For I—I care for him!'

Tull snarled. 'You love-sick fool! Tell your secrets. There'll be a way to teach you what you've never learned. ... Come men, out of here!'

'Mormon, the young man stays,' said the rider.

Like a shot his voice halted Tull.

'What!'

'He stays.'

'Who'll keep him? He's my prisoner!' cried Tull, hotly. 'Stranger, again I tell you—don't mix here. You've meddled enough. Go your way now or—'

'Listen! ... He stays.'

Absolute certainty, beyond any shadow of doubt, breathed in the rider's low voice.

'Who are you? We are seven here.'

The rider dropped his sombrero and made a rapid movement, singular in that it left him somewhat crouched, arms bent and stiff, with the big black gun-sheaths swung round to the fore.

'*Lassiter!*'

It was Venters's wondering, thrilling cry that bridged the fateful connection between the rider's singular position and the dreaded name.

Tull put out a groping hand. The life of his eyes dulled to the gloom with which men of his fear saw the approach of death. But death, while it hovered over him, did not descend, for the rider waited for the twitching fingers, the downward flash of hand that did not come. Tull, gathering himself together, turned to the horses, attended by his pale comrades.

CHAPTER TWO
Cottonwoods

Venters appeared too deeply moved to speak the gratitude his face expressed. And Jane turned upon the rescuer and gripped his hands. Her smiles and tears seemingly dazed him. Presently, as something like calmness returned, she went to Lassiter's weary horse.

'I will water him myself,' she said, and she led the horse to a trough under a huge old cottonwood. With nimble fingers she loosened the bridle and removed the bit. The horse snorted and bent his head. The trough was of solid stone, hollowed out, moss-covered and green and wet and cool, and the clear brown water that fed it spouted and splashed from a wooden pipe.

'He has brought you far to-day?'

'Yes, ma'am, a matter of over sixty miles, mebbe seventy.'

'A long ride—a ride that—Ah, he is blind!'

'Yes, ma'am,' replied Lassiter.

'What blinded him?'

'Some men once roped an' tied him, an' then held white-iron close to his eyes.'

'Oh! Men? You mean devils. … Were they your enemies—Mormons?'

'Yes, ma'am.'

'To take revenge on a horse! Lassiter, the men of my creed are unnaturally cruel. To my everlasting sorrow I confess it. They have been driven, hated, scourged till their hearts have hardened. But we women hope and pray for the time when our men will soften.'

'Beggin' your pardon, ma'am—that time will never come.'

'Oh, it will! … Lassiter, do you think Mormon women wicked? Has your hand been against them, too?'

'No. I believe Mormon women are the best and noblest, the most long-sufferin', and the blindest, unhappiest women on earth.'

'Ah!' She gave him a grave, thoughtful look. 'Then you will break bread with me?'

Lassiter had no ready response, and he uneasily shifted his weight from one leg to another, and turned his sombrero round and round in his hands. 'Ma'am,' hė began, presently, 'I reckon your kindness of heart makes you overlook things. Perhaps I ain't well known hereabouts, but back up North there's Mormons who'd rest uneasy in their graves at the idea of me sittin' to table with you.'

'I dare say. But—will you do it, anyway?' she asked.

'Mebbe you have a brother or relative who might drop in an' be offended, an' I wouldn't want to—'

'I've not a relative in Utah that I know of. There's no one with a right to question my actions.' She turned smilingly to Venters. 'You will come in, Bern, and Lassiter will come in. We'll eat and be merry while we may.'

'I'm only wonderin' if Tull an' his men'll raise a storm down in the village,' said Lassiter, in his last weakening stand.

'Yes, he'll raise the storm—after he has prayed,' replied Jane. 'Come.'

She led the way, with a bridle of Lassiter's horse over her arm. They entered a grove and walked down a wide path shaded by great low-branching cottonwoods. The last rays of the setting sun sent golden bars through the leaves. The grass was deep and rich, welcome contrast to sage-tired eyes. Twittering quail darted across the path, and from a tree-top somewhere a robin sang its evening song, and on the still air floated the freshness and murmur of flowing water.

The home of Jane Withersteen stood in a circle of cottonwoods, and was a flat, long, red-stone structure with a covered court in the center through which flowed a lively stream of amber-colored water. In the massive blocks of stone and heavy timbers and solid doors and shutters showed the hand of a man who had built against pillage and time; and in the flowers and mosses lining the stone-bedded stream, in the bright colors of rugs and blankets on the court floor, and the cozy corner with hammock and books, and the clean-linened table, showed the grace of a daughter who lived for happiness and the day at hand.

Jane turned Lassiter's horse loose in the thick grass. 'You will want him to be near you,' she said, 'or I'd have him taken to the alfalfa fields.' At her call appeared women who began at once to bustle about, hurrying to and fro, setting the table. Then Jane, excusing herself, went within.

She passed through a huge low-ceiled chamber, like the inside of a fort, and into a smaller one where a bright wood-fire blazed in an old open fireplace, and from this into her own room. It had the same comfort as was manifested in the home-like outer court; moreover, it was warm and rich in soft hues.

Seldom did Jane Withersteen enter her room without looking into her mirror. She knew she loved the reflection of that beauty which since early childhood she had never been allowed to forget. Her relatives and friends, and later a horde of Mormon and Gentile suitors, had fanned the flame of natural vanity in her. So that at twenty-eight she scarcely thought at all of her wonderful influence for good in the little community where her father had left her practically its beneficent landlord; but cared most for the dream and the assurance and the allurement of her beauty. This time, however, she gazed into her glass with more than the usual happy motive, without the usual slight conscious smile. For she was thinking of more than the desire to be fair in her own eyes, in those of her friend; she wondered if she were to seem fair in the eyes of this Lassiter, this man whose name had crossed the long, wild brakes of stone and plains of sage, this gentle-voiced, sad-faced man who was a hater and a killer of Mormons. It was not now her usual half-conscious vain obsession that actuated her as she hurriedly changed her riding-dress to one of white, and then looked long at the stately form with its gracious contours, at the fair face with its strong chin and full firm lips, at the dark–blue, proud, and passionate eyes.

'If by some means I can keep him here a few days, a week—he will never kill another Mormon,' she mused. 'Lassiter! … I shudder when I think of that name, of him. But when I look at the man I forget who he is—I almost like him. I remember only that he saved Bern. He has suffered. I wonder what it was—did he love a Mormon woman once? How splendidly he championed us poor misunderstood souls! Somehow he knows—much.'

Jane Withersteen joined her guests and bade them to her board. Dismissing her woman, she waited upon them with her own hands. It was a bountiful supper and a strange company. On her right sat the ragged and half-starved Venters; and though blind eyes could have seen what he counted for in the sum of her happiness, yet he looked the gloomy outcast his allegiance had made him, and about him there was the shadow of the ruin presaged by Tull. On her left sat the black-leather-garbed Lassiter looking like a man in a dream. Hunger was not with him, nor composure, nor speech, and when he twisted in frequent unquiet movements the heavy guns that he had not removed knocked against the tablelegs. If it had been otherwise possible to forget the presence of Lassiter those telling little jars would have rendered it unlikely. And Jane Withersteen talked and smiled and laughed with all the dazzling play of lips and eyes that a beautiful, daring woman could summon to her purpose.

When the meal ended, and the men pushed back their chairs, she leaned closer to Lassiter and looked square into his eyes.

'Why did you come to Cottonwoods?'

Her question seemed to break a spell. The rider arose as if he had just remembered himself and had tarried longer than his wont.

'Ma'am, I have hunted all over southern Utah and Nevada for—somethin'. An' through your name I learned where to find it—here in Cottonwoods.'

'My name! Oh, I remember. You did know my name when you spoke first. Well, tell me where you heard it and from whom?'

'At the little village—Glaze, I think it's called—some fifty miles or more west of here. An' I heard it from a Gentile, a rider who said you'd know where to tell me to find—'

'What?' she demanded, imperiously, as Lassiter broke off.

'Milly Erne's grave,' he answered low, and the words came with a wrench.

Venters wheeled in his chair to regard Lassiter in amazement, and Jane slowly raised herself in white, still wonder.

'Milly Erne's grave?' she echoed, in a whisper. 'What do you know of Milly Erne, my best-beloved friend—who died in my arms? What were you to her?'

'Did I claim to be anythin'?' he inquired. 'I know people—relatives—who have long wanted to know where she's buried. That's all.'

'Relatives? She never spoke of relatives, except a brother who was shot in Texas. Lassiter, Milly Erne's grave is in a secret burying-ground on my property.'

'Will you take me there? ... You'll be offendin' Mormons worse than by breakin' bread with me.'

'Indeed yes, but I'll do it. Only we must go unseen. Tomorrow perhaps.'

'Thank you, Jane Withersteen,' replied the rider, and he bowed to her and stepped backward out of the court.

'Will you not stay—sleep under my roof?' she asked.

'No, ma'am, an' thanks again. I never sleep indoors. An' even if I did there's that gatherin' storm in the village below. No, no. I'll go to the sage. I hope you won't suffer none for your kindness to me.'

'Lassiter,' said Venters, with a half-bitter laugh, 'my bed, too, is the sage. Perhaps we may meet out there.'

'Mebbe so. But the sage is wide an' I won't be near. Good night.'

At Lassiter's low whistle the black horse whinnied, and carefully picked his blind way out of the grove. The rider did not bridle him, but walked beside him, leading him by touch of hand, and together they passed slowly into the shade of the cottonwoods.

'Jane, I must be off soon,' said Venters. 'Give me my guns. If I'd had my guns—'

'Either my friend or the Elder of my church would be lying dead,' she interposed.

'Tull would be—surely.'

'Oh, you fierce-blooded, savage youth! Can't I teach you forebearance, mercy? Bern, it's divine to forgive your enemies. "Let not the sun go down upon the wrath."'

'Hush! Talk to me no more of mercy or religion—after today. Today this strange coming of Lassiter left me still a man, and now I'll die a man! ... Give me my guns.'

Silently she went into the house, to return with a heavy cartridge-belt and gun-filled sheath and a long rifle; these she handed to him, and as he buckled on the belt she stood before him in silent eloquence.

'Jane,' he said, in gentler voice, 'don't look so. I'm not going out to murder your churchman. I'll try to avoid him and all his men. But can't you see I've reached the end of my rope? Jane, you're a wonderful woman. Never was there a woman so unselfish and good. Only you're blind in one way. ... Listen!'

From behind the grove came the clicking sound of horses in a rapid trot.

'Some of your riders,' he continued. 'It's getting time for the night shift. Let us go out to the bench in the grove and talk there.'

It was still daylight in the open, but under the spreading cottonwoods shadows were obscuring the lanes. Venters drew Jane off from one of these into a shrublined trail, just wide enough for the two to walk abreast, and in a roundabout way led her far from the house to a knoll on the edge of the grove. Here in a secluded nook was a bench from which, through an opening in the tree-tops, could be seen the sage slope and the wall of rock and the dim lines of cañons. Jane had not spoken since Venters had shocked her with his first harsh speech; but all the way she had clung to his arm, and now, as he stopped and laid his rifle against the bench, she still clung to him.

'Jane, I'm afraid I must leave you.'

'Bern!' she cried.

'Yes, it looks that way. My position is not a happy one—I can't feel right—I've lost all—'

'I'll give you anything you—'

'Listen, please. When I say loss I don't mean what you think. I mean loss of good-will, good name—that which would have enabled me to stand up in this village without bitterness. Well, it's too late. ... Now, as to the future, I think you'd do best to give me up. Tull is implacable. You ought to see from his intention today that—But you can't see. Your blindness—your damned religion! ... Jane, forgive me—I'm sore within and something rankles. Well, I fear that invisible hand will turn its hidden work to your ruin.'

'Invisible hand? Bern!'

'I mean your Bishop.' Venters said it deliberately and would not release her as she started back. 'He's the law. The edict went forth to ruin me. Well, look at me! It'll now go forth to compel you to the will of the Church.'

'You wrong Bishop Dyer. Tull is hard, I know. But then he has been in love with me for years.'

'Oh, your faith and your excuses! You can't see what I know—and if you did see it you'd not admit it to save your life. That's the Mormon of you. These elders and bishops will do absolutely any deed to go on building up the power and wealth of their church, their empire. Think of what they've done to the Gentiles here, to me—think of Milly Erne's fate!'

'What do you know of her story?'

'I know enough—all, perhaps, except the name of the Mormon who brought her here. But I must stop this kind of talk.'

She pressed his hand in response. He helped her to a seat beside him on the bench. And he respected a silence that he divined was full of woman's deep emotion, beyond his understanding.

It was the moment when the last ruddy rays of the sunset brightened momentarily before yielding to twilight. And for Venters the outlook before him was in some sense similar to a feeling of his future, and with searching eyes he studied the beautiful purple, barren waste of sage. Here was the unknown and the perilous. The whole scene impressed Venters as a wild, austere, and mighty manifestation of nature. And as it somehow reminded him of his prospect in life, so it suddenly resembled the woman near him, only in her there were greater beauty and peril, a mystery more unsolvable, and something nameless that numbed his heart and dimmed his eye.

'Look! A rider!' exclaimed Jane, breaking the silence. 'Can that be Lassiter?'

Venters moved his glance once more to the west. A horseman showed dark on the sky-line, then merged into the color of the sage.

'It might be. But I think not—that fellow was coming in. One of your riders, more likely. Yes, I see him clearly now. And there's another.'

'I see them, too.'

'Jane, your riders seem as many as the bunches of sage. I ran into five yesterday 'way down near the trail to Deception Pass. They were with the white herd.'

'You still go to that cañon? Bern, I wish you wouldn't. Oldring and his rustlers live somewhere down there.'

'Well, what of that?'

'Tull has already hinted of your frequent trips into Deception Pass.'

'I know.' Venters uttered a short laugh. 'He'll make a rustler of me next. But, Jane, there's no water for fifty miles after I leave here, and the nearest is in the cañon. I must drink and water my horse. There! I see more riders. They are going out.'

'The red herd is on the slope, towards the Pass.'

Twilight was fast falling. A group of horsemen crossed the dark line of low ground to become more distinct as they climbed the slope. The silence broke to a clear call from an incoming rider, and, almost like the peal of a hunting-horn, floated back the answer. The outgoing riders moved swiftly, came sharply into sight as they topped a ridge to show wild and black above the horizon, and then passed down, dimming into the purple of the sage.

'I hope they don't meet Lassiter,' said Jane.

'So do I,' replied Venters. 'By this time the riders of the night shift know what happened today. But Lassiter will likely keep out of their way.'

'Bern, who is Lassiter? He's only a name to me—a terrible name.'

'Who is he? I don't know, Jane. Nobody I ever met knows him. He talks a little like a Texan, like Milly Erne. Did you note that?'

'Yes. How strange of him to know of her! And she lived here ten years and has been dead two. Bern, what do you know of Lassiter? Tell me what he has done—why you spoke of him to Tull—threatening to become another Lassiter yourself?'

'Jane, I only heard things, rumors, stories, most of which I disbelieved. At Glaze his name was known, but none of the riders or ranchers I knew there ever met him. At Stone Bridge I never heard him mentioned. But at Sterling and villages north of there he was spoken of often. I've never been in a village which he had been known to visit. There were many conflicting stories about him and his doings. Some said he had shot up this and that Mormon village, and others denied it. I'm inclined to believe he has, and you know how Mormons hide the truth. But there was one feature about Lassiter upon which all agree—that he was what riders in this country call a gunman. He's a man with marvelous quickness and accuracy in the use of a Colt. And now that I've seen him I know more. Lassiter was born without fear. I watched him with eyes which saw him my friend. I'll never forget the moment I recognized him from what had been told me of his crouch before the draw. It was then I yelled his name. I believe that yell saved Tull's life. At any rate, I know this, between Tull and death then there was not the breadth of the littlest hair. If he or any of his men had moved a finger downward ...'

Venters left his meaning unspoken, but at the suggestion Jane shuddered.

The pale afterglow in the west darkened with the merging of twilight into night. The sage now spread out black and gloomy. One dim star glimmered in the southwest sky. The sound of trotting horses had ceased, and there was silence broken only by a faint, dry pattering of cottonwood leaves in the soft night wind.

Into this peace and calm suddenly broke the high-keyed yelp of a coyote, and from far off in the darkness came the faint answering note of a trailing mate.

'Hello! the sage-dogs are barking,' said Venters.

'I don't like to hear them,' replied Jane. 'At night, sometimes, when I lie awake, listening to the long mourn or breaking bark or wild howl, I think of you asleep somewhere in the sage, and my heart aches.'

'Jane, you couldn't listen to sweeter music, nor could I have a better bed.'

'Just think! Men like Lassiter and you have no home, no comfort, no rest, no place to lay your weary heads. Well! ... Let us be patient. Tull's anger may cool, and time may help us. You might do some service to the village—who can tell?

Suppose you discovered the long-unknown hiding place of Oldring and his band, and told it to my riders? That would disarm Tull's ugly hints and put you in favor. For years my riders have trailed the tracks of stolen cattle. You know as well as I how dearly we've paid for our ranges in this wild country. Oldring drives our cattle down into that network of deceiving cañons, and somewhere far to the north or east he drives them up and out to Utah markets. If you will spend time in Deception Pass try to find the trails.'

'Jane, I've thought of that. I'll try.'

'I must go now. And it hurts, for now I'll never be sure of seeing you again. But tomorrow, Bern?'

'Tomorrow surely. I'll watch for Lassiter and ride in with him.'

'Good night.'

Then she left him and moved away, a white, gliding shape that soon vanished in the shadows.

Venters waited until the faint slam of a door assured him she had reached the house; and then, taking up his rifle, he noiselessly slipped through the bushes, down the knoll, and on under the dark trees to the edge of the grove. The sky was now turning from gray to blue; stars had begun to lighten the earlier blackness; and from the wide flat sweep before him blew a cool wind, fragrant with the breath of sage. Keeping close to the edge of the cottonwoods, he went swiftly and silently westward. The grove was long, and he had not reached the end when he heard something that brought him to a halt. Low padded thuds told him horses were coming his way. He sank down in the gloom, waiting, listening. Much before he had expected, judging from sound, to his amazement he descried horsemen near at hand. They were riding along the border of the sage, and instantly he knew the hoofs of the horses were muffled. Then the pale starlight afforded him indistinct sight of the riders. But his eyes were keen and used to the dark, and by peering closely he recognized the huge bulk and black-bearded visage of Oldring and the lithe, supple form of the rustler's lieutenant, a masked rider. They passed on; the darkness swallowed them. Then, farther out on the sage, a dark, compact body of horsemen went by, almost without sound, almost like specters, and they, too, melted into the night.

CHAPTER THREE
Amber Spring

No unusual circumstance was it for Oldring and some of his men to visit Cottonwoods in the broad light of day, but for him to prowl about in the dark with the hoofs of his horses muffled meant that mischief was brewing. Moreover, to Venters the presence of the masked rider with Oldring seemed especially ominous. For about this man there was mystery; he seldom rode through the village, and when he did ride through it was swiftly; riders seldom met him by day on the sage; but wherever he rode there always followed deeds as dark and mysterious as the mask he wore. Oldring's band did not confine themselves to the rustling of cattle.

Venters lay low in the shade of the cottonwoods, pondering this chance meeting, and not for many moments did he consider it safe to move on. Then, with sudden impulse, he turned the other way and went back along the grove. When he reached the path leading to Jane's home he decided to go down to the village. So he hurried onward, with quick soft steps. Once beyond the grove he entered the one and only street. It was wide, lined with tall poplars, and under each row of trees, inside the foot-path, were ditches where ran the water from Jane Withersteen's spring.

Between the trees twinkled lights of cottage candles, and far down flared bright windows of the village stores. When Venters got closer to these he saw knots of men standing together in earnest conversation. The usual lounging on the corners and benches and steps was not in evidence. Keeping in the shadow, Venters went closer and closer until he could hear voices. But he could not distinguish what was said. He recognized many Mormons, and looked hard for Tull and his men, but looked in vain. Venters concluded that the rustlers had not passed along the village street. No doubt these earnest men were discussing Lassiter's coming. But Venters felt positive that Tull's intention toward himself that day had not been and would not be revealed.

So Venters, seeing there was little for him to learn, began retracing his steps. The church was dark, Bishop Dyer's home next to it was also dark, and likewise Tull's cottage. Upon almost any night at this hour there would be lights here, and Venters marked the unusual omission.

As he was about to pass out of the street to skirt the grove, he once more slunk down at the sound of trotting horses. Presently he descried two mounted men riding toward him. He hugged the shadow of a tree. Again the starlight, brighter now, aided him, and he made out Tull's stalwart figure, and beside him the short, frog-like shape of the rider Jerry. They were silent, and they rode on to disappear.

Venters went his way with busy, gloomy mind, revolving events of the day, trying to reckon those brooding in the night. His thoughts overwhelmed him. Up in that dark grove dwelt a woman who had been his friend. And he skulked about her home, gripping a gun stealthily as an Indian, a man without place or people or purpose. Above her hovered the shadow of grim, hidden, secret power. No queen could have given more royally out of a bounteous store than Jane Withersteen gave her people, and likewise to those unfortunates whom her people hated. She asked only the divine right of all women—freedom; to love and to live as her heart willed. And yet prayer and her hope were vain.

'For years I've seen a storm clouding over her and the village of Cottonwoods,' muttered Venters, as he strode on. 'Soon it'll burst. I don't like the prospect.' That night the villagers whispered in the street—and night-riding rustlers muffled horses—and Tull was at work in secret—and out there in the sage hid a man who meant something terrible—Lassiter!

Venters passed the black cottonwoods, and, entering the sage, climbed the gradual slope. He kept his direction in line with a western star. From time to time he stopped to listen and heard only the usual familiar bark of coyote and sweep of wind and rustle of sage. Presently a low jumble of rocks loomed up darkly somewhat to his right, and, turning that way, he whistled softly. Out of the rocks glided a dog that leaped and whined about him. He climbed over rough, broken rock, picking his way carefully, and then went down. Here it was darker, and sheltered from the wind. A white object guided him. It was another dog, and this one was asleep, curled up between a saddle and a pack. The animal awoke and thumped his tail in greeting. Venters placed the saddle for a pillow, rolled in his blankets, with his face upward to the stars. The white dog snuggled close to him. The other whined and pattered a few yards to the rise of ground and there crouched on guard. And in that wild covert Venters shut his eyes under the great white stars and intense vaulted blue, bitterly comparing their loneliness to his own, and fell asleep.

When he awoke, day had dawned and all about him was bright steel-gray. The air had a cold tang. Arising, he greeted the fawning dogs and stretched his cramped body, and then, gathering together bunches of dead sage sticks, he lighted a fire. Strips of dried beef held to the blaze for a moment served him and the dogs. He drank from a canteen. There was nothing else in his outfit; he had grown used to a scant fare. Then he sat over the fire, palms outspread, and waited. Waiting had been his chief occupation for months, and he scarcely knew what he waited for, unless it was the passing of the hours. But now he sensed action in the immediate present; the day promised another meeting with Lassiter and Jane, perhaps news of the rustlers; on the morrow he meant to take the trail to Deception Pass.

And while he waited he talked to his dogs. He called them Ring and Whitie; they were sheep-dogs, half collie, half deer-hound, superb in build, perfectly trained. It seemed that in his fallen fortunes these dogs understood the nature of their value to him, and governed their affection and faithfulness accordingly. Whitie watched him with somber eyes of love, and Ring, crouched on the little rise of ground above, kept tireless guard. When the sun rose, the white dog took the place of the other, and Ring went to sleep at his master's feet.

By and by Venters rolled up his blankets and tied them and his meager pack together, then climbed out to look for his horse. He saw him, presently, a little way off in the sage, and went to fetch him. In that country, where every rider boasted of a fine mount and was eager for a race, where thoroughbreds dotted the wonderful grazing ranges, Venters rode a horse that was sad proof of his misfortunes.

Then, with his back against a stone, Venters faced the east, and stick in hand and idle blade, he waited. The glorious sunlight filled the valley with purple fire. Before him, to left, to right, waving, rolling, sinking, rising, like low swells of a purple sea, stretched the sage. Out of the grove of cottonwoods, a green patch on the purple, gleamed the dull red of Jane Withersteen's old stone house. And from these extended the wide green of the village gardens and orchards marked by the graceful poplars; and farther down shone the deep, dark richness of the alfalfa fields. Numberless red and black and white dots speckled the sage, and these were cattle and horses.

So, watching and waiting, Venters let the time wear away. At length he saw a horse rise above a ridge, and he knew it to be Lassiter's black. Climbing to the highest rock, so that he would show against the skyline, he stood and waved his hat. The almost instant turning of Lassiter's horse attested to the quickness of that rider's eye. Then Venters climbed down, saddled his horse, tied on his pack, and with a word to his dogs, was about to ride out to meet Lassiter, when he concluded to wait for him there, on higher ground, where the outlook was commanding.

It had been long since Venters had experienced friendly greeting from a man. Lassiter's warmed in him something that had grown cold from neglect. And when he had returned it, with a strong grip of the iron hand that held his, and met the gray eyes, he knew that Lassiter and he were to be friends.

'Venters, let's talk awhile before we go down there,' said Lassiter, slipping his bridle. 'I ain't in no hurry. Them's sure fine dogs you've got.' With a rider's eye he took in the points of Venters's horse, but did not speak his thought. 'Well, did anythin' come off after I left you last night?'

Venters told him about the rustlers.

'I was snug hid in the sage,' replied Lassiter, 'an' didn't see or hear no one. Oldrin's got a high hand here, I reckon. It's no news up in Utah how he holes in cañons an' leaves no track.' Lassiter was silent a moment. 'Me an' Oldrin' wasn't exactly strangers some years back when he drove cattle into Bostil's Ford, at the head of the Rio Virgin. But he got harassed there an' now he drives some place else.'

'Lassiter, you knew him? Tell me, is he Mormon or Gentile?'

'I can't say. I've knowed Mormons who pretended to be Gentiles.'

'No Mormon ever pretended that unless he was a rustler,' declared Venters.

'Mebbe so.'

'It's a hard country for any one, but hardest for Gentiles. Did you ever know or hear of a Gentile prospering in a Mormon community?'

'I never did.'

'Well, I want to get out of Utah. I've a mother living in Illinois. I want to go home. It's eight years now.'

The older man's sympathy moved Venters to tell his story. He had left Quincy, run off to seek his fortune in the gold fields, had never gotten any farther than Salt Lake City, wandered here and there as helper, teamster, shepherd, and drifted southward over the divide and across the barrens and up the rugged plateau through the passes to the last border settlements. Here he became a rider of the sage, had stock of his own, and for a time prospered, until chance threw him in the employ of Jane Withersteen.

'Lassiter, I needn't tell you the rest.'

'Well, it'd be no news to me. I know Mormons. I've seen their women's strange love an' patience an' sacrifice an' silence an' what I call madness for their idea of God. An' over against that I've seen the tricks of the men. They work hand in hand, all together, an' in the dark. No man can hold out against them, unless he takes to packin' guns. For Mormons are slow to kill. That's the only good I ever seen in their religion. Venters, take this from me, these Mormons ain't just right in their minds. Else could a Mormon marry one woman when he already had a wife, an' call it duty?'

'Lassiter, you think as I think,' returned Venters.

'How'd it come then that you never throwed a gun on Tull or some of them?' inquired the rider, curiously.

'Jane pleaded with me, begged me to be patient, to overlook. She even took my guns from me. I lost all before I knew it,' replied Venters, with the red color in his face. 'But, Lassiter, listen. Out of the wreck I saved a Winchester, two Colts, and plenty of shells. I packed these down into Deception Pass. There, almost every day for six months, I have practiced with my rifle till the barrel burnt my hands. Practiced the draw—the firing of a Colt, hour after hour!'

'Now that's interestin' to me,' said Lassiter, with a quick uplift of his head and a concentration of his gray gaze on Venters. 'Could you throw a gun before you began that practicin'?'

'Yes. And now ...' Venters made a lightning-swift movement.

Lassiter smiled, and then his bronzed eyelids narrowed till his eyes seemed mere gray slits. 'You'll kill Tull!' He did not question; he affirmed.

'I promised Jane Withersteen I'd try to avoid Tull. I'll keep my word. But sooner or later Tull and I will meet. As I feel now, if he even looks at me I'll draw!'

'I reckon so. There'll be hell down there, presently.' He paused a moment and flicked a sage-brush with his quirt. 'Venters, seein' as you're considerable worked up, tell me Milly Erne's story.'

Venters's agitation stilled to the trace of suppressed eagerness in Lassiter's query.

'Milly Erne's story? Well, Lassiter, I'll tell you what I know. Milly Erne had been in Cottonwoods years when I first arrived there, and most of what I tell you happened before my arrival. I got to know her pretty well. She was a slip of a woman, and crazy on religion. I conceived an idea that I never mentioned—I thought she was at heart more Gentile than Mormon. But she passed as a Mormon, and certainly she had the Mormon woman's locked lips. You know, in every Mormon village there are women who seem mysterious to us, but about Milly there was more than the ordinary mystery. When she came to Cottonwoods she had a beautiful little girl whom she loved passionately. Milly was not known openly in Cottonwoods as a Mormon wife. That she really was a Mormon wife I have no doubt. Perhaps the Mormon's other wife or wives would not acknowledge Milly. Such things happen in these villages. Mormon wives wear yokes, but they get jealous. Well, whatever had brought Milly to this country—love or madness of religion—she repented of it. She gave up teaching the village school. She quit the church. And she began to fight Mormon upbringing for her baby girl. Then the Mormons put on the screws—slowly, as is their way. At last the child disappeared. Lost, was the report. The child was stolen, I know that. So do you. That wrecked Milly Erne. But she lived on in hope. She became a slave. She worked her heart and soul and life out to get back her child. She never heard of it again. Then she sank. ... I can see her now, a frail thing, so transparent you could almost look through her—white like ashes—and her eyes! ... Her eyes have always haunted me. She had one real friend—Jane Withersteen. But Jane couldn't mend a broken heart, and Milly died.'

For moments Lassiter did not speak, or turn his head.

'The man!' he exclaimed, presently, in husky accents.

'I haven't the slightest idea who the Mormon was,' replied Venters; 'nor has any Gentile in Cottonwoods.'

'Does Jane Withersteen know?'

'Yes. But a red-hot running iron couldn't burn that name out of her!'

Without further speech Lassiter started off, walking his horse, and Venters followed with his dogs. Half a mile down the slope they entered a luxuriant growth of willows, and soon came into an open space carpeted with grass like deep green velvet. The rushing of water and singing of birds filled their ears. Venters led his comrade to a shady bower and showed him Amber Spring. It was a magnificent outburst of clear, amber water pouring from a dark, stone-lined hole. Lassiter knelt and drank, lingered there to drink again. He made no comment, but Venters did not need words. Next to his horse a rider of the sage loved a spring. And this spring was the most beautiful and remarkable known to the upland riders of southern Utah. It was the spring that made old Withersteen a feudal lord and now enabled his daughter to return the toll which her father had exacted from the toilers of the sage.

The spring gushed forth in a swirling torrent, and leaped down joyously to make its swift way along a willow-skirted channel. Moss and ferns and lilies overhung its green banks. Except for the rough-hewn stones that held and directed the water, this willow thicket and glade had been left as nature had made it.

Below were artificial lakes, three in number, one above the other in banks of raised earth; and round about them rose the lofty green-foliated shafts of poplar trees. Ducks dotted the glassy surface of the lakes; a blue heron stood motionless on a water-gate; kingfishers darted with shrieking flight along the shady banks; a white hawk sailed above; and from the trees and shrubs came the song of robins and catbirds. It was all in strange contrast to the endless slopes of lonely sage and the wild rock environs beyond. Venters thought of the woman who loved the birds and the green of the leaves and the murmur of water.

Next on the slope, just below the third and largest lake, were corrals and a wide stone barn and open sheds and coops and pens. Here were clouds of dust, and cracking sounds of hoofs, and romping colts and hee-hawing burros. Neighing horses trampled to the corral fences. And from the little windows of the barn projected bobbing heads of bays and blacks and sorrels. When the two men entered the immense barnyard, from all around the din increased. This welcome, however, was not seconded by the several men and boys who vanished on sight.

Venters and Lassiter were turning toward the house when Jane appeared in the lane leading a horse. In riding-skirt and blouse she seemed to have lost some of her statuesque proportions, and looked more like a girl rider than the mistress of Withersteen. She was bright, smiling, and her greeting was warmly cordial.

'Good news,' she announced. 'I've been to the village. All is quiet. I expected—I don't know what. But there's no excitement. And Tull has ridden out on his way to Glaze.'

'Tull gone?' inquired Venters, with surprise. He was wondering what could have taken Tull away. Was it to avoid another meeting with Lassiter that he went? Could it have any connection with the probable nearness of Oldring and his gang?

'Gone, yes, thank goodness,' replied Jane. 'Now I'll have peace for a while. Lassiter, I want you to see my horses. You are a rider, and you must be a judge of horseflesh. Some of mine have Arabian blood. My father got his best strain in Nevada from Indians who claimed their horses were bred down from the original stock left by the Spaniards.'

'Well, ma'am, the one you've been ridin' takes my eye,' said Lassiter, as he walked round the racy, clean-limbed, and fine-pointed roan.

'Where are the boys?' she asked, looking about. 'Jerd, Paul, where are you? Here, bring out the horses.'

The sound of dropping bars inside the barn was the signal for the horses to jerk their heads in the windows, to snort and stamp. Then they came pounding out of the door, a file of thoroughbreds, to plunge about the barnyard, heads and tails up, manes flying. They halted afar off, squared away to look, came slowly forward with whinnies for their mistress, and doubtful snorts for the strangers and their horses.

'Come—come—come,' called Jane, holding out her hands. 'Why Bells—Wrangle, where are your manners? Come, Black Star—come, Night. Ah, you beauties! My racers of the sage!'

Only two came up to her; those she called Night and Black Star. Venters never looked at them without delight. The first was soft dead black, the other glittering black, and they were perfectly matched in size, both being high and long-bodied, wide through the shoulders, with lithe, powerful legs. That they were a woman's pets showed in the gloss of skin, the fineness of mane. It showed, too, in the light of big eyes and the gentle reach of eagerness.

'I never seen their like,' was Lassiter's encomium, 'an' in my day I've seen a sight of horses. Now, ma'am, if you was wantin' to make a long an' fast ride across the sage—say to elope—'

Lassiter ended there with dry humor, yet behind that was meaning. Jane blushed and made arch eyes at him.

'Take care, Lassiter, I might think that a proposal,' she replied, gaily. 'It's dangerous to propose elopement to a Mormon woman. Well, I was expecting you. Now will be a good hour to show you Milly Erne's grave. The day-riders have gone, and the night-riders haven't come in. Bern, what do you make of that? Need I worry? You know I have to be made to worry.'

'Well, it's not usual for the night shift to ride in so late,' replied Venters, slowly, and his glance sought Lassiter's. 'Cattle are usually quiet after dark. Still, I've known even a coyote to stampede your white herd.'

'I refuse to borrow trouble. Come,' said Jane.

They mounted, and, with Jane in the lead, rode down the lane, and, turning off into a cattle trail, proceeded westward. Venters's dogs trotted behind them. On this side of the ranch the outlook was different from that on the other; the immediate foreground was rough and the sage more rugged and less colorful; there were no dark-blue lines of cañons to hold the eye, nor any up-rearing rock walls. It was a long roll and slope into gray obscurity. Soon Jane left the trail and rode into the sage, and presently she dismounted and threw her bridle. The men did likewise. Then, on foot, they followed her, coming out at length on the rim of a low escarpment. She passed by several little ridges of earth to halt before a faintly defined mound. It lay in the shade of a sweeping sage-brush close to the edge of the promontory; and a rider could have jumped his horse over it without recognizing a grave.

'Here!'

She looked sad as she spoke, but she offered no explanation for the neglect of an unmarked, uncared-for grave. There was a little bunch of pale, sweet lavender daisies, doubtless planted there by Jane.

'I only come here to remember and to pray,' she said. 'But I leave no trail!'

A grave in the sage! How lonely this resting-place of Milly Erne! The cottonwoods or the alfalfa fields were not in sight, nor was there any rock or ridge or cedar to lend contrast to the monotony. Gray slopes, tinging the purple, barren and wild, with the wind waving the sage, swept away to the dim horizon.

Lassiter looked at the grave and then out into space. At that moment he seemed a figure of bronze.

Jane touched Venters's arm and led him back to the horses.

'Bern!' cried Jane, when they were out of hearing. 'Suppose Lassiter were Milly's husband—the father of that little girl lost so long ago!'

'It might be, Jane. Let us ride on. If he wants to see us again he'll come.'

So they mounted and rode out to the cattle trail and began to climb. From the height of the ridge, where they had started down, Venters looked back. He did not see Lassiter, but his glance, drawn irresistibly farther out on the gradual slope, caught sight of a moving cloud of dust.

'Hello, a rider!'

'Yes, I see,' said Jane.

'That fellow's riding hard. Jane, there's something wrong.'

'Oh yes, there must be. …. How he rides!'

The horse disappeared in the sage, and then puffs of dust marked his course.

'He's short-cut on us—he's making straight for the corrals.'

Venters and Jane galloped their steeds and reined in at the turning of the lane. This lane led down to the right of the grove. Suddenly into its lower entrance flashed a bay horse. Then Venters caught the fast rhythmic beat of pounding hoofs. Soon his keen eyes recognized the swing of the rider in his saddle.

'It's Judkins, your Gentile rider!' he cried. 'Jane, when Judkins rides like that it means hell!'

CHAPTER FOUR
Deception Pass

The rider thundered up and almost threw his foam-flecked horse in the sudden stop. He was of giant form, and with fearless eyes.

'Judkins, you're all bloody!' cried Jane, in affright. 'Oh, you've been shot!'

'Nothin' much, Miss Withersteen. I got a nick in the shoulder. I'm some wet an' the hoss's been throwin' lather, so all this ain't blood.'

'What's up?' queried Venters, sharply.

'Rustlers sloped off with the red herd.'

'Where are my riders?' demanded Jane.

'Miss Withersteen, I was alone all night with the herd. At daylight this mornin' the rustlers rode down. They began to shoot at me on sight. They chased me hard an' far, burnin' powder all the time, but I got away.'

'Jud, they meant to kill you,' declared Venters.

'Now I wonder,' returned Judkins. 'They wanted me bad. An' it ain't regular for rustlers to waste time chasin' one rider.'

'Thank Heaven you got away,' said Jane. 'But my riders—where are they?'

'I don't know. The night-riders weren't there last night when I rode down, an' this mornin' I met no day-riders.'

'Judkins! Bern, they've been set upon—killed by Oldring's men!'

'I don't think so,' replied Venters, decidedly. 'Jane, your riders haven't gone out in the sage.'

'Bern, what do you mean?' Jane Withersteen turned deathly pale.

'You remember what I said about the unseen hand?'

'Oh! … Impossible!'

'I hope so. But I fear—' Venters finished, with a shake of his head.

'Bern, you're bitter; but that's only natural. We'll wait to see what's happened to my riders. Judkins, come to the house with me. Your wound must be attended to.'

'Jane, I'll find out where Oldring drives the herd,' vowed Venters.

'No, no! Bern, don't risk it now—when the rustlers are in such shooting mood.'

'I'm going. Jud, how many cattle in that red herd?'

'Twenty-five hundred head.'

'Whew! What on earth can Oldring do with so many cattle? Why, a hundred head is a big steal. I've got to find out.'

'Don't go,' implored Jane.

· 'Bern, you want a hoss thet can run. Miss Withersteen, if it's not too bold of me to advise, make him take a fast hoss or don't let him go.'

'Yes, yes, Judkins. He must ride a horse that can't be caught. Which one—Black Star—Night?'

'Jane, I won't take either,' said Venters, emphatically. 'I wouldn't risk losing one of your favorites.'

'Wrangle, then?'

'Thet's the hoss,' replied Judkins. 'Wrangle can outrun Black Star an' Night. You'd never believe it, Miss Withersteen, but I know. Wrangle's the biggest an' fastest hoss on the sage.'

'Oh no, Wrangle can't beat Black Star. But, Bern, take Wrangle, if you will go. Ask Jerd for anything you need. Oh, be watchful, careful. … God speed you!'

She clasped his hand, turned quickly away, and went down the lane with the rider.

Venters rode to the bar, and, leaping off, shouted for Jerd. The boy came running. Venters sent him for meat, bread, and dried fruits, to be packed in saddle-bags. His own horse he turned loose into the nearest corral. Then he went for Wrangle. The giant sorrel had earned his name for a trait the opposite of amiability. He came readily out of the barn, but once in the yard he broke from Venters, and plunged about with ears laid back. Venters had to rope him, and then he kicked down a section of fence, stood on his hind legs, crashed down and fought the rope. Jerd returned to lend a hand.

'Wrangle don't git enough work,' said Jerd, as the big saddle went on. 'He's unruly when he's corralled, an' wants to run. Wait till he smells the sage!'

'Jerd, this horse is an iron-jawed devil. I never straddled him but once. Run? Say, he's swift as wind!'

When Venters's boot touched the stirrup the sorrel bolted, giving him the rider's flying mount. The swing of this fiery horse recalled to Venters days that were not really long past, when he rode into the sage as the leader of Jane Withersteen's riders. Wrangle pulled hard on a tight rein. He galloped out of the lane, down the shaky border of the grove, and hauled up at the watering-trough, where he pranced and champed his bit. Venters got off and filled his canteen while the horse drank. The dogs, Ring and Whitie, came trotting up for their drink. Then Venters remounted and turned Wrangle toward the sage.

A wide, white trail wound away down the slope. One keen, sweeping glance told Venters that there was neither man nor horse nor steer within the limit of his vision, unless they were lying down in the sage. Ring loped in the lead and Whitie loped in the rear. Wrangle settled gradually into an easy swinging canter, and Venters's thoughts, now that the rush and flurry of the start were past, and the long miles stretched before him, reverted to a calm reckoning of late singular coincidences.

There was the night ride of Tull's, which, viewed in the light of subsequent events, had a look of his covert machinations; Oldring and his Masked Rider and his rustlers riding muffled horses; the report that Tull had ridden out that morning with his man Jerry on the trail to Glaze, the strange disappearance of Jane Withersteen's riders, the unusually determined attempt to kill the one Gentile still in her employ, an intention frustrated, no doubt, only by Judkins's magnificent riding of her racer, and lastly the driving of the red herd. These events, to Venters's color of mind, had a dark relationship. Remembering Jane's accusation of bitterness, he tried hard to put aside his rancor in judging Tull. But it was bitter knowledge that made him see the truth. He had felt the shadow of an unseen hand; he had watched till he saw its dim outline, and then he had traced it to a man's hate, to the rivalry of a Mormon Elder, to the power of a Bishop, to the long, far-reaching arm of a terrible creed. That unseen hand had made its first move against Jane Withersteen. Her riders had been called in, leaving her without help to drive seven thousand head of cattle. But to Venters it seemed extraordinary that the power which had called in these riders had left so many cattle to be driven by rustlers and harried by wolves. For hand in glove with that power was an insatiate greed; they were one and the same.

'What can Oldring do with twenty-five hundred head of cattle?' muttered Venters. 'Is he a Mormon? Did he meet Tull last night? It looks like a black plot to me. But Tull and his churchmen wouldn't ruin Jane Withersteen unless the Church was to profit by that ruin. Where does Oldring come in? I'm going to find out about these things.'

Wrangle did twenty-five miles in three hours and walked little of the way. When he had gotten warmed up he had been allowed to choose his own gait. The afternoon had well advanced when Venters struck the trail of the red herd and found where it had grazed the night before. Then Venters rested the horse and used his eyes. Near at hand were a cow and a calf and several yearlings, and farther out in the sage some struggling steers. He caught a glimpse of coyotes skulking near the cattle. The slow, sweeping gaze of the rider failed to find other living things within the field of sight. The sage about him was breast-high to his horse, oversweet with its warm, fragrant breath, gray where it waved to the light, darker where the wind left it still, and beyond the wonderful haze-purple lent by distance. Far across that wide waste began the slow lift of uplands through which Deception Pass cut its tortuous many-cañoned way.

Venters raised the bridle of his horse and followed the broad cattle trail. The crushed sage resembled the path of a monster snake. In a few miles of travel he passed several cows and calves that had escaped the drive. Then he stood on the last high bench of the slope with the floor of the valley beneath. The opening of the cañon showed in a break of the sage, and the cattle trail paralleled it as far as he could see. That trail led to an undiscovered point where Oldring drove cattle into the pass, and many a rider who had followed it had never returned. Venters satisfied himself that the rustlers had not deviated from their usual course, and then he turned at right angles off the cattle trail and made for the head of the pass.

The sun lost its heat and wore down to the western horizon, where it changed from white to gold and rested like a huge ball about to roll on its golden shadows down the slope. Venters watched the lengthening of the rays and bars, and marveled at his own league-long shadow. The sun sank. There was instant shading of brightness about him, and he saw a kind of cold purple bloom creep ahead of him to cross the cañon, to mount the opposite slope and chase and darken and bury the last golden flare of sunlight.

Venters rode into a trail that he always took to get down into the cañon. He dismounted and found no tracks but his own made several days previous. Nevertheless he sent the dog Ring ahead and waited. In a little while Ring returned. Whereupon Venters led his horse on to the break in the ground.

The opening into Deception Pass was one of the remarkable natural phenomena in a country remarkable for vast slopes of sage, uplands insulated by gigantic red walls, and deep cañons of mysterious source and outlet. Here the valley floor was level, and here opened a narrow chasm, a ragged vent in yellow walls of stone. The trail down the five hundred feet of sheer depth always tested Venters's nerve. It was bad going for even a burro. But Wrangle, as Venters led him, snorted defiance or disgust rather than fear, and, like a hobbled horse on the jump, lifted his ponderous iron-shod fore hoofs and crashed down over the first rough step. Venters warmed to greater admiration of the sorrel; and, giving him a loose bridle, he stepped down foot by foot. Oftentimes the stones and shale started by Wrangle buried Venters to his knees; again he was hard put to it to dodge a rolling boulder;

there were times when he could not see Wrangle for dust, and once he and the horse rode a sliding shelf of yellow, weathered cliff. It was a trail on which there could be no stops, and, therefore, if perilous, it was at least one that did not take long in the descent.

Venters breathed lighter when that was over, and felt a sudden assurance in the success of his enterprise. For at first it had been a reckless determination to achieve something at any cost, and now it resolved itself into an adventure worthy of all his reason and cunning, and keenness of eye and ear.

Piñon pines clustered in little clumps along the level floor of the pass. Twilight had gathered under the walls. Venters rode into the trail and up the cañon. Gradually the trees and caves and objects low down turned black, and this blackness moved up the walls till night enfolded the pass, while day still lingered above. The sky darkened; and stars began to show, at first pale and then bright. Sharp notches of the rim-wall, biting like teeth into the blue, were landmarks by which Venters knew where his camping site lay. He had to feel his way through a thicket of slender oaks to a spring where he watered Wrangle and drank himself. Here he unsaddled and turned Wrangle loose, having no fear that the horse would leave the thick, cool grass adjacent to the spring. Next he satisfied his own hunger, fed Ring and Whitie, and, with them curled beside him, composed himself to await sleep.

There had been a time when night in the high altitude of these Utah uplands had been satisfying to Venters. But that was before the oppression of enemies had made the change in his mind. As a rider guarding the herd he had never thought of the night's wildness and loneliness; as an outcast, now when the full silence set in, and the deep darkness, and trains of radiant stars shone cold and calm, he lay with an ache in his heart. For a year he had lived as a black fox, driven from his kind. He longed for the sound of a voice, the touch of a hand. In the daytime there was riding from place to place, and the gun practice to which something drove him, and other tasks that at least necessitated action; at night, before he won sleep, there was strife in his soul. He yearned to leave the endless sage slopes, the wilderness of cañons; and it was in the lonely night that this yearning grew unbearable. It was then that he reached forth to feel Ring or Whitie, immeasurably grateful for the love and companionship of two dogs.

On this night the same old loneliness beset Venters, the old habit of sad thought and burning unquiet had its way. But from it evolved a conviction that his useless life had undergone a subtle change. He had sensed it first when Wrangle swung him up to the high saddle, he knew it now when he lay in the gateway of Deception Pass. He had no thrill of adventure, rather a gloomy perception of great hazard, perhaps death. He meant to find Oldring's retreat. The rustlers had fast horses, but none that could catch Wrangle. Venters knew no rustlers could creep upon

him at night when Ring and Whitie guarded his hiding-place. For the rest, he had
eyes and ears, and a long rifle and an unerring aim, which he meant to use.
Strangely his foreshadowing of change did not hold a thought of the killing of
Tull. It related only to what was to happen to him in Deception Pass; and he could
no more lift the veil of that mystery than tell where the trails led to in that
unexplored cañon. Moreover, he did not care. And at length, tired out by stress
of thought, he fell asleep.

When his eyes unclosed, day had come again, and he saw the rim of the opposite
wall tipped with the gold of sunrise. A few moments sufficed for the morning's
simple camp duties. Near at hand he found Wrangle, and to his surprise the horse
came to him. Wrangle was one of the horses that left his viciousness in the home
corral. What he wanted was to be free of mules and burros and steers, to roll in
dust-patches, and then to run down the wide, open, windy sage-plains, and at
night browse and sleep in the cool wet grass of a spring-hole. Jerd knew the sorrel
when he said of him, 'Wait till he smells the sage!'

Venters saddled and led him out of the oak thicket, and, leaping astride, rode
up the cañon, with Ring and Whitie trotting behind. An old grass-grown trail
followed the course of a shallow wash where flowed a thin stream of water. The
cañon was a hundred rods wide; its yellow walls were perpendicular; it had
abundant sage and a scant growth of oak and piñon. For five miles it held to a
comparatively straight bearing, and then began a heightening of rugged walls and
a deepening of the floor. Beyond this point of sudden change in the character of
the cañon Venters had never explored, and here was the real door to the intricacies
of Deception Pass.

He reined Wrangle to a walk, halted now and then to listen, and then proceeded
cautiously with shifting and alert gaze. The cañon assumed proportions that
dwarfed those of its first ten miles. Venters rode on and on, not losing in the
interest of his wide surroundings any of his caution or keen search for tracks or
sight of living thing. If there ever had been a trail here, he could not find it. He
rode through sage and clumps of piñon trees and grassy plots where long-petaled
purple lilies bloomed. He rode through a dark constriction of the pass no wider
than the lane in the grove at Cottonwoods. And he came out into a great
amphitheater into which jutted huge towering corners of a confluence of inter-
section cañons.

Venters sat his horse, and, with a rider's eye, studied this wild cross-cut of huge
stone gullies. Then he went on, guided by the course of running water. If it had
not been for the main stream of water flowing north he would never have been
able to tell which of those many openings was a continuation of the pass. In
crossing this amphitheater he went by the mouths of five cañons, fording little
streams that flowed into the larger one. Gaining the outlet which he took to be

the pass, he rode on again under overhanging walls. One side was dark in shade, the other light in sun. This narrow passageway turned and twisted and opened into a valley that amazed Venters.

Here again was a sweep of purple sage richer than upon the higher levels. The valley was miles long, several wide, and enclosed by unscalable walls. But it was the background of this valley that so forcibly struck him. Across the sage-flat rose a strange upflinging of yellow rocks. He could not tell which were close and which were distant. Scrawled mounds of stone, like mountain waves, seemed to roll up to steep bare slopes and towers.

In this plain of sage Venters flushed birds and rabbits, and when he had proceeded about a mile he caught sight of the bobbing white tails of a herd of running antelope. He rode along the edge of the stream which wound toward the western end of the slowly looming mounds of stone. The high slope retreated out of sight behind the nearer projection. To Venters the valley appeared to have been filled in by a mountain of melted stone that had hardened in strange shapes of rounded outline. He followed the stream till he lost it in a deep rut. Therefore Venters quit the dark slit which baffled further search in that direction, and rode out along the curved edge of stone where it met the sage. It was not long before he came to a low place, and here Wrangle readily climbed up.

All about him was ridgy roll of wind-smoothed, rain-washed rock. Not a tuft of grass or a bunch of sage colored the dull rust-yellow. He saw where, to the right, this uneven flow of stone ended in a blunt wall. Leftward, from the hollow that lay at his feet, mounted a gradual slow-swelling slope to a great height topped by leaning, cracked, and ruined crags. Not for some time did he grasp the wonder of that acclivity. It was no less than a mountainside, glistening in the sun like polished granite, with cedar-trees springing as if by magic out of the denuded surface. Winds had swept it clear of weathered shale, and rains had washed it free of dust. Far up the curved slope its beautiful lines broke to meet the vertical rim-wall, to lose its grace in a different order and color of rock, a stained yellow cliff of cracks and caves and seamed crags. And straight before Venters was a scene less striking but more significant to his keen survey. For beyond a mile of the bare, hummocky rock began the valley of sage, and the mouths of cañons, one of which surely was another gateway into the pass.

He got off his horse, and, giving the bridle to Ring to hold, he commenced a search for the cleft where the stream ran. He was not successful and concluded the water dropped into an underground passage. Then he returned to where he had left Wrangle, and led him down off the stone to the sage. It was a short ride to the opening cañons. There was no reason for a choice of which one to enter. The one he rode into was a clear, sharp shift in yellow stone a thousand feet deep, with wonderful wind-worn caves low down and high above buttressed and turreted ramparts. Farther on Venters came into a region where deep indentations marked the line of cañon walls. These were huge, cove-like blind pockets extending back to a sharp corner with a dense growth of underbrush and trees.

Venters penetrated into one of these offshoots, and, as he had hoped, he found abundant grass. He had to bend the oak saplings to get his horse through. Deciding to make this a hiding-place if he could find water, he worked back to the limit of the shelving walls. In a little cluster of silver spruces he found a spring. This enclosed nook seemed an ideal place to leave his horse and to camp at night, and from which to make stealthy trips on foot. The thick grass hid his trail; the dense growth of oaks in the opening would serve as a barrier to keep Wrangle in, if, indeed, the luxuriant browse would not suffice for that. So Venters, leaving Whitie with the horse, called Ring to his side, and, rifle in hand, worked his way out to the open. A careful photographing in mind of the formation of the bold outlines of rim-rock assured him he would be able to return to his retreat, even in the dark.

Bunches of scattered sage covered the center of the cañon, and among these Venters threaded his way with the step of an Indian. At intervals he put his hand on the dog and stopped to listen. There was a drowsy hum of insects, but no other sound disturbed the warm midday stillness. Venters saw ahead a turn, more abrupt than any yet. Warily he rounded this corner, once again to halt bewildered.

The cañon opened fan-shaped into a great oval of green and gray growths. It was the hub of an oblong wheel, and from it, at regular distances, like spokes, ran the outgoing cañons. Here a dull red color predominated over the fading yellow. The corners of wall bluntly rose, scarred and scrawled, to taper into towers and serrated peaks and pinnacled domes.

Venters pushed on more heedfully than ever. Toward the center of this circle the sage-brush grew smaller and farther apart. He was about to sheer off to the right, where thickets and jumbles of fallen rock would afford him cover, when he ran right upon a broad cattle trail. Like a road it was, more than a trail; and the cattle tracks were fresh. What surprised him more, they were wet! He pondered over this feature. It had not rained. The only solution to this puzzle was that the cattle had been driven through water, and water deep enough to wet their legs.

Suddenly Ring growled low. Venters rose cautiously and looked over the sage. A band of straggling horsemen were riding across the oval. He sank down, startled and trembling. 'Rustlers!' he muttered. Hurriedly he glanced about for a place to hide. Near at hand there was nothing but sage-brush. He dared not risk crossing the open patches to reach the rocks. Again he peeped over the sage. The rustlers—four—five—seven—eight in all, were approaching, but not directly in line with him. That was relief for a cold deadness which seemed to be creeping inward along his veins. He crouched down with bated breath and held the bristling dog.

He heard the click of iron-shod hoofs on stone, the coarse laughter of men, and then voices gradually dying away. Long moments passed. Then he rose. The rustlers were riding into a cañon. Their horses were tired, and they had several pack animals; evidently they had traveled far. Venters doubted that they were the rustlers who had driven the red herd. Oldring's band had split. Venters watched these horsemen disappear under a bold cañon wall.

The rustlers had come from the northwest side of the oval. Venters kept a steady gaze in that direction, hoping, if there were more, to see from what cañon they rode. A quarter of an hour went by. Reward for his vigilance came when he descried three more mounted men, far over to the north. But out of what cañon they had ridden it was too late to tell. He watched the three ride across the oval and round the jutting red corner where the others had gone.

'Up that cañon!' exclaimed Venters. 'Oldring's den! I've found it!'

A knotty point for Venters was the fact that the cattle tracks all pointed west. The broad trail came from the direction of the cañon into which the rustlers had ridden, and undoubtedly the cattle had been driven out of it across the oval. There were no tracks pointing the other way. It had been in his mind that Oldring had driven the red herd toward the rendezvous, and not from it. Where did that broad trail come down into the pass, and where did it lead? Venters knew he wasted time in pondering the question, but it held a fascination not easily dispelled. For many years Oldring's mysterious entrance and exit to Deception Pass had been all-absorbing topics to sage-riders.

All at once the dog put an end to Venters's pondering. Ring sniffed the air, turned slowly in his tracks with a whine, and then growled. Venters wheeled. Two horsemen were within a hundred yards, coming straight at him. One, lagging behind the other, was Oldring's Masked Rider.

Venters cunningly sank, slowly trying to merge into sage-brush. But, guarded as his action was, the first horse detected it. He stopped short, snorted, and shot up his ears. The rustler bent forward, as if keenly peering ahead. Then, with a swift sweep, he jerked a gun from its sheath and fired.

The bullet zipped through the sage-brush. Flying bits of wood struck Venters, and the hot, stinging pain seemed to lift him in one leap. Like a flash the blue barrel of his rifle gleamed level and he shot once—twice.

The foremost rustler dropped his weapon and toppled from his saddle, to fall with his foot catching in a stirrup. The horse snorted wildly and plunged away, dragging the rustler through the sage.

The Masked Rider huddled over his pommel, slowly swaying to one side, and then, with a faint, strange cry, slipped out of the saddle.

CHAPTER FIVE
The Masked Rider

Venters looked quickly from the fallen rustlers to the cañon where the others had disappeared. He calculated on the time needed for running horses to return to the open, if their riders heard shots. He waited breathlessly. But the estimated time dragged by and no riders appeared. Venters began presently to believe that the rifle report had not penetrated into the recesses of the cañon, and felt safe for the immediate present.

He hurried to the spot where the first rustler had been dragged by his horse. The man lay in deep grass, dead, jaw fallen, eyes protruding—a sight that sickened Venters. The first man at whom he had ever aimed a weapon he had shot through the heart. With the clammy sweat oozing from every pore Venters dragged the rustler in among some boulders and covered him with slabs of rock. Then he smoothed out the crushed trail in grass and sage. The rustler's horse had stopped a quarter of a mile off and was grazing.

When Venters rapidly strode toward the Masked Rider not even the cold nausea that gripped him could wholly banish curiosity. For he had shot Oldring's infamous lieutenant, whose face had never been seen. Venters experienced a grim pride in the feat. What would Tull say to this achievement of the outcast who rode too often to Deception Pass?

Venters's curious eagerness and expectation had not prepared him for the shock he received when he stood over a slight, dark figure. The rustler wore the black mask that had given him his name, but he had no weapons. Venters glanced at the drooping horse; there were no gun-sheaths on the saddle.

'A rustler who didn't pack guns!' muttered Venters. 'He wears no belt. He couldn't pack guns in that rig . ... Strange!'

A low, gasping intake of breath and a sudden twitching of body told Venters the rider still lived.

'He's alive! ... I've got to stand here and watch him die. And I shot an unarmed man.'

Shrinkingly Venters removed the rider's wide sombrero and the black cloth mask. This action disclosed bright chestnut hair, inclined to curl, and a white, youthful face. Along the lower line of cheek and jaw was a clear demarcation, where the brown of tanned skin met the white that had been hidden from the sun.

'Oh, he's only a boy! ... What! Can he be Oldring's Masked Rider?'

The boy showed signs of returning consciousness. He stirred; his lips moved; a small brown hand clenched in his blouse.

Venters knelt with a gathering horror of his deed. His bullet had entered the rider's right breast, high up to the shoulder. With hands that shook, Venters untied a black scarf and ripped open the blood-wet blouse.

First he saw a gaping hole, dark red against a whiteness of skin, from which welled a slender red stream. Then the graceful, beautiful swell of a woman's breast!

'A woman!' he cried. 'A girl! ... I've killed a girl!'

She suddenly opened her eyes that transfixed Venters. They were fathomless blue. Consciousness of death was there, a blended terror and pain, but no consciousness of sight. She did not see Venters. She stared into the unknown.

Then came a spasm of vitality. She writhed in a torture of reviving strength, and in her convulsions she almost tore from Venter's grasp. Slowly she relaxed and sank partly back. The ungloved hand sought the wound, and pressed so hard that her wrist half buried itself in her bosom. Blood trickled between her spread fingers. And she looked at Venters with eyes that saw him.

He cursed himself and the unerring aim of which he had been so proud. He had seen that look in the eyes of a crippled antelope which he was about to finish with his knife. But in her it had infinitely more—a revelation of mortal spirit. The instinctive clinging to life was there, and the driving helplessness and the terrible accusation of the stricken.

'Forgive me! I didn't know!' burst out Venters.

'You shot me—you've killed me!' she whispered, in panting gasps. Upon her lips appeared a fluttering, bloody froth. By that Venters knew the air in her lungs was mixing with blood. 'Oh, I knew—it would—come—some day! ... Oh, the burn! ... Hold me—I'm sinking—it's all dark. ... Ah, God! ... Mercy—'

Her rigidity loosened in one long quiver and she lay back limp, still, white as snow, with closed eyes.

Venters thought then that she died. But the faint pulsation of her breast assured him that life yet lingered. Death seemed only a matter of moments, for the bullet had gone clear through her. Nevertheless, he tore sage-leaves from a bush, and, pressing them tightly over her wounds, he bound the black scarf round her shoulder, tying it securely under her arm. Then he closed the blouse, hiding from his sight that blood-stained, accusing breast.

'What—now?' he questioned, with flying mind. 'I must get out of here. She's dying—but I can't leave her.'

He rapidly surveyed the sage to the north and made out no animate object. Then he picked up the girl's sombrero and mask. This time the mask gave him as great a shock as when he first removed it from her face. For in the woman he had forgotten the rustler, and this black strip of felt-cloth established the identity of Oldring's Masked Rider. Venters had solved the mystery. He slipped his rifle under her, and, lifting her carefully upon it, he began to retrace his steps. The dog trailed in his shadow. And the horse, that had stood drooping by, followed without a call. Venters chose the deepest tufts of grass and clumps of sage on his return. From time to time he glanced over his shoulder. He did not rest. His concern was to avoid jarring the girl and to hide his trail. Gaining the narrow cañon, he turned and held close to the wall till he reached his hiding-place. When he entered the dense thicket of oaks he was hard put to it to force a way through. But he held his burden almost upright, and by slipping sidewise and bending the saplings he got in. Through sage and grass he hurried to the grove of silver spruces.

He laid the girl down, almost fearing to look at her. Though marble pale and cold, she was living. Venters then appreciated the tax that long carry had been to his strength. He sat down to rest. Whitie sniffed at the pale girl and whined and crept to Venters's feet. Ring lapped the water in the runway of the spring.

Presently Venters went out to the opening, caught the horse, and, leading him through the thicket, unsaddled him and tied him with a long halter. Wrangle left his browsing long enough to whinny and toss his head. Venters felt that he could not rest easily till he had secured the other rustler's horse; so, taking his rifle and calling for Ring, he set out. Swiftly yet watchfully he made his way through the cañon to the oval and out to the cattle trail. What few tracks might have betrayed him he obliterated, so only an expert tracker could have trailed him. Then, with many a wary backward glance across the sage, he started to round up the rustler's horse. This was unexpectedly easy. He led the horse to lower ground, out of sight from the opposite side of the oval, along the shadowy western wall, and so on into his cañon and secluded camp.

The girl's eyes were open; a feverish spot burned in her cheeks; she moaned something unintelligible to Venters, but he took the movement of her lips to mean that she wanted water. Lifting her head, he tipped the canteen to her lips. After that she again lapsed into unconsciousness or a weakness which was its counterpart. Venters noted, however, that the burning flush had faded into the former pallor.

The sun set behind the high cañon rim, and a cool shade darkened the walls. Venters fed the dogs and put a halter on the dead rustler's horse. He allowed Wrangle to browse free. This done, he cut spruce boughs and made a lean-to for the girl. Then, gently lifting her upon a blanket, he folded the sides over her. The other blanket he wrapped about his shoulders and found a comfortable seat against a spruce-tree that upheld the little shack. Ring and Whitie lay near at hand, one asleep, the other watchful.

Venters dreaded the night's vigil. At night his mind was active, and this time he had to watch and think and feel beside a dying girl whom he had all but murdered. A thousand excuses he invented for himself, yet not one made any difference in his act or his self-reproach.

It seemed to him that when night fell black he could see her white face so much more plainly.

'She'll go, presently,' he said, 'and be out of agony—thank God!'

Every little while certainty of her death came to him with a shock; and then he would bend over and lay his ear on her breast. Her heart still beat.

The early night blackness cleared to the cold starlight. The horses were not moving, and no sound disturbed the deathly silence of the cañon.

'I'll bury her here,' thought Venters, 'and let her grave be as much a mystery as her life was.'

For the girl's few words, the look of her eyes, the prayer, had strangely touched Venters.

'She was only a girl,' he soliloquized. 'What was she to Oldring? Rustlers don't have wives nor sisters nor daughters. She was bad—that's all. But somehow... well, she may not have willingly become the companion of rustlers. That prayer of hers to God for mercy! ... Life is strange and cruel. I wonder if other members of Oldring's gang are women? Likely enough. But what was his game? Oldring's Masked Rider! A name to make villagers hide and lock their doors. A name credited with a dozen murders, a hundred forays, and a thousand stealings of cattle. What part did the girl have in this? It may have served Oldring to create mystery.'

Hours passed. The white stars moved across the narrow strip of dark-blue sky above. The silence awoke to the low hum of insects. Venters watched the immovable white face, and as he watched, hour by hour waiting for death, the infamy of her passed from his mind. He thought only of the sadness, the truth of the moment. Whoever she was—whatever she had done—she was young and she was dying.

The after-part of the night wore on interminably. The starlight failed and the gloom blackened to the darkest hour. 'She'll die at the gray of dawn,' muttered Venters, remembering some old woman's fancy. The blackness paled to gray, and the gray lightened and day peeped over the eastern rim. Venters listened at the breast of the girl. She still lived. Did he only imagine that her heart beat stronger, ever so slightly, but stronger? He pressed his ear closer to her breast. And he rose with his own pulse quickening.

'If she doesn't die soon—she's got a chance—the barest chance—to live,' he said.

He wondered if the internal bleeding had ceased. There was no more film of blood upon her lips. But no corpse could have been whiter. Opening her blouse, he untied the scarf, and carefully picked away the sage-leaves from the wound in her shoulder. It had closed. Lifting her lightly, he ascertained that the same was true of the hole where the bullet had come out. He reflected on the fact that clean wounds closed quickly in the healing upland air. He recalled instances of riders who had been cut and shot, apparently to fatal issues; yet the blood had clotted, the wounds closed, and they had recovered. He had no way to tell if internal hemorrhage still went on, but he believed that it had stopped. Otherwise she would surely not have lived so long. He marked the entrance of the bullet and concluded that it had just touched the upper lobe of her lung. Perhaps the wound in the lung had also closed. As he began to wash the blood stains from her breast and carefully rebandage the wound, he was vaguely conscious of a strange, grave happiness in the thought that she might live.

Broad daylight and a hint of sunshine high on the cliff-rim to the west brought him to consideration of what he had better do. And while busy with his few camp tasks he revolved the thing in his mind. It would not be wise for him to remain long in his present hiding place. And if he intended to follow the cattle trail and try to find the rustlers he had better make a move at once. For he knew that rustlers, being riders, would not make much of a day's or night's absence from camp for one or two of their number; but when the missing ones failed to show up in reasonable time there would be a search. And Venters was afraid of that.

'A good tracker could trail me,' he muttered. 'And I'd be cornered here. Let's see. Rustlers are a lazy set when they're not on the ride. I'll risk it. Then I'll change my hiding-place.'

He carefully cleaned and reloaded his guns. When he rose to go he bent a long glance down upon the unconscious girl. Then, ordering Whitie and Ring to keep guard, he left the camp.

The safest cover lay close under the wall of the cañon, and here through the dense thickets Venters made his slow, listening advance toward the oval. Upon gaining the wide opening he decided to cross it and follow the left wall till he came to the cattle trail. He scanned the oval as keenly as if hunting for antelope. Then, stooping, he stole from one cover to another, taking advantage of rocks and bunches of sage, until he had reached the thickets under the opposite wall. Once there, he exercised extreme caution in his surveys of the ground ahead, but increased his speed when moving. Dodging from bush to bush, he passed the mouths of two cañons, and in the entrance of a third cañon he crossed a wash of swift, clear water, to come abruptly upon the cattle trail.

It followed the low bank of the wash, and, keeping it in sight, Venters hugged the line of sage and thicket. Like the curves of a serpent, the cañon wound for a mile or more and then opened into a valley. Patches of red showed clear against the purple of sage, and farther out on the level dotted strings of red led away to the wall of rock.

'Ha, the red herd!' exclaimed Venters.

Then dots of white and black told him there were cattle of other colors in this enclosed valley. Oldring, the rustler, was also a rancher. Venters's calculating eye took count of stock that outnumbered the red herd.

'What a range!' went on Venters. 'Water and grass enough for fifty thousand head, and no riders needed!'

After his first burst of surprise and rapid calculation Venters lost no time there, but slunk again into the sage on his back trail. With the discovery of Oldring's hidden cattle-range had come enlightenment on several problems. Here the rustler kept his stock; here was Jane Withersteen's red herd; here were the few cattle that had disappeared from the Cottonwoods slopes during the last two years. Until Oldring had driven the red herd his thefts of cattle for that time had not been more than enough to supply meat for his men. Of late no drives had been reported from Sterling or the villages north. And Venters knew that the riders had wondered at Oldring's inactivity in that particular field. He and his band had been active enough in their visits to Glaze and Cottonwoods; they always had gold; but of late the amount gambled away and drunk and thrown away in the villages had given rise to much conjecture. Oldring's more frequent visits had resulted in new saloons, and where there had formerly been one raid or shooting fray in the little hamlets there were now many. Perhaps Oldring had another range farther on up the pass, and from there drove the cattle to distant Utah towns where he was little known. But Venters came finally to doubt this. And, from what he had learned in the last few days, a belief began to form in Venters's mind that Oldring's intimidations of the villages and the mystery of the Masked Rider, with his alleged evil deeds, and the fierce resistance offered any trailing riders, and the rustling of cattle—these things were only the craft of the rustler-chief to conceal his real life and purpose and work in Deception Pass.

And like a scouting Indian Venters crawled through the sage of the oval valley, crossed trail after trail on the north side, and at last entered the cañon out of which headed the cattle trail, and into which he had watched the rustlers disappear.

If he had used caution before, now he strained every nerve to force himself to creeping stealth and to sensitiveness of ear. He crawled along so hidden that he could not use his eyes except to aid himself in the toilsome progress through the brakes and ruins of cliff-wall. Yet from time to time, as he rested, he saw the massive red walls growing higher and wilder, more looming and broken. He made note of the fact that he was turning and climbing. The sage and thickets of oak and brakes of alder gave place to piñon pine growing out of rocky soil. Suddenly a low, dull murmur assailed his ears. At first he thought it was thunder, then the slipping of a weathered slope of rock. But it was incessant, and as he progressed it filled out deeper and from a murmur changed into a soft roar.

'Falling water,' he said. 'There's volume to that. I wonder if it's the stream I lost.'

The roar bothered him, for he could hear nothing else. Likewise, however, no rustlers could hear him. Emboldened by this, and sure that nothing but a bird could see him, he arose from his hands and knees to hurry on. An opening in the piñons warned him that he was nearing the height of slope.

He gained it, and dropped low with a burst of astonishment. Before him stretched a short cañon with rounded stone floor bare of grass or sage or tree, and with curved, shelving walls. A broad rippling stream flowed toward him, and at the back of the cañon a waterfall burst from a wide rent in the cliff, and, bounding down in two green steps, spread into a long white sheet.

If Venters had not been indubitably certain that he had entered the right cañon his astonishment would not have been so great. There had been no breaks in the walls, no side cañons entering this one where the rustlers' tracks and the cattle trail had guided him, and, therefore, he could not be wrong. But here the cañon ended, and presumably the trails also.

'That cattle trail headed out of here,' Venters kept saying to himself. 'It headed out. Now what I want to know is how on earth did cattle ever get in here?'

If he could be sure of anything it was of the careful scrutiny he had given that cattle track, every hoofmark of which headed straight west. He was now looking east at an immense round boxed corner of cañon down which tumbled a thin, white veil of water, scarcely twenty yards wide. Somehow, somewhere, his calculations had gone wrong. For the first time in years he found himself doubting his rider's skill in finding tracks, and his memory of what he had actually seen. In his anxiety to keep under cover he must have lost himself in this offshoot of Deception Pass, and thereby, in some unaccountable manner, missed the cañon with the trails. There was nothing else for him to think. Rustlers could not fly, nor cattle jump down thousand-foot precipices. He was only proving what the sage-riders had long said of this labyrinthine system of deceitful cañons and valleys—trails led down into Deception Pass, but no rider had ever followed them.

On a sudden he heard above the soft roar of the waterfall an unusual sound that he could not define. He dropped flat behind a stone and listened. From the direction he had come swelled something that resembled a strange muffled pounding and splashing and ringing. Despite his nerve the chill sweat began to dampen his forehead. What might not be possible in this stone-walled maze of mystery? The unnatural sound passed beyond him as he lay gripping his rifle and fighting for coolness. Then from the open came the sound, now distinct and different. Venters recognized a hobble-bell of a horse, and the cracking of iron on submerged stones, and the hollow splash of hoofs in water.

Relief surged over him. His mind caught again at realities, and curiosity prompted him to peep from behind the rock.

In the middle of the stream waded a long string of packed burros driven by three superbly mounted men. Had Venters met these dark-clothed, dark-visaged, heavily armed men anywhere in Utah, let alone in this robbers' retreat, he would have recognized them as rustlers. The discerning eye of a rider saw the signs of a long, arduous trip. These men were packing in supplies from one of the northern villages. They were tired, and their horses were almost played out, and the burros plodded on, after the manner of their kind when exhausted, faithful and patient, but as if every weary, splashing, slipping step would be their last.

All this Venters noted in one glance. After that he watched with a thrilling eagerness. Straight at the waterfall the rustlers drove the burros, and straight through the middle, where the water spread into a fleecy, thin film like dissolving smoke. Following closely, the rustlers rode into this white mist, showing in bold black relief for an instant, and then they vanished.

Venters drew a full breath that rushed out in brief and sudden utterance.

'Good Heaven! Of all the holes for a rustler! … There's a cavern under that waterfall, and a passageway leading out to a cañon beyond. Oldring hides in there. He needs only to guard a trail leading down from the sage-flat above. Little danger of this outlet to the pass being discovered. I stumbled on it by luck, after I had given up. And now I know the truth of what puzzled me most—why that cattle trail was wet!'

He wheeled and ran down the slope, and out to the level of the sage-brush. Returning, he had no time to spare, only now and then, between dashes, a moment when he stopped to cast sharp eyes ahead. The abundant grass left no trace of his trail. Short work he made of the distance to the circle of cañons. He doubted that he would ever see it again; he knew he never wanted to; yet he looked at the red corners and towers with the eyes of a rider picturing landmarks never to be forgotten.

Here he spent a panting moment in a slow-circling gaze of the sage-oval and the gaps between the bluffs. Nothing stirred except the gentle wave of the tips of the brush. Then he pressed on past the mouths of several cañons and over ground new to him, now close under the eastern wall. This latter part proved to be easy traveling, well screened from possible observation from the north and west, and he soon covered it and felt safer in the deepening shade of his own cañon. Then the huge, notched bulge of red rim loomed over him, a mark by which he knew again the deep cove where his camp lay hidden. As he penetrated the thicket, safe again for the present, his thoughts reverted to the girl he had left there. The afternoon had far advanced. How would he find her? He ran into camp, frightening the dogs.

The girl lay with wide-open, dark eyes, and they dilated when he knelt beside her. The flush of fever shone in her cheeks. He lifted her and held water to her dry lips, and felt an inexplicable sense of lightness as he saw her swallow in a slow, choking gulp. Gently he laid her back.

'Who—are—you?' she whispered, haltingly.

'I'm the man who shot you,' he replied.

'You'll—not—kill me—now?'

'No, no.'

'What—will—you—do—with me?'

'When you get better—strong enough—I'll take you back to the cañon where the rustlers ride through the waterfall.'

As with a faint shadow from a flitting wing overhead, the marble whiteness of her face seemed to change.

'Don't—take—me—back—there!'

CHAPTER SIX
The Mill-Wheel of Steers

Meantime, at the ranch, when Judkins's news had sent Venters on the trail of the rustlers, Jane Withersteen led the injured man to her house and with skilled fingers dressed the gunshot wound in his arm.

'Judkins, what do you think happened to my riders?'

'I—I'd rather not say,' he replied.

'Tell me. Whatever you'll tell me I'll keep to myself. I'm beginning to worry about more than the loss of a herd of cattle. Venters hinted of—but tell me, Judkins.'

'Well, Miss Withersteen, I think as Venters thinks—your riders have been called in.'

'Judkins! ... By whom?'

'You know who handles the reins of your Mormon riders.'

'Do you dare insinuate that my churchmen have ordered in my riders?'

'I ain't insinuatin' nothin', Miss Withersteen,' answered Judkins, with spirit.

'I know what I'm talking about. I didn't want to tell you.'

'Oh, I can't believe that! I'll not believe it! Would Tull leave my herds at the mercy of rustlers and wolves just because—because—? No, no! It's unbelievable.'

'Yes, thet particular thing's onheard of around Cottonwoods. But, beggin' pardon, Miss Withersteen, there never was any other rich Mormon woman here on the border, let alone one thet's taken the bit between her teeth.'

That was a bold thing for the reserved Judkins to say, but it did not anger her. This rider's crude hint of her spirit gave her a glimpse of what others might think. Humility and obedience had been hers always. But had she taken the bit between her teeth? Still she wavered. And then, with a quick spurt of warm blood along her veins, she thought of Black Star when he got the bit fast between his iron jaws and ran wild in the sage. If she ever started to run! Jane smothered the glow and burn within her, ashamed of a passion for freedom that opposed her duty.

'Judkins, go to the village,' she said, 'and when you have learned anything definite about my riders please come to me at once.'

When he had gone Jane resolutely applied her mind to a number of tasks that of late had been neglected. Her father had trained her in the management of a hundred employees and the working of gardens and fields; and to keep record of the movement of cattle and riders. And beside the many duties she had added to this work was one of extreme delicacy, such as required all her tact and ingenuity. It was an unobtrusive, almost secret aid which she rendered to the Gentile families of the village. Though Jane Withersteen never admitted so to herself, it amounted to no less than a system of charity. But for her invention of numberless kinds of employment, for which there was no actual need, these families of Gentiles, who had failed in a Mormon community, would have starved.

In aiding these poor people Jane thought she deceived her keen churchmen, but it was a kind of deceit for which she did not pray to be forgiven. Equally as difficult was the task of deceiving the Gentiles, for they were as proud as they were poor. It had been a great grief to her to discover how these people hated her people; and it had been a source of great joy that through her they had come to soften in hatred. At any time this work called for a clearness of mind that precluded anxiety and worry; but under the present circumstances it required all her vigor and obstinate tenacity to pin her attention upon her task.

Sunset came, bringing with the end of her labor a patient calmness and power to wait that had not been hers earlier in the day. She expected Judkins, but he did not appear. Her house was always quiet; tonight, however, it seemed unusually so. At supper her women served her with a silent assiduity; it spoke what their sealed lips could not utter—the sympathy of Mormon women. Jerd came to her with the key of the great door of the stone stable, and to make his daily report about the horses. One of his daily duties was to give Black Star and Night and the other racers a ten-mile run. This day it had been omitted, and the boy grew confused in explanations that she had not asked for. She did inquire if he would return on the morrow, and Jerd, in mingled surprise and relief, assured her he would always work for her. Jane missed the rattle and trot, canter and gallop of the incoming riders on the hard trails. Dusk shaded the grove where she walked; the birds ceased singing; the wind sighed through the leaves of the cottonwoods, and the running water murmured down its stone-bedded channel. The glimmering of the first star was like the peace and beauty of the night. Her faith welled up in her heart and said that all would soon be right in her little world. She pictured Venters about his lonely camp-fire sitting between his faithful dogs. She prayed for his safety, for the success of his undertaking.

Early the next morning one of Jane's women brought in word that Judkins wished to speak to her. She hurried out, and in her surprise to see him armed with rifle and revolver, she forgot her intention to inquire about his wound.

'Judkins! Those guns? You never carried guns.'

'It's high time, Miss Withersteen,' he replied. 'Will you come into the grove? It ain't jest exactly safe for me to be seen here.'

She walked with him into the shade of the cottonwoods.

'What do you mean?'

'Miss Withersteen, I went to my mother's house last night. While there, someone knocked, an' a man asked for me. I went to the door. He wore a mask. He said I'd better not ride any more for Jane Withersteen. His voice was hoarse an' strange, disguised, I reckon, like his face. He said no more, an' ran off in the dark.'

'Did you know who he was?' asked Jane, in a low voice.

'Yes.'

Jane did not ask to know; she did not want to know; she feared to know. All her calmness fled at a single thought.

'Thet's why I'm packin' guns,' went on Judkins. 'For I'll never quit ridin' for you, Miss Withersteen, till you let me go.'

'Judkins, do you want to leave me?'

'Do I look thet way? Give me a hoss—a fast hoss, an' send me out on the sage.'

'Oh, thank you, Judkins! You're more faithful than my own people. I ought not accept your loyalty—you might suffer more through it. But what in the world can I do? My head whirls. The wrong to Venters—the stolen herd—these masks, threats, this coil in the dark! I can't understand! But I feel something dark and terrible closing in around me.'

'Miss Withersteen, it's all simple enough,' said Judkins, earnestly. 'Now please listen—an' beggin' your pardon—jest turn thet deaf Mormon ear aside, an' let me talk clear an' plain in the other. I went around to the saloons an' the stores an' the loafin' places yesterday. All your riders are in. There's talk of a vigilance band organized to hunt down rustlers. They call themselves "The Riders." Thet's the report—thet's the reason given for your riders leavin' you. Strange thet only a few riders of other ranchers joined the band! An' Tull's man, Jerry Card—he's the leader. I seen him an' his hoss. He ain't been to Glaze. I'm not easy to fool on the looks of a hoss thet's traveled the sage. Tull an' Jerry didn't ride to Glaze! ... Well, I met Blake an' Dorn, both good friends of mine, usually, as far as their Mormon lights will let 'em go. But these fellers couldn't fool me, an' they didn't try very hard. I asked them, straight out like a man, why they left you like thet. I didn't forget to mention how you nursed Blake's poor old mother when she was sick, an' how good you was to Dorn's kids. They looked ashamed, Miss Withersteen. An' they jest froze up—thet dark set look thet makes them strange an' different to me. But I could tell the difference between thet first natural twinge of conscience an' the later look of some secret thing. An' the difference I caught was thet they couldn't help themselves. They hadn't no say in the matter. They looked as if their bein' unfaithful to you was bein' faithful to a higher duty. An' there's the secret. Why, it's as plain as—as sight of my gun here.'

'Plain! ... My herds to wander in the sage—to be stolen! Jane Withersteen a poor woman! Her head to be brought low and her spirit broken! ... Why, Judkins, it's plain enough.'

'Miss Withersteen, let me get what boys I can gather, an' hold the white herd. It's on the slope now, not ten miles out—three thousand head, an' all steers. They're wild, an' likely to stampede at the pop of a jack-rabbit's ears. We'll camp right with them, an' try to hold them.'

'Judkins, I'll reward you some day for your service, unless all is taken from me. Get the boys and tell Jerd to give you pick of my horses, except Black Star and Night. But—do not shed blood for my cattle nor heedlessly risk your lives.'

Jane Withersteen rushed to the silence and seclusion of her room, and there could no longer hold back the bursting of her wrath. She went stone-blind in the fury of a passion that had never before showed its power. Lying upon her bed, sightless, voiceless, she was a writhing, living flame. And she tossed there while her fury burned and burned, and finally burned itself out.

Then, weak and spent, she lay thinking, not of the oppression that would break her, but of this new revelation of self. Until the last few days there had been little in her life to rouse passions. Her forefathers had been Vikings, savage chieftains who bore no cross and brooked no hindrance to their will. Her father had inherited that temper; and at times, like antelope fleeing before fire on the slope, his people fled from his red rages. Jane Withersteen realized that the spirit of wrath and war had lain dormant in her. She shrank from black depths hitherto unsuspected. The one thing in man or woman that she scorned above all scorn, and which she could not forgive, was hate. Hate headed a flaming pathway straight to hell. All in a flash, beyond her control there had been in her a birth of fiery hate. And the man who had dragged her peaceful and loving spirit to this degradation was a minister of God's word, an Elder of her church, the counselor of her beloved Bishop.

The loss of herds and ranges, even of Amber Spring and the Old Stone House, no longer concerned Jane Withersteen; she faced the foremost thought of her life, what she now considered the mightiest problem—the salvation of her soul.

She knelt by her bedside and prayed; she prayed as she had never prayed in all her life—prayed to be forgiven for her sin; to be immune from that dark, hot hate; to love Tull as her minister, though she could not love him as a man; to do her duty by her church and people and those dependent upon her bounty; to hold reverence of God and womanhood inviolate.

When Jane Withersteen rose from that storm of wrath and prayer for help she was serene, calm, sure—a changed woman. She would do her duty as she saw it, live her life as her own truth guided her. She might never be able to marry a man of her choice, but she certainly never would become the wife of Tull. Her churchmen might take her cattle and horses, ranges and fields, her corrals and stables, the house of Withersteen and the water that nourished the village of Cottonwoods; but they could not force her to marry Tull, they could not change her decision or break her spirit. Once resigned to further loss, and sure of herself, Jane Withersteen attained a peace of mind that had not been hers for a year. She forgave Tull, and felt a melancholy regret over what she knew he considered duty, irrespective of his personal feeling for her. First of all, Tull, as he was a man, wanted her for himself; and secondly, he hoped to save her and her riches for his church. She did not believe that Tull had been actuated solely by his minister's zeal to save her soul. She doubted her interpretation of one of his dark sayings— that if she were lost to him she might as well be lost to heaven. Jane Withersteen's common sense took arms against the binding limits of her religion; and she doubted that her Bishop, whom she had been taught had direct communication with God—would damn her soul for refusing to marry a Mormon. As for Tull and his churchmen, when they had harassed her, perhaps made her poor, they would find her unchangeable, and then she would get back most of what she had lost. So she reasoned, true at last to her faith in all men, and in their ultimate goodness.

The clank of iron hoofs upon the stone courtyard drew her hurriedly from her retirement. There, beside his horse, stood Lassiter, his dark apparel and the great black gun-sheaths contrasting singularly with his gentle smile. Jane's active mind took up her interest in him and her half-determined desire to use what charm she had to foil his evident design in visiting Cottonwoods. If she could mitigate his hatred of Mormons, or at least keep him from killing more of them, not only would she be saving her people, but also be leading back this blood-spiller to some semblance of the human.

'Mornin', ma'am,' he said, black sombrero in hand.

'Lassiter, I'm not an old woman, or even a madam,' she replied, with her bright smile. 'If you can't say Miss Withersteen—call me Jane.'

'I reckon Jane would be easier. First names are always handy for me.'

'Well, use mine, then. Lassiter, I'm glad to see you. I'm in trouble.'

Then she told him of Judkins's return, of the driving of the red herd, of Venters's departure on Wrangle, and the calling-in of her riders.

'"Pears to me you're some smilin' an' pretty for a woman with so much trouble,' he remarked.

'Lassiter! Are you paying me compliments? But, seriously, I've made up my mind not to be miserable. I've lost much, and I'll lose more. Nevertheless, I won't be sour, and I hope I'll never be unhappy—again.'

Lassiter twisted his hat round and round, as was his way, and took his time in replying.

'Women are strange to me. I got to back-trailin' myself from them long ago. But I'd like a game woman. Might I ask, seein' as how you take this trouble, if you're goin' to fight?'

'Fight! How? Even if I would, I haven't a friend except that boy who doesn't dare stay in the village.'

'I make bold to say, ma'am—Jane—that there's another, if you want him.'

'Lassiter! ... Thank you. But how can I accept you as a friend? Think! Why, you'd ride down into the village with those terrible guns and kill my enemies—who are also my churchmen.'

'I reckon I might be riled up to jest about that,' he replied, dryly.

She held out both hands to him.

'Lassiter! I'll accept your friendship—be proud of it—return it—if I may keep you from killing another Mormon.'

'I'll tell you one thing,' he said bluntly, as the gray lightning formed in his eyes. 'You're too good a woman to be sacrificed as you're goin' to be. ... No, I reckon you an' me can't be friends on such terms.'

In her earnestness she stepped closer to him, repelled yet fascinated by the sudden transition of his moods. That he would fight for her was at once horrible and wonderful.

'You came here to kill a man—the man whom Milly Erne—'

'The man who dragged Milly Erne to hell—put it that way! ... Jane Withersteen, yes, that's why I came here. I'd tell so much to no other livin' soul. ... There're things such a woman as you'd never dream of—so don't mention her again. Not till you tell me the name of the man!'

'Tell you! I? Never!'

'I reckon you will. An' I'll never ask you. I'm a man of strange beliefs an' ways of thinkin', an' I seem to see into the future an' feel things hard to explain. The trail I've been followin' for so many years was twisted an' tangled, but it's straightenin' out now. An', Jane Withersteen, you crossed it long ago to ease poor Milly's agony. That, whether you want or not, makes Lassiter your friend. But you cross it now strangely to mean somethin' to me—God knows what!—unless by your noble blindness to incite me to greater hatred of Mormon men.'

Jane felt swayed by a strength that far exceeded her own. In a clash of wills with this man she would go to the wall. If she were to influence him it must be wholly through womanly allurement. There was that about Lassiter which commanded her respect; she had abhorred his name; face to face with him, she found she feared only his deeds. His mystic suggestion, his foreshadowing of something that she was to mean to him, pierced deep into her mind. She believed fate had thrown in her way the lover or husband of Milly Erne. She believed that through her an evil man might be reclaimed. His allusion to what he called her blindness terrified her. Such a mistaken idea of his might unleash the bitter, fatal mood she sensed in him. At any cost she must placate this man; she knew the die was cast, and that if Lassiter did not soften to a woman's grace and beauty and wiles, then it would be because she could not make him.

'I reckon you'll hear no more such talk from me,' Lassiter went on, presently. 'Now, Miss Jane, I rode in to tell you that your herd of white steers is down on the slope behind them big ridges. An' I seen somethin' goin' on that'd be mighty interestin' to you, if you could see it. Have you a field-glass?'

'Yes, I have two glasses. I'll get them and ride out with you. Wait, Lassiter, please,' she said, and hurried within. Sending word to Jerd to saddle Black Star and fetch him to the court, she then went to her room and changed to the riding-clothes she always donned when going into the sage. In this male attire her mirror showed her a jaunty, handsome rider. If she expected some little meed of admiration from Lassiter, she had no cause for disappointment. The gentle smile that she liked, which made of him another person, slowly overspread his face.

'If I didn't take you for a boy!' he exclaimed. 'It's powerful queer what difference clothes make. Now I've been some scared of your dignity, like when the other night you was all in white, but in this rig—'

Black Star came pounding into the court, dragging Jerd half off his feet, and he whistled at Lassiter's black. But at sight of Jane all his defiant lines seemed to soften, and with tosses of his beautiful head he whipped his bridle.

'Down, Black Star, down,' said Jane.

He dropped his head, and, slowly lengthening, he bent one foreleg, then the other, and sank to his knees. Jane slipped her left foot in the stirrup, swung lightly into the saddle, and Black Star rose with a ringing stamp. It was not easy for Jane to hold him to a canter through the grove, and like the wind he broke when he saw the sage. Jane let him have a couple of miles of free running on the open trail, and then she coaxed him in and waited for her companion. Lassiter was not long in catching up, and presently they were riding side by side. It reminded her how she used to ride with Venters. Where was he now? She gazed far down the slope to the curved purple lines of Deception Pass, and involuntarily shut her eyes with a trembling stir of nameless fear.

'We'll turn off here,' Lassiter said, 'an' take to the sage a mile or so. The white herd is behind them big ridges.'

'What are you going to show me?' asked Jane. 'I'm prepared—don't be afraid.'

He smiled as if he meant that bad news came swiftly enough without being presaged by speech.

When they reached the lee of a rolling ridge Lassiter dismounted, motioning to her to do likewise. They left the horses standing, bridles down. Then Lassiter, carrying the field glasses, began to lead the way up the slow rise of ground. Upon nearing the summit he halted her with a gesture.

'I reckon we'd see more if we didn't show ourselves against the sky,' he said. 'I was here less than an hour ago. Then the herd was seven or eight miles south, an' if they ain't bolted yet—'

'Lassiter! ... Bolted?'

'That's what I said. Now let's see.'

Jane climbed a few more paces behind him and then peeped over the ridge. Just beyond began a shallow swale that deepened and widened into a valley and then swung to the left. Following the undulating sweep of sage, Jane saw the straggling lines and then the great body of the white herd. She knew enough about steers, even at a distance of four or five miles, to realize that something was in the wind. Bringing her field-glass into use, she moved it slowly from left to right, which action swept the whole herd into range. The stragglers were restless; the more compactly massed steers were browsing. Jane brought the glass back to the big sentinels of the herd, and she saw them trot with quick steps, stop short and toss wide horns, look everywhere, and then trot in another direction.

'Judkins hasn't been able to get his boys together yet,' said Jane. 'But he'll be there soon. I hope not too late. Lassiter, what's frightening those big leaders?'

'Nothin' jest on the minute,' replied Lassiter. 'Them steers are quietin' down. They've been scared, but not bad yet. I reckon the whole herd has moved a few miles this way since I was here.'

'They didn't browse that distance—not in less than an hour. Cattle aren't sheep.'

'No, they jest run it, an' that looks bad.'

'Lassiter, what frightened them?' repeated Jane, impatiently.

'Put down your glass. You'll see at first better with a naked eye. Now look along them ridges on the other side of the herd, the ridges where the sun shines bright on the sage . … . That's right. Now look an' look hard an' wait.'

Long-drawn moments of straining sight rewarded Jane with nothing save the low, purple rim of ridge and the shimmering sage.

'It's begun again!' whispered Lassiter, and he gripped her arm. 'Watch. … There, did you see that?'

'No, no. Tell me what to look for?'

'A white flash—a kind of pin-point of quick light—a gleam as from sun shinin' on somethin' white.'

Suddenly Jane's concentrated gaze caught a fleeting glint. Quickly she brought her glass to bear on the spot. Again the purple sage, magnified in color and size and wave, for long moments irritated her with its monotony. Then from out of the sage on the ridge flew up a broad, white object, flashed in the sunlight and vanished. Like magic it was, and bewildered Jane.

'What on earth is that?'

'I reckon there's someone behind that ridge throwin' up a sheet or a white blanket to reflect the sunshine.'

'Why?' queried Jane, more bewildered than ever.

'To stampede the herd,' replied Lassiter, and his teeth clicked.

'Ah!' She made a fierce, passionate movement, clutched the glass tightly, shook as with the passing of a spasm, and then dropped her head. Presently she raised it to greet Lassiter with something like a smile. 'My righteous brethren are at work again,' she said, in scorn. She had stifled the leap of her wrath, but for perhaps the first time in her life a bitter derision curled her lips. Lassiter's cool gray eyes seemed to pierce her. 'I said I was prepared for anything; but that was hardly true. But why would they—anybody stampede my cattle?'

'That's a Mormon's godly way of bringin' a woman to her knees.'

'Lassiter, I'll die before I ever bend my knees. I might be led; I won't be driven. Do you expect the herd to bolt?'

'I don't like the looks of them big steers. But you can never tell. Cattle sometimes stampede as easily as buffalo. Any little flash or move will start them. A rider gettin' down an' walkin' toward them sometimes will make them jump an' fly. Then again nothin' seems to scare them. But I reckon that white flare will do the biz. It's a new one on me, an' I've seen some ridin' an' rustlin'. It jest takes one of them God-fearin' Mormons to think of devilish tricks.'

'Lassiter, might not this trick be done by Oldring's men?' asked Jane, ever grasping at straws.

'It might be, but it ain't,' replied Lassiter. 'Oldrin's an honest thief. He don't skulk behind ridges to scatter your cattle to the four winds. He rides down on you, an' if you don't like it you can throw a gun.'

Jane bit her tongue to refrain from championing men who at the very moment were proving to her that they were little and mean compared even with rustlers.

'Look! ... Jane, them leadin' steers have bolted! They're drawin' the stragglers, an' that'll pull the whole herd.'

Jane was not quick enough to catch the details called out by Lassiter, but she saw the line of cattle lengthening. Then, like a stream of white bees pouring from a huge swarm, the steers stretched out from the main body. In a few moments, with astonishing rapidity, the whole herd got into motion. A faint roar of trampling hoofs came to Jane's ears, and gradually swelled; low, rolling clouds of dust began to rise above the sage.

'It's a stampede, an' a hummer,' said Lassiter.

'Oh, Lassiter! The herd's running with the valley! It leads into the cañon! There's a straight jump-off!'

'I reckon they'll run into it, too. But that's a good many miles yet. An' Jane, this valley swings round almost north before it goes east. That stampede will pass within a mile of us.'

The long, white, bobbing line of steers streaked swiftly through the sage, and a funnel-shaped dust-cloud arose at a low angle. A dull rumbling filled Jane's ears.

'I'm thinkin' of millin' that herd,' said Lassiter. His gray glance swept up the slope to the west. 'There's some specks an' dust way off toward the village. Mebbe that's Judkins an' his boys. It ain't likely he'll get here in time to help. You'd better hold Black Star here on this high ridge.'

He ran to his horse and, throwing off saddle-bags and tightening the cinches, he leaped astride and galloped straight down across the valley.

Jane went for Black Star and, leading him to the summit of the ridge, she mounted and faced the valley with excitement and expectancy. She had heard of milling stampeded cattle, and knew it was a feat accomplished by only the most daring riders.

The white herd was now strung out in a line two miles long. The dull rumble of thousands of hoofs deepened into continuous low thunder, and as the steers swept swiftly closer the thunder became a heavy roll. Lassiter crossed in a few moments the level of the valley to the eastern rise of ground and there waited the coming of the herd. Presently, as the head of the white line reached a point opposite to where Jane stood, Lassiter spurred his black into a run.

Jane saw him take a position on the off side of the leaders of the stampede, and there he rode. It was like a race. They swept on down the valley, and when the end of the white line neared Lassiter's first stand the head had begun to swing round to the west. It swung slowly and stubbornly, yet surely, and gradually assumed a long, beautiful curve of moving white. To Jane's amaze she saw the leaders swinging, turning till they headed back toward her and up the valley. Out to the right of these wild, plunging steers ran Lassiter's black, and Jane's keen eye appreciated the fleet stride and sure-footedness of the blind horse. Then it seemed that the herd moved in a great curve, a huge half-moon, with the points of head and tail almost opposite, and a mile apart. But Lassiter relentlessly crowded the leaders, sheering them to the left, turning them little by little. And the dust-blinded wild followers plunged on madly in the tracks of their leaders. This ever-moving, ever-changing curve of steers rolled toward Jane, and when below her, scarce half a mile, it began to narrow and close into a circle. Lassiter had ridden parallel with her position, turned toward her, then aside, and now he was riding directly away from her, all the time pushing the head of that bobbing line inward.

It was then that Jane, suddenly understanding Lassiter's feat, stared and gasped at the riding of this intrepid man. His horse was fleet and tireless, but blind. He had pushed the leaders around and around till they were about to turn in on the inner side of the end of that line of steers. The leaders were already running in a circle; the end of the herd was still running almost straight. But soon they would be wheeling. Then, when Lassiter had the circle formed, how would he escape? With Jane Withersteen prayer was as ready as praise; and she prayed for this man's safety. A circle of dust began to collect. Dimly, as through a yellow veil, Jane saw Lassiter press the leaders inward to close the gap in the sage. She lost sight of him in the dust; again she thought she saw the black, riderless now, rear and drag himself and fall. Lassiter had been thrown—lost! Then he reappeared running out of the dust into the sage. He had escaped, and she breathed again.

Spellbound, Jane Withersteen watched this stupendous mill-wheel of steers. Here was the milling of the herd. The white running circle closed in upon the open space of sage. And the dust circles closed above into a pall. The ground quaked and the incessant thunder of pounding hoofs rolled on. Jane felt deafened, yet she thrilled to a new sound. As the circle of sage lessened the steers began to bawl, and when it closed entirely there came a great upheaval in the center, and a terrible thumping of heads and clicking of horns. Bawling, climbing, goring, the great mass of steers on the inside wrestled in a crashing din, heaved and groaned under the pressure. Then came a deadlock. The inner strife ceased, and the hideous roar and crash. Movement went on in the outer circle, and that, too, gradually stilled. The white herd had come to a stop, and the pall of yellow dust began to drift away on the wind.

Jane Withersteen waited on the ridge, with full and grateful heart. Lassiter appeared, making his weary way toward her through the sage. And up on the slope

Judkins rode into sight with his troop of boys. For the present, at least, the white herd would be looked after.

When Lassiter reached her and laid his hand on Black Star's mane, Jane could not find speech.

'Killed—my—hoss,' he panted.

'Oh! I'm sorry,' cried Jane. 'Lassiter! I know you can't replace him, but I'll give you any one of my racers—Bells, or Night, even Black Star.'

'I'll take a fast hoss, Jane, but not one of your favorites,' he replied. 'Only—will you let me have Black Star now an' ride him over there an' head off them fellers who stampeded the herd?'

He pointed to several moving specks of black and puffs of dust in the purple sage.

'I can head them off with this hoss, an' then—'

'Then, Lassiter?'

'They'll never stampede no more cattle.'

'Oh! No! No! … Lassiter, I won't let you go!'

But a flush of fire flamed in her cheeks, and her trembling hands shook Black Star's bridle, and her eyes fell before Lassiter's.

CHAPTER SEVEN
The Daughter of Withersteen

'Lassiter will you be my rider?' Jane had asked him.

'I reckon so,' he had replied.

Few as the words were, Jane knew how infinitely much they implied. She wanted him to take charge of her cattle and horses and ranges, and save them if that were possible. Yet, though she could not have spoken aloud all she meant, she was perfectly honest with herself. Whatever the price to be paid, she must keep Lassiter close to her; she must shield from him the man who had lured Milly Erne to Cottonwoods. In her fear she so controlled her mind that she did not whisper this Mormon's name to her own soul, she did not even think it. Besides, beyond this thing she regarded as a sacred obligation thrust upon her, was the need of a helper, of a friend, of a champion in this critical time. If she could rule this gun-man, as Venters had called him, if she could even keep him from shedding blood, what strategy to play his name and his presence against the game of oppression her churchmen were waging against her? Never would she forget the effect upon Tull and his men when Venters shouted Lassiter's name. If she could not wholly control Lassiter, then what she could do might put off the fatal day.

One of her safe racers was a dark bay, and she called him Bells because of the way he struck his iron shoes on the stones. When Jerd led out this slender, beautifully built horse Lassiter suddenly became all eyes. A rider's love of a thoroughbred shone in them. Round and round Bells he walked, plainly weakening all the time in his determination not to take one of Jane's favorite racers.

'Lassiter, you're half horse, and Bells sees it already,' said Jane, laughing. 'Look at his eyes. He likes you. He'll love you, too. How can you resist him? Oh, Lassiter, but Bells can run! It's nip and tuck between him and Wrangle, and only Black Star can beat him. He's too spirited a horse for a woman. Take him. He's yours.'

'I jest am weak where a hoss is concerned,' said Lassiter. 'I'll take him, an' I'll take your orders, ma'am.'

'Well, I'm glad, but never mind the ma'am. Let it still be Jane.'

From that hour, it seemed, Lassiter was always in the saddle, riding early and late; and coincident with his part in Jane's affairs the days assumed their old tranquillity. Her intelligence told her this was only the lull before the storm, but her faith would not have it so.

She resumed her visits to the village, and upon one of these she encountered Tull. He greeted her as he had before any trouble came between them, and she, responsive to peace if not quick to forget, met him halfway with manner almost cheerful. He regretted the loss of her cattle; he assured her that the vigilantes which had been organized would soon rout the rustlers; when that had been accomplished her riders would likely return to her.

'You've done a headstrong thing to hire this man Lassiter,' Tull went on, severely. 'He came to Cottonwoods with evil intent.'

'I had to have somebody. And perhaps making him my rider may turn out best in the end for the Mormons of Cottonwoods.'

'You mean to stay his hand?'

'I do—if I can.'

'A woman like you can do anything with a man. That would be well, and would atone in some measure for the errors you have made.'

He bowed and passed on. Jane resumed her walk with conflicting thoughts. She resented Elder Tull's cold, impassive manner that looked down upon her as one who had incurred his just displeasure. Otherwise he would have been the same calm, dark-browed, impenetrable man she had known for ten years. In fact, except when he had revealed his passion in the matter of the seizing of Venters, she had never dreamed he could be other than the grave, reproving preacher. He stood out now a strange, secretive man. She would have thought better of him if he had picked up the threads of their quarrel where they had parted. Was Tull what he appeared to be? The question flung itself involuntarily over Jane Withersteen's inhibitive habit of faith without question. And she refused to answer it. Tull could not fight in the open. Venters had said, Lassiter had said, that her Elder shirked fight and worked in the dark. Just now in this meeting Tull had ignored the fact that he had sued, exhorted, demanded that she marry him. He made no mention of Venters. His manner was that of the minister who had been outraged, but who overlooked the frailties of a woman. Beyond question he seemed unutterably aloof from all knowledge of pressure being brought to bear upon her, absolutely guiltless of any connection with secret power over riders, with night journeys, with rustlers and stampedes of cattle. And that convinced her again of unjust suspicions. But it was convincement through an obstinate faith. She shuddered as she accepted it, and that shudder was the nucleus of a terrible revolt.

Jane turned into one of the wide lanes leading from the main street and entered a huge, shady yard. Here were sweet-smelling clover, alfalfa, flowers, and vegetables, all growing in happy confusion. And like these fresh green things were the dozens of babies, tots, toddlers, noisy urchins, laughing girls, a whole multitude of children of one family. For Collier Brandt, the father of all this numerous progeny, was a Mormon with four wives.

The big house where they lived was old, solid, picturesque, the lower part built of logs, the upper of rough clapboards, with vines growing up the outside stone chimneys. There were many wooden-shuttered windows, and one pretentious window of glass, proudly curtained in white. As this house had four mistresses, it likewise had four separate sections, not one of which communicated with another, and all had to be entered from the outside.

In the shade of a wide, low, vine-roofed porch Jane found Brandt's wives entertaining Bishop Dyer. They were motherly women, of comparatively similar ages, and plain-featured, and just at this moment anything but grave. The Bishop was rather tall, of stout build, with iron-gray hair and beard, and eyes of light blue. They were merry now; but Jane had seen them when they were not, and then she feared him as she had feared her father.

The women flocked around her in welcome.

'Daughter of Withersteen,' said the Bishop, gaily, as he took her hand, 'you have not been prodigal of your gracious self of late. A Sabbath without you at service! I shall reprove Elder Tull.'

'Bishop, the guilt is mine. I'll come to you and confess,' Jane replied, lightly; but she felt the undercurrent of her words.

'Mormon love-making!' exclaimed the Bishop, rubbing his hands. 'Tull keeps you all to himself.'

'No. He is not courting me.'

'What? The laggard! If he does not make haste, I'll go a-courting myself up to the Withersteen House.'

There was laughter and further bantering by the Bishop, and then mild talk of village affairs, after which he took his leave, and Jane was left with her friend, Mary Brandt.

'Jane, you're not yourself. Are you sad about the rustling of the cattle? But you have so many, you are so rich.'

Then Jane confided in her, telling much, yet holding back her doubts and fears.

'Oh, why don't you marry Tull and be one of us?'

'But, Mary, I don't love Tull,' said Jane, stubbornly.

'I don't blame you for that. But, Jane Withersteen, you've got to choose between the love of man and love of God. Often we Mormon women have to do that. It's not easy. The kind of happiness you want I wanted once. I never got it, nor will you, unless you throw away your soul. We've all watched your affair with Venters in fear and trembling. Some dreadful thing will come of it. You don't want him hanged or shot—or treated worse, as that Gentile boy was treated in Glaze for fooling round a Mormon woman. Marry Tull. It's your duty as a Mormon. You'll feel no rapture as his wife—but think of Heaven! Mormon women don't marry for what they expect on earth. Take up the cross, Jane. Remember your father founded Amber Spring, built these old houses, brought Mormons here, and fathered them. You are the daughter of Withersteen!'

Jane left Mary Brandt and went to call upon other friends. They received her with the same glad welcome as had Mary, lavished upon her the pent-up affection of Mormon women, and let her go with her ears ringing of Tull, Venters, Lassiter, of duty to God and glory in Heaven.

'Verily,' murmured Jane, 'I don't know myself when, through all this, I remain unchanged—nay, more fixed of purpose.'

She returned to the main street and bent her thoughtful steps toward the center of the village. A string of wagons drawn by oxen was lumbering along. These 'sage-freighters,' as they were called, hauled grain and flour and merchandise from Sterling; and Jane laughed suddenly in the midst of her humility at the thought that they were her property, as was one of the three stores for which they freighted goods. The water that flowed along the path at her feet, and turned into each cottage-yard to nourish garden and orchard, also was hers, no less her private property because she chose to give it free. Yet in this village of Cottonwoods, which her father had founded and which she maintained, she was not her own mistress; she was not to abide by her own choice of a husband. She was the daughter of Withersteen. Suppose she proved it, imperiously! But she quelled that proud temptation at its birth.

Nothing could have replaced the affection which the village people had for her; no power could have made her happy as the pleasure her presence gave. As she went on down the street, past the stores with their rude platform entrances, and the saloons, where tired horses stood with bridles dragging, she was again assured of what was the bread and wine of life to her—that she was loved. Dirty boys playing in the ditch, clerks, teamsters, riders, loungers on the corners, ranchers on dusty horses, little girls running errands, and women hurrying to the stores all looked up at her coming with glad eyes.

Jane's various calls and wandering steps at length led her to the Gentile quarter of the village. This was at the extreme southern end, and here some thirty Gentile families lived in huts and shacks and log-cabins and several dilapidated cottages. The fortunes of these inhabitants of Cottonwoods could be read in their abodes. Water they had in abundance, and therefore grass and fruit-trees and patches of alfalfa and vegetable gardens. Some of the men and boys had a few stray cattle, others obtained such intermittent employment as the Mormons reluctantly tendered them. But none of the families was prosperous, many were very poor, and some lived only by Jane Withersteen's beneficence.

As it made Jane happy to go among her own people, so it saddened her to come in contact with these Gentiles. Yet that was not because she was unwelcome; here she was gratefully received by the women, passionately by the children. But poverty and idleness, with their attendant wretchedness and sorrow, always hurt her. That she could alleviate this distress more now than ever before proved the adage that it was an ill wind that blew nobody good. While her Mormon riders were in her employ she had found few Gentiles who could stay with her, and now she was able to find employment for all the men and boys. No little shock was it to have man after man tell her that he dare not accept her kind offer.

'It won't do,' said one Carson, an intelligent man who had seen better days. 'We've had our warning. Plain and to the point! Now there's Judkins, he packs guns, and he can use them, and so can the daredevil boys he's hired. But they've little responsibility. Can we risk having our homes burned in our absence?'

Jane felt the stretching and chilling of the skin of her face as the blood left it.

'Carson, you and the others rent these houses?' she asked.

'You ought to know, Miss Withersteen. Some of them are yours.'

'I know? … Carson, I never in my life took a day's labor for rent or a yearling calf or a bunch of grass, let alone gold.'

'Bivens, your store-keeper, sees to that.'

'Look here, Carson,' went on Jane, hurriedly, and now her cheeks were burning. 'You and Black and Willet pack your goods and move your families up to my cabins in the grove. They're far more comfortable than these. Then go to work for me. And if aught happens to you there I'll give you money—gold enough to leave Utah!'

The man choked and stammered, and then, as tears welled into his eyes, he found the use of his tongue and cursed. No gentle speech could ever have equaled that curse in eloquent expression of what he felt for Jane Withersteen. How strangely his look and tone reminded her of Lassiter!

'No, it won't do,' he said, when he had somewhat recovered himself. 'Miss Withersteen, there are things that you don't know, and there's not a soul among us who can tell you.'

'I seem to be learning many things, Carson. Well, then, will you let me aid you—say till better times?'

'Yes, I will,' he replied, with his face lighting up. 'I see what it means to you, and you know what it means to me. Thank you! And if better times ever come I'll be only too happy to work for you.'

'Better times will come. I trust God and have faith in man. Good day, Carson.'

The lane opened out upon the sage-enclosed alfalfa fields, and the last habitation, at the end of that lane of hovels, was the meanest. Formerly it had been a shed; now it was a home. The broad leaves of a wide-spreading cottonwood sheltered the sunken roof of weathered boards. Like an Indian hut, it had one floor. Round about it were a few scanty rows of vegetables, such as the hand of a weak woman had time and strength to cultivate. This little dwelling-place was just outside the village limits, and the widow who lived there had to carry her water from the nearest irrigation ditch. As Jane Withersteen entered the unfenced yard a child saw her, shrieked with joy, and came tearing toward her with curls flying. This child was a little girl of four called Fay. Her name suited her, for she was an elf, a sprite, a creature so fairy-like and beautiful that she seemed unearthly.

'Muvver sended for oo,' cried Fay, as Jane kissed her, 'an' oo never tome.'

'I didn't know, Fay; but I've come now.'

Fay was a child of outdoors, of the garden and ditch and field, and she was dirty and ragged. But rags and dirt did not hide her beauty. The one thin little bedraggled garment she wore half covered her fine, slim body. Red as cherries were her cheeks and lips; her eyes were violet blue, and the crown of her childish loveliness was the curling golden hair. All the children of Cottonwoods were Jane Withersteen's friends; she loved them all. But Fay was dearest to her. Fay had few playmates, for among the Gentile children there were none near her age, and the Mormon children were forbidden to play with her. So she was a shy, wild, lonely child.

'Muvver's sick,' said Fay, leading Jane toward the door of the hut.

Jane went in. There was only one room, rather dark and bare, but it was clean and neat. A woman lay upon a bed.

'Mrs Larkin, how are you?' asked Jane, anxiously.

'I've been pretty bad for a week, but I'm better now.'

'You haven't been here all alone—with no one to wait on you?'

'Oh no! My women neighbors are kind. They take turns coming in.'

'Did you send for me?'

'Yes, several times.'

'But I had no word—no messages ever got to me.'

'I sent the boys, and they left word with your women that I was ill and would you please come.'

A sudden deadly sickness seized Jane. She fought the weakness, as she fought to be above suspicious thoughts, and it passed, leaving her conscious of her utter impotence. That, too, passed as her spirit rebounded. But she had again caught a glimpse of dark underhand domination, running its secret lines this time into her own household. Like a spider in the blackness of night an unseen hand had begun to run these dark lines, to turn and twist them about her life, to plait and weave a web. Jane Withersteen knew it now, and in the realization further coolness and sureness came to her, and the fighting courage of her ancestors.

'Mrs Larkin, you're better, and I'm so glad,' said Jane. 'But may I not do something for you—a turn at nursing, or send you things, or take care of Fay?'

'You're so good. Since my husband's been gone what would have become of Fay and me but for you? It was about Fay that I wanted to speak to you. This time I thought surely I'd die, and I was worried about Fay. Well, I'll be around all right shortly, but my strength's gone and I won't live long. So I may as well speak now. You remember you've been asking me to let you take Fay and bring her up as your daughter?'

'Indeed yes, I remember. I'll be happy to have her. But I hope the day—'

'Never mind that. The day'll come—sooner or later. I refused your offer, and now I'll tell you why.'

'I know why,' interposed Jane. 'It's because you don't want her to be brought up as a Mormon.'

'No, it wasn't altogether that.' Mrs Larkin raised her thin hand and laid it appealingly on Jane's. 'I don't like to tell you. But—it's this: I told all my friends what you wanted. They know you, care for you, and they said for me to trust Fay to you. Women will talk, you know. It got to the ears of Mormons—gossip of your love for Fay and your wanting her. And it came straight back to me, in jealousy, perhaps, that you wouldn't take Fay as much for love of her as because of your religious duty to bring up another girl for some Mormon to marry.'

'That's a damnable lie!' cried Jane Withersteen.

'It was what made me hesitate,' went on Mrs Larkin, 'but I never believed it at heart. And now I guess I'll let you—'

'Wait! Mrs Larkin, I may have told little white lies in my life, but never a lie that mattered, that hurt anyone. Now believe me. I love little Fay. If I had her near me I'd grow to worship her. When I asked for her I thought only of that love . . . . Let me prove this. You and Fay come to live with me. I've such a big house, and I'm so lonely. I'll help nurse you, take care of you. When you're better you can work for me. I'll keep little Fay and bring her up—without Mormon teaching. When she's grown, if she should want to leave me, I'll send her, and not empty-handed, back to Illinois where you came from. I promise you.'

'I knew it was a lie,' replied the mother, and she sank back upon her pillow with something of peace in her white, worn face. 'Jane Withersteen, may Heaven bless you! I've been deeply grateful to you. But because you're a Mormon I never felt close to you till now. I don't know much about religion as religion, but your God and my God are the same.'

CHAPTER EIGHT
Surprise Valley

Back in that strange cañon, which Venters had found indeed a valley of surprises, the wounded girl's whispered appeal, almost a prayer, not to take her back to the rustlers crowned the events of the last few days with a confounding climax. That she should not want to return to them staggered Venters. Presently, as logical thought returned, her appeal confirmed his first impression—that she was more unfortunate than bad—and he experienced a sensation of gladness. If he had known before that Oldring's Masked Rider was a woman his opinion would have been formed and he would have considered her abandoned. But his first knowledge had come when he lifted a white face quivering in a convulsion of agony; he had heard God's name whispered by blood-stained lips; through her solemn and awful eyes he had caught a glimpse of her soul. And just now had come the entreaty to him, 'Don't—take—me—back—there!'

Once for all Venters's quick mind formed a permanent conception of this poor girl. He based it, not upon what the chances of life had made her, but upon the revelation of dark eyes that pierced the infinite, upon a few pitiful, halting words that betrayed failure and wrong and misery, yet breathed the truth of a tragic fate rather than a natural leaning to evil.

'What's your name?' he inquired.

'Bess,' she answered.

'Bess what?'

'That's enough—just Bess.'

The red that deepened in her cheeks was not all the flush of fever. Venters marveled anew, and this time at the tint of shame in her face, at the momentary drooping of long lashes. She might be a rustler's girl, but she was still capable of shame; she might be dying, but she still clung to some little remnant of honor.

'Very well, Bess. It doesn't matter,' he said. 'But this matters—what shall I do with you?'

'Are—you—a rider?' she whispered.

'Not now. I was once. I drove the Withersteen herds. But I lost my place—lost all I owned—and now I'm—I'm a sort of outcast. My name's Bern Venters.'

'You won't—take me—to Cottonwoods—or Glaze? I'd be—hanged.'

'No, indeed. But I must do something with you. For it's not safe for me here. I shot that rustler who was with you. Sooner or later he'll be found, and then my tracks. I must find a safer hiding-place where I can't be trailed.'

'Leave me—here.'

'Alone—to die!'

'Yes.'

'I will not.' Venters spoke shortly with a kind of ring in his voice.

'What—do you want—to do—with me?' Her whispering grew difficult, so low and faint that Venters had to stoop to hear her.

'Why, let's see,' he replied, slowly. 'I'd like to take you some place where I could watch by you, nurse you, till you're all right again.'

'And—then?'

'Well, it'll be time to think of that when you're cured of your wound. It's a bad one. And—Bess, if you don't want to live—if you don't fight for life—you'll never—'

'Oh! I want—to live! I'm afraid—to die. But I'd rather die—than go back—to—to—'

'To Oldring?' asked Venters, interrupting her in turn.

Her lips moved in an affirmative.

'I promise not to take you back to him or to Cottonwoods or to Glaze.'

The mournful earnestness of her gaze suddenly shone with unutterable gratitude and wonder. And as suddenly Venters found her eyes beautiful as he had never seen or felt beauty. They were as dark blue as the sky at night. Then the flashing changed to a long, thoughtful look, in which there was wistful, unconscious searching of his face, a look that trembled on the verge of hope and trust.

'I'll try—to live,' she said. The broken whisper just reached his ears. 'Do what—you want—with me.'

'Rest then—don't worry—sleep,' he replied.

Abruptly he arose, as if her words had been decision for him, and with a sharp command to the dogs he strode from the camp. Venters was conscious of an indefinite conflict of change within him. It seemed to be a vague passing of old moods, a dim coalescing of new forces, a moment of inexplicable transition. He was both cast down and uplifted. He wanted to think and think of the meaning, but he resolutely dispelled emotion. His imperative need at present was to find a safe retreat, and this called for action.

So he set out. It still wanted several hours before dark. This trip he turned to the left and wended his skulking way southward a mile or more to the opening of the valley, where lay the strange scrawled rocks. He did not, however, venture boldly out into the open sage, but clung to the right-hand wall and went along that till its perpendicular line broke into the long incline of bare stone.

Before proceeding farther he halted, studying the strange character of this slope and realizing that a moving black object could be seen far against such background. Before him ascended a gradual swell of smooth stone. It was hard, polished and full of pockets worn by centuries of eddying rain-water. A hundred yards up began a line of grotesque cedar-trees, and they extended along the slope clear to its most southerly end. Beyond that end Venters wanted to get, and he concluded the cedars, few as they were, would afford some cover.

Therefore he climbed swiftly. The trees were farther up than he had estimated, though he had from long habit made allowance for the deceiving nature of distances in that country. When he gained the cover of cedars he paused to rest and look, and it was then he saw how the trees sprang from holes in the bare rock. Ages of rain had run down the slope, circling, eddying in depressions, wearing deep round holes. There had been dry seasons, accumulations of dust, windblown seeds, and cedars rose wonderfully out of solid rock. But these were not beautiful cedars. They were gnarled, twisted into weird contortions, as if growth were torture, dead at the tops, shrunken, gray, and old. Theirs had been a bitter fight, and Venters felt a strange sympathy for them. This country was hard on trees—and men.

He slipped from cedar to cedar, keeping them between him and the open valley. As he progressed, the belt of trees widened, and he kept to its upper margin. He passed shady pockets half full of water, and, as he marked the location for possible future need, he reflected that there had been no rain since the winter snows. From one of these shady holes a rabbit hopped out and squatted down, laying its ears flat.

Venters wanted fresh meat now more than when he had only himself to think of. But it would not do to fire his rifle there. So he broke off a cedar branch and threw it. He crippled the rabbit, which started to flounder up the slope. Venters did not wish to lose the meat, and he never allowed crippled game to escape, to die lingeringly in some covert. So after a careful glance below, and back toward the cañon, he began to chase the rabbit.

The fact that rabbits generally ran uphill was not new to him. But it presently seemed singular why this rabbit, that might have escaped downward, chose to ascend the slope. Venters knew then that it had a burrow higher up. More than once he jerked over to seize it, only in vain, for the rabbit by renewed effort eluded his grasp. Thus the chase continued on up the bare slope. The farther Venters climbed the more determined he grew to catch his quarry. At last, panting and sweating, he captured the rabbit at the foot of a steeper grade. Laying his rifle on the bulge of rising stone, he killed the animal and slung it from his belt.

Before starting down he waited to catch his breath. He had climbed far up that wonderful smooth slope, and had almost reached the base of yellow cliff that rose skyward, a huge scarred and cracked bulk. It frowned down upon him as if to forbid further ascent. Venters bent over for his rifle, and, as he picked it up from where it leaned against the steeper grade, he saw several little nicks cut in the solid stone.

They were only a few inches deep and about a foot apart. Venters began to count them—one—two—three—four—on up to sixteen. That number carried his glance to the top of this first bulging bench of cliff-base. Above, after a more level offset, was still steeper slope, and the line of nicks kept on, to wind round a projecting corner of wall.

A casual glance would have passed by these little dents; if Venters had not known what they signified he would never have bestowed upon them the second glance. But he knew they had been cut there by hand, and, though age-worn, he recognized them as steps cut in the rock by the cliff-dwellers. With a pulse beginning to beat and hammer away his calmness, he eyed that indistinct line of steps, up to where the buttress of wall hid further sight of them. He knew that behind the corner of stone would be a cave or a crack which could never be suspected from below. Chance, that had sported with him of late, now directed him to a probable hiding-place. Again he laid aside his rifle, and, removing boots and belt, he began to walk up the steps. Like a mountain goat, he was agile, surefooted, and he mounted the first bench without bending to use his hands. The next ascent took grip of fingers as well as toes, but he climbed steadily, swiftly, to reach the projecting corner, and slipped around it. Here he faced a notch in the cliff. At the apex he turned abruptly into a ragged vent that split the ponderous wall clear to the top, showing a narrow streak of blue sky.

At the base this vent was dark, cool, and smelled of dry, musty dust. It zigzagged so that he could not see ahead more than a few yards at a time. He noticed tracks of wildcats and rabbits in the dusty floor. At every turn he expected to come upon a huge cavern full of little square stone houses, each with a small aperture like a staring dark eye. The passage lightened and widened, and opened at the foot of a narrow, steep, ascending chute.

Venters had a moment's notice of the rock, which was of the same smoothness and hardness as the slope below, before his gaze went irresistibly upward to the precipitous walls of this wide ladder of granite. These were ruined walls of yellow sandstone, and so split and splintered, so overhanging with great sections of balancing rim, so impending with tremendous crumbling crags, that Venters caught his breath sharply, and, appalled, he instinctively recoiled as if a step upward might jar the ponderous cliffs from their foundation. Indeed, it seemed that these ruined cliffs were but awaiting a breath of wind to collapse and come tumbling down. Venters hesitated. It would be a foolhardy man who risked his life under the leaning, waiting avalanches of rock in that gigantic split. Yet how many years had they leaned there without falling! At the bottom of the incline was an immense heap of weathered sandstone all crumbling to dust, but there were no huge rocks as large as houses, such as rested so lightly and frightfully above, waiting patiently and inevitably to crash down. Slowly split from the parent rock by the weathering process, and carved and sculptured by ages of wind and rain, they waited their moment. Venters felt how foolish it was for him to fear these broken walls; to fear that, after they had endured for thousands of years, the moment of his passing should be the one for them to slip. Yet he feared it.

'What a place to hide!' muttered Venters. 'I'll climb—I'll see where this thing goes. If only I can find water!'

With teeth tight shut he essayed the incline. And as he climbed he bent his eyes downward. This, however, after a little grew impossible; he had to look to obey his eager, curious mind. He raised his glance and saw light between row on row of shafts and pinnacles and crags that stood out from the main wall. Some leaned against the cliff, others against each other; many stood sheer and alone; all were crumbling, cracked, rotten. It was a place of yellow, ragged ruin. The passage narrowed as he went up; it became a slant, hard for him to stick on; it was smooth as marble. Finally he surmounted it, surprised to find the walls still several hundred feet high, and a narrow gorge leading down on the other side. This was a divide between two inclines, about twenty yards wide. At one side stood an enormous rock. Venters gave it a second glance, because it rested on a pedestal. It attracted closer attention. It was like a colossal pear of stone standing on its stem. Around the bottom were thousands of little nicks just distinguishable to the eye. They were marks of stone hatchets. The cliff-dwellers had chipped and chipped away at this boulder till it rested its tremendous bulk upon a mere pin-point of its surface. Venters pondered. Why had the little stone-men hacked away at that big boulder? It bore no semblance to a statue or an idol or a godhead or a sphinx.

Instinctively he put his hands on it and pushed; then his shoulder and heaved. The stone seemed to groan, to stir, to grate, and then to move. It tipped a little downward and hung balancing for a long instant, slowly returned, rocked slightly, groaned, and settled back to its former position.

Venters divined its significance. It had been meant for defense. The cliff-dwellers, driven by dreaded enemies to this last stand, had cunningly cut the rock until it balanced perfectly, ready to be dislodged by strong hands. Just below it leaned a tottering crag that would have toppled, starting an avalanche on an acclivity where no sliding mass could stop. Crags and pinnacles, splintered cliffs, and leaning shafts and monuments, would have thundered down to block forever the outlet to Deception Pass.

'That was a narrow shave for me,' said Venters, soberly. 'A balancing rock! The cliff-dwellers never had to roll it. They died, vanished, and here the rock stands, probably little changed. ... But it might serve another lonely dweller of the cliffs. I'll hide up here somewhere, if I can only find water.'

He descended the gorge on the other side. The slope was gradual, the space narrow, the course straight for many rods. A gloom hung between the upsweeping walls. In a turn the passage narrowed to scarce a dozen feet, and here was darkness of night. But light shone ahead; another abrupt turn brought day again, and then wide open space.

Above Venters loomed a wonderful arch of stone bridging the cañon rims, and through the enormous round portal gleamed and glistened a beautiful valley shining under sunset gold reflected by surrounding cliffs. He gave a start of surprise. The valley was a cove a mile long, half that wide, and its enclosing walls were smooth and stained, and curved inward, forming great caves. He decided that its floor was far higher than the level of Deception Pass and the intersecting cañons. No purple sage colored this valley floor. Instead there were the white of aspens, streaks of branch and slender trunk glistening from the green of leaves, and the darker green of oaks, and through the middle of this forest, from wall to wall, ran a winding line of brilliant green which marked the course of cottonwoods and willows.

'There's water here—and this is the place for me,' said Venters. 'Only birds can peep over those walls. I've gone Oldring one better.'

Venters waited no longer, and turned swiftly to retrace his steps. He named the cañon Surprise Valley and the huge boulder that guarded the outlet Balancing Rock. Going down he did not find himself attended by such fears as had beset him in the climb; still, he was not easy in mind and could not occupy himself with plans of moving the girl and his outfit until he had descended to the notch. There he rested a moment and looked about him. The pass was darkening with the approach of night. At the corner of the wall, where the stone steps turned, he saw a spur of rock that would serve to hold the noose of a lasso. He needed no more aid to scale that place. As he intended to make the move under cover of darkness, he wanted most to be able to tell where to climb up. So, taking several small stones with him, he stepped and slid down to the edge of the slope where he had left his rifle and boots. Here he placed the stones some yards apart. He left the rabbit lying upon the bench where the steps began. Then he addressed a keen-sighted, remembering gaze to the rim-wall above. It was serrated, and between two spears of rock, directly in line with his position, showed a zigzag crack that at night would let through the gleam of sky. This settled, he put on his belt and boots and prepared to descend. Some consideration was necessary to decide whether or not to leave his rifle there. On the return, carrying the girl and a pack, it would be added encumbrance; and after debating the matter he left the rifle leaning against the bench. As he went straight down the slope he halted every few rods to look up at his mark on the rim. It changed, but he fixed each change in his memory. When he reached the first cedar-tree, he tied his scarf upon a dead branch, and then hurried toward camp, having no more concern about finding his trail upon the return trip.

Darkness soon emboldened and lent him greater speed. It occurred to him, as he glided into the grassy glade near camp and heard the whinny of a horse, that he had forgotten Wrangle. The big sorrel could not be gotten into Surprise Valley. He would have to be left there.

Venters determined at once to lead the other horses out through the thicket and turn them loose. The farther they wandered from this cañon the better it would suit him. He easily descried Wrangle through the gloom, but the others were not in sight. Venters whistled low for the dogs, and when they came trotting to him he sent them out to search for the horses, and followed. It soon developed that they were not in the glade nor the thicket. Venters grew cold and rigid at the thought of rustlers having entered his retreat. But the thought passed, for the demeanor of Ring and Whitie reassured him. The horses had wandered away.

Under the clump of silver spruces hung a denser mantle of darkness, yet not so thick that Venters's night-practiced eyes could not catch the white oval of a still face. He bent over it with a slight suspension of breath that was both caution lest he frighten her and chill uncertainty of feeling lest he find her dead. But she slept, and he arose to renewed activity.

He packed his saddle-bags. The dogs were hungry, they whined about him and nosed his busy hands; but he took no time to feed them nor to satisfy his own hunger. He slung the saddle-bags over his shoulders and made them secure with his lasso. Then he wrapped the blankets closer about the girl and lifted her in his arms. Wrangle whinnied and thumped the ground as Venters passed him with the dogs. The sorrel knew he was being left behind, and was not sure whether he liked it or not. Venters went on and entered the thicket. Here he had to feel his way in pitch blackness and to wedge his progress between the close saplings. Time meant little to him now that he had started, and he edged along with slow side movement till he got clear of the thicket. Ring and Whitie stood waiting for him. Taking to the open aisles and patches of the sage, he walked guardedly, careful not to stumble or step in dust or strike against spreading sage-branches.

If he were burdened he did not feel it. From time to time, when he passed out of the black lines of shade into the wan starlight, he glanced at the white face of the girl lying in his arms. She had not awakened from her sleep or stupor. He did not rest until he cleared the black gate of the cañon. Then he leaned against a stone breast-high to him and gently released the girl from his hold. His brow and hair and the palms of his hands were wet, and there was a kind of nervous contraction of his muscles. They seemed to ripple and string tense. He had a desire to hurry and no sense of fatigue. A wind blew the scent of sage in his face. The first early blackness of night passed with the brightening of the stars. Somewhere back on his trail a coyote yelped, splitting the dead silence. Venters's faculties seemed singularly acute.

He lifted the girl again and pressed on. The valley afforded better traveling than the cañon. It was lighter, freer of sage, and there were no rocks. Soon, out of the pale gloom shone a still paler thing, and that was the low swell of slope. Venters mounted it, and his dogs walked beside him. Once upon the stone he slowed to snail pace, straining his sight to avoid the pockets and holes. Foot by foot he went up. The weird cedars, like great demons and witches chained to the rock and writhing in silent anguish, loomed up with wide and twisting naked arms. Venters crossed this belt of cedars, skirted the upper border, and recognized the tree he had marked, even before he saw his waving scarf.

Here he knelt and deposited the girl gently, feet first, and slowly laid her out full length. What he feared was to reopen one of her wounds. If he gave her a violent jar, or slipped and fell! But the supreme confidence so strangely felt that night admitted of no such blunders.

The slope before him seemed to swell into obscurity, to lose its definite outline in a misty, opaque cloud that shaded into the over-shadowing wall. He scanned the rim where the serrated points speared the sky, and he found the zigzag crack. It was dim, only a shade lighter than the dark ramparts; but he distinguished it, and that served.

Lifting the girl, he stepped upward, closely attending to the nature of the path under his feet. After a few steps he stopped to mark his line with the crack in the rim. The dogs clung closer to him. While chasing the rabbit this slope had appeared interminable to him; now, burdened as he was, he did not think of length or height or toil. He remembered only to avoid a misstep and to keep his direction.

He climbed on, with frequent stops to watch the rain, and before he dreamed of gaining the bench he bumped his knees into it, and saw, in the dim gray light, his rifle and the rabbit. He had come straight up without mishap or swerving off his course, and his shut teeth unlocked.

As he laid the girl down in the shallow hollow of the little ridge, with her white face upturned, she opened her eyes. Wide, staring, black, at once like both the night and the stars, they made her face seem still whiter.

'Is—it—you?' she asked, faintly.

'Yes,' replied Venters.

'Oh! Where—are we?'

'I'm taking you to a safe place where no one will ever find you. I must climb a little here and call the dogs. Don't be afraid. I'll soon come for you.'

She said no more. Her eyes watched him steadily for a moment and then closed. Venters pulled off his boots and then felt for the little steps in the rock. The shade of the cliff above obscured the point he wanted to gain, but he could see dimly a few feet before him. What he had attempted with care he now went at with surpassing lightness. Buoyant, rapid, sure, he attained the corner of wall and slipped around it. Here he could not see a hand before his face, so he groped along, found a little flat space, and there removed the saddle-bags. The lasso he took back with him to the corner and looped the noose over the spur of rock.

'Ring—Whitie—come,' he called softly.

Low whines came up from below.

'Here! Come, Whitie—Ring,' he repeated, this time sharply.

Then followed scraping of claws and pattering of feet; and out of the gray gloom below him swiftly climbed the dogs to reach his side and pass beyond.

Venters descended, holding to the lasso. He tested its strength by throwing all his weight upon it. Then he gathered the girl up, and holding her securely in his left arm, he began to climb, at every few steps jerking his right hand upward along the lasso. It sagged at each forward movements he made, but he balanced himself lightly during the interval when he lacked the support of a taut rope. He climbed as if he had wings, the strength of a giant, and knew not the sense of fear. The sharp corner of cliff seemed to cut out of the darkness. He reached it and the protruding shelf, and then, entering the black shade of the notch, he moved blindly but surely to the place where he had left the saddle-bags. He heard the dogs, though he could not see them. Once more he carefully placed the girl at his feet. Then, on hands and knees, he went over the little flat space, feeling for stones. He removed a number, and, scraping the deep dust into a heap, he unfolded the outer blanket from around the girl and laid her upon this bed. Then he went down the slope again for his boots, rifle, and the rabbit, and, bringing also his lasso with him, he made short work of that trip.

'Are—you—there?' The girl's voice came low from the blackness.

'Yes,' he replied, and was conscious that his laboring breast made speech difficult.

'Are we—in a cave?'

'Yes.'

'Oh, listen! ... The waterfall! ... I hear it! You've brought me back!'

Venters heard a murmuring moan that one moment swelled to a pitch almost softly shrill and the next lulled to a low, almost inaudible sigh.

'That's—wind blowing—in the—cliffs,' he panted. 'You're far—from Oldring's—cañon.'

The effort it cost him to speak made him conscious of extreme lassitude following upon great exertion. It seemed that when he lay down and drew his blanket over him the action was the last before utter prostration. He stretched inert, wet, hot, his body one great strife of throbbing, stinging nerves and bursting veins. And there he lay for a long while before he felt that he had begun to rest.

Rest came to him that night, but no sleep. Sleep he did not want. The hours of strained effort were now as if they had never been, and he wanted to think. Earlier in the day he had dismissed an inexplicable feeling of change; but now, when there was no longer demand on his cunning and strength and he had time to think, he could not catch the illusive thing that had sadly perplexed as well as elevated his spirit.

Above him, through a V-shaped cleft in the dark rim of the cliff, shone the lustrous stars that had been his lonely accusers for a long, long year. Tonight they were different. He studied them. Larger, whiter, more radiant they seemed; but that was not the difference he meant. Gradually it came to him that the distinction was not one he saw, but one he felt. In this he divined as much of the baffling change as he thought would be revealed to him then. And as he lay there, with the singing of the cliff-winds in his ears, the white stars above the dark, bold vent, the difference which he felt was that he was no longer alone.

CHAPTER NINE
Silver Spruce and Aspens

The rest of that night seemed to Venters only a few moments of starlight, a dark overcasting of sky, an hour or so of gray gloom, and then the lighting of dawn.

When he had bestirred himself, feeding the hungry dogs and breaking his long fast, and had repacked his saddle bags, it was clear daylight, though the sun had not tipped the yellow wall in the east. He concluded to make the climb and descent into Surprise Valley in one trip. To that end he tied his blanket upon Ring and gave Whitie the extra lasso and the rabbit to carry. Then, with the rifle and saddle-bags slung upon his back, he took up the girl. She did not awaken from heavy slumber.

That climb up under the rugged, menacing brows of the broken cliffs, in the face of a grim, leaning boulder that seemed to be weary of its age-long wavering, was a tax on strength and nerve that Venters felt equally with something sweet and strangely exulting in its accomplishment. He did not pause until he gained the narrow divide and there he rested. Balancing Rock loomed huge, cold in the gray light of dawn, a thing without life, yet it spoke silently to Venters: 'I am waiting to plunge down, to shatter and crash, roar and boom, to bury your trail, and close forever the outlet to Deception Pass!'

On the descent of the other side Venters had easy going, but was somewhat concerned because Whitie appeared to have succumbed to temptation, and while carrying the rabbit was also chewing on it. And Ring evidently regarded this as an injury to himself, especially as he had carried the heavier load. Presently he snapped at one end of the rabbit and refused to let go. But his action prevented Whitie from further misdoing, and then the two dogs pattered down, carrying the rabbit between them.

Venters turned out of the gorge, and suddenly paused stock-still, astounded at the scene before him. The curve of the great stone bridge had caught the sunrise, and through the magnificent arch burst a glorious stream of gold that shone with a long slant down into the center of Surprise Valley. Only through the arch did any sunlight pass, so that all the rest of the valley lay still asleep, dark green, mysterious, shadowy, merging its level into walls as misty and soft as morning clouds.

Venters then descended, passing through the arch, looking up at its tremendous height and sweep. It spanned the opening to Surprise Valley, stretching in almost perfect curve from rim to rim. Even in his hurry and concern Venters could not but feel its majesty, and the thought came to him that the cliff-dwellers must have regarded it as an object of worship.

Down, down, down Venters strode, more and more feeling the weight of his burden as he descended, and still the valley lay below him. As all other cañons and coves and valleys had deceived him, so had this deep, nesting oval. At length he passed beyond the slope of weathered stone that spread fan-shape from the arch, and encountered a grassy terrace running to the right and about on a level with the tips of the oaks and cottonwoods below. Scattered here and there upon this shelf were clumps of aspens, and he walked through them into a glade that surpassed, in beauty and adaptability for a wild home, any place he had ever seen. Silver spruces bordered the base of a precipitous wall that rose loftily. Caves indented its surface, and there were no detached ledges or weathered sections that might dislodge a stone. The level ground, beyond the spruces, dropped down into a little ravine. This was one dense line of slender aspens from which came the low splashing of water. And the terrace, lying open to the west, afforded unobstructed view of the valley of green tree-tops.

For his camp Venters chose a shady, grassy plot between the silver spruces and the cliff. Here, in the stone wall, had been wonderfully carved by wind or washed by water several deep caves above the level of the terrace. They were clean, dry, roomy. He cut spruce boughs and made a bed in the largest cave and laid the girl there. The first intimation that he had of her being aroused from sleep or lethargy was a low call for water.

He hurried down into the ravine with his canteen. It was a shallow, grass-green place with aspens growing up everywhere. To his delight he found a tiny brook of swift-running water. Its faint tinge of amber reminded him of the spring at Cottonwoods, and the thought gave him a little shock. The water was so cold it made his fingers tingle as he dipped the canteen. Having returned to the cave, he was glad to see the girl drink thirstily. This time he noted that she could raise her head slightly without his help.

'You were thirsty,' he said. 'It's good water. I've found a fine place. Tell me—how do you feel?'

'There's pain—here,' she replied, and moved her hand to her left side.

'Why, that's strange! Your wounds are on your right side. I believe you're hungry. Is the pain a kind of dull ache—a gnawing?'

'It's like—that.'

'Then it's hunger.' Venters laughed, and suddenly caught himself with a quick breath and felt again the little shock. When had he laughed? 'It's hunger,' he went on. 'I've had that gnaw many a time. I've got it now. But you mustn't eat. You can have all the water you want, but no food just yet.'

'Won't I—starve?'

'No, people don't starve easily. I've discovered that. You must lie perfectly still and rest and sleep—for days.'

'My hands—are dirty; my face feels—so hot and sticky; my boots hurt.' It was her longest speech as yet, and it trailed off in a whisper.

'Well, I'm a fine nurse!'

It annoyed him that he had never thought of these things. But then, awaiting her death and thinking of her comfort were vastly different matters. He unwrapped the blanket which covered her. What a slender girl she was! No wonder he had been able to carry her miles and pack her up that slippery ladder of stone. Her boots were soft, fine leather, reaching clear to her knees. He recognized the make as one of a bootmaker in Sterling. Her spurs, that he had stupidly neglected to remove, consisted of silver frames and gold chains, and the rowels, large as silver dollars, were fancifully engraved. The boots slipped off rather hard. She wore heavy woollen rider's stockings, half length, and these were pulled up over the ends of her short trousers. Venters took off the stockings to note her little feet were red and swollen. He bathed them. Then he removed his scarf and bathed her face and hands.

'I must see your wounds now,' he said, gently.

She made no reply, but watched him steadily as he opened her blouse and untied the bandage. His strong fingers trembled a little as he removed it. If the wounds had reopened! A chill struck him as he saw the angry red bullet-mark, and a tiny stream of blood winding from it down her white breast. Very carefully he lifted her to see that the wound in her back had closed perfectly. Then he washed the blood from her breast, bathed the wound, and left it unbandaged, open to the air.

Her eyes thanked him.

'Listen,' he said earnestly. 'I've had some wounds, and I've seen many. I know a little about them. The hole in your back has closed. If you lie still three days the one in your breast will close and you'll be safe. The danger from hemorrhage will be over.'

He had spoken with earnest sincerity, almost eagerness.

'Why—do you—want me—to get well?' she asked, wonderingly.

The simple question seemed unanswerable except on grounds of humanity. But the circumstances under which he had shot this strange girl, the shock and realization, the waiting for death, the hope, had resulted in a condition of mind wherein Venters wanted her to live more than he had ever wanted anything. Yet he could not tell why. He believed the killing of the rustler and the subsequent excitement had disturbed him. For how else could he explain the throbbing of his brain, the heat of his blood, the undefined sense of full hours, charged, vibrant with pulsating mystery where once they had dragged in loneliness?

'I shot you,' he said, slowly, 'and I want you to get well so I shall not have killed a woman. But—for your own sake, too—'

A terrible bitterness darkened her eyes, and her lips quivered.

'Hush,' said Venters. 'You've talked too much already.'

In her unutterable bitterness he saw a darkness of mood that could not have been caused by her present weak and feverish state. She hated the life she had led, that she probably had been compelled to lead. She had suffered some unforgivable wrong at the hands of Oldring. With that conviction Venters felt a flame throughout his body, and it marked the rekindling of fierce anger and ruthlessness. In the past long year he had nursed resentment. He had hated the wilderness—the loneliness of the uplands. He had waited for something to come to pass. It had come. Like an Indian stealing horses he had skulked into the recesses of the cañons. He had found Oldring's retreat; he had killed a rustler; he had shot an unfortunate girl, then had saved her from this unwitting act, and he meant to save her from the consequent wasting of blood, from fever and weakness. Starvation he had to fight for her and for himself. Where he had been sick at the letting of blood, now he remembered it in grim, cold calm. And as he lost that softness of nature, so he lost his fear of men. He would watch for Oldring, biding his time, and he would kill this great black-bearded rustler who had held a girl in bondage, who had used her to his infamous ends.

Venters surmised this much of the change in him—idleness had passed; keen, fierce vigor flooded his mind and body; all that had happened to him at Cottonwoods seemed remote and hard to recall; the difficulties and perils of the present absorbed him, held him in a kind of spell.

First, then, he fitted up the little cave adjoining the girl's room for his own comfort and use. His next work was to build a fireplace of stones and to gather a store of wood. That done, he spilled the contents of his saddle-bags upon the grass and took stock. His outfit consisted of a small-handled axe, a hunting-knife, a large number of cartridges for rifle or revolver, a tin plate, a cup, and a fork and spoon, a quantity of dried beef and dried fruits, and small canvas bags containing tea, sugar, salt, and pepper. For him alone this supply would have been bountiful to begin a sojourn in the wilderness, but he was no longer alone. Starvation in the uplands was not an unheard-of thing; he did not, however, worry at all on that score, and feared only his possible inability to supply the needs of a woman in a weakened and extremely delicate condition.

If there was no game in the valley—a contingency he doubted—it would not be a great task for him to go by night to Oldring's herd and pack out a calf. The exigency of the moment was to ascertain if there were game in Surprise Valley. Whitie still guarded the dilapidated rabbit, and Ring slept near by under a spruce. Venters called Ring and went to the edge of the terrace, and there halted to survey the valley.

He was prepared to find it larger than his unstudied glances had made it appear; for more than a casual idea of dimensions and a hasty conception of oval shape and singular beauty he had not had time. Again the felicity of the name he had given the valley struck him forcibly. Around the red perpendicular walls, except under the great arc of stone, ran a terrace fringed at the cliff-base by silver spruces; below that first terrace sloped another wider one densely overgrown with aspens, and the center of the valley was a level circle of oaks and alders, with the glittering green line of willows and cottonwood dividing it in half. Venters saw a number and variety of birds flitting among the trees. To his left, facing the stone bridge, an enormous cavern opened in the wall; and low down, just above the tree-tops, he made out a long shelf of cliff-dwellings, with little black, staring windows or doors. Like eyes they were, and seemed to watch him. The few cliff-dwellings he had seen—all ruins—had left him with haunting memory of age and solitude and of something past. He had come, in a way, to be a cliff-dweller himself, and those silent eyes would look down upon him, as if in surprise that after thousands of years a man had invaded the valley.

Venters felt sure that he was the only white man who had ever walked under the shadow of the wonderful stone bridge, down into that wonderful valley with its circle of caves and its terraced rings of silver spruce and aspens.

The dog growled below and rushed into the forest. Venters ran down the declivity to enter a zone of light shade streaked with sunshine. The oak-trees were slender, none more than half a foot thick, and they grew close together, intermingling their branches. Ring came running back with a rabbit in his mouth. Venters took the rabbit and, holding the dog near him, stole softly on. There were fluttering of wings among the branches and quick bird-notes, and rustling of dead leaves and rapid patterings. Venters crossed well-worn trails marked with fresh tracks; and when he had stolen on a little farther he saw many birds and running quail, and more rabbits than he could count. He had not penetrated the forest of oaks for a hundred yards, had not approached anywhere near the line of willows and cottonwoods which he knew grew along a stream. But he had seen enough to know that Surprise Valley was the home of many wild creatures.

Venters returned to camp. He skinned the rabbits, and gave the dogs the one they had quarreled over, and the skin of this he dressed and hung up to dry, feeling that he would like to keep it. It was a particularly rich, furry pelt with a beautiful white tail. Venters remembered that but for the bobbing of that white tail catching his eye he would not have espied the rabbit, and he would never have discovered Surprise Valley. Little incidents of chance like this had turned him here and there in Deception Pass; and now they had assumed to him the significance and direction of destiny.

His good fortune in the matter of game at hand brought to his mind the necessity of keeping it in the valley. Therefore he took the axe and cut bundles of aspens and willows, and packed them up under the bridge to the narrow outlet of the gorge. Here he began fashioning a fence, by driving aspens into the ground and lacing them fast with willows. Trip after trip he made down for more building material, and the afternoon had passed when he finished the work to his satisfaction. Wildcats might scale the fence, but no coyote could come in to search for prey, and no rabbits or other small game could escape from the valley.

Upon returning to camp he set about getting his supper at ease, around a fine fire, without hurry or fear of discovery. After hard work that had definite purpose, this freedom and comfort gave him peculiar satisfaction. He caught himself often, as he kept busy round the camp-fire, stopping to glance at the quiet form in the cave, and at the dogs stretched cozily near him, and then out across the beautiful valley. The present was not yet real to him.

While he ate, the sun set beyond a dip in the rim of the curved wall. As the morning sun burst wondrously through a grand arch into this valley, in a golden, slanting shaft, so the evening sun, at the moment of setting, shone through a gap of cliffs, sending down a broad red burst to brighten the oval with a blaze of fire. To Venters both sunrise and sunset were unreal.

A cool wind blew across the oval, waving the tips of oaks, and, while the light lasted, fluttering the aspen leaves into millions of facets of red, and sweeping the graceful spruces. Then with the wind soon came a shade and a darkening, and suddenly the valley was gray. Night came there quickly after the sinking of the sun. Venters went softly to look at the girl. She slept, and her breathing was quiet and slow. He lifted Ring into the cave, with stern whisper for him to stay there on guard. Then he drew the blanket carefully over her and returned to the camp-fire.

Though exceedingly tired, he was yet loath to yield to lassitude, but this night it was not from listening, watching vigilance; it was from a desire to realize his position. The details of his wild environment seemed the only substance of a strange dream. He saw the darkening rims, the gray oval turning black, the undulating surface of forest, like a rippling lake, and the spear-pointed spruces. He heard the flutter of aspen-leaves and the soft, continuous splash of falling water. The melancholy note of a cañon bird broke clear and lonely from the high cliffs. Venters had no name for this night singer, and he had never seen one; but the few notes, always pealing out just at darkness, were as familiar to him as the cañon silence. Then they ceased, and the rustle of leaves and the murmur of water hushed in a growing sound that Venters fancied was not of earth. Neither had he a name for this, only it was inexpressibly wild and sweet. The thought came that it might be a moan of the girl in her last outcry of life, and he felt a tremor shake him. But no! This sound was not human, though it was like despair. He began to doubt his sensitive perceptions, to believe that he half-dreamed what he thought he heard. Then the sound swelled with the strengthening of the breeze, and he realized it was the singing of the wind in the cliffs.

By and by a drowsiness overcame him, and Venters began to nod, half asleep, with his back against a spruce. Rousing himself and calling Whitie, he went to the cave. The girl lay barely visible in the dimness. Ring crouched beside her, and the patting of his tail on the stone assured Venters that the dog was awake and faithful to his duty. Venters sought his own bed of fragrant boughs; and as he lay back, somehow grateful for the comfort and safety, the night seemed to steal away from him and he sank softly into intangible space and rest and slumber.

Venters awakened to the sound of melody that he imagined was only the haunting echo of dream music. He opened his eyes to another surprise of this valley of beautiful surprises. Out of his cave he saw the exquisitely fine foliage of the silver spruces crossing a round space of blue morning sky; and in this lacy leafage fluttered a number of gray birds with black and white stripes and long tails. They were mocking-birds, and they were singing as if they wanted to burst their throats. Venters listened. One long, silver-tipped branch drooped almost to his cave, and upon it, within a few yards of him, sat one of the graceful birds. Venters saw the swelling and quivering of its throat in song. He arose, and when he slid down out of his cave the birds fluttered and flew farther away.

Venters stepped before the opening of the other cave and looked in. The girl was awake, with wide eyes and listening look, and she had a hand on Ring's neck.

'Mocking-birds!' she said.

'Yes,' replied Venters, 'and I believe they like our company.'

'Where are we?'

'Never mind now. After a little I'll tell you.'

'The birds woke me. When I heard them—and saw the shiny trees—and the blue sky—and then a blaze of gold dropping down—I wondered—'

She did not complete her fancy, but Venters imagined he understood her meaning. She appeared to be wandering in mind. Venters felt her face and hands and found them burning with fever. He went for water, and was glad to find it almost as cold as if flowing with ice. That water was the only medicine he had, and he put faith in it. She did not want to drink, but he made her swallow, and then he bathed her face and head and cooled her wrists.

The day began with a heightening of the fever. Venters spent the time reducing her temperature, cooling her hot cheeks and temples. He kept close watch over her, and at the least indication of restlessness, that he knew led to tossing and rolling of the body, he held her tightly, so no violent move could reopen her wounds. Hour after hour she babbled and laughed and cried and moaned in delirium; but whatever her secret was she did not reveal it. Attended by something somber for Venters, the day passed. At night in the cool winds the fever abated and she slept.

The second day was a repetition of the first. On the third he seemed to see her wither and waste away before his eyes. That day he scarcely went from her side for a moment, except to run for fresh, cool water; and he did not eat. The fever broke on the fourth day and left her spent and shrunken, a slip of a girl with life only in her eyes. They hung upon Venters with a mute observance, and he found hope in that.

To rekindle the spark that had nearly flickered out, to nourish the little life and vitality that remained in her, was Venters's problem. But he had little resource other than the meat of the rabbits and quail; and from these he made broths and soups as best he could, and fed her with a spoon. It came to him that the human body, like the human soul, was a strange thing and capable of recovering from terrible shocks. For almost immediately she showed faint signs of gathering strength. There was one more waiting day, in which he doubted, and spent long hours by her side as she slept, and watched the gentle swell of her breast rise and fall in breathing, and the wind stir the tangled chestnut curls. On the next day he knew that she would live.

Upon realizing it he abruptly left the cave and sought his accustomed seat against the trunk of a big spruce, where once more he let his glance stray along the sloping terraces. She would live, and the somber gloom lifted out of the valley, and he felt relief that was pain. Then he roused to the call of action, to the many things he needed to do in the way of making camp fixtures and utensils, to the necessity of hunting food, and the desire to explore the valley.

But he decided to wait a few more days before going far from camp, because he fancied that the girl rested easier when she could see him near at hand. And on the first day her languor appeared to leave her in a renewed grip of life. She awoke stronger from each short slumber; she ate greedily, and she moved about in her bed of boughs; and always, it seemed to Venters, her eyes followed him. He knew now that her recovery would be rapid. She talked about the dogs, about the caves, the valley, about how hungry she was, till Venters silenced her, asking her to put off further talk till another time. She obeyed, but she sat up in her bed, and her eyes roved to and fro, and always back to him.

Upon the second morning she sat up when he awakened her, and would not permit him to bathe her face and feed her, which actions she performed for herself. She spoke little, however, and Venters was quick to catch in her the first intimations of thoughtfulness and curiosity and appreciation of her situation. He left camp and took Whitie out to hunt for rabbits. Upon his return he was amazed and somewhat anxiously concerned to see his invalid sitting with her back to a corner of the cave and her bare feet swinging out. Hurriedly he approached, intending to advise her to lie down again, to tell her that perhaps she might overtax her strength. The sun shone upon her, glinting on the little head with its tangle of bright hair and the small, oval face with its pallor, and dark-blue eyes underlined by dark-blue circles. She looked at him and he looked at her. In that exchange of glances he imagined each saw the other in some different guise. It seemed impossible to Venters that this frail girl could be Oldring's Masked Rider. It flashed over him that he had made a mistake which presently she would explain.

'Help me down,' she said.

'But—are you well enough?' he protested. 'Wait—a little longer.'

'I'm weak—dizzy. But I want to get down.'

He lifted her—what a light burden now!—and stood her upright beside him, and supported her as she essayed to walk with halting steps. She was like a stripling of a boy; the bright, small head scarcely reached his shoulder. But now, as she clung to his arm, the rider's costume she wore did not contradict, as it had done at first, his feeling of her femininity. She might be the famous Masked Rider of the uplands, she might resemble a boy; but her outline, her little hands and feet, her hair, her big eyes and tremulous lips, and especially a something that Venters felt as a subtle essence rather than what he saw, proclaimed her sex.

She soon tired. He arranged a comfortable seat for her under the spruce that overspread the camp-fire.

'Now tell me—everything,' she said.

He recounted all that had happened from the time of his discovery of the rustlers in the cañon up to the present moment.

'You shot me—and now you've saved my life?'

'Yes. After almost killing you I've pulled you through.'

'Are you glad?'

'I should say so!'

Her eyes were unusually expressive, and they regarded him steadily; she was unconscious of that mirroring of her emotions, and they shone with gratefulness and interest and wonder and sadness.

'Tell me—about yourself?' she asked.

He made this a briefer story, telling of his coming to Utah, his various occupations till he became a rider, and then how the Mormons had practically driven him out of Cottonwoods, an outcast.

Then, no longer able to withstand his own burning curiosity, he questioned her in turn.

'Are you Oldring's Masked Rider?'

'Yes,' she replied, and dropped her eyes.

'I knew it—I recognized your figure—and mask, for I saw you once. Yet I can't believe it! ... But you never were really that rustler, as we riders knew him? A thief—a marauder—a kidnapper of women—a murderer of sleeping riders!'

'No! I never stole—or harmed any one—in all my life. I only rode and rode—'

'But why—why?' he burst out. 'Why the name? I understand Oldring made you ride. But the black mask—the mystery—the things laid to your hands—the threats in your infamous name—the night-riding credited to you—the evil deeds deliberately blamed on you and acknowledged by rustlers—even Oldring himself! Why? Tell me why!'

'I never knew that,' she answered low. Her drooping head straightened, and the large eyes, larger now and darker, met Venters's with a clear, steadfast gaze in which he read truth. It verified his own conviction.

'Never knew? That's strange! Are you a Mormon?'

'No.'

'Is Oldring a Mormon?'

'No.'

'Do you—care for him?'

'Yes. I hate his men—his life—sometimes I almost hate him!'

Venters paused in his rapid-fire questioning, as if to brace himself to ask for a truth that would be abhorrent for him to confirm, but which he seemed driven to hear.

'What are—what *were* you to Oldring?'

Like some delicate thing suddenly exposed to blasting heat, the girl wilted; her head dropped, and into her white, wasted cheeks crept the red of shame.

Venters would have given anything to recall that question. It seemed so different—his thought when spoken. Yet her shame established in his mind something akin to the respect he had strangely been hungering to feel for her.

'D—n that question!—forget it!' he cried, in a passion of pain for her and anger at himself. 'But once and for all—tell me—I know it, yet I want to hear you say so—you couldn't help yourself?'

'Oh no.'

'Well, that makes it all right with me,' he went on, honestly. 'I—I want you to feel that ... you see—we've been thrown together—and—and I want to help you—not hurt you. I thought life had been cruel to me, but when I think of yours I feel mean and little for my complaining. Anyway, I was a lonely outcast. And now! ... I don't see very clearly what it all means. Only we are here—together.

We've got to stay here, for long, surely till you are well. But you'll never go back to Oldring. And I'm sure helping you will help me, for I was sick in mind. There's something now for me to do. And if I can win back your strength—then get you away, out of this wild country—help you somehow to a happier life—just think how good that'll be for me!'

CHAPTER TEN
Love

During all these waiting days Venters, with the exception of the afternoon when he had built the gate in the gorge, had scarcely gone out of sight of camp and never out of hearing. His desire to explore Surprise Valley was keen, and on the morning after his long talk with the girl he took his rifle and, calling Ring, made a move to start. The girl lay back in a rude chair of boughs he had put together for her. She had been watching him, and when he picked up the gun and called the dog Venters thought she gave a nervous start.

'I'm only going to look over the valley,' he said.

'Will you be gone long?'

'No,' he replied, and started off. The incident set him thinking of his former impression that, after her recovery from fever, she did not seem at ease unless he was close at hand. It was fear of being alone, due, he concluded, most likely to her weakened condition. He must not leave her much alone.

As he strode down the sloping terrace, rabbits scampered before him, and the beautiful valley quail, as purple in color as the sage on the uplands, ran fleetly along the ground into the forest. It was pleasant under the trees, in the goldflecked shade, with the whistle of quail and twittering of birds everywhere. Soon he had passed the limit of his former excursions and entered new territory. Here the woods began to show open glades and brooks running down from the slope, and presently he emerged from shade into the sunshine of a meadow. The shaking of the high grass told him of the running of animals, what species he could not tell, but from Ring's manifest desire to have a chase they were evidently some kind wilder than rabbits. Venters approached the willow and cottonwood belt that he had observed from the height of slope. He penetrated it to find a considerable stream of water and great half-submerged mounds of brush and sticks, and all about him were old and new gnawed circles at the base of the cottonwoods.

'Beaver!' he exclaimed. 'By all that's lucky! The meadow's full of beaver! How did they ever get here?'

Beaver had not found a way into the valley by the trail of the cliff-dwellers, of that he was certain; and he began to have more than curiosity as to the outlet or inlet of the stream. When he passed some dead water, which he noted was held by a beaver-dam, there was a current in the stream, and it flowed west. Following its course, he soon entered the oak forest again, and passed through to find himself before massed and jumbled ruins of cliff-wall. There were tangled thickets of wild plum-trees and other thorny growths that made passage extremely laborsome. He found innumerable tracks of wildcats and foxes. Rustlings in the thick undergrowth told him of stealthy movements of these animals. At length his further advance appeared futile, for the reason that the stream disappeared in a split at the base of immense rocks over which he could not climb. To his relief he concluded that though beaver might work their way up the narrow chasm where the water rushed, it would be impossible for men to enter the valley there.

This western curve was the only part of the valley where the walls had been split asunder, and it was a wildly rough and inaccessible corner. Going back a little way, he leaped the stream and headed toward the southern wall. Once out of the oaks he found again the low terrace of aspens, and above that the wide, open terrace fringed by silver spruces. This side of the valley contained the wind or water worn caves. As he pressed on, keeping to the upper terrace, cave after cave opened out of the cliff; now a large one, now a small one. Then yawned, quite suddenly and wonderfully above him, the great cavern of the cliff-dwellers.

It was still a goodly distance, and he tried to imagine, if it appeared so huge from where he stood, what it would be when he got there. He climbed the terrace and then faced a long, gradual ascent of weathered rock and dust, which made climbing too difficult for attention to anything else. At length he entered a zone of shade, and looked up. He stood just within the hollow of a cavern so immense that he had no conception of its real dimensions. The curved roof, stained by ages of leakage, with buff and black and rust-colored streaks, swept up and loomed higher and seemed to soar to the rim of the cliff. Here again was a magnificent arch, such as formed the grand gateway to the valley, only in this instance it formed the dome of a cave instead of the span of a bridge.

Venters passed onward and upward. The stones he dislodged rolled down with strange, hollow crack and roar. He had climbed a hundred rods inward, and yet he had not reached the base of the shelf where the cliff-dwellings rested, a long half circle of connected stone house, with little dark holes that he had fancied were eyes. At length he gained the base of the shelf, and here found steps cut in the rock. These facilitated climbing, and as he went up he thought how easily this vanished race of men might once have held that stronghold against an army. There was only one possible place to ascend, and this was narrow and steep.

Venters had visited cliff-dwellings before, and they had been in ruins, and of no great character or size but this place was of proportions that stunned him, and it had not been desecrated by the hand of man, nor had it been crumbled by the hand of time. It was a stupendous tomb. It had been a city. It was just as it had been left by its builders. The little houses were there, the smoke-blackened stains of fires, the pieces of pottery scattered about cold hearths, the stone hatchets; and stone pestles and mealing-stones lay beside round holes polished by years of grinding maize—lay there as if they had been carelessly dropped yesterday. But the cliff-dwellers were gone!

Dust! They were dust on the floor or at the foot of the shelf, and their habitations and utensils endured. Venters felt the sublimity of that marvelous vaulted arch, and it seemed to gleam with a glory of something that was gone. How many years had passed since the cliff-dwellers gazed out across the beautiful valley as he was gazing now? How long had it been since women ground grain in those polished holes? What time had rolled by since men of an unknown race lived, loved, fought, and died there? Had an enemy destroyed them? Had disease destroyed them, or only that greatest destroyer—time? Venters saw a long line of blood-red hands painted low down upon the yellow roof of stone. Here was strange portent, if not an answer to his queries. The place oppressed him. It was light, but full of a transparent gloom. It smelled of dust and musty stone, of age and disuse. It was sad. It was solemn. It had the look of a place where silence had become master and was now irrevocable and terrible and could not be broken. Yet, at the moment, from high up in the carved crevices of the arch, floated down the low, strange wail of wind—a knell indeed for all that had gone.

Venters, sighing, gathered up an armful of pottery, such pieces as he thought strong enough and suitable for his own use, and bent his steps toward camp. He mounted the terrace at an opposite point to which he had left. He saw the girl looking in the direction he had gone. His footsteps made no sound in the deep grass, and he approached close without her being aware of his presence. Whitie lay on the ground near where she sat, and he manifested the usual actions of welcome, but the girl did not notice them. She seemed to be oblivious to everything near at hand. She made a pathetic figure drooping there, with her sunny hair contrasting so markedly with her white, wasted cheeks and her hands listlessly clasped and her little bare feet propped in the framework of the rude seat. Venters could have sworn and laughed in one breath at the idea of the connection between this girl and Oldring's Masked Rider. She was the victim of more than accident of fate—a victim to some deep plot the mystery of which burned him. As he stepped forward with a half-formed thought that she was absorbed in watching for his return, she turned her head and saw him. A swift start, a change rather than rush of blood under her white cheeks, a flashing of big eyes that fixed their glance upon him, transformed her face in that single instant of turning; and he knew she had been watching for him, that his return was the one thing in her mind. She did not smile; she did not flush, she did not look glad. All these would have meant little compared to her indefinite expression. Venters grasped the peculiar, vivid, vital something that leaped from her face. It was as if she had been in a dead, hopeless clamp of inaction and feeling, and had been suddenly shot through and through with quivering animation. Almost it was as if she had returned to life.

And Venters thought with lightning swiftness, 'I've saved her—I've unlinked her from that old life—she was watching as if I were all she had left on earth—she belongs to me!' The thought was startlingly new. Like a blow it was in an unprepared moment. The cheery salutation he had ready for her died unborn and he tumbled the pieces of pottery awkwardly on the grass, while some unfamiliar, deep-seated emotion, mixed with pity and glad assurance of his power to succor her, held him dumb.

'What a load you had!' she said. 'Why, they're pots and crocks! Where did you get them?'

Venters laid down his rifle, and, filling one of the pots from his canteen, he placed it on the smoldering camp-fire.

'Hope it'll hold water,' he said, presently. 'Why, there's an enormous cliff dwelling just across here. I got the pottery there. Don't you think we needed something? That tin cup of mine has served to make tea, broth, soup—everything.'

'I noticed we hadn't a great deal to cook in.'

She laughed. It was the first time. He liked that laugh, and though he was tempted to look at her, he did not want to show his surprise or his pleasure.

'Will you take me over there, and all around in the valley—pretty soon when I'm well?' she added.

'Indeed I shall. It's a wonderful place. Rabbits so thick you can't step without kicking one out. And quail, beaver, foxes, wildcats. We're in a regular den. But—haven't you ever seen a cliff-dwelling?'

'No. I've heard about them, though. The—the men say the Pass is full of old houses and ruins.'

'Why, I should think you'd have run across one in all your riding around,' said Venters. He spoke slowly, choosing his words carefully, and he essayed a perfectly casual manner, and pretended to be busy sorting pieces of pottery. She must have no cause again to suffer shame for curiosity of his. Yet never in all his days had he been so eager to hear the details of anyone's life.

'When I rode—I rode like the wind,' she replied, 'and never had time to stop for anything.'

'I remember that day I—I met you in the Pass—how dusty you were, how tired your horse looked. Were you always riding?'

'Oh, no. Sometimes not for months, when I was shut up in the cabin.'

Venters tried to subdue a hot tingling.

'You were shut up, then?' he asked, carelessly.

'When Oldring went away on his long trips—he was gone for months sometimes—he shut me up in the cabin.'

'What for?'

'Perhaps to keep me from running away. I always threatened that. Mostly, though, because the men got drunk at the villages. But they were always good to me. I wasn't afraid.'

'A prisoner! That must have been hard on you.'

'I liked that. As long as I can remember I've been locked up there at times, and those times were the only happy ones I ever had. It's a big cabin, high up on a cliff, and I could look out. Then I had dogs and pets I had tamed, and books. There was a spring inside, and food stored, and the men brought me fresh meat. Once I was there one whole winter.'

It now required deliberation on Venters's part to persist in his unconcern and to keep at work. He wanted to look at her, to volley questions at her.

'As long as you can remember—you've lived in Deception Pass?' he went on.

'I've a dim memory of some other place, and women and children; but I can't make anything of it. Sometimes I think till I'm weary.'

'Then you can read—you have books?'

'Oh yes, I can read, and write, too, pretty well. Oldring is educated. He taught me, and years ago an old rustler lived with us, and he had been something different once. He was always teaching me.'

'So Oldring takes long trips,' mused Venters. 'Do you know where he goes?'

'No. Every year he drives cattle north of Sterling—then does not return for months. I heard him accused once of living two lives—and he killed the man. That was at Stone Bridge.'

Venters dropped his apparent task and looked up with an eagerness he no longer strove to hide.

'Bess,' he said, using her name for the first time, 'I suspected Oldring was something besides a rustler. Tell me, what's his purpose here in the Pass? I believe much that he has done was to hide his real work here.'

'You're right. He's more than a rustler. In fact, as the men say, his rustling cattle is now only a bluff. There's gold in the cañons!'

'Ah!'

'Yes, there's gold, not in great quantities, but gold enough for him and his men. They wash for gold week in and week out. Then they drive a few cattle and go into the villages to drink and shoot and kill—to bluff the riders.'

'Drive a few cattle! But, Bess, the Withersteen herd, the red herd—twenty-five hundred head! That's not a few. And I tracked them into a valley near here.'

'Oldring never stole the red herd. He made a deal with Mormons. The riders were to be called in, and Oldring was to drive the herd and keep it till a certain time—I don't know when—then drive it back to the range. What his share was I didn't hear.'

'Did you hear *why* that deal was made?' queried Venters.

'No. But it was a trick of Mormons. They're full of tricks. I've heard Oldring's men tell about Mormons. Maybe the Withersteen woman wasn't minding her halter! I saw the man who made the deal. He was a little, queer-shaped man, all humped up. He sat his horse well. I heard one of our men say afterward there was no better rider on the sage than this fellow. What was the name? I forget.'

'Jerry Card?' suggested Venters.

'That's it. I remember—it's a name easy to remember—and Jerry Card appeared to be on fair terms with Oldring's men.'

'I shouldn't wonder,' replied Venters, thoughtfully. Verification of his suspicions in regard to Tull's underhand work—for the deal with Oldring made by Jerry Card assuredly had its inception in the Mormon Elder's brain, and had been accomplished through his orders—revived in Venters a memory of hatred that had been smothered by press of other emotions. Only a few days had elapsed since the hour of his encounter with Tull, yet they had been forgotten and now seemed far off, and the interval one that now appeared large and profound with incalculable change in his feelings. Hatred of Tull still existed in his heart; but it had lost its white heat. His affection for Jane Withersteen had not changed in the least; nevertheless, he seemed to view it from another angle and see it as another thing—what, he could not exactly define. The recalling of these two feelings was to Venters like getting glimpses into a self that was gone; and the wonder of them—perhaps the change which was too illusive for him—was the fact that a strange irritation accompanied the memory and a desire to dismiss it from mind. And straightaway he did dismiss it, to return to thoughts of his significant present.

'Bess, tell me one more thing,' he said. 'Haven't you known any women—any young people?'

'Sometimes there were women with the men; but Oldring never let me know them. And all the young people I ever saw in my life was when I rode fast through the villages.'

Perhaps that was the most puzzling and thought-provoking thing she had yet said to Venters. He pondered, more curious the more he learned, but he curbed his inquisitive desires, for he saw her shrinking on the verge of that shame, the causing of which had occasioned him such self-reproach. He would ask no more. Still he had to think, and he found it difficult to think clearly. This sad-eyed girl was so utterly different from what it would have been reason to believe such a remarkable life would have made her. On this day he had found her simple and frank, as natural as any girl he had ever known. About her there was something sweet. Her voice was low and well modulated. He could not look into her face, meet her steady, unabashed, yet wistful eyes, and think of her as the woman she had confessed herself. Oldring's Masked Rider sat before him, a girl dressed as a man. She had been made to ride at the head of infamous forays and drives. She had been imprisoned for many months of her life in an obscure cabin. At times the most vicious of men had been her companions; and the vilest of women, if they had not been permitted to approach her, had, at least, cast their shadows over her. But—but in spite of all this—there thundered at Venters some truth that lifted its voice higher than the clamoring facts of dishonor, some truth that was the very life of her beautiful eyes; and it was innocence.

In the days that followed, Venters balanced perpetually in mind this haunting conception of innocence over against the cold and sickening fact of an unintentional yet actual gift. How could it be possible for the two things to be true? He believed the latter to be true, and he would not relinquish his conviction of the former; and these conflicting thoughts augmented the mystery that appeared to be a part of Bess. In those ensuing days, however, it became clear as clearest light that Bess was rapidly regaining strength; that, unless reminded of her long association with Oldring, she seemed to have forgotten it; that, like an Indian who lives solely from moment to moment, she was utterly absorbed in the present.

Day by day Venters watched the white of her face slowly change to brown, and the wasted cheeks fill out by imperceptible degrees. There came a time when he could just trace the line of demarcation between the part of her face once hidden by a mask and that left exposed to wind and sun. When that line disappeared in clear bronze tan it was as if she had been washed clean of the stigma of Oldring's Masked Rider. The suggestion of the mask always made Venters remember; now that it was gone he seldom thought of her past. Occasionally he tried to piece together the several stages of strange experience and to make a whole. He had shot a masked outlaw the very sight of whom had been ill omen to riders; he had carried off a wounded woman whose bloody lips quivered in prayer; he had nursed what seemed a frail, shrunken boy; and now he watched a girl whose face had become strangely sweet, whose dark-blue eyes were ever upon him without boldness, without shyness, but with a steady, grave, and growing light. Many times Venters found the clear gaze embarrassing to him, yet, like wine, it had an exhilarating effect. What did she think when she looked at him so? Almost he believed she had no thought at all. All about her and the present there in Surprise Valley, and the dim yet subtly impending future, fascinated Venters and made him thoughtful as all his lonely vigils in the sage had not.

Chiefly it was the present that he wished to dwell upon; but it was the call of the future which stirred him to action. No idea had he of what that future had in store for Bess and him. He began to think of improving Surprise Valley as a place to live in, for there was no telling how long they would be compelled to stay there. Venters stubbornly resisted the entering into his mind of an insistent thought that, clearly realized, might have made it plain to him that he did not want to leave Surprise Valley at all. But it was imperative that he consider practical matters; and whether or not he was destined to stay long there, he felt the immediate need of a change of diet. It would be necessary for him to go farther afield for a variety of meat, and also that he soon visit Cottonwoods for a supply of food.

It occurred again to Venters that he could go to the cañon where Oldring kept his cattle, and at little risk he could pack out some beef. He wished to do this, however, without letting Bess know of it till after he had made the trip. Presently he hit upon the plan of going while she was asleep.

That very night he stole out of camp, climbed up under the stone bridge, and entered the outlet to the Pass. The gorge was full of luminous gloom. Balancing Rock loomed dark and leaned over the pale descent. Transformed in the shadowy light, it took shape and dimensions of a spectral god waiting—waiting for the moment to hurl himself down upon the tottering walls and close forever the outlet to Deception Pass. At night more than by day Venters felt something fearful and fateful in that rock, and that it had leaned and waited through a thousand years to have somehow to deal with his destiny.

'Old man, if you must roll, wait till I get back to the girl, and then roll!' he said, aloud, as if the stones were indeed a god.

And those spoken words, in their grim note to his ear, as well as contents to his mind, told Venters that he was all but drifting on a current which he had not power nor wish to stem.

Venters exercised his usual care in the matter of hiding tracks from the outlet, yet it took him scarcely an hour to reach Oldring's cattle. Here sight of many calves changed his original intention, and instead of packing out meat he decided to take a calf out alive. He roped one, securely tied its feet, and swung it up over his shoulder. Here was an exceedingly heavy burden, but Venters was powerful—he could take up a sack of grain and with ease pitch it over a pack-saddle—and he made long distance without resting. The hardest work came in the climb up to the outlet and on through to the valley. When he had accomplished it, he became fired with another idea that again changed his intention. He would not kill the calf, but keep it alive. He would go back to Oldring's herd and pack out more calves. Thereupon he secured the calf in the best available spot for the moment and turned to make a second trip.

When Venters got back to the valley with another calf, it was close upon daybreak. He crawled into his cave and slept late. Bess had no inkling that he had been absent from camp nearly all night, and only remarked solicitously that he appeared to be more tired than usual, and more in the need of sleep. In the afternoon Venters built a gate across a small ravine near camp, and here corralled the calves; and he succeeded in completing his task without Bess being any the wiser.

That night he made two more trips to Oldring's range, and again on the following night, and yet another on the next. With eight calves in his corral, he concluded that he had enough; but it dawned upon him then that he did not want to kill one. 'I've rustled Oldring's cattle,' he said, and laughed. He noted then that all the calves were red. 'Red!' he exclaimed. 'From the red herd. I've stolen Jane Withersteen's cattle! ... That's about the strangest thing yet.'

One more trip he undertook to Oldring's valley, and this time he roped a yearling steer and killed it and cut out a small quarter of beef. The howling of coyotes told him he need have no apprehension that the work of his knife would be discovered. He packed the beef back to camp and hung it upon a spruce-tree. Then he sought his bed.

On the morrow he was up bright and early, glad that he had a surprise for Bess. He could hardly wait for her to come out. Presently she appeared and walked under the spruce. Then she approached the camp-fire. There was a tinge of healthy red in the bronze of her cheeks, and her slender form had begun to round out in graceful lines.

'Bess, didn't you say you were tired of rabbit?' inquired Venters. 'And quail and beaver?'

'Indeed I did.'

'What would you like?'

'I'm tired of meat, but if we have to live on it I'd like some beef.'

'Well, how does that strike you?' Venters pointed to the quarter hanging from the spruce tree. 'We'll have fresh beef for a few days, then we'll cut the rest into strips and dry it.'

'Where did you get that?' asked Bess, slowly.

'I stole that from Oldring.'

'You went back to the cañon—you risked—' While she hesitated the tinge of bloom faded out of her cheeks.

'It wasn't any risk, but it was hard work.'

'I'm sorry I said I was tired of rabbit. Why! How—When did you get that beef?'

'Last night.'

'While I was asleep?'

'Yes.'

'I woke last night sometime—but I didn't know.'

Her eyes were widening, darkening with thought, and whenever they did so the steady, watchful, seeing gaze gave place to the wistful light. In the former she saw as the primitive woman without thought; in the latter she looked inward, and her gaze was the reflection of a troubled mind. For long Venters had not seen that dark change, that deepening of blue, which he thought was beautiful and sad. But now he wanted to make her think.

'I've done more than pack in that beef,' he said. 'For five nights I've been working while you slept. I've got eight calves corralled near a ravine. Eight calves, all alive and doing fine!'

'You went five nights!'

All that Venters could make of the dilation of her eyes, her slow pallor, and her exclamation, was fear—fear for herself or for him.

'Yes. I didn't tell you, because I knew you were afraid to be alone.'

'Alone?' She echoed his word, but the meaning of it was nothing to her. She had not even thought of being left alone. It was not, then, fear for herself, but for him. This girl, always slow of speech and action, now seemed almost stupid. She put forth a hand that might have indicated the groping of her mind. Suddenly she stepped swiftly to him, with a look and touch that drove from him any doubt of her quick intelligence or feeling.

'Oldring has men watch the herds—they would kill you. You must never go again!'

When she had spoken, the strength and the blaze of her died, and she swayed towards Venters.

'Bess, I'll not go again,' he said, catching her.

She leaned against him, and her body was limp and vibrated to a long, wavering tremble. Her face was upturned to his. Woman's face, woman's eyes, woman's lips—all acutely and blindly and sweetly and terribly truthful in their betrayal! But as her fear was instinctive, so was her clinging to this one and only friend.

Venters gently put her from him and steadied her upon her feet; and all the while his blood raced wild, and a thrilling tingle unsteadied his nerve, and something—that he had seen and felt in her—that he could not understand—seemed very close to him, warm and rich as a fragrant breath, sweet as nothing had ever before been sweet to him.

With all his will Venters strove for calmness and thought and judgment unbiased by pity, and reality unswayed by sentiment. Bess's eyes were still fixed upon him with all her soul bright in that wistful light. Swiftly, resolutely he put out of mind all of her life except what had been spent with him. He scorned himself for the intelligence that made him still doubt. He meant to judge her as she had judged him. He was face to face with the inevitableness of life itself. He saw destiny in the dark, straight path of her wonderful eyes. Here was the simplicity, the sweetness of a girl contending with new and strange and enthralling emotions; here the living truth of innocence; here the blind terror of a woman confronted with the thought of death to her savior and protector. All this Venters saw, but, besides, there was in Bess's eyes a slow-dawning consciousness that seemed about to break out in glorious radiance.

'Bess, are you thinking?' he asked.

'Yes—oh yes!'

'Do you realize we are here alone—man and woman?'

'Yes.'

'Have you thought that we may make our way out to civilization, or we may have to stay here—alone—hidden from the world all our lives?'

'I never thought—till now.'

'Well, what's your choice—to go—or to stay here—alone with me?'

'Stay!' New-born thought of self, ringing vibrantly in her voice, gave her answer singular power.

Venters trembled, and then swiftly turned his gaze from her face—from her eyes. He knew what she had only half divined—that she loved him.

CHAPTER ELEVEN
Faith and Unfaith

At Jane Withersteen's home the promise made to Mrs Larkin to care for little Fay had begun to be fulfilled. Like a gleam of sunlight through the cottonwoods was the coming of the child to the gloomy house of Withersteen. The big, silent halls echoed with childish laughter. In the shady court, where Jane spent many of the hot July days, Fay's tiny feet pattered over the stone flags and splashed in the amber stream. She prattled incessantly. What difference, Jane thought, a child made in her home! It had never been a real home, she discovered. Even the tidiness and neatness she had so observed, and upon which she had insisted to her women, became, in the light of Fay's smile, habits that now lost their importance. Fay littered the court with Jane's books and papers, and other toys her fancy improvised, and many a strange craft went floating down the little brook.

And it was owing to Fay's presence that Jane Withersteen came to see more of Lassiter. The rider had for the most part kept to the sage. He rode for her, but he did not seek her except on business; and Jane had to acknowledge in pique that her overtures had been made in vain. Fay, however, captured Lassiter the moment he first laid eyes on her.

Jane was present at the meeting, and there was something about it which dimmed her sight and softened her toward this foe of her people. The rider had clanked into the court, a tired yet wary man, always looking for the attack upon him that was inevitable and might come from any quarter; and he had walked right upon little Fay. The child had been beautiful even in her rags and amid the surroundings of the hovel in the sage, but now, in a pretty white dress, with her shining curls brushed and her face clean and rosy, she was lovely. She left her play and looked up at Lassiter.

If there was not an instinct for all three of them in that meeting, an unreasoning tendency toward a closer intimacy, then Jane Withersteen believed she had been subject to a queer fancy. She imagined any child would have feared Lassiter. And Fay Larkin had been a lonely, a solitary elf of the sage, not at all an ordinary child, and exquisitely shy with strangers. She watched Lassiter with great, round, grave eyes, but showed no fear. The rider gave Jane a favorable report of cattle and horses; and as he took the seat to which she invited him, little Fay edged as much as half an inch nearer. Jane replied to his look of inquiry and told Fay's story. The rider's gray, earnest gaze troubled her. Then he turned to Fay and smiled in a way that made Jane doubt her sense of the true relation of things. How could Lassiter smile so at a child when he had made so many children fatherless? But he did smile, and to the gentleness she had seen a few times he added something that was infinitely sad and sweet. Jane's intuition told her that Lassiter had never been a father; but if life ever so blessed him he would be a good one. Fay, also, must have found that smile singularly winning. For she edged closer and closer, and then, by way of feminine capitulation, went to Jane, from whose side she bent a beautiful glance upon the rider.

Lassiter only smiled at her.

Jane watched them, and realized that now was the moment she should seize, if she was ever to win this man from his hatred. But the step was not easy to take. The more she saw of Lassiter the more she respected him, and the greater her respect the harder it became to lend herself to mere coquetry. Yet as she thought of her great motive, of Tull, and of that other whose name she had schooled herself never to think of in connection with Milly Erne's avenger, she suddenly found she had no choice. And her creed gave her boldness far beyond the limit to which vanity would have led her.

'Lassiter, I see so little of you now,' she said, and was conscious of heat in her cheeks.

'I've been ridin' hard,' he replied.

'But you can't live in the saddle. You come in sometimes. Won't you come here to see me—oftener?'

'Is that an order?'

'Nonsense! I simply ask you to come to see me when you find time.'

'Why?'

The query once heard was not so embarrassing to Jane as she might have imagined. Moreover, it established in her mind a fact that there existed actually other than selfish reasons for her wanting to see him. And as she had been bold, so she determined to be both honest and brave.

'I've reasons—only one of which I need mention,' she answered. 'If it's possible I want to change you toward my people. And on the moment I can conceive of little I wouldn't do to gain that end.'

How much better and freer Jane felt after that confession! She meant to show him that there was one Mormon who could play a game or wage a fight in the open.

'I reckon,' said Lassiter, and he laughed.

It was the best in her, if the most irritating, that Lassiter always aroused.

'Will you come?' She looked into his eyes, and for the life of her could not quite subdue an imperiousness that rose with her spirit. 'I never asked so much of any man—except Bern Venters.'

''Pears to me that you'd run no risk, or Venters, either. But mebbe that doesn't hold good for me.'

'You mean it wouldn't be safe for you to be often here ? You look for ambush in the cottonwoods?'

'Not that so much.'

At this juncture little Fay sidled over to Lassiter.

'Has oo a little dirl?' she inquired.

'No, lassie,' replied the rider.

Whatever Fay seemed to be searching for in Lassiter's sun-reddened face and quiet eyes she evidently found. 'Oo tan tum to see me,' she added, and with that, shyness gave place to friendly curiosity. First his sombrero with its leather band and silver ornaments commanded her attention; next his quirt, and then the clinking, silver spurs. These held her for some time, but presently, true to childish fickleness, she left off playing with them to look for something else. She laughed in glee as she ran her little hands down the slippery, shiny surface of Lassiter's leather chaps. Soon she discovered one of the hanging gun-sheaths, and she dragged it up and began tugging at the huge black handle of the gun. Jane Withersteen repressed an exclamation. What significance there was to her in the little girl's efforts to dislodge that heavy weapon! Jane Withersteen saw Fay's play and her beauty and her love as most powerful allies to her own woman's part in a game that suddenly had acquired a strange zest and a hint of danger. And as for the rider, he appeared to have forgotten Jane in the wonder of this lovely child playing about him. At first he was much the shyer of the two. Gradually her confidence overcame his backwardness, and he had the temerity to stroke her golden curls with a great hand. Fay rewarded his boldness with a smile, and when he had gone to the extreme of closing that great hand over her little brown one, she said, simple, 'I like oo!'

Sight of his face then made Jane oblivious for the time of his character as a hater of Mormons. Out of the mother longing that swelled her breast she divined the child hunger in Lassiter.

He returned the next day, and the next; and upon the following he came both at morning and at night. Upon the evening of this fourth day Jane seemed to feel the breaking of a brooding struggle in Lassiter. During all these visits he had scarcely a word to say, though he watched her and played absent-mindedly with Fay. Jane had contented herself with silence. Soon little Fay substituted for the expression of regard, 'I like oo,' a warmer and more generous one, 'I love oo.'

Thereafter Lassiter came oftener to see Jane and her little protégée. Daily he grew more gentle and kind, and gradually developed a quaintly merry mood. In the morning he lifted Fay upon his horse and let her ride as he walked beside her to the edge of the sage. In the evening he played with the child at an infinite variety of games she invented, and then, oftener than not, he accepted Jane's invitation to supper. No other visitor came to Withersteen House during those days. So that in spite of watchfulness he never forgot, Lassiter began to show he felt at home there. After the meal they walked into the grove of cottonwoods or up by the lakes, and little Fay held Lassiter's hand as much as she held Jane's. Thus a strange relationship was established, and Jane liked it. At twilight they always returned to the house, where Fay kissed them and went in to her mother. Lassiter and Jane were left alone.

Then, if there were anything that a good woman could do to win a man and still preserve her self-respect, it was something which escaped the natural subtlety of a woman determined to allure. Jane's vanity, that after all was not great, was soon satisfied with Lassiter's silent admiration. And her honest desire to lead him from his dark, blood-stained path would never have blinded her to what she owed herself. But the driving passion of her religion, and its call to save Mormons' lives, one life in particular, bore Jane Withersteen close to an infringement of her

womanhood. In the beginning she had reasoned that her appeal to Lassiter must
be through the senses. With whatever means she possessed in the way of
adornment she enhanced her beauty. And she stooped to artifices that she knew
were unworthy of her, but which she deliberately chose to employ. She made of
herself a girl in every variable mood wherein a girl might be desirable. In those
moods she was not above the methods of an inexperienced though natural flirt.
She kept close to him whenever opportunity afforded; and she was forever
playfully, yet passionately underneath the surface, fighting him for possession of
the great black guns. These he would never yield to her. And so in that manner
their hands were often and long in contact. The more of simplicity that she sensed
in him the greater the advantage she took.

She had a trick of changing—and it was not altogether voluntary—from
this gay, thoughtless, girlish coquettishness to the silence and the brooding,
burning mystery of a woman's mood. The strength and passion and fire of her
were in her eyes, and she so used them that Lassiter had to see this depth in her,
this haunting promise more fitted to her years than to the flaunting guise
of a willful girl.

The July days flew by. Jane reasoned that if it were possible for her to be happy
during such a time, then she was happy. Little Fay completely filled a long aching
void in her heart. In fettering the hands of this Lassiter she was accomplishing
the greatest good of her life, and to do good even in a small way rendered
happiness to Jane Withersteen. She had attended the regular Sunday services of
her church; otherwise she had not gone to the village for weeks. It was unusual
that none of her churchmen or friends had called upon her of late; but it was
neglect for which she was glad. Judkins and his boy riders had experienced no
difficulty in driving the white herd. So these warm July days were free of worry,
and soon Jane hoped she had passed the crisis; and for her to hope was presently
to trust, and then to believe. She thought often of Venters, but in a dreamy,
abstract way. She spent hours teaching and playing with little Fay. And the activity
of her mind centered around Lassiter. The direction she had given her will seemed
to blunt any branching off of thought from that straight line. The mood came to
obsess her.

In the end, when her awakening came, she learned that she had built better
than she knew. Lassiter, though kinder and gentler than ever, had parted with his
quaint humor and his coldness and his tranquillity to become a restless and
unhappy man. Whatever the power of his deadly intent toward Mormons,
that passion now had a rival, and one equally burning and consuming. Jane
Withersteen had one moment of exultation before the dawn of a strange uneasiness. What if she had made of herself a lure, at tremendous cost to him and to
her, and all in vain!

That night in the moonlit grove she summoned all her courage and, turning suddenly in the path, she faced Lassiter and leaned close to him, so that she touched him and her eyes looked up to his.

'Lassiter! … Will you do anything for me?'

In the moonlight she saw his dark, worn face change, and by that change she seemed to feel him immovable as a wall of stone.

Jane slipped her hands down to the swinging gun-sheaths, and when she had locked her fingers around the huge, cold handles of the guns, she trembled as with a chilling ripple over all her body.

'May I take your guns?'

'Why?' he asked, and for the first time to her his voice carried a harsh note. Jane felt his hard, strong hands close around her wrists. It was not wholly with intent that she leaned toward him, for the look of his eyes and the feel of his hands made her weak.

'It's no trifle—no woman's whim—it's deep—as my heart. Let me take them?'

'Why?'

'I want to keep you from killing more men—Mormons. You must let me save you from more wickedness—more wanton bloodshed—' Then the truth forced itself falteringly from her lips. 'You must—let—me—help me to keep my vow to Milly Erne. I swore to her—as she lay dying—that if ever any one came here to avenge her—I swore I would stay his hand. Perhaps I—I alone can save the—the man who—who—Oh, Lassiter! … I feel that if I can't change you— then soon you'll go out to kill—and you'll kill by instinct—and among the Mormons you kill will be the one—who … Lassiter, if you care a little for me—let me—for my sake—let me take your guns!'

As if her hands had been those of a child, he unclasped their clinging grip from the handles of his guns, and, pushing her away, he turned his gray face to her in one look of terrible realization and then strode off into the shadows of cottonwoods.

When the first shock of her futile appeal to Lassiter had passed, Jane took his cold, silent condemnation and abrupt departure not so much as a refusal to her entreaty as a hurt and stunned bitterness for her attempt at his betrayal. Upon further thought and slow consideration of Lassiter's past actions, she believed he would return and forgive her. The man could not be hard to a woman, and she doubted that he could stay away from her. But at the point where she had hoped to find him vulnerable she now began to fear he was proof against all persuasion. The iron and stone quality that she had early suspected in him had actually cropped out as an impregnable barrier. Nevertheless, if Lassiter remained in Cottonwoods she would never give up her hope and desire to change him. She would change him if she had to sacrifice everything dear to her except hope of heaven. Passionately devoted as she was to her religion, she had yet refused to marry a

Mormon. But a situation had developed wherein self paled in the great white light of religious duty of the highest order. That was the leading motive, the divinely spiritual one; but there were other motives, which, like tentacles, aided in drawing her will to the acceptance of a possible abnegation. And through the watches of that sleepless night Jane Withersteen, in fear and sorrow and doubt, came finally to believe that if she must throw herself into Lassiter's arms to make him abide by 'Thou shalt not kill!' she would yet do well.

In the morning she expected Lassiter at the usual hour, but she was not able to go at once to the court, so she sent little Fay. Mrs Larkin was ill and required attention. It appeared that the mother, from the time of her arrival at Withersteen House, had relaxed and was slowly losing her hold on life. Jane had believed that absence of worry and responsibility coupled with good nursing and comfort would mend Mrs Larkin's broken health. Such, however, was not the case.

When Jane did get out to the court, Fay was there alone, and at the moment embarking on a dubious voyage down the stoned-lined amber stream upon a craft of two brooms and a pillow. Fay was as delightfully wet as she could possibly get.

Clatter of hoofs distracted Fay and interrupted the scolding she was gleefully receiving from Jane. The sound was not the light-spirited trot that Bells made when Lassiter rode him into the outer court. This was slower and heavier, and Jane did not recognize in it any of the other horses. The appearance of Bishop Dyer startled Jane. He dismounted with his rapid, jerky motion, flung the bridle, and, as he turned toward the inner court and stalked up on the stone flags, his boots rang. In his authoritative front, and in the red anger unmistakably flaming in his face, he reminded Jane of her father.

'Is that the Larkin pauper?' he asked bruskly, without any greeting to Jane.

'It's Mrs Larkin's little girl,' replied Jane, slowly.

'I hear you intend to raise the child?'

'Yes.'

'Of course you mean to give her Mormon bringing-up?'

'No!'

His questions had been swift. She was amazed at a feeling that someone else was replying for her.

'I've come to say a few things to you.' He stopped to measure her with stern, speculative eye.

Jane Withersteen loved this man. From earliest childhood she had been taught to revere and love bishops of her church. And for ten years Bishop Dyer had been the closest friend and counselor of her father, and for the greater part of that period her own friend and Scriptural teacher. Her interpretation of her creed and her religious activity in fidelity to it, her acceptance of mysterious and holy

Mormon truths, were all invested in this Bishop. Bishop Dyer as an entity was next to God. He was God's mouthpiece to the little Mormon community at Cottonwoods. God revealed himself in secret to this mortal.

And Jane Withersteen suddenly suffered a paralyzing affront to her consciousness of reverence by some strange, irresistible twist of thought wherein she saw this Bishop as a man. And the train of thought hurdled the rising, crying protests of that other self whose poise she had lost. It was not her Bishop who eyed her in curious measurement. It was a man who tramped into her presence without removing his hat, who had no greeting for her, who had no semblance of courtesy. In looks, as in action, he made her think of a bull stamping cross-grained into a corral. She had heard of Bishop Dyer forgetting the minister in the fury of a common man, and now she was to feel it. The glance by which she measured him in turn momentarily veiled the divine in the ordinary. He looked a rancher; he was booted, spurred, and covered with dust; he carried a gun at his hip, and she remembered that he had been known to use it. But during the long moment while he watched her there was nothing commonplace in the slow-gathering might of his wrath.

'Brother Tull has talked to me,' he began. 'It was your father's wish that you marry Tull, and my order. You refused him?'

'Yes.'

'You would not give up your friendship with that tramp Venters?'

'No.'

'But you'll do as *I* order!' he thundered. 'Why, Jane Withersteen, you are in danger of becoming a heretic! You can thank your Gentile friends, for that. You face the damning of your soul to perdition.'

In the flux and reflux of the whirling torture of Jane's mind, that new daring spirit of hers vanished in the old habitual order of her life. She was a Mormon, and the Bishop regained ascendance.

'It's well I got you in time, Jane Withersteen. What would your father have said to these goings-on of yours? He would have put you in a stone cage on bread and water. He would have taught you something about Mormonism. Remember, you're a *born* Mormon. There have been Mormons who turned heretic—damn their souls!—but no born Mormon ever left us yet. Ah, I see your shame. Your faith is not shaken. You are only a wild girl.' The Bishop's tone softened. 'Well, it's enough that I got to you in time. ... Now tell me about this Lassiter. I hear strange things.'

'What do you wish to know?' queried Jane.

'About this man. You hired him?'

'Yes, he's riding for me. When my riders left me I had to have any one I could get.'

'Is it true what I hear—that he's a gun-man, a Mormon-hater, steeped in blood?'

'True—terribly true, I fear.'

'But what's he doing here in Cottonwoods? This place isn't notorious enough for such a man. Sterling and the villages north, where there's universal gun-packing and fights every day—where there are more men like him, it seems to me they would attract him most. We're only a wild, lonely border settlement. It's only recently that the rustlers have made killings here. Nor have there been saloons till lately, nor the drifting in of outcasts. Has not this gun-man some special mission here?'

Jane maintained silence.

'Tell me,' ordered Bishop Dyer, sharply.

'Yes,' she replied.

'Do you know what it is?'

'Yes.'

'Tell me that.'

'Bishop Dyer, I don't want to tell.'

He waved his hand in an imperative gesture of command. The red once more leaped to his face, and in his steel-blue eyes glinted a pin-point of curiosity.

'That first day,' whispered Jane, 'Lassiter said he came here to find—Milly Erne's grave!'

With downcast eyes Jane watched the swift flow of the amber water. She saw it and tried to think of it, of the stones, of the ferns; but, like her body, her mind was in a leaden vise. Only the Bishop's voice could release her. Seemingly there was silence of longer duration than all her former life.

'For what—else?' When Bishop Dyer's voice did cleave the silence it was high, curiously shrill, and on the point of breaking. It released Jane's tongue, but she could not lift her eyes.

'To kill the man who persuaded Milly Erne to abandon her home and her husband—and her God!'

With wonderful distinctness Jane Withersteen heard her own clear voice. She heard the water murmur at her feet and flow on to the sea; she heard the rushing of all the waters in the world. They filled her ears with low, unreal murmurings—these sounds that deadened her brain and yet could not break the long and terrible silence. Then, from somewhere—from an immeasurable distance—came a slow, guarded, clinking, clanking step. Into her it shot electrifying life. It released the weight upon her numbed eyelids. Lifting her eyes she saw—ashen, shaken, stricken—not the Bishop but the man! And beyond him, from round the corner came that soft, silvery step. A long black boot with a gleaming spur swept into sight—and then Lassiter! Bishop Dyer did not see, did not hear: he stared at Jane in the throes of sudden revelation.

'Ah, I understand!' he cried, in hoarse accents. 'That's why you made love to this Lassiter—to bind his hands!'

It was Jane's gaze riveted upon the rider that made Bishop Dyer turn. Then clear sight failed her. Dizzily, in a blur, she saw the Bishop's hand jerk to his hip. She saw gleam of blue and spout of red. In her ears burst a thundering report. The court floated in darkening circles around her, and she fell into utter blackness.

The darkness lightened, turned to slow-drifting haze, and lifted. Through a thin film of blue smoke she saw the rough-hewn timbers of the court roof. A cool, damp touch moved across her brow. She smelled powder, and it was that which galvanized her suspended thought. She moved, to see that she lay prone upon the stone flags with her head on Lassiter's knee, and he was bathing her brow with water from the stream. The same swift glance, shifting low, brought into range of her sight a smoking gun and splashes of blood.

'*Ah-h!*' she moaned, and was drifting, sinking again into darkness, when Lassiter's voice arrested her.

'It's all right, Jane. It's all right.'

'Did—you—kill—him?' she whispered.

'Who? That fat party who was here? No. I didn't kill him.'

'Oh! ... Lassiter!'

'Say! It was queer for you to faint. I thought you were such a strong woman, not faintish like that. You're all right now—only some pale. I thought you'd never come to. But I'm awkward round women folks. I couldn't think of anythin'.'

'Lassiter! ... the gun there! ... the blood!'

'So that's troublin' you. I reckon it needn't. You see it was this way. I come round the house an' seen that fat party an' heard him talkin' loud. Then he seen me, an' very impolite goes straight for his gun. He oughtn't have tried to throw a gun on me—whatever his reason was. For that's meetin' me on my own grounds. I've seen runnin' molasses that was quicker'n him. Now I didn't know who he was, visitor or friend or relation of yours, though I seen he was a Mormon all over, an' I couldn't get serious about shootin'. So I winged him—put a bullet through his arm as he was pullin' at his gun. An' he dropped the gun there, an' a little blood. I told him he'd introduced himself sufficient, an' to please move out of my vicinity. An' he went.'

Lassiter spoke with slow, cool, soothing voice, in which there was a hint of levity, and his touch, as he continued to bathe her brow, was gentle and steady. His impassive face, and the kind, gray eyes, further stilled her agitation.

'He drew on you first, and you deliberately shot to cripple him—you wouldn't kill him—you—*Lassiter?*'

'That's about the size of it.'

Jane kissed his hand.

All that was calm and cool about Lassiter instantly vanished.

'Don't do that! I won't stand it! An' I don't care a d——n who that fat party was.'

He helped Jane to her feet and to a chair. Then with the wet scarf he had used to bathe her face he wiped the blood from the stone flags and, picking up the gun, he threw it upon a couch. With that he began to pace the court, and his silver spurs jangled musically, and the great gun-sheaths softly brushed against his leather chaps.

'So—it's true—what I heard him say?' Lassiter asked, presently halting before her. 'You made love to me—to bind my hands?'

'Yes,' confessed Jane. It took all her woman's courage to meet the gray storm of his glance.

'All these days that you've been so friendly an' like a pardner—all these evenin's that have been so bewilderin' to me—your beauty—an'— an' the way you looked an' came close to me—they were woman's tricks to bind my hands?'

'Yes.'

'An' your sweetness that seemed so natural, an' your throwin' little Fay an' me so much together—to make me love the child—all that was for the same reason?'

'Yes.'

Lassiter flung his arms—a strange gesture for him.

'Mebbe it wasn't much in your Mormon thinkin', for you to play that game. But to bring the child in—that was hellish!'

Jane's passionate, unheeding zeal began to loom darkly.

'Lassiter, whatever my intention in the beginning, Fay loves you dearly—and I—I've grown to—to like you.'

'That's powerful kind of you, now,' he said. Sarcasm and scorn made his voice that of a stranger. 'An' you sit there an' look me straight in the eyes! You're a wonderful strange woman, Jane Withersteen.'

'I'm not ashamed, Lassiter. I told you I'd try to change you.'

'Would you mind tellin' me just what you tried?'

'I tried to make you see beauty in me and be softened by it. I wanted you to care for me so that I could influence you. It wasn't easy. At first you were stone-blind. Then I hoped you'd love little Fay, and through that come to feel the horror of making children fatherless.'

'Jane Withersteen, either you're a fool or noble beyond my understandin'. Mebbe you're both. I know you're blind. What you meant is one thing—what you *did* was to make me love you.'

'Lassiter!'

'I reckon I'm a human bein', though I never loved any one but my sister, Milly Erne. That was long—'

'Oh, are you Milly's brother?'

'Yes, I was, an' I loved her. There never was anyone but her in my life till now. Didn't I tell you that long ago I back-trailed myself from women? I was a Texas ranger till—till Milly left home, an' then I became somethin' else—Lassiter! For years I've been a lonely man set on one thing. I came here an' met you. An' now I'm not the man I was. The change was gradual, an' I took no notice of it. I understand now that never-satisfied longin' to see you, listen to you, watch you, feel you near me. It's plain now why you were never out of my thoughts. I've had no thoughts but of you. I've lived an' breathed for you. An' now when I know what it means—what you've done—I'm burnin' up with hell's fire!'

'Oh, Lassiter—no—no—you don't love me that way!' Jane cried.

'If that's what love is, then I do.'

'Forgive me! I didn't mean to make you love me like that. Oh, what a tangle of our lives! You—Milly Erne's brother! And I—heedless, mad to melt your heart toward Mormons. Lassiter, I may be wicked, but not wicked enough to hate. If I couldn't hate Tull, could I hate you?'

'After all, Jane, mebbe you're only blind—Mormon blind. That only can explain what's close to selfishness—'

'I'm not selfish. I despise the very word. If I were free—'

'But you're not free. Not free of Mormonism. An' in playin' this game with me you've been unfaithful.'

'Unfaithful!' faltered Jane.

'Yes, I said unfaithful. You're faithful to your Bishop an' unfaithful to yourself. You're false to your womanhood an' true to your religion. But for a savin' innocence you'd have made yourself low an' vile—betrayin' yourself, betrayin' me—all to bind my hands an keep me from snuffin' out Mormon life. It's your damned Mormon blindness.'

'Is it vile—is it blind—is it only Mormonism to save human life? No, Lassiter, that's God's law, divine, universal for all Christians.'

'The blindness I mean is blindness that keeps you from seein' the truth. I've known many good Mormons. But some are blacker than hell. You won't see that even when you know it. Else, why all this blind passion to save the life of that—that. ...'

Jane shut out the light, and the hands she held over her eyes trembled and quivered against her face.

'Blind—yes, an' let me make it clear an' simple to you,' Lassiter went on, his voice losing its tone of anger. 'Take, for instance, that idea of yours last night when you wanted my guns. It was good an' beautiful, an' showed your heart—but—

why, Jane, it was crazy. Mind I'm assumin' that life to me is as sweet as to any other man. An' to preserve that life is each man's first an' closest thought. Where would any man be on this border without guns? Where, especially, would Lassiter be? Well, I'd be under the sage with thousands of other men now livin' an' sure better men than me. Gun-packin' in the West since the Civil War has growed into a kind of moral law. An' out here on this border it's the difference between a man an' somethin' not a man. Look what your takin' Venters's guns from him all but made him! Why, your churchmen carry guns. Tull has killed a man an' drawed on others. Your Bishop has shot a half dozen men, an' it wasn't through prayers of his that they recovered. An' today he'd have shot me if he'd been quick enough on the draw. Could I walk or ride down into Cottonwoods without my guns? This is a wild time, Jane Withersteen, this year of our Lord eighteen seventy-one.'

'No time—for a woman!' exclaimed Jane, brokenly. 'Oh, Lassiter, I feel helpless—lost—and don't know where to turn. If I *am* blind—then—I need some one—a friend—you, Lassiter—more than ever!'

'Well, I didn't say nothin' about goin' back on you, did I?'

CHAPTER TWELVE
The Invisible Hand

Jane received a letter from Bishop Dyer, not in his own handwriting, which stated that the abrupt termination of their interview had left him in some doubt as to her future conduct. A slight injury had incapacitated him from seeking another meeting at present, the letter went on to say, and ended with a request which was virtually a command, that she call upon him at once.

The reading of the letter acquainted Jane Withersteen with the fact that something within her had all but changed. She sent no reply to Bishop Dyer nor did she go to see him. On Sunday she remained absent from the service—for the second time in years—and though she did not actually suffer there was a dead-lock of feelings deep within her, and the waiting for a balance to fall on either side was almost as bad as suffering. She had a gloomy expectancy of untoward circumstances, and with it a keen-edged curiosity to watch developments. She had a half-formed conviction that her future conduct—as related to her churchmen— was beyond her control and would be governed by their attitude toward her.

Something was changing in her, forming, waiting for decision to make it a real and fixed thing. She had told Lassiter that she felt helpless and lost in the fateful tangle of their lives; and now she feared that she was approaching the same chaotic condition of mind in regard to her religion. It appalled her to find that she questioned phases of that religion. Absolute faith had been her serenity. Though leaving her faith unshaken, her serenity had been disturbed, and now it was broken by open war between her and her ministers. That something within her—a whisper—which she had tried in vain to hush had become a ringing voice, and it called to her to wait. She had transgressed no laws of God. Her churchmen, however invested with the power and the glory of a wonderful creed, however they sat in inexorable judgment of her, must now practice toward her the simple, common, Christian virtue they professed to preach, 'Do unto others as you have others do unto you!'

Jane Withersteen, waiting in darkness of mind, remained faithful still. But it was darkness that must soon be pierced by light. If her faith were justified, if her churchmen were trying only to intimidate her, the fact would soon be manifest, as would their failure, and then she would redouble her zeal toward them and toward what had been the best work of her life—work for the welfare and happiness of those among whom she lived. Mormon and Gentile alike. If that secret, intangible power closed its toils round her again, if that great invisible hand moved here and there and everywhere, slowly paralyzing her with its mystery and its inconceivable sway over her affairs, then she would know beyond doubt that it was not chance, nor jealousy, nor intimidation, nor ministerial wrath at her revolt, but a cold and calculating policy thought out long before she was born, a dark, immutable will of whose empire she and all that was hers was but an atom.

Then might come her ruin. Then might come her fall into black storm. Yet she would rise again, and to the light. God would be merciful to a driven woman who had lost her way.

A week passed. Little Fay played and prattled and pulled at Lassiter's big black guns. The rider came to Withersteen House oftener than ever. Jane saw a change in him, though it did not relate to his kindness and gentleness. He was quieter and more thoughtful. While playing with Fay or conversing with Jane he seemed to be possessed of another self that watched with cool, roving eyes, that listened, listened always as if the murmuring amber stream brought messages, and the moving leaves whispered something. Lassiter never rode Bells into the court any more, nor did he come by the lane or the paths. When he appeared it was suddenly and noiselessly out of the dark shadow of the grove.

'I left Bells out in the sage,' he said one day at the end of that week. 'I must carry water to him.'

'Why not let him drink at the trough or here?' asked Jane, quickly.

'I reckon it'll be safer for me to slip through the grove. I've been watched when I rode in from the sage.'

'Watched? By whom?'

'By a man who thought he was well hid. But my eyes are pretty sharp. An', Jane,' he went on, almost in a whisper, 'I reckon it'd be a good idea for us to talk low. You're spied on here by your women.'

'Lassiter!' she whispered in turn. 'That's hard to believe. My women love me.'

'What of that?' he asked. 'Of course they love you. But they're Mormon women.'

Jane's old, rebellious loyalty clashed with her doubt.

'I won't believe it,' she replied, stubbornly.

'Well then, just act natural an' talk natural, an' pretty soon—give them time to hear us—pretend to go over there to the table, an' then quick-like make a move for the door an' open it.'

'I will,' said Jane, with heightened color. Lassiter was right; he never made mistakes; he would not have told her unless he positively knew. Yet Jane was so tenacious of faith that she had to see with her own eyes, and so constituted that to employ even such small deceit toward her women made her ashamed, and angry for her shame as well as theirs. Then a singular thought confronted her that made her hold up this simple ruse—which hurt her, though it was well justified— against the deceit she had wittingly and eagerly used toward Lassiter. The difference was staggering in its suggestion of that blindness of which he had accused her. Fairness and justice and mercy, that she had imagined were anchor-cables to hold fast her soul to righteousness, had not been hers in the strange, biased duty that had so exalted and confounded her.

Presently Jane began to act her little part, to laugh and play with Fay, to talk of horses and cattle to Lassiter. Then she made deliberate mention of a book in which she kept records of all pertaining to her stock, and she walked slowly toward the table, and when near the door she suddenly whirled and thrust it open. Her sharp action nearly knocked down a woman who had undoubtedly been listening.

'Hester,' said Jane, sternly, 'you may go home, and you need not come back.'

Jane shut the door and returned to Lassiter. Standing unsteadily, she put her hand on his arm. She let him see that doubt had gone, and how this stab of disloyalty pained her.

'Spies! My own women! ... Oh, miserable!' she cried, with flashing, tearful eyes.

'I hate to tell you,' he replied. By that she knew he had long spared her. 'It's begun again—that work in the dark.'

'Nay, Lassiter—it never stopped!'

So bitter certainty claimed her at last, and trust fled Withersteen House and fled forever. The women who owed much to Jane Withersteen changed not in love for her, nor in devotion to their household work, but they poisoned both by a thousand acts of stealth and cunning and duplicity. Jane broke out once and caught them in strange, stone-faced, unhesitating falsehood. Thereafter she broke out no more. She forgave them because they were driven. Poor, fettered, and sealed Hagars, how she pitied them! What terrible thing bound them and locked their lips, when they showed neither consciousness of guilt toward their benefactress nor distress at the slow wearing apart of long-established and dear ties?

'The blindness again!' cried Jane Withersteen. 'In my sisters as in me! … Oh, God!'

There came a time when no words passed between Jane and her women. Silently they went about their household duties, and secretly they went about the underhand work to which they had been bidden. The gloom of the house and the gloom of its mistress, which darkened even the bright spirit of little Fay, did not pervade these women. Happiness was not among them, but they were aloof from gloom. They spied and listened; they received and sent secret messengers; and they stole Jane's books and records, and finally the papers that were deeds of her possessions. Through it all they were silent, rapt in a kind of trance. Then one by one, without leave or explanation or farewell, they left Withersteen House, and never returned.

Coincident with this disappearance Jane's gardeners and workers in the alfalfa fields and stable men quit her, not even asking for their wages. Of all her Mormon employees about the great ranch only Jerd remained. He went on with his duty, but talked no more of the change than if it had never occurred.

'Jerd,' said Jane, 'what stock you can't take care of turn out in the sage. Let your first thought be for Black Star and Night. Keep them in perfect condition. Run them every day and watch them always.'

Though Jane Withersteen gave with such liberality, she loved her possessions. She loved the rich, green stretches of alfalfa, and the farms, and the grove, and the old stone house, and the beautiful, ever-faithful amber spring, and every one of a myriad of horses and colts and burros and fowls down to the smallest rabbit that nipped her vegetables; but she loved best her noble Arabian steeds. In common with all riders of the upland sage Jane cherished two material things—the cold, sweet, brown water that made life possible in the wilderness and the horses which were a part of that life. When Lassiter asked her what he would be without his guns he was assuming that his horse was part of himself. So Jane loved Black Star and Night because it was her nature to love all beautiful creatures—perhaps all living things; and then she loved them because she herself was of the sage and in her had been born and bred the rider's instinct to rely on his four-footed brother. And when Jane gave Jerd the order to keep her favorites trained down to the day it was a half-conscious admission that presaged a time when she would need her fleet horses.

Jane had now, however, no leisure to brood over the coils that were closing round her. Mrs Larkin grew weaker as the August days began; she required constant care; there was little Fay to look after; and such household work as was imperative. Lassiter put Bells in the stable with the other racers, and directed his efforts to a closer attendance upon Jane. She welcomed the change. He was always at hand to help, and it was her fortune to learn that his boast of being awkward around women had its root in humility and was not true.

His great, brown hands were skilled in a multiplicity of ways which a woman might have envied. He shared Jane's work, and was of especial help to her in nursing Mrs Larkin. The woman suffered most at night, and this often broke Jane's rest. So it came about that Lassiter would stay by Mrs Larkin during the day, when she needed care, and Jane would make up the sleep she lost in night-watches. Mrs Larkin at once took kindly to the gentle Lassiter, and, without ever asking who or what he was, praised him to Jane. 'He's a good man and loves children,' she said. How sad to hear this truth spoken of a man whom Jane thought lost beyond all redemption! Yet ever and ever Lassiter towered above her, and behind or through his black, sinister figure shone something luminous that strangely affected Jane. Good and evil began to seem incomprehensibly blended in her judgment. It was her belief that evil could not come forth from good; yet here was a murderer who dwarfed in gentleness, patience, and love any man she had ever known.

She had almost lost track of her more outside concerns when early one morning Judkins presented himself before her in the courtyard.

Thin, hard, burnt, bearded, with the dust and sage thick on him, with his leather wrist-bands shining from use, and his boots worn through on the stirrup side, he looked the rider of riders. He wore two guns and carried a Winchester.

Jane greeted him with surprise and warmth, set meat and bread and drink before him; and called Lassiter out to see him. The men exchanged glances, and the meaning of Lassiter's keen inquiry and Judkins's bold reply, both unspoken, was not lost upon Jane.

'Where's your hoss?' asked Lassiter, aloud.

'Left him down the slope,' answered Judkins. 'I footed it in a ways, an' slept last night in the sage. I went to the place you told me you 'most always slept, but didn't strike you.'

'I moved up some, near the spring, an' now I go there nights.'

'Judkins—the white herd?' queried Jane, hurriedly.

'Miss Withersteen, I make proud to say I've not lost a steer. Fer a good while after thet stampede Lassiter milled we hed no trouble. Why, even the sage dogs left us. But it's begun agin—thet flashin' of lights over ridge tips, an' queer puffin' of smoke, an' then at night strange whistles an' noises. But the herd's acted magnificent. An' my boys, say, Miss Withersteen, they're only kids, but I ask no better riders. I got the laugh in the village fer takin' them out. They're a wild lot, an' you know boys hev more nerve than grown men, because they don't know what danger is. I'm not denyin' there's danger. But they glory in it, an' mebbe I like it myself—anyway, we'll stick. We're goin' to drive the herd on the far side of the first break of Deception Pass. There's a great round valley over there, an' no ridges or piles of rocks to aid these stampeders. The rains are due. We'll hev plenty of water fer a while. An' we can hold thet herd from anybody except Oldrin'. I come in fer supplies. I'll pack a couple of burros an' drive out after dark tonight.'

'Judkins, take what you want from the store-room. Lassiter will help you. I—I can't thank you enough … but—wait.'

Jane went to the room that had once been her father's, and from a secret chamber in the thick stone wall she took a bag of gold, and, carrying it back to the court, she gave it to the rider.

'There, Judkins, and understand that I regard it as little for your loyalty. Give what is fair to your boys, and keep the rest. Hide it. Perhaps that would be wisest.'

'Oh … Miss Withersteen!' ejaculated the rider. 'I couldn't earn so much in—in ten years. It's not right—I oughtn't take it.'

'Judkins, you know I'm a rich woman. I tell you I've few faithful friends. I've fallen upon evil days. God only knows what will become of me and mine! So take the gold.'

She smiled in understanding of his speechless gratitude, and left him with Lassiter. Presently she heard him speaking low at first, then in louder accents emphasized by the thumping of his rifle on the stones. 'As infernal a job as even you, Lassiter, ever heerd of.'

'Why, son,' was Lassiter's reply, 'this breakin' of Miss Withersteen may seem bad to you, but it ain't bad—yet. Some of these wall-eyed fellers who look jest as if they was walkin' in the shadow of Christ himself, right down the sunny road, now they can think of things an' do things that are really hell-bent.'

Jane covered her ears and ran to her own room, and there like a caged lioness she paced to and fro till the coming of little Fay reversed her dark thoughts.

The following day, a warm and muggy one threatening rain, while Jane was resting in the court, a horseman clattered through the grove and up to the hitching-rack. He leaped off and approached Jane with the manner of a man determined to execute a difficult mission, yet fearful of its reception. In the gaunt, wiry figure and the lean, brown face Jane recognized one of her Mormon riders, Blake. It was he of whom Judkins had long since spoken. Of all the riders ever in her employ Blake owed her the most, and as he stepped before her, removing his hat and making manly efforts to subdue his emotion, he showed that he remembered.

'Miss Withersteen, mother's dead,' he said.

'Oh—Blake!' exclaimed Jane, and she could say no more.

'She died free from pain in the end, and she's buried—resting at last, thank God! ... I've come to ride for you again, if you'll have me. Don't think I mentioned mother to get your sympathy. When she was living and your riders quit, I had to also. I was afraid of what might be done—said to her. ... Miss Withersteen, we can't talk of—of what's going on now—'

'Blake, do you know?'

'I know a great deal. You understand, my lips are shut. But without explanation or excuse I offer my services. I'm a Mormon—I hope a good one. But—there are some things! ... It's no use, Miss Withersteen, I can't say any more—what I'd like to. But will you take me back?'

'Blake! ... You know what it means?'

'I don't care. I'm sick of—of—I'll show you a Mormon who'll be true to you!'

'But, Blake—how terribly you might suffer for that!'

'Maybe. Aren't you suffering now?'

'God knows indeed I am!'

'Miss Withersteen, it's a liberty on my part to speak so, but I know you pretty well—know you'll never give in. I wouldn't if I were you. And I—I must—Something makes me tell you the worst is yet to come. That's all. I absolutely can't say more. Will you take me back—let me ride for you—show everybody what I mean?'

'Blake, it makes me happy to hear you. How my riders hurt me when they quit!' Jane felt the hot tears well to her eyes and splash down upon her hands. 'I thought so much of them—tried so hard to be good to them. And not one was true. You've made it easy to forgive. Perhaps many of them really feel as you do, but dare not return to me. Still, Blake, I hesitate to take you back. Yet I want you so much.'

'Do it, then. If you're going to make your life a lesson to Mormon women, let me make mine a lesson to the men. Right is right. I believe in you, and here's my life to prove it.'

'You hint it may mean your life!' said Jane, breathless and low.

'We won't speak of that. I want to come back. I want to do what every rider aches in his secret heart to do for you. ... Miss Withersteen, I hoped it'd not be necessary to tell you that my mother on her deathbed told me to have courage. She knew how the thing galled me—she told me to come back. ... Will you take me?'

'God bless you, Blake! Yes, I'll take you back. And will you—will you accept gold from me?'

'Miss Withersteen!'

'I just gave Judkins a bag of gold. I'll give you one. If you will not take it you must not come back. You might ride for me a few months—weeks—days till the storm breaks. Then you'd have nothing, and be in disgrace with your people. We'll forearm you against poverty, and me against endless regret. I'll give you gold which you can hide—till some future time.'

'Well, if it pleases you,' replied Blake. 'But you know I never thought of pay. Now, Miss Withersteen, one thing more. I want to see this man Lassiter. Is he here?'

'Yes, but, Blake—what—Need you see him? Why?' asked Jane, instantly worried. 'I can speak to him—tell him about you.'

'That won't do. I want to—I've got to tell him myself. Where is he?'

'Lassiter is with Mrs Larkin. She is ill. I'll call him,' answered Jane, and going to the door she softly called for the rider. A faint, musical jingle preceded his step—then his tall form crossed the threshold.

'Lassiter, here's Blake, an old rider of mine. He has come back to me and he wishes to speak to you.'

Blake's brown face turned exceedingly pale.

'Yes, I had to speak to you,' he said, swiftly. 'My name's Blake. I'm a Mormon and a rider. Lately I quit Miss Withersteen. I've come to beg her to take me back. Now I don't know you, but I know—what you are. So I've this to say to your face. It would never occur to this woman to imagine—let alone suspect me to be a spy. She couldn't think it might just be a low plot to come here and shoot you in the back. Jane Withersteen hasn't that kind of a mind. ... Well, I've not come for that. I want to help her—to pull a bridle along with Judkins and—and you. The thing is—do you believe me?'

'I reckon I do,' replied Lassiter. How this slow, cool speech contrasted with Blake's hot, impulsive words! 'You might have saved some of your breath. See here, Blake, cinch this in your mind. Lassiter has met some square Mormons! An' mebbe —'

'Blake,' interrupted Jane, nervously anxious to terminate a colloquy that she perceived was an ordeal for him. 'Go at once and fetch me a report of my horses.'

'Miss Withersteen! ... You mean the big drove—down in the sage-cleared fields?'

'Of course,' replied Jane. 'My horses are all there, except the blooded stock I keep here.'

'Haven't you heard—then?'

'Heard? No! What's happened to them?'

'They're gone, Miss Withersteen, gone these ten days past. Dorn told me, and I rode down to see for myself.'

'Lassiter—did you know?' asked Jane, whirling to him.

'I reckon so. ... But what was the use to tell you?'

It was Lassiter turning away his face and Blake studying the stone flags at his feet that brought Jane to the understanding of what she betrayed. She strove desperately, but she could not rise immediately from such a blow.

'My horses! My horses! What's become of them?'

'Dorn said the riders report another drive by Oldring. ... And I trailed the horses miles down the slope toward Deception Pass.'

'My red herd's gone! My horses gone! The white herd will go next. I can stand that. But if I lost Black Star and Night, it would be like parting with my own flesh and blood. Lassiter—Blake—am I in danger of losing my racers?'

'A rustler—or—or anybody stealin' hosses of yours would most of all want the blacks,' said Lassiter. His evasive reply was affirmation enough. The other rider nodded gloomy acquiescence.

'Oh! Oh!' Jane Withersteen choked, with violent utterance.

'Let me take charge of the blacks?' asked Blake. 'One more rider won't be any great help to Judkins. But I might hold Black Star and Night, if you put such store on their value.'

'Value! Blake, I love my racers. Besides, there's another reason why I mustn't lose them. You go to the stables. Go with Jerd every day when he runs the horses, and don't let them out of your sight. If you would please me—win my gratitude, guard my black racers.'

When Blake had mounted and ridden out of the court Lassiter regarded Jane with the smile that was becoming rarer as the days sped by.

"Pears to me, as Blake says, you do put some store on them hosses. Now I ain't gainsayin' that the Arabians are the handsomest hosses I ever seen. But Bells can beat Night, an' run neck an' neck with Black Star.'

'Lassiter, don't tease me now. I'm miserable—sick. Bells is fast, but he can't stay with the blacks, and you know it. Only Wrangle can do that.'

'I'll bet that big raw-boned brute can more'n show his heels to your black racers. Jane, out there in the sage, on a long chase, Wrangle could kill your favorites.'

'No, no,' replied Jane, impatiently. 'Lassiter, why do you say that so often? I know you've teased me at times, and I believe it's only kindness. You're always trying to keep my mind off worry. But you mean more by this repeated mention of my racers?'

'I reckon so.' Lassiter paused, and for the thousandth time in her presence moved his black sombrero round and round, as if counting the silver pieces on the band. 'Well, Jane, I've sort of read a little that's passin' in your mind.'

'You think I might fly from my home—from Cottonwoods—from the Utah border?'

'I reckon. An' if you ever do an' get away with the blacks I wouldn't like to see Wrangle left here on the sage. Wrangle could catch you. I know Venters had him.

But you can never tell. Mebbe he hasn't got him now. ... Besides—things are happenin', an' somethin' of the same queer nature might have happened to Venters.'

'God knows you're right! ... Poor Bern, how long he's gone! In my trouble I've been forgetting him. But, Lassiter, I've little fear for him. I've heard my riders say he's as keen as a wolf. ... As to your reading my thoughts—well, your suggestion makes an actual thought of what was only one of my dreams. I believe I dreamed of flying from this wild borderland, Lassiter. I've strange dreams. I'm not always practical and thinking of my many duties, as you said once. For instance—if I dared—if I dared I'd ask you to saddle the blacks and ride away with me—and hide me.'

'Jane!'

The rider's sunburnt face turned white. A few times Jane had seen Lassiter's cool calm broken—when he had met little Fay, when he had learned how and why he had come to love both child and mistress, when he had stood beside Milly Erne's grave. But one and all they could not be considered in the light of his present agitation. Not only did Lassiter turn white—not only did he grow tense, not only did he lose his coolness, but also he suddenly, violently, hungrily took her into his arms and crushed her to his breast.

'Lassiter!' cried Jane, trembling. It was an action for which she took sole blame. Instantly, as if dazed, weakened, he released her. 'Forgive me!' went on Jane. 'I'm always forgetting your—your feelings. I thought of you as my faithful friend. I'm always making you out more than human ... only, let me say—I meant that—about riding away. I'm wretched, sick of this—this—Oh, something bitter and black grows on my heart!'

'Jane, the hell—of it,' he replied, with deep intake of breath, 'is you *can't* ride away. Mebbe realizin' it accounts for my grabbin' you—that way, as much as the crazy boy's rapture your words gave me. I don't understand myself. ... But the hell of this game is—you *can't* ride away.'

'Lassiter! ... What on earth do you mean? I'm an absolutely free woman.'

'You ain't absolutely anythin' of the kind . ... I reckon I've got to tell you!'

'Tell me all. It's uncertainty that makes me a coward. It's faith and hope—blind love, if you will, that makes me miserable. Every day I awake believing—still believing. The day grows, and with it doubts, fears, and that black bat hate that bites hotter and hotter into my heart. Then comes night—I pray—I pray for all, and for myself—I sleep—and I awake free once more, trustful, faithful, to believe—to hope! Then, Oh, my God! I grow and live a thousand years till night again! ... But if you want to see me a woman, tell me why I can't ride away—tell me what more I'm to lose—tell me the worst.'

'Jane, you're watched. There's no single move of yours, except when you're hid in your house, that ain't seen by sharp eyes. The cottonwood grove's full of creepin', crawlin' men. Like Indians in the grass. When you rode, which wasn't often lately, the sage was full of sneakin' men. At night they crawl under your windows, into the court, an' I reckon into the house. Jane Withersteen, you know, never locked a door! This here grove's a hummin' bee-hive of mysterious happenin's. Jane, it ain't so much that these spies keep out of my way as me keepin' out of theirs. They're goin' to try to kill me. That's plain. But mebbe I'm as hard to shoot in the back as in the face. So far I've seen fit to watch only. This all means, Jane, that you're a marked woman. You can't get away—not now. Mebbe later, when you're broken, you might. But that's sure doubtful. Jane, you're to lose the cattle that's left—your home an' ranch—an' Amber Spring. You can't even hide a sack of gold! For it couldn't be slipped out of the house, day or night, an' hid or buried, let alone be rid off with. You may lose all. I'm tellin' you, Jane, hopin' to prepare you, if the worst does come. I told you once before about that strange power I've got to feel things.'

'Lassiter, what can I do?'

'Nothin', I reckon, except know what's comin' an' wait an' be game. If you'd let me make a call on Tull, an' a long-deferred call on—'

'Hush! … Hush!' she whispered.

'Well, even that wouldn't help you any in the end.'

'What does it mean? Oh, what does it mean? I am my father's daughter—a Mormon, yet I can't see! I've not failed in religion—in duty. For years I've given with a free and full heart. When my father died I was rich. If I'm still rich it's because I couldn't find enough ways to become poor. What am I, what are my possessions to set in motion such intensity of secret oppression?'

'Jane, the mind behind it all is an empire builder.'

'But, Lassiter, I would give freely—all I own to avert this—this wretched thing. If I gave—that would leave me with faith still. Surely my—my churchmen think of my soul? If I lose my trust in them—'

'Child, be still!' said Lassiter, with a dark dignity that had in it something of pity. 'You are a woman, fine an' big an' strong, an' your heart matches your size. But in mind you're a child. I'll say a little more—then I'm done. I'll never mention this again. Among many thousands of women you're one who has bucked against your churchmen. They tried you out, an' failed of persuasion, an' finally of threats. You meet now the cold steel of a will as far from Christlike as the universe is wide. You're to be broken. Your body's to be held, given to some man, made, if possible, to bring children into the world. But your soul? … What do they care for your soul?'

CHAPTER THIRTEEN
Solitude and Storm

In his hidden valley Venters awakened from sleep, and his ears rang with innumerable melodies from full-throated mocking-birds, and his eyes opened wide upon the glorious golden shaft of sunlight shining through the great stone bridge. The circle of cliffs surrounding Surprise Valley lay shrouded in morning mist, a dim blue low down along the terraces, a creamy, moving cloud along the ramparts. The oak forest in the center was a plumed and tufted oval of gold.

He saw Bess under the spruces. Upon her complete recovery of strength she always rose with the dawn. At the moment she was feeding the quail she had tamed. And she had begun to tame the mocking-birds. They fluttered among the branches overhead, and some left off their songs to flit down and shyly hop near the twittering quail. Little gray and white rabbits crouched in the grass, now nibbling, now laying long ears flat and watching the dogs.

Venters's swift glance took in the brightening valley, and Bess and her pets, and Ring and Whitie. It swept over all to return again and rest upon the girl. She had changed. To the dark trousers and blouse she had added moccasins of her own make, but she no longer resembled a boy. No eye could have failed to mark the rounded contours of a woman. The change had been to grace and beauty. A glint of warm gold gleamed from her hair, and a tint of red shone in the clear dark brown of cheeks. The haunting sweetness of her lips and eyes, that earlier had been illusive, a promise, had become a living fact. She fitted harmoniously into that wonderful setting; she was like Surprise Valley—wild and beautiful.

Venters leaped out of his cave to begin the day.

He had postponed his journey to Cottonwoods until after the passing of the summer rains. The rains were due soon. But until their arrival and the necessity for his trip to the village he sequestered in a far corner of mind all thought of peril, of his past life, and almost that of the present. It was enough to live. He did not want to know what lay hidden in the dim and distant future. Surprise Valley had enchanted him. In this home of the cliff-dwellers there were peace and quiet and solitude, and another thing, wondrous as the golden morning shaft of sunlight, that he dared not ponder over long enough to understand.

The solitude he had hated when alone he had now come to love. He was assimilating something from this valley of gleams and shadows. From this strange girl he was assimilating more.

The day at hand resembled many days gone before. As Venters had no tools with which to build, or to till the terraces, he remained idle. Beyond the cooking of the simple fare there were no tasks. And as there were no tasks, there was no system. He and Bess began one thing, to leave it; to begin another, to leave that; and then do nothing but lie under the spruces and watch the great cloud-sails majestically move along the ramparts, and dream and dream. The valley was a golden, sunlit world. It was silent. The sighing wind and the twittering quail and the singing birds, even the rare and seldom-occurring hollow crack of a sliding weathered stone, only thickened and deepened that insulated silence.

Venters and Bess had vagrant minds.

'Bess, did I tell you about my horse Wrangle?' inquired Venters.

'A hundred times,' she replied.

'Oh, have I? I'd forgotten. I want you to see him. He'll carry us both.'

'I'd like to ride him. Can he run?'

'Run? He's a demon. Swiftest horse on the sage! I hope he'll stay in that cañon.'

'He'll stay.'

They left camp to wander along the terraces, into the aspen ravines, under the gleaming walls. Ring and Whitie wandered in the fore, often turning, often trotting back, open-mouthed and solemn-eyed and happy. Venters lifted his gaze to the grand archway over the entrance to the valley, and Bess lifted hers to follow his, and both were silent. Sometimes the bridge held their attention for a long time. Today a soaring eagle attracted them.

'How he sails!' exclaimed Bess. 'I wonder where his mate is?'

'She's at the nest. It's on the bridge in a crack near the top. I see her often. She's almost white.'

They wandered on down the terrace, into the shady, sun-flecked forest. A brown bird fluttered crying from a bush. Bess peeped into the leaves.

'Look! A nest and four little birds. They're not afraid of us. See how they open their mouths. They're hungry.'

Rabbits rustled the dead brush and pattered away. The forest was full of a drowsy hum of insects. Little darts of purple, that were running quail, crossed the glades. And a plaintive, sweet peeping came from the coverts. Bess's soft step disturbed a sleeping lizard that scampered away over the leaves. She gave chase and caught it, a slim creature of nameless color but of exquisite beauty.

'Jewel eyes,' she said. 'It's like a rabbit—afraid. We wont eat you. There—go.'

Murmuring water drew their steps down into a shallow shaded ravine where a brown brook brawled softly over mossy stones. Multitudes of strange, gray frogs with white spots and black eyes lined the rocky bank and leaped only at close approach. Then Venters's eye descried a very thin, very long green snake coiled round a sapling. They drew closer and closer till they could have touched it. The snake had no fear and watched them with scintillating eyes.

'It's pretty,' said Bess. 'How tame! I thought snakes always ran.'

'No. Even the rabbits didn't run here till the dogs chased them.'

On and on they wandered to the wild jumble of massed and broken fragments of cliff at the west end of the valley. The roar of the disappearing stream dinned in their ears. Into this maze of rocks they threaded a tortuous way, climbing, descending, halting to gather wild plums and great lavender lilies, and going on at the will of fancy. Idle and keen perceptions guided them equally.

'Oh, let us climb there!' cried Bess, pointing upward to a small space of terrace left green and shady between huge abutments of broken cliff. And they climbed to the nook and rested and looked out across the valley to the curling column of blue smoke from their campfire. But the cool shade and the rich grass and the fine view were not what they had climbed for. They could not have told, although whatever had drawn them was all-satisfying. Light, sure-footed as a mountain goat, Bess pattered down at Venters's heels; and they went on, calling the dogs, eyes dreamy and wide, listening to the wind and the bees and the crickets and the birds.

Part of the time Ring and Whitie led the way, then Venters, then Bess; and the direction was not an object. They left the sun-streaked shade of the oaks, brushed the long grass of the meadows, entered the green and fragrant swaying willows, to stop, at length, under the huge old cottonwoods where the beavers were busy.

Here they rested and watched. A dam of brush and logs and mud and stones backed the stream into a little lake. The round, rough beaver houses projected from the water. Like the rabbits, the beavers had become shy. Gradually, however, as Venters and Bess knelt low, holding the dogs, the beavers emerged to swim with logs and gnaw at cottonwoods and pat mud walls with their paddle-like tails, and, glossy and shiny in the sun, to go on with their strange, persistent industry. They were the builders. The lake was a mud-hole, and the immediate environment a scarred and dead region, but it was a wonderful home of wonderful animals.

'Look at that one—he puddles in the mud,' said Bess. 'And there! See him dive! Hear them gnawing! I'd think they'd break their teeth. How's it they can stay out of the water and under the water?'

And she laughed.

Then Venters and Bess wandered farther, and, perhaps not all unconsciously this time, wended their slow steps to the cave of the cliff-dwellers, where she liked best to go.

The tangled thicket and the long slant of dust and little chips of weathered rock and the steep bench of stone and the worn steps all were arduous work for Bess in the climbing. But she gained the shelf, gasping, hot of cheek, glad of eye, with her hand in Venters's. Here they rested. The beautiful valley glittered below with its millions of wind-turned leaves bright-faced in the sun, and the mighty bridge towered heavenward, crowned with blue sky. Bess, however, never rested for long. Soon she was exploring, and Venters followed; she dragged forth from corners and shelves a multitude of crudely fashioned and painted pieces of pottery, and he carried them. They peeped down into the dark holes of the kivas, and Bess gleefully dropped a stone and waited for the long-coming hollow sound to rise. They peeped into the little globular houses, like mud-wasp nests, and wondered if these had been store-places for grain, or baby cribs, or what; and they crawled into the larger houses and laughed when they bumped their heads on the low roofs, and they dug in the dust of the floors. And they brought from dust and darkness armloads of treasure which they carried to the light. Flints and stones and strange curved sticks and pottery they found; and twisted grass rope that crumbled in their hands, and bits of whitish stone which crushed to powder at a touch and seemed to vanish in the air.

'That white stuff was bone,' said Venters, slowly. 'Bones of a cliff-dweller.'

'No!' exclaimed Bess.

'Here's another piece. Look! … Whew! dry, powdery smoke! That's bone.'

Then it was that Venters's primitive, childlike mood, like a savage's, seeing, yet unthinking, gave way to the encroachment of civilized thought. The world had not been made for a single day's play or fancy or idle watching. The world was old. Nowhere could be gotten a better idea of its age than in this gigantic silent tomb. The gray ashes in Venters's hand had once been bone of a human being like himself. The pale gloom of the cave had shadowed people long ago. He saw that Bess had received the same shock—could not in moments such as this escape her feeling, living, thinking destiny.

'Bern, people have lived here,' she said, with wide, thoughtful eyes.

'Yes,' he replied.

'How long ago?'

'A thousand years and more.'

'What were they?'

'Cliff-dwellers. Men who had enemies and made their homes high out of reach.'

'They had to fight?'

'Yes.'

'They fought for—what?'

'For life. For their homes, food, children, parents—for their women!'

'Has the world changed any in a thousand years?'

'I don't know—perhaps very little.'

'Have men?'

'I hope so—I think so.'

'Things crowd into my mind,' she went on, and the wistful light in her eyes told Venters the truth of her thoughts. 'I've ridden the border of Utah. I've seen people—know how they live—but they must be few of all who are living. I had my books and I studied them. But all that doesn't help me any more. I want to go out into the big world and see it. Yet I want to stay here more. What's to become of us? Are we cliff-dwellers? We're alone here. I'm happy when I don't think. These—these bones that fly into dust—they make me sick and a little afraid. Did the people who lived here once have the same feelings as we have? What was the good of their living at all? They're gone! What's the meaning of it all—of us?'

'Bess, you ask more than I can tell. It's beyond me. Only there was laughter here once—and now there's silence. There was life—and now there's death. Men cut these little steps, made these arrow-heads and mealing-stones, plaited the ropes we found, and left their bones to crumble in our fingers. As far as time is concerned it might all have been yesterday. We're here today. Maybe we're higher in the scale of human beings—in intelligence. But who knows? We can't be any higher in the things for which life is lived at all.'

'What are they?'

'Why—I suppose relationship, friendship—love.'

'Love!'

'Yes. Love of man for woman—love of woman for man. That's the nature, the meaning, the best of life itself.'

She said no more. Wistfulness of glance deepened into sadness.

'Come, let us go,' said Venters.

Action brightened her. Beside him, holding his hand, she slipped down the shelf, ran down the long, steep slant of sliding stones, out of the cloud of dust, and likewise out of the pale gloom.

'We beat the slide,' she cried.

The miniature avalanche cracked and roared, and rattled itself into an inert mass at the base of the incline. Yellow dust like the gloom of the cave, but not so changeless, drifted away on the wind; the roar clapped in echo from the cliff, returned, went back, and came again to die in the hollowness. Down on the sunny terrace there was a different atmosphere. Ring and Whitie leaped around Bess. Once more she was smiling, gay, and thoughtless, with the dream-mood in the shadow of her eyes.

'Bess, I haven't seen that since last summer. Look!' said Venters, pointing to the scalloped edge of rolling purple clouds that peeped over the western wall. 'We're in for a storm.'

'Oh, I hope not. I'm afraid of storms.'

'Are you? Why?'

'Have you ever been down in one of these walled-up pockets in a bad storm?'

'No, now I think of it, I haven't.'

'Well, it's terrible. Every summer I get scared to death and hide somewhere in the dark. Storms up on the sage are bad, but nothing to what they are down here in the cañons. And in this little valley—why, echoes can rap back and forth so quick they'll split our ears.'

'We're perfectly safe here, Bess.'

'I know. But that hasn't anything to do with it. The truth is I'm afraid of lightning and thunder, and thunder-claps hurt my head. If we have a bad storm, will you stay close by me?'

'Yes.'

When they got back to camp the afternoon was closing, and it was exceedingly sultry. Not a breath of air stirred the aspen leaves, and when these did not quiver the air was indeed still. The dark-purple clouds moved almost imperceptibly out of the west.

'What have we for supper?' asked Bess.

'Rabbit.'

'Bern, can't you think of another new way to cook rabbit?' went on Bess, with earnestness.

'What do you think I am—a magician?' retorted Venters.

'I wouldn't dare tell you. But, Bern, do you want me to turn into a rabbit?'

There was a dark-blue, merry flashing of eyes and a parting of lips; then she laughed. In that moment she was naïve and wholesome.

'Rabbit seems to agree with you,' replied Venters. 'You are well and strong—and growing very pretty.'

Anything in the nature of compliment he had never before said to her, and just now he responded to a sudden curiosity to see its effect. Bess stared as if she had not heard aright, slowly blushed, and completely lost her poise in happy confusion.

'I'd better go right away,' he continued, 'and fetch supplies from Cottonwoods.'

A startlingly swift change in the nature of her agitation made him reproach himself for his abruptness.

'No, no, don't go!' she said. 'I didn't mean—that about the rabbit. I—I was only trying to be—funny. Don't leave me all alone!'

'Bess, I must go sometime.'

'Wait then. Wait till after the storms.'

The purple cloud-bank darkened the lower edge of the setting sun, crept up and up, obscuring its fiery red heart, and finally passed over the last ruddy crescent of its upper rim.

The intense dead silence awakened to a long, low, rumbling roll of thunder.
'Oh!' cried Bess, nervously.

'We've had big black clouds before this without rain,' said Venters. 'But there's no doubt about that thunder. The storms are coming. I'm glad. Every rider on the sage will hear that thunder with glad ears.'

Venters and Bess finished their simple meal and the few tasks around the camp, then faced the open terrace, the valley, and the west, to watch and await the approaching storm.

It required keen vision to see any movement whatever in the purple clouds. By infinitesimal degrees the dark cloud-line merged upward into the golden-red haze of the afterglow of sunset. A shadow lengthened from under the western wall across the valley. As straight and rigid as steel rose the delicate spear-pointed silver spruces; the aspen leaves, by nature pendant and quivering, hung limp and heavy; no slender blade of grass moved. A gentle splashing of water came from the ravine. Then again from out of the west sounded the low, dull, and rumbling roll of thunder.

A wave, a ripple of light, a trembling and turning of the aspen leaves, like the approach of a breeze on the water, crossed the valley from the west; and the lull and the deadly stillness and the sultry air passed away on a cool wind.

The night bird of the cañon, with his clear and melancholy notes, announced the twilight. And from all along the cliffs rose the faint murmur and moan and mourn of the wind singing in the caves. The bank of clouds now swept hugely out of the western sky. Its front was purple and black, with gray between, a bulging, mushrooming, vast thing instinct with storm. It had a dark, angry, threatening aspect. As if all the power of the winds were pushing and piling behind, it rolled ponderously across the sky. A red flare burned out instantaneously, flashed from west to east, and died. Then from the deepest black of the purple cloud burst boom. It was like the bowling of a huge boulder along the crags and ramparts, and seemed to roll on and fall into the valley to bound and bang and boom from cliff to cliff.

'Oh!' cried Bess, with her hands over her ears. 'What did I tell you?'

'Why, Bess, be reasonable!' said Venters.

'I'm a coward.'

'Not quite that, I hope. It's strange you're afraid. I love a storm.'

'I tell you a storm down in these cañons is an awful thing. I know Oldring hated storms. His men were afraid of them. There was one who went deaf in a bad storm, and never could hear again.'

'Maybe I've lots to learn, Bess. I'll lose my guess if this storm isn't bad enough. We're going to have heavy wind first, then lightning and thunder, then the rain. Let's stay out as long as we can.'

The tips of the cottonwoods and the oaks waved to the east, and the rings of aspens along the terraces twinkled their myriad of bright faces in fleet and glancing gleam. A low roar rose from the leaves of the forest, and the spruces swished in the rising wind. It came in gusts, with light breezes between. As it increased in strength the lulls shortened in length till there was a strong and steady blow all the time, and violent puffs at intervals, and sudden whirling currents. The clouds spread over the valley, rolling swiftly and low, and twilight faded into a sweeping darkness. Then the singing of the wind in the caves drowned the swift roar of rustling leaves; then the song swelled to a mourning, moaning wail; then with the gathering power of the wind the wail changed to a shriek. Steadily the wind strengthened and constantly the strange sound changed.

The last bit of blue sky yielded to the onsweep of clouds. Like angry surf the pale gleams of gray, amid the purple of that scudding front, swept beyond the eastern rampart of the valley. The purple deepened to black. Broad sheets of lightning flared over the western wall. There were not yet any ropes or zigzag streaks darting down through the gathering darkness. The storm center was still beyond Surprise Valley.

'Listen! ... Listen!' cried Bess, with her lips close to Venters's ear. 'You'll hear Oldring's knell!'

'What's that?'

'Oldring's knell. When the wind blows a gale in the caves it makes what the rustlers call Oldring's knell. They believe it bodes his death. I think he believes so, too. It's not like any sound on earth ... It's beginning. Listen!'

The gale swooped down with a hollow unearthly howl. It yelled and pealed and shrilled and shrieked. It was made up of a thousand piercing cries. It was a rising and moving sound. Beginning at the western break of the valley, it rushed along each gigantic cliff, whistling into the caves and cracks, to mount in power, to bellow a blast through the great stone bridge. Gone, as into an engulfing roar of surging waters, it seemed to shoot back and begin all over again.

It was only wind, thought Venters. Here sped and shrieked the sculptor that carved out the wonderful caves in the cliffs. It was only a gale, but as Venters listened, as his ears became accustomed to the fury and strife, out of it all or through it or above it pealed low and perfectly clear and persistently uniform a strange sound that had no counterpart in all the sounds of the elements. It was not of earth or of life. It was the grief and agony of the gale. A knell of all upon which it blew!

Black night enfolded the valley. Venters could not see his companion, and knew of her presence only through the tightening hold of her hand on his arm. He felt the dogs huddle closer to him. Suddenly the dense, black vault overhead split asunder to a blue-white, dazzling streak of lightning. The whole valley lay vividly clear and luminously bright in his sight. Up-reared, vast and magnificent, the stone bridge glimmered like some grand god of storm in the lightning's fire. Then all flashed black again—blacker than pitch—a thick, impenetrable coalblackness. And there came a ripping, crashing report. Instantly an echo resounded with clapping crash. The initial report was nothing to the echo. It was a terrible, living, reverberating, detonating crash. The wall threw the sound across, and could have made no greater roar if it had slipped in avalanche. From cliff to cliff the echo went in crashing retort and banged in lessening power, and boomed in thinner volume, and clapped weaker and weaker till a final clap could not reach across to waiting cliff.

In the pitchy darkness Venters led Bess, and, groping his way, by feel of hand found the entrance to her cave and lifted her up. On the instant a blinding flash of lightning illumined the cave and all about him. He saw Bess's face white now, with dark, frightened eyes. He saw the dogs leap up, and he followed suit. The golden glare vanished; all was black; then came the splitting crack and the infernal din of echoes.

Bess shrank closer to him and closer, found his hands, and pressed them tightly over her ears, and dropped her face upon his shoulder, and hid her eyes.

Then the storm burst with a succession of ropes and streaks and shafts of lightning, playing continuously, filling the valley with a broken radiance; and the cracking shots followed each other swiftly till the echoes blended in one fearful, deafening crash.

Venters looked out upon the beautiful valley—beautiful now as never before—mystic in its transparent, luminous gloom, weird in the quivering, golden haze of lightning. The dark spruces were tipped with glimmering lights; the aspens bent low in the winds, as waves in a tempest at sea; the forest of oaks tossed wildly and shone with gleams of fire. Across the valley the huge cavern of the cliff-dwellers yawned in the glare, every little black window as clear as at noonday; but the night and storm added to their tragedy. Flung arching to the black clouds, the great stone bridge seemed to bear the brunt of the storm. It caught the full fury of the rushing wind. It lifted its noble crown to meet the lightnings. Venters thought of the eagles and their lofty nest in a niche under the arch. A driving pall of rain, black as the clouds, came sweeping on to obscure the bridge and the gleaming walls and the shining valley. The lightning played incessantly, streaking down through opaque darkness of rain. The roar of the wind, with its strange knell and the recrashing echoes, mingled with the roar of the flooding rain, and all seemingly were deadened and drowned in a world of sound.

In the dimming pale light Venters looked down upon the girl. She had sunk into his arms, upon his breast, burying her face. She clung to him. He felt the softness of her, and the warmth, and the quick heave of her breast. He saw the dark, slender, graceful outline of her form. A woman lay in his arms! And he held her closer. He who had been alone in the sad, silent watches of the night was not now and never must be again alone. He who had yearned for the touch of a hand felt the long tremble and the heartbeat of a woman. By what strange chance had she come to love him! By what change—by what marvel had she grown into a treasure!

No more did he listen to the rush and roar of the thunder-storm. For with the touch of clinging hands and the throbbing bosom he grew conscious of an inward storm—the tingling of new chords of thought, strange music of unheard, joyous bells, sad dreams dawning to wakeful delight, dissolving doubt, resurging hope, force, fire, and freedom, unutterable sweetness of desire. A storm in his breast—a storm of real love.

CHAPTER FOURTEEN
West Wind

When the storm abated Venters sought his own cave, and late in the night, as his blood cooled and the stir and throb and thrill subsided, he fell asleep.

With the breaking of dawn his eyes unclosed. The valley lay drenched and bathed, a burnished oval of glittering green. The rain-washed walls glistened in the morning light. Waterfalls of many forms poured over the rims. One, a broad, lacy sheet, thin as smoke, slid over the western notch and struck a ledge in its downward fall, to bound into broader leap, to burst far below into white and gold and rosy mist.

Venters prepared for the day, knowing himself a different man.

'It's a glorious morning,' said Bess, in greeting.

'Yes. After the storm the west wind,' he replied.

'Last night was I—very much of a baby?' she asked, watching him.

'Pretty much.'

'Oh, I couldn't help it!'

'I'm glad you were afraid.'

'Why?' she asked, in slow surprise.

'I'll tell you some day,' he answered, soberly. Then around the camp-fire and through the morning meal he was silent; afterward he strolled thoughtfully off alone along the terrace. He climbed a great yellow rock raising its crest among the spruces, and there he sat down to face the valley and the west.

'I love her!'

Aloud he spoke—unburdened his heart—confessed his secret. For an instant the golden valley swam before his eyes, and the walls waved, and all about him whirled with tumult within.

'I love her! ... I understand now.'

Reviving memory of Jane Withersteen and thought of the complications of the present amazed him with proof of how far he had drifted from his old life. He discovered that he hated to take up the broken threads, to delve into dark problems and difficulties. In this beautiful valley he had been living a beautiful dream. Tranquillity had come to him, and the joy of solitude, and interest in all the wild creatures and crannies of this incomparable valley—and love. Under the shadow of the great stone bridge God had revealed himself to Venters.

'The world seems very far away,' he muttered, 'but it's there—and I'm not yet done with it. Perhaps I never shall be ... Only—how glorious it would be to live here always and never think again!'

Whereupon the resurging reality of the present, as if in irony of his wish, steeped him instantly in contending thought. Out of it all he presently evolved these things: he must go to Cottonwoods; he must bring supplies back to Surprise Valley; must cultivate the soil and raise corn and stock, and, most imperative of all, he must decide the future of the girl who loved him and whom he loved. The first of these things required tremendous effort, the last one, concerning Bess, seemed simply and naturally easy of accomplishment. He would marry her. Suddenly, as from roots of poisonous fire, flamed up the forgotten truth concerning her. It seemed to wither and shrivel up all his joy on its hot, tearing way to his heart. She had been Oldring's Masked Rider. To Venters's question, 'What were you to Oldring?' she had answered with scarlet shame and drooping head.

'What do I care who she is or what she was!' he cried, passionately. And he knew it was not his old self speaking. It was this softer, gentler man who had awakened to new thoughts in the quiet valley. Tenderness, masterful in him now, matched the absences of joy and blunted the knife-edge of entering jealousy. Strong and passionate effort of will, surprising to him, held back the poison from piercing his soul.

'Wait ... Wait!' he cried, as if calling. His hand pressed his breast, and he might have called to the pang there. 'Wait! It's all so strange—so wonderful. Anything can happen. Who am I to judge her? I'll glory in my love for her. But I can't tell it—can't give up to it.'

Certainly he could not then decide her future. Marrying her was impossible in

Surprise Valley and in any village south of Sterling. Even without the mask she had once worn she would easily have been recognized as Oldring's Rider. No man who had ever seen her would forget her, regardless of his ignorance as to her sex. Then more poignant than all other argument was the fact that he did not want to take her away from Surprise Valley. He resisted all thought of that. He had brought her to the most beautiful and wildest place of the uplands; he had saved her, nursed her back to strength, watched her bloom as one of the valley lilies; he knew her life there to be pure and sweet—she belonged to him, and he loved her. Still these were not all the reasons why he did not want to take her away. Where could they go? He feared the rustlers—he feared the riders—he feared the Mormons. And if he should ever succeed in getting Bess safely away from these immediate perils, he feared the sharp eyes of women and their tongues, the big outside world with its problems of existence. He must wait to decide her future, which, after all, was deciding his own. But between her future and his something hung impending. Like Balancing Rock, which waited darkly over the steep gorge, ready to close forever the outlet to Deception Pass, that nameless thing, as certain yet intangible as fate, must fall and close forever all doubts and fears of the future.

'I've dreamed,' muttered Venters, as he rose. 'Well, why not? ... To dream is happiness! But let me just once see this clearly, wholly; then I can go on dreaming till the things fall. I've got to tell Jane Withersteen. I've dangerous trips to take. I've work here to make comfort for this girl. She's mine. I'll fight to keep her safe from that old life. I've already seen her forget it. I love her. And if a beast ever rises in me I'll burn my hand off before I lay it on her with shameful intent. And, by God! Sooner or later I'll kill the man who hid her and kept her in Deception Pass!'

As he spoke the west wind softly blew in his face. It seemed to soothe his passion. That west wind was fresh, cool, fragrant, and it carried a sweet, strange burden of far-off things—tidings of life in other climes, of sunshine asleep on other walls—of other places where reigned peace. It carried, too, sad truth of human hearts and mystery—of promise and hope unquenchable. Surprise Valley was only a little niche in the wide world whence blew that burdened wind. Bess was only one of millions at the mercy of unknown motive in nature and life. Content had come to Venters in the valley; happiness had breathed in the slow, warm air; love as bright as light had hovered over the walls and descended to him; and now on the west wind came a whisper of the eternal triumph of faith over doubt.

'How much better I am for what has come to me!' he exclaimed. 'I'll let the future take care of itself. Whatever falls, I'll be ready.'

Venters retraced his steps along the terrace back to camp, and found Bess in the old familiar seat, waiting and watching for his return.

'I went off by myself to think a little,' he explained.

'You never looked that way before. What—what is it? Won't you tell me?'

'Well, Bess, the fact is I've been dreaming a lot. This valley makes a fellow dream. So I forced myself to think. We can't live this way much longer. Soon I'll simply have to go to Cottonwoods. We need a whole pack train of supplies. I can get —'

'Can you go safely?' she interrupted.

'Why, I'm sure of it. I'll ride through the Pass at night. I haven't any fear that Wrangle isn't where I left him. And once on him—Bess, just wait till you see that horse!'

'Oh, I want to see him—to ride him. But—but, Bern, this is what troubles me,' she said. 'Will—will you come back?'

'Give me four days. If I'm not back in four days you'll know I'm dead. For that only shall keep me.'

'Oh!'

'Bess, I'll come back. There's danger—I wouldn't lie to you—but I can take care of myself.'

'Bern, I'm sure—oh, I'm sure of it! All my life I've watched hunted men. I can tell what's in them. And I believe you can ride and shoot and see with any rider of the sage. It's not—not that I—fear.'

'Well, what is it, then?'

'Why—why—why should you come back at all?'

'I couldn't leave you here alone.'

'You might change your mind when you get to the village—among old friends —'

'I won't change my mind. As for old friends —' He uttered a short, expressive laugh.

'Then—there—there must be a—a woman!' Dark red mantled the clear tan of temple and cheek and neck. Her eyes were eyes of shame, upheld a long moment by intense, straining search for the verification of her fear. Suddenly they drooped, her head fell to her knees, her hands flew to her hot cheeks.

'Bess—look here,' said Venters, with a sharpness due to the violence with which he checked his quick, surging emotion.

As if compelled against her will—answering to an irresistible voice—Bess raised her head, looked at him with sad, dark eyes, and tried to whisper with tremulous lips.

'There's no woman,' went on Venters, deliberately holding her glance with his. 'Nothing on earth, barring the chances of life, can keep me away.'

Her face flashed and flushed with the glow of a leaping joy; but like the vanishing of a gleam it disappeared to leave her as he had never beheld her.

'I am nothing—I am lost—I am nameless!'

'Do you *want* me to come back?' he asked, with sudden stern coldness. 'Maybe *you* want to go back to Oldring!'

That brought her erect, trembling and ashy pale, with dark, proud eyes and mute lips refuting his insinuation.

'Bess, I beg your pardon. I shouldn't have said that. But you angered me. I intend to work—to make a home for you here—to be a—a brother to you as long as ever you need me. And you must forget what you are—were—I mean, and be happy. When you remember that old life you are bitter, and it hurts me.'

'I was happy—I shall be very happy. Oh, you're so good that—that it kills me! If I think, I can't believe it. I grow sick with wondering *why*. I'm only a—*let me say it*—only a lost, nameless—girl of the rustlers. *Oldring's Girl*, they called me. That you should save me—be so good and kind—want to make me happy—why, it's beyond belief. No wonder I'm wretched at the thought of your leaving me. But I'll be wretched and bitter no more. I promise you. If only I could repay you even a little—'

'You've repaid me a hundredfold. Will you believe me?'

'Believe you! I couldn't do else.'

'Then listen! … Saving you, I saved myself. Living here in this valley with you, I've found myself. I've learned to think while I was dreaming. I never troubled myself about God. But God, or some wonderful spirit, has whispered to me here. I absolutely deny the truth of what you say about yourself. I can't explain it. There are things too deep to tell. Whatever the terrible wrongs you've suffered, God holds you blameless. I see that—feel that in you every moment you are near me. I've a mother and a sister 'way back in Illinois. If I could I'd take you to them—tomorrow.'

'*If it were true!* Oh, I might—I might lift my head!' she cried.

'Lift it then—you child. For I swear it's true.'

She did lift her head with the singular wild grace always a part of her actions, with that old unconscious intimation of innocence which always tortured Venters, but now with something more—a spirit rising from the depths that linked itself to his brave words.

'I've been thinking—too,' she cried, with quivering smile and swelling breast. 'I've discovered myself—too. I'm young—I'm alive—I'm so full—oh! I'm a woman!'

'Bess, I believe I can claim credit of that last discovery—before you,' Venters said, and laughed.

'Oh, there's more—there's something I must tell you.'

'Tell it, then.'

'When will you go to Cottonwoods?'

'As soon as the storms are past, or the worst of them.'

'I'll tell you before you go. I can't now. I don't know how I shall then. But it must be told. I'd never let you leave me without knowing. For in spite of what you say there's a chance you mightn't come back.'

Day after day the west wind blew across the valley. Day after day the clouds clustered gray and purple and black. The cliffs sang and the caves rang with Oldring's knell, and the lightning flashed, the thunder rolled, the echoes crashed and crashed, and the rains flooded the valley. Wild flowers sprang up everywhere, swaying with the lengthening grass of the terraces, smiling wanly from shady nooks, peeping wondrously from year-dry crevices of the walls. The valley bloomed into a paradise. Every single moment, from the breaking of the gold bar through the bridge at dawn on to the reddening of rays over the western wall, was one of colorful change. The valley swam in thick, transparent haze, golden at dawn, warm and white at noon, purple in the twilight. At the end of every storm a rainbow curved down into the leaf-bright forest to shine and fade and leave lingeringly some faint essence of its rosy iris in the air.

Venters walked with Bess, once more in a dream, and watched the lights change on the walls, and faced the wind from out of the west.

Always it brought softly to him strange, sweet tidings of far-off things. It blew from a place that was old and whispered of youth. It blew down the grooves of time. It brought a story of the passing hours. It breathed low of fighting men and praying women. It sang clearly the song of love. That ever was the burden of its tidings—youth in the shady woods, waders through the wet meadows, boy and girl at the hedgerow stile, bathers in the booming surf, sweet, idle hours on grassy, windy hills, long strolls down moonlit lanes—everywhere in far-off lands, fingers locked and bursting hearts and longing lips—from all the world tidings of unquenchable love.

Often, in these hours of dreams he watched the girl, and asked himself of what was she dreaming? For the changing light of the valley reflected its gleam and its color and its meaning in the changing light of her eyes. He saw in them infinitely more than he saw in his dreams. He saw thought and soul and nature—strong vision of life. All tidings the west wind blew from distance and age he found deep in those dark-blue depths, and found them mysteries solved. Under their wistful shadow he softened, and in the softening felt himself grow a sadder, a wiser, and a better man.

While the west wind blew its tidings, filling his heart full, teaching him a man's part, the days passed, the purple clouds changed to white, and the storms were over for that summer.

'I must go now,' he said.

'When?' she asked.

'At once—tonight.'

'I'm glad the time has come. It dragged at me. Go—for you'll come back the sooner.'

Late in the afternoon, as the ruddy sun split its last flame in the ragged notch of the western wall, Bess walked with Venters along the eastern terrace, up the long, weathered slope, under the great stone bridge. They entered the narrow gorge to climb around the fence long before built there by Venters. Farther than this she had never been. Twilight had already fallen in the gorge. It brightened to waning shadow in the wider ascent. He showed her Balancing Rock, of which he had often told her, and explained its sinister leaning over the outlet. Shuddering, she looked down the long, pale incline with its closed-in, toppling walls.

'What an awful trail! Did you carry me up here?'

'I did, surely,' replied he.

'It frightens me, somehow. Yet I never was afraid of trails. I'd ride anywhere a horse could go, and climb where he couldn't. But there's something fearful here. I feel as—as if the place was watching me.'

'Look at this rock. It's balanced here—balanced perfectly. You know I told you the cliff-dwellers cut the rock, and why. But they're gone and the rock waits. Can't you see—feel how it waits here? I moved it once, and I'll never dare again. A strong heave would start it. Then it would fall and bang, and smash that crag, and jar the walls, and close forever the outlet to Deception Pass!'

'Ah! When you come back I'll steal up here and push and push with all my might to roll the rock and close forever the outlet to the Pass!' She said it lightly, but in the undercurrent of her voice was a heavier note, a ring deeper than any ever given mere play of words.

'Bess … You can't dare me! Wait till I come back with supplies—then roll the stone.'

'I—was—in—fun.' Her voice now throbbed low. 'Always you must be free to go when you will. Go now … this place presses on me—stifles me.'

'I'm going—but you had something to tell me?'

'Yes … Will you—come back?'

'I'll come if I live.'

'But—but you mightn't come?'

'That's possible, of course. It'll take a good deal to kill me. A man couldn't have a faster horse or keener dog. And, Bess, I've guns, and I'll use them if I'm pushed. But don't worry.'

'I've faith in you. I'll not worry until after four days. Only—because you mightn't come—I must tell you—'

She lost her voice. Her pale face, her great, glowing, earnest eyes, seemed to stand alone out of the gloom of the gorge. The dog whined, breaking the silence.

'I *must* tell you—because you mightn't come back,' she whispered. 'You *must* know what—what I think of your goodness—of you. Always I've been tongue-tied. I seemed not to be grateful. It was deep in my heart. Even now—if I were other than I am—I couldn't tell you. But I'm nothing—only a rustler's girl—nameless—infamous. You've saved me—and I'm—I'm yours to do with as you like ... With all my heart and soul—I love you!'

CHAPTER FIFTEEN
Shadows on the Sage-Slope

In the cloudy, threatening, waning summer days shadows lengthened down the sage-slope, and Jane Withersteen likened them to the shadows gathering and closing in around her life.

Mrs Larkin died, and little Fay was left an orphan with no known relative. Jane's love redoubled. It was the saving brightness of a darkening hour. Fay turned now to Jane in childish worship. And Jane at last found full expression for the mother-longing in her heart. Upon Lassiter, too, Mrs Larkin's death had some subtle reaction. Before, he had often, without explanation, advised Jane to send Fay back to any Gentile family that would take her in. Passionately and reproach-fully and wonderingly Jane had refused even to entertain such an idea. And now Lassiter never advised it again, grew sadder and quieter in his contemplation of the child, and infinitely more gentle and loving. Sometimes Jane had a cold, inexplanable sensation of dread when she saw Lassiter watching Fay. What did the rider see in the future? Why did he, day by day, grow more silent, calmer, cooler, yet sadder in prophetic assurance of something to be?

No doubt, Jane thought, the rider, in his almost superhuman power of foresight, saw behind the horizon the dark, lengthening shadows that were soon to crowd and gloom over him and her and little Fay. Jane Withersteen awaited the long-deferred breaking of the storm with a courage and embittered calm that had come to her in her extremity. Hope had not died. Doubt and fear, subservient to her will, no longer gave her sleepless nights and tortured days. Love remained. All that she had loved she now loved the more. She seemed to feel that she was defiantly flinging the wealth of her love in the face of misfortune and of hate. No day passed but she prayed for all—and most fervently for her enemies. It troubled her that she had lost, or had never gained, the whole control of her mind. In some measure reason and wisdom and decision were locked in a chamber of her brain, awaiting a key. Power to think of some things was taken from her. Meanwhile, abiding a day of judgment, she fought ceaselessly to deny the bitter drops in her cup, to tear back the slow, the intangibly slow growth of a hot, corrosive lichen eating into her heart.

On the morning of August 10th, Jane, while waiting in the court for Lassiter, heard a clear, ringing report of a rifle. It came from the grove, somewhere toward the corrals. Jane glanced out in alarm. The day was dull, windless, soundless. The leaves of the cottonwoods drooped, as if they had foretold the doom of Withersteen House and were now ready to die and drop and decay. Never had Jane seen such shade. She pondered on the meaning of the report. Revolver shots had of late cracked from different parts of the grove—spies taking snap-shots of Lassiter from a cowardly distance! But a rifle report meant more. Riders seldom used rifles. Judkins and Venters were the exceptions she called to mind. Had the men who hounded her hidden in her grove, taken to the rifle to rid her of Lassiter, her last friend? It was probable—it was likely. And she did not share his cool assumption that his death would never come at the hands of a Mormon. Long had she expected it. His constancy to her, his singular reluctance to use the fatal skill for which he was famed—both now plain to all Mormons—laid him open to inevitable assassination. Yet what charm against ambush and aim and enemy he seemed to bear about him! No, Jane reflected, it was not charm; only a wonderful training of eye and ear, and sense of impending peril. Nevertheless that could not forever avail against secret attack.

That moment a rustling of leaves attracted her attention; then the familiar clinking accompaniment of a slow, soft, measured step, and Lassiter walked into the court.

'Jane, there's a fellow out there with a long gun,' he said, and, removing his sombrero, showed his head bound in a bloody scarf.

'I heard the shot; I knew it was meant for you. Let me see—you can't be badly injured?'

'I reckon not. But mebbe it wasn't a close call! … I'll sit here in this corner where nobody can see me from the grove.' He untied the scarf and removed it to show a long, bleeding furrow above his left temple.

'It's only a cut,' said Jane. 'But how it bleeds! Hold your scarf over it just a moment till I come back.'

She ran into the house and returned with bandages; and while she bathed and dressed the wound Lassiter talked.

'That fellow had a good chance to get me. But he must have flinched when he pulled the trigger. As I dodged down I saw him run through the trees. He had a rifle. I've been expectin' that kind of gun play. I reckon now I'll have to keep a little closer hid myself. These fellers all seem to get chilly or shaky when they draw a bead on me, but one of them might jest happen to hit me.'

'Won't you go away—leave Cottonwoods as I've begged you to—before someone does happen to hit you?' she appealed to him.

'I reckon I'll stay.'

'But, oh, Lassiter—your blood will be on my hands!'

'See here, lady, look at your hands now, right now. Aren't they fine, firm, white hands? Aren't they bloody now? Lassiter's blood! That's a queer thing to stain your beautiful hands. But if you could only see deeper you'd find a redder color of blood. Heart color, Jane!'

'Oh! ... My friend!'

'No, Jane, I'm not one to quit when the game grows hot, no more than you. This game, though, is new to me, an' I don't know the moves yet, else I wouldn't have stepped in front of that bullet.'

'Have you no desire to hunt the man who fired at you—to find him—and—kill him?'

'Well, I reckon I haven't any great hankerin' for that.'

'Oh, the wonder of it! ... I knew—I prayed—I trusted. Lassiter, I almost gave—all myself to soften you to Mormons. Thank God, and thank you, my friend ... But, selfish woman that I am, this is no great test. What's the life of one of those sneaking cowards to such a man as you? I think of your great hate toward him who—I think of your life's implacable purpose. Can it be—'

'Wait! ... Listen!' he whispered. 'I hear a hoss.'

He rose noiselessly, with his ear to the breeze. Suddenly he pulled his sombrero down over his bandaged head and, swinging his gun-sheaths round in front, he stepped into the alcove.

'It's a hoss—comin' fast,' he added.

Jane's listening ear soon caught a faint, rapid, rhythmic beat of hoofs. It came from the sage. It gave her a thrill that she was at a loss to understand. The sound rose stronger, louder. Then came a clear, sharp difference when the horse passed from the sage trail to the hard-packed ground of the grove. It became a ringing run—swift in its bell-like clatterings, yet singular in longer pause than usual between the hoof-beats of a horse.

'It's Wrangle! ... It's Wrangle!' cried Jane Withersteen. 'I'd know him from a million horses!'

Excitement and thrilling expectancy flooded out all Jane Withersteen's calm. A tight band closed round her breast as she saw the giant sorrel flit in reddish-brown flashes across the openings in the green. Then he was pounding down the lane—thundering into the court—crashing his great iron-shod hoofs on the stone flags. Wrangle it was surely, but shaggy and wild-eyed, and sage-streaked, with dust-caked lather staining his flanks. He reared and crashed down and plunged. The rider leaped off, threw the bridle, and held hard on a lasso looped round Wrangle's head and neck. Jane's heart sank as she tried to recognize Venters in the rider. Something familiar struck her in the lofty stature, in the sweep of the powerful shoulders. But this bearded, long-haired, unkempt man, who wore ragged clothes patched with pieces of skin, and boots that showed bare legs and feet—this dusty, dark and wild rider could not possibly be Venters.

'Whoa, Wrangle, old boy! Come down. Easy now. So—so—so. You're home, old boy, and presently you can have a drink of water you'll remember.'

In the voice Jane knew the rider to be Venters. He tied Wrangle to the hitching-rack and turned to the court.

'Oh, Bern! ... You wild man!' she exclaimed.

'Jane—Jane, it's good to see you! Hello, Lassiter! Yes, it's Venters.'

Like rough iron his hard hand crushed Jane's. In it she felt the difference she saw in him. Wild, rugged, unshorn—yet how splendid! He had gone away a boy—he had returned a man. He appeared taller, wider of shoulder, deeper-chested, more powerfully built. But was that only her fancy—he had always been a young giant—was the change one of spirit? He might have been absent for years, proven by fire and steel, grown like Lassiter, strong and cool and sure. His eyes—were they keener, more flashing than before?—met hers with clear, frank, warm regard, in which perplexity was not, nor discontent, nor pain.

'Look at me long as you like,' he said, with a laugh. 'I'm not much to look at. And, Jane, neither you nor Lassiter, can brag. You're paler than I ever saw you. Lassiter, here, he wears a bloody bandage under his hat. That reminds me. Someone took a flying shot at me down in the sage. It made Wrangle run some ... Well, perhaps you've more to tell me than I've got to tell you.'

Briefly, in few words, Jane outlined the circumstances of her undoing in the weeks of his absence.

Under his beard and bronze she saw his face whiten in terrible wrath.

'Lassiter—what held you back?'

No time in the long period of fiery moments and sudden shocks had Jane Witersteen ever beheld Lassiter as calm and serene and cool as then.

'Jane had gloom enough without my addin' to it by shootin' up the village,' he said.

As strange as Lassiter's coolness was Venters's curious, intent scrutiny of them both, and under it Jane felt a flaming tide wave from bosom to temples.

'Well—you're right,' he said, with slow pause. 'It surprises me a little, that's all.'

Jane sensed then a slight alteration in Venters, and what it was, in her own confusion, she could not tell. It had always been her intention to acquaint him with the deceit she had fallen to in her zeal to move Lassiter. She did not mean to spare herself. Yet now, at the moment, before these riders, it was an impossibility to explain.

Venters was speaking somewhat haltingly, without his former frankness. 'I found Oldring's hiding-place and your red herd. I learned—I know—I'm sure there was a deal between Tull and Oldring.' He paused and shifted his position and his gaze. He looked as if he wanted to say something that he found beyond him. Sorrow and pity and shame seemed to contend for mastery over him. Then he raised himself and spoke with effort. 'Jane, I've cost you too much. You've almost ruined yourself for me. It was wrong, for I'm not worth it. I never deserved such friendship. Well, maybe it's not too late. You must give me up. Mind, I haven't changed. I am just the same as ever. I'll see Tull while I'm here, and tell him to his face.'

'Bern, it's too late,' said Jane.

'I'll *make* him believe!' cried Venters, violently.

'You ask me to break our friendship?'

'Yes. If you don't, I shall!'

'Forever?'

'Forever!'

Jane sighed. Another shadow had lengthened down the sage-slope to cast further darkness upon her. A melancholy sweetness pervaded her resignation. The boy who had left her had returned a man, nobler, stronger, one in whom she divined something unbending as steel. There might come a moment later when she would wonder why she had not fought against his will, but just now she yielded to it. She liked him as well—nay, more, she thought, only her emotions were deadened by the long, menacing wait for the bursting storm.

Once before she had held out her hand to him—when she gave it; now she stretched it tremblingly forth in acceptance of the decree circumstance had laid upon them. Venters bowed over it, kissed it, pressed it hard, and half stifled a sound very like a sob. Certain it was that when he raised his head tears glistened in his eyes.

'Some—women—have a hard lot,' he said, huskily. Then he shook his powerful form, and his rags lashed about him. 'I'll say a few things to Tull—when I meet him.'

'Bern—you'll not draw on Tull? Oh, that must not be! Promise me—'

'I promise you this,' he interrupted, in stern passion that thrilled while it terrorized her. 'If you say one more word for that plotter I'll kill him as I would a mad coyote!'

Jane clasped her hands. Was this fire-eyed man the one whom she had once made as wax to her touch? Had Venters become Lassiter and Lassiter Venters?

'I'll—say no more,' she faltered.

'Jane, Lassiter once called you blind,' said Venters. 'It must be true. But I won't upbraid you. Only don't rouse the devil in me by praying for Tull! I'll try to keep cool when I meet him. That's all. Now there's one more thing I want to ask of you—the last. I've found a valley down in the Pass. It's a wonderful place. I intend to stay there. It's so hidden I believe no one can find it. There's good water, and browse, and game. I want to raise corn and stock. I need to take in supplies. Will you give them to me?'

'Assuredly. The more you take the better you'll please me—and perhaps the less my—my enemies will get.'

'Venters, I reckon you'll have trouble packin' anythin' away,' put in Lassiter.

'I'll go at night.'

'Mebbe that wouldn't be best. You'd sure be stopped. You'd better go early in the mornin'—say, just after dawn. That's the safest time to move round here.'

'Lassiter, I'll be hard to stop,' returned Venters, darkly.

'I reckon so.'

'Bern,' said Jane, 'go first to the riders' quarters and get yourself a complete outfit. You're a—a sight. Then help yourself to whatever else you need—burros, packs, grain, dried fruits, and meat. You must take coffee and sugar and flour—all kinds of supplies. Don't forget corn and seeds. I remember how you used to starve. Please—please take all you can pack away from here. I'll make a bundle for you, which you musn't open till you're in the valley. How I'd like to see it! To judge by you and Wrangle, how wild it must be!'

Jane walked down into the outer court and approached the sorrel. Upstarting, he laid back his ears and eyed her.

'Wrangle—dear old Wrangle,' she said, and put a caressing hand on his matted mane. 'Oh, he's wild, but he knows me! Bern, can he run as fast as ever?'

'Run? Jane, he's done sixty miles since last night at dark, and I could make him kill Black Star right now in a ten-mile race.'

'He never could,' protested Jane. 'He couldn't even if he was fresh.'

'I reckon mebbe the best hoss'll prove himself yet,' said Lassiter, 'an', Jane, if it ever comes to that race I'd like you to be on Wrangle.'

'I'd like that, too,' rejoined Venters. 'But, Jane, maybe Lassiter's hint is extreme. Bad as your prospects are, you'll surely never come to the running point.'

'Who knows!' she replied, with mournful smile.

'No, no, Jane, it can't be so bad as all that. Soon as I see Tull there'll be a change in your fortunes. I'll hurry down to the village … Now don't worry.'

Jane retired to the seclusion of her room. Lassiter's subtle forecasting of disaster, Venters's forced optimism, neither remained in mind. Material loss weighed nothing in the balance with other losses she was sustaining. She wondered dully at her sitting there, hands folded listlessly, with a kind of numb deadness to the passing of time and the passing of her riches. She thought of Venters's friendship. She had not lost that, but she had lost him. Lassiter's friendship—that was more than love—it would endure, but soon he, too, would be gone. Little Fay slept dreamlessly upon the bed, her golden curls streaming over the pillow. Jane had the child's worship. Would she lose that, too? And if she did, what then would be left? Conscience thundered at her that there was left her religion. Conscience thundered that she should be grateful on her knees for this baptism of fire; that through misfortune, sacrifice, and suffering her soul might be fused pure gold. But the old, spontaneous, rapturous spirit no more exalted her. She wanted to be a woman—not a martyr. Like the saint of old who mortified his flesh, Jane Withersteen had in her the temper for heroic martyr-dom, if by sacrificing herself she could save the souls of others. But here the damnable verdict blistered her that the more she sacrificed herself the blacker grew the souls of her churchmen. There was something terribly wrong with her soul, something terribly wrong with her churchmen and her religion. In the whirling gulf of her thought there was yet one shining light to guide her, to sustain her in her hope; and it was that, despite her errors and her frailties and her blindness, she had one absolute and unfaltering hold on ultimate and supreme justice. That was love. 'Love your enemies as yourself!' was a divine word, entirely free from any church or creed.

Jane's meditations were disturbed by Lassiter's soft, tinkling step in the court. Always he wore the clinking spurs. Always he was in readiness to ride. She passed out and called him into the huge, dim hall.

'I think you'll be safer here. The court is too open,' she said.

'I reckon,' replied Lassiter. 'An' it's cooler here. The day's sure muggy. Well, I went down to the village with Venters.'

'Already! Where is he?' queried Jane, in quick amaze.

'He's at the corrals. Blake's helpin' him get the burros an' packs ready. That Blake is a good fellow.'

'Did—did Bern meet Tull?'

'I guess he did,' answered Lassiter, and he laughed dryly.

'Tell me! Oh, you exasperate me! You're so cool, so calm! For heaven's sake, tell me what happened!'

'First time I've been in the village for weeks,' went on Lassiter, mildly. 'I reckon there ain't been more of a show for a long time. Me an' Venters walkin' down the road! It was funny. I ain't sayin' anybody was particular glad to see us. I'm not much thought of hereabouts, an' Venters he sure looks like what you called him, a wild man. Well, there was some runnin' of folks before we got to the stores. Then everybody vamoosed except some surprised rustlers in front of a saloon.

Venters went right in the stores an' saloons, an' of course I went along. I don't know which tickled me the most—the actions of many fellers we met, or Venters's nerve. Jane, I was downright glad to be along. You see *that* sort of thing is my element, an' I've been away from it for a spell. But we didn't find Tull in one of them places. Some Gentile feller at last told Venters he'd find Tull in that long buildin' next to Parson's store. It's a kind of meetin'-room; and sure enough, when we peeped in, it was half full of men.

'Venters yelled: "Don't anybody pull guns! We ain't come for that!" Then he tramped in, an' I was some put to keep alongside him. There was a hard, scrapin' sound of feet, a loud cry, an' then some whisperin', an' after that stillness you could cut with a knife. Tull was there, an' that fat party who once tried to throw a gun on me, an' other important-lookin' men, an' that little frog-legged feller who was with Tull the day I rode in here. I wish you could have seen their faces, 'specially Tull's an' the fat party's. But there ain't no use of me tryin' to tell you how they looked.

'Well, Venters an' I stood there in the middle of the room, with that batch of men all in front of us, an' not a blamed one of them winked an eyelash or moved a finger. It was natural, of course, for me to notice many of them packed guns. That's a way of mine, first noticin' them things. Venters spoke up, an' his voice sort of chilled an' cut, an' he told Tull he had a few things to say.'

Here Lassiter paused while he turned his sombrero round and round, in his familiar habit, and his eyes had the look of a man seeing over again some thrilling spectacle, and under his red bronze there was strange animation.

'Like a shot, then, Venters told Tull that the friendship between you an' him was all over, an' he was leaving your place. He said you'd both of you broken off in the hope of propitiatin' your people, but you hadn't changed your mind otherwise, an' never would.

'Next he spoke up for you. I ain't goin' to tell you what he said. Only—no other woman who ever lived ever had such tribute! You had a champion, Jane, an' never fear that those thick-skulled men don't know you now. It couldn't be otherwise. He spoke the ringin', lightnin' truth. ... Then he accused Tull of the underhand, miserable robbery of a helpless woman. He told Tull where the red herd was, of a deal made with Oldrin', that Jerry Card had made the deal. I thought Tull was goin' to drop, an' that little frog-legged cuss, he looked some limp an' white. But Venters's voice would have kept anybody's legs from bucklin'. I was stiff myself. He went on an' called Tull—called him every bad name ever known to a rider, an' them some. He cursed Tull. I never heard a man get such a cursin'. He laughed in scorn at the idea of Tull bein' a minister. He said Tull an' a few more dogs of hell builded their empire out of the hearts of such innocent an' God-fearin' women as Jane Withersteen. He called Tull a binder of women, a callous beast who hid behind a mock mantle of righteousness—an' the last an' lowest coward on the face of the earth. To prey on weak women through their religion—that was the last unspeakable crime!

'Then he finished, an' by this time he'd almost lost his voice. But his whisper was enough. "Tull," he said, "*she* begged me not to draw on you today. *She* would pray for you if you burned her at the stake. ... But listen! ... I swear if you and I ever come face to face again, I'll kill you!"

'We backed out of the door then, an' up the road. But nobody follered us.'

Jane found herself weeping passionately. She had not been conscious of it till Lassiter ended his story, and she experienced exquisite pain and relief in shedding tears. Long had her eyes been dry, her grief deep; long had her emotions been dumb. Lassiter's story put her on the rack; the appalling nature of Venters's act and speech had no parallel as an outrage; it was worse than bloodshed. Men like Tull had been shot, but had one ever been so terribly denounced in public? Over-mounting her horror, an uncontrollable, quivering passion shook her very soul. It was sheer human glory in the deed of a fearless man. It was hot, primitive instinct to live—to fight. It was a kind of mad joy in Venters's chivalry. It was close to the wrath that had first shaken her in the beginning of this war waged upon her.

'Well, well, Jane, don't take it that way,' said Lassiter, in evident distress. 'I had to tell you. There's some things a feller jest can't keep. It's strange you give up on hearin' that, when all this long time you've been the gamest woman I ever seen. But I don't know women. Mebbe there's reason for you to cry. I know this—nothin' ever rang in my soul an' so filled it as what Venters did. I'd like to have done it, but—I'm only good for throwin' a gun, an' it seems you hate that. ... Well, I'll be goin' now.'

'Where?'

'Venters took Wrangle to the stable. The sorrel's shy a shoe, an' I've got to help hold the big devil an' put on another.'

'Tell Bern to come for the pack I want to give him—and—and to say good-bye,' called Jane, as Lassiter went out.

Jane passed the rest of that day in a vain endeavor to decide what and what not to put in the pack for Venters. This task was the last she would ever perform for him, and the gifts were the last she would ever make him. So she picked and chose and rejected, and chose again, and often paused in sad revery, and began again, till at length she filled the pack.

It was about sunset, and she and Fay had finished supper and were sitting in the court, when Venters's quick steps rang on the stones. She scarcely knew him, for he had changed the tattered garments, and she missed the dark beard and long hair. Still he was not the Venters of old. As he came up the steps she felt

herself pointing to the pack, and heard herself speaking words that were meaningless to her. He said good-bye; he kissed her, released her, and turned away. His
tall figure blurred in her sight, grew dim through dark, streaked vision, and then
he vanished.

Twilight fell around Withersteen House, and dusk and night. Little Fay slept;
but Jane lay with strained, aching eyes. She heard the wind moaning in the
cottonwoods and mice squeaking in the walls. The night was interminably long,
yet she prayed to hold back the dawn. What would another day bring forth? The
blackness of her room seemed blacker for the sad, entering gray of morning light.
She heard the chirp of awakening birds, and fancied she caught a faint clatter of
hoofs. Then low, dull, distant, throbbed a heavy gunshot. She had expected it,
was waiting for it; nevertheless, an electric shock checked her heart, froze the very
living fiber of her bones. That vise-like hold on her faculties apparently did not
relax for a long time, and it was a voice under her windows that released her.

'Jane! ... Jane!' softly called Lassiter.

She answered somehow.

'It's all right. Venters got away. I thought mebbe you'd heard that shot, an' I
was worried some.'

'What was it—who fired?'

'Well—some fool feller tried to stop Venters out there in the sage—an' he only
stopped lead! ... I think it'll be all right. I haven't seen or heard of any other fellers
around. Venters'll go through safe. An', Jane, I've got Bells saddled, an' I'm going
to trail Venters. Mind, I won't show myself unless he falls foul of somebody an'
needs me. I want to see if this place where he's goin' is safe for him. He says
nobody can track him there. I never seen the place yet I couldn't track a man to.
Now, Jane, you stay indoors while I'm gone, an' keep close watch on Fay. Will
you?'

'Yes! Oh yes!'

'An' another thing, Jane,' he continued, then paused for long—'another
thing—if you ain't here when I come back—if you're *gone*—don't fear, I'll trail
you—I'll find you.'

'My dear Lassiter, where could I be gone—as you put it?' asked Jane, in a
curious surprise.

'I reckon you might be somewhere. Mebbe tied in an old barn—or corralled
in some gulch—or chained in a cave! *Milly Erne was*—till she gave in! Mebbe that's
news to you ... Well, if you're gone I'll hunt for you.'

'No, Lassiter,' she replied, sadly and low. 'If I'm gone just forget the unhappy
woman whose blinded selfish deceit you repaid with kindness and love.'

She heard a deep, muttering curse, under his breath, and then the silvery
tinkling of his spurs as he moved away.

Jane entered upon the duties of that day with a settled, gloomy calm. Disaster hung in the dark clouds, in the shade, in the humid west wind. Blake, when he reported, appeared without his usual cheer; and Jerd wore a harassed look of a worn and worried man. And when Judkins put in appearance, riding a lame horse, and dismounted with the cramp of a rider, his dust-covered figure and his darkly grim, almost dazed expression told Jane of dire calamity. She had no need of words.

'Miss Withersteen, I have to report—loss of the—white herd,' said Judkins, hoarsely.

'Come, sit down; you look played out,' replied Jane, solicitously. She brought him brandy and food, and while he partook of refreshments, of which he appeared badly in need, she asked no questions.

'No one rider—could hev done more—Miss Withersteen,' he went on, presently.

'Judkins, don't be distressed. You've done more than any other rider. I've long expected to lose the white herd. It's no surprise. It's in line with other things that are happening. I'm grateful for your service.'

'Miss Withersteen, I knew how you'd take it. But if anythin', that makes it harder to tell. You see, a feller wants to do so much fer you, an' I'd got fond of my job. We hed the herd a ways off to the north of the break in the valley. There was a big level an' pools of water an' tip-top browse. But the cattle was in a high nervous condition. Wild—as wild as antelope! You see, they'd been so scared they never slept. I ain't a-goin' to tell you of the many tricks that were pulled off out there in the sage. But there wasn't a day fer weeks thet the herd didn't get started to run. We allus managed to ride 'em close an' drive 'em back an' keep 'em bunched. Honest, Miss Withersteen, them steers was *thin*. They was *thin* when water and grass was everywhere. *Thin* at this season—thet'll tell you how your steers was pestered. Fer instance, one night a strange runnin' streak of fire run right through the herd. That streak was a coyote—*with an oiled an' blazin' tail!* Fer I shot it an' found out. We hed hell with the herd that night, an' if the sage an' grass hedn't been wet—we, hosses, steers, an' all would hev burned up. But I said I wasn't goin' to tell you any of the tricks. ... Strange now, Miss Withersteen, when the stampede did come it was from natural cause—jest a whirlin' devil of dust. You've seen the like often. An' this wasn't no big whirl, fer the dust was mostly settled. It had dried out in a little swale, an' ordinarily no steer would ever hev run fer it. But the herd was nervous an' wild. An' jest as Lassiter said, when that bunch of white steers got to movin' they was as bad as buffalo. I've seen some buffalo stampedes back in Nebraska, an' this bolt of the steers was the same kind.

'I tried to mill the herd jest as Lassiter did. But I wasn't equal to it, Miss Withersteen. I don't believe the rider lives who could hev turned thet herd. We kept along of the herd fer miles, an' more'n one of my boys tried to get the steers a-millin'. It wasn't no use. We got off level ground, goin' down, an' then the steers ran somethin' fierce. We left the little gullies an' washes level-full of dead steers. Finally I saw the herd was makin' to pass a kind of low pocket between ridges. There was a hog-back—as we used to call 'em—a pile of rocks stickin' up, and I saw the herd was goin' to split round it, or swing out to the left. An' I wanted 'em to go to the right so mebbe we'd be able to drive 'em into the pocket. So, with all my boys except three, I rode hard to turn the herd a little to the right. We couldn't budge 'em. They went on, an' split round the rocks, an' the most of 'em was turned sharp to the left by a deep wash we hedn't seen—had no chance to see.

'The other three boys—Jimmy Vail, Joe Wills, an' thet little Cairns boy—a nervy kid! they, with Cairns leadin', tried to buck thet herd round to the pocket. It was a wild, fool idee. I couldn't do nothin'. The boys got hemmed in between the steers an' the wash—thet they hedn't no chance to see, either. Vail an' Wills was run down right before our eyes. An' Cairns, who rode a fine hoss, he did some ridin' I never seen equaled, an' would hev beat the steers if there'd been any room to run in. I was high up an' could see how the steers kept spillin' by twos and threes over into the wash. Cairns put his hoss to a place thet was too wide fer any hoss, an' broke his neck an' the hoss's too. We found that out after, an' as fer Vail an' Wills—two thousand steers ran over the poor boys. There was't much left to pack home fer buryin'! … An', Miss Withersteen, thet all happened yesterday, an' I believe, if the white herd didn't run over the wall of the Pass, it's runnin' yet.'

On the morning of the second day after Judkins's recital, during which time Jane remained indoors a prey to regret and sorrow for the boy riders, and a new and now strangely insistent fear for her own person, she again heard what she had missed more than she dared honestly confess—the soft, jingling step of Lassiter. Almost overwhelming relief surged through her, a feeling as akin to joy as any she could have been capable of in those gloomy hours of shadow, and one that suddenly stunned her with the significance of what Lassiter had come to mean to her. She had begged him, for his own sake, to leave Cottonwoods. She might yet beg that, if her weakening courage permitted her to dare absolute loneliness and helplessness, but she realized now that if she were left alone her life would become one long, hideous nightmare.

When his soft steps clinked into the hall, in answer to her greeting, and his tall, black-garbed form filled the door, she felt an inexpressible sense of immediate safety. In his presence she lost her fear of the dim passageways of Withersteen House and of every sound. Always it had been that, when he entered the court or the hall, she had experienced a distinctly sickening but gradually lessening shock at sight of the huge black guns swinging at his sides. This time the sickening shock again visited her, it was, however, because a revealing flash of thought told her that it was not alone. Lassiter who was thrillingly welcome, but also his fatal weapons. They meant so much. How she had fallen—how broken and spiritless must she be—to have still the same old horror of Lassiter's guns and his name, yet feel somehow a cold, shrinking protection in their law and might and use.

'Did you trail Venters—find this wonderful valley?' she asked, eagerly.

'Yes, an' I reckon it's sure a wonderful place.'

'Is he safe there?'

'That's been botherin' me some. I tracked him an' part of the trail was the hardest I ever tackled. Mebbe there's a rustler or somebody in this country who's as good at trackin' as I am. If that's so Venters ain't safe.'

'Well—tell me all about Bern and his valley.'

To Jane's surprise Lassiter showed disinclination for further talk about his trip. He appeared to be extremely fatigued. Jane reflected that one hundred and twenty miles, with probably a great deal of climbing on foot, all in three days, was enough to tire any rider. Moreover, it presently developed that Lassiter had returned in a mood of singular sadness and preoccupation. She put it down to a moodiness over the loss of her white herd and the now precarious condition of her fortune.

Several days passed, and, as nothing happened, Jane's spirits began to brighten. Once in her musings she thought that this tendency of hers to rebound was as sad as it was futile. Meanwhile, she had resumed her walks through the grove with little Fay.

One morning she went as far as the sage. She had not seen the slope since the beginning of the rains, and now it bloomed a rich deep purple. There was a high wind blowing, and the sage tossed and waved and colored beautifully from light to dark. Clouds scudded across the sky and their shadows sailed darkly down the sunny slope.

Upon her return toward the house she went by the lane to the stables, and she had scarcely entered the great open space with its corrals and sheds when she saw Lassiter hurriedly approaching. Fay broke from her and, running to a corral fence, began to pat and pull the long, hanging ears of a drowsy burro.

One look at Lassiter armed her for a blow.

Without a word he led her across the wide yard to the rise of the ground upon which the stable stood.

'Jane—look!' he said, and pointed to the ground.

Jane glanced down, and again, and upon steadier vision made out splotches of blood on the stones, and broad, smooth marks in the dust, leading out toward the sage.

'What made these?' she asked.

'I reckon somebody has dragged dead or wounded men out to where there was hosses in the sage.'

'Dead—or—wounded—men!'

'I reckon—Jane, are you strong? Can you bear up?'

His hands were gently holding hers, and his eyes—suddenly she could no longer look into them. 'Strong?' she echoed, trembling. 'I—I will be.'

Up on the stone-flag drive, nicked with the marks made by the iron-shod hoofs of her racers, Lassiter led her, his grasp ever growing firmer.

'Where's Blake—and—and Jerd?' she asked, haltingly.

'I don't know where Jerd is. Bolted, most likely,' replied Lassiter, as he took her through the stone door.

'But Blake—poor Blake! He's gone forever! … Be prepared, Jane.'

With a cold prickling of her skin, with a queer thrumming in her ears, with fixed and staring eyes, Jane saw a gun lying at her feet with chamber swung and empty, and discharged shells scattered near.

Outstretched upon the stable floor lay Blake, ghastly white—dead—one hand clutching a gun and the other twisted in his bloody blouse.

'Whoever the thieves were, whether your people or rustlers—Blake killed some of them!' said Lassiter

'Thieves?' whispered Jane.

'I reckon. Hoss-thieves! … Look!' Lassiter waved his hand toward the stalls.

The first stall—Bells's stall—was empty. All the stalls were empty. No racer whinnied and stamped greeting to her. Night was gone! Black Star was gone!

CHAPTER SIXTEEN
Gold

As Lassiter had reported to Jane, Venters 'went through' safely, and after a toilsome journey reached the peaceful shelter of Surprise Valley. When finally he lay wearily down under the silver spruces, resting from the strain of dragging packs and burros up the slope and through the entrance to Surprise Valley, he had leisure to think, and a great deal of the time went in regretting that he had not been frank with his loyal friend, Jane Withersteen.

But, he kept continually recalling, when he had stood once more face to face with her and had been shocked at the change in her and had heard the details of her adversity, he had not had the heart to tell her of the closer interest which had entered his life. He had not lied; yet he had kept silence.

Bess was in transports over the stores of supplies and the outfit he had packed from Cottonwoods. He had certainly brought a hundred times more than he had gone for; enough, surely, for years, perhaps to make permanent home in the valley. He saw no reason why he need ever leave there again.

After a day of rest he recovered his strength and shared Bess's pleasure in rummaging over the endless packs, and began to plan for the future. And in this planning, his trip to Cottonwoods, with its revived hate of Tull and consequent unleashing of fierce passions, soon faded out of mind. By slower degrees his friendship for Jane Withersteen and his contrition drifted from the active preoccupation of his present thought to a place in memory, with more and more infrequent recalls.

And as far as the state of his mind was concerned, upon the second day after his return, the valley, with its golden hues and purple shades, the speaking west wind and the cool, silent night, and Bess's watching eyes with their wonderful light, so wrought upon Venters that he might never have left them at all.

That very afternoon he set to work. Only one thing hindered him upon beginning, though it in no wise checked his delight, and that was that in the multiplicity of tasks planned to make a paradise out of the valley he could not choose the one with which to begin. He had to grow into the habit of passing from one dreamy pleasure to another, like a bee going from flower to flower in the valley, and he found his wandering habit likely to extend to his labors. Nevertheless, he made a start.

At the outset he discovered Bess to be both a considerable help in some ways and a very great hindrance in others. Her excitement and joy were spurs, inspirations; but she was utterly impracticable in her ideas, and she flitted from one plan to another with bewildering vacillation. Moreover, he fancied that she grew more eager, youthful, and sweet; and he marked that it was far easier to watch her and listen to her than it was to work. Therefore he gave her tasks that necessitated her going often to the cave where he had stored his packs.

Upon the last of these trips, when he was some distance down the terrace and out of sight of camp, he heard a scream, and then the sharp barking of the dogs.

For an instant he straightened up, amazed. Danger for her had been absolutely out of his mind. She had seen a rattlesnake—or a wildcat. Still she would not have been likely to scream at sight of either; and the barking of the dogs was ominous. Dropping his work, he dashed back along the terrace. Upon breaking through a clump of aspens he saw the dark form of a man in the camp. Cold, then hot, Venters burst into frenzied speed to reach his guns. He was cursing himself for a thoughtless fool when the man's tall form became familiar and he recognized Lassiter. Then the reversal of emotions changed his run to a walk; he tried to call out, but his voice refused to carry; when he reached camp there was Lassiter staring at the white–faced girl. By that time Ring and Whitie had recognized him.

'Hello, Venters! I'm makin' you a visit,' said Lassiter, slowly. 'An' I'm some surprised to see you've a—a young feller for company.'

One glance had sufficed for the keen rider to read Bess's real sex, and for once his cool calm had deserted him. He stared till the white of Bess's cheeks flared into crimson. That, if it were needed, was the concluding evidence of her femininity; for it went fittingly with her sun-tinted hair and darkened, dilated eyes, the sweetness of her mouth, and the striking symmetry of her slender shape.

'Heavens! Lassiter!' panted Venters, when he caught his breath. 'What relief—it's only you! How—in the name of all—that's wonderful—did you ever get here?'

'I trailed you. We—I wanted to know where you was, if you had a safe place. So I trailed you.'

'Trailed me!' cried Venters, bluntly.

'I reckon. It was some of a job after I got to them smooth rocks. I was all day trackin' you up to them little cut steps in the rock. The rest was easy.'

'Where's your hoss? I hope you hid him.'

'I tied him in them queer cedars down on the slope. He can't be seen from the valley.'

'That's good. Well, well! I'm completely dumbfounded. It was my idea that no man could track me in here.'

'I reckon. But if there's a tracker in these uplands as good as me he can find you.'

'That's bad. That'll worry me. But, Lassiter, now you're here I'm glad to see you. And—my companion here is not a young fellow! … Bess, this is a friend of mine. He saved my life once.'

The embarrassment of the moment did not extend to Lassiter. Almost at once his manner, as he shook hands with Bess, relieved Venters and put the girl at ease. After Venters's words and one quick look at Lassiter, her agitation stilled, and, though she was shy, if she were conscious of anything out of the ordinary in the situation, certainly she did not show it.

'I reckon I'll only stay a little while,' Lassiter was saying. 'An' if you don't mind troublin', I'm hungry. I fetched some biscuits along, but they're gone. Venters, this place is sure the wonderfullest ever seen. Them cut steps on the slope! That outlet into the gorge! An' it's like climbin' up through hell into heaven to climb through that gorge into this valley! There's a queer-lookin' rock at the top of the passage. I didn't have time to stop. I'm wonderin' how you ever found this place. It's sure interestin'.'

During the preparation and eating of dinner Lassiter listened mostly, as was his wont, and occasionally he spoke in his quaint and dry way. Venters noted, however, that the rider showed an increasing interest in Bess. He asked her no questions, and only directed his attention to her while she was occupied and had no opportunity to observe his scrutiny. It seemed to Venters that Lassiter grew more and more absorbed in his study of Bess, and that he lost his coolness in some strange, softening sympathy. Then, quite abruptly, he arose and announced the necessity for his early departure. He said good-bye to Bess in a voice gentle and somewhat broken, and turned hurriedly away. Venters accompanied him, and they had traversed the terrace, climbed the weathered slope, and passed under the stone bridge before either spoke again.

Then Lassiter put a great hand on Venters's shoulder and wheeled him to meet a smoldering fire of gray eyes.

'Lassiter, I couldn't tell Jane! I couldn't,' burst out Venters, reading his friend's mind. 'I tried. But I couldn't. She wouldn't understand, and she has troubles enough. And I love the girl!'

'Venters, I reckon this beats me. I've seen some queer things in my time, too. This girl—who is she?'

'I don't know.'

'Don't know! What is she, then?'

'I don't know that, either. Oh, it's the strangest story you ever heard. I must tell you. But you'll never believe.'

'Venters, women were always puzzles to me. But for all that, if this girl ain't a child, an' as innocent, I'm no fit person to think of virtue an' goodness in anybody. Are you goin' to be square with her?'

'I am—so help me God!'

'I reckoned so. Mebbe my temper oughtn't led me to make sure. But, man, she's a woman in all but years. She's sweeter'n the sage.'

'Lassiter, I know, I know. And the *hell* of it is that in spite of her innocence and charm she's—she's not what she seems!'

'I wouldn't want to—of course, I couldn't call you a liar, Venters,' said the older man.

'What's more, she was Oldring's Masked Rider!'

Venters expected to floor his friend with that statement, but he was not in any way prepared for the shock his words gave. For an instant he was astounded to see Lassiter stunned; then his own passionate eagerness to unbosom himself, to tell the wonderful story, precluded any other thought.

'Son, tell me all about this,' presently said Lassiter as he seated himself on a stone and wiped his moist brow.

Thereupon Venters began his narrative at the point where he had shot the rustler and Oldring's Masked Rider, and he rushed through it, telling all, not holding back even Bess's unreserved avowal of her love or his deepest emotions.

'That's the story,' he said, concluding. 'I love her, though I've never told her. If I did tell her I'd be ready to marry her, and that seems impossible in this country. I'd be afraid to risk taking her anywhere. So I intend to do the best I can for her here.'

'The longer I live the stranger life is,' mused Lassiter, with downcast eyes. 'I'm reminded of somethin' you once said to Jane about hands in her game of life. There's that unseen hand of power, an' Tull's black hand, an' my red one, an' your indifferent one, an' the girl's little brown, helpless one. An', Venters, there's another one that's all-wise an' all-wonderful. *That's* the hand guidin' Jane Withersteen's game of life! ... Your story's one to daze a far clearer head than mine. I can't offer no advice, even if you asked for it. Mebbe I can help you. Anyway, I'll hold Oldrin' up when he comes to the village, an' find out about this girl. I knew the rustler years ago. He'll remember me.'

'Lassiter, if I ever meet Oldring I'll kill him!' cried Venters, with sudden intensity.

'I reckon that'd be perfectly natural,' replied the rider.

'Make him think Bess is dead—as she is to him and that old life.'

'Sure, sure, son. Cool down now. If you're goin' to begin pullin' guns on Tull an' Oldrin' you want to be cool. I reckon, though, you'd better keep hid here. Well, I must be leavin'.'

'One thing, Lassiter. You'll not tell Jane about Bess? Please don't!'

'I reckon not. But I wouldn't be afraid to bet that after she'd got over anger at your secrecy—Venters, she'd be furious once in her life!—she'd think more of you. I don't mind sayin' for myself that I think you're a good deal of a man.'

In the further ascent Venters halted several times with the intention of saying good-bye, yet he changed his mind and kept on climbing till they reached Balancing Rock. Lassiter examined the huge rock, listened to Venters's idea of its position and suggestion, and curiously placed a strong hand upon it.

'Hold on!' cried Venters. 'I heaved at it once and have never gotten over my scare.'

'Well, you do seem uncommon nervous,' replied Lassiter, much amused. 'Now, as for me, why I always had the funniest notion to roll stones! When I was a kid I did it, an' the bigger I got the bigger stones I'd roll. Ain't that funny? Honest— even now I often get off my hoss just to tumble a big stone over a precipice, an' watch it drop, an' listen to it bang an' boom. I've started some slides in my time, an' don't you forget it. I never seen a rock I wanted to roll as bad as this one! Wouldn't there jest be roarin' crashin' hell down that trail?'

'You'd close the outlet forever!' exclaimed Venters. 'Well, good-bye, Lassiter. Keep my secret and don't forget me. And be mighty careful how you get out of the valley below. The rustlers' cañon isn't more than three miles up the Pass. Now you've tracked me here, I'll never feel safe again.'

In his descent to the valley, Venters's emotion, roused to stirring pitch by the recital of his love story, quieted gradually, and in its place came a sober, thoughtful mood. All at once he saw that he was serious, because he would never more regain his sense of security while in the valley. What Lassiter could do another skillful cracker might duplicate. Among the many riders with whom Venters had ridden he recalled no one who could have taken his trail at Cottonwoods and have followed it to the edge of the bare slope in the pass, let alone up that glistening smooth stone. Lassiter, however, was not an ordinary rider. Instead of hunting cattle tracks he had likely spent a goodly portion of his life tracking men. It was not improbable that among Oldring's rustlers there was one who shared Lassiter's gift for trailing. And the more Venters dwelt on this possibility the more perturbed he grew.

Lassiter's visit, moreover, had a disquieting effect upon Bess, and Venters fancied that she entertained the same thought as to future seclusion. The breaking of their solitude, though by a well-meaning friend, had not only dispelled all its dream and much of its charm, but had instilled a canker of fear. Both had seen the footprint in the sand.

Venters did no more work that day. Sunset and twilight gave way to night, and the canõn bird whistled its melancholy notes, and the wind sang softly in the cliffs, and the camp-fire blazed and burned down to red embers. To Venters a subtle difference was apparent in all of these, or else the shadowy change had been in him. He hoped that on the morrow this slight depression would have passed away.

In that measure, however, he was doomed to disappointment. Furthermore, Bess reverted to a wistful sadness that he had not observed in her since her recovery. His attempt to cheer her out of it resulted in dismal failure, and consequently in a darkening of his own mood. Hard work relieved him; still, when the day had passed, his unrest returned. Then he set to deliberate thinking, and there came to him the startling conviction that he must leave Surprise Valley and take Bess with him. As a rider he had taken many chances, and as an adventurer in Deception Pass he had unhesitatingly risked his life; but now he would run no preventable hazard of Bess's safety and happiness, and he was too keen not to see that hazard. It gave him a pang to think of leaving the beautiful valley just when he had the means to establish a permanent and delightful home there. One flashing thought tore in hot temptation through his mind—why not climb up into the gorge, roll Balancing Rock down the trail, and close forever the outlet to Deception Pass? 'That was the beast in me—showing his teeth!' muttered Venters, scornfully. 'I'll just kill him good and quick! I'll be fair to this girl, if it's the last thing I do on earth!'

Another day went by, in which he worked less and pondered more and all the time covertly watched Bess. Her wistfulness had deepened into downright unhappiness, and that made his task to tell her all the harder. He kept the secret another day, hoping by some chance she might grow less moody, and to his exceeding anxiety she fell into far deeper gloom. Out of his own secret and the torment of it he divined that she, too, had a secret and the keeping of it was torturing her. As yet he had no plan thought out in regard to how or when to leave the valley, but he decided to tell her the necessity of it and to persuade her to go. Furthermore, he hoped his speaking out would induce her to unburden her own mind.

'Bess, what's wrong with you?' he asked.

'Nothing,' she answered, with averted face.

Venters took hold of her and gently, though masterfully, forced her to meet his eyes.

'You can't look at me and lie,' he said. 'Now—what's wrong with you? You're keeping something from me. Well, I've got a secret, too, and I intend to tell it presently.'

'Oh—I *have* a secret. I was crazy to tell you when you came back. That's why I was so silly about everything. I kept holding my secret back—gloating over it. But when Lassiter came I got an idea—that changed my mind. Then I hated to tell you.'

'Are you going to now?'

'Yes—yes. I was coming to it. I tried yesterday, but you were so cold. I was afraid. I couldn't keep it much longer.'

'Very well, most mysterious lady, tell your wonderful secret.'

'You needn't laugh,' she retorted, with a first glimpse of reviving spirit. 'I can take the laugh out of you in one second.'

'It's a go.'

She ran through the spruces to the cave, and returned carrying something which was manifestly heavy. Upon nearer view he saw that whatever she held with such evident importance, had been bound up in a black scarf he well remembered. That alone was sufficient to make him tingle with curiosity.

'Have you any idea what I did in your absence?' she asked.

'I imagine you lounged about, waiting and watching for me,' he replied, smiling. 'I've my share of conceit, you know.'

'You're wrong. I worked. Look at my hands.' She dropped on her knees close to where he sat, and, carefully depositing the black bundle, she held out her hands. The palms and inside of her fingers were white, puckered, and worn.

'Why, Bess, you've been fooling in the water,' he said.

'Fooling? Look here! With deft fingers she spread open the black scarf, and the bright sun shone upon a dull, glittering heap of gold.

'Gold!' he ejaculated.

'Yes, gold! See, pounds of gold! I found it—washed it out of the stream—picked it out grain by grain, nugget by nugget!'

'Gold!' he cried.

'Yes. Now—now laugh at my secret!'

For a long minute Venters gazed. Then he stretched forth a hand to feel if the gold was real.

'*Gold!*' he almost shouted. 'Bess, there are hundreds—thousands of dollars' worth here!'

He leaned over to her, and put his hand, strong and clenching now, on hers. 'Is there more where this came from?' he whispered.

'Plenty of it, all the way up the stream to the cliff. You know I've often washed for gold. Then I've heard the men talk. I think there's no great quantity of gold here, but enough for—for a fortune for *you*.'

'That—was—your—secret!'

'Yes. I hate gold. For it makes men mad. I've seen them drunk with joy and dance and fling themselves around. I've seen them curse and rave. I've seen them fight like dogs and roll in the dust. I've seen them kill each other for gold.'

'Is that why you hated to tell me?'

'Not—not altogether.' Bess lowered her head. 'It was because I knew you'd never stay here long after you found gold.'

'You were afraid I'd leave you?'

'Yes.'

'Listen! ... You great, simple child! Listen ... You sweet, wonderful, wild, blue-eyed girl! I was tortured by my secret. It was that I knew we—*we* must leave the valley. We can't stay here much longer. I couldn't think how we'd get away—out of the country—or how we'd live, if we ever got out. I'm a beggar. That's why I kept my secret. I'm poor. It takes money to make way beyond Sterling. We couldn't ride horses or burros or walk forever. So while I knew we must go, I was distracted over how to go and what to do. *Now!* We've gold! Once beyond Sterling, we'll be safe from rustlers. We've no others to fear.

'Oh! Listen! Bess!' Venters now heard his voice ringing high and sweet, and he felt Bess's cold hands in his crushing grasp as she leaned toward him pale, breathless. 'This is how much I'd leave you! You made me live again! I'll take you away—far away from this wild country. You'll begin a new life. You'll be happy. You shall see cities, ships, people. You shall have anything your heart craves. All the shame and sorrow of your life shall be forgotten—as if they had never been. This is how much I'd leave you here alone—you sad-eyed girl. I love you! Didn't you know it? How could you fail to know it? I love you! I'm free! I'm a man—a man you've made—no more a beggar! ... Kiss me! This is how much I'd leave you here alone—you beautiful, strange, unhappy girl. But I'll make you happy.

What—what do I care for—your past! I love you! I'll take you home to Illinois—to my mother. Then I'll take you to far places. I'll make up all you've lost. Oh, I know you love me—knew it before you told me. And it changed my life. And you'll go with me, not as my companion as you are here, nor my sister, but, Bess, darling! … As *my wife!*'

CHAPTER SEVENTEEN
Wrangle's Race Run

The plan eventually decided upon by the lovers was for Venters to go to the village, secure a horse and some kind of a disguise for Bess, or at least less striking apparel than her present garb, and to return post–haste to the valley. Meanwhile, she would add to their store of gold. Then they would strike the long and perilous trail to ride out of Utah. In the event of his inability to fetch back a horse for her, they intended to make the giant sorrel carry double. The gold, a little food, saddle blankets, and Venters's guns were to compose the light outfit with which they would make the start.

'I love this beautiful place,' said Bess. 'It's hard to think of leaving it.'

'Hard! Well, I should think so,' replied Venters. 'Maybe—in years—' But he did not complete in words his thought that it might be possible to return after many years of absence and change.

Once again Bess bade Venters farewell under the shadow of Balancing Rock, and this time it was with whispered hope and tenderness and passionate trust. Long after he had left her, all down through the outlet to the Pass, the clinging clasp of her arms, the sweetness of her lips, and the sense of a new and exquisite birth of character in her remained hauntingly and thrillingly in his mind. The girl who had sadly called herself nameless and nothing had been marvelously transformed in the moment of his avowal of love. It was something to think over, something to warm his heart, but for the present it had absolutely to be forgotten so that all his mind could be addressed to the trip so fraught with danger.

He carried only his rifle, revolver, and a small quantity of bread and meat; and thus lightly burdened, he made swift progress down the slope and out into the valley. Darkness was coming on, and he welcomed it. Stars were blinking when he reached his old hiding-place in the split of canõn wall, and by their aid he slipped through the dense thickets to the grassy enclosure. Wrangle stood in the center of it with his head up, and he appeared black and of gigantic proportions in the dim light. Venters whistled softly, began a slow approach, and then called. The horse snorted and, plunging away with dull, heavy sound of hoofs, he disappeared in the gloom. 'Wilder than ever!' muttered Venters. He followed the sorrel into the narrowing split between the walls, and presently had to desist because he could not see a foot in advance. As he went back toward the open Wrangle jumped out of an ebony shadow of cliff and like a thunderbolt shot huge and black past him down into the starlit glade. Deciding that all attempts to catch Wrangle at night would be useless, Venters repaired to the shelving rock where he had hidden saddle and blanket, and there went to sleep.

The first peep of day found him stirring, and as soon as it was light enough to distinguish objects, he took his lasso off his saddle and went out to rope the sorrel. He espied Wrangle at the lower end of the cove and approached him in a perfectly natural manner. When he got near enough, Wrangle evidently recognized him, but was too wild to stand. He ran up the glade and on into the narrow lane between the walls. This favored Venters's speedy capture of the horse, so coiling his noose ready to throw, he hurried on. Wrangle let Venters get to within a hundred feet and then he broke. But as he plunged by, rapidly getting into his stride, Venters made a perfect throw with the rope. He had time to brace himself for the shock; nevertheless, Wrangle threw him and dragged him several yards before halting.

'You wild devil,' said Venters, as he slowly pulled Wrangle up. 'Don't you know me? Come now—old fellow—so—so—'

Wrangle yielded to the lasso and then to Venters's strong hand. He was as straggly and wild-looking as a horse left to roam free in the sage. He dropped his long ears and stood readily to be saddled and bridled. But he was exceedingly sensitive, and quivered at every touch and sound. Venters led him to the thicket, and, bending the close saplings to let him squeeze through, at length reached the open. Sharp survey in each direction assured him of the usual lonely nature of the cañon; then he was in the saddle, riding south.

Wrangle's long, swinging canter was a wonderful ground-gainer. His stride was almost twice that of an ordinary horse, and his endurance was equally remarkable. Venters pulled him in occasionally, and walked him up the stretches of rising ground and along the soft washes. Wrangle had never yet shown any indication of distress while Venters rode him. Nevertheless, there was now reason to save the horse; therefore Venters did not resort to the hurry that had characterized his former trip. He camped at the last water in the Pass. What distance that was to Cottonwoods he did not know; he calculated, however, that it was in the neighborhood of fifty miles.

Early in the morning he proceeded on his way, and about the middle of the forenoon reached the constricted gap that marked the southerly end of the Pass, and through which led the trail up to the sage-level. He spied out Lassiter's tracks in the dust, but no others, and dismounting, he straightened out Wrangle's bridle and began to lead him up the trail. The short climb, more severe on beast than on man, necessitated a rest on the level above, and during this he scanned the wide purple reaches of slope.

Wrangle whistled his pleasure at the smell of the sage. Remounting, Venters headed up the white trail with the fragrant wind in his face. He had proceeded for perhaps a couple of miles when Wrangle stopped with a suddenness that threw Venters heavily against the pommel.

'What's wrong, old boy?' called Venters, looking down for a loose shoe or a snake or a foot lamed by a picked-up stone. Unrewarded, he raised himself from his scrutiny. Wrangle stood stiff, head high, with his long ears erect. Thus guided, Venters swiftly gazed ahead to make out a dust-clouded, dark group of horsemen riding down the slope. If they had seen him, it apparently made no difference in their speed or direction.

'Wonder who they are!' exclaimed Venters. He was not disposed to run. His cool mood tightened under grip of excitement as he reflected that, whoever the approaching riders were, they could not be friends. He slipped out of the saddle and led Wrangle behind the tallest sage-brush. It might serve to conceal them until the riders were close enough for him to see who they were; after that he would be indifferent to how soon they discovered him.

After looking to his rifle and ascertaining that it was in working order, he watched, and as he watched, slowly the force of a bitter fierceness, long dormant, gathered ready to flame into life. If those riders were not rustlers he had forgotten how rustlers looked and rode. On they came, a small group, so compact and dark that he could not tell their number. How unusual that their horses did not see Wrangle! But such failure, Venters decided, was owing to the speed with which they were traveling. They moved at a swift canter affected more by rustlers than by riders. Venters grew concerned over the possibility that these horsemen would actually ride down on him before he had a chance to tell what to expect. When they were within three hundred yards he deliberately led Wrangle out into the trail.

Then he heard shouts, and the hard scrape of sliding hoofs, and saw horses rear and plunge back with up-flung heads and flying manes. Several little white puffs of smoke appeared sharply against the black background of riders and horses, and shots rang out. Bullets struck far in front of Venters, and whipped up the dust and then hummed low into the sage. The range was great for revolvers, but whether the shots were meant to kill or merely to check advance, they were enough to fire that waiting ferocity in Venters. Slipping his arm through the bridle, so that Wrangle could not get away, Venters lifted his rifle and pulled the trigger twice.

He saw the first horseman lean sideways and fall. He saw another lurch in his saddle and heard a cry of pain. Then Wrangle, plunging in fright, lifted Venters and nearly threw him. He jerked the horse down with a powerful hand and leaped into the saddle. Wrangle pulled again, dragging his bridle, that Venters had not had time to throw in place. Bending over with a swift movement, he secured it and dropped the loop over the pommel. Then, with grinding teeth, he looked to see what the issue would be.

The band had scattered so as not to afford such a broad mark for bullets. The riders faced Venters, some with red-belching guns. He heard a sharper report, and just as Wrangle plunged again he caught the whizz of a leaden missile that would have hit him but for Wrangle's sudden jump. A swift, hot wave, turning cold, passed over Venters. Deliberately he picked out the one rider with a carbine, and killed him. Wrangle snorted shrilly and bolted into the sage. Venters let him run a few rods, then with iron arm checked him.

Five riders, surely rustlers, were left. One leaped out of the saddle to secure his fallen comrade's carbine. A shot from Venters, which missed the man but sent the dust flying over him, made him run back to his horse. Then they separated. The crippled rider went one way; the one frustrated in his attempt to get the carbine rode another; Venters thought he made out a third rider, carrying a strange-appearing bundle and disappearing in the sage. But in the rapidity of action and vision he could not discern what it was. Two riders with three horses swung out to the right. Afraid of the long rifle—a burdensome weapon seldom carried by rustlers or riders—they had been put to rout.

Suddenly Venters discovered that one of the two men last noted was riding Jane Withersteen's horse Bells—the beautiful bay racer she had given to Lassiter. Venters uttered a savage outcry. Then the small, wiry, frog-like shape of the second rider, and the ease and grace of his seat in the saddle—things so strikingly incongruous—grew more and more familiar in Venters's sight.

'*Jerry Card!*' cried Venters.

It was indeed Tull's right-hand man. Such a white-hot wrath inflamed Venters that he fought himself to see with clearer gaze.

'It's Jerry Card!' he exclaimed, instantly. '*And he's riding Black Star and leading Night!*'

The long-kindling, stormy fire in Venters's heart burst into flame. He spurred Wrangle, and as the horse lengthened his stride Venters slipped cartridges into the magazine of his rifle till it was once again full. Card and his companion were now half a mile or more in advance, riding easily down the slope. Venters marked the smooth gait, and understood it when Wrangle galloped out of the sage into the broad cattle trail, down which Venters had once tracked Jane Withersteen's red herd. This hard-packed trail, from years of use, was as clean and smooth as a road. Venters saw Jerry Card look back over his shoulder; the other rider did likewise. Then the three racers lengthened their stride to the point where the swinging canter was ready to break into a gallop.

'Wrangle, the race's on,' said Venters, grimly. 'We'll canter with them and gallop with them and run with them. We'll let them set the pace.'

Venters knew he bestrode the strongest, swiftest, most tireless horse ever ridden by any rider across the Utah uplands. Recalling Jane Withersteen's devoted assurance that Night could run neck and neck with Wrangle, and Black Star could show his heels to him, Venters wished that Jane were there to see the race to recover her blacks and in the unqualified superiority of the giant sorrel. Then Venters found himself thankful that she was absent, for he meant that race to end in Jerry Card's death. The first flush, the raging of Venters's wrath, passed, to leave him in sullen, almost cold possession of his will. It was a deadly mood, utterly foreign to his nature, engendered, fostered, and released by the wild passions of wild men in a wild country. The strength in him then—the thing rife in him that was not hate, but something as remorseless—might have been the fiery fruition of a whole lifetime of vengeful quest. Nothing could have stopped him.

Venters thought out the race shrewdly. The rider on Bells would probably drop behind and take to the sage. What he did was of little moment to Venters. To stop Jerry Card, his evil, hidden career as well as his present flight, and then to catch the blacks—that was all that concerned Venters. The cattle trail wound for miles and miles down the slope. Venters saw with a rider's keen vision ten, fifteen, twenty miles of clear purple sage. There were no on-coming riders or rustlers to aid Card. His only chance to escape lay in abandoning the stolen horses and creeping away in the sage to hide. In ten miles Wrangle could run Black Star and Night off their feet, and in fifteen he could kill them outright. So Venters held the sorrel in, letting Card make the running. It was a long race that would save the blacks.

In a few miles of that swinging canter Wrangle had crept appreciably closer to the three horses. Jerry Card turned again, and when he saw how the sorrel had gained, he put Black Star to a gallop. Night and Bells, on either side of him, swept into his stride.

Venters loosened the rein on Wrangle and let him break into a gallop. The sorrel saw the horses ahead and wanted to run. But Venters restrained him. And in the gallop he gained more than in the canter. Bells was fast in that gait, but Black Star and Night had been trained to run. Slowly Wrangle closed the gap down to a quarter of a mile, and crept closer and closer.

Jerry Card wheeled once more. Venters distinctly saw the red flash of his red face. This time he looked long. Venters laughed. He knew what passed in Card's mind. The rider was trying to make out what horse it happened to be that thus gained on Jane Withersteen's peerless racers. Wrangle had so long been away from the village that not improbably Jerry had forgotten. Besides, whatever Jerry's qualifications for his fame as the greatest rider of the sage, certain it was that his best point was not far-sightedness. He had not recognized Wrangle. After what must have been a searching gaze he got his comrade to face about. This action gave Venters amusement. It spoke so surely of the fact that neither Card nor the rustler actually knew their danger. Yet if they kept to the trail—and the last thing such men would do would be to leave it—they were both doomed.

This comrade of Card's whirled far around in his saddle, and he even shaded his eyes from the sun. He, too, looked long. Then, all at once, he faced ahead again and, bending lower in the saddle, began to fling his right arm up and down. That flinging Venters knew to be the lashing of Bells. Jerry also became active. And the three racers lengthened out into a run.

'Now, Wrangle!' cried Venters. 'Run, you big devil! Run!'

Venters laid the reins on Wrangle's neck and dropped the loop over the pommel. The sorrel needed no guiding on that smooth trail. He was surer-footed in a run than at any other fast gait, and his running gave the impression of something devilish. He might now have been actuated by Venters's spirit; undoubtedly his savage running fitted the mood of his rider. Venters bent forward, swinging with the horse, and gripped his rifle. His eye measured the distance between him and Jerry Card.

In less than two miles of running Bells began to drop behind the blacks, and Wrangle began to overhaul him. Venters anticipated that the rustler would soon take to the sage. Yet he did not. Not improbably he reasoned that the powerful sorrel could more easily overtake Bells in the heavier going outside of the trail. Soon only a few hundred yards lay between Bells and Wrangle. Turning in his saddle, the rustler began to shoot, and the bullets beat up little whiffs of dust. Venters raised his rifle, ready to take snap shots, and waited for favorable opportunity when Bells was out of line with the forward horses. Venters had it in him to kill these men as if they were skunk-bitten coyotes, but also he had restraint enough to keep from shooting one of Jane's beloved Arabians.

No great distance was covered, however, before Bells swerved to the left, out of line with Black Star and Night. Then Venters, aiming high and waiting for the pause between Wrangle's great strides, began to take snap shots at the rustler. The fleeing rider presented a broad target for rifle, but he was moving swiftly forward and bobbing up and down. Moreover, shooting from Wrangle's back was shooting from a thunderbolt. And added to that was the danger of a low-placed bullet taking effect on Bells. Yet, despite these considerations, making the shot exceedingly difficult, Venters's confidence, like his implacability, saw a speedy and fatal termination of that rustler's race. On the sixth shot the rustler threw up his arms and took a flying tumble off his horse. He rolled over and over, hunched himself to a half-erect position, fell, and then dragged himself into the sage. As Venters went thundering by he peered keenly into the sage, but caught no sign of the man. Bells ran a few hundred yards, slowed up, and had stopped when Wrangle passed him.

Again Venters began slipping fresh cartridges into the magazine of his rifle, and his hand was so sure and steady that he did not drop a single cartridge. With the eye of a rider and the judgment of a marksman he once more measured the distance between him and Jerry Card. Wrangle had gained, bringing him into rifle range. Venters was hard put to it now not to shoot, but thought it better to withhold his fire. Jerry, who, in anticipation of a running fusillade, had huddled himself into a little twisted ball on Black Star's neck, now surmising that this pursuer would make sure of not wounding one of the blacks, rose to his natural seat in the saddle.

In his mind perhaps, as certainly as in Venters's, this moment was the beginning of the real race.

Venters leaned forward to put his hand on Wrangle's neck; then backward to put it on his flank. Under the shaggy, dusty hair trembled and vibrated and rippled a wonderful muscular activity. But Wrangle's flesh was still cold. What a cold-blooded brute, thought Venters, and felt in him a love for the horse he had never given to any other. It would not have been humanly possible for any rider, even though clutched by hate or revenge or a passion to save a loved one or fear of his own life, to be astride the sorrel, to swing with his swing, to see his magnificent stride and hear the rapid thunder of his hoofs, to ride him in that race and not glory in the ride.

So, with his passion to kill still keen and unabated, Venters lived out that ride, and drank a rider's sage-sweet cup of wildness to the dregs.

When Wrangle's long mane, lashing in the wind, stung Venters in the cheek, the sting added a beat to his flying pulse. He bent a downward glance to try to see Wrangle's actual stride, and saw only twinkling, darting streaks and the white rush of the trail. He watched the sorrel's savage head, pointed level, his mouth still closed and dry, but his nostrils distended as if he were snorting unseen fire. Wrangle was the horse for a race with death. Upon each side Venters saw the sage merged into a sailing, colorless wall. In front sloped the lay of ground with its purple breadth split by the white trail. The wind, blowing with heavy, steady blast into his face, sickened him with enduring, sweet odor, and filled his ears with a hollow, rushing roar.

Then for the hundredth time he measured the width of space separating him from Jerry Card. Wrangle had ceased to gain. The blacks were proving their fleetness. Venters watched Jerry Card, admiring the little rider's horsemanship. He had the incomparable seat of the upland rider, born in the saddle. It struck Venters that Card had changed his position, or the position of the horses. Presently Venters remembered positively that Jerry had been leading Night on the right-hand side of the trail. The racer was now on the side to the left. No—it was Black Star. But, Venters argued in amaze, Jerry had been mounted on Black Star. Another clearer, keener gaze assured Venters that Black Star was really riderless. Night now carried Jerry Card.

'He's changed from one to the other!' ejaculated Venters, realizing the astounding feat with unstinted admiration. 'Changed at full speed! Jerry Card, that's what you've done unless I'm drunk on the smell of sage. But I've got to see the trick before I believe it.'

Thenceforth, while Wrangle sped on, Venters glued his eyes to the little rider. Jerry Card rode as only he could ride. Of all the daring horsemen of the uplands, Jerry was the one rider fitted to bring out the greatness of the blacks in that long race. He had them on a dead run, but not yet at the last strained and killing pace. From time to time he glanced backward, as a wise general in retreat calculating his chances and the power and speed of pursuers, and the moment for the last desperate burst. No doubt, Card, with his life at stake, gloried in that race, perhaps more wildly than Venters. For he had been born to the sage and the saddle and the wild. He was more than half horse. Not until the last call—the sudden upflashing instinct of self-preservation—would he lose his skill and judgment and nerve and the spirit of that race. Venters seemed to read Jerry's mind. That little crime-stained rider was actually thinking of his horses, husbanding their speed, handling them with knowledge of years, glorying in their beautiful, swift, racing stride, and wanting them to win the race when his own life hung suspended in quivering balance. Again Jerry whirled in his saddle and the sun flashed red on his face. Turning, he drew Black Star closer and closer toward Night, till they ran side by side, as one horse. Then Card raised himself in the saddle, slipped out of the stirrups, and, somehow twisting himself, leaped upon Black Star. He did not even lose the swing of the horse. Like a leech he was there in the other saddle, and as the horses separated, his right foot, that had been apparently doubled under him, shot down to catch the stirrup. The grace and dexterity and daring of that rider's act won something more than admiration from Venters.

For the distance of a mile Jerry rode Black Star and then changed back to Night. But all Jerry's skill and the running of the blacks could avail little more against the sorrel.

Venters peered far ahead, studying the lay of the land. Straightaway for five miles the trail stretched, and then it disappeared in hummocky ground. To the right, some few rods, Venters saw a break in the sage, and this was the rim of Deception Pass. Across the dark cleft gleamed the red of the opposite wall. Venters imagined that the trail went down into the Pass somewhere north of those ridges. And he realized that he must and would overtake Jerry Card in this straight course of five miles.

Cruelly he struck his spurs into Wrangle's flanks. A light touch of spur was sufficient to make Wrangle plunge. And now, with a ringing, wild snort, he seemed to double up in muscular convulsions and to shoot forward with an impetus that almost unseated Venters. The sage blurred by, the trail flashed by, and the wind robbed him of breath and hearing. Jerry Card turned once more. And the way he shifted to Black Star showed he had to make his last desperate running. Venters aimed to the side of the trail and sent a bullet puffing the dust beyond Jerry. Venters hoped to frighten the rider and get him to take to the sage. But Jerry returned the shot, and his ball struck dangerously close in the dust at Wrangle's flying feet. Venters held his fire then, while the rider emptied his revolver. For a mile, with Black Star leaving Night behind and doing his utmost, Wrangle did not gain; for another mile he gained little, if at all. In the third he caught up with the now galloping Night and began to gain rapidly on the other black.

Only a hundred yards now stretched between Black Star and Wrangle. The giant sorrel thundered on—and on—and on. In every yard he gained a foot. He was whistling through his nostrils, wringing wet, flying lather, and as hot as fire. Savage as ever, strong as ever, fast as ever, but each tremendous stride jarred Venters out of the saddle! Wrangle's power and spirit and momentum had begun to run him off his legs. Wrangle's great race was nearly won—and run. Venters seemed to see the expanse before him as a vast, sheeted, purple plain sliding under him. Black Star moved in it as a blur. The rider, Jerry Card, appeared a mere dot bobbing dimly. Wrangle thundered on—on—on! Venters felt the increase in quivering, straining shock after every leap. Flecks of foam flew into Venters's eyes, burning him, making him see all the sage as red. But in that red haze he saw, or seemed to see, Black Star suddenly riderless and with broken gait. Wrangle thundered on to change his pace with a violent gallop. Then Venters pulled him hard. From run to gallop, gallop to canter, canter to trot, trot to walk, and walk to stop, the great sorrel ended his race.

Venters looked back. Black Star stood riderless in the trail. Jerry Card had taken to the sage. Far up the white trail Night came trotting faithfully down. Venters leaped off, still half blind, reeling dizzily. In a moment he had recovered sufficiently to have a care for Wrangle. Rapidly he took off the saddle and bridle. The sorrel was reeking, heaving, whistling, shaking. But he had still the strength to stand, and for him Venters had no fears.

As Venters ran back to Black Star he saw the horse stagger on shaking legs into the sage and go down in a heap. Upon reaching him Venters removed the saddle and bridle. Black Star had been killed on his legs, Venters thought. He had no hope for the stricken horse. Black Star lay flat, covered with bloody froth, mouth wide, tongue hanging, eyes glaring, and all his beautiful body in convulsions.

Unable to stay there to see Jane's favorite racer die, Venters hurried up the trail to meet the other black. On the way he kept a sharp lookout for Jerry Card. Venters imagined the rider would keep well out of range of the rifle, but, as he would be lost on the sage without a horse, not improbably he would linger in the vicinity on the chance of getting back one of the blacks. Night soon came trotting up, hot and wet and run out. Venters led him down near the others, and, unsaddling him, let him loose to rest. Night wearily lay down in the dust and rolled, proving himself not yet spent.

Then Venters sat down to rest and think. Whatever the risk, he was compelled to stay where he was, or comparatively near, for the night. The horses must rest and drink. He must find water. He was now seventy miles from Cottonwoods, and, he believed, close to the cañon where the cattle trail must surely turn off and go down into the Pass. After a while he rose to survey the valley.

He was very near to the ragged edge of a deep cañon into which the trail turned. The ground lay in uneven ridges divided by washes, and those sloped into the cañon. Following the cañon line, he saw where its rim was broken by other intersecting cañon, and farther down red walls and yellow cliffs leading toward a deep blue cleft that he made sure was Deception Pass. Walking out a few rods to a promontory, he found where the trail went down. The descent was gradual, along a stone-walled trail, and Venters felt sure that this was the place where Oldring drove cattle into the Pass. There was, however, no indication at all that he ever had driven cattle out at this point. Oldring had many holes to his burrow.

In searching round in the little hollows Venters, much to his relief, found water. He composed himself to rest and eat some bread and meat, while he waited for a sufficient time to elapse so that he could safely give the horses a drink. He judged the hour to be somewhere around noon. Wrangle lay down to rest and Night followed suit. So long as they were down Venters intended to make no move. The longer they rested the better, and the safer it would be to give them water. By and by he forced himself to go over to where Black Star lay, expecting to find him dead. Instead he found the racer partially if not wholly recovered. There was recognition, even fire, in his big black eyes. Venters was overjoyed. He sat by the black for a long time. Black Star presently labored to his feet with a heave and a groan, shook himself, and snorted for water. Venters repaired to the little pool he had found, filled his sombrero, and gave the racer a drink. Black Star gulped it at one draught, as if it were but a drop, and pushed his nose into the hat and snorted for more. Venters now led Night down to drink, and after a further time Black Star also. Then the blacks began to graze.

The sorrel had wandered off down the sage between the trail and the cañon. Once or twice he disappeared in little swales. Finally Venters concluded Wrangle had grazed far enough, and, taking his lasso, he went to fetch him back. In crossing from one ridge to another he saw where the horse had made a muddy pool of water. It occurred to Venters then that Wrangle had drunk his fill, and did not seem the worse for it, and might be anything but easy to catch. And, true enough, he could not come within roping reach of the sorrel. He tried for an hour, and gave up in disgust. Wrangle did not seem so wild as simply perverse. In a quandary Venters returned to the other horses, hoping much, yet doubting more, that when Wrangle had grazed to suit himself he might be caught.

As the afternoon wore away Venters's concern diminished, yet he kept close watch on the blacks and the trail and the sage. There was no telling of what Jerry Card might be capable. Venters sullenly acquiesced to the idea that the rider had been too quick and too shrewd for him. Strangely and doggedly, however, Venters clung to his foreboding of Card's downfall.

The wind died away; the red sun topped the far distant western rise of slope; and the long, creeping purple shadows lengthened. The rims of the cañons gleamed crimson and the deep clefts appeared to belch forth blue smoke. Silence enfolded the scene.

It was broken by a horrid, long-drawn scream of a horse and the thudding of heavy hoofs. Venters sprang erect and wheeled south. Along the cañon rim, near the edge, came Wrangle, once more in thundering flight.

Venters gasped in amazement. Had the wild sorrel gone mad? His head was high and twisted, in a most singular position for a running horse. Suddenly Venters descried a frog-like shape clinging to Wrangle's neck. Jerry Card! Somehow he had straddled Wrangle and now stuck like a huge burr. But it was his strange position and the sorrel's wild scream that shook Venters's nerves. Wrangle was pounding toward the turn where the trail went down. He plunged onward like a blind horse. More than one of his leaps took him to the very edge of the precipice.

Jerry Card was bent forward with his teeth fast in the front of Wrangle's nose! Venters saw it, and there flashed over him a memory of this trick of a few desperate riders. He even thought of one rider who had worn off his teeth in this terrible hold to break or control desperate horses. Wrangle had indeed gone mad. The marvel was what guided him. Was it the half-brute, the more than half-horse instinct of Jerry Card? Whatever the mystery, it was true. And in a few more rods Jerry would have the sorrel turning into the trail leading down into the cañon.

'No—Jerry!' whispered Venters, stepping forward and throwing up the rifle.

He tried to catch the little humped, frog-like shape over the sights. It was moving too fast; it was too small. Yet Venters shot once ... twice ... the third time ... four times ... five! All wasted shots and precious seconds!

With a deep-muttered curse Venters caught Wrangle through the sights and pulled the trigger. Plainly he heard the bullet thud. Wrangle uttered a horrible strangling sound. In swift death action he whirled, and with one last splendid leap he cleared the cañon rim. And he whirled downward with the little frog-like shape clinging to his neck!

There was a pause which seemed never ending, a shock, and an instant's silence.

Then up rolled a heavy crash, a long roar of sliding rocks dying away in distant echo, then silence unbroken.

Wrangle's race was run.

CHAPTER EIGHTEEN
Oldring's Knell

Some forty hours or more later Venters created a commotion in Cottonwoods by riding down the main street on Black Star and leading Bells and Night. He had come upon Bells grazing near the body of a dead rustler, the only incident of his quick ride into the village.

Nothing was farther from Venters's mind than bravado. No thought came to him of the defiance and boldness of riding Jane Withersteen's racers straight into the arch-plotter's stronghold. He wanted men to see the famous Arabians; he wanted men to see them dirty and dusty, bearing all the signs of having been driven to their limit; he wanted men to see and to know that the thieves who had ridden them out into the sage had not ridden them back. Venters had come for that and for more—he wanted to meet Tull face to face; if not Tull, then Dyer; if not Dyer, then anyone in the secret of these master conspirators. Such was Venters's passion. The meeting with the rustlers, the unprovoked attack upon him, the spilling of blood, the recognition of Jerry Card and the horses, the race, and that last plunge of mad Wrangle—all these things, fuel on fuel to the smoldering fire, had kindled and swelled and leaped into living flame. He could have shot Dyer in the midst of his religious services at the altar; he could have killed Tull in front of wives and babes.

He walked the three racers down the broad, green-bordered village road. He heard the murmur of running water from Amber Spring. Bitter waters for Jane Withersteen! Men and women stopped to gaze at him and the horses. All knew him; all knew the blacks and the bay. As well as if it had been spoken, Venters read in the faces of men the intelligence that Jane Withersteen's Arabians had been known to have been stolen. Venters reined in and halted before Dyer's residence. It was a low, long, stone structure resembling Withersteen House. The spacious front yard was green and luxuriant with grass and flowers; gravel walks led to the huge porch; a well-trimmed hedge of purple sage separated the yard from the church grounds; birds sang in the trees; water flowed musically along the walks; and there were glad, careless shouts of children. For Venters the beauty of this home, and the serenity and its apparent happiness, all turned red and black. For Venters a shade over-spread the lawn, the flowers, the old vine-clad stone house. In the music of the singing birds, in the murmur of the running water, he heard an ominous sound. Quiet beauty—sweet music—innocent laughter! By what monstrous abortion of fate did these abide in the shadow of Dyer?

Venters rode on and stopped before Tull's cottage. Women stared at him with white faces and then flew from the porch. Tull himself appeared at the door, bent low, craning his neck. His dark face flashed out of sight; the door banged; a heavy bar dropped with a hollow sound.

Venters shook Black Star's bridle, and, sharply trotting, led the other horses to the center of the village. Here at the intersecting streets and in front of the stores he halted once more. The usual lounging atmosphere of that prominent corner was not now in evidence. Riders and ranchers and villagers broke up what must have been absorbing conversation. There was a rush of many feet, and then the walk was lined with faces.

Venters's glance swept down the line of silent stone-faced men. He recognized many riders and villagers, but none of those he had hoped to meet. There was no expression in the faces turned toward him. All of them knew him, most were inimical, but there were few who were not burning with curiosity and wonder in regard to the return of Jane Withersteen's racers. Yet all were silent. Here were the familiar characteristics—masked feeling—strange secretiveness—expressionless expression of mystery and hidden power.

'Has anybody here seen Jerry Card?' queried Venters, in a loud voice.

In reply there came not a word, not a nod or shake of head, not so much as dropping eye or twitching lip—nothing but a quiet, stony stare.

'Been under the knife? You've a fine knife-wielder here—one Tull, I believe! … Maybe you've all had your tongues cut out?'

This passionate sarcasm of Venters brought no response, and the stony calm was as oil on the fire within him.

'I see some of you pack guns, too!' he added, in biting scorn. In the long, tense pause, strung keenly as a tight wire, he sat motionless on Black Star. 'All right,' he went on. 'Then let some of you take this message to Tull. Tell him I've seen Jerry Card! ... Tell him Jerry Card *will never return!*'

Thereupon, in the same dead calm, Venters backed Black Star away from the curb, into the street, and out of range. He was ready now to ride up to Withersteen House and turn the racers over to Jane.

'Hello, Venters!' a familiar voice cried, hoarsely, and he saw a man running toward him. It was the rider Judkins who came up and gripped Venters's hand. 'Venters, I could hev dropped when I seen them hosses. But thet sight ain't a marker to the looks of you. What's wrong? Hev you gone crazy? You must be crazy to ride in here this way—with them hosses—talkin' thet way about Tull an' Jerry Card.'

'Jud, I'm not crazy—only mad clean through,' replied Venters.

'Wal, now, Bern, I'm glad to hear some of your old self in your voice. Fer when you come up you looked like the corpse of a dead rider with fire fer eyes. You hed thet crowd too stiff fer throwin' guns. Come, we've got to hev a talk. Let's go up the lane. We ain't much safe here.'

Judkins mounted Bells and rode with Venters up to the cottonwood grove. Here they dismounted and went among the trees.

'Let's hear from you first,' said Judkins. 'You fetched back them hosses. Thet *is* the trick. An', of course, you got Jerry the same as you got Horne.'

'Horne!'

'Sure. He was found dead yesterday all chewed by coyotes, an' he'd been shot plumb center.'

'Where was he found?'

'At the split down the trail—you know where Oldrin's cattle trail runs off north from the trail to the pass.'

'That's where I met Jerry and the rustlers. What was Horne doing with them? I thought Horne was an honest cattle-man.'

'Lord—Bern, don't ask me thet! I'm all muddled now tryin' to figure things.'

Venters told of the fight and the race with Jerry Card and its tragic conclusion.

'I knowed it! I knowed all along that Wrangle was the best hoss!' exclaimed Judkins, with his lean face working and his eyes lighting. 'Thet was a race! Lord, I'd like to hev seen Wrangle jump the cliff with Jerry. An' thet was good-bye to the grandest hoss an' rider ever on the sage! ... But, Bern, after you got the hosses why'd you want to bolt right in Tull's face?'

'I want him to know. An' if I can get to him I'll—'

'You can't get near Tull,' interrupted Judkins. 'Thet vigilante bunch hev taken to bein' bodyguard for Tull an' Dyer, too.'

'Hasn't Lassiter made a break yet?' inquired Venters, curiously.

'Naw!' replied Judkins, scornfully. 'Jane turned his head. He's mad in love over her—follers her like a dog. He ain't no more Lassiter! He's lost his nerve; he doesn't look like the same feller. It's village talk. Everybody knows it. He hasn't thrown a gun, an' he won't!'

'Jud, I'll bet he does,' replied Venters, earnestly. 'Remember what I say. This Lassiter is something more than a gun-man. Jud, he's big—he's great! ... I feel that in him. God help Tull and Dyer when Lassiter does go after them. For horses and riders and stone walls won't save them.'

'Wal, hev it your way, Bern. I hope you're right. Nat'rully I've been some sore on Lassiter fer gittin' soft. But I ain't denyin' his nerve, or whatever's great in him thet sort of paralyzes people. No later 'n this mornin' I seen him saunterin' down the lane, quiet an' slow. An' like his guns he comes black—*black*, thet's Lassiter. Wal, the crowd on the corner never batted an eye, an' I'll gamble my hoss thet there wasn't one who hed a heartbeat till Lassiter got by. He went in Shell's saloon, an' as there wasn't no gun play I had to go in, too. An' there, darn my pictures, if Lassiter wasn't standin' to the bar, drinkin' an' talkin' with Oldrin'.

'*Oldring!*' whispered Venters. His voice, as all fire and pulse within him, seemed to freeze.

'Let go my arm!' exclaimed Judkins. 'Thet's my bad arm. Sure it was Oldrin'. What the hell's wrong with you, anyway? Venters, I tell you somethin's wrong. You're whiter'n a sheet. You can't be *scared* of the rustler. I don't believe you've got a scare in you. Wal, now, jest let me talk. You know I like to talk, an' if I'm slow I allus git there sometime. As I said, Lassiter was talkin' chummy with Oldrin'. There wasn't no hard feelin's. An' the gang wasn't payin' no pertic'lar attention. But like a cat watchin' a mouse I hed my eyes on them two fellers. It was strange to me, thet confab. I'm gittin' to think a lot, fer a feller who doesn't know much. There's been some queer deals lately an' this seemed to me the queerest. These men stood to the bar alone, an' so close their big gun-hilts butted together. I seen Oldrin' was some surprised at first, an' Lassiter was cool as ice. They talked, an' presently at somethin' Lassiter said the rustler bawled out a curse, an' then he jest fell up against the bar, an' sagged there. The gang in the saloon looked around an' laughed, an' thet's about all. Finally Oldrin' turned, and it was easy to see somethin' had shook him. Yes, sir, thet big rustler—you know he's as broad as he is long, an' the powerfulest build of a man—yes, sir, the nerve had been taken out of him. Then, after a little, he began to talk an' said a lot to Lassiter, an' by an' by it didn't take much of an eye to see thet Lassiter was gittin' hit hard. I never seen him anyway but cooler 'n ice—till then. He seemed to be hit harder 'n Oldrin', only he didn't roar out thet way. He jest kind of sunk in, an' looked an' looked, an' he didn't see a livin' soul in thet saloon. Then he sort of come to, an' shakin' hands—mind you, *shakin' hands* with Oldrin'—he went out. I couldn't help thinkin' how easy even a boy could hev dropped the great gun-man then! ... Wal, the rustler stood at the bar fer a long time, an' he was seein' things far off, too; then he come to an' roared for whisky, an' gulped a drink thet was big enough to drown me.'

'Is Oldring here now?' whispered Venters. He could not speak above a whisper. Judkins's story had been meaningless to him.

'He's at Shell's yet. Bern, I hevn't told you yet thet the rustlers hev been raisin' hell. They shot up Stone Bridge an' Glaze, an' fer three days they've been here drinkin' an' gamblin' an' throwin' of gold. These rustlers hev a pile of gold. If it was gold dust or nugget gold I'd hev reason to think, but it's new coin gold, as if it had jest come from the United States treasury. An' the coin's genuine. Thet's all been proved. The truth is Oldrin's on a rampage. A while back he lost his Masked Rider, an' they say he's wild about thet. I'm wonderin' if Lassiter could hev told the rustler anythin' about thet little masked, hard-ridin' devil! Ride! He was most as good as Jerry Card. An', Bern, I've been wonderin' if you know—'

'Judkins, you're a good fellow,' interrupted Venters. 'Some day I'll tell you a story. I've no time now. Take the horses to Jane.'

Judkins stared, and then, muttering to himself, he mounted Bells, and stared again at Venters, and then, leading the other horses, he rode into the grove and disappeared.

Once, long before, on the night Venters had carried Bess through the cañon and up into Surprise Valley, he had experienced the strangeness of faculties singularly, tinglingly acute. And now the same sensation recurred. But it was different in that he felt cold, frozen, mechanical, incapable of free thought, and all about him seemed unreal, aloof, remote. He hid his rifle in the sage, marking its exact location with extreme care. Then he faced down the lane and strode toward the center of the village. Perceptions flashed upon him, the faint, cold touch of the breeze, a cold, silvery tinkle of flowing water, a cold sun shining out of a cold sky, song of birds and laugh of children, coldly distant. Cold and intangible were all things in earth and heaven. Colder and tighter stretched the skin over his face; colder and harder grew the polished butts of his guns; colder and steadier became his hands as he wiped the clammy sweat from his face or reached low to his gun-sheaths. Men meeting him in the walk gave him wide berth. In front of Bevin's store a crowd melted apart for his passage, and their faces and whispers were faces and whispers of a dream. He turned a corner to meet Tull face to face, eye to eye. As once before he had seen this man pale to a ghastly, livid white, so again he saw the change. Tull stopped in his tracks, with right hand raised and shaking. Suddenly it dropped, and he seemed to glide aside, to pass out of Venters's sight. Next he saw many horses with bridles down—all clean-limbed, dark bays or blacks—rustlers' horses! Loud voices and boisterous laughter, rattle of dice and scrape of chair and clink of gold, burst in mingled din from an open doorway. He stepped inside.

With the sight of smoke-hazed room and drinking, cursing, gambling, dark-visaged men, reality once more dawned upon Venters.

His entrance had been unnoticed, and he bent his gaze upon the drinkers at the bar. Dark-clothed, dark-faced men they all were, burned by the sun, bow-legged as were most riders of the sage, but neither lean nor gaunt. Then Venters's gaze passed to the tables, and swiftly it swept over the hard-featured gamesters, to alight upon the huge, shaggy, black head of the rustler chief.

'*Oldring!* he cried, and to him his voice seemed to split a bell in his ears.

It stilled the din.

That silence suddenly broke to the scrape and crash of Oldring's chair as he rose; and then, while he passed, a great gloomy figure, again the thronged room stilled in silence yet deeper.

'Oldring, a word with you!' continued Venters.

'Ho! What's this?' boomed Oldring, in frowning scrutiny.

'Come outside, alone. A word for you—*from your Masked Rider!*'

Oldring kicked a chair out of his way and lunged forward with a stamp of heavy boot that jarred the floor. He waved down his muttering, rising men.

Venters backed out of the door and waited, hearing, as no sound had ever before struck into his soul, the rapid, heavy steps of the rustler.

Oldring appeared, and Venters had one glimpse of his great breadth and bulk, his gold-buckled belt with hanging guns, his high-top boots with gold spurs. In that moment Venters had a strange, unintelligible curiosity to see Oldring alive. The rustler's broad brow, his large black eyes, his sweeping beard, as dark as the wing of a raven, his enormous width of shoulder and depth of chest, his whole splendid presence so wonderfully charged with vitality and force and strength, seemed to afford Venters an unutterable fiendish joy because for that magnificent manhood and life he meant cold and sudden death.

'Oldring, Bess is alive! But she's dead to you—dead to the life you made her lead—dead as you will be in one second!'

Swift as lightning Venters glance dropped from Oldring's rolling eyes to his hands. One of them, the right, swept out, then toward his gun—and Venters shot him through the heart.

Slowly Oldring sank to his knees, and the hand, dragging at his gun, fell away. Venters's strangely acute faculties grasped the meaning of that limp arm, of the swaying hulk, of the gasp and heave, of the quivering beard. But was that awful spirit in the black eyes only one of vitality?

'Man—why—didn't—you—wait? Bess—was—' Oldring's whisper died under his beard, and with a heavy lurch he fell forward.

Bounding swiftly away, Venters fled around the corner, across the street, and, leaping a hedge, he ran through the yard, orchard, and garden to the sage. Here, under cover of the tall brush, he turned west and ran on to the place where he had hidden his rifle. Securing that, he again set out into a run, and circling through the sage, came up behind Jane Withersteen's stable and corrals. With laboring, dripping chest, and pain as of a knife thrust in his side, he stopped to regain his breath, and while resting his eyes roved around in search of a horse. Doors and windows of the stable were open wide and had a deserted look. One dejected, lonely burro stood in the near corral. Strange indeed was the silence brooding over the once happy, noisy home of Jane Withersteen's pets.

He went into the corral, exercising care to leave no tracks, and led the burro to the watering-trough. Venters, though not thirsty, drank till he could drink no more. Then, leading the burro over hard ground, he struck into the sage and down the slope.

He strode swiftly, turning from time to time to scan the slope for riders. His head just topped the level of sage-brush, and the burro could not have been seen at all. Slowly the green of Cottonwoods sank behind the slope, and at last a wavering line of purple sage met the blue of sky.

To avoid being seen, to get away, to hide his trail—these were the sole ideas in his mind as he headed for Deception Pass; and he directed all his acuteness of eye and ear, and the keenness of a rider's judgment for distance and ground, to stern accomplishment of the task. He kept to the sage far to the left of the trail leading into the Pass. He walked ten miles and looked back a thousand times. Always the graceful, purple wave of sage remained wide and lonely, a clear, undotted waste. Coming to a stretch of rocky ground, he took advantage of it to cross the trail and then continued down on the right. At length he persuaded himself that he would be able to see riders mounted on horses before they could see him on the little burro, and he rode bareback.

Hour by hour the tireless burro kept to his faithful, steady trot. The sun sank and the long shadows lengthened down the slope. Moving veils of purple twilight crept out of the hollows and, mustering and forming on the levels, soon merged and shaded into night. Venters guided the burro nearer to the trail, so that he could see its white line from the ridges, and rode on through the hours.

Once down in the Pass without leaving a trail, he would hold himself safe for the time being. When late in the night he reached the break in the sage, he sent the burro down ahead of him, and started an avalanche that all but buried the animal at the bottom of the trail. Bruised and battered as he was, he had a moment's elation, for he had hidden his tracks. Once more he mounted the burro and rode on. The hour was the blackest of the night when he made the thicket which inclosed his old camp. Here he turned the burro loose in the grass near the spring, and then lay down on his old bed of leaves.

He felt only vaguely, as outside things, the ache and burn and throb of the muscles of his body. But a dammed-up torrent of emotion at last burst its bounds, and the hour that saw his release from immediate action was one that confounded him in the reaction of his spirit. He suffered without understanding why. He caught glimpses into himself, into unlit darkness of soul. The fire that had blistered him and the cold which had frozen him now united in one torturing possession of his mind and heart, and like a fiery steed with ice-shod feet, ranged his being, ran rioting through his blood, trampling the resurging good, dragging ever at the evil.

Out of the subsiding chaos came a clear question. What had happened? He had left the valley to go to Cottonwoods. Why? It seemed that he had gone to kill a man—Oldring! The name riveted his consciousness upon the one man of all men upon earth whom he had wanted to meet. He had met the rustler. Venters recalled the smoky haze of the saloon, the dark-visaged men, the huge Oldring. He saw him step out of the door, a splendid specimen of manhood, a handsome giant with purple-black and sweeping beard. He remembered inquisitive gaze of falcon eyes. He heard himself repeating: '*Oldring, Bess is alive! But she's dead to you,*' and he felt himself jerk, and his ears throbbed to the thunder of a gun, and he saw the giant sink slowly to his knees. Was that only the vitality of him—that awful light in the eyes—only the hard-dying life of a tremendously powerful brute? A broken whisper, strange as death: *Man—why—didn't—you wait! Bess—was—*And Oldring plunged face forward, dead.

'I killed him,' cried Venters, in remembering shock. 'But it wasn't *that*. Ah, the look in his eyes and his whisper!'

Herein lay the secret that had clamored to him through all the tumult and stress of his emotions. What a look in the eyes of a man shot through the heart! It had been neither hate nor ferocity nor fear of men nor fear of death. It had been no passionate, glinting spirit of a fearless foe, willing shot for shot, life for life, but lacking physical power. Distinctly recalled now, never to be forgotten, Venters saw in Oldring's magnificent eyes the rolling of great, glad surprise—softness— love! Then came a shadow and the terrible superhuman striving of his spirit to speak. Oldring, shot through the heart, had fought and forced back death, not for a moment in which to shoot or curse, but to whisper strange words.

What words for a dying man to whisper! Why had not Venters waited? For what? That was no plea for life. It was a regret that there was not a moment of life left in which to speak. Bess was—Herein lay renewed torture for Venters. What had Bess been to Oldring? The old question, like a specter, stalked from its grave to haunt him. He had overlooked, he had forgiven, he had loved, and he had forgotten; and now, out of the mystery of a dying man's whisper rose again that perverse, unsatisfied, jealous uncertainty. Bess had loved that splendid, black crowned giant—by her own confession she had loved him; and in Venters's soul again flamed up the jealous hell. Then into the clamoring hell burst the shot that had killed Oldring, and it rang in a wild, fiendish gladness, a hateful, vengeful joy. That passed to the memory of the love and light in Oldring's eyes and the mystery in his whisper. So the changing, swaying emotions fluctuated in Venters's heart.

This was the climax of his year of suffering and the crucial struggle of his life. And when the gray dawn came he rose, a gloomy, almost heartbroken man, but victor over evil passions. He could not change the past; and, even if he had not loved Bess with all his soul, he had grown into a man who would not change the future he had planned for her. Only, and once for all, he must know the truth, know the worst, stifle all these insistent doubts and subtle hopes and jealous fancies, and kill the past by knowing truly what Bess had been to Oldring. For that matter, he knew—he had always known, but he must hear it spoken. Then, when they had safely gotten out of that wild country to take up a new and an absorbing life, she would forget, she would be happy, and through that, in the years to come, he could not but find life worth living.

All day he rode slowly and cautiously up the Pass, taking time to peer around corners, to pick out hard ground and grassy patches, and to make sure there was no one in pursuit. In the night sometime he came to the smooth, scrawled rocks dividing the valley, and here set the burro at liberty. He walked beyond, climbed the slope and the dim, starlit gorge. Then, weary to the point of exhaustion, he crept into a shallow cave and fell asleep.

In the morning, when he descended the trail, he found the sun was pouring a golden stream of light through the arch of the great stone bridge. Surprise Valley, like a valley of dreams, lay mystically soft and beautiful, awakening to the golden flood which rolling away its slumberous bands of mist, brightening its walled faces.

While yet far off he discerned Bess moving under the silver spruces, and soon the barking of the dogs told him that they had seen him. He heard the mocking-birds singing in the trees, and then the twittering of the quail. Ring and Whitie came bounding toward him, and behind them ran Bess, her hands outstretched.

'Bern! You're back! You're back!' she cried, in joy that rang of her loneliness.

'Yes, I'm back,' he said, as she rushed to meet him.

She had reached out for him when suddenly, as she saw him closely, something checked her, and as quickly all her joy fled, and with it her color, leaving her pale and trembling.

'Oh! What's happened?'

'A good deal has happened, Bess. I don't need to tell you what. And I'm played out. Worn out in mind more than body.'

'Dear—you look strange to me!' faltered Bess.

'Never mind that. I'm all right. There's nothing for you to be scared about. Things are going to turn out just as we have planned. As soon as I'm rested we'll make a break to get out of the country. Only now, right now, I must know the truth about you.'

'Truth about me?' echoed Bess, shrinkingly. She seemed to be casting back into her mind for a forgotten key. Venters himself, as he saw her, received a pang.

'Yes—the truth. Bess, don't misunderstand. I haven't changed that way. I love you still. I'll love you more afterward. Life will be just as sweet—sweeter to us. We'll be—be married as soon as ever we can. We'll be happy—but there's a devil in me. A perverse, jealous devil! Then I've queer fancies. I forgot for a long time. Now all those fiendish little whispers of doubt and faith and fear and hope come torturing me again. I've got to kill them with the truth.'

'I'll tell you anything you want to know,' she replied frankly.

'Then, by Heaven! we'll have it over and done with! ... Bess—did Oldring love you?'

'Certainly he did.'

'Did—you love him?'

'Of course. I told you so.'

'How can you tell it so lightly?' cried Venters, passionately. 'Haven't you any sense of—of—' He choked back speech. He felt the rush of pain and passion. He seized her in rude, strong hands and drew her close. He looked straight into her dark-blue eyes. They were shadowing with the old wistful light, but they were as clear as the limpid water of the spring. They were earnest, solemn in unutterable love and faith and abnegation. Venters shivered. He knew he was looking into her soul. He knew she could not lie in that moment; but that she might tell the truth, looking at him with those eyes, almost killed his belief in purity.

'What are—what were you to—to Oldring?' he panted, fiercely.

'I am his daughter,' she replied, instantly.

Venters slowly let go of her. There was a violent break in the force of his feeling—then creeping blankness.

'What—was it—you said?' he asked, in a kind of dull wonder.

'I am his daughter.'

'Oldring's daughter?' queried Venters, with life gathering in his voice.

'Yes.'

With a passionately awakening start he grasped her hands and drew her close.

'All the time—you've been Oldring's daughter?'

'Yes, of course all the time—always.'

'But Bess, you told me—you let me think—I made out you were—a—so—so ashamed.'

'It is my shame,' she said, with voice deep and full, and now the scarlet fired her cheek. 'I told you—I'm nothing—nameless—just Bess, Oldring's girl!'

'I know—I remember. But I never thought—' he went on, hurriedly, huskily. 'That time—when you lay dying—you prayed—you—somehow I got the idea you were bad.'

'Bad?' she asked, with a little laugh.

She looked up with a faint smile of bewilderment and the absolute unconsciousness of a child. Venters gasped in the gathering might of the truth. She did not understand his meaning.

'Bess! Bess!' He clasped her in his arms, hiding her eyes against his breast. She must not see his face in that moment. And he held her while he looked out across the valley. In his dim and blinded sight, in the blur of golden light and moving mist, he saw Oldring. She was the rustler's nameless daughter. Oldring had loved her. He had so guarded her, so kept her from women and men and knowledge of life that her mind was as a child's. That was part of the secret—part of the mystery. That was the wonderful truth. Not only was she not bad, but good, pure, innocent above all innocence in the world—the innocence of lonely girlhood.

He saw Oldring's magnificent eyes, inquisitive, searching—softening. He saw them flare in amaze, in gladness, with love, then suddenly strain in terrible effort of will. He heard Oldring whisper and saw him sway like a log and fall. Then a million bellowing, thundering voices—gunshots of conscience, thunderbolts of remorse—dinned horribly in his ears. He had killed Bess's father. Then a rushing wind filled his ears like the moan of wind in the cliffs, a knell indeed—Oldring's knell.

He dropped to his knees and hid his face against Bess, and grasped her with hands of a drowning man.

'My God! ... My God! ... Oh, Bess! ... Forgive me! Never mind what I've done—what I've thought. But forgive me. I'll give you my life. I'll live for you. I'll love you. Oh, I do love you as no man ever loved a woman. I want you to know—to remember that I fought a fight for you—however blind I was. I thought—I thought—never mind what I thought—but I loved you—I asked you to marry me. Let that—let me have that to hug to my heart. Oh, Bess, I was driven! And I might have known! I could not rest nor sleep till I had this mystery solved. God! how things work out!'

'Bern, you're weak—trembling—you talk wildly.' cried Bess. 'You've overdone your strength. There's nothing to forgive. There's no mystery except your love for me. You have come back to me!'

And she clasped his head tenderly in her arms and pressed it closely to her throbbing breast.

CHAPTER NINETEEN
Fay

At the home of Jane Withersteen Little Fay was climbing Lassiter's knee.

'Does oo love me?' she asked.

Lassiter, who was as serious with Fay as he was gentle and loving, assured her in earnest and elaborate speech that he was her devoted subject. Fay looked thoughtful and appeared to be debating the duplicity of men or searching for a supreme test to prove this cavalier.

'Does oo love my new muvver?' she asked, with a bewildering suddenness.

Jane Withersteen laughed, and for the first time in many a day she felt a stir of her pulse and warmth in her cheek.

It was a still drowsy summer of afternoon, and the three were sitting in the shade of the wooded knoll that faced the sage-slope. Little Fay's brief spell of unhappy longing for her mother—the childish, mystic gloom—had passed, and now where Fay was there were prattle and laughter and glee. She had emerged from sorrow to be the incarnation of joy and loveliness. She had grown supernaturally sweet and beautiful. For Jane Withersteen, the child was an answer to prayer, a blessing, a possession infinitely more precious than all she had lost. For Lassiter, Jane divined that little Fay had become a religion.

'Does oo love my new muvver?' repeated Fay.

Lassiter's answer to this was a modest and sincere affirmative.

'Why don't oo marry my new muvver an' be my favver?'

Of the thousands of questions put by little Fay to Lassiter that was the first he had been unable to answer.

'Fay—Fay, don't ask questions like that,' said Jane.

'Why?'

'Because,' replied Jane. And she found it strangely embarrassing to meet the child's gaze. It seemed to her that Fay's violet eyes looked through her with piercing wisdom.

'Oo love him, don't oo?'

'Dear child—run and play,' said Jane, 'but don't go too far. Don't go from this little hill.'

Fay pranced off wildly, joyous over freedom that had not been granted her for weeks.

'Jane, why are children more sincere than grown-up persons?' asked Lassiter.

'Are they?'

'I reckon so. Little Fay there—she sees things as they appear on the face. An Indian does that. So does a dog. An' an Indian an' a dog are most of the time right in what they see. Mebbe a child is always right.'

'Well, what does Fay see?' asked Jane.

'I reckon you know. I wonder what goes on in Fay's mind when she sees part of the truth with the wise eyes of a child, an' wantin' to know more, meets with strange falseness from you? Wait! You are false in a way, though you're the best woman I ever knew. What I want to say is this. Fay has taken you're pretendin' to—to care for me for the thing it looks on the face. An' her little formin' mind asks questions. An' the answers she gets are different from the looks of things. So she'll grow up, gradually takin' on that falseness, an' be like the rest of women, an' men, too. An' the truth of this falseness to life is proved by your appearin' to love me when you don't. Things aren't what they seem.'

'Lassiter, you're right. A child should be told the absolute truth. But—is that possible? I haven't been able to do it, and all my life I've loved the truth, and I've prided myself upon being truthful. Maybe that was only egotism. I'm learning much, my friend. Some of those blinding scales have fallen from my eyes. And—as to caring for you, I think I care a great deal. How much, how little, I couldn't say. My heart is almost broken, Lassiter. So now is not a good time to judge of affection. I can still play and be merry with Fay. I can still dream. But when I attempt serious thought I'm dazed. I don't think. I don't care any more. I don't pray! ... Think of that my friend! But in spite of my numb feeling I believe I'll rise out of all this dark agony a better woman, with greater love of man and God. I'm on the rack now; I'm senseless to all but pain, and growing dead to that. Sooner or later I shall rise out of this stupor. I'm waiting the hour.'

'It'll soon come, Jane,' replied Lassiter, soberly. 'Then I'm afraid for you. Years are terrible things, an' for years you've been bound. Habit of years is strong as life itself. Somehow, though, I believe as you—that you'll come out of it all a finer woman. I'm waitin' too. An' I'm wonderin'—I reckon, Jane, that marriage between us is out of all human reason?'

'Lassiter! ... My dear friend! ... It's impossible for us to marry.'

'Why—as Fay says?' inquired Lassiter, with gentle persistence.

'Why! I never thought why. But it's not possible. I am Jane, daughter of Withersteen. My father would rise out of his grave. I'm of Mormon birth. I'm being broken. But I'm still a Mormon woman. And you—you are Lassiter!'

'Mebbe I'm not so much Lassiter as I used to be.'

'What was it you said? Habit of years is strong as life itself! You can't change the one habit—the purpose of your life. For you still pack those black guns! You still nurse your passion for blood.'

A smile, like a shadow, flickered across his face.

'No.'

'Lassiter, I lied to you. But I beg of you—don't you lie to me. I've great respect for you. I believe you're softened toward most, perhaps all, my people except— But when I speak of your purpose, your hate, your guns, I have only him in mind. I don't believe you've changed.'

For answer he unbuckled the heavy cartridge-belt, and laid it with the heavy, swing gun-sheaths in her lap.

'Lassiter!' Jane whispered, as she gazed from him to the black, cold guns. Without them he appeared shorn of strength, defenseless, a smaller man. Was she Delilah? Swiftly, conscious of only one motive—refusal to see this man called craven by his enemies—she rose, and with blundering fingers buckled the belt round his waist where it belonged.

'Lassiter, *I* am the coward.'

'Come with me out of Utah—where I can put away my guns an' be a man,' he said. 'I reckon I'll prove it to you then! Come! You've got Black Star back, an' Night an' Bells. Let's take the racers an' little Fay, an' ride out of Utah. The hosses an' the child are all you have left. Come!'

'No, no, Lassiter. I'll never leave Utah. What would I do in the world with my broken fortunes and my broken heart? I'll never leave these purple slopes I love so well.'

'I reckon I ought to've knowed that. Presently you'll be livin' down here in a hovel, an' presently Jane Withersteen will be a memory. I only wanted to have a chance to show you how a man—any man—can be better 'n he was. If we left Utah I could prove—I reckon I could prove this thing you call love. It's strange, an' hell an' heaven at once, Jane Withersteen. 'Pears to me that you've thrown away your big heart on love—love of religion an' duty an' church-men, an' riders an' poor families an' poor children! Yet you can't see what love is—how it changes a person! ... Listen, an' in tellin' you Milly Erne's story I'll show you how love changed her.

'Milly an' me was children when our family moved from Missouri to Texas, an' we growed up in Texas ways same as if we'd been born there. We had been poor, an' there we prospered. In time the little village where we went became a town, an' strangers an' new families kept movin' in. Milly was the belle them days. I can see her now, a little girl no bigger 'n a bird, an' as pretty. She had the finest eyes, dark blue-black when she was excited, an' beautiful all the time. You remember Milly's eyes! An' she had light-brown hair with streaks of gold, an' a mouth that every feller wanted to kiss.

'An' about the time Milly was the prettiest an' the sweetest, along came a young minister who began to ride some of a race with the other fellers for Milly. An' he won. Milly had always been strong on religion, an' when she met Frank Erne she went in heart an' soul for the salvation of souls. Fact was, Milly, through study of the Bible an' attendin' church an' revivals, went a little out of her head. It didn't worry the old folks none, an' the only worry to me was Milly's ever-lastin' prayin' an' workin' to save my soul. She never converted me, but we was the best of comrades, an' I reckon no brother an' sister ever loved each other better. Well, Frank Erne an' me hit up a great friendship. He was a strappin' feller, good to look at, an' had the most pleasin' ways. His religion never bothered me, for he could hunt an' fish an' ride an' be a good feller. After buffalo once, he come pretty near to savin' my life. We got to be thick as brothers, an' he was the only man I ever seen who I thought was good enough for Milly. An' the day they were married I got drunk for the only time in my life.

'Soon after that I left home—it seems Milly was the only one who could keep me home—an' I went to the bad, as to prosperin'. I saw some pretty hard life in the Pan Handle, an' then I went North. In them days Kansas an' Nebraska was as bad, come to think of it, as these days right here on the border of Utah. I got to be pretty handy with guns. An' there wasn't many riders as could beat me ridin'. An' I can say all modest-like that I never seen the white man who could track a hoss or a steer or a man with me. Afore I knowed it two years slipped by, an' all at once I got homesick, an' pulled a bridle south.

'Things at home had changed. I never got over that home-comin'. Mother was dead an' in her grave. Father was a silent, broken man, killed already on his feet. Frank Erne was a ghost of his old self, through with workin', through with preachin', almost through with livin', an' Milly was gone! ... It was a long time before I got the story. Father had no mind left, an' Frank Erne was *afraid* to talk. So I had to pick up what'd happened from different people.

'It 'pears that soon after I left home another preacher come to the little town. An' he an' Frank become rivals. This feller was different from Frank. He preached some other kind of religion, and he was quick an' passionate, where Frank was slow an' mild. He went after people, women specially. In looks he couldn't compare to Frank Erne, but he had power over women. He had a voice, an' he talked an' talked an' preached an' preached. Milly fell under his influence. She became mightily interested in his religion. Frank had patience with her, as was his way, an' let her be as interested as she liked. All religions were devoted to one God, he said, an' it wouldn't hurt Milly none to study a different point of view. So the new preacher often called on Milly, an' sometimes in Frank's absence. Frank was a cattle-man between Sundays.

'Along about this time an incident come off that I couldn't get much light on. A stranger come to town, an' was seen with the preacher. This stranger was a big man with an eye like blue ice, an' a beard of gold. He had money, an' he 'peared a man of mystery, an' the town went to buzzin' when he disappeared about the same time as a young woman known to be mightily interested in the new preacher's religion. Then, presently, along comes a man from somewheres in Illinois, an' he up an' spots this preacher as a famous Mormon proselyter. That ri'led Frank Erne as nothin' ever before, an' from rivals they come to be bitter enemies. An' it ended in Frank goin' to the meetin'-house where Milly was listenin', an' before her an' everybody else he called that preacher—called him, well, almost as hard as Venters called Tull here sometime back. An' Frank followed up that call with a hoss-whippin', an' he drove the proselyter out of town.

'People noticed, so 'twas said, that Milly's sweet disposition changed. Some said it was because she would soon become a mother, an' others said she was pinin' after the new religion. An' there was women who said right out that she was pinin' after the Mormon. Anyway, one mornin' Frank rode in from one of his trips, to find Milly gone. He had no real near neighbors—livin' a little out of town—but those who was nearest said a wagon had gone by in the night, an' they thought it stopped at her door. Well, tracks always tell, an' there was the wagon tracks an' hoss tracks an' man tracks. The news spread like wildfire that Milly had run off from her husband. Everybody but Frank believed it an' wasn't slow in tellin' why she run off. Mother had always hated that strange streak of Milly's, takin' up with the new religion as she had, an' she believed Milly ran off with the Mormon. That hastened mother's death, an' she died unforgivin'. Father wasn't the kind to bow down under disgrace or misfortune, but he had surpassin' love for Milly, an' the loss of her broke him.

'From the minute I heard of Milly's disappearance I never believed she went off of her own free will. I knew Milly, an' I knew she *couldn't* have done that. I stayed at home awhile, tryin' to make Frank Erne talk. But if he knowed anythin' then he wouldn't tell it. So I set out to find Milly. An' I tried to get on the trail of that proselyter. I knew if I ever struck a town he'd visited that I'd get a trail. I knew, too, that nothin' short of hell would stop his proselytin'. An' I rode from town to town. I had a blind faith that somethin' was guidin' me. An' as the weeks an' months went by I growed into a strange sort of a man, I guess. Anyway, people were afraid of me. Two years after that, way over in a corner of Texas, I struck a town where my man had been. He'd jest left. People said he came to that town *without* a woman. I back-trailed my man through Arkansas an' Mississippi, an' the old trail got hot again in Texas. I found the town where he first went after leavin' home. An' here I got track of Milly. I found a cabin where she had given birth to her baby. There was no way to tell whether she'd been kept a prisoner or not. The feller who owned the place was a mean, silent sort of a skunk, an' as I was leavin' I jest took a chance an' left my mark on him. Then I went home again.

'It was to find that I hadn't any home, no more. Father had been dead a year. Frank Erne still lived in the house where Milly had left him. I stayed with him awhile, an' I grew old watchin' him. His farm had gone to weed, his cattle had strayed or been rustled, his house weathered till it wouldn't keep out rain nor wind. An' Frank set on the porch an' whittled sticks, an' day by day wasted away. There was times when he ranted about like a crazy man, but mostly he was always sittin' an' starin' with eyes that made a man curse. I figured Frank had a secret fear that I needed to know. An' when I told him I'd trailed Milly for near three years an' had got trace of her, an' saw where she'd had her baby, I thought he would drop dead at my feet. An' when he'd come round more natural-like he begged me to *give up* the trail. But he wouldn't explain. So I let him alone, an' watched him day an' night.

'An' I found there was one thing still precious to him, an' it was a little drawer where he kept his papers. This was in the room where he slept. An' it 'peared he seldom slept. But after bein' patient I got the contents of that drawer an' found two letters from Milly. One was a long letter written a few months after her disappearance. She had been bound an' gagged an' dragged away from her home by three men, an' she named them—Hurd, Metzger, Slack. They was strangers to her. She was taken to the little town where I found trace of her two years after. But she didn't send the letter from that town. There she was penned in. 'Peared that the proselyter, who had, of course, come on the scene, was not runnin' any risks of losin' her. She went on to say that for a time she was out of her head, an' when she got right again all that kept her alive was the baby. It was a beautiful baby, she said, an' all she thought an' dreamed of was somehow to get baby back to its father, an' then she'd thankfully lay down and die. An' the letter ended abrupt, in the middle of a sentence, an' it wasn't signed.

'The second letter was written more than two years after the first. It was from Salt Lake City. It simply said that Milly had heard her brother was on her trail. She asked Frank to tell her brother to give up the search because if he didn't she would suffer in a way too horrible to tell. She didn't beg. She just stated a fact an' made the simple request. An' she ended that letter by sayin' she would soon leave Salt Lake City with the man she had come to love, an' would never be heard of again.

'I recognized Milly's handwritin', an' I recognized her way of puttin' things. But that second letter told me of some great change in her. Ponderin' over it, I felt at last she'd either come to love that feller an' his religion, or some terrible fear made her lie an' say so. I couldn't be sure which. But, of course, I meant to find out. I'll say here, if I'd known Mormons then as I do now I'd left Milly to her fate. For mebbe she was right about what she'd suffer if I kept on her trail. But I was young an' wild them days. First I went to the town where she'd first been taken, an' I went to the place where she'd been kept. I got that skunk who owned the place, an' took him out in the woods, an' made him tell all he knowed. That wasn't much as to length, but it was pure hell's-fire in substance. This time I left him some incapacitated for any more skunk work short of hell. Then I hit the trail for Utah.

'That was fourteen years ago. I saw the incomin' of most of the Mormons. It was a wild country an' a wild time. I rode from town to town, village to village, ranch to ranch, camp to camp, I never stayed long in one place. I never had but one idea. I never rested. Four years went by, an' I knowed every trail in northern Utah. I kept on an' as time went by, an' I'd begun to grow old in my search, I had firmer, blinder faith in whatever was guidin' me. Once I read about a feller who sailed the seven seas an' traveled the world, an' he had a story to tell, an' whenever he seen the man to whom he must tell that story he knowed him on sight. I was like that, only I had a question to ask. An' always I knew the man of whom I must ask. So I never really lost the trail, though for years it was the dimmest trail ever followed by any man.

'Then come a change in my luck. Along in Central Utah I rounded up Hurd, an' I whispered somethin' in his ear, an' watched his face, an' then throwed a gun against his bowels. An' he died with his teeth so tight shut that I couldn't have pried them open with a knife. Slack an' Metzger that same year both heard me whisper the same question, an' neither would they speak a word when they lay dyin'. Long before I'd learned no man of this breed or class—or God knows what—would give up any secrets! I had to see in a man's fear of death the connections with Milly Erne's fate. An' as the years passed at long intervals I would find such a man.

'So as I drifted on the long trail down into southern Utah my name preceded me, an' I had to meet a people prepared for me, an' ready with guns. They made me a gun-man. An' that suited me. In all this time signs of the proselyter an' the giant with the blue-ice eyes an' the gold beard seemed to fade dimmer out of the trail. Only twice in ten years did I find a trace of the mysterious man who had visited the proselyter at my home village. What he had to do with Milly's fate was beyond all hope for me to hear, unless my guidin' spirit led me to him! As for the other man, I knew, as sure as I breathed an' the stars shone an' the wind blew, that I'd meet him some day.

'Eighteen years I've been on the trail. An' it led me to the last lonely villages of the Utah border. Eighteen years! ... I feel pretty old now. I was only twenty when I hit that trail. Well, as I told you, back here a ways a Gentile said Jane Withersteen could tell me about Milly Erne an' show me her grave!'

The low voice ceased, and Lassiter slowly turned his sombrero round and round, and appeared to be counting the silver ornaments on the band. Jane, leaning toward him, sat as if petrified, listening intently, waiting to hear more. She could have shrieked, but power of tongue and lips were denied her. She saw only this sad, gray, passion-worn man, and she heard only the faint rustling of the leaves.

'Well, I came to Cottonwoods,' went on Lassiter, 'an' you showed me Milly's grave. An' though your teeth have been shut tighter'n them of all the dead men lyin' back along that trail, jest the same you told me the secret I've lived these eighteen years to hear! Jane, I said you'd tell me without ever me askin'. I didn't need to ask my question here. The day, you remember, when that fat party throwed a gun on me in your court, an'—'

'Oh! Hush!' whispered Jane, blindly holding up her hands.

'*I seen in your face that Dyer, now a bishop, was the proselyter who ruined Milly Erne!*'

For an instant Jane Withersteen's brain was a whirling chaos, and she recovered to find herself grasping at Lassiter like one drowning. And as if by a lightning stroke she sprang from her dull apathy into exquisite torture.

'*It's a lie!* Lassiter! No, no!' she moaned. 'I swear—you're wrong!'

'Stop! You'd perjure yourself! But I'll spare you that. You poor woman! Still blind! Still faithful! ... Listen. I *know*. Let that settle it. An' I give up my purpose!'

'What is it—you say?'

'I give up my purpose. I've come to see an' feel differently. I can't help poor Milly. An' I've outgrowed revenge. I've come to see I can be no judge for men. I can't kill a man jest for hate. Hate ain't the same with me since I loved you and little Fay.'

'Lassiter! You mean you won't kill him?' Jane whispered.

'No.'

'For my sake?'

'I reckon. I can't understand, but I'll respect your feelin's.'

'Because you—oh, because you love me? ... Eighteen years! You were that terrible Lassiter! And *now*—because you love me?'

'That's it, Jane.'

'Oh, you'll make me love you! How can I help but love you? My heart must be stone. But—oh, Lassiter, wait, wait! Give me time. I'm not what I was. Once it was so easy to love. Now it's easy to hate. Wait! My faith in God—*some* God—still lives. By it I see happier times for you, poor passion-swayed wanderer! For me—a miserable, broken woman. I loved your sister Milly. I *will* love you. I can't have fallen so low—I can't be so abandoned by God—that I've no love left to give you. Wait! Let us forget Milly's sad life. Ah, I knew it as no one else on earth! There's one thing I shall tell you—if you are at my death-bed, but I can't speak now.'

'I reckon I don't want to hear no more,' said Lassiter.

Jane leaned against him; as if some pent-up force had rent its way out, she fell into a paroxysm of weeping. Lassiter held her in silent sympathy. By degrees she regained composure, and she was rising, sensible of being relieved of a weighty burden, when a sudden start on Lassiter's part alarmed her.

'I heard hosses—hosses with muffled hoofs!' he said; and he got up guardedly.

'Where's Fay?' asked Jane, hurriedly glancing round the shady knoll. The bright-haired child, who had appeared to be close all the time, was not in sight.

'Fay!' called Jane.

No answering shout of glee. No patter of flying feet. Jane saw Lassiter stiffen.

'*Fay—oh—Fay!*' Jane almost screamed.

The leaves quivered and rustled; a lonesome cricket chirped in the grass; a bee hummed by. The silence of the waning afternoon breathed hateful portent. It terrified Jane. When had silence been so infernal?

'She's—only—strayed—out—of—earshot,' faltered Jane, looking at Lassiter.

Pale, rigid as a statue, the rider stood, not in listening, searching posture, but in one of doomed certainty. Suddenly he grasped Jane with an iron hand, and, turning his face from her gaze, he strode with her from the knoll.

'See—Fay played here last—a house of stones an' sticks ... An' here's a corral of pebbles with leaves for hosses,' said Lassiter, stridently, and pointed to the ground. 'Back an' forth she trailed ... See, she's buried somethin'—a dead grasshopper—there's a tombstone ... here she went, chasin' a lizard—see the tiny streaked trail ... she pulled bark off this cottonwood ... look in the dust of the path—the letters you taught her—she's drawn pictures of birds an' hosses an' people ... Look, a cross! Oh, Jane, *your* cross!'

Lassiter dragged Jane on, and as if from a book read the meaning of little Fay's trail. All the way down the knoll. through the shrubbery, round and round a cottonwood. Fay's vagrant fancy left records of her sweet musings and innocent play. Long had she lingered round a bird-nest to leave therein the gaudy wing of a butterfly. Long had she played beside the running stream, sending adrift vessels freighted with pebbly cargo. Then she had wandered through the deep grass, her tiny feet scarcely turning a fragile blade, and she had dreamed beside some old faded flowers. Thus her steps led her into the broad lane. The little dimpled imprints of her bare feet showed clean-cut in the dust; they went a little way down the lane; and then, at a point where they stopped, the great tracks of a man led out from the shrubbery and returned.

CHAPTER TWENTY
Lassiter's Way

Footprints told the story of little Fay's abduction. In anguish Jane Withersteen turned speechlessly to Lassiter, and, confirming her fears, she saw him gray-faced, aged all in a moment, stricken as if by a mortal blow.

Then all her life seemed to fall about her in wreck and ruin.

'It's all over,' she heard her voice whisper. 'It's ended. I'm going—I'm going—'

'Where?' demanded Lassiter, suddenly looming darkly over her.

'To—to those cruel men—'

'Speak names!' thundered Lassiter.

'To Bishop Dyer—to Tull,' went on Jane, shocked into obedience.

'Well—what for?'

'I want little Fay. I can't live without her. They've stolen her as they stole Milly Erne's child. I must have little Fay. I want only her. I give up. I'll go and tell Bishop Dyer—I'm broken. I'll tell him I'm ready for the yoke—only give me back Fay—and—I'll marry Tull!'

'*Never!*' hissed Lassiter.

His long arm leaped at her. Almost running, he dragged her under the cottonwoods, across the court, into the huge hall of Withersteen House, and he shut the door with a force that jarred the heavy walls. Black Star and Night and Bells, since their return, had been locked in this hall, and now they stamped on the stone floor.

Lassiter released Jane and like a dizzy man swayed from her with a hoarse cry and leaned shaking against a table where he kept his rider's accoutrements. He began to fumble in his saddle-bags. His action brought a clinking, metallic sound—the rattling of gun-cartridges. His fingers trembled as he slipped cartridges into an extra belt. But as he buckled it over the one he habitually wore his hands became steady. This second belt contained two guns, smaller than the black ones swinging low, and he slipped them round so that his coat hid them. Then he fell to swift action. Jane Withersteen watched him, fascinated but uncomprehending; and she saw him rapidly saddle Black Star and Night. Then he drew her into the light of the huge window, standing over her, gripping her arm with fingers like cold steel.

'Yes, Jane, it's ended—but you're not goin' to Dyer! ... *I'm goin' instead!*'

Looking at him—he was so terrible of aspect—she could not comprehend his words. Who was this man with the face gray as death, with eyes that would have made her shriek had she the strength, with the strange, ruthlessly bitter lips? Where was the gentle Lassiter? What was this presence in the hall, about him, about her—this cold, invisible presence?

'Yes, it's ended, Jane,' he was saying, so awfully quiet and cool and implacable, 'an' I'm goin' to make a little call. I'll lock you in here, an' when I get back have the saddle-bags full of meat an' bread. An' be ready to ride!'

'Lassiter!' cried Jane.

Desperately she tried to meet his gray eyes, in vain; desperately she tried again, fought herself as feeling and thought resurged in torment, and she succeeded; and then she knew.

'No—no—no!' she wailed. 'You said you'd foregone your vengeance. You promised not to kill Bishop Dyer.'

'If you want to talk to me about him—leave off the Bishop. I don't understand that name, or its use.'

'Oh, hadn't you foregone your vengeance on—on Dyer?'

'Yes.'

'But—your actions—your words—your guns—your terrible looks! ... They don't seem foregoing vengeance?'

'Jane, now it's justice.'

'You'll—kill him?'

'If God lets me live another hour! If not God—then the devil who drives me!'

'You'll kill him—for yourself—for your vengeful hate?'

'No!'

'For Milly Erne's sake?'

'No.'

'For little Fay's?'

'No!'

'Oh—for whose?'

'*For yours!*'

'His blood on my soul!' whispered Jane, and she fell to her knees. This was the long-pending hour of fruition. And the habit of years—the religious passion of her life—leaped from lethargy, and the long months of gradual drifting to doubt were as if they had never been. 'If you spill his blood it'll be on my soul—and on my father's. Listen.' And she clasped his knees, and clung there as he tried to raise her. 'Listen. Am I nothing to you?'

'Woman—don't trifle at words! I love you! An' I'll soon prove it!'

'I'll give myself to you—I'll ride away with you—marry you, if only you'll spare him?'

His answer was a cold, ringing, terrible laugh.

'Lassiter—I'll love you. Spare him!'

'No!'

She sprang up in despairing, breaking spirit, and encircled his neck with her arms, and held him in an embrace that he strove vainly to loosen. 'Lassiter, would you kill me? I'm fighting my last fight for the principles of my youth—love of religion, love of father. You don't know—you can't guess the truth, and I can't speak it! I'm losing all. I'm changing. All I've gone through is nothing to this hour. Pity me—help me in my weakness. You're strong again—oh, so cruelly, coldly strong! You're killing me. I see you—feel you as some other Lassiter! My master, be merciful—spare him!'

His answer was a ruthless smile.

She clung closer to him, and leaned her panting breast on him, and lifted her face to his. 'Lassiter, *I do love you!* It's leaped out of my agony. It comes suddenly with a terrible blow of truth. You are a man! I never knew it till now. Some wonderful change came to me when you buckled on these guns and showed that gray, awful face. I loved you then. All my life I've loved, but never as now. No woman can love like a broken woman. If it were not for one thing—just one thing—and yet! I *can't* speak it—I'd glory in your manhood—the lion in you that means to slay for me. Believe me—and spare Dyer. Be merciful—great as it's in you to be great ... Oh, listen and believe—I have nothing, but I'm a woman—a beautiful woman, Lassiter—a passionate, loving woman—and I love you! Take me—hide me in some wild place—and love me and mend my broken heart. Spare him and take me away.'

She lifted her face closer and closer to his, until their lips nearly touched, and she hung upon his neck, and with strength almost spent pressed and still pressed her palpitating body to his.

'Kiss me!' she whispered, blindly.

'No—not at your price!' he answered. His voice had changed or she had lost clearness of hearing.

'Kiss me! ... Are you a man? Kiss me and save me!'

'Jane, you never played fair with me. But now you're blisterin' your lips—blackenin' your soul with lies!'

'By the memory of my mother—by my Bible—no! No, I have no Bible! But by my hope of heaven I swear I love you!'

Lassiter's gray lips formed soundless words that meant even her love could not avail to bend his will. As if the hold of her arms was that of a child's he loosened it and stepped away.

'Wait! Don't go! Oh, hear a last word! … May a more just and merciful God than the God I was taught to worship judge me—forgive me—save me! For I can no longer keep silent! … Lassiter, in pleading for Dyer I've been pleading more for my father. My father was a Mormon master, close to the leaders of the church. It was my father who sent Dyer out to proselyte. It was my father who had the blue-ice eye and the beard of gold. It was my father you got trace of in the past years. Truly, Dyer ruined Milly Erne—dragged her from her home—to Utah—to Cottonwoods. *But it was for my father!* If Milly Erne was ever wife of a Mormon that Mormon was my father! I never knew—never will know whether or not she was a wife. Blind I may be, Lassiter—fanatically faithful to a false religion I may have been, but I know justice, and my father is beyond human justice. Surely he is meeting just punishment—somewhere. Always it has appalled me—the thought of your killing Dyer for my father's sins. So I have prayed!'

'Jane, the past is dead. In my love for you I forgot the past. This thing I'm about to do ain't for myself or Milly or Fay. It's not because of anythin' that ever happened in the past, but for what is happenin' right *now. It's for you!* … An' listen. Since I was a boy I've never thanked God for anythin'. If there is a God—an' I've come to believe it—I thank Him now for the years that made me Lassiter! … I can reach down an' feel these big guns, an' know what I can do with them. An', Jane, only one of the miracles Dyer professes to believe in can save him!'

Again for Jane Withersteen came the spinning of her brain in darkness, and as she whirled in endless chaos she seemed to be falling at the feet of a luminous figure—a man—Lassiter—who had saved her from herself, who could not be changed, who would slay rightfully. Then she slipped into utter blackness.

When she recovered from her faint she became aware that she was lying on a couch near the window in her sitting-room. Her brow felt damp and cold and wet; someone was chafing her hands; she recognized Judkins, and then saw that his lean, hard face wore the hue and look of excessive agitation.

'Judkins!' Her voice broke weakly.

'Aw, Miss Withersteen, you're comin' round fine. Now jest lay still a little. You're all right; everythin's all right.'

'Where is—he?'

'Who?'

'Lassiter!'

'You needn't worry none about him.'

'Where is he? Tell me—instantly.'

'Wal, he's in the other room patchin' up a few triflin' bullet-holes.'

'*Ah! … Bishop Dyer?*'

'When I seen him last—a matter of half an hour ago, he was on his knees. He was some busy, *but* he wasn't prayin'!'

'How strangely you talk! I'll sit up. I'm—well, strong again. Tell me. Dyer on his knees! What was he doing?'

'Wal, beggin' your pardon fer blunt talk, Miss Withersteen, Dyer was on his knees an' *not* prayin'. You remember his big, broad hands? You've seen 'em raised in blessin' over old gray men an' little curly-headed children like—like Fay Larkin! Come to think of thet, I disremember ever hearin' of his liftin' his big hands in blessin' over a *woman*. Wal, when I seen him last—jest a little while ago—he was on his knees, *not* prayin', as I remarked—an' he was pressin' his big hands over some bigger wounds.'

'Man, you drive me mad! Did Lassiter kill Dyer?'

'Yes.'

'Did he kill Tull?'

'No. Tull's out of the village with most of his riders. He's expected back before evenin'. Lassiter will hev to git away before Tull an' his riders come in. It's sure death fer him here. An' wuss for you, too, Miss Withersteen. There'll be some of an uprisin' when Tull gits back.'

'I shall ride away with Lassiter. Judkins, tell me all you saw—all you know about this killing.' She realized, without wonder or amaze, how Judkins's one word, affirming the death of Dyer—that the catastrophe had fallen—had completed the change whereby she had been molded or beaten or broken into another woman. She felt calm, slightly cold, strong as she had not been strong since the first shadow fell upon her.

'I jest saw about all of it, Miss Withersteen, an' I'll be glad to tell you if you'll only hev patience with me,' said Judkins, earnestly. 'You see, I've been pecooliarly interested, an' nat'rully I'm some excited. An' I talk a lot thet mebbe ain't necessary, but I can't help thet.

'I was at the meetin'-house where Dyer was holdin' court. You know he allus acts as magistrate an' judge when Tull's away. An' the trial was fer tryin' what's left of my boy riders—thet helped me hold your cattle—fer a lot of hatched-up things the boys never did. We're used to thet, an' the boys wouldn't hev minded bein' locked up fer a while, or hevin' to dig ditches, or whatever the judge laid down. You see, I divided the gold you give me among all my boys, an' they all hid it, an' they all feel rich. Howsomever, court was adjourned before the judge passed sentence. Yes, ma'am, court was adjourned some strange an' quick, much as if lightnin' hed struck the meetin'-house.

'I hed trouble attendin' the trial, but I got in. There was a good many people there, all my boys, an' Judge Dyer with his several clerks. Also he hed with him the five riders who've been guardin' him pretty close of late. They was Carter, Wright, Jengessen, an' two new riders from Stone Bridge. I didn't hear their names, but I heard they was handy men with guns an' they looked more like rustlers than riders. Anyway, there they was, the five all in a row.

'Judge Dyer was tellin' Willie Kern, one of my best an' steadiest boys—Dyer was tellin' him how there was a ditch opened near Willie's home lettin' water through his lot, where it hadn't ought to go. An' Willie was tryin' to git a word in to prove he wasn't at home all the day it happened—which was true, as I know—but Willie couldn't git a word in, an' then Judge Dyer went on layin' down the law. An' all at once he happened to look down the long room. An' if ever any man turned to stone he was thet man.

'Nat'rully I looked back to see what hed acted so powerful strange on the judge. An' there, half-way up the room, in the middle of the wide aisle, stood Lassiter! All white an' black he looked an' I can't think of anythin' he resembled, onless it's death. Venters made thet same room some still an' chilly when he called Tull; but this was different. I give my word, Miss Withersteen, thet I went cold to my very marrow. I don't know why. But Lassiter has a way about him thet's awful. He spoke a word—a name—I couldn't understand it, though he spoke clear as a bell. I was too excited, mebbe. Judge Dyer must hev understood it, an' a lot more thet was mystery to me, fer he pitched forward out of his chair right on to the platform.

'Then them five riders, Dyer's bodyguards, they jumped up, an' two of them thet I found out afterward were the strangers from Stone Bridge, they piled right out of a winder, so quick you couldn't catch your breath. It was plain they wasn't Mormons.

'Jengessen, Carter, an' Wright eyed Lassiter, for what must hev been a second an' seemed like an hour, an' they went white an' strung. But they didn't weaken nor lose their nerve.

'I hed a good look at Lassiter. He stood sort of stiff, bendin' a little, an' both his arms were crooked, an' his hands looked like a hawk's claws. But there ain't no tellin' how his eyes looked. I know this, though, an' thet is his eyes could read the mind of any man about to throw a gun. An' in watchin' him, of course, I couldn't see the three men go fer their guns. An' though I was lookin' right at Lassiter—lookin' hard—I couldn't see how he drawed. He was quicker'n eyesight—thet's all. But I seen the red spurtin' of his guns, an' heard his shots jest the very littlest instant before I heard the shots of the riders. An' when I turned, Wright an' Carter was down, an' Jengessen, who's tough like a steer, was pullin' the trigger of a wabblin' gun. But it was plain he was shot through, plumb center. An' sudden he fell with a crash, an' his gun clattered on the floor.

'Then there was a hell of a silence. Nobody breathed. Sartin I didn't, anyway. I saw Lassiter slip a smokin' gun back in a belt. But he hadn't throwed either of the big black guns, an' I thought thet strange. An' all this was happenin' quick—you can't imagine how quick.

'There come a scrapin' on the floor an' Dyer got up, his face like lead. I wanted to watch Lassiter, but Dyer's face, onct I seen it like thet, glued my eyes. I seen him go fer his gun—why, I could hev done better, quicker—an' then there was a thunderin' shot from Lassiter, an' it hit Dyer's right arm, an' his gun went off as it dropped. He looked at Lassiter like a cornered sage-wolf, an' sort of howled, an' reached down fer his gun. He'd jest picked it off the floor an' was raisin' it when another thunderin' shot almost tore thet arm off—so it seemed to me. The gun dropped again an' he went down on his knees, kind of flounderin' after it. It was some strange an' terrible to see his awful earnestness. Why would such a man cling so to life? Anyway, he got the gun with left hand an' was raisin' it, pullin' trigger in his madness, when the third thunderin' shot hit his left arm, an' he dropped the gun again. But thet left arm wasn't useless yet, fer he grabbed up the gun, an' with a shakin' aim thet would hev been pitiful to me—in any other man—he began to shoot. One wild bullet struck a man twenty feet from Lassiter. An' it killed thet man, as I seen afterward. Then come a bunch of thunderin' shots—nine I calkilated after, fer they come so quick I couldn't count them—an' I knew Lassiter hed turned the black guns loose on Dyer.

'I'm tellin' you straight, Miss Withersteen, fer I want you to know. Afterward you'll git over it. I've seen some soul-rackin' scenes on this Utah border, but this was the awfulest. I remember I closed my eyes, an' fer a minute I thought of the strangest things, out of place there, such as you'd never dream would come to mind. I saw the sage, an' runnin' hosses—an' thet's the beautifulest sight to me—an' I saw dim things in the dark, an' there was a kind of hummin' in my ears. An' I remember distinctly—fer it was what made all these things whirl out of my mind an' opened my eyes—I remember distinctly it was the smell of gunpowder.

'The court had about adjourned fer thet judge. He was on his knees, an' he wasn't prayin'. He was gaspin' an' trying' to press his big, floppin', crippled hands over his body. Lassiter had sent all those last thunderin' shots through his body. Thet was Lassiter's way.

'An' Lassiter spoke, an' if I ever forgit his words I'll never forgit the sound of his voice.

' "*Proselyter*, I reckon you'd better call quick on thet God who reveals Hisself to you on earth, because He won't be visitin' the place you're goin' to!"

'An' then I seen Dyer look at his big, hangin' hands thet wasn't big enough fer the last work he set them to. An' he looked up at Lassiter. An' then he stared horrible at somethin' thet wasn't Lassiter, nor anyone there, nor the room, nor the branches of purple sage peepin' into the winder. Whatever he seen, it was with the look of a man who *discovers* somethin' too late. Thet's a terrible look! ... An' with a horrible *understandin'* cry he slid forward on his face.'

Judkins paused in his narrative, breathing heavily while he wiped his perspiring brow.

'Thet's about all,' he concluded. 'Lassiter left the meetin'-house an' I hurried to catch up with him. He was bleedin' from three gunshots, none of them much to bother him. An' we come right up here. I found you layin' in the hall, an' I hed to work some over you.'

Jane Withersteen offered up no prayer for Dyer's soul.

Lassiter's step sounded in the hall—the familiar soft, silver-clinking step—and she heard it with thrilling new emotions in which was a vague joy in her very fear of him. The door opened, and she saw him, the old Lassiter, slow, easy, gentle, cool, yet not exactly the same Lassiter. She rose, and for a moment her eyes blurred and swam in tears.

'Are you—all—all right?' she asked, tremulously.

'I reckon.'

'Lassiter, I'll ride away with you. Hide me till danger is past—till we are forgotten—then take me where you will. Your people shall be my people, and your God my God!'

He kissed her hand with the quaint grace and courtesy that came to him in rare moments.

'Black Star an' Night are ready,' he said, simply.

His quiet mention of the black racers spurred Jane to action. Hurrying to her room, she changed to her rider's suit, packed her jewelry, and the gold that was left, and all the woman's apparel for which there was space in the saddle-bags, and then returned to the hall. Black Star stamped his iron-shod hoofs and tossed his beautiful head, and eyed her with knowing eyes.

'Judkins, I give Bells to you,' said Jane. 'I hope you will always keep him and be good to him.'

Judkins mumbled thanks that he could not speak fluently, and his eyes flashed.

Lassiter strapped Jane's saddle-bags upon Black Star, and led the racers out into the court.

'Judkins, you ride with Jane out into the sage. If you see any riders comin' shout quick twice. An', Jane, *don't look back!* I'll catch up soon. We'll get to the break into the Pass before midnight, an' then wait until the mornin' to go down.'

Black Star bent his graceful neck and bowed his noble head, and his broad shoulders yielded as he knelt for Jane to mount.

She rode out of the court beside Judkins, through the grove, across the wide lane into the sage, and she realized that she was leaving Withersteen House forever, and she did not look back. A strange, dreamy, calm peace pervaded her soul. Her doom had fallen upon her, but, instead of finding life no longer worth living she found it doubly significant, full of sweetness as the western breeze, beautiful and unknown as the sage-slope stretching its purple sunset shadows before her. She became aware of Judkins's hand touching hers; she heard him speak a husky good-bye; then into the place of Bells shot the dead-black, keen, racy nose of Night, and she knew Lassiter rode beside her.

'Don't—look—back!' he said, and his voice, too, was not clear.

Facing straight ahead, seeing only the waving, shadowy sage, Jane held out her gauntleted hand, to feel it enclosed in strong clasp. So she rode on without a backward glance at the beautiful grove of Cottonwoods. She did not seem to think of the past, of what she left forever, but of the color and mystery and wildness of the sage-slope leading down to Deception Pass, and of the future. She watched the shadows lengthen down the slope; she felt the cool west wind sweeping by from the rear; and she wondered at low, yellow clouds sailing swiftly over her and beyond.

'Don't—look—back!' said Lassiter.

Thick-driving belts of smoke traveled by on the wind, and with it came a strong, pungent odor of burning wood.

Lassiter had fired Withersteen House! But Jane did not look back.

A misty veil obscured the clear, searching gaze she had kept steadfastly upon the purple slope and the dim lines of cañons. It passed, as passed the rolling clouds of smoke, and she saw the valley deepening into the shades of twilight. Night came on, swift as the fleet racers, and stars peeped out to brighten and grow, and the huge, windy, eastern heave of sage-level paled under a rising moon and turned to silver. Blanched in moonlight, the sage yet seemed to hold its hue of purple and was infinitely more wild and lonely. So the night hours wore on, and Jane Withersteen never once looked back.

CHAPTER TWENTY-ONE
Black Star and Night

The time had come for Venters and Bess to leave their retreat. They were at great pains to choose the few things they would be able to carry with them on the journey out of Utah.

'Bern, whatever kind of a pack's this, anyhow?' questioned Bess, rising from her work with reddened face.

Venters, absorbed in his own task, did not look up at all, and in reply said he had brought so much from Cottonwoods that he did not recollect the half of it.

'A woman packed this!' Bess exclaimed.

He scarcely caught her meaning, but the peculiar tone of her voice caused him instantly to rise, and he saw Bess on her knees before an open pack which he recognized as the one given him by Jane.

'By George!' he ejaculated, guiltily, and then at sight of Bess's face he laughed outright.

'A woman packed this,' she repeated, fixing woeful, tragic eyes on him.

'Well, is that a crime?'

'There—there *is* a woman, after all!'

'Now Bess—'

'You've lied to me!'

Then and there Venters found it imperative to postpone work for the present. All her life Bess had been isolated, but she had inherited certain elements of the eternal feminine.

'But there *was* a woman and you *did* lie to me,' she kept repeating, after he had explained.

'What of that? Bess, I'll get angry at you in a moment. Remember you've been pent up all your life. I venture to say that if you'd been out in the world you'd have had a dozen sweethearts and had told many a lie before this.'

'I wouldn't anything of the kind,' declared Bess, indignantly.

'Well—perhaps not a lie. But you'd have had the sweethearts. You couldn't have helped that—being so pretty.'

This remark appeared to be a very clever and fortunate one; and the work of selecting and then of stowing all the packs in the cave went on without further interruption.

Venters closed up the opening of the cave with a thatch of willows and aspens, so that not even a bird or a rat could get in to the sacks of grain. And this work was in order with the precaution habitually observed by him. He might not be able to get out of Utah, and have to return to the valley. But he owed it to Bess to make the attempt, and in case they were compelled to turn back he wanted to find that fine store of food and grain intact. te The outfit of implements and utensils he packed away in another cave.

'Bess, we have enough to live here all our lives,' he said once, dreamily.

'Shall I go roll Balancing Rock?' she asked, in light speech, but with deep-blue fire in her eyes.

'No—no.'

'Ah, you don't forget the gold and the world,' she signed.

'Child, you forget the beautiful dresses and the travel—and everything.'

'Oh, I want to go. But I want to stay!'

'I feel the same way.'

They let the eight calves out of the corral, and kept only two of the burros Venters had brought from Cottonwoods. These they intended to hide. Bess freed all her pets—the quail and rabbits and foxes.

The last sunset and twilight and night were both the sweetest and saddest they had ever spent in Surprise Valley. Morning brought keen exhilaration and excitement. When Venters had saddled the two burros, strapped on the light packs and the two canteens, the sunlight was dispersing the lazy shadows from the valley. Taking a last look at the caves and the silver spruces, Venters and Bess made a reluctant start, leading the burros. Ring and Whitie looked keen and knowing. Something seemed to drag at Venters's feet and he noticed Bess lagged behind. Never had the climb from terrace to bridge appeared so long.

Not till they reached the opening of the gorge did they stop to rest and take one last look at the valley. The tremendous arch of stone curved clear and sharp in outline against the morning sky. And through it streaked the golden shaft. The valley seemed an enchanted circle of glorious veils of gold and wraiths of white and silver haze and dim, blue, moving shade—beautiful and wild and unreal as a dream.

'We—we—can—th—think of it—always—re—re—member,' sobbed Bess.

'Hush! Don't cry. Our valley has only fitted us for a better life somewhere. Come!'

They entered the gorge and he closed the willow gate. From rosy, golden morning light they passed into cool, dense gloom. The burros pattered up the trail with little hollow-cracking steps. And the gorge widened to narrow outlet and the gloom lightened to gray. At the divide they halted for another rest. Venters's keen, remembering gaze searched Balancing Rock, and the long incline, and the cracked toppling walls, but failed to note the slightest change.

The dogs led the descent; then came Bess leading her burro; then Venters leading his. Bess kept her eyes bent downward. Venters, however, had an irresistible desire to look upward at Balancing Rock. It had always haunted him, and now he wondered if he were really to get through the outlet before the huge stone thundered down. He fancied that would be a miracle. Every few steps he answered to the strange, nervous fear and turned to make sure the rock still stood like a giant statue. And, as he descended, it grew dimmer in his sight. It changed form; it swayed; it nodded darkly; and at last, in his heightened fancy, he saw it heave and roll. As in a dream when he felt himself falling yet knew he would never fall, so he saw this long-standing thunderbolt of the little stone-men plunge down to close forever the outlet to Deception Pass.

And while he was giving way to unaccountable dread imaginations the descent was accomplished without mishap.

'I'm glad that's over,' he said, breathing more freely. 'I hope I'm by that hanging rock for good and all. Since almost the moment I first saw it I've had an idea that it was waiting for me. Now, when it does fall, if I'm thousands of miles away, I'll hear it.'

With the first glimpses of the smooth slope leading down to the grotesque cedars and out to the Pass, Venters's cool nerve returned. One long survey to the left, then one to the right, satisfied his caution. Leading the burros down to the spur of the rock, he halted at the steep incline.

'Bess, here's the bad place, the place I told you about, with the cut steps. You start down, leading your burro. Take your time and hold on to him if you slip. I've got a rope on him and a half-hitch on this point of rock, so I can let him down safely. Coming up here was a killing job. But it'll be easy going down.'

Both burros passed down the difficult stairs cut by the cliff-dwellers, and did it without a misstep. After that the descent down the slope and over the mile of scrawled, ribbed, and ridged rock required only careful guidance, and Venters got the burros to level ground in a condition that caused him to congratulate himself.

'Oh, if we only had Wrangle!' exclaimed Venters. 'But we're lucky. That's the worst of our trail passed. We've only men to fear now. If we get up in the sage we can hide and slip along like coyotes.'

They mounted and rode west through the valley and entered the canõn. From time to time Venters walked, leading his burro. When they got by all the canõns and gullies opening into the Pass they went faster and with fewer halts. Venters did not confide in Bess the alarming fact that he had seen horses and smoke less than a mile up one of the intersecting canõns. He did not talk at all. And long after he had passed this canõn and felt secure once more in the certainty that they had been unobserved he never relaxed his watchfulness. But he did not walk any more, and he kept the burros at a steady trot. Night fell before they reached the last water in the Pass and they made camp by starlight. Venters did not want the burros to stray, so he tied them with long halters in the grass near the spring. Bess, tired out and silent, laid her head in a saddle and went to sleep between the two dogs. Venters did not close his eyes. The canõn silence appeared full of the low, continuous hum of insects. He listened until the hum grew into a roar, and then, breaking the spell, once more he heard it low and clear. He watched the stars and the moving shadows, and always his glance returned to the girl's dimly pale face. And he remembered how white and still it had once looked in the starlight. And again stern thought fought his strange fancies. Would all his labor and his love be for naught? Would he lose her, after all? Did calamity lurk on that long upland trail through the sage? Why should his heart swell and throb with nameless fear? He listened to the silence, and told himself that in the broad light of day he could dispel this leaden-weighted dread.

At the first hint of gray over the eastern rim he awoke Bess, saddled the burros, and began the day's travel. He wanted to get out of the Pass before there was any chance of riders coming down. They gained the break as the first red rays of the rising sun colored the rim.

For once, so eager was he to get up to level ground, he did not send Ring or Whitie in advance. Encouraging Bess to hurry, pulling at his patient, plodding burro, he climbed the soft, steep trail.

Brighter and brighter grew the light. He mounted the last broken edge of rim to have the sun-fired, purple sage-slope burst upon him as a glory. Bess panted up to his side, tugging on the halter of her burro.

'We're up!' he cried, joyously. 'There's not a dot on the sage. We're safe. We'll not be seen! Oh, Bess—'

Ring growled and sniffed the keen air and bristled. Venters clutched at his rifle. Whitie sometimes made a mistake, but Ring never. The dull thud of hoofs almost deprived Venters of power to turn and see from where disaster threatened. He felt his eyes dilate as he stared at Lassiter leading Black Star and Night out of the sage, with Jane Withersteen, in rider's costume, close beside them.

For an instant Venters felt himself whirl dizzily in the center of vast circles of sage. He recovered partially, enough to see Lassiter standing with a glad smile and Jane riveted in astonishment.

'Why, Bern!' she exclaimed. 'How good it is to see you! We're riding away, you see. The storm burst—and I'm a ruined woman! ... I thought you were alone.'

Venters, unable to speak for consternation, and bewildered out of all sense of what he ought or ought not to do, simply stared at Jane.

'Son, where are you bound for?' asked Lassiter.

'Not safe—where I was. I'm—we're going out of Utah—back East,' he found tongue to say.

'I reckon this meetin's the luckiest thing that ever happened to you an' to me—an' to Jane—an' to Bess,' said Lassiter, coolly.

'*Bess!*' cried Jane, with a sudden leap of blood to her pale cheek.

It was entirely beyond Venters to see any luck in that meeting.

Jane Withersteen took one flashing, woman's glance at Bess's scarlet face, at her slender, shapely form.

'Venters! is this a girl—a woman?' she questioned, in a voice that stung.

'Yes.'

'Did you have her in that wonderful valley?'

'Yes, but Jane—'

'All the time you were gone?'

'Yes, but I couldn't tell—'

'Was it for *her* you asked me to give you supplies? Was it for *her* that you wanted to make your valley a paradise?'

'Oh—Jane—'

'Answer me.'

'Yes.'

'Oh, you liar!' And with these passionate words Jane Withersteen succumbed to fury. For the second time in her life she fell into the ungovernable rage that had been her father's weakness. And it was worse than his, for she was a jealous woman—jealous even of her friends.

As best he could, he bore the brunt of her anger. It was not only his deceit to her that she visited upon him, but her betrayal by religion, by life itself.

Her passion, like fire at white heat, consumed itself in little time. Her physical strength failed, and still her spirit attempted to go on in magnificent denunciation of those who had wronged her. Like a tree cut deep into its roots, she began to quiver and shake, and her anger weakened into despair. And her ringing voice sank into a broken, husky whisper. Then, spent and pitiable, upheld by Lassiter's arm, she turned and hid her face in Black Star's mane.

Numb as Venters was when at length Jane Withersteen lifted her head and looked at him, he yet suffered a pang.

'Jane, the girl is innocent!' he cried.

'Can you expect me to believe that?' she asked, with weary, bitter eyes.

'I'm not that kind of a liar. And you know it. If I lied—if I kept silent when honor should have made me speak, it was to spare you. I came to Cottonwoods to tell you. But I couldn't add to your pain. I intended to tell you I had come to love this girl. But, Jane, I hadn't forgotten how good you were to me. I haven't changed at all toward you. I prize your friendship as I always have. But, however it may look to you—don't be unjust. The girl is innocent. Ask Lassiter.'

'Jane, she's jest as sweet an' innocent as little Fay,' said Lassiter. There was a faint smile upon his face and a beautiful light.

Venters saw, and knew that Lassiter saw, how Jane Withersteen's tortured soul wrestled with hate and threw it—with scorn, doubt, suspicion, and overcame all.

'Bern, if in my misery I accused you unjustly, I crave forgiveness,' she said. 'I'm not what I once was. Tell me—who is this girl?'

'Jane, she is Oldring's daughter, and his Masked Rider. Lassiter will tell you how I shot her for a rustler, saved her life—all the story. It's a strange story, Jane, as wild as the sage. But it's true—true as her innocence. That you must believe!'

'Oldring's Masked Rider! Oldring's daughter!' exclaimed Jane. 'And she's innocent! You ask me to believe much. If this girl is—is what you say, how could she be going away with the man who killed her father?'

'Why did you tell that?' cried Venters, passionately.

Jane's question had roused Bess out of stupefaction. Her eyes suddenly darkened and dilated. She stepped toward Venters and held up both hands as if to ward off a blow.

'Did—did you kill Oldring?'

'I did, Bess, and I hate myself for it. But you know I never dreamed he was your father. I thought he'd wronged you. I killed him when I was madly jealous.'

For a moment Bess was shocked into silence.

'But he was my father!' she broke out, at last. 'And now I must go back—I can't go with you. It's all over—that beautiful dream. Oh, I *knew* it couldn't come true. You can't take me now.'

'If you forgive me, Bess, it'll all come right in the end!' implored Venters.

'It can't be right. I'll go back. After all, I loved him. He was good to me. I can't forget that.'

'If you go back to Oldring's men I'll follow you, and then they'll kill me,' said Venters, hoarsely.

'Oh no, Bern, you'll not come. Let me go. It's best for you to forget me. I've brought you only pain and dishonor.'

She did not weep. But the sweet bloom and life died out of her face. She looked haggard and sad, all at once stunted; and her hands dropped listlessly; and her head drooped in slow, final acceptance of a hopeless fate.

'Jane, look there!' cried Venters, in despairing grief. 'Need you have told her? Where was all your kindness of heart? This girl has had a wretched, lonely life. And I'd found a way to make her happy. You've killed it. You've killed something sweet and pure and hopeful, just as sure as you breathe.'

'Oh, Bern! It was a slip. I never thought—I never thought!' replied Jane. 'How could I tell she didn't know?'

Lassiter suddenly moved forward, and with the beautiful light on his face now strangely luminous, he looked at Jane and Venters and then let his soft, bright gaze rest on Bess.

'Well, I reckon you've all had your say, an' now it's Lassiter's turn. Why, I was jest prayin' for this meetin'. Bess, jest look here.'

Gently he touched her arm and turned her to face the others, and then outspread his great hand to disclose a shiny, battered gold locket.

'Open it,' he said, with a singularly rich voice.

Bess complied, but listlessly.

'Jane—Venters—come closer,' went on Lassiter. 'Take a look at the picture. Don't you know the woman?'

Jane, after one glance, drew back.

'Milly Erne!' she cried, wonderingly.

Venters, with tingling pulse, with something growing on him, recognized in the faded miniature portrait the eyes of Milly Erne.

'Yes, that's Milly,' said Lassiter, softly. 'Bess, did you ever see her face—look hard—with all your heart an' soul?'

'The eyes seem to haunt me,' whispered Bess. 'Oh, I can't remember—they're eyes of my dreams—but—but—'

Lassiter's strong arm went round her and he bent his head.

'Child, I thought you'd remember her eyes. They're the same beautiful eyes you'd see if you looked in a mirror or a clear spring. They're your mother's eyes. You are Milly Erne's child. Your name is Elizabeth Erne. You're not Oldring's daughter. You're the daughter of Frank Erne, a man once my best friend. Look! Here's his picture beside Milly's. He was handsome, an' as fine an' gallant a Southern gentleman as I ever seen. Frank come of an old family. You come of the best of blood, lass, an' blood tells.'

Bess slipped through his arm to her knees and hugged the locket to her bosom, and lifted wonderful, yearning eyes.

'It—can't—be—true!'

'Thank God, lass, it is true,' replied Lassiter. 'Jane an' Bern here—they both recognize Milly. They see Milly in you. They're so knocked out they can't tell you, that's all.'

'Who are you?' whispered Bess.

'I reckon I'm Milly's brother an' your uncle! … Uncle Jim! Ain't that fine?'

'Oh, I can't believe—Don't raise me! Bern, let me kneel. I see truth in your face—in Miss Withersteen's. But let me hear it all—on my knees. Tell me how it's true!'

'Well, Elizabeth, listen,' said Lassiter. 'Before you was born your father made a mortal enemy of a Mormon named Dyer. They was both ministers an' come to be rivals. Dyer stole your mother away from her home. She gave birth to you in Texas eighteen years ago. Then she was taken to Utah, from place to place, an' finally to the last border settlement—Cottonwoods. You was about three years old when you was taken away from Milly. She never knew what had become of you. But she lived a good while hopin' and prayin' to have you again. Then she gave up an' died. An' I may as well put in here your father died ten years ago. Well, I spent my time tracin' Milly, an' some months back I landed in Cottonwoods. An' jest lately I learned all about you. I had a talk with Oldrin' an' told him you was dead, an' he told me what I had so long been wantin' to know. It was Dyer, of course, who stole you from Milly. Part reason he was sore because Milly refused to give you Mormon teachin', but mostly he still hated Frank Erne so infernally that he made a deal with Oldrin' to take you an' bring you up as an infamous rustler an' rustler's girl. The idea was to break Frank Erne's heart if he ever came to Utah—to show him his daughter with a band of low rustlers. Well—Oldrin' took you, brought you up from childhood, an' then made you his Masked Rider. He made you infamous. He kept that part of the contract, but he learned to love you as a daughter an' never let any but his own men know you was a girl. I heard him say that with my own ears, an' I saw his big eyes grow dim. He told me how he had guarded you always, kept you locked up in his absence, was always at your side or near you on those rides that made you famous on the sage. He said he an' an old rustler whom he trusted had taught you how to read an' write. They selected the books for you. Dyer had wanted you brought up the vilest of the vile! An' Oldrin' brought you up the innocentest of the innocent. He said you didn't know what vileness was. I can hear his big voice tremble now as he said it. He told me how the men—rustlers an' outlaws—who from time to time tried to approach you familiarly—he told me how he shot them dead. I'm tellin' you this 'specially because you've showed such shame—sayin' you was nameless an' all that. Nothin' on earth can be wronger than that idea of yours. An' the truth of it is here. Oldrin' swore to me that if Dyer died, releasin' the contract, he intended to hunt up your father an' give you back to him. It seems Oldrin' wasn't all bad, an' he sure loved you.'

Venters leaned forward in passionate remorse.

'Oh, Bess! I know Lassiter speaks the truth. For when I shot Oldring he dropped to his knees and fought with unearthly power to speak. And he said: "Man—why—didn't—you—wait? Bess was—" Then he fell dead. And I've been haunted by his look and words. Oh, Bess, what a strange, splendid thing for Oldring to do! It all seems impossible. But, dear, you really are not what you thought.'

'Elizabeth Erne!' cried Jane Withersteen. 'I loved your mother and I see her in you!'

What had been incredible from the lips of men became, in the tone, look, and gesture of a woman, a wonderful truth for Bess. With little tremblings of all her slender body she rocked to and fro on her knees. The yearning wistfulness of her eyes changed to solemn splendor of joy. She believed. She was realizing happiness. And as the process of thought was slow, so were the variations of her expression. Her eyes reflected the transformation of her soul. Dark, brooding, hopeless belief—clouds of gloom—drifted, paled, vanished in glorious light. An exquisite rose flush—a glow—shone from her face as she slowly began to rise from her knees. A spirit uplifted her. All that she had held as base dropped from her.

Venters watched her in joy too deep for words. By it he divined something of what Lassiter's revelation meant to Bess, but he knew he could only faintly understand. That moment when she seemed to be lifted by some spiritual transfiguration was the most beautiful moment of his life. She stood with parted, quivering lips, with hands tightly clasping the locket to her heaving breast. A new conscious pride of worth dignified the old, wild, free grace and poise.

'Uncle Jim!' she said, tremulously, with a different smile from any Venters had ever seen on her face.

Lassiter took her into his arms.

'I reckon. It's powerful fine to hear that,' replied Lassiter, unsteadily.

Venters, feeling his eyes grow hot and wet, turned away, and found himself looking at Jane Withersteen. He had almost forgotten her presence. Tenderness and sympathy were fast hiding traces of her agitation. Venters read her mind—felt the reaction of her noble heart—saw the joy she was beginning to feel at the happiness of others. And suddenly blinded, choked by his emotions, he turned from her also. He knew what she would do presently; she would make some magnificent amend for her anger; she would give some manifestation of her love; probably all in a moment, as she had loved Milly Erne, so would she love Elizabeth Erne.

' 'Pears to me, folks, that we'd better talk a little serious now,' remarked Lassiter, at length. 'Time flies.'

'You're right,' replied Venters, instantly. 'I'd forgotten time—place—danger. Lassiter, you're riding away. Jane's leaving Withersteen House?'

'Forever,' replied Jane.

'I fired Withersteen House,' said Lassiter.

'Dyer?' questioned Venters, sharply.

'I reckon where Dyer's gone there won't be any kidnappin' of girls.'

'Ah! I knew it. I told Judkins—And Tull?' went on Venters, passionately.

'Tull wasn't around when I broke loose. By now he's likely on our trail with his riders.'

'Lassiter, you're going into the Pass to hide till all this storm blows over?'

'I reckon that's Jane's idea. I'm thinkin' the storm'll be a powerful long time blowin' over. I was comin' to join you in Surprise Valley. You'll go back now with me?'

'No. I want to take Bess out of Utah. Lassiter, Bess found gold in the valley. We've a saddle-bag full of gold. If we can reach Sterling—'

'Man! how're you ever goin' to do that? Sterlin' is a hundred miles.'

'My plan is to ride on, keeping a sharp lookout. Somewhere up the trail we'll take to the sage and go round Cottonwoods and then hit the trail again.'

'It's a bad plan. You'll kill the burros in two days.'

'Then we'll walk.'

'That's more bad an' worse. Better go back down the Pass with me.'

'Lassiter, this girl has been hidden all her life in that lonely place,' went on Venters. 'Oldring's men are hunting me. We'd not be safe there any longer. Even if we would be I'd take this chance to get her out. I want to marry her. She shall have some of the pleasures—of life—see cities and people. We've gold—we'll be rich. Why, life opens sweet for both of us. And, by Heaven! I'll get her out or lose my life in the attempt!'

'I reckon if you go on with them burros you'll lose your life all right. Tull will have riders all over this sage. You can't get out on them burros. It's a fool idea. That's not doin' best by the girl. Come with me an' take chances on the rustlers.'

Lassiter's cool arguments made Venters waver, not in determination to go, but in hope of success.

'Bess, I want you to know. Lassiter says the trip's almost useless now. I'm afraid he's right. We've got about one chance in a hundred to go through. Shall we take it? Shall we go on?'

'We'll go on,' replied Bess.

'That settles it, Lassiter.'

Lassiter spread wide his hands, as if to signify he could do no more, and his face clouded.

Venters felt a touch on his elbow. Jane stood beside him with a hand on his arm. She was smiling. Something radiated from her, and like an electric current accelerated the motion of his blood.

'Bern, you'd be right to die rather than not take Elizabeth out of Utah—out of this wild country. You must do it. You'll show her the great world, with all its wonders. Think how little she has seen! Think what delight is in store for her! You have gold; you will be free; you will make her happy. What a glorious prospect! I share it with you. I'll think of you—dream of you—pray for you.'

'Thank you, Jane,' replied Venters, trying to steady his voice. 'It looks bright. Oh, if we were only across that wide, open waste of sage!'

'Bern, the trip's as good as made. It'll be safe—easy. It'll be a glorious ride,' she said, softly.

Venters stared. Had Jane's troubles made her insane? Lassiter, too, acted queerly, all at once beginning to turn his sombrero round with hands that actually shook.

'You are a rider. She is a rider. This will be the ride of your lives,' added Jane, in that same soft undertone, almost as if she were musing to herself.

'Jane!' he cried.

'I give you Black Star and Night!'

'*Black Star and Night!*' he echoed.

'It's done. Lassiter, put our saddle-bags on the burros.'

Only when Lassiter moved swiftly to execute her bidding did Venters's clogged brain grasp at literal meanings. He leaped to catch Lassiter's busy hands.

'No, no! What are you doing?' he demanded, in a kind of fury. 'I won't take her racers. What do you think I am? It'd be monstrous. Lassiter! stop it, I say! … You've got her to save. You've miles and miles to go. Tull is trailing you. There are rustlers in the Pass. Give me back that saddle-bag!'

'Son—cool down,' returned Lassiter, in a voice he might have used to a child. But the grip with which he tore away Venters's grasping hands was that of a giant. 'Listen—you fool boy! Jane's sized up the situation. The burros'll do for us. We'll sneak along an' hide. I'll take your dogs an' your rifle. Why, it's the trick. The blacks are yours, an' sure as I can throw a gun you're goin' to ride safe out of the sage.'

'Jane—stop him—please stop him,' gasped Venters. 'I've lost my strength. I can't do—anything. This's hell for me! Can't you see that? I've ruined you—it was through me you lost all. You've only Black Star and Night left. You love these horses. Oh! I know how you must love them now! And—you're trying to give them to me. To help me out of Utah! To save the girl I love!'

'That will be my glory.'

Then in the white, rapt face, in the unfathomable eyes, Venters saw Jane Withersteen in a supreme moment. This moment was one wherein she reached up to the height for which her noble soul had ever yearned. He, after disrupting the calm tenor of her peace, after bringing down on her head the implacable hostility of her churchmen, after teaching her a bitter lesson of life—he was to be her salvation. And he turned away again, this time shaken to the core of his soul. Jane Withersteen was the incarnation of selflessness. He experienced wonder and terror, exquisite pain and rapture. What were all the shocks life had dealt him compared to the thought of such loyal and generous friendship?

And instantly, as if by some divine insight, he knew himself in the remaking—

tried, found wanting; but stronger, better, surer—and he wheeled to Jane Witherseen, eager, joyous, passionate, wild, exalted. He bent to her; he left tears and kisses on her hands.

'Jane, I—I can't find words—now,' he said. 'I'm beyond words. Only—I understand. And I'll take the blacks.'

'Don't be losin' no more time,' cut in Lassiter. 'I ain't certain, but I think I seen a speck up the sage-slope. Mebbe I was mistaken. But, anyway, we must all be movin'. I've shortened the stirrups on Black Star. Put Bess on him.'

Jane Withersteen held out her arms.

'Elizabeth Erne!' she cried, and Bess flew to her.

How inconceivably strange and beautiful it was for Venters to see Bess clasped to Jane Withersteen's breast!

Then he leaped astride Night.

'Venters, ride straight on up the slope,' Lassiter was saying, 'an' if you don't meet any riders keep on till you're a few miles from the village, then cut off in the sage an' go round to the trail. But you'll most likely meet riders with Tull. Jest keep right on till you're just out of gunshot an' then make your cut-off into the sage. They'll ride after you, but it won't be no use. You can ride, an' Bess can ride. When you're out of reach turn on round to the west, an' hit the trail somewhere. Save the hosses all you can, but don't be afraid. Black Star and Night are good for a hundred miles before sundown, if you have to push them. You can get to Sterlin' by night if you want. But better make it along about tomorrow mornin'. When you get through the notch on the Glaze trail, swing to the right. You'll be able to see both Glaze an' Stone Bridge. Keep away from them villages. You won't run no risk of meetin' any of Oldrin's rustlers from Sterlin' on. You'll find water in them deep hollows north of the Notch. There's an old trail there, not much used, an' it leads to Sterlin'. That's your trail. An' one thing more. If Tull pushes you—or keeps on persistent-like, for a few miles—jest let the blacks out an' lose him an' his riders.'

'Lassiter, may we meet again!' said Venters, in a deep voice.

'Son, it ain't likely—it ain't likely. Well, Bess Oldrin'—Masked Rider—Elizabeth Erne—now you climb on Black Star. I've heard you could ride. Well, every rider loves a good hoss. An', lass, there never was but one that could beat Black Star.'

'Ah, Lassiter, there never was any horse that could beat Black Star,' said Jane, with the old pride.

'I often wondered—mebbe Venters rode out that race when he brought back the blacks. Son, was Wrangle the best hoss?'

'No, Lassiter,' replied Venters. For this lie he had his reward in Jane's quick smile.

'Well, well, my hoss-sense ain't always right. An' here I'm talkin' a lot, wastin' time. It ain't so easy to find an' lose a pretty niece all in one hour! Elizabeth— good-bye!'

'Oh, Uncle Jim! ... Good-bye!'

'Elizabeth Erne, be happy! Good-bye,' said Jane.

'Good-bye—oh—good-bye!'

In lithe, supple action Bess swung up to Black Star's saddle.

'Jane Withersteen! ... Good-bye!' called Venters hoarsely.

'Bern—Bess—riders of the purple sage—good-bye!'

TWENTY-TWO
Riders of the Purple Sage

Black Star and Night, answering to spur, swept swiftly westward along the white, slow-rising, sage-bordered trail. Venters heard a mournful howl from Ring, but Whitie was silent. The blacks settled into their fleet, long-striding gallop. The wind sweetly fanned Venters's hot face. From the summit of the first low-swelling ridge he looked back. Lassiter waved his hand; Jane waved her scarf. Venters replied by standing in his stirrups and holding high his sombrero. Then the dip of the ridge hid them. From the height of the next he turned once more. Lassiter, Jane, and the burros had disappeared. They had gone down into the Pass. Venters felt a sensation of irreparable loss.

'Bern—look!' called Bess, pointing up the long slope.

A small, dark, moving dot split the line where purple sage met blue sky. That dot was a band of riders.

'Pull the black, Bess.'

They slowed from gallop to canter, then to trot. The fresh and eager horses did not like the check.

'Bern, Black Star has great eyesight.'

'I wonder if they're Tull's riders. They might be rustlers. But it's all the same to us."

The black dot grew to a dark patch moving under low dust-clouds. It grew all the time, though very slowly. There were long periods when it was in plain sight, and intervals when it dropped behind the sage. The blacks trotted for half an hour, for another half-hour, and still the moving patch appeared to stay on the horizon line. Gradually, however, as time passed, it began to enlarge, to creep down the slope, to encroach upon the intervening distance.

'Bess, what do you make them out?' asked Venters. 'I don't think they're rustlers.'

'They're sage-riders,' replied Bess. 'I see a white horse and several grays. Rustlers seldom ride any horses but bays and blacks.'

'That white horse is Tull's. Pull the black, Bess. I'll get down and cinch up. We're in for some riding. Are you afraid?'

'Not now,' answered the girl, smiling.

'You needn't be. Bess, you don't weigh enough to make Black Star know you're on him. I won't be able to stay with you. You'll leave Tull and his riders as if they were standing still.'

'How about you?'

'Never fear. If I can't stay with you I can still laugh at Tull.'

'Look, Bern! They've stopped on that ridge. They see us.'

'Yes. But we're too far yet for them to make out who we are. They'll recognize the blacks first. We've passed most of the ridges and the thickest sage. Now, when I give the word, let Black Star go and ride!'

Venters calculated that a mile or more still intervened between them and the riders. They were approaching at a swift canter. Soon Venters recognized Tull's white horse, and concluded that the riders had likewise recognized Black Star and Night. But it would be impossible for Tull yet to see that the blacks were not ridden by Lassiter and Jane. Venters noted that Tull and the line of horsemen, perhaps ten or twelve in number, stopped several times and evidently looked hard down the slope. It must have been a puzzling circumstance for Tull. Venters laughed grimly at the thought of what Tull's rage would be when he finally discovered the trick. Venters meant to sheer out into the sage before Tull could possibly be sure who rode the blacks.

The gap closed to a distance of half a mile. Tull halted. His riders came up and formed a dark group around him. Venters thought he saw him wave his arms, and was certain of it when the riders dashed into the sage, to right and left of the trail. Tull had anticipated just the move held in mind by Venters.

'Now Bess!' shouted Venters. 'Strike north. Go round those riders and turn west.'

Black Star sailed over the low sage, and in few leaps got into his stride and was running. Venters spurred Night after him. It was hard going in the sage. The horses could run as well there, but keen eyesight and judgment must constantly be used by the riders in choosing ground. And continuous swerving from aisle to aisle between the brush, and leaping little washes and mounds of the pack-rats, and breaking through sage, made rough riding. When Venters had turned into a long aisle he had time to look up at Tull's riders. They were now strung out into an extended line riding northeast. And, as Venters and Bess were holding due north, this meant, if the horses of Tull and his riders had the speed and the staying power, they would head the blacks and turn them back down the slope. Tull's men were not saving their mounts; they were driving them desperately. Venters feared only an accident to Black Star or Night, and skillful riding would mitigate possibility of that. One glance ahead served to show him that Bess could pick a course through the sage as well as he. She looked neither back nor at the running riders, and bent forward over Black Star's neck and studied the ground ahead.

It struck Venters, presently, after he had glanced up from time to time, that Bess was drawing away from him as he had expected. He had, however, only thought of the light weight Black Star was carrying and of his superior speed; he saw now that the black was being ridden as never before, except when Jerry Card lost the race to Wrangle. How easily, gracefully, naturally, Bess sat at her saddle! She could ride! Suddenly Venters remembered she had said she could ride. But he had not dreamed she was capable of such superb horsemanship. Then all at once, flashing over him, thrilling him, came the recollection that Bess was Oldring's Masked Rider.

He forgot Tull—the running riders—the race. He let Night have a free rein and felt him lengthen out to suit himself, knowing he would keep to Black Star's course, knowing that he had been chosen by the best rider now on the upland sage. For Jerry Card was dead. And fame had rivaled him with only one rider, and that was the slender girl who now swung so easily with Black Star's stride. Venters had abhorred her notoriety, but now he took passionate pride in her skill, her daring, her power over a horse. And he delved into his memory, recalling famous rides which he had heard related in the villages and round the camp-fires. Oldring's Masked Rider! Many times this strange rider, at once well known and unknown, had escaped pursuers by matchless riding. He had run the gauntlet of vigilantes down the main street of Stone Bridge, leaving dead horses and dead rustlers behind. He had jumped his horse over the Gerber Wash, a deep, wide ravine separating the fields of Glaze from the wild sage. He had been surrounded north of Sterling; and he had broken through the line. How often had been told the story of day stampedes, of night raids, of pursuit, and then how the Masked Rider, swift as the wind, was gone in the sage! A fleet, dark horse—a slender, dark form—a black mask—a driving run down the slope—a dot on the purple sage—a shadowy, muffled steed disappearing in the night!

And this Masked Rider of the uplands had been Elizabeth Erne!

The sweet sage wind rushed in Venters's face and sang a song in his ears. He heard the dull, rapid beat of Night's hoofs; he saw Black Star drawing away, farther and farther. He realized both horses were swinging to the west. Then gunshots in the rear reminded him of Tull. Venters looked back. Far to the side, dropping behind, trooped the riders. They were shooting. Venters saw no puffs of dust, heard no whistling bullets. He was out of range. When he looked back again Tull's riders had given up pursuit. The best they could do, no doubt, had been to get near enough to recognize who really rode the blacks. Venters saw Tull drooping in his saddle.

Then Venters pulled Night out of his running stride. Those few miles had scarcely warmed the black, but Venters wished to save him. Bess turned, and, though she was far away, Venters caught the white glint of her waving hand. He held Night to a trot and rode on, seeing Bess and Black Star, and the sloping upward stretch of sage, and from time to time the receding black riders behind. Soon they disappeared behind a ridge, and he turned no more. They would go back to Lassiter's trail and follow it, and follow in vain. So Venters rode on, with the wind growing sweeter to taste and smell, and the purple sage richer and the sky bluer in his sight; and the song in his ears ringing. By and by Bess halted to wait for him, and he knew she had come to the trail. When he reached her it was to smile at sight of her standing with arms round Black Star's neck.

'Oh, Bern! I love him!' she cried. 'He's beautiful; he knows; and how he can run! I've had fast horses. But Black Star! … Wrangle never beat him!'

'I'm wondering if I didn't dream that. Bess, the blacks are grand. What it must have cost Jane—ah!—well, when we get out of this wild country with Star and Night, back to my old home in Illinois, we'll buy a beautiful farm with meadows and springs and cool shade. There we'll turn the horses free—free to roam and browse and drink—never to feel a spur again—never to be ridden!'

'I would like that,' said Bess.

They rested. Then, mounting, they rode side by side up the white trail. The sun rose higher behind them. Far to the left a low line of green marked the site of Cottonwoods. Venters looked once and looked no more. Bess gazed only straight ahead. They put the blacks to the long, swinging rider's canter, and at times pulled them to a trot, and occasionally to a walk. The hours passed, the miles slipped behind, and the wall of rock loomed in the fore. The Notch opened wide. It was a rugged, stony pass, but with level and open trail, and Venters and Bess ran the blacks through it. An old trail led off to the right, taking the line of the wall, and this Venters knew to be the trail mentioned by Lassiter.

The little hamlet, Glaze, a white and green patch in the vast waste of purple, lay miles down a slope much like the Cottonwoods slope, only this descended to the west. And miles farther west a faint green spot marked the location of Stone Bridge. All the rest of that world was seemingly smooth, undulating sage, with no ragged lines of canõns to accentuate its wildness.

'Bess, we're safe—we're free!' said Venters. 'We're alone on the sage. We're half way to Sterling.'

'Ah! I wonder how it is with Lassiter and Miss Withersteen.'

'Never fear, Bess. He'll outwit Tull. He'll get away and hide her safely. He might climb into Surprise Valley, but I don't think he'll go so far.'

'Bern, will we ever find any place like our beautiful valley?'

'No. But, dear, listen. We'll go back some day, after years—ten years. Then we'll be forgotten. And our valley will be just as we left it.'

'What if Balancing Rock falls and closes the outlet to the Pass?'

'I've thought of that. I'll pack in ropes and ropes. And if the outlet's closed we'll climb up the cliffs and over them to the valley and go down on rope ladders. It could be done. I know just where to make the climb, and I'll never forget.'

'Oh, yes, let us go back!'

'It's something sweet to look forward to. Bess, it's like all the future looks to me.'

'Call me—Elizabeth,' she said shyly.

'Elizabeth Erne! It's a beautiful name. But I'll never forget Bess. Do you know—have you thought that very soon—by this time tomorrow—you will be Elizabeth Venters?'

So they rode on down the old trail. And the sun sloped to the west, and a golden sheen lay on the sage. The hours sped now; the afternoon waned. Often they rested the horses. The glisten of a pool of water in a hollow caught Venters's eye, and here he unsaddled the blacks and let them roll and drink and browse. When he and Bess rode up out of the hollow the sun was low, a crimson ball, and the valley seemed veiled in purple fire and smoke. It was that short time when the sun appeared to rest before setting, and silence, like a cloak of invisible life, lay heavy on all that shimmering world of sage.

They watched the sun begin to bury its red curve under the dark horizon.

'We'll ride on till late,' he said. 'Then you can sleep a little, while I watch and graze the horses. And we'll ride into Sterling early tomorrow. We'll be married! … We'll be in time to catch the stage. We'll tie Black Star and Night behind—and then—for a country not wild and terrible like this!'

'Oh, Bern! … But look! The sun is setting on the sage—the last time for us till we dare come again to the Utah border. Ten years! Oh, Bern, look, so you will never forget!'

Slumbering, fading purple fire burned over the undulating sage ridges. Long streaks and bars and shafts and spears fringed the far western slope. Drifting, golden veils mingled with low, purple shadows. Colors and shades changed in slow, wondrous transformation.

Suddenly Venters was startled by a low, rumbling roar—so low that it was like the roar in a sea-shell.

'Bess, did you hear anything?' he whispered.

'No.'

'Listen! ... Maybe I only imagined ... *Ah!*'

Out of the east or north, from remote distance, breathed an infinitely low, continuously long sound—deep, weird, detonating, thundering, deadening—dying.

TWENTY-THREE
The Fall of Balancing Rock

Through tear-blurred sight Jane Withersteen watched Venters and Elizabeth Erne and the black racers disappear over the ridge of sage.

'They're gone!' said Lassiter. 'An' they're safe now. An' there'll be a day of their comin' happy lives but what they'll remember Jane Withersteen an'—an' Uncle Jim! ... I reckon, Jane, we'd better be on our way.'

The burros obediently wheeled and started down the break with little, cautious steps, but Lassiter had to leash the whining dogs and lead them. Jane felt herself bound in a feeling that was neither listlessness nor indifference, yet which rendered her incapable of interest. She was still strong in body, but emotionally tired. That hour at the entrance to Deception Pass had been the climax of her suffering—the flood of her wrath—the last of her sacrifice—the supremity of her love—and the attainment of peace. She thought that if she had little Fay she would not ask any more of life.

Like an automaton she followed Lassiter down the steep trail of dust and bits of weathered stone; and when the little slides moved with her or piled around her knees she experienced no alarm. Vague relief came to her in the sense of being enclosed between dark stone walls, deep hidden from the glare of sun, from the glistening sage. Lassiter lengthened the stirrup straps on one of the burros and bade her mount and ride close to him. She was to keep the burro from cracking his little hard hoofs on stones. Then she was riding on between dark, gleaming walls. There were quiet and rest and coolness in this cañon. She noted indifferently that they passed close under shady, bulging shelves of cliff, through patches of grass and sage and thicket and groves of slender trees, and over white, pebbly washes, and around masses of broken rock. The burros trotted tirelessly; the dogs, once more free, pattered tirelessly; and Lassiter led on with never a stop, and at every open place he looked back. The shade under the walls gave place to sunlight. And presently they came to a dense thicket of slender trees, through which they passed to rich, green grass and water. Here Lassiter rested the burros for a little while, but he was restless, uneasy, silent, always listening, peering under the trees. She dully reflected that enemies were behind them—before them; still the thought awakened no dread or concern or interest.

At his bidding she mounted and rode on close to the heels of his burro. The cañon narrowed; the walls lifted their rugged rims higher; and the sun shone down hot from the center of the blue stream of sky above. Lassiter traveled slower, with more exceeding care as to the ground he chose, and he kept speaking low to the dogs. They were now hunting-dogs—keen, alert, suspicious, sniffing the warm breeze. The monotony of the yellow walls broke in change of color and smooth surface, and the rugged outline of rims grew craggy. Splits appeared in deep breaks, and gorges running at right angles, and then the Pass opened wide at a junction of intersecting cañons.

Lassiter dismounted, led his burro, called the dogs close, and proceeded at snail pace through dark masses of rock and dense thickets under the left wall. Long he watched and listened before venturing to cross the mouths of side cañons. At length he halted, tied his burro, lifted a warning hand to Jane, and then slipped away among the boulders, and, followed by the stealthy dogs, disappeared from sight. The time he remained absent was neither short nor long to Jane Withersteen.

When he reached her side again he was pale, and his lips were set in a hard line, and his gray eyes glittered coldly. Bidding her dismount, he led the burros into a covert of stones and cedars, and tied them.

'Jane, I've run into the fellers I've been lookin' for, an' I'm goin' after them,' he said.

'Why?' she asked.

'I reckon I won't take time to tell you.'

'Couldn't we slip by without being seen?'

'Likely enough. But that ain't my game. An' I'd like to know, in case I don't come back, what you'll do.'

'What can I do?'

'I reckon you can go back to Tull. Or stay in the Pass an' be taken off by rustlers. Which'll you do?'

'I don't know. I can't think very well. But I believe I'd rather be taken off by rustlers.'

Lassiter sat down, put his head in his hands, and remained for a few moments in what appeared to be deep and painful thought. When he lifted his face it was haggard, lined, cold as sculptured marble.

'I'll go. I only mentioned that chance of my not comin' back. I'm pretty sure to come.'

'Need you risk so much? Must you fight more? Haven't you shed enough blood?'

'I'd like to tell you why I'm goin',' he continued, in coldness he had seldom used to her. She remarked it, but it was the same to her as if he had spoken with his old gentle warmth. 'But I reckon I won't. Only, I'll say that mercy an' goodness, such as is in you, though they're the grand things in human nature, can't be lived up to on this Utah border. Life's hell out here. You think—or you used to think—that your religion made this life heaven. Mebbe them scales on your eyes has dropped now, Jane, I wouldn't have you no different, an' that's why I'm goin' to try to hide you somewhere in this Pass. I'd like to hide many more women, for I've come to see there are more like you among your people. An' I'd like you to see jest how hard an' cruel this border life is. It's bloody. You'd think churches an' churchmen would make it better. They make it worse. You give names to things—bishops, elders, ministers, Mormonism, duty, faith, glory. You dream— or you're driven mad. I'm a man, an' I know. I name fanatics, followers, blind women, oppressors, thieves, ranchers, rustlers, riders. An' we have—what you've lived through these last months. It can't be helped. But it can't last always. An' remember this—some day the border'll be better, cleaner, for the ways of men like Lassiter!'

She saw him shake his tall form erect, look at her strangely and steadfastly, and then, noiselessly, stealthily slip away amid the rocks and trees. Ring and Whitie, not being bidden to follow, remained with Jane. She felt extreme weariness, yet somehow it did not seem to be of her body. And she sat down in the shade and tried to think. She saw a creeping lizard, cactus flowers, the drooping burros, the resting dogs, an eagle high over a yellow crag. Once the meanest flower, a color, the flight of a bee, or any living thing had given her deepest joy. Lassiter had gone off, yielding to his incurable blood lust, probably to his own death; and she was sorry, but there was no feeling in her sorrow.

Suddenly from the mouth of the cañon just beyond her rang out a clear, sharp report of a rifle. Echoes clapped. Then followed a piercingly high yell of anguish, quickly breaking. Again echoes clapped, in grim imitation. Dull revolver shots— hoarse yells—pound of hoofs—shrill neighs of horses—commingling of echoes—and again silence! Lassiter must be busily engaged, thought Jane, and no chill trembled over her, no blanching tightened her skin. Yes, the border was a bloody place. But life had always been bloody. Men were blood-spillers. Phases of the history of the world flashed through her mind—Greek and Roman wars, dark, medieval times, the crimes in the name of religion. On sea, on land, everywhere—shooting, stabbing, cursing, clashing, fighting men! Greed, power, oppression, fanaticism, love, hate, revenge, justice, freedom—for these, men killed one another.

She lay there under the cedars, gazing up through the delicate lacelike foliage at the blue sky, and she thought and wondered and did not care.

More rattling shots disturbed the noonday quiet. She heard a sliding of weathered rock, a hoarse shout of warning, a yell of alarm, again the clear, sharp crack of the rifle, and another cry that was a cry of death. Then rifle reports pierced a dull volley of revolver shots. Bullets whizzed over Jane's hiding-place; one struck a stone and whined away in the air. After that, for a time, succeeded desultory shots; and then they ceased under long, thundering fire from heavier guns.

Sooner or later, then, Jane heard the cracking of horses' hoofs on the stones, and the sound came nearer and nearer. Silence intervened until Lassiter's soft, jingling step assured her of his approach. When he appeared he was covered with blood.

'All right, Jane,' he said. 'I come back. An' don't worry.'

With water from a canteen he washed the blood from his face and hands.

'Jane, hurry now. Tear my scarf in two, an' tie up these places. That hole through my hand is some inconvenient, worse'n this cut over my ear. There—you're doin' fine! Not a bit nervous—no tremblin'. I reckon I ain't done your courage justice. I'm glad you're brave jest now—you'll need to be. Well, I was hid pretty good, enough to keep them from shootin' me deep, but they was slingin' lead close all the time. I used up all the rifle shells, an' then I went after them. Mebbe you heard. It was then I got hit. I had to use up every shell in my own guns, an' they did, too, as I seen. Rustlers an' Mormons, Jane! An' now I'm packin' five bullet holes in my carcass, an' guns without shells. Hurry, now.'

He unstrapped the saddle-bags from the burros, slipped the saddles and let them lie, turned the burros loose, and, calling the dogs, led the way through stones and cedars to an open where two horses stood.

'Jane, are you strong?' he asked.

'I think so. I'm not tired,' Jane replied.

'I don't mean that way. Can you bear up?'

'I think I can bear anything.'

'I reckon you look a little cold an' thick. So I'm preparing you.'

'For what?'

'I didn't tell you why I jest had to go after them fellers. I couldn't tell you. I believe you'd have died. But I can tell you now—if you'll bear up under a shock?'

'Go on, my friend.'

'*I've got little Fay!* Alive—bad hurt—but she'll live!'

Jane Withersteen's dead-locked feeling, rent by Lassiter's deep, quivering voice, leaped into an agony of sensitive life.

'Here,' he added, and showed her where little Fay lay on the grass.

Unable to speak, unable to stand, Jane dropped on her knees. By that long, beautiful golden hair Jane recognized the beloved Fay. But Fay's loveliness was gone. Her face was drawn and looked old with grief. But she was not dead—her heart beat—and Jane Withersteen gathered strength and lived again.

'You see I jest had to go after Fay,' Lassiter was saying, as he knelt to bathe her little pale face. 'But I reckon I don't want no more choices like the one I had to make. There was a crippled feller in that bunch, Jane. Mebbe Venters crippled him. Anyway, that's why they were holdin' up here. I seen little Fay first thing, an' was hard put to it to figure out a way to get her. An' I wanted hosses, too. I had to take chances. So I crawled close to their camp. One feller jumped a hoss with little Fay, an' when I shot him, of course she dropped. She's stunned an' bruised—she fell right on her head. Jane, she's comin' to! She ain't bad hurt!'

Fay's long lashes fluttered; her eyes opened. At first they seemed glazed over. They looked dazed by pain. Then they quickened, darkened, to shine with intelligence—bewilderment—memory—and sudden wonderful joy.

'Muvver—Jane!' she whispered.

'Oh, little Fay, little Fay!' cried Jane, lifting, clasping the child to her.

'*Now*, we've got to rustle!' said Lassiter, in grim coolness. 'Jane, look down the Pass!'

Across the mounds of rock and sage Jane caught sight of a band of riders filing out of the narrow neck of the Pass; and in the lead was a white horse, which, even at a distance of a mile or more, she knew.

'Tull!' she almost screamed.

'I reckon. But, Jane, we've still got the game in our hands. They're ridin' tired hosses. Venters likely give them a chase. He wouldn't forget that. An' we've fresh hosses.'

Hurriedly he strapped on the saddle-bags, gave quick glance to girths and cinches and stirrups, then leaped astride.

'Lift little Fay up,' he said.

With shaking arms Jane complied.

'Get back your nerve, woman! This's life or death now. Mind that. Climb up! Keep your wits. Stick close to me. Watch where your hoss's goin' an' ride!'

Somehow Jane mounted; somehow found strength to hold the reins, to spur, to cling on, to ride. A horrible quaking, craven fear possessed her soul. Lassiter led the swift flight across the wide space, over washes, through sage, into a narrow canõn where the rapid clatter of hoofs rapped sharply from the walls. The wind roared in her ears; the gleaming cliffs swept by; trail and sage and grass moved under her. Lassiter's bandaged, blood-stained face turned to her; he shouted encouragement; he looked back down the Pass; he spurred his horse. Jane clung on, spurring likewise. And the horses settled from hard, furious gallop into a long-striding, driving run. She had never ridden at anything like that pace; desperately she tried to get the swing of the horse, to be of some help to him in that race, to see the best of the ground and guide him into it. But she failed of everything except to keep her seat in the saddle, and to spur and spur. At times she closed her eyes, unable to bear sight of Fay's golden curls streaming in the wind. She could not pray; she could not rail; she no longer cared for herself. All of life, of good, of use in the world, of hope in heaven centered in Lassiter's ride with little Fay to safety. She would have tried to turn the iron-jawed brute she rode; she would have given herself to that relentless, dark-browed Tull. But she knew Lassiter would turn with her, so she rode on and on.

Whether that run was of moments or hours Jane Withersteen could not tell. Lassiter's horse covered her with froth that blew back in white streams. Both horses ran their limit, were allowed to slow down in time to save them, and went on dripping, heaving, staggering.

'Oh, Lassiter, we must run—we must run!'

He looked back, saying nothing. The bandage had blown from his head, and blood trickled down his face. He was bowing under the strain of injuries, of the ride, of his burden. Yet how cool and gray he looked—how intrepid!

The horses walked, trotted, galloped, ran, to fall again to walk. Hours sped or dragged. Time was an instant—an eternity. Jane Withersteen felt hell pursuing her, and dared not look back for fear she would fall from her horse.

'Oh, Lassiter! Is he coming?'

The grim rider looked over his shoulder, but said no word. Little Fay's golden hair floated on the breeze. The sun shone; the walls gleamed; the sage glistened. And then it seemed the sun vanished, the walls shaded, the sage paled. The horses walked—trotted—galloped—ran—to fall again to walk. Shadows gathered under shelving cliffs. The canõn turned, brightened, opened into long, wide, wall-enclosed valley. Again the sun, lowering in the west, reddened the sage. Far ahead round, scrawled stone appeared to block the Pass.

'Bear up, Jane, bear up!' called Lassiter. 'It's our game, if you don't weaken.'

'Lassiter! Go on—*alone*! Save little Fay!'

'Only with you!'

'Oh!—I'm a coward—a miserable coward! I can't fight or think or hope or pray! I'm lost! Oh, Lassiter, look back! Is he coming? I'll not—hold out—'

'Keep your breath, woman, an' ride not for yourself or for me, but for Fay!'

A last breaking run across the sage brought Lassiter's horse to a walk.

'He's done,' said the rider.

'Oh, no—no!' moaned Jane.

'Look back, Jane, look back. Three—four miles we've come across this valley, an' no Tull yet in sight. Only a few more miles!'

Jane looked back over the long stretch of sage, and found the narrow gap in the wall, out of which came a file of dark horses with a white horse in the lead. Sight of the riders acted upon Jane as a stimulant. The weight of cold, horrible terror lessened. And, gazing forward at the dogs, at Lassiter's limping horse, at the blood on his face, at the rocks growing nearer, last at Fay's golden hair, the ice left her veins, and slowly, strangely, she gained hold of strength that she believed would see her to the safety Lassiter promised. And, as she gazed, Lassiter's horse stumbled and fell.

He swung his legs and slipped from the saddle.

'Jane, take the child,' he said, and lifted Fay up. Jane clasped her with arms suddenly strong.

'They're gainin',' went on Lassiter, as he watched the pursuing riders. 'But we'll beat 'em yet.'

Turning with Jane's bridle in his hand, he was about to start when he saw the saddle-bag on the fallen horse.

'I've jest about got time,' he muttered, and with swift fingers that did not blunder or fumble he loosened the bag and threw it over his shoulder. Then he started to run, leading Jane's horse, and he ran, and trotted, and walked, and ran again. Close ahead now Jane saw a rise of bare rock. Lassiter reached it, searched along the base, and, finding a low place, dragged the weary horse up and over round, smooth stone. Looking backward, Jane saw Tull's white horse not a mile distant, with riders strung out in a long line behind him. Looking forward, she saw more valley to the right, and to the left a towering cliff. Lassiter pulled the horse and kept on.

Little Fay lay in her arms with wide-open eyes—eyes which were still shadowed by pain, but no longer fixed, glazed in terror. The golden curls blew across Jane's lips; the little hands feebly clasped her arm; a ghost of a troubled, trustful smile hovered round the sweet lips. And Jane Withersteen awoke to the spirit of a lioness.

Lassiter was leading the horse up a smooth slope toward cedar-trees of twisted and bleached appearance. Among these he halted.

'Jane, give me the girl an' get down,' he said. As if it wrenched him he unbuckled the empty black guns with a strange air of finality. He then received Fay in his arms and stood a moment looking backward. Tull's white horse mounted the ridge of round stone, and several bays or blacks followed. 'I wonder what he'll think when he sees them empty guns. Jane, bring your saddle-bag and climb after me.'

A glistening, wonderful bare slope, with little holes, swelled up and up to lose itself in a frowning yellow cliff. Jane closely watched her steps and climbed behind Lassiter. He moved slowly. Perhaps he was only husbanding his strength. But she saw drops of blood on the stone, and then she knew. They climbed and climbed without looking back. Her breast labored; she began to feel as if little points of fiery steel were penetrating her side into her lungs. She heard the panting of Lassiter and the quicker panting of the dogs.

'Wait—here,' he said.

Before her rose a bulge of stone, nicked with little cut steps, and above that a corner of yellow wall, and overhanging that a vast, ponderous cliff.

The dogs pattered up, disappeared round the corner. Lassiter mounted the steps with Fay, and he swayed like a drunken man, and he too disappeared. But instantly he returned alone, and half ran, half slipped down to her.

Then from below pealed up hoarse shouts of angry men. Tull and several of his riders had reached the spot where Lassiter had parted with his guns.

'You'll need that breath—mebbe!' said Lassiter, facing downward, with glittering eyes.

'Now, Jane, the last pull,' he went on. 'Walk up them little steps. I'll follow an' steady you. Don't think. Jest go. Little Fay's above. Her eyes are open. She jest said to me, "*Where's muvver Jane?*"'

Without a fear or a tremor or a slip or a touch of Lassiter's hand Jane Withersteen walked up that ladder of cut steps.

He pushed her round the corner of wall. Fay lay with wide staring eyes, in the shade of a gloomy wall. The dogs waited. Lassiter picked up the child and turned into a dark cleft. It zigzagged. It widened. It opened. Jane was amazed at a wonderfully smooth and steep incline leading up between ruined, splintered, toppling walls. A red haze from the setting sun filled this passage. Lassiter climbed with slow, measured steps, and blood dripped from him to make splotches on the white stone. Jane tried not to step in his blood, but was compelled, for she found no other footing. The saddle-bag began to drag her down; she gasped for breath; she thought her heart was bursting. Slower, slower yet the rider climbed, whistling as he breathed. The incline widened. Huge pinnacles and monuments of stone stood alone, leaning fearfully. Red sunset haze shone through cracks where the wall had split. Jane did not look high, but she felt the overshadowing of broken rims above. She felt it was a fearful, menacing place. And she climbed on in heartrending effort. And she fell beside Lassiter and Fay at the top of the incline in a narrow, smooth divide.

He staggered to his feet—staggered to a huge, leaning rock that rested on a small pedestal. He put his hand on it—the hand that had been shot through—and Jane saw blood drip from the ragged hole. Then he fell.

'Jane—I—can't—do—it!' he whispered.

'What?'

'Roll the—stone! ... All my—life I've loved—to roll stones—an' now I—can't!'

'What of it? You talk strangely. Why roll that stone?'

'I planned to—fetch you here—to roll this stone. See! It'll smash the crags—loosen the walls—close the outlet!'

As Jane Withersteen gazed down that long incline, walled in by crumbling cliffs, awaiting only the slightest jar to make them fall asunder, she saw Tull appear at the bottom and begin to climb. A rider followed him—another—and another.

'See! Tull! The riders!'

'Yes—they'll get us—now.'

'Why? Haven't you got strength left to roll the stone?'

'Jane—it ain't that—I've lost my nerve!'

'*You!* ... Lassiter!'

'I wanted to roll it—meant to—but I—can't. Venters's valley is down behind here. We could—live there. But if I roll the stone—we're shut in for always I don't dare. I'm thinkin' of you!'

'Lassiter! Roll the stone!' she cried.

He arose, tottering, but with set face, and again he placed the bloody hand on the Balancing Rock. Jane Withersteen gazed from him down the passageway. Tull was climbing. Almost, she thought, she saw his dark, relentless face. Behind him more riders climbed. What did they mean for Fay—for Lassiter—for herself?

'*Roll the stone! ... Lassiter, I love you!*'

Under all his deathly pallor, and the blood, and the iron of seared cheek and lined brow, worked a great change. He placed both hands on the rock and then leaned his shoulder there and braced his powerful body.

'ROLL THE STONE!'

It stirred, it groaned, it grated, it moved; and with a slow grinding, as of wrathful relief, began to lean. It had waited ages to fall, and now was slow in starting. Then, as if suddenly instinct with life, it leaped hurtlingly down to alight on the steep incline, to bound more swiftly into the air, to gather momentum, to plunge into the lofty leaning crag below. The crag thundered into atoms. A wave of air—a splitting shock! Dust shrouded the sunset red of shaking rims; dust shrouded Tull as he fell on his knees with uplifted arms. Shafts and monuments and sections of wall fell majestically.

From the depths there arose a long-drawn rumbling roar. The outlet to Deception Pass closed forever.

THE LAST OF THE PLAINSMEN

1

The Arizona Desert

One afternoon, far out on the sun-baked waste of sage, we made camp near a clump of withered piñon trees. The cold desert wind came down upon us with the sudden darkness. Even the Mormons, who were finding the trail for us across the drifting sands, forgot to sing and pray at sundown. We huddled round the campfire, a tired and silent little group. When out of the lonely, melancholy night some wandering Navajos stole like shadows to our fire, we hailed their advent with delight. They were good-natured Indians, willing to barter a blanket or bracelet; and one of them, a tall, gaunt fellow, with the bearing of a chief, could speak a little English.

'How,' said he, in a deep chest voice.

'Hello, Noddlecoddy,' greeted Jim Emmett, the Mormon guide.

'Ugh!' answered the Indian.

'Big paleface—Buffalo Jones—big chief—buffalo man,' introduced Emmett, indicating Jones.

'How.' The Navajo spoke with dignity, and extended a friendly hand.

'Jones big white chief—rope buffalo—tie up tight,' continued Emmett, making motions with his arm, as if he were whirling a lasso.

'No big—heap small buffalo,' said the Indian, holding his hand level with his knee, and smiling broadly.

Jones, erect, rugged, brawny, stood in the full light of the campfire. He had a dark, bronzed, inscrutable face; a stern mouth and square jaw, keen eyes, half-closed from years of searching the wide plains, and deep furrows wrinkling his cheeks. A strange stillness enfolded his features—the tranquility earned from a long life of adventure.

He held up both muscular hands to the Navajo, and spread out his fingers.

'Rope buffalo—heap big buffalo—heap many—one sun.'

The Indian straightened up, but kept his friendly smile.

'Me big chief,' went on Jones, 'me go far north—Land of Little Sticks—Naza! Naza!—rope musk-ox; rope White Manitou of Great Slaves—Naza! Naza!'

'Naza!' replied the Navajo, pointing to the North Star; 'no—no.'

'Yes—me big paleface—me come long way toward setting sun—go cross Big Water—go Buckskin—Siwash—chase cougar.'

The cougar, or mountain lion, is a Navajo god and the Navajos hold him in as much fear and reverence as do the Great Slave Indians the musk-ox.

'No kill cougar,' continued Jones, as the Indian's bold features hardened. 'Run cougar horseback—run long way—dogs chase cougar long time—chase cougar up tree! Me big chief—me climb tree—climb high up—lasso cougar—rope cougar—tie cougar all tight.'

The Navajo's solemn face relaxed.

'White man heap fun. No.'

'Yes,' cried Jones, extending his great arms. 'Me strong; me rope cougar—me tie cougar; ride off wigwam, keep cougar alive.'

'No,' replied the savage vehemently.

'Yes,' protested Jones, nodding earnestly.

'No,' answered the Navajo, louder, raising his dark head.

'Yes!' shouted Jones.

'BIG LIE!' the Indian thundered.

Jones joined good-naturedly in the laugh at his expense. The Indian had crudely voiced a skepticism I had heard more delicately hinted in New York, and singularly enough, which had strengthened on our way West, as we met ranchers, prospectors and cowboys. But those few men I had fortunately met, who really knew Jones, more than overbalanced the doubt and ridicule cast upon him. I recalled a scarred old veteran of the plains, who had talked to me in true Western bluntness:

'Say, young feller, I heerd yer couldn't git acrost the cañon fer the deep snow on the north rim. Wal, ye're lucky. Now, yer hit the trail fer New York, an' keep goin'! Don't ever tackle the desert, 'specially with them Mormons. They've got water on the brain, wusser 'n religion. It's two hundred an' fifty miles from Flagstaff to Jones range, an' only two drinks on the trail. I know this hyar Buffalo Jones. I knowed him way back in the seventies, when he was doin' them ropin' stunts thet made him famous as the preserver of the American bison. I know about that crazy trip of his'n to the Barren Lands, after musk-ox. An' I reckon I kin guess what he'll do over there in the Siwash. He'll rope cougars—sure he will—an' watch 'em jump. Jones would rope the devil, an' tie him down if the lasso didn't burn. Oh! he's hell on ropin' things. An' he's wusser 'n hell on men, an' hosses, an' dogs.'

All that my well-meaning friend suggested made me, of course, only the more eager to go with Jones. Where I had once been interested in the old buffalo hunter, I was now fascinated. And now I was with him in the desert and seeing him as he was, a simple, quiet man, who fitted the mountains and the silences and the long reaches of distance.

'It does seem hard to believe—all this about Jones,' remarked Judd, one of Emmett's men. 'How could a man have the strength and the nerve? And isn't it cruel to keep wild animals in captivity? Isn't it against God's word?'

Quick as speech could flow, Jones quoted: 'And God said, "Let us make man in our image, and give him dominion over the fish of the sea, the fowls of the air, over all the cattle, and over every creeping thing that creepeth upon the earth"!'

'Dominion—over all the beasts of the field!' repeated Jones, his big voice rolling out. He clenched his huge fists, and spread wide his long arms. 'Dominion! That was God's word!' The power and intensity of him could be felt. Then he relaxed, dropped his arms, and once more grew calm. But he had shown a glimpse of the great, strange and absorbing passion of his life. Once he had told me how, when a mere child, he had hazarded limb and neck to capture a fox squirrel, how he had held on to the vicious little animal, though it bit his hand through; how he had never learned to play the games of boyhood; that when the youths of the little Illinois village were at play, he roamed the prairies, or the rolling, wooded hills, or watched a gopher hole. That boy was father of the man: for sixty years an enduring passion for dominion over wild animals had possessed him, and made his life an endless pursuit.

Our guests, the Navajos, departed early, and vanished silently in the gloom of the desert. We settled down again into a quiet that was broken only by the low chant-like song of a praying Mormon. Suddenly the hounds bristled, and old Moze, a surly and aggressive dog, rose and barked at some real or imaginary desert prowler. A sharp command from Jones made Moze crouch down, and the other hounds cowered close together.

'Better tie up the dogs,' suggested Jones. 'Like as not coyotes run down here from the hills.'

The hounds were my especial delight. But Jones regarded them with considerable contempt. When all was said, this was no small wonder, for that quintet of long-eared canines would have tried the patience of a saint. Old Moze was a Missouri hound that Jones had procured in that State of uncertain qualities; and the dog had grown old over coontrails. He was black and white, grizzled and battle-scarred; and if ever a dog had an evil eye, Moze was that dog. He had a way of wagging his tail—an indeterminate, equivocal sort of wag, as if he realized his ugliness and knew he stood little chance of making friends, but was still hopeful and willing. As for me, the first time he manifested this evidence of a good heart under a rough coat, he won me forever.

To tell of Moze's derelictions up to that time would take more space than would a history of the whole trip; but the enumeration of several incidents will at once stamp him as a dog of character, and will establish the fact that even if his progenitors had never taken any blue ribbons, they had at least bequeathed him fighting blood. At Flagstaff we chained him in the yard of a livery stable. Next morning we found him hanging by his chain on the other side of an eight-foot fence. We took him down, expecting to have the sorrowful duty of burying him; but Moze shook himself, wagged his tail, and then pitched into the livery stable dog. As a matter of fact, fighting was his forte. He whipped all of the dogs in Flagstaff; and when our bloodhounds came on from California, he put three of them *hors de combat* at once, and subdued the pup with a savage growl. His crowning feat, however, made even the stoical Jones open his mouth in amaze. We had taken Moze to the El Tovar at the Grand Cañon, and finding it impossible to get over to the north rim, we left him with one of Jones's men, called Rust, who was working on the cañon trail. Rust's instructions were to bring Moze to Flagstaff in two weeks. He brought the dog a little ahead of time, and roared his appreciation of the relief it was to get the responsibility off his hands. And he related many strange things, most striking of which was how Moze had broken his chain and plunged into the raging Colorado River, and tried to swim it just above the terrible Sockdolager Rapids. Rust and his fellow-workmen watched the dog disappear in the yellow, wrestling, turbulent whirl of waters, and had heard his knell in the booming roar of the falls. Nothing but a fish could live in that current; nothing but a bird could scale those perpendicular marble walls. That night, however, when the men crossed on the tramway, Moze met them with a wag of his tail. He had crossed the river, and he had come back!

To the four reddish-brown, big-framed bloodhounds I had given the names of Don, Tige, Jude and Ranger; and by dint of persuasion, had succeeded in establishing some kind of family relation between them and Moze. This night I tied up the bloodhounds, after bathing and salving their sore feet; and I left Moze free, for he grew fretful and surly under restraint.

The Mormons, prone, dark, blanketed figures, lay on the sand. Jones was crawling into his bed. I walked a little way from the dying fire, and faced the north, where the desert stretched, mysterious and illimitable. How solemn and still it was! I drew in a great breath of the cold air, and thrilled with a nameless sensation. Something was there, away to the northward; it called to me from out of the dark and gloom; I was going to meet it.

I lay down to sleep with the great blue expanse open to my eyes. The stars were very large, and wonderfully bright, yet they seemed so much farther off than I had ever seen them. The wind softly sifted the sand. I hearkened to the tinkle of the cowbells on the hobbled horses. The last thing I remembered was old Moze creeping close to my side, seeking the warmth of my body.

When I awakened, a long, pale line showed out of the dun-colored clouds in the east. It slowly lengthened, and tinged to red. Then the morning broke, and the slopes of snow on the San Francisco peaks behind us glowed a delicate pink.

The Mormons were up and doing with the dawn. They were stalwart men, rather silent, and all workers. It was interesting to see them pack for the day's journey. They traveled with wagons and mules, in the most primitive way, which Jones assured me was exactly as their fathers had crossed the plains fifty years before, on the trail to Utah.

All morning we made good time, and as we descended into the desert, the air became warmer, the scrubby cedar growth began to fail, and the bunches of sage were few and far between. I turned often to gaze back at the San Francisco peaks. The snowcapped tips glistened and grew higher, and stood out in startling relief. Some one said they could be seen two hundred miles across the desert, and were a landmark and a fascination to all travelers thither-ward.

I never raised my eyes to the north that I did not draw my breath quickly and grow chill with awe and bewilderment with the marvel of the desert. The scaly red ground descended gradually; bare red knolls, like waves, rolled away northward; black buttes reared their flat heads; long ranges of sand flowed between them like streams, and all sloped away to merge into gray, shadowy obscurity, into wild and desolate, dreamy and misty nothingness.

'Do you see those white sand dunes there, more to the left?' asked Emmett. 'The Little Colorado runs in there. How far does it look to you?'

'Thirty miles, perhaps,' I replied, adding ten miles to my estimate.

'It's seventy-five. We'll get there day after to-morrow. If the snow in the mountains has begun to melt, we'll have a time getting across.'

That afternoon, a hot wind blew in my face, carrying fine sand that cut and blinded. It filled my throat, sending me to the water cask till I was ashamed. When I fell into my bed at night, I never turned. The next day was hotter; the wind blew harder; the sand stung sharper.

About noon the following day, the horses whinnied, and the mules roused out of their tardy gait. 'They smell water,' said Emmett. And despite the heat, and the sand in my nostrils, I smelled it, too. The dogs, poor foot-sore fellows, trotted on ahead down the trail. A few more miles of hot sand and gravel and red stone brought us around a low mesa to the Little Colorado.

It was a wide stream of swiftly running, reddish-muddy water. In the channel, cut by floods, little streams trickled and meandered in all directions. The main part of the river ran in close to the bank we were on. The dogs lolled in the water; the horses and mules tried to run in, but were restrained; the men drank, and bathed their faces. According to my Flagstaff adviser, this was one of the two drinks I would get on the desert, so I availed myself heartily of the opportunity. The water was full of sand, but cold and gratefully thirst-quenching.

The Little Colorado seemed no more to me than a shallow creek; I heard nothing sullen or menacing in its musical flow.

'Doesn't look bad, eh?' queried Emmett, who read my thought. 'You'd be surprised to learn how many men and Indians, horses, sheep and wagons are buried under that quicksand.'

The secret was out, and I wondered no more. At once the stream and wet bars of sand took on a different color. I removed my boots, and waded out to a little bar. The sand seemed quite firm, but water oozed out around my feet; and when I stepped, the whole bar shook like jelly. I pushed my foot through the crust, and the cold, wet sand took hold, and tried to suck me down.

'How can you ford this stream with horses?' I asked Emmett.

'We must take our chances,' replied he. 'We'll hitch two teams to one wagon, and run the horses. I've forded here at worse stages than this. Once a team got stuck, and I had to leave it; another time the water was high, and washed me downstream.'

Emmett sent his son into the stream on a mule. The rider lashed his mount, and plunging, splashing, crossed at a pace near a gallop. He returned in the same manner, and reported one bad place near the other side.

Jones and I got on the first wagon and tried to coax up the dogs, but they would not come. Emmett had to lash the four horses to start them; and other Mormons riding alongside, yelled at them, and used their whips. The wagon bowled into the water with a tremendous splash. We were wet through before we had gone twenty feet. The plunging horses were lost in yellow spray; the stream rushed through the wheels; the Mormons yelled. I wanted to see, but was lost in a veil of yellow mist. Jones yelled in my ear, but I could not hear what he said. Once the wagon wheels struck a stone or log, almost lurching us overboard. A muddy splash blinded me. I cried out in my excitement, and punched Jones in the back. Next moment, the keen exhilaration of the ride gave way to horror. We seemed to drag, and almost stop. Some one roared: 'Horse down!' One instant of painful suspense, in which imagination pictured another tragedy added to the record of this deceitful river—a moment filled with intense feeling, and sensation of splash, and yell, and fury of action: then the three able horses dragged their comrade out of the quick-sand. He regained his feet, and plunged on. Spurred by fear, the horses increased their efforts, and amid clouds of spray, galloped the remaining distance to the other side.

Jones looked disgusted. Like all plainsmen, he hated water. Emmett and his men calmly unhitched. No trace of alarm, or even of excitement showed in their bronzed faces.

'We made that fine and easy,' remarked Emmett.

So I sat down and wondered what Jones and Emmett, and these men would consider really hazardous. I began to have a feeling that I would find out; that experience for me was but in its infancy; that far across the desert the something which had called me would show hard, keen, perilous life. And I began to think of reserve powers of fortitude and endurance.

The other wagons were brought across without mishap; but the dogs did not come with them. Jones called and called. The dogs howled and howled. Finally I waded out over the wet bars and little streams to a point several hundred yards nearer the dogs. Moze was lying down, but the others were whining and howling in a state of great perturbation. I called and called. They answered, and even ran into the water, but did not start across.

'Hyah, Moze! hyah, you Indian!' I yelled, losing my patience. 'You've already swum the Big Colorado, and this is only a brook. Come on!'

This appeal evidently touched Moze, for he barked, and plunged in. He made the water fly, and when carried off his feet, breasted the current with energy and power. He made shore almost even with me, and wagged his tail. Not to be out-done, Jude, Tige and Don followed suit, and first one and then another was swept off his feet and carried downstream. They landed below me. This left Ranger, the pup, alone on the other shore. Of all the pitiful yelps ever uttered by a frightened and lonely puppy, his were the most forlorn I had ever heard. Time after time he plunged in, and with many bitter howls of distress, went back. I kept calling, and at last, hoping to make him come by a show of indifference, I started away. This broke his heart. Putting up his head, he let out a long, melancholy wail, which for aught I knew might have been a prayer, and then consigned himself to the yellow current. Ranger swam like a boy learning. He seemed to be afraid to get wet. His forefeet were continually pawing the air in front of his nose. When he struck the swift place, he went downstream, like a flash, but still kept swimming valiantly. I tried to follow along the sand-bar, but found it impossible. I encouraged him by yelling. He drifted far below, stranded on an island, crossed it, and plunged in again, to make shore almost out of my sight. And when at last I got to dry sand, there was Ranger, wet and disheveled, but consciously proud and happy.

After lunch we entered upon the seventy-mile stretch from the Little to the Big Colorado.

Imagination had pictured the desert for me as a vast, sandy plain, flat and monotonous. Reality showed me desolate mountains gleaming bare in the sun, long lines of red bluffs, white sand dunes, and hills of blue clay, areas of level ground—in all, a many-hued, boundless world in itself, wonderful and beautiful, fading all around into the purple haze of deceiving distance.

Thin, clear, sweet, dry, the desert air carried a languor, a dreaminess, tidings of far-off things, and an enthralling promise. The fragrance of flowers, the beauty and grace of women, the sweetness of music, the mystery of life—all seemed to float on that promise. It was the air breathed by the lotus-eaters, when they dreamed, and wandered no more.

Beyond the Little Colorado, we began to climb again. The sand was thick; the horses labored; the drivers shielded their faces. The dogs began to limp and lag. Ranger had to be taken into a wagon; and then, one by one, all of the other dogs except Moze. He refused to ride, and trotted along with his head down.

Far to the front the pink cliffs, the ragged mesas, the dark, volcanic spurs of the Big Colorado stood up and beckoned us onward. But they were a far hundred miles across the shifting sands, and baked clay, and ragged rocks. Always in the rear rose the San Francisco peaks, cold and pure, startlingly clear and close in the rare atmosphere.

We camped near another water hole, located in a deep, yellow-colored gorge, crumbling to pieces, a ruin of rock, and silent as the grave. In the bottom of the cañon was a pool of water, covered with green scum. My thirst was effectually quenched by the mere sight of it. I slept poorly, and lay for hours watching the great stars. The silence was painfully oppressive. If Jones had not begun to give a respectable imitation of the exhaust pipe on a steamboat, I should have been compelled to shout aloud, or get up; but this snoring would have dispelled anything. The morning came gray and cheerless. I got up stiff and sore, with a tongue like a rope.

All day long we ran the gauntlet of the hot, flying sand. Night came again, a cold, windy night. I slept well until a mule stepped on my bed, which was conducive to restlessness. At dawn, cold, gray clouds tried to blot out the rosy east. I could hardly get up. My lips were cracked; my tongue swollen to twice its natural size; my eyes smarted and burned. The barrels and kegs of water were exhausted. Holes that had been dug in the dry sand of a dry stream-bed the night before in the morning yielded a scant supply of muddy alkali water, which went to the horses.

Only twice that day did I rouse to anything resembling enthusiasm. We came to a stretch of country showing the wonderful diversity of the desert land. A long range of beautiful rounded clay dunes bordered the trail. So symmetrical were they that I imagined them works of sculptors. Light blue, dark blue, clay blue, marine blue, cobalt blue—every shade of blue was there, but no other color. The other time that I awoke to sensations from without was when we came to the top of a ridge. We had been passing through red-lands. Jones called the place a strong, specific word which really was illustrative of the heat amid those scaling red ridges. We came out where the red changed abruptly to gray. I seemed always to see things first, and I cried out: 'Look! here are a red lake and trees!'

'No, lad, not a lake,' said old Jim, smiling at me; 'that's what haunts the desert traveler. It's only a mirage!'

So I awoke to the realization of that illusive thing, the mirage, a beautiful lie, false as stairs of sand. Far northward a clear rippling lake sparkled in the sunshine. Tall, stately trees, with waving green foliage, bordered the water. For a long moment it lay there, smiling in the sun, a thing almost tangible; and then it faded. I felt a sense of actual loss. So real had been the illusion that I could not believe I was not soon to drink and wade and dabble in the cool waters. Disappointment was keen. This is what maddens the prospector or sheep-herder lost in the desert. Was it not a terrible thing to be dying of thirst, to see sparkling water, almost to smell it, and then realize suddenly that all was only a lying trick of the desert, a lure, a delusion? I ceased to wonder at the Mormons, and their search for water, their talk of water. But I had not realized its true significance. I had not known what water was. I had never appreciated it. So it was my destiny to learn that water is the greatest thing on earth. I hung over a three-foot hole in a dry stream-bed, and watched it ooze and seep through the sand, and fill up—oh, so slowly; and I felt it loosen my parched tongue, and steal through all my dry body with strength and life. Water is said to constitute three fourths of the universe. However that may be, on the desert it is the whole world, and all of life.

Two days passed by, all hot sand and wind and glare. The Mormons sang no more at evening; Jones was silent; the dogs were limp as rags.

At Moncáupie Wash we ran into a sandstorm. The horses turned their backs to it, and bowed their heads patiently. The Mormons covered themselves. I wrapped a blanket round my head and hid behind a sage bush. The wind, carrying the sand, made a strange hollow roar. All was enveloped in a weird yellow opacity. The sand seeped through the sage bush and swept by with a soft, rustling sound, not unlike the wind in the rye. From time to time I raised a corner of my blanket and peeped out. Where my feet had stretched was an enormous mound of sand. I felt the blanket, weighted down, slowly settle over me.

Suddenly as it had come, the sandstorm passed. It left a changed world for us. The trail was covered; the wheels hub-deep in sand; the horses, walking sand dunes. I could not close my teeth without grating harshly on sand.

We journeyed onward, and passed long lines of petrified trees, some a hundred feet in length, lying as they had fallen, thousands of years before. White ants crawled among the ruins. Slowly climbing the sandy trail, we circled a great red bluff with jagged peaks, that had seemed an interminable obstacle. A scant growth of cedar and sage again made its appearance. Here we halted to pass another night. Under a cedar I heard the plaintive, piteous bleat of an animal. I searched, and presently found a little black and white lamb, scarcely able to stand. It came readily to me, and I carried it to the wagon.

'That's a Navajo lamb,' said Emmett. 'It's lost. There are Navajo Indians close by.'

' "Away in the desert we heard its cry," ' quoted one of the Mormons.

Jones and I climbed the red mesa near camp to see the sunset. All the western world was ablaze in golden glory. Shafts of light shot toward the zenith, and bands of paler gold, tinging to rose, circled away from the fiery, sinking globe. Suddenly the sun sank, the gold changed to gray, then to purple, and shadows formed in the deep gorge at our feet. So sudden was the transformation that soon it was night, the solemn, impressive night of the desert. A stillness that seemed too sacred to break clasped the place; it was infinite; it held the bygone ages, and eternity.

More days, and miles, miles, miles! The last day's ride to the Big Colorado was unforgettable. We rode toward the head of a gigantic red cliff pocket, a veritable inferno, immeasurably hot, glaring, awful. It towered higher and higher above us. When we reached a point of this red barrier, we heard the dull rumbling roar of water, and we came out, at length, on a winding trail cut in the face of a bluff overhanging the Colorado River. The first sight of most famous and much-heralded wonders of nature is often disappointing; but never can this be said of the blood-hued Rio Colorado. If it had beauty, it was beauty that appalled. So riveted was my gaze that I could hardly turn it across the river, where Emmett proudly pointed out his lonely home—an oasis set down amidst beetling red cliffs. How grateful to the eye was the green of alfalfa and cottonwood! Going round the bluff trail, the wheels had only a foot of room to spare; and the sheer descent into the red, turbid, congested river was terrifying.

I saw the constricted rapids, where the Colorado took its plunge into the box-like head of the Grand Cañon of Arizona; and the deep, reverberating boom of the river, at flood height, was a fearful thing to hear. I could not repress a shudder at the thought of crossing above that rapid.

The bronze walls widened as we proceeded, and we got down presently to a level, where a long wire cable stretched across the river. Under the cable ran a rope. On the other side was an old scow moored to the bank.

'Are we going across in that?' I asked Emmett, pointing to the boat.

'We'll all be on the other side before dark,' he replied cheerily.

I felt that I would rather start back alone over the desert than trust myself in such a craft, on such a river. And it was all because I had had experience with bad rivers, and thought I was a judge of dangerous currents. The Colorado slid with a menacing roar out of a giant split in the red wall, and whirled, eddied, bulged on toward its confinement in the iron-ribbed cañon below.

In answer to shots fired, Emmett's man appeared on the other side, and rode down to the ferry landing. Here he got into a skiff, and rowed laboriously upstream for a long distance before he started across, and then swung into the current. He swept down rapidly, and twice the skiff whirled, and completely turned round; but he reached our bank safely. Taking two men aboard he rowed upstream again, close to the shore, and returned to the opposite side in much the same manner in which he had come over.

The three men pushed out the scow, and grasping the rope overhead, began to pull. The big craft ran easily. When the current struck it, the wire cable sagged, the water boiled and surged under it, raising one end, and then the other. Nevertheless, five minutes were all that were required to pull the boat over.

It was a rude, oblong affair, made of heavy planks loosely put together, and it leaked. When Jones suggested that we get the agony over as quickly as possible, I was with him, and we embarked together. Jones said he did not like the looks of the tackle; and when I thought of his by no means small mechanical skill, I had not added a cheerful idea to my consciousness. The horses of the first team had to be dragged upon the scow, and once on, they reared and plunged.

When we started, four men pulled the rope, and Emmett sat in the stern, with the tackle guys in hand. As the current hit us, he let out the guys, which maneuver caused the boat to swing stern down stream. When it pointed obliquely, he made fast the guys again. I saw that this served two purposes: the current struck, slid alongside, and over the stern, which mitigated the danger, and at the same time helped the boat across.

To look at the river was to court terror, but I had to look. It was an infernal thing. It roared in hollow, sullen voice, as a monster growling. It had a voice, this river, and one strangely changeful. It moaned as if in pain—it whined, it cried. Then at times it would seem strangely silent. The current was so complex and mutable as human life. It boiled, beat and bulged. The bulge itself was an incomprehensible thing, like a roaring lift of the waters from a submarine explosion. Then it would smooth out, and run like oil. It shifted from one channel to another, rushed to the center of the river, then swung close to one shore or the other. Again it swelled near the boat, in great, boiling, hissing eddies.

'Look! See where it breaks through the mountain!' yelled Jones in my ear.

I looked upstream to see the stupendous granite walls separated in a gigantic split that must have been made by a terrible seismic disturbance; and from this gap poured the dark, turgid, mystic flood.

I was in a cold sweat when we touched shore, and I jumped long before the boat was properly moored.

Emmett was wet to the waist where the water had surged over him. As he sat rearranging some tackle I remarked to him that of course he must be a splendid swimmer, or he would not take such risks.

'No, I can't swim a stroke,' he replied; 'and it wouldn't be any use if I could. Once in there a man's a goner.'

'You've had bad accidents here?' I questioned.

'No, not bad. We only drowned two men last year. You see, we had to tow the boat up the river, and row across, as then we hadn't the wire. Just above, on this side, the boat hit a stone, and the current washed over her, taking off the team and two men.'

'Didn't you attempt to rescue them?' I asked, after waiting a moment.

'No use. They never came up.'

'Isn't the river high now?' I continued, shuddering as I glanced out at the whirling logs and drifts.

'High, and coming up. If I don't get the other teams over to-day I'll wait until she goes down. At this season she rises and lowers every day or so, until June; then comes the big flood, and we don't cross for months.'

I sat for three hours watching Emmett bring over the rest of his party, which he did without accident, but at the expense of great effort. And all the time in my ears dinned the roar, the boom, the rumble of this singularly rapacious and purposeful river—a river of silt, a red river of dark, sinister meaning, a river with terrible work to perform, a river which never gave up its dead.

2
The Range

After a much-needed rest at Emmett's, we bade good-bye to him and his hospitable family, and under the guidance of his man once more took to the wind-swept trail. We pursued a southwesterly course now, following the lead of the craggy red wall that stretched on and on for hundreds of miles into Utah. The desert, smoky and hot, fell away to the left, and in the foreground a dark, irregular line marked the Grand Cañon cutting through the plateau.

The wind whipped in from the vast, open expanse, and meeting an obstacle in the red wall, turned north and raced past us. Jones's hat blew off, stood on its rim, and rolled. It kept on rolling, thirty miles an hour, more or less; so fast, at least, that we were a long time catching up to it with a team of horses. Possibly we never would have caught it had not a stone checked its flight. Further manifestation of the power of the desert wind surrounded us on all sides. It had hollowed out huge stones from the cliffs, and tumbled them to the plain below; and then, sweeping sand and gravel low across the desert floor, had cut them deeply, until they rested on slender pedestals, thus sculptoring grotesque and striking monuments to the marvelous persistence of this element of nature.

Late that afternoon, as we reached the height of the plateau, Jones woke up and shouted: 'Ha! there's Buckskin!'

Far southward lay a long, black mountain, covered with patches of shining snow. I could follow the zigzag line of the Grand Cañon splitting the desert plateau, and saw it disappear in the haze round the end of the mountain. From this I got my first clear impression of the topography of the country surrounding our objective point. Buckskin mountain ran its blunt end eastward to the cañon—in fact, formed a hundred miles of the north rim. As it was nine thousand feet high it still held the snow, which had occasioned our lengthy desert ride to get back of the mountain. I could see the long slopes rising out of the desert to meet the timber.

As we bowled merrily down grade I noticed that we were no longer on stony ground, and that a little scant silvery grass had made its appearance. Then little branches of green, with a blue flower, smiled out of the clayish sand.

All of a sudden Jones stood up, and let out a wild Comanche yell. I was more startled by the yell than by the great hand he smashed down on my shoulder, and for the moment I was dazed.

'There! look! look! the buffalo! Hi! Hi! Hi!'

Below us, a few miles on a rising knoll, a big herd of buffalo shone black in the gold of the evening sun. I had not Jones's incentive, but I felt enthusiasm born of the wild and beautiful picture, and added my yell to his. The huge, burly leader of the herd lifted his head, and after regarding us for a few moments calmly went on browsing.

The desert had fringed away into a grand rolling pastureland, walled in by the red cliffs, the slopes of Buckskin, and further isolated by the cañon. Here was a range of twenty-four hundred square miles without a foot of barb-wire, a pasture fenced in by natural forces, with the splendid feature that the buffalo could browse on the plain in winter, and go up into the cool foothills of Buckskin in summer.

From another ridge we saw a cabin dotting the rolling plain, and in half an hour we reached it. As we climbed down from the wagon a brown and black dog came dashing out of the cabin, and promptly jumped at Moze. His selection showed poor discrimination, for Moze whipped him before I could separate them. Hearing Jones heartily greeting some one, I turned in his direction, only to be distracted by another dog fight. Don had tackled Moze for the seventh time. Memory rankled in Don, and he needed a lot of whipping, some of which he was getting when I rescued him.

Next moment I was shaking hands with Frank and Jim, Jones's ranchmen. At a glance I liked them both. Frank was short and wiry, and had a big, ferocious mustache, the effect of which was softened by his kindly brown eyes. Jim was tall, a little heavier; he had a careless, tidy look; his eyes were searching, and though he appeared a young man, his hair was white.

'I shore am glad to see you all,' said Jim, in slow, soft, Southern accent.

'Get down, get down,' was Frank's welcome—a typically Western one, for we had already gotten down; 'an' come in. You must be worked out. Sure you've come a long way.' He was quick of speech, full of nervous energy, and beamed with hospitality.

The cabin was the rudest kind of log affair, with a huge stone fireplace in one end, deer antlers and coyote skins on the wall, saddles and cowboys' traps in a corner, a nice, large, promising cupboard, and a table and chairs. Jim threw wood on a smoldering fire, that soon blazed and crackled cheerily.

I sank down into a chair with a feeling of blessed relief. Ten days of desert ride behind me! Promise of wonderful days before me, with the last of the old plainsmen! No wonder a sweet sense of ease stole over me, or that the fire seemed a live and joyously welcoming thing, or that Jim's deft maneuvers in preparation of supper roused in me a rapt admiration.

'Twenty calves this spring!' cried Jones, punching me in my sore side. 'Ten thousand dollars worth of calves!'

He was now altogether a changed man; he looked almost young; his eyes danced, and he rubbed his big hands together while he plied Frank with questions. In strange surroundings—that is, away from his native wilds, Jones had been a silent man; it had been almost impossible to get anything out of him. But now I saw that I should come to know the real man. In a very few moments he had talked more than on all the desert trip, and what he said, added to the little I had already learned, put me in possession of some interesting information as to his buffalo.

Some years before he had conceived the idea of hybridizing buffalo with black Galloway cattle; and with the characteristic determination and energy of the man, he at once set about finding a suitable range. This was difficult, and took years of searching. At last the wild north rim of the Grand Cañon, a section unknown except to a few Indians and mustang hunters, was settled upon. Then the gigantic task of transporting the herd of buffalo by rail from Montana to Salt Lake was begun. The two hundred and ninety miles of desert lying between the home of the Mormons and Buckskins Mountain was an obstacle almost insurmountable. The journey was undertaken and found even more trying than had been expected. Buffalo after buffalo died on the way. Then Frank, Jones's right-hand man, put into execution a plan he had been thinking of—namely, to travel by night. It succeeded. The buffalo rested in the day and traveled by easy stages by night, with the result that the big herd was transported to the ideal range.

Here, in an environment strange to their race, but peculiarly adaptable, they thrived and multiplied. The hybrid of the Galloway cow and buffalo proved a great success. Jones called the new species 'Cattalo.' The cattalo took the hardiness of the buffalo, and never required artificial food or shelter. He would face the desert storm or blizzard and stand stock still in his tracks until the weather cleared. He became quite domestic, could be easily handled, and grew exceedingly fat on very little provender. The folds of his stomach were so numerous that they digested even the hardest and flintiest of corn. He had fourteen ribs on each side, while domestic cattle had only thirteen; thus he could endure rougher work and longer journeys to water. His fur was so dense and glossy that it equaled that of the unplucked beaver or otter, and was fully as valuable as the buffalo robe. And not to be overlooked by any means was the fact that his meat was delicious.

Jones had to hear every detail of all that had happened since his absence in the East, and he was particularly inquisitive to learn all about the twenty cattalo calves. He called different buffalo by name; and designated the calves by descriptive terms, such as 'Whiteface' and 'Crosspatch.' He almost forgot to eat, and kept Frank too busy to get anything into his own mouth. After supper he calmed down.

'How about your other man—Mr. Wallace, I think you said?' asked Frank.

'We expected to meet him at Grand Cañon Station, and then at Flagstaff. But he didn't show up. Either he backed out or missed us. I'm sorry; for when we get up on Buckskin, among the wild horses and cougars, we'll be likely to need him.'

'I reckon you'll need me, as well as Jim,' said Frank dryly, with a twinkle in his eye. 'The buffs are in good shape an' can get along without me for a while.'

'That'll be fine. How about cougar sign on the mountain?'

'Plenty. I've got two spotted near Oak Spring. Comin' over two weeks ago I tracked them in the snow along the trail for miles. We'll ooze over that way, as it's goin' toward the Siwash. The Siwash breaks of the cañon—there's the place for lions. I met a wild-horse wrangler not long back, an' he was tellin' me about Old Tom an' the colts he'd killed this winter.'

Naturally, I here expressed a desire to know more of Old Tom.

'He's the biggest cougar ever known of in these parts. His tracks are bigger than a horse's an' have been seen on Buckskin for twelve years. This wrangler—his name is Clark—said he'd turned his saddle horse out to graze near camp, an' Old Tom sneaked in an' downed him. The lions over there are sure a bold bunch. Well, why shouldn't they be? No one ever hunted them. You see, the mountain is hard to get at. But now you're here, if it's big cats you want we sure can find them. Only be easy, be easy. You've all the time there is. An' any job on Buckskin will take time. We'll look the calves over, an' you must ride the range to harden up. Then we'll ooze over toward Oak. I expect it'll be boggy, an' I hope the snow melts soon.'

'The snow hadn't melted on Greenland point,' replied Jones. 'We saw that with a glass from the El Tovar. We wanted to cross that way, but Rust said Bright Angel Creek was breast high to a horse, and that creek is the trail.'

'There's four feet of snow on Greenland,' said Frank. 'It was too early to come that way. There's only about three months in the year the cañon can be crossed at Greenland.'

'I want to get in the snow,' returned Jones. 'This bunch of long-eared canines I brought never smelled a lion track. Hounds can't be trained quick without snow. You've got to see what they're trailing, or you can't break them.'

Frank looked dubious. ''Pears to me we'll have trouble gettin' a lion without lion dogs. It takes a long time to break a hound off of deer, once he's chased them. Buckskin is full of deer, wolves, coyotes, and there's wild horses. We couldn't go a hundred feet without crossin' trails.'

'How's the hound you and Jim fetched in last year? Has he got a good nose? Here he is—I like his head. Come here, Bowser—what's his name?'

'Jim named him Sounder, because he sure has a voice. It's great to hear him on a trail. Sounder has a nose that can't be fooled, an' he'll trail anythin'; but I don't know if he ever got up a lion.'

Sounder wagged his bushy tail and looked up affectionately at Frank. He had a fine head, great brown eyes, very long ears and curly brownish-black hair. He was not demonstrative, looked rather askance at Jones, and avoided the other dogs.

'That dog will make a great lion-chaser,' said Jones, decisively, after his study of Sounder. 'He and Moze will keep us busy, once they learn we want lions.'

'I don't believe any dog-trainer could teach them short of six months,' replied Frank. 'Sounder is no spring chicken; an' that black and dirty white cross between a cayuse an' a barb-wire fence is an old dog. You can't teach old dogs new tricks.'

Jones smiled mysteriously, a smile of conscious superiority, but said nothing.

'We'll shore hev a storm to-morrow,' said Jim, relinquishing his pipe long enough to speak. He had been silent, and now his meditative gaze was on the west, through the cabin window, where a dull afterglow faded under the heavy laden clouds of night and left the horizon dark.

I was very tired when I lay down, but so full of excitement that sleep did not soon visit my eyelids. The talk about buffalo, wild-horse hunters, lions and dogs, the prospect of hard riding and unusual adventure; the vision of Old Tom that had already begun to haunt me, filled my mind with pictures and fancies. The other fellows dropped off to sleep, and quiet reigned. Suddenly a succession of queer, sharp barks came from the plain, close to the cabin. Coyotes were paying us a call, and judging from the chorus of yelps and howls from our dogs, it was not a welcome visit. Above the medley rose one big, deep, full voice that I knew at once belonged to Sounder. Then all was quiet again. Sleep gradually benumbed my senses. Vague phrases dreamily drifted to and fro in my mind: 'Jones's wild range—Old Tom—Sounder—great name—great voice—Sounder! Sounder! Sound—'

Next morning I could hardly crawl out of my sleeping-bag. My bones ached, my muscles protested excruciatingly, my lips burned and bled, and the cold I had contracted on the desert clung to me. A good brisk walk round the corrals, and then breakfast, made me feel better.

'Of course you can ride?' queried Frank.

My answer was not given from an overwhelming desire to be truthful. Frank frowned a little, as it wondering how a man could have the nerve to start out on a jaunt with Buffalo Jones without being a good horseman. To be unable to stick on the back of a wild mustang, or a cayuse, was an unpardonable sin in Arizona. My frank admission was made relatively, with my mind on what cowboys held as a standard of horsemanship.

The mount Frank trotted out of the corral for me was a pure white, beautiful mustang, nervous, sensitive, quivering. I watched Frank put on the saddle, and when he called me I did not fail to catch a covert twinkle in his merry brown eyes. Looking away toward Buckskin Mountain, which was coincidentally in the direction of home, I said to myself: 'This may be where you get on, but most certainly it is where you get off!'

Jones was already riding far beyond the corral, as I could see by a cloud of dust; and I set off after him, with the painful consciousness that I must have looked to Frank and Jim much as Central Park equestrians had often looked to me. Frank shouted after me that he would catch up with us out on the range. I was not in any great hurry to overtake Jones, but evidently my horse's inclinations differed from mine; at any rate, he made the dust fly, and jumped the little sage bushes.

Jones, who had tarried to inspect one of the pools—formed of running water from the corrals—greeted me as I came up with this cheerful observation:

'What in thunder did Frank give you that white nag for? The buffalo hate white horses—anything white. They're liable to stampede off the range, or chase you into the cañon.'

I replied grimly that, as it was certain something was going to happen, the particular circumstance might as well come off quickly.

We rode over the rolling plain with a cool, bracing breeze in our faces. The sky was dull and mottled with a beautiful cloud effect that presaged wind. As we trotted along Jones pointed out to me and descanted upon the nutritive value of three different kinds of grass, one of which he called the Buffalo Pea, noteworthy for a beautiful blue blossom. Soon we passed out of sight of the cabin, and could see only the billowy plain, the red tips of the stony wall, and the black-fringed crest of Buckskin. After riding a while we made out some cattle, a few of which were on the range, browsing in the lee of a ridge. No sooner had I marked them than Jones let out another Comanche yell.

'Wolf!' he yelled; and spurring his big bag, he was off like the wind.

A single glance showed me several cows running as if bewildered, and near them a big white wolf pulling down a calf. Another white wolf stood not far off. My horse jumped as if he had been shot; and the realization darted upon me that here was where the certain something began. Spot—the mustang had one black spot in his pure white—snorted like I imagined a blooded horse might, under dire insult. Jones's bay had gotten about a hundred paces the start. I lived to learn that Spot hated to be left behind; moreover, he would not be left behind; he was the swiftest horse on the range, and proud of the distinction. I cast one unmentionable word on the breeze toward the cabin and Frank, then put mind and muscle to the sore task of remaining with Spot. Jones was born on a saddle, and had been taking his meals in a saddle for about sixty-three years, and the bay horse could run. Run is not a felicitous word—he flew. And I was rendered mentally deranged for the moment to see that hundred paces between the bay and Spot materially lessen at every jump. Spot lengthened out, seemed to go down near the ground, and cut the air like a highgeared auto. If I had not heard the fast rhythmic beat of his hoofs, and had not bounced high into the air at every jump, I would have been sure I was riding a bird. I tried to stop him. As well might I have tried to pull in the *Lusitania* with a thread. Spot was out to overhaul that bay, and in spite of me, he was doing it. The wind rushed into my face and sang in my ears. Jones seemed the nucleus of a sort of haze, and he grew larger and larger. Presently he became clearly defined in my sight; the violent commotion under me subsided; I once more felt the saddle, and then I realized that Spot had been content to stop alongside of Jones, tossing his head and champing his bit.

'Well, by George! I didn't know you were in the stretch,' cried my companion. 'That was a fine little brush. We must have come several miles. I'd have killed those wolves if I'd brought a gun. The big one that had the calf was a bold brute. He never let go until I was within fifty feet of him. Then I almost rode him down. I don't think the calf was much hurt. But those blood-thirsty devils will return, and like as not get the calf. That's the worst of cattle raising. Now, take the buffalo. Do you suppose those wolves could have gotten a buffalo calf out from under the mother? Never. Neither could a whole band of wolves. Buffalo stick close together, and the little ones do not stray. When danger threatens, the herd closes in and faces it and fights. That is what is grand about the buffalo and what made them once roam the prairies in countless, endless droves.'

From the highest elevation in that part of the range we viewed the surrounding ridges, flats and hollows, searching for the buffalo. At length we spied a cloud of dust rising from behind an undulating mound, then big black dots hove in sight.

'Frank has rounded up the herd, and is driving it this way. We'll wait,' said Jones.

Though the buffalo appeared to be moving fast, a long time elapsed before they reached the foot of our outlook. They lumbered along in a compact mass, so dense that I could not count them, but I estimated the number at seventy-five. Frank was riding zigzag behind them, swinging his lariat and yelling. When he espied us he reined in his horse and waited. Then the herd slowed down, halted and began browsing.

'Look at the cattalo calves,' cried Jones, in ecstatic tones. 'See how shy they are, how close they stick to their mothers.'

The little dark-brown fellows were plainly frightened. I made several unsuccessful attempts to photograph them, and gave it up when Jones told me not to ride too close and that it would be better to wait till we had them in the corral.

He took my camera and instructed me to go on ahead, in the rear of the herd. I heard the click of the instrument as he snapped a picture, and then suddenly heard him shout in alarm: 'Look out! look out! pull your horse!'

Thundering hoof-beats pounding the earth accompanied his words. I saw a big bull, with head down, tail raised, charging my horse. He answered Frank's yell of command with a furious grunt. I was paralyzed at the wonderfully swift action of the shaggy brute, and I sat helpless. Spot wheeled as if he were on a pivot and plunged out of the way with a celerity that was astounding. The buffalo stopped, pawed the ground, and angrily tossed his huge head. Frank rode up to him, yelled, and struck him with the lariat, whereupon he gave another toss of his horns, and then returned to the herd.

'It was that darned white nag,' said Jones. 'Frank, it was wrong to put an inexperienced man on Spot. For that matter, the horse should never be allowed to go near the buffalo.'

'Spot knows the buffs; they'd never get to him,' replied Frank. But the usual spirit was absent from his voice, and he glanced at me soberly. I knew I had turned white, for I felt the peculiar cold sensation in my face.

'Now, look at that, will you?' cried Jones. 'I don't like the looks of that.'

He pointed to the herd. They stopped browsing, and were uneasily shifting to and fro. The bull lifted his head; the others slowly grouped together.

'Storm! Sandstorm!' exclaimed Jones, pointing desertward. Dark yellow clouds like smoke were rolling, sweeping, bearing down upon us. They expanded, blossoming out like gigantic roses, and whirled and merged into one another, all the time rolling on and blotting out the light.

'We've got to run. That storm may last two days,' yelled Frank to me. 'We've had some bad ones lately. Give your horse free rein, and cover your face.'

A roar, resembling an approaching storm at sea, came on puffs of wind, as the horse got into their stride. Long streaks of dust whipped up in different places; the silver-white grass bent to the ground; round bunches of sage went rolling before us. The puffs grew longer, steadier, harder. Then a shrieking blast howled on our trail, seeming to swoop down on us with a yellow, blinding pall. I shut my eyes and covered my face with a handkerchief. The sand blew so thick that it filled my gloves, pebbles struck me hard enough to sting through my coat.

Fortunately, Spot kept to an easy swinging lope, which was the most comfortable motion for me. But I began to get numb, and could hardly stick on the saddle. Almost before I had dared to hope, Spot stopped. Uncovering my face, I saw Jim in the doorway of the lee side of the cabin. The yellow, streaky, whistling clouds of sand split on the cabin and passed on, leaving a small, dusty space of light.

'Shore Spot do hate to be beat,' yelled Jim, as he helped me off. I stumbled into the cabin and fell upon a buffalo robe and lay there absolutely spent. Jones and Frank came in a few minutes apart, each anathematizing the gritty, powdery sand.

All day the desert storm raged and roared. The dust sifted through the numerous cracks in the cabin, burdened our clothes, spoiled our food and blinded our eyes. Wind, snow, sleet and rainstorms are discomforting enough under trying circumstances; but all combined, they are nothing to the choking, stinging, blinding sandstorm.

'Shore it'll let up by sundown,' averred Jim. And sure enough the roar died away about five o'clock, the wind abated and the sand settled.

Just before supper, a knock sounded heavily on the cabin door. Jim opened it to admit one of Emmett's sons and a very tall man whom none of us knew. He was a sand-man. All that was not sand seemed a space or two of corduroy, a big bone-handled knife, a prominent square jaw and bronzed cheek and flashing eyes.

'Get down—get down, an' come in, stranger,' said Frank cordially.

'How do you do, sir,' said Jones.

'Colonel Jones, I've been on your trail for twelve days,' announced the stranger, with a grim smile. The sand streamed off his coat in little white streaks.

Jones appeared to be casting about in his mind.

'I'm Grant Wallace,' continued the newcomer. 'I missed you at the El Tovar, at Williams and at Flagstaff, where I was one day behind. Was half a day late at the Little Colorado, saw your train cross Moncaupie Wash, and missed you because of the sandstorm there. Saw you from the other side of the Big Colorado as you rode out from Emmett's along the red wall. And here I am. We've never met till now, which obviously isn't my fault.'

The Colonel and I fell upon Wallace's neck. Frank manifested his usual alert excitation, and said: 'Well, I guess he won't hang fire on a long cougar chase.' And Jim—slow, careful Jim, dropped a plate with the exclamation: 'Shore it do beat hell!' The hounds sniffed round Wallace, and welcomed him with vigorous tails.

Supper that night, even if we did grind sand with our teeth, was a joyous occasion. The biscuits were flaky and light; the bacon fragrant and crisp. I produced a jar of blackberry jam, which by subtle cunning I had been able to secrete from the Mormons on that dry desert ride, and it was greeted with acclamations of pleasure. Wallace, divested of his sand guise, beamed with the gratification of a hungry man once more in the presence of friends and food. He made large cavities in Jim's great pot of potato stew, and caused biscuits to vanish in a way that would not have shamed a Hindoo magician. The grand cañon he dug in my jar of jam, however, could not have been accomplished by legerdemain.

Talk became animated on dogs, cougars, horses and buffalo. Jones told of our experience out on the range, and concluded with some salient remarks.

'A tame wild animal is the most dangerous of beasts. My old friend, Dick Rock, a great hunter and guide out of Idaho, laughed at my advice, and got killed by one of his three-year-old bulls. I told him they knew him just well enough to kill him, and they did. My friend, A. H. Cole, of Oxford, Nebraska, tried to rope a Weetah that was too tame to be safe, and the bull killed him. Same with General Bull, a member of the Kansas Legislature, and two cowboys who went into a corral to tie up a tame elk at the wrong time. I pleaded with them not to undertake it. They had not studied animals as I had. That tame elk killed all of them. He had to be shot in order to get General Bull off his great antlers. You see, a wild animal must learn to respect a man. The way I used to teach the Yellowstone Park bears to be respectful and safe neighbors was to rope them around the front paw, swing them up on a tree clear of the ground, and whip them with a long pole. It was a dangerous business, and looks cruel, but it is the only way I could find to make the bears good. You see, they eat scraps around the hotels and get so tame they will steal everything but red-hot stoves, and will cuff the life out of those who try to shoo them off. But after a bear mother has had a licking, she not only becomes a good bear for the rest of her life, but she tells all her cubs about it with a good smack of her paw, for emphasis, and teaches them to respect peaceable citizens generation after generation.

'One of the hardest jobs I ever tackled was that of supplying the buffalo for Bronx Park. I rounded up a magnificent 'king' buffalo bull, belligerent enough to fight a battleship. When I rode after him the cowmen said I was as good as killed. I made a lance by driving a nail into the end of a short pole and sharpening it. After he had chased me, I wheeled my broncho, and hurled the lance into his back, ripping a wound as long as my hand. That put the fear of Providence into him and took the fight all out of him. I drove him uphill and down, and across cañons at a dead run for eight miles single-handed, and loaded him on a freight car; but he came near getting me once or twice, and only quick broncho work and lance play saved me.

'In the Yellowstone Park all our buffaloes have become docile, excepting the huge bull which led them. The Indians call the buffalo leader the "Weetah", the master of the herd. It was sure death to go near this one. So I shipped in another Weetah, hoping that he might whip some of the fight out of old Manitou, the Mighty. They came together head on, like a railway collision, and ripped up over a square mile of landscape, fighting till night came on, and then on into the night.

'I jumped into the field with them, chasing them with my biograph, getting a series of moving pictures of that bullfight which was sure the real thing. It was a ticklish thing to do, though knowing that neither bull dared take his eyes off his adversary for a second, I felt reasonably safe. The old Weetah beat the new champion out that night, but the next morning they were at it again, and the new buffalo finally whipped the old one into submission. Since then his spirit has remained broken, and even a child can approach him safely—but the new Weetah is in turn a holy terror.

'To handle buffalo, elk and bear, you must get into sympathy with their methods of reasoning. No tenderfoot stands any show, even with the tame animals of the Yellowstone.'

The old buffalo hunter's lips were no longer locked. One after another he told reminiscences of his eventful life, in a simple manner; yet so vivid and gripping were the unvarnished details that I was spellbound.

'Considering what appears the impossibility of capturing a full-grown buffalo, how did you earn the name of preserver of the American bison?' inquired Wallace.

'It took years to learn how, and ten more to capture the fifty-eight that I was able to keep. I tried every plan under the sun. I roped hundreds, of all sizes and ages. They would not live in captivity. If they could not find an embankment over which to break their necks, they would crash their skulls on stones. Failing any means like that, they would lie down, will themselves to die, and die. Think of a savage wild nature that could will its heart to cease beating! But it's true. Finally I found I could keep only calves under three months of age. But to capture them so young entailed time and patience. For the buffalo fight for their young, and when I say fight, I mean till they drop. I almost always had to go alone, because I could neither coax nor hire any one to undertake it with me. Sometimes I would be weeks getting one calf. One day I captured eight—eight little buffalo calves! Never will I forget that day as long as I live!'

'Tell us about it,' I suggested, in a matter of fact, round-the-campfire voice. Had the silent plainsman ever told a complete and full story of his adventures? I doubted it. He was not the man to eulogize himself.

A short silence ensued. The cabin was snug and warm; the ruddy embers glowed; one of Jim's pots steamed musically and fragrantly. The hounds lay curled in the cozy chimney corner.

Jones began to talk again, simply and unaffectedly, of his famous exploit; and as he went on so modestly, passing lightly over features we recognized as wonderful, I allowed the fire of my imagination to fuse for myself all the toil, patience, endurance, skill, herculean strength and marvelous courage and unfathomable passion which he slighted in his narrative.

3
The Last Herd

Over gray No-Man's-Land stole down the shadows of night. The undulating prairie shaded dark to the western horizon, rimmed with a fading streak of light. Tall figures, silhouetted sharply against the last golden glow of sunset, marked the rounded crest of a grassy knoll.

'Wild hunter!' cried a voice in sullen rage, 'buffalo or no, we halt here. Did Adams and I hire to cross the Staked Plains? Two weeks in No-Man's-Land, and now we're facing the sand! We've one keg of water, yet you want to keep on. Why, man, you're crazy! You didn't tell us you wanted buffalo alive. And here you've got us looking death in the eye!'

In the grim silence that ensued the two men unhitched the team from the long, light wagon, while the buffalo hunter staked out his wiry, lithe-limbed racehorses. Soon a fluttering blaze threw a circle of light, which shone on the agitated face of Rude and Adams, and the cold, iron-set visage of their brawny leader.

'It's this way,' began Jones, in slow, cool voice: 'I engaged you fellows, and you promised to stick by me. We've had no luck. But I've finally found sign—old sign, I'll admit—of the buffalo I'm looking for—the last herd on the plains. For two years I've been hunting this herd. So have other hunters. Millions of buffalo have been killed and left to rot. Soon this herd will be gone, and then the only buffalo in the world will be those I have given ten years of the hardest work in capturing. This is the last herd, I say, and my last chance to capture a calf or two. Do you imagine I'd quit? You fellows go back if you want, but I keep on.'

'We can't go back. We're lost. We'll have to go with you. But, man, thirst is not the only risk we run. This is Comanche country. And if that herd is in here the Indians have it spotted.'

'That worries me some,' replied the plainsman, 'but we'll keep on.'

They slept. The night wind swished the grasses; dark storm clouds blotted out the northern stars; the prairie wolves mourned dismally.

Day broke cold, wan, threatening, under a leaden sky. The hunters traveled thirty miles by noon, and halted in a hollow where a stream flowed in wet season. Cottonwood trees were bursting into green; thickets of prickly thorn, dense and matted, showed bright spring buds.

'What is it?' suddenly whispered Rude.

The plainsman lay in strained posture, his ear against the ground.

'Hide the wagon and horses in the clump of cottonwoods,' he ordered, tersely. Springing to his feet, he ran to the top of the knoll above the hollow, where he again placed his ear to the ground.

Jones's practiced ear had detected the quavering rumble of far-away, thundering hoofs. He searched the wide waste of plain with his powerful glass. To the southwest, miles distant, a cloud of dust mushroomed skyward. 'Not buffalo,' he muttered, 'maybe wild horses.' He watched and waited. The yellow cloud rolled forward, enlarging, spreading out, and drove before it a darkly indistinct, moving mass. As soon as he had one good look at this he ran back to his comrades.

'Stampede! Wild horses! Indians! Look to your rifles and hide!'

Wordless and pale, the men examined their Sharps, and made ready to follow Jones. He slipped into the thorny brake and, flat on his stomach, wormed his way like a snake far into the thickly interlaced web of branches. Rude and Adams crawled after him. Words were superfluous. Quiet, breathless, with beating hearts, the hunters pressed close to the dry grass. A long, low, steady rumble filled the air, and increased in volume till it became a roar. Moments, endless moments, passed. The roar filled out like a flood slowly released from its confines to sweep down with the sound of doom. The ground began to tremble and quake: the light faded; the smell of dust pervaded the thicket, then a continuous streaming roar, deafening as persistent roll of thunder, pervaded the hiding place. The stampeding horses had split round the hollow. The roar lessened. Swiftly as a departing snow-squall rushing on through the pines, the thunderous thud and tramp of hoofs died away.

The trained horses hidden in the cottonwoods never stirred. 'Lie low! lie low!' breathed the plainsman to his companions.

Throb of hoofs again became audible, not loud and madly pounding as those that had passed, but low, muffled, rhythmic. Jones's sharp eye, through a peephole in the thicket, saw a cream-colored mustang bob over the knoll, carrying an Indian. Another and another, then a swiftly following, close-packed throng appeared. Bright red feathers and white gleamed; weapons glinted; gaunt, bronzed savages leaned forward on racy, slender mustangs.

The plainsman shrank closer to the ground. 'Apache!' he exclaimed to himself, and gripped his rifle. The band galloped down to the hollow, and slowing up, piled single file over the bank. The leader, a short, squat chief, plunged into the brake not twenty yards from the hidden men. Jones recognized the cream mustang; he knew the somber, sinister, broad face. It belonged to the Red Chief of the Apaches.

'Geronimo!' murmured the plainsman through his teeth.

Well for the Apache that no falcon savage eye discovered aught strange in the little hollow! One look at the sand of the stream bed would have cost him his life. But the Indians crossed the thicket too far up; they cantered up the slope and disappeared. The hoof-beats softened and ceased.

'Gone?' whispered Rude.

'Gone. But wait,' whispered Jones. He knew the savage nature, and he knew how to wait. After a long time, he cautiously crawled out of the thicket and searched the surroundings with a plainsman's eye. He climbed the slope and saw the clouds of dust, the near one small, the far one large, which told him all he needed to know.

'Comanches?' queried Adams, with a quaver in his voice. He was new to the plains.

'Likely,' said Jones, who thought it best not to tell all he knew. Then he added to himself: 'We've no time to lose. There's water back here somewhere. The Indians have spotted the buffalo, and were running the horses away from the water.'

The three got under way again, proceeding carefully, so as not to raise the dust, and headed due southwest. Scantier and scantier grew the grass; the hollows were washes of sand; steely gray dunes, like long, flat, ocean swells, ribbed the prairie. The gray day declined. Late into the purple night they traveled, then camped without fire.

In the gray morning Jones climbed a high ride and scanned the southwest. Low dun-colored sandhills waved from him down and down, in slow, deceptive descent. A solitary and remote waste reached out into gray infinitude. A pale lake, gray as the rest of that gray expanse, glimmered in the distance.

'Mirage!' he muttered, focusing his glass, which only magnified all under the dead gray, steely sky. 'Water must be somewhere; but can that be it? It's too pale and elusive to be real. No life—a blasted, staked plain! Hello!'

A thin, black, wavering line of wild fowl, moving in beautiful, rapid flight, crossed the line of his vision. 'Geese flying north, and low. There's water here,' he said. He followed the flock with his glass, saw them circle over the lake, and vanish in the gray sheen.

'It's water.' He hurried back to camp. His haggard and worn companions scorned his discovery. Adams siding with Rude, who knew the plains, said: 'Mirage! the lure of the desert!' Yet dominated by a force too powerful for them to resist, they followed the buffalo-hunter. All day the gleaming lake beckoned them onward, and seemed to recede. All day the drab clouds scudded before the cold north wind. In the gray twilight, the lake suddenly lay before them, as if it had opened at their feet. The men rejoiced, the horses lifted their noses and sniffed the damp air.

The whinnies of the horses, the clank of harness, and splash of water, the whirr of ducks did not blur out of Jones's keen ear a sound that made him jump. It was the thump of hoofs, in a familiar beat, beat, beat. He saw a shadow moving up a ridge. Soon, outlined black against the yet light sky, a lone buffalo cow stood like a statue. A moment she held toward the lake, studying the danger, then went out of sight over the ridge.

Jones spurred his horse up the ascent, which was rather long and steep, but he mounted the summit in time to see the cow join eight huge, shaggy buffalo. The hunter reined in his horse, and standing high in his stirrups, held his hat at arm's length over his head. So he thrilled to a moment he had sought for two years. The last herd of American bison was near at hand. The cow would not venture far from the main herd; the eight stragglers were the old broken-down bulls that had been expelled, at this season, from the herd by younger and more vigorous bulls. The old monarchs saw the hunter at the same time his eyes were gladdened by sight of them, and lumbered away after the cow, to disappear in the gathering darkness. Frightened buffalo always make straight for their fellows; and this knowledge contented Jones to return to the lake, well satisfied that the herd would not be far away in the morning, within easy striking distance by daylight.

At dark the storm which had threatened for days, broke in a fury of rain, sleet and hail. The hunters stretched a piece of canvas over the wheels of the north side of the wagon, and wet and shivering, crawled under it to their blankets. During the night the storm raged with unabated strength.

Dawn, forbidding and raw, lightened to the whistle of the sleety gusts. Fire was out of the question. Chary of weight, the hunters had carried no wood, and the buffalo chips they used for fuel were lumps of ice. Grumbling, Adams and Rude ate a cold breakfast, while Jones, munching a biscuit, faced the biting blast from the crest of the ridge. The middle of the plain below held a ragged, circular mass, as still as stone. It was the buffalo herd, with every shaggy head to the storm. So they would stand, never budging from their tracks, till the blizzard of sleet was over.

Jones, though eager and impatient, restrained himself, for it was unwise to begin operations in the storm. There was nothing to do but wait. Ill fared the hunters that day. Food had to be eaten uncooked. The long hours dragged by with the little group huddled under icy blankets. When darkness fell, the sleet changed to drizzling rain. This blew over at midnight, and a colder wind, penetrating to the very marrow of the sleepless men, made their condition worse. In the after part of the night, the wolves howled mournfully.

With a gray, misty light appearing in the east, Jones threw off his stiff, ice-incased blanket, and crawled out. A gaunt gray wolf, the color of the day and the sand and the lake, sneaked away, looking back. While moving and threshing about to warm his frozen blood, Jones munched another biscuit. His men crawled from under the wagon, and made an unfruitful search for the whisky. Fearing it, Jones had thrown the bottle away. The men cursed. The patient horses drooped sadly, and shivered in the lee of the improvised tent. Jones kicked the inch-thick casing of ice from his saddle. Kentuck, his racer, had been spared on the whole trip for this day's work. The thoroughbred was cold, but as Jones threw the saddle over him, he showed that he knew the chase ahead, and was eager to be off. At last, after repeated efforts with his benumbed fingers, Jones got the girths tight. He tied a bunch of soft cords to the saddle and mounted.

'Follow as fast as you can,' he called to his surly men. 'The buffs will run north against the wind. This is the right direction for us; we'll soon leave the sand. Stick to my trail and come a-humming.'

From the ridge he met the red sun, rising bright, and a keen northeasterly wind that lashed like a whip. As he had anticipated, his quarry had moved northward. Kentuck let out into a swinging stride, which in an hour had the loping herd in sight. Every jump now took him upon higher ground, where the sand failed, and the grass grew thicker and began to bend under the wind.

In the teeth of the nipping gale Jones slipped close upon the herd without alarming even a cow. More than a hundred little reddish-black calves leisurely loped in the rear. Kentuck, keen to his work, crept on like a wolf, and the hunter's great fist clenched the coiled lasso. Before him expanded a boundless plain. A situation long cherished and dreamed of had become a reality. Kentuck, fresh and strong, was good for all day. Jones gloated over the little red bulls and heifers, as a miser gloats over gold and jewels. Never before had he caught more than two in one day, and often it had taken days to capture one. This was the last herd, this the last opportunity toward perpetuating a grand race of beasts. And with born instinct he saw ahead the day of his life.

At a touch, Kentuck closed in, and the buffalo, seeing him, stampeded into the heaving roll so well known to the hunter. Racing on the right flank of the herd,

Jones selected a tawny heifer and shot the lariat after her. It fell true, but being stiff and kinky from the sleet, failed to tighten, and the quick calf leaped through the loop to freedom.

Undismayed the pursuer quickly recovered his rope. Again he whirled and sent the loop. Again it circled true, and failed to close; again the agile heifer bounded through it. Jones whipped the air with the stubborn rope. To lose a chance like that was worse than boy's work.

The third whirl, running a smaller loop, tightened the coil round the frightened calf just back of its ears. A pull on the bridle brought Kentuck to a halt in his tracks, and the baby buffalo rolled over and over in the grass. Jones bounced from his seat and jerked loose a couple of the soft cords. In a twinkling his big knee crushed down on the calf, and his big hands bound it helpless.

Kentuck neighed. Jones saw his black ears go up. Danger threatened. For a moment the hunter's blood turned chill, not from fear, for he never felt fear, but because he thought the Indians were returning to ruin his work. His eye swept the plain. Only the gray forms of wolves flitted through the grass, here, there, all about him. Wolves! They were as fatal to his enterprise as savages. A trooping pack of prairie wolves had fallen in with the herd and hung close on the trail, trying to cut a calf away from its mother. The gray brutes boldly trotted to within a few yards of him, and slyly looked at him, with pale, fiery eyes. They had already scented his captive. Precious time flew by; the situation, critical and baffling, had never before been met by him. There lay his little calf tied fast, and to the north ran many others, some of which he must—he would have. To think quickly had meant the solving of many a plainsman's problem. Should he stay with his prize to save it, or leave it to be devoured?

'Ha! you old gray devils!' he yelled, shaking his fist at the wolves. 'I know a trick or two.' Slipping his hat between the legs of the calf, he fastened it securely. This done, he vaulted on Kentuck, and was off with never a backward glance. Certain it was that the wolves would not touch anything, alive or dead, that bore the scent of a human being.

The bison scoured away a long half-mile in the lead, sailing northward like a cloud-shadow over the plain. Kentuck, mettlesome, over-eager, would have run himself out in short order, but the wary hunter, strong to restrain as well as impel, with the long day in his mind, kept the steed in his easy stride, which, springy and stretching, overhauled the herd in the course of several miles.

A dash, a whirl, a shock, a leap, horse and hunter working in perfect accord, and a fine big calf, bellowing lustily, struggled desperately for freedom under the remorseless knee. The big hands toyed with him; and then, secure in the double knots, the calf lay still, sticking out his tongue and rolling his eyes, with the coat of the hunter tucked under his bonds to keep away the wolves.

The race had but begun; the horse had but warmed to his work; the hunter had but tasted of sweet triumph. Another hopeful of a buffalo mother, negligent in danger, truant from his brothers, stumbled and fell in the enmeshing loop. The hunter's vest, slipped over the calf's neck, served as danger signal to the wolves. Before the lumbering buffalo missed their loss, another red and black baby kicked helplessly on the grass and sent up vain, weak calls, and at last lay still, with the hunter's boot tied to his cords.

Four! Jones counted them aloud, and in his mind, and kept on! Fast, hard work, covering upward of fifteen miles, had begun to tell on herd, horse and man, and all slowed down to the call for strength. The fifth time Jones closed in on his game, he encountered different circumstances such as called forth his cunning.

The herd had opened up; the mothers had fallen back to the rear; the calves hung almost out of sight under the shaggy sides of protectors. To try them out Jones darted close and threw his lasso. It struck a cow. With activity incredible in such a huge beast, she lunged at him. Kentuck, expecting just such a move, wheeled to safety. This duel, ineffectual on both sides, kept up for a while, and all the time, man and herd were jogging rapidly to the north.

Jones could not let well enough alone; he acknowledged this even as he swore he must have five. Emboldened by his marvelous luck, and yielding headlong to the passion within, he threw caution to the winds. A lame old cow with a red calf caught his eye; in he spurred his willing horse and slung his rope. It stung the haunch of the mother. The mad grunt she vented was no quicker than the velocity with which she plunged and reared. Jones had but time to swing his leg over the saddle when the hoofs beat down. Kentuck rolled on the plain, flinging his rider from him. The infuriated buffalo lowered her head for the fatal charge on the horse, when the plainsman, jerking out his heavy Colts, shot her dead in her tracks.

Kentuck got to his feet unhurt, and stood his ground, quivering but ready, showing his steadfast courage. He showed more, for his ears lay back, and his eyes had the gleam of the animal that strikes back.

The calf ran round its mother. Jones lassoed it, and tied it down, being compelled to cut a piece from his lasso, as the cords on the saddle had given out. He left his other boot with baby number five. The still heaving, smoking body of the victim called forth the stern, intrepid hunter's pity for a moment. Spill of blood he had not wanted. But he had not been able to avoid it; and mounting again with close-shut jaw and smoldering eye, he galloped to the north.

Kentuck snorted; the pursuing wolves shied off in the grass; the pale sun began to slant westward. The cold iron stirrups froze and cut the hunter's bootless feet.

When once more he came hounding the buffalo, they were considerably winded. Short-tufted tails, raised stiffly, gave warning. Snorts, like puffs of escaping steam, and deep grunts from cavernous chests evinced anger and impatience that might, at any moment, bring the herd to a defiant stand.

He whizzed the shortened noose over the head of a calf that was laboring painfully to keep up, and had slipped down, when a mighty grunt told him of peril. Never looking to see whence it came, he sprang into the saddle. Fiery Kentuck jumped into action, then hauled up with a shock that almost threw himself and rider. The lasso, fast to the horse, and its loop end round the calf, had caused the sudden check.

A maddened cow bore down on Kentuck. The gallant horse straightened in a jump, but dragging the calf pulled him in a circle, and in another moment he was running round and round the howling, kicking pivot. Then ensued a terrible race, with horse and bison describing a twenty-foot circle. Bang! Bang! The hunter fired two shots, and heard the spats of the bullets. But they only augmented the frenzy of the beast. Faster Kentuck flew, snorting in terror; closer drew the dusty, bouncing pursuer; the calf spun like a top; the lasso strung tighter than wire. Jones strained to loosen the fastening, but in vain. He swore at his carelessness in dropping his knife by the last calf he had tied. He thought of shooting the rope, yet dared not risk the shot. A hollow sound turned him again, with the Colts leveled. Bang! Dust flew from the ground beyond the bison.

The two charges left in the gun were all that stood between him and eternity. With a desperate display of strength Jones threw his weight in a backward pull, and hauled Kentuck up. Then he leaned far back in the saddle, and shoved the Colts out beyond the horse's flank. Down went the broad head, with its black, glistening horns. Bang! She slid forward with a crash, plowing the ground with hoofs and nose—spouted blood, uttered a hoarse cry, kicked and died.

Kentuck, for once completely terrorized, reared and plunged from the cow, dragging the calf. Stern command and iron arm forced him to a standstill. The calf, nearly strangled, recovered when the noose was slipped, and moaned a feeble protest against life and captivity. The remainder of Jones's lasso went to bind number six, and one of his socks went to serve as reminder to the persistent wolves.

'Six! On! On! Kentuck! On!' Weakening, but unconscious of it, with bloody hands and feet, without lasso, and with only one charge in his revolver, hatless, coatless, vestless, bootless, the wild hunter urged on the noble horse. The herd had gained miles in the interval of the fight. Game to the backbone, Kentuck lengthened out to overhaul it, and slowly the rolling gap lessened and lessened. A long hour thumped away, with the rumble growing nearer.

Once again the lagging calves dotted the grassy plain before the hunter. He dashed beside a burly calf, grasped its tail, stopped his horse, and jumped. The calf went down with him, and did not come up. The knotted, blood-stained hands, like claws of steel, bound the hind legs close and fast with a leathern belt, and left between them a torn and bloody sock.

'Seven! On! Old Faithful! We *must* have another! the last! This is your day.'

The blood that flecked the hunter was not all his own.

The sun slanted westwardly toward the purpling horizon; the grassy plain gleamed like a ruffled sea of glass; the gray wolves loped on.

When next the hunger came within sight of the herd, over a wavy ridge, changes in its shape and movement met his gaze. The calves were almost done; they could run no more; their mothers faced the south,and trotted slowly to and fro; the bulls were grunting, herding, piling close. It looked as if the herd meant to stand and fight.

This mattered little to the hunter who had captured seven calves since dawn. The first limping calf he reached tried to elude the grasping hand and failed. Kentuck had been trained to wheel to the right or left, in whichever way his rider leaned; and as Jones bent over and caught an upraised tail, the horse turned to strike the calf with both front hoofs. The calf rolled; the horse plunged down; the rider sped beyond to the dust. Though the calf was tired, he still could bellow, and he filled the air with robust bawls.

Jones all at once saw twenty or more buffalo dash in at him with fast, twinkling, short legs. With the thought of it, he was in the air to the saddle. As the black, round mounds charged from every direction, Kentuck let out with all there was left in him. He leaped and whirled, pitched and swerved, in a roaring, clashing, dusty mêlée. Beating hoofs threw the turf, flying tails whipped the air, and everywhere were dusky, sharp-pointed heads, tossing low. Kentuck squeezed out unscathed. The mob of bison, bristling, turned to lumber after the main herd. Jones seized his opportunity and rode after them, yelling with all his might. He drove them so hard that soon the little fellows lagged paces behind. Only one or two old cows straggled with the calves.

Then wheeling Kentuck, he cut between the herd and a calf, and rode it down. Bewildered, the tously little bull bellowed in great affright. The hunter seized the stiff tail, and calling to his horse, leaped off. But his strength was far spent, and the buffalo, larger than his fellows, threshed about and jerked in terror. Jones threw it again and again. But it struggled up, never once ceasing its loud demands for help. Finally the hunter tripped it up and fell upon it with his knees.

Above the rumble of retreating hoofs, Jones heard the familiar short, quick, jarring pound on the turf. Kentuck neighed his alarm and raced to the right. Bearing down on the hunter, hurtling through the air, was a giant furry mass, instinct with fierce life and power—a buffalo cow robbed of her young.

With his senses almost numb, barely able to pull and raise the Colt, the plainsman willed to live, and to keep his captive. His leveled arm wavered like a leaf in a storm.

Bang! Fire, smoke, a shock, a jarring crash, and silence!

The calf stirred beneath him. He put out a hand to touch a warm, furry coat. The mother had fallen beside him. Lifting a heavy hoof, he laid it over the neck of the calf to serve as additional weight. He lay still and listened. The rumble of the herd died away in the distance.

The evening waned. Still the hunter lay quiet. From time to time the calf struggled and bellowed. Lank, gray wolves appeared on all sides; they prowled about with hungry howls, and shoved black-tipped noses through the grass. The sun sank, and the sky paled to opal blue. A star shone out, then another, and another. Over the prairie slanted the first dark shadow of night.

Suddenly the hunter laid his ear to the ground, and listened. Faint beats, like throbs of a pulsing heart, shuddered from the soft turf. Stronger they grew, till the hunter raised his head. Dark forms approached, voices broke the silence; the creaking of a wagon scared away the wolves.

'This way!' shouted the hunter weakly.

'Ha! here he is. Hurt?' cried Rude, vaulting the wheel.

'Tie up this calf. How many—did you find?' The voice grew fainter.

'Seven—alive, and in good shape, and all your clothes.'

But the last words fell on unconscious ears.

4
The Trail

"Frank, what'll we do about horses?' asked Jones. 'Jim'll want the bay, and of course you'll want to ride Spot. The rest of our nags will only do to pack the outfit.'

'I've been thinkin',' replied the foreman. 'You sure will need good mounts. Now it happens that a friend of mine is just at this time at House Rock Valley, an outlyin' post of one of the big Utah ranches. He is gettin' in the horses off the range, an' he has some crackin' good ones. Let's ooze over there—it's only thirty miles—an' get some horses from him.'

We were all eager to act upon Frank's suggestion. So plans were made for three of us to ride over and select our mounts. Frank and Jim would follow with the pack train, and if all went well, on the following evening we would camp under the shadow of Buckskin.

Early next morning we were on our way. I tried to find a soft place on Old Baldy, one of Frank's pack horses. He was a horse that would not have raised up at the trumpet of doom. Nothing under the sun, Frank said, bothered Old Baldy but the operation of shoeing. We made the distance to the outpost by noon, and found Frank's friend a genial and obliging cowboy, who said we could have all the horses we wanted.

While Jones and Wallace strutted round the big corral, which was full of vicious, dusty, shaggy horses and mustangs, I sat high on the fence. I heard them talking about points and girth and stride, and a lot of terms that I could not understand. Wallace selected a heavy sorrel, and Jones a big bay, very like Jim's. I had observed, way over in the corner of the corral, a bunch of cayuses, and among them a clean-limbed black horse. Edging round on the fence I got a closer view, and then cried out that I had found my horse. I jumped down and caught him, much to my surprise, for the other horses were wild, and had kicked viciously. The black was beautifully built, wide-chested and powerful, but not heavy. His coat glistened like sheeny black satin, and he had a white face and white feet and a long mane.

'I don't know about giving you Satan—that's his name,' said the cowboy. 'The foreman rides him often. He's the fastest, the best climber, and the best dis-positioned horse on the range.

'But I guess I can let you have him,' he continued, when he saw my disappointed face.

'By George!' exclaimed Jones. 'You've got it on us this time.'

'Would you like to trade?' asked Wallace, as his sorrel tried to bite him. 'That black looks sort of fierce.'

I led my prize out of the corral, up to the little cabin nearby, where I tied him, and proceeded to get acquainted after a fashion of my own. Though not versed in horse-lore, I knew that half the battle was to win his confidence. I smoothed his silky coat, and patted him, and then surreptitiously slipped a lump of sugar from my pocket. This sugar, which I had purloined in Flagstaff, and carried all the way across the desert, was somewhat disreputably soiled, and Satan sniffed at it disdainfully. Evidently he had never smelled or tasted sugar. I pressed it into his mouth. He munched it, and then looked me over with some interest. I handed him another lump. He took it and rubbed his nose against me. Satan was mine!

Frank and Jim came along early in the afternoon. What with packing, changing saddles and shoeing the horses, we were all busy. Old Baldy would not be shod, so we let him off till a more opportune time. By four o'clock we were riding toward the slopes of Buckskin, now only a few miles away, standing up higher and darker.

'What's that for?' inquired Wallace, pointing to a long, rusty, wire-wrapped, double-barreled blunderbuss of a shotgun, stuck in the holster of Jones's saddle.

The Colonel, who had been having a fine time with the impatient and curious hounds, did not vouchsafe any information on that score. But very shortly we were destined to learn the use of this incongruous firearm. I was riding in advance of Wallace, and a little behind Jones. The dogs—excepting Jude, who had been kicked and lamed—were ranging along before their master. Suddenly, right before me, I saw an immense jack-rabbit; and just then Moze and Don caught sight of it. In fact, Moze bumped his blunt nose into the rabbit. When it leaped into scared action, Moze yelped, and Don followed suit. Then they were after it in wild, clamoring pursuit. Jones let out the stentorian blast, now becoming familiar, and spurred after them. He reached over, pulled the shotgun out of the holster and fired both barrels at the jumping dogs.

I expressed my amazement in strong language, and Wallace whistled.

Don came sneaking back with his tail between his legs, and Moze, who had cowered as if stung, circled round ahead of us. Jones finally succeeded in getting him back.

'Come in hyah! You measly rabbit dogs! What do you mean chasing off that way? We're after lions. Lions! understand?'

Don looked thoroughly convinced of his error, but Moze, being more thick-headed, appeared mystified rather than hurt or frightened.

'What size shot do you use?' I asked.

'Number ten. They don't hurt much at seventy-five yards,' replied our leader. 'I use them as sort of a long arm. You see, the dogs must be made to know what we're after. Ordinary means would never do in a case like this. My idea is to break them off coyotes, wolves and deer, and when we cross a lion trail, let them go. I'll teach them sooner than you'd think. Only we must get where we can see what they're trailing. Then I can tell whether to call them back or not.'

The sun was gilding the rim of the desert ramparts when we began the ascent of the foothills of Buckskin. A steep trail wound zigzag up the mountain. We led our horses, as it was a long, hard climb. From time to time, as I stopped to catch my breath, I gazed away across the growing void to the gorgeous Pink Cliffs, far above and beyond the red wall which had seemed so high, and then out toward the desert. The irregular ragged crack in the plain, apparently only a thread of broken ground, was the Grand Cañon. How unutterably remote, wild, grand was that world of red and brown, of purple pall, of vague outline!

Two thousand feet, probably, we mounted to what Frank called Little Buckskin. In the west a copper glow, ridged with lead-colored clouds, marked where the sun had set. The air was very thin and icy cold. At the first clump of piñon pines, we made dry camp. When I sat down it was as if I had been anchored. Frank solicitously remarked that I looked 'sort of beat.' Jim built a roaring fire and began getting supper. A snow squall came on the rushing wind. The air grew colder, and though I hugged the fire, I could not get warm. When I had satisfied my hunger, I rolled out my sleeping-bag and crept into it. I stretched my aching limbs and did not move again. Once I awoke, drowsily feeling the warmth of the fire, and I heard Frank say: 'He's asleep, dead to the world!'

'He's all in,' said Jones. 'Riding's what did it. You know how a horse tears a man to pieces.'

'Will he be able to stand it?' asked Frank, with as much solicitude as if he were my brother. 'When you get out after anythin'—well, you're hell. An' think of the country we're goin' into. I know you've never seen the breaks of the Siwash, but I have, an' it's the worst an' roughest country I ever saw. Breaks after breaks, like the ridges on a washboard, headin' on the south slope of Buckskin, an' runnin' down, side by side, miles an' miles, deeper an' deeper, till they run into that awful hole. It will be a killin' trip on men, horses an' dogs. Now, Mr Wallace, he's been campin' an' roughin' with the Navajos for months; he's in some kind of shape, but—'

Frank concluded his remark with a doubtful pause.

'I'm some worried, too,' replied Jones. 'But he would come. He stood the desert well enough; even the Mormons said that.'

In the ensuing silence the fire sputtered, the glare fitfully merged into dark shadows under the weird piñons, and the wind moaned through the short branches.

'Wal,' drawled a slow, soft voice, 'shore I reckon you're hollerin' too soon. Frank's measly trick puttin' him on Spot showed me. He rode out on Spot, an' he rode in on Spot. Shore he'll stay.'

It was not all the warmth of the blankets that glowed over me then. The voices died away dreamily, and my eyelids dropped sleepily tight. Late in the night I sat up suddenly, roused by some unusual disturbance. The fire was dead; the wind swept with a rush through the piñons. From the black darkness came the staccato chorus of coyotes. Don barked his displeasure; Sounder made the welkin ring, and old Moze growled low and deep, grumbling like muttered thunder. Then all was quiet, and I slept.

Dawn, rosy red, confronted me when I opened my eyes. Breakfast was ready; Frank was packing Old Baldy; Jones talked to his horse as he saddled him; Wallace came stooping his giant figure under the piñons; the dogs, eager and soft-eyed, sat around Jim and begged. The sun peeped over the Pink Cliffs; the desert still lay asleep, tranced in a purple and golden-streaked mist.

'Come, come!' said Jones, in his big voice. 'We're slow; here's the sun.'

'Easy, easy,' replied Frank, 'we've all the time there is.'

When Frank threw the saddle over Satan I interrupted him and said I would care for my horse hence forward. Soon we were under way, the horses fresh, the dogs scenting the keen, cold air.

The trail rolled over the ridges of piñon and scrubby pine. Occasionally we could see the black, ragged crest of Buckskin above us. From one of these ridges I took my last long look back at the desert, and engraved on my mind a picture of the red wall, and the many-hued ocean of sand. The trail; narrow and indistinct, mounted the last slow-rising slope; the piñons failed, and the scrubby pines became abundant. At length we reached the top, and entered the great arched aisles of Buckskin Forest. The ground was flat as a table. Magnificent pine trees, far apart, with branches high and spreading, gave the eye glad welcome. Some of these monarchs were eight feet thick at the base and two hundred feet high. Here and there one lay, gaunt and prostrate, a victim of the wind. The smell of pitch pine was sweetly overpowering.

'When I went through here two weeks ago, the snow was a foot deep, an' I bogged in places,' said Frank. 'The sun has been oozin' round here some. I'm afraid Jones won't find any snow on this end of Buckskin.'

Thirty miles of winding trail, brown and springy from its thick mat of pine needles, shaded always by the massive, seamy-barked trees, took us over the extremity of Buckskin. Then we faced down into the head of a ravine that ever grew deeper, stonier and rougher. I shifted from side to side, from leg to leg in my saddle, dismounted and hobbled before Satan, mounted again, and rode on. Jones called the dogs and complained to them of the lack of snow. Wallace sat his horse comfortably, taking long pulls at his pipe and long gazes at the shaggy sides of the ravine. Frank, energetic and tireless, kept the pack-horses in the trail. Jim jogged on silently. And so we rode down to Oak Spring.

The spring was pleasantly situated in a grove of oaks and piñons, under the shadow of three cliffs. Three ravines opened here into an oval valley. A rude cabin of roughhewn logs stood near the spring.

'Get down, get down,' sang out Frank. 'We'll hang up here. Beyond Oak is No-Man's-Land. We take our chances on water after we leave here.'

When we had unsaddled, unpacked, and got a fire roaring on the wide stone hearth of the cabin, it was once again night.

'Boys,' said Jones after supper, 'we're now on the edge of lion country. Frank saw lion sign in here only two weeks ago; and though the snow is gone, we stand a show of finding tracks in the sand and dust. To-morrow morning, before the sun gets a chance at the bottom of these ravines, we'll be up and doing. We'll each take a dog and search in different directions. Keep the dog in leash, and when he opens up, examine the ground carefully for tracks. If a dog opens on any track that you are sure isn't a lion's, punish him. And when a lion-track is found, hold the dog in, wait and signal. We'll use a signal I have tried and found far-reaching and easy to yell. Waa-hoo! That's it. Once yelled it means come. Twice means come quickly. Three times means come—danger!'

In one corner of the cabin was a platform of poles, covered with straw. I threw the sleeping-bag on this, and was soon stretched out. Misgivings as to my strength worried me before I closed my eyes. Once on my back, I felt I could not rise; my chest was sore; my cough deep and rasping. It seemed I had scarcely closed my eyes when Jones's impatient voice recalled me from sweet oblivion.

'Frank, Frank, it's daylight. Jim—boys!' he called.

I tumbled out in a gray, wan twilight. It was cold enough to make the fire acceptable, but nothing like the morning before on Buckskin.

'Come to the festal board,' drawled Jim, almost before I had my boots laced.

'Jones,' said Frank, 'Jim an' I'll ooze round here to-day. There's lots to do, an' we want to have things hitched right before we strike for the Siwash. We've got to shoe Old Baldy, an' if we can't get him locoed, it'll take all of us to do it.'

The light was still gray when Jones led off with Don, Wallace with Sounder and I with Moze. Jones directed us to separate, follow the dry stream beds in the ravines, and remember his instructions given the night before.

The ravine to the right, which I entered, was choked with huge stones fallen from the cliff above, and piñons growing thick; and I wondered apprehensively how a man could evade a wild animal in such a place, much less chase it.

Old Moze pulled on his chain and sniffed at coyote and deer tracks. And every time he evinced interest in such, I cut him with a switch, which, to tell the truth, he did not notice.

I thought I heard a shout, and holding Moze tight, I waited and listened.

'Waa-hoo—waa-hoo!' floated on the air, rather deadened as if it had come from round the triangular cliff that faced into the valley. Urging and dragging Moze, I ran down the ravine as fast as I could, and soon encountered Wallace coming from the middle ravine.

'Jones,' he said excitedly, 'this way—there's the signal again.'

We dashed in haste for the mouth of the third ravine, and came suddenly upon Jones, kneeling under a piñon tree.

'Boys, look!' he exclaimed, as he pointed to the ground. There, clearly defined in the dust, was a cat track as big as my spread hand, and the mere sight of it sent a chill up my spine. 'There's a lion track for you; made by a female, a two-year-old; but I can't say if she passed here last night. Don won't take the trail. Try Moze.'

I led Moze to the big, round imprint, and put his nose down into it. The old hound sniffed and sniffed, then lost interest.

'Cold!' ejaculated Jones. 'No go. Try Sounder. Come, old boy, you've the nose for it.'

He urged the reluctant hound forward. Sounder needed not to be shown the trail; he stuck his nose in it, and stood very quiet for a long moment; then he quivered slightly, raised his nose and sought the next track. Step by step he went slowly, doubtfully. All at once his tail wagged stiffly.

'Look at that!' cried Jones in delight. 'He's caught a scent when the others couldn't. Hyah, Moze, get back. Keep Moze and Don back; give him room.'

Slowly Sounder paced up the ravine, as carefully as if he were traveling on thin ice. He passed the dusty, open trail to a scaly ground with little bits of grass, and he kept on.

We were electrified to hear him give vent to a deep bugle-blast note of eagerness.

'By George, he's got it, boys!' exclaimed Jones, as he lifted the stubborn, struggling hound off the trail. 'I know that bay. It means a lion passed here this morning. And we'll get him up as sure as you're alive. Come, Sounder. Now for the horses.'

As we ran pell-mell into the little glade, where Jim sat mending some saddle trapping, Frank rode up the trail with the horses.

'Well, I heard Sounder,' he said with his genial smile. 'Somethin's comin' off, eh? You'll have to ooze round some to keep up with that hound.'

I saddled Satan with fingers that trembled in excitement, and pushed my little Remington automatic into the rifle holster.

'Boys, listen,' said our leader. 'We're off now in the beginning of a hunt new to you. Remember—no shooting, no blood-letting, except in self-defense. Keep as close to me as you can. Listen for the dogs, and when you fall behind or separate, yell out the signal cry. Don't forget this. We're bound to lose each other. Look out for the spikes and branches on the trees. If the dogs split, whoever follows the one that trees the lion must wait there till the rest come up. Off now! Come, Sounder; Moze, you rascal, hyah! Come, Don, come, Puppy, and take your medicine.'

Except Moze, the hounds were all trembling and running eagerly to and fro. When Sounder was loosed, he led them in a bee-line to the trail, with us cantering after. Sounder worked exactly as before, only he followed the lions tracks a little farther up the ravine before he bayed. He kept going faster and faster, occasionally letting out one deep, short yelp. The other hounds did not give tongue, but eager, excited, baffled, kept at his heels. The ravine was long, and the wash at the bottom, up which the lion had proceeded, turned and twisted round bowlders large as houses, and led through dense growths of some short, rough shrub. Now and then the lion tracks showed plainly in the sand. For five miles or more Sounder led us up the ravine, which began to contract and grow steep. The dry stream bed got to be full of thickets of poplar—tall, straight, branchless saplings, about the size of a man's arm, and growing so close we had to press them aside to let our horses through.

Presently Sounder slowed up and appeared at fault. We found him puzzling over an open, grassy patch, and after nosing it for a little while, he began skirting the edge.

'Cute dog!' declared Jones. 'That Sounder will make a lion chaser. Our game has gone up here somewhere.'

Sure enough, Sounder directly gave tongue from the side of the ravine. It was climb for us now. Broken shale, rocks of all dimensions, piñons down and piñons up made ascending no easy problem. We had to dismount and lead the horses, thus losing ground. Jones forged ahead and reached the top of the ravine first. When Wallace and I got up, breathing heavily, Jones and the hounds were out of sight. But Sounder kept voicing his clear call, giving us our direction. Off we flew, over ground that was still rough, but enjoyable going compared to the ravine slopes. The ridge was sparsely covered with cedar and piñon, through which, far ahead, we pretty soon spied Jones. Wallace signaled, and our leader answered twice. We caught up with him on the brink of another ravine deeper and craggier than the first, full of dead, gnarled piñon and splintered rocks.

'This gulch is the largest of the three that head in at Oak Spring,' said Jones. 'Boys, don't forget your direction. Always keep a feeling where camp is, always sense it every time you turn. The dogs have gone down. That lion is in here somewhere. Maybe he lives down in the high cliffs near the spring and came up here last night for a kill he's buried somewhere. Lions never travel far. Hark! Hark! There's Sounder and the rest of them! They've got the scent; they've all got it! Down, boys, down, and ride!'

With that he crashed into the cedar in a way that showed me how impervious he was to slashing branches, sharp as thorns, and steep descent and peril. Wallace's big sorrel plunged after him and the rolling stones cracked. Suffering as I was by this time, with cramp in my legs, and torturing pain, I had to choose between holding my horse in or falling off; so I chose the former and accordingly got behind.

Dead cedar and piñon trees lay everywhere, with their contorted limbs reaching out like the arms of a devil-fish. Stones blocked every opening. Making the bottom of the ravine after what seemed an interminable time, I found the tracks of Jones and Wallace. A long 'Waa-hoo!' drew me on; then the mellow bay of a hound floated up the ravine. Satan made up time in the sandy stream bed, but kept me busily dodging overhanging branches. I became aware, after a succession of efforts to keep from being strung on piñons, that the sand before me was clean and trackless. Hauling Satan up sharply, I waited irresolutely and listened. Then from high up the ravine side wafted down a medley of yelps and barks.

'Waa-hoo, waa-hoo!' ringing down the slope, pealed against the cliff behind me, and sent the wild echoes flying.

Satan, of his own accord, headed up the incline. Surprised at this, I gave him free rein. How he did climb! Not long did it take me to discover that he picked out easier going than I had. Once I saw Jones crossing a ledge far above me, and I yelled our signal cry. The answer returned clear and sharp; then its echo cracked under the hollow cliff, and crossing and recrossing the ravine, it died at last far away, like the muffled peal of a bell-buoy. Again I heard the blended yelping of the hounds, and closer at hand. I saw a long, low cliff above, and decided that the hounds were running at the base of it. Another chorus of yelps, quicker, wilder than the others, drew a yell from me. Instinctively I knew the dogs had jumped game of some kind. Satan knew it as well as I, for he quickened his pace and sent the stones clattering behind him.

I gained the base of the yellow cliff, but found no tracks in the dust of ages that had crumbled in its shadow, nor did I hear the dogs. Considering how close they had seemed, this was strange. I halted and listened. Silence reigned supreme. The ragged cracks in the cliff walls could have harbored many a watching lion, and I cast an apprehensive glance into their dark confines. Then I turned my horse to get round the cliff and over the ridge. When I again stopped, all I could hear was the thumping of my heart and the labored panting of Satan. I came to a break in the cliff, a steep place of weathered rock, and I put Satan to it. He went up with a will. From the narrow saddle of the ridge-crest I tried to take my bearings. Below me slanted the green of piñon, with the bleached treetops standing like spears, and uprising yellow stones. Fancying I heard a gunshot, I leaned a straining ear against the soft breeze. The proof came presently in the unmistakable report of Jones's blunderbuss. It was repeated almost instantly, giving reality to the direction, which was down the slope of what I concluded must be the third ravine. Wondering what was the meaning of the shots, and chagrined because I was out of the race, but calmer in mind, I let Satan stand.

Hardly a moment elapsed before a sharp bark tingled in my ears. It belonged to old Moze. Soon I distinguished a rattling of stones and the sharp, metallic clicks of hoofs striking rocks. Then into a space below me loped a beautiful deer, so large that at first I took it for an elk. Another sharp bark, nearer this time, told the tale of Moze's dereliction. In a few moments he came in sight, running with his tongue out and his head high.

'Hyah, you old gladiator! hyah! hyah!' I yelled and yelled again. Moze passed over the saddle on the trail of the deer, and his short bark floated back to remind me how far he was from a lion dog.

Then I divined the meaning of the shotgun reports. The hounds had crossed a fresher trail than that of the lion, and our leader had discovered it. Despite a keen appreciation of Jones's task, I gave way to amusement, and repeated Wallace's paradoxical formula: 'Pet the lions and shoot the hounds.'

So I headed down the ravine, looking for a blunt, bold crag, which I had descried from camp. I found it before long, and profiting by past failures to judge of distance, gave my first impression a great stretch, and then decided that I was more than two miles from Oak.

Long after two miles had been covered, and I had begun to associate Jim's biscuits with a certain soft seat near a ruddy fire, I was apparently still the same distance from my landmark crag. Suddenly a slight noise brought me to a halt. I listened intently. Only an indistinct rattling of small rocks disturbed the impressive stillness. It might have been the weathering that goes on constantly, and it might have been an animal. I inclined to the former idea till I saw Satan's ears go up. Jones had told me to watch the ears of my horse, and short as had been my acquaintance with Satan, I had learned that he always discovered things more quickly than I. So I waited patiently.

From time to time a rattling roll of pebbles, almost musical, caught my ear. It came from the base of the wall of yellow cliff that barred the summit of all those ridges. Satan threw up his head and nosed the breeze. The delicate, almost stealthy sounds, the action of my horse, the waiting drove my heart to extra work. The breeze quickened and fanned my cheek, and borne upon it came the faint and far away bay of a hound. It came again and again, each time nearer. Then on a stronger puff of wind rang the clear, deep, mellow call that had given Sounder his beautiful name. Never it seemed had I heard music so blood-stirring. Sounder was on the trail of something, and he had it headed my way. Satan heard, shot up his long ears, and tried to go ahead; but I restrained and soothed him into quiet.

Long moments I sat there, with the poignant consciousness of the wildness of the scene, of the significant rattling of the stones and of the bell-tongued hound baying incessantly, sending warm joy through my veins, the absorption in sensations new, yielding only to the hunting instinct when Satan snorted and quivered. Again the deep-toned bay rang into the silence with its stirring thrill of life. And a sharp rattling of stones just above brought another snort from Satan.

Across an open space in the piñons a gray form flashed. I leaped off Satan and knelt to get a better view under the trees. I soon made out another deer passing along the base of the cliff. Mounting again, I rode up to the cliff to wait for Sounder.

A long time I had to wait for the hound. It proved that the atmosphere was as deceiving in regard to sound as to sight. Finally Sounder came running along the wall. I got off to intercept him. The crazy fellow—he had never responded to my overtures of friendship—uttered short, sharp yelps of delight, and actually leaped into my arms. But I could not hold him. He darted upon the trail again and paid no heed to my angry shouts. With a resolve to overhaul him, I jumped on Satan and whirled after the hound.

The black stretched out with such a stride that I was at pains to keep my seat. I dodged the jutting rocks and projecting snags; felt stinging branches in my face and the rush of sweet, dry wind. Under the crumbling walls, over slopes of weathered stone and droppings of shelving rock, round protruding noses of cliff, over and under piñons Satan thundered. He came out on the top of the ridge, at the narrow back I had called a saddle. Here I caught a glimpse of Sounder far below, going down into the ravine from which I had ascended some time before. I called to him, but I might as well have called to the wind.

Weary to the point of exhaustion, I once more turned Satan toward camp. I lay forward on his neck and let him have his will. Far down the ravine I awoke to strange sounds, and soon recognized the cracking of iron-shod hoofs against stone; then voices. Turning an abrupt bend in the sandy wash, I ran into Jones and Wallace.

'Fall in! Line up in the sad procession!' said Jones. 'Tige and the pup are faithful. The rest of the dogs are somewhere between the Grand Cañon and the Utah desert.'

I related my adventures, and tried to spare Moze and Sounder as much as conscience would permit.

'Hard luck!' commented Jones. 'Just as the hounds jumped the cougar—Oh! they bounced him out of the rocks all right—don't you remember, just under that cliff wall where you and Wallace came up to me? Well, just as they jumped him, they ran right into fresh deer tracks. I saw one of the deer. Now that's too much for any hounds, except those trained for lions. I shot at Moze twice, but couldn't turn him. He has to be hurt, they've all got to be hurt to make them understand.'

Wallace told of a wild ride somewhere in Jones's wake, and of sundry knocks and bruises he had sustained, of pieces of corduroy he had left decorating the cedars and of a most humiliating event, where a gaunt and bare piñon snag had penetrated under his belt and lifted him, mad and kicking, off his horse.

'These Western nags will hang you on a limb every chance they get,' declared Jones, 'and don't you overlook that. Well, there's the cabin. We'd better stay here a few days or a week and break in the dogs and horses, for this day's work was applepie to what we'll get in the Siwash.'

I groaned inwardly, and was remorselessly glad to see Wallace fall off his horse and walk on one leg to the cabin. When I got my saddle off Satan, had given him a drink and hobbled him, I crept into the cabin and dropped like a log. I felt as if every bone in my body was broken and my flesh was raw. I got gleeful gratification from Wallace's complaints, and Jones's remark that he had a stitch in his back. So ended the first chase after cougars.

5

Oak Spring

Moze and Don and Sounder straggled into camp next morning, hungry, footsore and scarred; and as they limped in, Jones met them with characteristic speech: 'Well, you decided to come in when you got hungry and tired? Never thought of how you fooled me, did you? Now, the first thing you get is a good licking.'

He tied them in a little log pen near the cabin and whipped them soundly. And the next few days while Wallace and I rested, he took them out separately and deliberately ran them over coyote and deer trails. Sometimes we heard his stentorian yell as a forerunner to the blast from his old shotgun. Then again we heard the shots unheralded by the yell. Wallace and I waxed warm under the collar over this peculiar method of training dogs, and each of us made dire threats. But in justice to their implacable trainer, the dogs never appeared to be hurt: never a spot of blood flecked their glossy coats, nor did they ever come home limping. Sounder grew wise, and Don gave up but Moze appeared not to change.

'All hands ready to rustle,' sang out Frank one morning. 'Old Baldy's got to be shod.'

This brought us all, except Jones, out of the cabin, to see the object of Frank's anxiety tied to a nearby oak. At first I failed to recognize Old Baldy. Vanished was the slow, sleepy, apathetic manner that had characterized him; his ears lay back on his head; fire flashed from his eyes. When Frank threw down a kit-bag, which emitted a metallic clanking, Old Baldy sat back on his haunches, planted his forefeet deep in the ground and plainly as a horse could speak, said 'No!'

'Sometimes he's bad, and sometimes worse,' growled Frank.

'Shore he's plumb bad this mornin',' replied Jim.

Frank got the three of us to hold Baldy's head and pull him up, then he ventured to lift a hind foot over his knee. Old Baldy straightened out his leg and sent Frank sprawling into the dirt. Twice again Frank patiently tried to hold a hind leg, with the same result; and then he lifted a forefoot. Baldy uttered a very intelligible snort, bit through Wallace's glove, yanked Jim off his feet, and scared me so that I let go his forelock. Then he broke the rope which held him to the tree. There was a plunge, a scattering of men, though Jim still valiantly held on to Baldy's head, and a thrashing of scrub piñon, where Baldy reached out vigorously with his hind feet. But for Jim, he would have escaped.

'What's all the row?' called Jones from the cabin. Then from the door, taking in the situation, he yelled: 'Hold on, Jim! Pull down on the ornery old cayuse!'

He leaped into action with a lasso in each hand, one whirling round his head. The slender rope straightened with a whiz and whipped round Baldy's legs as he kicked viciously. Jones pulled it tight, then fastened it with nimble fingers to the tree.

'Let go! Let go, Jim!' he yelled, whirling the other lasso. The loop flashed and fell over Baldy's head and tightened round his neck. Jones threw all the weight of his burly form on the lariat, and Baldy crashed to the ground, rolled, tussled, screamed, and then lay on his back, kicking the air with three free legs. 'Hold this!' ordered Jones, giving the tight rope to Frank. Whereupon he grabbed my lasso from the saddle, roped Baldy's two forefeet, and pulled him down on his side. This lasso he fastened to a scrub cedar.

'He's chokin'!' said Frank.

'Likely he is,' replied Jones shortly. 'It'll do him good.' But with his big hands he drew the coil loose and slipped it down over Baldy's nose, where he tightened it again.

'Now, go ahead,' he said, taking the rope from Frank.

It had all been done in a twinkling. Baldy lay there groaning and helpless, and when Frank once again took hold of the wicked leg, he was almost passive. When the shoeing operation had been neatly and quickly attended to and Baldy released from his uncomfortable position he struggled to his feet with heavy breaths, shook himself, and looked at his master.

'How'd you like being hog-tied?' queried his conqueror, rubbing Baldy's nose. 'Now, after this you'll have some manners.'

Old Baldy seemed to understand, for he looked sheepish, and lapsed once more into his listless, lazy unconcern.

'Where's Jim's old cayuse, the pack-horse?' asked our leader.

'Lost. Couldn't find him his morning, an' had a deuce of a time findin' the rest of the bunch. Old Baldy was cute. He hid in a bunch of piñons an' stood quiet so his bell wouldn't ring. I had to trail him.'

'Do the horses stray far when they are hobbled?' inquired Wallace.

'If they keep jumpin' all night they can cover some territory. We're now on the edge of the wild horse country, and our nags know this as well as we. They smell the mustangs, an' would break their necks to get away. Satan and the sorrel were ten miles from camp when I found them this mornin'. An' Jim's cayuse went farther, an' we never will get him. He'll wear his hobbles out, then away with the wild horses. Once with them, he'll never be caught again.'

On the sixth day of our stay at Oak we had visitors, whom Frank introduced as the Stewart brothers and Lawson, wild-horse wranglers. They were still, dark men, whose facial expression seldom varied; tall and lithe and wiry as the mustangs they rode. The Stewarts were on their way to Kanab, Utah, to arrange for the sale of a drove of horses they had captured and corraled in a narrow cañon back in the Siwash. Lawson said he was at our service, and was promptly hired to look after our horses.

'Any cougar signs back in the breaks?' asked Jones.

'Wal, there's a cougar on every deer trail,' replied the elder Stewart, 'an' two for every pinto in the breaks. Old Tom himself downed fifteen colts fer us this spring.'

'Fifteen colts! That's wholesale murder. Why don't you kill the butcher?'

'We've tried more'n onct. It's a turrible busted up country, them brakes. No man knows it, an' the cougars do. Old Tom ranges all the ridges and brakes, even up on the slopes of Buckskin; but he lives down there in them holes, an' Lord knows, no dog I ever seen could follow him. We tracked him in the snow, an' had dogs after him, but none could stay with him, except two as never cum back. But we've nothin' agin Old Tom like Jeff Clarke, a hoss rustler, who has a string of pintos corraled north of us. Clarke swears he ain't raised a colt in two years.'

'We'll put that old cougar up a tree,' exclaimed Jones.

'If you kill him we'll make you all a present of a mustang, an' Clarke, he'll give you two each,' replied Stewart. 'We'd be gettin' rid of him cheap.'

'How many wild horses on the mountain now?'

'Hard to tell. Two or three hundred, mebbe. There's almost no ketchin' them an' they're growin' all the time. We ain't had no luck this spring. The bunch in corral we got last year.'

'Seen anythin' of the White Mustang?' inquired Frank. 'Ever get a rope near him?'

'No nearer'n we hev fer six years back. He can't be ketched. We seen him an' his band of blacks a few days ago, headin' fer a water-hole down where Nail Cañon runs into Kanab Cañon. He's so cunnin' he'll never water at any of our trap corrals. An' we believe he can go without water fer two weeks, unless mebbe he hes a secret hole we've never trailed him to.'

'Would we have any chance to see this White Mustang and his band?' questioned Jones.

'See him? Why, thet'd be easy. Go down Snake Gulch, camp at Singin' Cliffs, go over into Nail Cañon, an' wait. Then send some one slippin' down to the water-hole at Kanab Cañon, an' when the band cums in to drink—which I reckon will be in a few days now—hev them drive the mustangs up. Only be sure to hev them get ahead of the White Mustang, so he'll hev only one way to cum, fer he sure is knowin'. He never makes a mistake. Mebbe you'll get to see him cum by like a white streak. Why, I've heerd thet mustang's hoofs ring like bells on the rocks a mile away. His hoofs are harder'n any iron shoe as was ever made. But even if you don't get to see him, Snake Gulch is worth seein'.'

I learned later from Stewart that the White Mustang was a beautiful stallion of the wildest strain of mustang blue blood. He had roamed the long reaches between the Grand Cañon and Buckskin toward its southern slope for years; he had been the most sought-for horse by all the wranglers, and had become so shy and experienced that nothing but a glimpse was ever obtained of him. A singular fact was that he never attached any of his own species to his band, unless they were coal black. He had been known to fight and kill other stallions, but he kept out of the well-wooded and watered country frequented by other bands, and ranged the brakes of the Siwash as far as he could range. The usual method, indeed the only successful way to capture wild horses, was to build corrals round the water-holes. The wranglers lay out night after night watching. When the mustangs came to drink—which was always after dark—the gates would be closed on them. But the trick had never been tried on the White Mustang, for the simple reason that he never approached one of these traps.

'Boys,' said Jones, 'seeing we need breaking in, we'll give the White Mustang a little run.'

This was most pleasureable news, for the wild horses fascinated me. Besides, I saw from the expression on our leader's face that an uncapturable mustang was an object of interest to him.

Wallace and I had employed the last few warm sunny afternoons in riding up and down the valley below Oak, where there was a fine, level stretch. Here I wore out my soreness of muscle, and gradually overcame my awkwardness in the saddle. Frank's remedy of maple sugar and red pepper had rid me of my cold, and with the return of strength, and the coming of confidence, full, joyous appreciation of wild environment and life made me unspeakably happy. And I noticed that my companions were in like condition of mind, though self-contained where I was exuberant. Wallace galloped his sorrel and watched the crags; Jones talked more kindly to the dogs; Jim baked biscuits indefatigably, and smoked in contented silence; Frank said always: 'We'll ooze along easy like, for we've all the time there is.' Which sentiment, whether from reiterated suggestion, or increasing confidence in the practical cowboy, or charm of its free import, gradually won us all.

'Boys,' said Jones, as we sat round the campfire, 'I see you're getting in shape. Well, I've worn off the wire edge myself. And I have the hounds coming fine. They mind me now, but they're mystified. For the life of them they can't understand what I mean. I don't blame them. Wait till, by good luck, we get a cougar in a tree. When Sounder and Don see that, we've lion dogs, boys! we've lion dogs! But Moze is a stubborn brute. In all my years of animal experience, I've never discovered any other way to make animals obey than by instilling fear and respect into their hearts. I've been fond of buffalo, horses and dogs, but sentiment never ruled me. When animals must obey, they must—that's all, and no mawkishness! But I never trusted a buffalo in my life. If I had I wouldn't be here to-night. You all know how many keepers of tame wild animals get killed. I could tell you dozens of tragedies. And I've often thought, since I got back from New York, of that woman I saw with her troop of African lions. I dream about those lions, and see them leaping over her head. What a grand sight that was! But the public is fooled. I read somewhere that she trained those lions by love. I don't believe it. I saw her use a whip and a steel spear. Moreover, I saw many things that escaped most observers—how she entered the cage, how she maneuvered among them, how she kept a compelling gaze on them! It was an admirable, a great piece of work. Maybe she loves those huge yellow brutes, but her life was in danger every moment while she was in that cage, and she knew it. Some day, one of her pets—likely the King of Beasts she pets the most—will rise up and kill her. That is as certain as death.'

6

The White Mustang

For thirty miles down Nail Cañon we marked, in every dusty trail and sandy wash, the small, oval, sharply defined tracks of the White Mustang and his band.

The cañon had been well named. It was long, straight and square sided; its bare walls glared steel-gray in the sun, smooth, glistening surfaces that had been polished by wind and water. No weathered heaps of shale, no crumbled piles of stone obstructed its level floor. And, softly toning its drab austerity, here grew the white sage, waving in the breeze, the Indian Paint Brush, with vivid vermilion flower, and patches of fresh, green grass.

'The White King, as we Arizona wild-hoss wranglers calls this mustang, is mighty pertickler about his feed, an' he ranged along here last night, easy like, browsin' on this white sage,' said Stewart. Infected by our intense interest in the famous mustang, and ruffled slightly by Jones's manifest surprise and contempt that no one had captured him, Stewart had volunteered to guide us. 'Never knowed him to run in this way fer water; fact is, never knowed Nail Cañon hed a fork. It splits down here, but you'd think it was only a crack in the wall. An' thet cunnin' mustang hes been foolin' us fer years about this water-hole.'

The fork of Nail Cañon, which Stewart had decided we were in, had been accidentally discovered by Frank, who, in search of our horses one morning, had crossed a ridge, to come suddenly upon the blind, box-like head of the cañon. Stewart knew the lay of the ridges and run of the cañons as well as any man could know a country where, seemingly, every rod was ridged and bisected, and he was of the opinion that we had stumbled upon one of the White Mustang's secret passages, by which he had so often eluded his pursuers.

Hard riding had been the order of the day, but still we covered ten more miles by sundown. The cañon apparently closed in on us, so camp was made for the night. The horses were staked out, and supper made ready while the shadows were dropping; and when darkness settled thick over us, we lay under our blankets.

Morning disclosed the White Mustang's secret passage. It was a narrow cleft, splitting the cañon wall, rough, uneven, tortuous and choked with fallen rocks— no more than a wonderful crack in solid stone, opening into another cañon. Above us the sky seemed a winding, flowing stream of blue. The walls were so close in places that a horse with pack would have been blocked, and a rider had to pull his legs up over the saddle. On the far side, the passage fell very suddenly for several hundred feet to the floor of the other cañon. No hunter could have seen it, or suspected it from that side.

'This is Grand Cañon country, an' nobody knows what he's goin' to find,' was Frank's comment.

'Now we're in Nail Cañon proper,' said Stewart, 'an' I know my bearin's. I can climb out a mile below an' cut across to Kanab Cañon, an' slip up into Nail Cañon agin, ahead of the mustangs, an' drive 'em up. I can't miss 'em, fer Kanab Cañon is impassable down a little ways. The mustangs will hev to run this way. So all you need do is go below the break, where I climb out, an' wait. You're sure goin' to get a look at the White Mustang. But wait. Don't expect him before noon, an' after thet, any time till he comes. Mebbe it'll be a couple of days, so keep a good watch.'

Then taking our man Lawson, with blankets and a knapsack of food, Stewart rode off down the cañon.

We were early on the march. As we proceeded the cañon lost its regularity and smoothness; it became crooked as a rail fence, narrower, higher, rugged and broken. Pinnacled cliffs, cracked and leaning, menaced us from above. Mountains of ruined wall had tumbled into fragments.

It seemed that Jones, after much survey of different corners, angles and points in the cañon floor, chose his position with much greater care than appeared necessary for the ultimate success of our venture—which was simply to see the

White Mustang, and if good fortune attended us, to snap some photographs of this wild king of horses. It flashed over me that, with his ruling passion strong within him, our leader was laying some kind of trap for that mustang, was indeed bent on his capture.

Wallace, Frank and Jim were stationed at a point below the break where Stewart had evidently gone up and out. How a horse could have climbed that streaky white slide was a mystery. Jones's instructions to the men were to wait until the mustangs were close upon them, and then yell and shout and show themselves.

He took me to a jutting corner of cliff, which hid us from the others, and here he exercised still more care in scrutinizing the lay of the ground. A wash from ten to fifteen feet wide, and as deep, ran through the cañon in a somewhat meandering course. At the corner which consumed so much of his attention, the dry ditch ran along the cliff wall about fifty feet out; between it and the wall was good level ground; on the other side huge rocks and shale made it hummocky, practically impassable for a horse. It was plain the mustangs, on their way up, would choose the inside of the wash; and here in the middle of the passage, just round the jutting corner, Jones tied our horses to good, strong bushes. His next act was significant. He threw out his lasso and, dragging every crook out of it, carefully recoiled it, and hung it loose over the pommel of his saddle.

'The White Mustang may be yours before dark,' he said with the smile that came so seldom. 'Now I placed our horses there for two reasons. The mustangs won't see them till they're right on them. Then you'll see a sight and have a chance for a great picture. They will halt; the stallion will prance, whistle and snort for a fight, and then they'll see the saddles and be off. We'll hide across the wash, down a little way, and at the right time we'll shout and yell to drive them up.'

By piling sagebrush round a stone, we made a hiding-place. Jones was extremely cautious to arrange the bunches in natural positions. 'A Rocky Mountain Big Horn is the only four-footed beast,' he said, 'that has a better eye than a wild horse. A cougar has an eye, too; he's used to lying high up on the cliffs and looking down for his quarry so as to stalk it at night; but even a cougar has to take second to a mustang when it comes to sight.'

The hours passed slowly. The sun baked us; the stones were too hot to touch; flies buzzed behind our ears; tarantulas peeped at us from holes. The afternoon slowly waned.

At dark we returned to where we had left Wallace and the cowboys. Frank had solved the problem of water supply, for he had found a little spring trickling from a cliff, which, by skillful management, produced enough drink for the horses. We had packed our water for camp use.

'You take the first watch to-night,' said Jones to me after supper. 'The mustangs might try to slip by our fire in the night and we must keep a watch for them. Call Wallace when your time's up. Now, fellows, roll in.'

When the pink of dawn was shading white, we were at our posts. A long, hot day—interminably long, deadening to the keenest interest—passed, and still no mustangs came. We slept and watched again, in the grateful cool of night, till the third day broke.

The hours passed; the cool breeze changed to hot; the sun blazed over the cañon wall; the stones scorched; the flies buzzed. I fell asleep in the scant shade of the sage bushes and awoke, stifled and moist. The old plainsman, never weary, leaned with his back against a stone and watched, with narrow gaze, the cañon below. The steely walls hurt my eyes; the sky was like hot copper. Though nearly wild with heat and aching bones and muscles and the long hours of wait—wait—wait, I was ashamed to complain, for there sat the old man, still and silent. I routed out a hairy tarantula from under a stone and teased him into a frenzy with my stick, and tried to get up a fight between him and a scallop-backed horned-toad that blinked wonderingly at me. Then I espied a green lizard on a stone. The beautiful reptile was about a foot in length, bright green, dotted with red, and he had diamonds for eyes. Nearby a purple flower blossomed, delicate and pale, with a bee sucking at its golden heart. I observed then that the lizard had his jewel eyes upon the bee; he slipped to the edge of the stone, flicked out a long, red tongue, and tore the insect from its honeyed perch. Here were beauty, life and death; and I had been weary for something to look at, to think about, to distract me from the wearisome wait!

'Listen!' broke in Jones's sharp voice. His neck was stretched, his eyes were closed, his ear was turned to the wind.

With thrilling, reawakened eagerness, I strained my hearing. I caught a faint sound, then lost it.

'Put your ear to the ground,' said Jones.

I followed his advice, and detected the rhythmic beat of galloping horses.

'The mustangs are coming, sure as you're born!' exclaimed Jones.

'There! See the cloud of dust!' cried he a minute later.

In the first bent of the cañon below, a splintered ruin of rock now lay under a rolling cloud of dust. A white flash appeared, a line of bobbing black objects, and more dust; then with a sharp pounding of hoofs, into clear vision shot a dense black band of mustangs, and well in front swung the White King.

'Look! Look! I never saw the beat of that—never in my born days!' cried Jones. 'How they move! yet that white fellow isn't half-stretched out. Get your picture before they pass. You'll never see the beat of that.'

With long manes and tails flying, the mustangs came on apace and passed us in a trampling roar, the white stallion in the front. Suddenly a shrill, whistling blast, unlike any sound I had ever heard, made the cañon fairly ring. The white stallion plunged back, and his band closed in behind him. He had seen our saddle horses.

Then trembling, whinnying, and with arched neck and high-poised head, bespeaking his mettle, he advanced a few paces, and again whistled his shrill note of defiance. Pure creamy white he was, and built like a racer. He pranced, struck his hoofs hard and cavorted; then, taking sudden fright, he wheeled.

It was then, when the mustangs were pivoting, with the white in the lead, that Jones jumped upon the stone, fired his pistol and roared with all his strength. Taking his cue, I did likewise. The band huddled back again, uncertain and frightened, then broke up the cañon.

Jones jumped the ditch with surprising agility, and I followed close at his heels. When we reached our plunging horses, he shouted: 'Mount, and hold this passage. Keep close in by that big stone at the turn so they can't run you down, or stampede you. If they head your way, scare them back.'

Satan quivered, and when I mounted, reared and plunged. I had to hold him in hard, for he was eager to run. At the cliff wall I was at some pains to check him. He kept champing his bit and stamping his feet.

From my post I could see the mustangs flying before a cloud of dust. Jones was turning in his horse behind a large rock in the middle of the cañon, where he evidently intended to hide. Presently successive yells and shots from our comrades blended in a roar which the narrow box cañon augmented and echoed from wall to wall. High the White Mustang reared, and above the roar whistled his snort of furious terror. His band wheeled with him and charged back, their hoofs ringing like hammers on iron.

The crafty old buffalo-hunter had hemmed the mustangs in a circle and had left himself free in the center. It was a wily trick, born of his quick mind and experienced eye.

The stallion, closely crowded by his followers, moved swiftly. I saw that he must pass near the stone. Thundering, crashing, the horses came on. Away beyond them I saw Frank and Wallace. Then Jones yelled to me: 'Open up! open up!'

I turned Satan into the middle of the narrow passage, screaming at the top of my voice and discharging my revolver rapidly.

But the wild horses thundered on. Jones saw that they would not now be balked, and he spurred his bay directly in their path. The big horse, courageous as his intrepid master, dove forward.

Then followed confusion for me. The pound of hoofs, the snorts, a screaming neigh that was frightful, the mad stampede of the mustangs with a whirling cloud of dust, bewildered and frightened me so that I lost sight of Jones. Danger threatened and passed me almost before I was aware of it. Out of the dust a mass of tossing manes, foam-flecked black horses, wild eyes and lifting hoofs rushed at me. Satan, with a presence of mind that shamed mine, leaped back and hugged the wall. My eyes were blinded by dust; the smell of dust choked me. I felt a strong rush of wind and a mustang grazed my stirrup. Then they had passed, on the wings of the dust-laden breeze.

But not all, for I saw that Jones had, in some inexplicable manner, cut the White Mustang and two of his blacks out of the band. He had turned them back again and was pursuing them. The bay he rode had never before appeared to much advantage, and now, with his long, lean, powerful body in splendid action, imbued with the relentless will of his rider, what a picture he presented! How he did run! With all that, the White Mustang made him look dingy and slow. Nevertheless, it was a critical time in the wild career of that king of horses. He had been penned in a space two hundred by five hundred yards, half of which was separated from him by a wide ditch, a yawning chasm that he had refused; and behind him, always keeping on the inside, wheeled the yelling hunter, who savagely spurred his bay and whirled a deadly lasso. He had been cut off and surrounded; the very nature of the rocks and trails of the cañon threatened to end his freedom or his life. Certain it was he preferred to end the latter, for he risked death from the rocks as he went over them in long leaps.

Jones could have roped either of the two blacks, but he hardly noticed them. Covered with dust and splotches of foam, they took their advantage, turned on the circle toward the passage way and galloped by me out of sight. Again Wallace, Frank and Jim let out strings of yells and volleys. The chase was narrowing down. Trapped, the White Mustang King had no chance. What a grand spirit he showed! Frenzied as I was with excitement, the thought occurred to me that this was an unfair battle, that I ought to stand aside and let him pass. But the blood and lust of primitive instinct held me fast. Jones, keeping back, met his every turn. Yet always with lithe and beautiful stride the stallion kept out of reach of the whirling lariat.

'Close in!' yelled Jones, and his voice, powerful with a note of triumph, bespoke the knell of the king's freedom.

The trap closed in. Back and forth at the upper end the White Mustang worked; then rendered desperate by the closing in, he circled round nearer to me. Fire shone in his wild eyes. The wily Jones was not to be outwitted; he kept in the middle, always on the move, and he yelled to me to open up. I lost my voice again, and fired my last shot. Then the White Mustang burst into a dash of daring, despairing speed. It was his last magnificent effort. Straight for the wash at the upper end he pointed his racy, spirited head, and his white legs stretched far apart, twinkled and stretched again. Jones galloped to cut him off, and the yells he emitted were demoniacal. It was a long, straight race for the mustang, a short curve for the bay.

That the white stallion gained was as sure as his resolve to elude capture, and he never swerved a foot from his course. Jones might have headed him, but manifestly he wanted to ride with him, as well as to meet him, so in case the lasso went true, a terrible shock might be averted.

Up went Jones's arm as the space shortened, and the lasso ringed his head. Out it shot, lengthened like a yellow, striking snake, and fell just short of the flying white tail.

The White Mustang, fulfilling his purpose in a last heroic display of power, sailed into the air, up and up, and over the wide wash like a white streak. Free! the dust rolled in a cloud from under his hoofs, and he vanished.

Jones's superb horse, crashing down on his haunches, just escaped sliding into the hole.

I awoke to the realization that Satan had carried me, in pursuit of the thrilling chase, all the way across the circle without my knowing it.

Jones calmly wiped the sweat from his face, calmly coiled his lasso, and calmly remarked:

'In trying to capture wild animals a man must never be too sure. Now what I thought my strong point was my weak point—the wash. I made sure no horse could ever jump that hole.'

7

Snake Gulch

Not far from the scene of our adventures with the White Streak, as we facetiously and appreciatively named the mustang, a deep, flat cave indented the cañon wall. By reason of its sandy floor and close proximity to Frank's trickling spring, we decided to camp in it. About dark, Lawson and Stewart straggled in on spent horses, and found awaiting them a bright fire, a hot supper and cheery comrades.

'Did yu fellars git to see him?' was the tall ranger's first question.

'Did we get to see him?' echoed five lusty voices as one. 'We did!'

It was after Frank, in his plain, blunt speech, had told of our experience, that the long Arizonian gazed fixedly at Jones.

'Did yu acktully tech the hair of thet mustang with a rope?'

In all his days Jones never had a greater compliment. By way of reply, he moved his big hand to a button of his coat, and, fumbling over it, unwound a string of long, white hairs, then said: 'I pulled these out of his tail with my lasso; it missed his left hind hoof about six inches.'

There were six of the hairs, pure, glistening white, and over three feet long. Stewart examined them in expressive silence, then passed them along; and when they reached me, they stayed.

The cave, lighted up by a blazing fire, appeared to me a forbidding, uncanny place. Small, peculiar round holes, and dark cracks, suggestive of hidden vermin, gave me a creepy feeling; and although not over-sensitive on the subject of crawling, creeping things, I voiced my disgust.

'Say, I don't like the idea of sleeping in this hole. I'll bet it's full of spiders, snakes and centipedes and other poisonous things.'

Whatever there was in my inoffensive declaration to rouse the usually slumbering humor of the Arizonians, and the thinly veiled ridicule of Colonel Jones, and a mixture of both in my once loyal California friend, I am not prepared to state. Maybe it was the dry, sweet, cool air of Nail Cañon; maybe my suggestion awoke ticklish associations that worked themselves off thus; maybe it was the first instance of my committing myself to a breach of camp etiquette. Be that as it may, my innocently expressed sentiment gave rise to bewildering dissertations on entomology, and most remarkable and startling tales from first-hand experience.

'Like as not,' began Frank in matter-of-fact tone. 'Them's tarantuler holes all right. An' scorpions, centipedes an' rattlers always rustle with tarantulers. But we never mind them—not us fellers! We're used to sleepin' with them. Why, I often wake up in the night to see a big tarantuler on my chest, an' see him wink. Ain't thet so, Jim?'

'Shore as hell,' drawled faithful, slow Jim.

'Reminds me how fatal the bite of a centipede is,' took up Colonel Jones, complacently. 'Once I was sitting in camp with a hunter, who suddenly hissed out: 'Jones, for God's sake don't budge! There's a centipede on your arm!' He pulled his Colt, and shot the blamed centipede off as clean as a whistle. But the bullet hit a steer in the leg; and would you believe it, the bullet carried so much poison that in less than two hours the steer died of blood poisoning. Centipedes are so poisonous they leave a blue trail on flesh just by crawling over it. Look there!'

He bared his arm, and there on the brown-corded flesh was a blue trail of something, that was certain. It might have been made by a centipede.

'This is a likely place for them,' put in Wallace, emitting a volume of smoke and gazing round the cave walls with the eye of a connoisseur. 'My archaeological pursuits have given me great experience with centipedes, as you may imagine, considering how many old tombs, caves and cliff-dwellings I have explored. This Algonkian rock is about the right stratum for centipedes to dig in. They dig somewhat after the manner of the fluviatile long-tailed decapod crustaceans, of the genera *Thoracostraca*, the common crawfish, you know. From that, of course, you can imagine, if a centipede can bite rock, what a biter he is.'

I began to grow weak, and did not wonder to see Jim's long pipe fall from his lips. Frank looked queer around the gills, so to speak, but the gaunt Steward never batted an eye.

'I camped here two years ago,' he said, 'an' the cave was alive with rock-rats, mice, snakes, horned-toads, lizards an' a big Gila monster, besides bugs, scorpions, rattlers, an' as fer tarantulers an' centipedes—say! I couldn't sleep fer the noise they made fightin'.'

'I seen the same,' concluded Lawson, as nonchalant as a wild-horse wrangler well could be. 'An' as fer me, now I allus lays perfickly still when the centipedes an' tarantulers begin to drop from their holes in the roof, same as them holes up there. An' when they light on me, I never move, nor even breathe fer about five minutes. Then they take a notion I'm dead an' crawl off. But sure, if I'd breathed I'd been a goner!'

All of this was playfully intended for the extinction of an unoffending and impressionable tenderfoot.

With an admiring glance at my tormentors, I rolled out my sleeping-bag and crawled into it, vowing I would remain there even if devil-fish, armed with pikes, invaded our cave.

Late in the night I awoke. The bottom of the cañon and the outer floor of our cave lay bathed in white, clear moonlight. A dense, gloomy black shadow veiled the opposite cañon wall. High up the pinnacles and turrets pointed toward a resplendent moon. It was a weird, wonderful scene of beauty entrancing, of breathless, dreaming silence that seemed not of life. Then a hoot-owl lamented dismally, his call fitting the scene and the dead stillness; the echoes resounded from cliff to cliff, strangely mocking and hollow, at last reverberating low and mournful in the distance.

How long I lay there enraptured with the beauty of night and mystery of shade, thrilling at the lonesome lament of the owl, I have no means to tell; but I was awakened from my trance by the touch of something crawling over me. Promptly I raised my head. The cave was as light as day. There, sitting sociably on my sleeping-bag was a great black tarantula, as large as my hand.

For one still moment, notwithstanding my contempt for Lawson's advice, I certainly acted upon it to the letter. If ever I was quiet, and if ever I was cold, the time was then. My companions snored in blissful ignorance of my plight. Slight rustling sounds attracted my wary gaze from the old black sentinel on my knee. I saw other black spiders running to and fro on the silver, sandy floor. A giant, as large as a soft-shell crab, seemed to be meditating an assault upon Jones's ear. Another, grizzled and shiny with age or moonbeams—I could not tell which—

pushed long, tentative feelers into Wallace's cap. I saw black spots darting over the roof. It was not a dream; the cave was alive with tarantulas!

Not improbably my strong impression that the spider on my knee deliberately winked at me was the result of memory, enlivening imagination. But it sufficed to bring to mind, in one rapid, consoling flash, the irrevocable law of destiny—that the deeds of the wicked return unto them again.

I slipped back into my sleeping bag, with a keen consciousness of its nature, and carefully pulled the flap in place, which almost hermetically sealed me up.

'Hey! Jones! Wallace! Frank! Jim!' I yelled, from the depths of my safe refuge.

Wondering cries gave me glad assurance that they had awakened from their dreams.

'The cave's alive with tarantulas!' I cried, trying to hide my unholy glee.

'I'll be durned if it ain't!' ejaculated Frank.

'Shore it beats hell!' added Jim, with a shake of his blanket.

'Look out, Jones, there's one on your pillow!' shouted Wallace.

Whack! A sharp blow proclaimed the opening of hostilities.

Memory stamped indelibly every word of that incident; but innate delicacy prevents the repetition of all save the old warrior's concluding remarks: '! ! !——place I was ever in! Tarantulas by the million—centipedes, scorpions, bats! Rattlesnakes, too, I'll swear. Look out, Wallace! there, under your blanket!'

From the shuffling sounds which wafted sweetly into my bed, I gathered that my long friend from California must have gone through motions creditable to a contortionist. An ensuing explosion from Jones proclaimed to the listening world that Wallace had thrown a tarantula upon him. Further fearful language suggested the thought that Colonel Jones had passed on the inquisitive spider to Frank. The reception accorded the unfortunate tarantula, no doubt scared out of its wits, began with a wild yell from Frank and ended in pandemonium.

While the confusion kept up, with whacks and blows and threshing about, with language such as never before had disgraced a group of old campers, I choked with rapture, and reveled in the sweetness of revenge.

When quiet reigned once more in the black and white cañon, only one sleeper lay on the moon-silvered sand of the cave.

At dawn, when I opened sleepy eyes, Frank, Jim, Stewart and Lawson had departed, as pre-arranged, with the outfit, leaving the horses belonging to us and rations for the day. Wallace and I wanted to climb the divide at the break, and go home by way of Snake Gulch, and the Colonel acquiesced with the remark that his sixty-three years had taught him there was much to see in the world. Coming to undertake it, we found the climb—except for a slide of weathered rock—no great task, and we accomplished it in half an hour, with breath to spare and no mishap to horses.

But descending into Snake Gulch, which was only a mile across the sparsely cedared ridge, proved to be tedious labor. By virtue of Satan's patience and skill, I forged ahead; which advantage, however, meant more risk for me because of the stones set in motion above. They rolled and bumped and cut into me, and I sustained many a bruise trying to protect the sinewy slender legs of my horse. The descent ended without serious mishap.

Snake Gulch had a character and sublimity which cast Nail Cañon into the obscurity of forgetfulness. The great contrast lay in the diversity of structure. The rock was bright red, with parapet of yellow, that leaned, heaved, bulged outward. These emblazoned cliff walls, two thousand feet high, were cracked from turret to base; they bowled out at such an angle that we were afraid to ride under them. Mountains of yellow rock hung balanced, ready to tumble down at the first angry breath of the gods. We rode among carved stones, pillars, obelisks and sculptured ruined walls of a fallen Babylon. Slides reaching all the way across and far up the cañon wall obstructed our passage. On every stone silent green lizards sunned themselves, gliding swiftly as we came near to their marble homes.

We came into a region of wind-worn caves, of all sizes and shapes, high and low on the cliffs; but strange to say, only on the north side of the cañon they appeared with dark mouths open and uninviting. One, vast and deep, though far off, menaced us as might the cave of a tawny-maned king of beasts; yet it impelled, fascinated and drew us on.

'It's a long, hard climb,' said Wallace to the Colonel, as we dismounted.

'Boys, I'm with you,' came the reply. And he was with us all the way, as we clambered over the immense blocks and threaded a passage between them and pulled weary legs up, one after the other. So steep lay the jumble of cliff fragments that we lost sight of the cave long before we got near it. Suddenly we rounded a stone, to halt and gasp at the thing looming before us.

The dark portal of death or hell might have yawned there. A gloomy hole, large enough to admit a church, had been hollowed in the cliff by ages of nature's chiseling.

'Vast sepulcher of Time's past, give up thy dead!' cried Wallace, solemnly.

'Oh! dark Stygian cave forlorn!' quoted I, as feelingly as my friend.

Jones hauled us down from the clouds.

'Now, I wonder what kind of a prehistoric animal holed in here,' said he.

Forever the one absorbing interest! If he realized the sublimity of this place, he did not show it.

The floor of the cave ascended from the very threshold. Stony ridges circled from wall to wall. We climbed till we were two hundred feet from the opening, yet we were not half-way to the dome. Our horses, browsing in the sage far below, looked like ants. So steep did the ascent become that we desisted; for if one of us had slipped on the smooth incline, the result would have been terrible. Our voices rang clear and hollow from the walls. We were so high that the sky was blotted out by the overhanging square, cornice-like top of the door; and the light was weird, dim, shadowy, opaque. It was a gray tomb.

'Waa-hoo!' yelled Jones with all the power of his wide, leather lungs.

Thousands of devilish voices rushed at us, seemingly on puffs of wind. Mocking, deep echoes bellowed from the ebon shades at the back of the cave, and the walls, taking them up, hurled them on again in fiendish concatenation.

We did not again break the silence of that tomb, where the spirits of ages lay in dusty shrouds; and we crawled down as if we had invaded a sanctuary and invoked the wrath of the gods.

We all proposed names: Montezuma's Amphitheater being the only rival of Jones's selection, Echo Cave, which we finally chose.

Mounting our horses again, we made twenty miles of Snake Gulch by noon, when we rested for lunch. All the way up we had played the boy's game of spying for sights, with the honors about even. It was a question if Snake Gulch ever before had such a raking over. Despite its name, however, we discovered no snakes.

From the sandy niche of a cliff where we lunched Wallace espied a tomb, and heralded his discovery with a victorious whoop. Digging in old ruins roused in him much the same spirit that digging in old books roused in me. Before we reached him, he had a big bowie-knife buried deep in the red, sandy floor of the tomb.

This one-time sealed house of the dead had been constructed of small stones, held together by a cement, the nature of which, Wallace explained, had never become clear to civilization. It was red in color and hard as flint, harder than the rocks it glued together. The tomb was half-round in shape, and its floor was a projecting shelf of cliff rock. Wallace unearthed bits of pottery, bone and finely braided rope, all of which, to our great disappointment, crumbled to dust in our fingers. In the case of the rope, Wallace assured us, this was a sign of remarkable antiquity.

In the next mile we traversed, we found dozens of these old cells, all demolished except a few feet of the walls, all despoiled of their one-time possessions. Wallace thought these depredations were due to Indians of our own time. Suddenly we came upon Jones, standing under a cliff, with his neck craned to a desperate angle.

'Now, what's that?' demanded he, pointing upward.

High on the cliff wall appeared a small, round protuberance. It was of the unmistakably red color of the other tombs; and Wallace, more excited than he had been in the cougar chase, said it was a sepulcher, and he believed it had never been opened.

From an elevated point of rock, as high up as I could well climb, I decided both questions with my glass. The tomb resembled nothing so much as a mud-wasp's nest, high on a barn wall. The fact that it had never been broken open quite carried Wallace away with enthusiasm.

'This is no mean discovery, let me tell you that,' he declared. 'I am familiar with the Aztec, Toltec and Pueblo ruins, and here I find no similarity. Besides, we are out of their latitude. An ancient race of people—very ancient indeed—lived in this cañon. How long ago, it is impossible to tell.'

'They must have been birds,' said the practical Jones. 'Now, how'd that tomb ever get there? Look at it, will you?'

As near as we could ascertain, it was three hundred feet from the ground below, five hundred from the rim wall above, and could not possibly have been approached from the top. Moreover, the cliff wall was as smooth as a wall of human make.

'There's another one,' called out Jones.

'Yes, and I see another; no doubt there are many of them,' replied Wallace. 'In my mind, only one thing possible accounts for their position. You observe they appear to be about level with each other. Well, once the cañon floor ran along that line, and in the ages gone by it has lowered, washed away by the rains.'

This conception staggered us, but it was the only one conceivable. No doubt we all thought at the same time of the little rainfall in that arid section of Arizona.

'How many years?' queried Jones.

'Years! What are years?' said Wallace. 'Thousands of years, ages have passed since the race who built these tombs lived.'

Some persuasion was necessary to drag our scientific friend from the spot, where obviously helpless to do anything else, he stood and gazed longingly at the isolated tombs. The cañon widened as we proceeded; and hundreds of points that invited inspection, such as overhanging shelves of rock, dark fissures, caverns and ruins had to be passed by, for lack of time.

Still, a more interesting and important discovery was to come, and the pleasure and honor of it fell to me. My eyes were sharp and peculiarly farsighted—the Indian sight, Jones assured me; and I kept them searching the walls in such places as my companions overlooked. Presently, under a large, bulging bluff, I saw a dark spot, which took the shape of a figure. This figure, I recollected, had been presented to my sight more than once, and now it stopped me. The hard climb up the slippery stones was fatiguing, but I did not hesitate, for I was determined to know. Once upon the ledge, I let out a yell that quickly set my companions in my direction. The figure I had seen was a dark, red devil, a painted image, rude, unspeakably wild, crudely executed, but painted by the hand of man. The whole surface of the cliff wall bore figures of all shapes—men, animals, birds and strange devices, some in red paint, mostly in yellow. Some showed the wear of time; others were clear and sharp.

Wallace puffed up to me, but he had wind enough left for another whoop. Jones puffed up also, and seeing the first thing a rude sketch of what might have been a deer or a buffalo, he commented thus: 'Darn me if I ever saw an animal like that! Boys, this is a find, sure as you're born. Because not even the Piutes ever spoke of these figures. I doubt if they know they're here. And the cowboys and wranglers, what few ever get by here in a hundred years, never saw these things. Beats anything I ever saw on the Mackenzie, or anywhere else.'

The meaning of some devices was as mystical as that of others was clear. Two blood-red figures of men, the larger dragging the smaller by the hair, while he waved aloft a blood-red hatchet or club, left little to conjecture. Here was the old battle of men, as old as life. Another group, two figures of which resembled the foregoing in form and action, battling over a prostrate form rudely feminine in outline, attested to an age when men was as susceptible as they are in modern times, but more forceful and original. An odd yellow Indian waved aloft a red hand, which striking picture suggested the idea that he was an ancient Macbeth, listening to the knocking at the gate. There was a character representing a great chief, before whom many figures lay prostrate, evidently slain or subjugated. Large red paintings, in the shape of bats, occupied prominent positions, and must have represented gods or devils. Armies of marching men told of that blight of nations old and young—war. These, and birds unnamable, and beasts unclassable, with dots and marks and hieroglyphics, recorded the history of a bygone people. Symbols they were of an era that had gone into the dim past, leaving only these marks, forever unintelligible; yet while they stood, century after century, ineffaceable, reminders of the glory, the mystery, the sadness of life.

'How could paint of any kind last so long?' asked Jones, shaking his head doubtfully.

'That is the unsolvable mystery,' returned Wallace. 'But the records are there. I am absolutely sure the paintings are at least a thousand years old. I have never seen any tombs or paintings similar to them. Snake Gulch is a find, and I shall some day study its wonders.'

Sundown caught us within sight of Oak Spring, and we soon trotted into camp to the welcoming chorus of the hounds. Frank and the others had reached the cabin some hours before. Supper was steaming on the hot coals with a delicious fragrance.

Then came the pleasantest time of the day, after a long chase or jaunt—the silent moments, watching the glowing embers of the fire; the speaking moments when a red-blooded story rang clear and true; the twilight moments, when the wood-smoke smelled sweet.

Jones seemed unusually thoughtful. I had learned that this preoccupation in him meant the stirring of old associations, and I waited silently. By and by Lawson snored mildly in a corner; Jim and Frank crawled into their blankets, and all was still. Wallace smoked his Indian pipe and hunted in firelit dreams.

'Boys,' said our leader finally, 'somehow the echoes dying away in that cave reminded me of the mourn of the big white wolves in the Barren Lands.'

Wallace puffed huge clouds of white smoke, and I waited, knowing that I was to hear at last the story of the Colonel's great adventure in the Northland.

8

Naza! Naza! Naza!

It was a waiting day at Fort Chippewayan. The lonesome, far-northern Hudson's Bay Trading Post seldom saw such life. Tepees dotted the banks of the Slave River and lines of blanketed Indians paraded its shores. Near the boat landing a group of chiefs, grotesque in semi-barbaric, semi-civilized splendor, but black-browed, austere-eyed, stood in savage dignity with folded arms and high-held heads. Lounging on the grassy bank were white men, traders, trappers and officials of the post.

All eyes were on the distant curve of the river where, as it lost itself in a fine-fringed bend of dark green, white-glinting waves danced and fluttered. A June sky lay blue in the majestic stream; ragged, spear-topped, dense green trees massed down to the water; beyond rose bold, bald-knobbed hills, in remote purple relief.

A long Indian arm stretched south. The waiting eyes discerned a black speck on the green, and watched it grow. A flatboat, with a man standing to the oars, bore down swiftly.

Not a red hand, nor a white one, offered to help the voyager in the difficult landing. The oblong, clumsy, heavily laden boat surged with the current and passed the dock despite the boatman's efforts. He swung his craft in below upon a bar and roped it fast to a tree. The Indians crowded above him on the bank. The boatman raised his powerful form erect, lifted a bronzed face which seemed set in craggy hardness, and cast from narrow eyes a keen, cool glance on those above. The silvery gleam in his fair hair told of years.

Silence, impressive as it was ominous, broke only to the rattle of camping paraphernalia, which the voyager threw to a level, grassy bench on the bank.

Evidently this unwelcome visitor had journeyed from afar, and his boat, sunk deep into the water with its load of barrels, boxes and bags, indicated that the journey had only begun. Significant, too, were a couple of long Winchester rifles shining on a tarpaulin.

The cold-faced crowd stirred and parted to permit the passage of a tall, thin, gray personage of official bearing, in a faded military coat.

'Are you the musk-ox hunter?' he asked, in tones that contained no welcome.

The boatman greeted this peremptory interlocutor with a cool laugh—a strange laugh, in which the muscles of his face appeared not to play.

'Yes, I am the man,' he said.

'The chiefs of the Chippewayan and Great Slave tribes have been apprised of your coming. They have held council and are here to speak with you.'

At a motion from the commandant, the line of chieftains piled down to the level bench and formed a half-circle before the voyager. To a man who had stood before grim Sitting Bull and noble Black Thunder of the Sioux, and faced the falcon-eyed Geronimo, and glanced over the sights of a rifle at gorgeous-feathered, wild, free Comanches, this semi-circle of savages—lords of the north—was a sorry comparison. Bedaubed and betrinketed, slouchy, and slovenly, these low-statured chiefs belied in appearance their scorn-bright eyes and lofty mien. They made a sad group.

One who spoke in unintelligible language, rolled out a haughty, sonorous voice over the listening multitude. When he had finished, a half-breed interpreter, in the dress of a white man, spoke at a signal from the commandant.

'He says listen to the great orator of the Chippewayan. He has summoned all the chiefs of the tribes south of Great Slave Lake. He has held council. The cunning of the pale-face, who comes to take the musk-oxen, is well known. Let the pale-face hunter return to his own hunting-grounds; let him turn his face from the north. Never will the chiefs permit the white man to take musk-oxen alive from their country. The Ageter, the Musk-ox, is their god. He gives them food and fur. He will never come back if he is taken away, and the reindeer will follow him. The chiefs and their people would starve. They command the pale-face hunter to go back. They cry Naza! Naza! Naza!'

'Say, for a thousand miles I've heard that word Naza!' returned the hunter, with mingled curiosity and disgust. 'At Edmonton Indian runners started ahead of me, and every village I struck the redskins would crowd round me and an old chief would harangue at me, and motion me back, and point north with Naza! Naza! Naza! What does it mean?'

'No white man knows; no Indian will tell,' answered the interpreter. 'The traders think it means the Great Slave, the North Star, the North Spirit, the North Wind, the North Lights and Ageter, the musk-ox god.'

'Well, say to the chiefs to tell Ageter I have been four moons on the way after some of his little Ageters, and I'm going to keep on after them.'

'Hunter, you are most unwise,' broke in the commandant, in his officious voice. 'The Indians will never permit you to take a musk-ox alive from the north. They worship him, pray to him. It is a wonder you have not been stopped.'

'Who'll stop me?'

'The Indians. They will kill you if you do not turn back.'

'Faugh! to tell an American plainsman that!' The hunter paused a steady moment, with his eyelids narrowing over slits of blue fire. 'There is no law to keep me out, nothing but Indian superstition and the greed of the Hudson's Bay people. And I am an old fox, not to be fooled by pretty baits. For years the officers of this fur-trading company have tried to keep out explorers. Even Sir John Franklin, an Englishman, could not buy food of them. The policy of the company is to side with the Indians, to keep out traders and trappers. Why? So they can keep on cheating the poor savages out of clothing and food by trading a few trinkets and blankets, a little tobacco and rum for millions of dollars worth of furs. Have I failed to hire man after man, Indian after Indian, not to know why I cannot get a helper? Have I, a plainsman, come a thousand miles alone to be scared by you, or a lot of craven Indians? Have I been dreaming of musk-oxen for forty years, to slink south now, when I begin to feel the north? Not I.'

Deliberately every chief, with the sound of a hissing snake, spat in the hunter's face. He stood immovable while they perpetrated the outrage, then calmly wiped his cheeks, and in his strange, cool voice, addressed the interpreter.

'Tell them thus they show their true qualities, to insult in council. Tell them they are not chiefs, but dogs. Tell them they are not even squaws, only poor, miserable starved dogs. Tell them I turn my back on them. Tell them the paleface has fought real chiefs, fierce, bold, like eagles, and he turns his back on dogs. Tell them he is the one who could teach them to raise the musk-oxen and the reindeer, and to keep out the cold and the wolf. But they are blinded. Tell them the hunter goes north.'

Through the council of chiefs ran a low mutter, as of gathering thunder.

True to his word, the hunter turned his back on them. As he brushed by, his eye caught a gaunt savage slipping from the boat. At the hunter's stern call, the Indian leaped ashore, and started to run. He had stolen a parcel, and would have succeeded in eluding its owner but for an unforeseen obstacle, as striking as it was unexpected.

A white man of colossal stature had stepped in the thief's passage, and laid two great hands on him. Instantly the parcel flew from the Indian, and he spun in the air to fall into the river with a sounding splash. Yells signaled the surprise and alarm caused by this unexpected incident. The Indian frantically swam to the shore. Whereupon the champion of the stranger in a strange land lifted a bag, which gave forth a musical clink of steel, and throwing it with the camp articles on the grassy bench, he extended a huge, friendly hand.

'My name is Rea,' he said, in deep, cavernous tones.

'Mine is Jones,' replied the hunter, and right quickly did he grip the proffered hand. He saw in Rea a giant, of whom he was but a stunted shadow. Six and one-half feet Rea stood, with yard-wide shoulders, a hulk of bone and brawn. His ponderous, shaggy head rested on a bull neck. His broad face, with its low forehead, its close-shut mastiff under jaw, its big, opaque eyes, pale and cruel as those of a jaguar, marked him a man of terrible brute force.

'Free-trader!' called the commandant. 'Better think twice before you join fortunes with the musk-ox hunter.'

'To hell with you an' your rantin', dog-eared redskins!' cried Rea. 'I've run agin a man of my own kind, a man of my own country, an' I'm goin' with him.'

With this he thrust aside some encroaching, gaping Indians so unconcernedly and ungently that they sprawled upon the grass.

Slowly the crowd mounted and once more lined the bank.

Jones realized that by some late-turning stroke of fortune, he had fallen in with one of the few free-traders of the province. These free-traders, from the very nature of their calling—which was to defy the fur company, and to trap and trade on their own account—were a hardy and intrepid class of men. Rea's worth to Jones exceeded that of a dozen ordinary men. He knew the ways of the north, the language of the tribes, the habits of animals, the handling of dogs, the uses of food and fuel. Moreover, it soon appeared that he was a carpenter and blacksmith.

'There's my kit,' he said, dumping the contents of his bag. It consisted of a bunch of steel traps, some tools, a broken ax, a box of miscellaneous things such as trappers used, and a few articles of flannel. 'Thievin' redskins,' he added, in explanation of his poverty. 'Not much of an outfit. But I'm the man for you. Besides, I had a pal onct who knew you on the plains, called you 'Buff' Jones. Old Jim Bent he was.'

'I recollect Jim,' said Jones. 'He went down in Custer's last charge. So you were Jim's pal. That'd be a recommendation if you needed one. But the way you chucked the Indian overboard got me.'

Rea soon manifested himself as a man of few words and much action. With the planks Jones had on board he heightened the stern and bow of the boat to keep out the beating waves in the rapids; he fashioned a steering-gear and a less awkward set of oars, and shifted the cargo so as to make more room in the craft.

'Buff, we're in for a storm. Set up a tarpaulin an' make a fire. We'll pretend to camp to-night. These Indians won't dream we'd try to run the river after dark, and we'll slip by under cover.'

The sun glazed over; clouds moved up from the north; a cold wind swept the tips of the spruces, and rain commenced to drive in gusts. By the time it was dark not an Indian showed himself. They were housed from the storm. Lights twinkled in the tepees and the big log cabins of the trading company. Jones scouted round till pitchy black night, when a freezing, pouring blast sent him back to the protection of the tarpaulin. When he got there he found that Rea had taken it down and awaited him. 'Off!' said the free-trader; and with no more noise than a drifting feather the boat swung into the current and glided down till the twinkling fires no longer accentuated the darkness.

By night the river, in common with all swift rivers, had a sullen voice, and murmured its hurry, its restraint, its menace, its meaning. The two boatmen, one at the steering gear, one at the oars, faced the pelting rain and watched the dim, dark line of trees. The craft slid noiselessly onward into the gloom.

And into Jones's ears, above the storm, poured another sound, a steady, muffled rumble, like the roll of giant chariot wheels. It had come to be a familiar roar to him, and the only thing which, in his long life of hazard, had ever sent the cold, prickling, tight shudder over his warm skin. Many times on the Athabasca that rumble had presaged the dangerous and dreaded rapids.

'Hell Bend Rapids!' shouted Rea. 'Bad water, but no rocks.'

The rumble expanded to a roar, the roar to a boom that charged the air with heaviness, with a dreamy burr. The whole indistinct world appeared to be moving to the lash of wind, to the sound of rain, to the roar of the river. The boat shot down and sailed aloft, met shock on shock, breasted leaping dim white waves, and in a hollow, unearthly blend of watery sounds, rode on and on, buffeted, tossed, pitched into a black chaos that yet gleamed with obscure shrouds of light. Then the convulsive stream shrieked out a last defiance, changed its course abruptly to slow down and drown the sound of rapids in muffling distance. Once more the craft swept on smoothly, to the drive of the wind and the rush of the rain.

By midnight the storm cleared. Murky clouds split to show shining, blue-white stars and a fitful moon, that silvered the crests of the spruces and sometimes hid like a gleaming, black-threaded pearl behind the dark branches.

Jones, a plainsman all his days, wonderingly watched the moon-blanched water. He saw it shade and darken under shadowy walls of granite, where it swelled with hollow song and gurgle. He heard again the far-off rumble, faint on the night wind. High cliff banks appeared, walled out the mellow light, and the river suddenly narrowed. Yawning holes, whirlpools of a second, opened with a gurgling suck and raced with the boat.

On the craft flew. Far ahead, a long, declining plane of jumping frosted waves played dark and white with the moonbeams. The Slave plunged to his freedom, down his riven, stone-spiked bed, knowing no patient eddy, and white-wreathed his dark, shiny rocks in spume and spray.

9

The Land of the Musk-Ox

A far cry it was from bright June at Port Chippewayan to dim October on Great Slave Lake.

Two long, laborious months Rea and Jones threaded the crooked shores of the great inland sea, to halt at the extreme northern end, where a plunging outlet formed the source of a river. Here they found a stone chimney and fireplace standing among the darkened, decayed ruins of a cabin.

'We mustn't lose no time,' said Rea. 'I feel the winter in the wind. An' see how dark the days are gettin' on us.'

'I'm for hunting musk-oxen,' replied Jones.

'Man, we're facin' the northern night; we're in the land of the midnight sun. Soon we'll be shut in for seven months. A cabin we want, an' wood, an' meat.'

A forest of stunted spruce trees edged on the lake, and soon its dreary solitudes rang to the strokes of axes. The trees were small and uniform in size. Black stumps protruded, here and there, from the ground, showing work of the steel in time gone by. Jones observed that the living trees were no larger in diameter than the stumps, and questioned Rea in regard to the difference in age.

'Cut twenty-five, mebbe fifty years ago,' said the trapper.

'But the living trees are no bigger.'

'Trees an' things don't grow fast in the northland.'

They erected a fifteen-foot cabin round the stone chimney, roofed it with poles and branches of spruce, and a layer of sand. In digging near the fireplace Jones unearthed a rusty file and the head of a whisky keg. Upon which was a sunken word in unintelligible letters.

'We've found the place,' said Rea. 'Franklin built a cabin here in 1819. An' in 1833 Captain Back wintered here when he was in search of Captain Ross of the vessel *Fury*. It was those explorin' parties thet cut the trees. I seen Indian sign out there, made last winter, I reckon; but Indians never cut down no trees.'

The hunters completed the cabin, piled cords of firewood outside, stowed away the kegs of dried fish and fruits, the sacks of flour, boxes of crackers, canned meats and vegetables, sugar, salt, coffee, tobacco—all of the cargo; then took the boat apart and carried it up the bank, which labor took them less than a week.

Jones found sleeping in the cabin, despite the fire, uncomfortably cold, because of the wide chinks between the logs. It was hardly better than sleeping under the swaying spruces. When he essayed to stop up the cracks—a task by no means easy, considering the lack of material—Rea laughed his short 'Ho! Ho!' and stopped him with the word, 'Wait.' Every morning the green ice extended farther out into the lake; the sun paled dim and dimmer; the nights grew colder. On October 8th the thermometer registered several degrees below zero; it fell a little more next night and continued to fall.

'Ho! Ho!' cried Rea. 'She's struck the toboggan, an' presently she'll commence to slide. Come on, Buff, we've got work to do.'

He caught up a bucket, made for their hole in the ice, rebroke a six-inch layer, the freeze of a few hours, and filling his bucket, returned to the cabin. Jones had no inkling of the trapper's intention, and wonderingly he soused his bucket full of water and followed.

By the time he had reached the cabin, a matter of some thirty or forty good paces, the water no longer splashed from his pail, for a thin film of ice prevented. Rea stood fifteen feet from the cabin, his back to the wind, and threw the water. Some of it froze in the air, most of it froze on the logs. The simple plan of the trapper to incase the cabin with ice was easily divined. All day the men worked, ceasing only when the cabin resembled a glistening mound. It had not a sharp corner nor a crevice. Inside it was warm and snug, and as light as when the chinks were open.

A slight moderation of the weather brought the snow. Such snow! A blinding white flutter of great flakes, as large as feathers! All day they rustled softly; all night they swirled, sweeping, seeping, brushing against the cabin. 'Ho! Ho!' roared Rea. ''Tis good; let her snow, an' the reindeer will migrate. We'll have fresh meat.' The sun shone again, but not brightly. A nipping wind cut down out of the frigid north and crusted the snow. The third night following the storm, when the hunters lay snug under their blankets, a commotion outside aroused them.

'Indians,' said Rea, 'come north for reindeer.'

Half the night, shouting and yelling, barking of dogs, hauling of sleds and cracking of dried-skin tepees murdered sleep for those in the cabin. In the morning the level plain and edge of the forest held an Indian village. Caribou hides, strung on forked poles, constituted tent-like habitations with no distinguishable doors. Fires smoked in the holes in the snow. Not till late in the day did any life manifest itself round the tepees, and then a group of children, poorly clad in ragged pieces of blankets and skins, gaped at Jones. He saw their pinched, brown faces, staring, hungry eyes, naked legs and throats, and noted particularly their dwarfish size. When he spoke they fled precipitously a little way, then turned. He called again, and all ran except one small lad. Jones went into the cabin and came out with a handful of sugar in square lumps.

'Yellow Knife Indians,' said Rea. 'A starved tribe! We're in for it.'

Jones made motions to the lad, but he remained still, as if transfixed, and his black eyes stared wonderingly.

'Molar nasu (white man good),' said Rea.

The lad came out of his trance and looked back at his companions, who edged nearer. Jones ate a lump of sugar, then handed one to the little Indian. He took it gingerly, put it into his mouth and immediately jumped up and down.

'Hoppieshampoolie! Hoppieshampoolie!' he shouted to his brothers and sisters. They came on the run.

'Think he means sweet salt,' interpreted Rea. 'Of course these beggars never tasted sugar.'

The band of youngsters trooped round Jones, and after tasting the white lumps, shrieked in such delight that the braves and squaws shuffled out of the tepees.

In all his days Jones had never seen such miserable Indians. Dirty blankets hid all their person, except straggling black hair, hungry, wolfish eyes and moccasined feet. They crowded into the path before the cabin door and mumbled and stared and waited. No dignity, no brightness, no suggestion of friendliness marked this peculiar attitude.

'Starved!' exclaimed Rea. 'They've come to the lake to invoke the Great Spirit to send the reindeer. Buff, whatever you do, don't feed them. If you do, we'll have them on our hands all winter. It's cruel, but, man, we're in the north!'

Notwithstanding the practical trapper's admonition Jones could not resist the pleading of the children. He could not stand by and see them starve. After ascertaining there was absolutely nothing to eat in the tepees, he invited the little ones into the cabin, and made a great pot of soup, into which he dropped compressed biscuits. The savage children were like wildcats. Jones had to call in Rea to assist him in keeping the famished little aborigines from tearing each other to pieces. When finally they were all fed, they had to be driven out of the cabin.

'That's new to me,' said Jones. 'Poor little beggars!'

Rea doubtfully shook his shaggy head.

Next day Jones traded with the Yellow Knives. He had a goodly supply of baubles, besides blankets, gloves and boxes of canned goods, which he had brought for such trading. He secured a dozen of the large-boned, white and black Indian dogs—huskies, Rea called them—two long sleds with harness and several pairs of snowshoes. This trade made Jones rub his hands in satisfaction, for during all the long journey north he had failed to barter for such cardinal necessities to the success of his venture.

'Better have doled out the grub to them in rations,' grumbled Rea.

Twenty-four hours sufficed to show Jones the wisdom of the trapper's words, for in just that time the crazed, ignorant savages had glutted the generous store of food, which should have lasted them for weeks. The next day they were begging at the cabin door. Rea cursed and threatened them with his fists, but they returned again and again.

Days passed. All the time, in light and dark, the Indians filled the air with dismal chant and doleful incantations to the Great Spirit, and the tum! tum! tum! tum! of tomtoms, a specific feature of their wild prayer for food.

But the white monotony of the rolling land and level lake remained unbroken. The reindeer did not come. The days became shorter, dimmer, darker. The mercury kept on the slide.

Forty degrees below zero did not trouble the Indians. They stamped till they dropped, and sang till their voices vanished, and beat the tomtoms everlastingly. Jones fed the children once each day, against the trapper's advice.

One day, while Rea was absent, a dozen braves succeeded in forcing an entrance, and clamored so fiercely, and threatened so desperately, that Jones was on the point of giving them food when the door opened to admit Rea.

With a glance he saw the situation. He dropped the bucket he carried, threw the door wide open and commenced action. Because of his great bulk he seemed slow, but every blow of his sledge-hammer fist knocked a brave against the wall, or through the door into the snow. When he could reach two savages at once, by way of diversion, he swung their heads together with a crack. They dropped like dead things. Then he handled them as if they were sacks of corn, pitching them out into the snow. In two minutes the cabin was clear. He banged the door and slipped the bar in place.

'Buff, I'm goin' to get mad at these thievin' redskins some day,' he said gruffly. The expanse of his chest heaved slightly, like the slow swell of a calm ocean, but there was no other indication of unusual exertion.

Jones laughed, and again gave thanks for the comradeship of this strange man.

Shortly afterward, he went out for wood, and as usual scanned the expanse of the lake. The sun shone mistier and wanner, and frost feathers floated in the air. Sky and sun and plain and lake—all were gray. Jones fancied he saw a distant moving mass of darker shade than the gray background. He called the trapper.

'Caribou,' said Rea instantly. 'The vanguard of the migration. Hear the Indians! Hear their cry: "Aton! Aton!" they mean reindeer. The idiots have scared the herd with their infernal racket, an' no meat will they get. The caribou will keep to the ice, an' man or Indian can't stalk them there.'

For a few moments his companion surveyed the lake and shore with a plainsman's eye, then dashed within, to reappear with a Winchester in each hand. Through the crowd of bewailing, bemoaning Indians he sped, to the low, dying bank. The hard crust of snow upheld him. The gray cloud was a thousand yards out upon the lake and moving southeast. If the caribou did not swerve from this course they would pass close to a projecting point of land, a half-mile up the lake. So, keeping a wary eye upon them, the hunter ran swiftly. He had not hunted antelope and buffalo on the plains all his life without learning how to approach moving game. As long as the caribou were in action, they could not tell whether he moved or was motionless. In order to tell if an object was inanimate or not, they must stop to see, of which fact the keen hunter took advantage. Suddenly he saw the gray mass slow down and bunch up. He stopped running, to stand like a stump. When the reindeer moved again, he moved, and when they slackened again, he stopped and became motionless. As they kept to their course, he worked gradually closer and closer. Soon he distinguished gray, bobbing heads. When the leader showed signs of halting in his slow trot the hunter again became a statue. He saw they were easy to deceive; and, daringly confident of success, he encroached on the ice and closed up the gap till not more than two hundred yards separated him from the gray, bobbing, antlered mass.

Jones dropped on one knee. A moment only his eyes lingered admiringly on the wild and beautiful spectacle; then he swept one of the rifles to a level. Old habit made the little beaded sight cover first the stately leader. Bang! The gray monarch leaped straight forward, forehoofs up, antlered head back, to fall dead with a crash. Then for a few moments the Winchester spat a deadly stream of fire, and when emptied was thrown down for the other gun, which in the steady, sure hands of the hunter belched death to the caribou.

The herd rushed on, leaving the white surface of the lake gray with a struggling, kicking, bellowing heap. When Jones reached the caribou he saw several trying to rise on crippled legs. With his knife he killed these, not without some hazard to himself. Most of the fallen ones were already dead, and the others soon lay still. Beautiful gray creatures they were, almost white, with wide-reaching, symmetrical horns.

A medley of yells arose from the shore, and Rea appeared running with two sleds, with the whole tribe of Yellow Knives pouring out of the forest behind him.

'Buff, you're jest what old Jim said you was,' thundered Rea, as he surveyed the gray pile. 'Here's winter meat, an' I'd not have given a biscuit for all the meat I thought you'd get.'

'Thirty shots in less than thirty seconds,' said Jones, 'an' I'll bet every ball I sent touched hair. How many reindeer?'

'Twenty! twenty! Buff, or I've forgot how to count. I guess mebbe you can't handle them shootin' arms. Ho! here comes the howlin' redskins.'

Rea whipped out a bowie knife and began disemboweling the reindeer. He had not proceeded far in his task when the crazed savages were around him. Every one carried a basket or receptacle, which he swung aloft, and they sang, prayed, rejoiced on their knees. Jones turned away from the sickening scenes that convinced him these savages were little better than cannibals. Rea cursed them, and tumbled them over, and threatened them with the big bowie. An altercation ensued, heated on his side, frenzied on theirs. Thinking some treachery might befall his comrade, Jones ran into the thick of the group.

'Share with them, Rea, share with them.'

Whereupon the giant hauled out ten smoking carcasses. Bursting into a babel of savage glee and tumbling over one another, the Indians pulled the caribou to the shore.

'Thievin' fools!' growled Rea, wiping the sweat from his brow. 'Said they'd prevailed on the Great Spirit to send the reindeer. Why, they'd never smelled warm meat but for you. Now, Buff, they'll gorge every hair, hide an' hoof of their share in less than a week. Thet's the last we do for the damned cannibals. Didn't you see them eatin' of the raw innards?—faugh! I'm calculatin' we'll see no more reindeer. It's late for the migration. The big herd has driven southward. But we're lucky, thanks to your prairie trainin'. Come on now with the sleds, or we'll have a pack of wolves to fight.'

By loading three reindeer on each sled, the hunters were not long in transporting them to the cabin. 'Buff, there ain't much doubt about them keepin' nice and cool,' said Rea. 'They'll freeze, an' we can skin them when we want.'

That night the starved wolf dogs gorged themselves till they could not rise from the snow. Likewise the Yellow Knives feasted. How long the ten reindeer might have served the wasteful tribe, Rea and Jones never found out. The next day two Indians arrived with dog-trains, and their advent was hailed with another feast, and a pow-wow that lasted into the night.

'Guess we're goin' to get rid of our blasted hungry neighbors,' said Rea, coming in next morning with the water pail, 'an' I'll be durned, Buff, if I don't believe them crazy heathen have been told about you. Them Indians was messengers. Grab your gun, an' let's walk over and see.'

The Yellow Knives were breaking camp, and the hunters were at once conscious of the difference in their bearing. Rea addressed several braves, but got no reply. He laid his broad hand on the old wrinkled chief, who repulsed him, and turned his back. With a growl, the trapper spun the Indian round, and spoke as many words of the language as he knew. He got a cold response, which ended in the ragged old chief starting up, stretching a long, dark arm northward, and with eyes fixed in fanatical subjection, shouting: 'Naza! Naza! Naza!'

'Heathen!' Rea shook his gun in the faces of the messengers. 'It'll go bad with you to come Nazain' any longer on our trail. Come, Buff, clear out before I get mad.'

When they were once more in the cabin, Rea told Jones that the messengers had been sent to warn the Yellow Knives not to aid the white hunters in any way. That night the dogs were kept inside, and the men took turns in watching. Morning showed a broad trail southward. And with the going of the Yellow Knives the mercury dropped to fifty, and the long, twilight winter night fell.

So with this agreeable riddance and plenty of meat and fuel to cheer them, the hunters sat down in their snug cabin to wait many months for daylight.

Those few intervals when the wind did not blow were the only times Rea and Jones got out of doors. To the plainsman, new to the north, the dim gray world about him was of exceeding interest. Out of the twilight shone a wan, round, lusterless ring that Rea said was the sun. The silence and desolation were heart-numbing.

'Where are the wolves?' asked Jones of Rea.

'Wolves can't live on snow. They're farther south after caribou, or farther north after musk-ox.'

In those few still intervals Jones remained out as long as he dared, with the mercury sinking to sixty degrees. He turned from the wonder of the unreal, remote sun, to the marvel in the north—Aurora borealis—ever-present, ever-changing, ever-beautiful! and he gazed in rapt attention.

'Polar lights,' said Rea, as if he were speaking of biscuits. 'You'll freeze. It's gettin' cold.'

Cold it became, to the matter of seventy degrees. Frost covered the walls of the cabin and the roof, except just over the fire. The reindeer were harder than iron. A knife or an ax or a steel-trap burned as if it had been heated in fire, and stuck to the hand. The hunters experienced trouble in breathing; the air hurt their lungs.

The months dragged. Rea grew more silent day by day, and as he sat before the fire his wide shoulders sagged lower and lower. Jones, unaccustomed to the waiting, the restraint, the barrier of the north, worked on guns, sleds, harness, till he felt he would go mad. Then to save his mind he constructed a windmill of caribou hides and pondered over it trying to invent, to put into practical use an idea he had once conceived.

Hour after hour he lay under his blankets unable to sleep, and listened to the north wind. Sometimes Rea mumbled in his slumbers; once his giant form started up, and he muttered a woman's name. Shadows from the fire flickered on the walls, visionary, spectral shadows, cold and gray, fitting the north. At such times he longed with all the power of his soul to be among those scenes far southward, which he called home. For days Rea never spoke a word, only gazed into the fire, ate and slept. Jones, drifting far from his real self, feared the strange mood of the trapper and sought to break it, but without avail. More and more he reproached himself, and singularly on the one fact that, as he did not smoke himself, he had brought only a small store of tobacco. Rea, inordinate and inveterate smoker, had puffed away all the weed in clouds of white, then had relapsed into gloom.

10
Success and Failure

At last the marvel in the north dimmed, the obscure gray shade lifted, the hope in the south brightened, and the mercury climbed—reluctantly, with a tyrant's hate to relinquish power.

Spring weather at twenty-five below zero! On April 12th a small band of Indians made their appearance. Of the Dog tribe were they, an offcast of the Great Slaves, according to Rea, and as motley, staring and starved as the Yellow Knives. But they were friendly, which presupposed ignorance of the white hunters, and Rea persuaded the strongest brave to accompany them as guide northward after musk-oxen.

On April 16th, having given the Indians several caribou carcasses, and assuring them that the cabin was protected by white spirits, Rea and Jones, each with sled and train of dogs, started out after their guide, who was similarly equipped, over the glistening snow toward the north. They made sixty miles the first day, and pitched their Indian tepee on the shores of Artillery Lake. Traveling northeast, they covered its white waste of one hundred miles in two days. Then a day due north, over rolling, monotonously snowy plain, devoid of rock, tree or shrub, brought them into a country of the strangest, queerest little spruce trees, very slender, and none of them over fifteen feet in height. A primeval forest of saplings.

'Ditchen Nechila!' said the guide.

'Land of Sticks Little,' translated Rea.

An occasional reindeer was seen and numerous foxes and hares trotted off into the woods, evincing more curiosity than fear. All were silver white, even the reindeer, at a distance, taking the hue of the north. Once a beautiful creature, unblemished as the snow it trod, ran up a ridge and stood watching the hunters. It resembled a monster dog, only it was inexpressibly more wild looking.

'Ho! Ho! there you are!' cried Rea, reaching for his Winchester. 'Polar wolf! Them's the white devils we'll have hell with.'

As if the wolf understood, he lifted his white, sharp head and uttered a bark or howl that was like nothing so much as a haunting, unearthly mourn. The animal then merged into the white, as if he were really a spirit of the world whence his cry seemed to come.

In this ancient forest of youthful appearing trees, the hunters cut firewood to the full carrying capacity of the sleds. For five days the Indian guide drove his dogs over the smooth crust, and on the sixth day, about noon, halting in a hollow, he pointed to tracks in the snow and called out: 'Ageter! Ageter! Ageter!'

The hunters saw sharply defined hoof-marks, not unlike the tracks of reindeer, except that they were longer. The tepee was set up on the spot and the dogs unharnessed.

The Indian led the way with the dogs, and Rea and Jones followed, slipping over the hard crust without sinking in and traveling swiftly. Soon the guide, pointing, again let out the cry: 'Ageter!' at the same moment loosing the dogs.

Some few hundred yards down the hollow, a number of large black animals, not unlike the shaggy, humpy buffalo, lumbered over the snow. Jones echoed Rea's yell, and broke into a run, easily distancing the puffing giant.

The musk-oxen squared round to the dogs, and were soon surrounded by the yelping pack. Jones came up to find six old bulls uttering grunts of rage and shaking ram-like horns at their tormentors. Notwithstanding that for Jones this was the cumulation of years of desire, the crowning moment, the climax and fruition of long-harbored dreams, he halted before the tame and helpless beasts, with joy not unmixed with pain.

'It will be murder!' he exclaimed. 'It's like shooting down sheep.'

Rea came crashing up behind him and yelled: 'Get busy. We need fresh meat, an' I want the skins.'

The bulls succumbed to well-directed shots, and the Indian and Rea hurried back to camp with the dogs to fetch the sleds, while Jones examined with warm interest the animals he had wanted to see all his life. He found the largest bull approached within a third of the size of a buffalo. He was of a brownish-black color and very like a large, woolly ram. His head was broad, with sharp, small ears; the horns had wide and flattened bases and lay flat on the head, to run down back of the eyes, then curve forward to a sharp point. Like the bison, the musk-ox had short, heavy limbs, covered with very long hair, and small, hard hoofs with hairy tufts inside the curve of bone, which probably served as pads or checks to hold the hoof firm on ice. His legs seemed out of proportion to his body.

Two musk-oxen were loaded on a sled and hauled to camp in one trip. Skinning them was but short work for such expert hands. All the choice cuts of meat were saved. No time was lost in broiling a steak, which they found sweet and juicy, with a flavor of musk that was disagreeable.

'Now, Rea, for the calves,' exclaimed Jones, 'and then we're homeward bound.'

'I hate to tell this redskin,' replied Rea. 'He'll be like the others. But it ain't likely he'd desert us here. He's far from his base, with nothin' but thet old musket.' Rea then commanded the attention of the brave, and began to mangle the Great Slave and Yellow Knife languages. Of this mixture Jones knew but few words. 'Ageter nechila,' which Rea kept repeating, he knew, however, meant 'musk-oxen little.'

The guide stared, suddenly appeared to get Rea's meaning, then vigorously shook his head and gazed at Jones in fear and horror. Following this came an action as singular as inexplicable. Slowly rising, he faced the north, lifted his hand, and remained statuesque in his immobility. Then he began deliberately packing his blankets and traps on his sled, which had not been unhitched from the train of dogs.

'Jackoway ditchen hula,' he said, and pointed south.

'Jackoway ditchen hula,' echoed Rea. 'The damned Indian says "wife sticks none." He's goin' to quit us. What do you think of thet? His wife's out of wood. Jackoway out of wood, and here we are two days from the Arctic Ocean! Jones, the damned heathen don't go back!'

The trapper coolly cocked his rifle. The savage, who plainly saw and understood the action, never flinched. He turned his breast to Rea, and there was nothing in his demeanor to suggest his relation to a craven tribe.

'Good heavens, Rea, don't kill him!' exclaimed Jones, knocking up the leveled rifle.

'Why not, I'd like to know!' demanded Rea, as if he were considering the fate of a threatening beast. 'I reckon it'd be a bad thing for us to let him go.'

'Let him go,' said Jones. 'We are here on the ground. We have dogs and meat. We'll get our calves and reach the lake as soon as he does, and we might get there before.'

'Mebbe we will,' growled Rea.

No vacillation attended the Indian's mood. From a friendly guide, he had suddenly been transformed into a dark, sullen savage. He refused the musk-ox meat offered by Jones, and he pointed south and looked at the white hunters as if he asked them to go with him. Both men shook their heads in answer. The savage struck his breast a sounding blow and with his index finger pointed at the white of the north, he shouted dramatically: 'Naza! Naza! Naza!'

He then leaped upon his sled, lashed his dogs into a run, and without looking back disappeared over a ridge.

The musk-ox hunters sat long silent. Finally Rea shook his shaggy locks and roared. 'Ho! Ho! Jackoway out of wood! Jackoway out of wood! Jackoway out of wood!'

On the day following the desertion, Jones found tracks to the north of the camp, making a broad trail in which were numerous little imprints that sent him flying back to get Rea and the dogs. Musk-oxen in great numbers had passed in the night, and Jones and Rea had not trailed the herd a mile before they had it in sight. When the dogs burst into full cry, the musk-oxen climbed a high knoll and squared about to give battle.

'Calves! Calves! Calves!' cried Jones.

'Hold back! Hold back! Thet's a big herd, an' they'll show fight.'

As good fortune would have it, the herd split up into several sections, and one part, hard pressed by the dogs, ran down the knoll, to be cornered under the lee of a bank. The hunters, seeing this small number, hurried upon them to find three cows and five badly frightened little calves backed against the bank of snow, with small red eyes fastened on the barking, snapping dogs.

To a man of Jones's experience and skill, the capturing of the calves was a ridiculously easy piece of work. The cows tossed their heads, watched the dogs, and forgot their young. The first cast of the lasso settled over the neck of a little fellow. Jones hauled him out over the slippery snow and laughed as he bound the hairy legs. In less time than he had taken to capture one buffalo calf, with half the effort, he had all the little musk-oxen bound fast. Then he signaled this feat by pealing out an Indian yell of victory.

'Buff, we've got 'em,' cried Rea; 'an' now for the hell of it—gettin' 'em home. I'll fetch the sleds. You might as well down thet best cow for me. I can use another skin.'

Of all Jones's prizes of captured wild beasts—which numbered nearly every species common to western North America—he took greatest pride in the little musk-oxen. In truth, so great had been his passion to capture some of these rare and inaccessible mammals, that he considered the day's work the fulfillment of his life's purpose. He was happy. Never had he been so delighted as when, the very evening of their captivity, the musk-oxen, evincing no particular fear of him, began to dig with sharp hoofs into the snow for moss. And they found moss, and ate it, which solved Jones's greatest problem. He had hardly dared to think how to feed them, and here they were picking sustenance out of the frozen snow.

'Rea, will you look at that! Rea, will you look at that!' he kept repeating. 'See, they're hunting feed.'

And the giant, with his rare smile, watched him play with the calves. They were about two and a half feet high, and resembled long-haired sheep. The ears and horns were undiscernible, and their color considerably lighter than that of the matured beasts.

'No sense of fear of man,' said the life-student of animals. 'But they shrink from the dogs.'

In packing for the journey south, the captives were strapped on the sleds. This circumstance necessitated a sacrifice of meat and wood, which brought grave, doubtful shakes of Rea's great head.

Days of hastening over the icy snow, with short hours for sleep and rest, passed before the hunters awoke to the consciousness that they were lost. The meat they had packed had gone to feed themselves and the dogs. Only a few sticks of wood were left.

'Better kill a calf, an' cook meat while we've got a little wood left,' suggested Rea.

'Kill one of my calves? I'd starve first!' cried Jones.

The hungry giant said no more.

They headed southwest. All about them glared the grim monotony of the arctics. No rock or bush or tree made a welcome mark upon the hoary plain. Wonderland of frost, white marble desert, infinitude of gleaming silences!

Snow began to fall, making the dogs flounder, obliterating the sun by which they traveled. They camped to wait for clearing weather. Biscuits soaked in tea made their meal. At dawn Jones crawled out of the tepee. The snow had ceased. But where were the dogs? He yelled in alarm. Then little mounds of white, scattered here and there, became animated, heaved, rocked and rose to fall to pieces, exposing the dogs. Blankets of snow had been their covering.

Rea had ceased his 'Jackoway out of wood,' for a reiterated question: 'Where are the wolves?'

'Lost,' replied Jones in hollow humor.

Near the close of that day, in which they had resumed travel, from the crest of a ridge they descried a long, low, undulating dark line. It proved to be the forest of 'little sticks,' where, with grateful assurance of fire and of soon finding their old trail, they made camp.

'We've four biscuits left, an' enough tea for one drink each,' said Rea. 'I calculate we're two hundred miles from Great Slave Lake. Where are the wolves?'

At that moment the night wind wafted through the forest a long, haunting mourn. The calves shifted uneasily; the dogs raised sharp noses to sniff the air, and Rea, settling back against a tree, cried out: 'Ho! Ho!' Again the savage sound, a keen wailing note with the hunger of the northland in it, broke the cold silence. 'You'll see a pack of real wolves in a minute,' said Rea. Soon a swift pattering of feet down a forest slope brought him to his feet with a curse to reach a brawny hand for his rifle. White streaks crossed the black of the tree trunks; then indistinct forms, the color of snow, swept up, spread out and streaked to and fro. Jones thought the great, gaunt, pure white beasts the spectral wolves of Rea's fancy, for they were silent, and silent wolves must belong to dreams only.

'Ho! Ho!' yelled Rea. 'There's green-fire eyes for you, Buff. Hell itself ain't nothin' to these white devils. Get the calves in the tepee, an' stand ready to loose the dogs, for we've got to fight.'

Raising his rifle he opened fire upon the white foe. A struggling, rustling sound followed the shots. But whether it was the threshing about of wolves dying in agony, or the fighting of the fortunate ones over those shot, could not be ascertained in the confusion.

Following his example Jones also fired rapidly on the other side of the tepee. The same inarticulate, silently rustling wrestle succeeded this volley.

'Wait!' cried Rea. 'Be sparin' of cartridges.'

The dogs strained at their chains and bravely bayed the wolves. The hunters heaped logs and brush on the fire, which, blazing up, sent a bright light far into the woods. On the outer edge of that circle moved the white, restless, gliding forms.

'They're more afraid of fire than of us,' said Jones.

So it proved. When the fire burned and crackled they kept well in the background. The hunters had a long respite from serious anxiety, during which time they collected all the available wood at hand. But at midnight, when this had been mostly consumed, the wolves grew bold again.

'Have you any shots left for the 45–90, besides what's in the magazine?' asked Rea.

'Yes, a good handful.'

'Well, get busy.'

With careful aim Jones emptied the magazine into the gray, gliding, groping mass. The same rustling, shuffling, almost silent strife ensued.

'Rea, there's something uncanny about those brutes. A silent pack of wolves!'

'Ho! Ho!' rolled the giant's answer through the woods.

For the present the attack appeared to have been effectually checked. The hunters, sparingly adding a little of their fast diminishing pile of fuel to the fire, decided to lie down for much needed rest, but not for sleep. How long they lay there, cramped by the calves, listening for stealthy steps, neither could tell; it might have been moments and it might have been hours. All at once came a rapid rush of pattering feet, succeeded by a chorus of angry barks, then a terrible commingling of savage snarls, growls, snaps and yelps.

'Out!' yelled Rea. 'They're on the dogs!'

Jones pushed his cocked rifle ahead of him and straightened up outside the tepee. A wolf, large as a panther and white as the gleaming snow, sprang at him. Even as he discharged his rifle, right against the breast of the beast, he saw its dripping jaws, its wicked green eyes, like spurts of fire and felt its hot breath. It fell at his feet and writhed in the death struggle. Slender bodies of black and white, whirling and tussling together, sent out fiendish uproar. Rea threw a blazing stick of wood among them, which sizzled as it met the furry coats, and brandishing another he ran into the thick of the fight. Unable to stand the proximity of fire, the wolves bolted and loped off into the woods.

'What a huge brute!' exclaimed Jones, dragging the one he had shot into the light. It was a superb animal, thin, supple, strong, with a coat of frosty fur, very long and fine. Rea began at once to skin it, remarking that he hoped to find other pelts in the morning.

Though the wolves remained in the vicinity of camp, none ventured near. The dogs moaned and whined; their restlessness increased as dawn approached, and when the gray light came, Jones found that some of them had been badly lacerated by the fangs of the wolves. Rea hunted for dead wolves and found not so much as a piece of white fur.

Soon the hunters were speeding southward. Other than a disposition to fight among themselves, the dogs showed no evil effects of the attack. They were lashed to their best speed, for Rea said the white rangers of the north would never quit their trail. All day the men listened for the wild, lonesome, haunting mourn. But it came not.

A wonderful halo of white and gold, that Rea called a sun-dog, hung in the sky all afternoon, and dazzlingly bright over the dazzling world of snow, circled and glowed a mocking sun, brother of the desert mirage, beautiful illusion, smiling cold out of the polar blue.

The first pale evening star twinkled in the east when the hunters made camp on the shore of Artillery Lake. At dusk the clear, silent air opened to the sound of a long, haunting mourn.

'Ho! Ho!' called Rea. His hoarse, deep voice rang defiance to the foe.

While he built a fire before the tepee, Jones strode up and down, suddenly to whip out his knife and make for the tame little musk-oxen, now digging in the snow. Then he wheeled abruptly and held out the blade to Rea.

'What for?' demanded the giant.

'We've got to eat,' said Jones. 'And I can't kill one of them. I can't, so you do it.'

'Kill one of our calves?' roared Rea. 'Not till hell freezes over! I ain't commenced to get hungry. Besides, the wolves are going to eat us, calves and all.'

Nothing more was said. They ate their last biscuit. Jones packed the calves away in the tepee, and turned to the dogs. All day they had worried him; something was amiss with them, and even as he went among them a fierce fight broke out. Jones saw it was unusual, for the attacked dogs showed craven fear, and the attacking ones a howling, savage intensity that surprised him. Then one of the vicious brutes rolled his eyes, frothed at the mouth, shuddered and leaped in his harness, vented a hoarse howl and fell back shaking and retching.

'My God! Rea!' cried Jones in horror. 'Come here! Look! That dog is dying of rabies! Hydrophobia! The white wolves have hydrophobia!'

'If you ain't right!' exclaimed Rea. 'I seen a dog die of thet onct, an' he acted like this. An' thet one ain't all. Look, Buff! look at them green eyes! Didn't I say the white wolves was hell? We'll have to kill every dog we've got.'

Jones shot the dog, and soon afterward three more that manifested signs of the disease. It was an awful situation. To kill all the dogs meant simply to sacrifice his life and Rea's; it meant abandoning hope of ever reaching the cabin. Then to risk being bitten by one of the poisoned, maddened brutes, to risk the most horrible of agonizing deaths—that was even worse.

'Rea, we've one chance,' cried Jones, with pale face. 'Can you hold the dogs, one by one, while I muzzle them?'

'Ho! Ho!' replied the giant. Placing his bowie knife between his teeth, with gloved hands he seized and dragged one of the dogs to the campfire. The animal whined and protested, but showed no ill spirit. Jones muzzled his jaws tightly with strong cords. Another and another were tied up, then one which tried to snap at Jones was nearly crushed by the giant's grip. The last, a surly brute, broke out into mad ravings the moment he felt the touch of Jones's hands, and writhing, frothing, he snapped Jones's sleeve. Rea jerked him loose and held him in the air with one arm, while with the other he swung the bowie. They hauled the dead dogs out on the snow, and returning to the fire sat down to await the cry they expected.

Presently, as darkness fastened down tight, it came—the same cry, wild, haunting, mourning. But for hours it was not repeated.

'Better rest some,' said Rea; 'I'll call you if they come.'

Jones dropped to sleep as he touched his blankets. Morning dawned for him, to find the great, dark, shadowy figure of the giant nodding over the fire.

'How's this? Why didn't you call me?' demanded Jones.

'The wolves only fought a little over the dead dogs.'

On the instant Jones saw a wolf skulking up the bank. Throwing up his rifle, which he had carried out of the tepee, he took a snap-shot at the beast. It ran off on three legs, to go out of sight over the bank. Jones scrambled up the steep, slippery place, and upon arriving at the ridge, which took several moments of hard work, he looked everywhere for the wolf. In a moment he saw the animal, standing still some hundred or more paces down a hollow. With the quick report of Jones's second shot, the wolf fell and rolled over. The hunter ran to the spot to find the wolf was dead. Taking hold of a front paw, he dragged the animal over the snow to camp. Rea began to skin the animal, when suddenly he exclaimed:

'This fellow's hind foot is gone!'

'That's strange. I saw it hanging by the skin as the wolf ran up the bank. I'll look for it.'

By the bloody trail on the snow he returned to the place where the wolf had fallen, and thence back to the spot where its leg had been broken by the bullet. He discovered no sign of the foot.

'Didn't find it, did you?' said Rea.

'No, and it appears odd to me. The snow is so hard the foot could not have sunk.'

'Well, the wolf ate his foot, thet's what,' returned Rea. 'Look at them teeth marks!'

'Is it possible?' Jones stared at the leg Rea held up.

'Yes, it is. These wolves are crazy at times. You've seen thet. An' the smell of blood, an' nothin' else, mind you, in my opinion, made him eat his own foot. We'll cut him open.'

Impossible as the thing seemed to Jones—and he could not but believe further evidence of his own eyes—it was even stranger to drive a train of mad dogs. Yet that was what Rea and he did, and lashed them, beat them to cover many miles in the long day's journey. Rabies had broken out in several dogs so alarmingly that Jones had to kill them at the end of the run. And hardly had the sound of the shots died when faint and far away, but clear as a bell, bayed on the wind the same haunting mourn of a trailing wolf.

'Ho! Ho! where are the wolves?' cried Rea.

A waiting, watching, sleepless night followed. Again the hunters faced the south. Hour after hour, riding, running, walking, they urged the poor, jaded, poisoned dogs. At dark they reached the head of Artillery Lake. Rea placed the tepee between two huge stones. Then the hungry hunters, tired, grim, silent, desperate, awaited the familiar cry.

It came on the cold wind, the same haunting mourn, dreadful in its significance.

Absence of fire inspirited the wary wolves. Out of the pale gloom gaunt white forms emerged, agile and stealthy, slipping on velvet-padded feet, closer, closer, closer. The dogs wailed in terror.

'Into the tepee!' yelled Rea.

Jones plunged in after his comrade. The despairing howls of the dogs, drowned in more savage, frightful sounds, knelled one tragedy and foreboded a more terrible one. Jones looked out to see a white mass, like leaping waves of a rapid.

'Pump lead into thet!' cried Rea.

Rapidly Jones emptied his rifle into the white fray. The mass split; gaunt wolves leaped high to fall back dead; others wriggled and limped away; others dragged their hind quarters; others darted at the tepee.

'No more cartridges!' yelled Jones.

The giant grabbed the ax, and barred the door of the tepee. Crash! the heavy iron cleaved the skull of the first brute. Crash! it lamed the second. Then Rea stood in the narrow passage between the rocks, waiting with uplifted ax. A shaggy, white demon, snapping his jaws, sprang like a dog. A sodden, thudding blow met him and he slunk away without a cry. Another rabid beast launched his white body at the giant. Like a flash the ax descended. In agony the wolf fell, to spin round and round, running on his hind legs, while his head and shoulders and forelegs remained in the snow. His back was broken.

Jones crouched in the opening of the tepee, knife in hand. He doubted his senses. This was a nightmare. He saw two wolves leap at once. He heard the crash of the ax; he saw one wolf go down and the other slip under the swinging weapon to grasp the giant's hip. Jones's heard the rend of cloth, and then he pounced like a cat, to drive his knife into the body of the beast. Another nimble foe lunged at Rea, to sprawl broken and limp from the iron. It was a silent fight. The giant shut the way to his comrade and the calves; he made no outcry; he needed but one blow for every beast; magnificent, he wielded death and faced it—silent. He brought the white wild dogs of the north down with lightning blows, and when no more sprang to the attack, down on the frigid silence he rolled his cry: 'Ho! Ho!'

'Rea! Rea! how is it with you?' called Jones, climbing out.

'A torn coat—no more, my lad.'

Three of the poor dogs were dead; the fourth and last gasped at the hunters and died.

The wintry night became a thing of half-conscious past, a dream to the hunters, manifesting its reality only by the stark, stiff bodies of wolves, white in the gray morning.

'If we can eat, we'll make the cabin,' said Rea. 'But the dogs an' wolves are poison.'

'Shall I kill a calf?' asked Jones.

'Ho! Ho! when hell freezes over—if we must!'

Jones found one 45–90 cartridge in all the outfit, and with that in the chamber of his rifle, once more struck south. Spruce trees began to show on the barrens and caribou trails roused hope in the hearts of the hunters.

'Look! in the spruces,' whispered Jones, dropping the rope of his sled. Among the black trees gray objects moved.

'Caribou!' said Rea. 'Hurry! Shoot! Don't miss!'

But Jones waited. He knew the value of the last bullet. He had a hunter's patience. When the caribou came out in an open space, Jones whistled. It was then the rifle grew set and fixed; it was then the red fire belched forth.

At four hundred yards the bullet took some fraction of time to strike. What a long time that was! Then both hunters heard the spiteful spat of the lead. The caribou fell, jumped up, ran down the slope, and fell again to rise no more.

An hour of rest, with fire and meat, changed the world to the hunters; still glistening, it yet had lost its bitter cold, its deathlike clutch.

'What's this?' cried Jones.

Moccasin tracks of different sizes, all toeing north, arrested the hunters.

'Pointed north! Wonder what thet means?' Rea plodded on, doubtfully shaking his head.

Night again, clear, cold, silver, starlit, silent night! The hunters rested, listening ever for the haunting mourn. Day again, white, passionless, monotonous, silent day! The hunters traveled on—on—on, ever listening for the haunting mourn.

Another dusk found them within thirty miles of their cabin. Only one more day now.

Rea talked of his furs, of the splendid white furs he could not bring. Jones talked of his little musk-oxen calves and joyfully watched them dig for moss in the snow.

Vigilance relaxed that night. Outworn nature rebelled, and both hunters slept.

Rea awoke first, and kicking off the blankets, went out. His terrible roar of rage made Jones fly to his side.

Under the very shadow of the tepee, where the little musk-oxen had been tethered, they lay stretched out pathetically on crimson snow—stiff stone-cold, dead. Moccasin tracks told the story of the tragedy.

Jones leaned against his comrade.

The giant raised his huge fist.

'Jackoway out of wood! Jackoway out of wood!'

Then he choked.

The north wind, blowing through the thin, dark, weird spruce trees, moaned and seemed to sigh, 'Naza! Naza! Naza!'

11

On to the Siwash

'Who all was doin' the talkin' last night?' asked Frank next morning, when we were having a late breakfast. 'Cause I've a joke on somebody. Jim he talks in his sleep often, an' last night after you did finally get settled down, Jim he up in his sleep an' says: "Shore he's windy as hell! Shore he's windy as hell"!'

At this cruel exposure of his subjective wanderings, Jim showed extreme humiliation; but Frank's eyes fairly snapped with the fun he got out of telling it. The genial foreman loved a joke. The week's stay at Oak, in which we all became thoroughly acquainted, had presented Jim as always the same quiet character, easy, slow, silent, lovable. In his brother cowboy, however, we had discovered in addition to his fine, frank, friendly spirit, an overwhelming fondness for playing tricks. This boyish mischievousness, distinctly Arizonian, reached its acme whenever it tended in the direction of our serious leader.

Lawson had been dispatched on some mysterious errand about which my curiosity was all in vain. The order of the day was leisurely to get in readiness, and pack for our journey to the Siwash on the morrow. I watered my horse, played with the hounds, knocked about the cliffs, returned to the cabin, and lay down on my bed. Jim's hands were white with flour. He was kneading dough, and had several low, flat pans on the table. Wallace and Jones strolled in, and later Frank, and they all took various positions before the fire. I saw Frank, with the quickness of a sleight-of-hand performer, slip one of the pans of dough on the chair Jones had placed by the table. Jim did not see the action; Jones's and Wallace's backs were turned to Frank, and he did not know I was in the cabin. The conversation continued on the subject of Jones's big bay horse, which, hobbles and all, had gotten ten miles from camp the night before.

'Better count his ribs than his tracks,' said Frank, and went on talking as easily and naturally as if he had not been expecting a very entertaining situation.

But no one could ever foretell Colonel Jones's actions. He showed every intention of seating himself in the chair, then walked over to his pack to begin searching for something or other. Wallace, however, promptly took the seat; and what began to be funnier than strange, he did not get up. Not unlikely this circumstance was owing to the fact that several of the rude chairs had soft layers of old blanket tacked on them. Whatever were Frank's internal emotions, he presented a remarkably placid and commonplace exterior; but when Jim began to search for the missing pan of dough, the joker slowly sagged in his chair.

'Shore that beats hell!' said Jim. 'I had three pans of dough. Could the pup have taken one?'

Wallace rose to his feet, and the bread pan clattered to the floor, with a clang and a clank, evidently protesting against the indignity it had suffered. But the dough stayed with Wallace, a great white conspicuous splotch on his corduroys. Jim, Frank and Jones all saw it at once.

'Why—Mr Wal—lace—you set—in the dough!' exclaimed Frank, in a queer, strangled voice. Then he exploded, while Jim fell over the table.

It seemed that those two Arizona rangers, matured men though they were, would die of convulsions. I laughed with them, and so did Wallace, while he brought his bone-handled bowie knife into novel use. Buffalo Jones never cracked a smile, though he did remark about the waste of good flour.

Frank's face was a study for a psychologist when Jim actually apologized to Wallace for being so careless with his pans. I did not betray Frank, but I resolved to keep a still closer watch on him. It was partially because of this uneasy sense of his trickiness in the fringe of my mind that I made a discovery. My sleeping-bag rested on a raised platform in one corner, and at a favorable moment I examined the bag. It had not been tampered with, but I noticed a string running out through a chink between the logs. I found it came from a thick layer of straw under my bed, and had been tied to the end of a flatly coiled lasso. Leaving the thing as it was, I went outside and carelessly chased the hounds round the cabin. The string stretched along the logs to another chink, where it returned into the cabin at a point near where Frank slept. No great power of deduction was necessary to acquaint me with full details of the plot to spoil my slumbers. So I patiently awaited developments.

Lawson rode in near sundown with the carcasses of two beasts of some species hanging over his saddle. It turned out that Jones had planned a surprise for Wallace and me, and it could hardly have been a more enjoyable one, considering the time and place. We knew he had a flock of Persian sheep on the south slope of Buckskin, but had no idea it was within striking distance of Oak. Lawson had that day hunted up the shepherd and his sheep, to return to us with two sixty-pound Persian lambs. We feasted at supper-time on meat which was sweet, juicy, very tender and of as rare a flavor as that of the Rocky Mountain sheep.

My state after supper was one of huge enjoyment and with interest I awaited Frank's first spar for an opening. It came presently, in a lull of the conversation.

'Saw a big rattler run under the cabin to-day,' he said, as if he were speaking of one of Old Buddy's shoes. 'I tried to get a whack at him, but he oozed away too quick.'

'Shore I seen him often,' put in Jim. Good, old, honest Jim, led away by his trickster comrade! It was very plain. So I was to be frightened by snakes.

'These old cañon beds are ideal dens for rattlesnakes,' chimed in my scientific California friend. 'I have found several dens, but did not molest them as this is a particularly dangerous time of the year to meddle with the reptiles. Quite likely there's a den under the cabin.'

While he made this remarkable statement, he had the grace to hide his face in a huge puff of smoke. He, too, was in the plot. I waited for Jones to come out with some ridiculous theory or fact concerning the particular species of snake, but as he did not speak, I concluded they had wisely left him out of the secret. After mentally debating a moment, I decided, as it was a very harmless joke, to help Frank to the fulfillment of his enjoyment.

'Rattlesnakes!' I exclaimed. 'Heavens! I'd die if I heard one, let alone seeing it. A big rattler jumped at me one day, and I've never recovered from the shock.'

Plainly, Frank was delighted to hear of any antipathy and my unfortunate experience, and he proceeded to expatiate on the viciousness of rattlesnakes, particularly those of Arizona. If I had believed the succeeding stories, emanating from the fertile brains of those three fellows, I should have made certain that Arizona cañons were Brazilian jungles. Frank's parting shot, sent in a mellow, kind voice, was the best point in the whole trick. 'Now, I'd be nervous if I had a sleeping-bag like yours, because it's just the place for a rattler to ooze into.'

In the confusion and dim light of bedtime I contrived to throw the end of my lasso over the horn of a saddle hanging on the wall, with the intention of augmenting the noise I soon expected to create; and I placed my automatic rifle and .38 S. and W. Special within easy reach of my hand. Then I crawled into my bag and composed myself to listen. Frank soon began to snore, so brazenly, so fictitiously, that I wondered at the man's absorbed intensity in his joke; and I was at great pains to smother in my breast a violent burst of riotous merriment. Jones's snores, however, were real enough, and this made me enjoy the situation all the more; because if he did not show a mild surprise when the catastrophe fell, I would greatly miss my guess. I knew the three wily conspirators were wide-awake. Suddenly I felt a movement in the straw under me and a faint rustling. It was so soft, so sinuous, that if I had not known it was the lasso, I would assuredly have been frightened. I gave a little jump, such as one will make quickly in bed. Then the coil ran out from under the straw. How subtly suggestive of a snake! I made a slight outcry, a big jump, paused a moment for effectiveness—in which time Frank forgot to snore—then let out a tremendous yell, grabbed my guns, sent twelve thundering shots through the roof and pulled my lasso.

Crash! the saddle came down, to be followed by sounds not on Frank's programme and certainly not calculated upon by me. But they were all the more effective. I gathered that Lawson, who was not in the secret, and who was a nightmare sort of sleeper anyway, had knocked over Jim's table, with its array of pots and pans and then, unfortunately for Jones, had kicked that innocent person in the stomach.

As I lay there in my bag, the very happiest fellow in the wide world, the sound of my mirth was as the buzz of the wings of a fly to the mighty storm. Roar on roar filled the cabin.

When the three hypocrites recovered sufficiently from the startling climax to calm Lawson, who swore the cabin had been attacked by Indians; when Jones stopped roaring long enough to hear it was only a harmless snake that had caused the trouble, we hushed to repose once more—not, however, without hearing some trenchant remarks from the boiling Colonel anent fun and fools, and the indubitable fact that there was not a rattlesnake on Buckskin Mountain.

Long after this explosion had died away, I heard, or rather felt, a mysterious shudder or tremor of the cabin, and I knew that Frank and Jim were shaking with silent laughter. On my own score, I determined to find if Jones, in his strange make-up, had any sense of humor, or interest in life, or feeling, or love that did not center and hinge on four-footed beasts. In view of the rude awakening from what, no doubt, were pleasant dreams of wonderful white and green animals, combining the intelligence of man and strength of brutes—a new species creditable to his genius—I was perhaps unjust in my conviction as to his lack of humor. And as to the other question, whether or not he had any real human feeling for the creatures built in his own image, that was decided very soon and unexpectedly.

The following morning, as soon as Lawson got in with the horses, we packed and started. Rather sorry was I to bid good-by to Oak Spring. Taking the back trail of the Stewarts, we walked the horses all day up a slowly narrowing, ascending cañon. The hounds crossed coyote and deer trails continually, but made no break. Sounder looked up as if to say he associated painful reminiscences with certain kinds of tracks. At the head of the cañon we reached timber at about the time dusk gathered, and we located for the night. Being once again nearly nine thousand feet high, we found the air bitterly cold, making a blazing fire most acceptable.

In the haste to get supper we all took a hand, and some one threw upon our tarpaulin tablecloth a tin cup of butter mixed with carbolic acid—a concoction Jones had used to bathe the sore feet of the dogs. Of course I got hold of this, spread a generous portion on my hot biscuit, placed some red-hot beans on that, and began to eat like a hungry hunter. At first I thought I was only burned. Then I recognized the taste and burn of the acid and knew something was wrong.

Picking up the tin, I examined it, smelled the pungent odor, and felt a queer, numb sense of fear. This lasted only for a moment, as I well knew the use and power of the acid, and had not swallowed enough to hurt me. I was about to make known my mistake in a matter-of-fact way, when it flashed over me the accident could be made to serve a turn.

'Jones!' I cried hoarsely. 'What's in this butter?'

'Lord! you haven't eaten any of that. Why, I put carbolic acid in it.'

'Oh—oh—oh—I'm poisoned! I ate nearly all of it! Oh—I'm burning up! I'm dying!' With that I began to moan and rock to and fro and hold my stomach.

Consternation preceded shock. But in the excitement of the moment, Wallace—who, though badly scared, retained his wits—made for me with a can of condensed milk. He threw me back with no gentle hand, and was squeezing the life out of me to make me open my mouth, when I gave him a jab in his side. I imagined his surprise, as this peculiar reception of his first-aid-to-the-injured made him hold off to take a look at me, and in this interval I contrived to whisper to him: 'Joke! Joke! you idiot! I'm only shamming. I want to see if I can scare Jones and get even with Frank. Help me out! Cry! Get tragic!'

From that moment I shall always believe that the stage lost a great tragedian in Wallace. With a magnificent gesture he threw the can of condensed milk at Jones, who was so stunned he did not try to dodge. 'Thoughtless man! Murderer! it's too late!' cried Wallace, laying me back across his knees. 'It's too late. His teeth are locked. He's far gone. Poor boy! poor boy! Who's to tell his mother?'

I could see from under my hat-brim that the solemn, hollow voice had penetrated the cold exterior of the plainsman. He could not speak; he clasped and unclasped his big hands in helpless fashion. Frank was as white as a sheet. This was simply delightful to me. But the expression of miserable, impotent distress on old Jim's sun-browned face was more than I could stand, and I could no longer keep up the deception. Just as Wallace cried out to Jones to pray—I wished then I had not weakened so soon—I got up and walked to the fire.

'Jim, I'll have another biscuit, please.'

His under jaw dropped, then he nervously shoveled biscuits at me. Jones grabbed my hand and cried out with a voice that was new to me: 'You can eat? You're better? You'll get over it?'

'Sure. Why, carbolic acid never phases me. I've often used it for rattlesnake bites. I did not tell you, but that rattler at the cabin last night actually bit me, and I used carbolic to cure the poison.'

Frank mumbled something about horses, and faded into the gloom. As for Jones, he looked at me rather incredulously, and the absolute, almost childish gladness he manifested because I had been snatched from the grave, made me regret my deceit, and satisfied me forever on one score.

On awakening in the morning I found frost half an inch thick covered my sleeping-bag, whitened the ground, and made the beautiful spruce trees silver in hue as well as in name.

We were getting ready for an early start, when two riders, with pack-horses jogging after them, came down the trail from the direction of Oak Spring. They proved to be Jeff Clarke, the wild-horse wrangler mentioned by the Stewarts, and his helper. They were on the way into the breaks for a string of pintos. Clarke was a short, heavily bearded man, of jovial aspect. He said he had met the Stewarts going into Fredonia, and being advised of our destination, had hurried to come up with us. As we did not know, except in a general way, where we were making for, the meeting was a fortunate event.

Our camping site had been close to the divide made by the one of the long, wooded ridges sent off by Buckskin Mountain, and soon we were descending again. We rode half a mile down a timbered slope, and then out into a beautiful, flat forest of gigantic pines. Clarke informed us it was a level bench some ten miles long, running out from the slopes of Buckskin to face the Grand Cañon on the south, and the breaks of the Siwash on the west. For two hours we rode between the stately lines of trees, and the hoofs of the horses gave forth no sound. A long, silvery grass, sprinkled with smiling bluebells, covered the ground, except close under the pines, where soft red mats invited lounging and rest. We saw numerous deer, great gray mule deer, almost as large as elk. Jones said they had been crossed with elk once, which accounted for their size. I did not see a stump, or a burned tree, or a windfall during the ride.

Clarke led us to the rim of the cañon. Without any preparation—for the giant trees hid the open sky—we rode right out to the edge of the tremendous chasm. At first I did not seem to think; my faculties were benumbed; only the pure sensorial instinct of the savage who sees, but does not feel, made me take note of the abyss. Not one of our party had ever seen the cañon from this side, and not one of us said a word. But Clarke kept talking.

'Wild place this is hyar,' he said. 'Seldom any one but horse wranglers gits over this far. I've bed a bunch of wild pintos down in a cañon below fer two years. I reckon you can't find no better place fer camp than right hyar. Listen. Do you hear thet rumble? Thet's Thunder Falls. You can only see it from one place, an' thet far off, but thar's brooks you can git at to water the hosses. Fer thet matter, you can ride up the slopes an' git snow. If you can git snow close, it'd be better, fer thet's an all-fired bad trail down fer water.'

'Is this the cougar country the Stewarts talked about?' asked Jones.

'Reckon it is. Cougars is as thick in hyar as rabbits in a spring-hole cañon. I'm on the way now to bring up my pintos. The cougars hev cost me hundreds—I might say thousands of dollars. I lose hosses all the time; an' damn me, gentlemen,

I've never raised a colt. This is the greatest cougar country in the West. Look at those yellow crags! Thar's where the cougars stay. No one ever hunted 'em. It seems to me they can't be hunted. Deer and wild hosses by the thousand browse hyar on the mountain in summer, an' down in the breaks in winter. The cougars live fat. You'll find deer and wild-hoss carcasses all over this country. You'll find lions's dens full of bones. You'll find warm deer left for the coyotes. But whether you'll find the cougars, I can't say. I fetched dogs in hyar, an' tried to ketch Old Tom. I've put them on his trail an' never saw hide nor hair of them again. Jones, it's no easy huntin' hyar.'

'Well, I can see that,' replied our leader. 'I never hunted lions in such a country, and never knew any one who had. We'll have to learn how. We've the time and the dogs, all we need is the stuff in us.'

'I hope you fellars git some cougars, an' I believe you will. Whatever you do, kill Old Tom.'

'We'll catch him alive. We're not on a hunt to kill cougars,' said Jones.

'What!' exclaimed Clarke, looking from Jones to us. His rugged face wore a half-smile.

'Jones ropes cougars, an' ties them up,' replied Frank.

'I'm——— ———if he'll ever rope Old Tom,' burst out Clarke, ejecting a huge quid of tobacco. 'Why, man alive! it'd be the death of you to git near thet old villain. I never seen him, but I've seen his tracks fer five years. They're larger than any hoss tracks you ever seen. He'll weigh over three hundred, thet old cougar. Hyar, take a look at my man's hoss. Look at his back. See them marks? Wal, Old Tom made them, an' he made them right in camp last fall, when we were down in the cañon.'

The mustang to which Clarke called our attention was a sleek cream and white pinto. Upon his side and back were long regular scars, some an inch wide, and bare of hair.

'How on earth did he get rid of the cougar?' asked Jones.

'I don't know. Perhaps he got scared of the dogs. It took thet pinto a year to git well. Old Tom is a real lion. He'll kill a full-grown hoss when he wants, but a yearlin' colt is his especial likin'. You're sure to run acrost his trail, an' you'll never miss it. Wal, if I find any cougar sign down in the cañon, I'll build two fires so as to let you know. Though no hunter, I'm tolerably acquainted with the varmints. The deer an' hosses are rangin' the forest slopes now, an' I think the cougars come up over the rim rock at night an' go back in the mornin'. Anyway, if your dogs can follow the trails, you've got sport, an' more'n sport comin' to you. But take it from me—don't try to rope Old Tom.'

After all our disappointments in the beginning of the expedition, our hardship on the desert, our trials with the dogs and horses, it was real pleasure to make permanent camp with wood, water and feed at hand, a soul-stirring, ever-changing picture before us, and the certainty that we were in the wild lairs of the lions— among the Lords of the Crags!

While we were unpacking, every now and then I would straighten up and gaze out beyond. I knew the outlook was magnificent and sublime beyond words, but as yet I had not begun to understand it. The great pine trees, growing to the very edge of the rim, received their full quota of appreciation from me, as did the smooth, flower-decked aisles leading back into the forest.

The location we selected for camp was a large glade, fifty paces or more from the precipice—far enough, the cowboys averred, to keep our traps from being sucked down by some of the whirlpool winds, native to the spot. In the center of this glade stood a huge gnarled and blasted old pine, that certainly by virtue of hoary locks and bent shoulders had earned the right to stand aloof from his younger companions. Under this tree we placed all our belongings, and then, as Frank so felicitously expressed it, we were free to 'ooze round an' see things.'

I believe I had a sort of subconscious, selfish idea that some one would steal the cañon away from me if I did not hurry to make it mine forever; so I sneaked off, and sat under a pine growing on the very rim. At first glance, I saw below me, seemingly miles away, a wild chaos of red and buff mesas rising out of dark purple clefts. Beyond these reared a long, irregular tableland, running south almost to the extent of my vision, which I remembered Clarke had called Powell's Plateau. I remembered, also, that he had said it was twenty miles distant, was almost that many miles long, was connected to the mainland of Buckskin Mountain by a very narrow wooded dip of land called the Saddle, and that it practically shut us out of a view of the Grand Cañon proper. If that was true, what, then, could be the name of the cañon at my feet? Suddenly, as my gaze wandered from point to point, it was arrested by a dark, conical mountain, white-tipped, which rose in the notch of the Saddle. What could it mean? Were there such things as cañon mirages? Then the dim purple of its color told of its great distance from me; and then its familiar shape told I had come into my own again—I had found my old friend once more. For in all that plateau there was only one snow-capped mountain—the San Francisco Peak; and there, a hundred and fifty, perhaps two hundred miles away, far beyond the Grand Cañon, it smiled brightly at me, as it had for days and days across the desert.

Hearing Jones yelling for somebody or everybody, I jumped up to find a procession heading for a point farther down the rim wall, where our leader stood waving his arms. The excitement proved to have been caused by cougar signs at the head of the trail where Clarke had started down.

'They're here, boys, they're here,' Jones kept repeating, as he showed us different tracks. 'This sign is not so old. Boys, to-morrow we'll get up a lion, sure as you're born. And if we do, and Sounder sees him, then we've got a lion-dog! I'm afraid of Don. He has a fine nose; he can run and fight, but he's been trained to deer, and maybe I can't break him. Moze is still uncertain. If old Jude only hadn't been lamed! She would be the best of the lot. But Sounder is our hope. I'm almost ready to swear by him.'

All this was too much for me, so I slipped off again to be alone, and this time headed for the forest. Warm patches of sunlight, like gold, brightened the ground; dark patches of sky, like ocean blue, gleamed between the treetops. Hardly a rustle of wind in the fine-toothed green branches disturbed the quiet. When I got fully out of sight of camp, I started to run as if I were a wild Indian. My running had no aim; just sheer mad joy of the grand old forest, the smell of pine, the wild silence of beauty loosed the spirit in me so it had to run, and I ran with it till the physical being failed.

While resting on a fragrant bed of pine needles, endeavoring to regain control over a truant mind, trying to subdue the encroaching of the natural man on the civilized man, I saw gray objects moving under the trees. I lost them, then saw them, and presently so plainly that, with delight on delight, I counted seventeen deer pass through an open arch of dark green. Rising to my feet, I ran to get round a low mound. They saw me and bounded away with prodigiously long leaps. Bringing their forefeet together, stiff-legged under them, they bounced high, like rubber balls, yet they were graceful.

The forest was so open that I could watch them for a long way; and as I circled with my gaze, a glimpse of something white arrested my attention. A light, grayish animal appeared to be tearing at an old stump. Upon nearer view, I recognized a wolf, and he scented or sighted me at the same moment, and loped off into the shadows of the trees. Approaching the spot where I had marked him I found he had been feeding from the carcass of a horse. The remains had been only partly eaten, and were of an animal of the mustang build that had evidently been recently killed. Frightful lacerations under the throat showed where a lion had taken fatal hold. Deep furrows in the ground proved how the mustang had sunk his hoofs, reared and shaken himself. I traced roughly defined tracks fifty paces to the lee of a little bank, from which I concluded the lion had sprung.

I gave free rein to my imagination and saw the forest dark, silent, peopled by none but its savage denizens. The lion crept like a shadow, crouched noiselessly down, then leaped on his sleeping or browsing prey. The lonely night stillness split to a frantic snort and scream of terror, and the stricken mustang with his mortal enemy upon his back, dashed off with fierce, wild love of life. As he went he felt his foe crawl toward his neck on claws of fire; he saw the tawny body and the gleaming eyes; then the cruel teeth snapped with the sudden bite, and the woodland tragedy ended.

On the spot I conceived an antipathy toward lions. It was born of the frightful spectacle of what had once been a glossy, prancing mustang, of the mute, sickening proof of the survival of the fittest, of the law that levels life.

Upon telling my camp-fellows about my discovery, Jones and Wallace walked out to see it, while Jim told me the wolf I had seen was a 'lofer,' one of the giant buffalo wolves of Buckskin; and if I would watch the carcass in the mornings and evenings, I would 'shore as hell get a plunk at him.'

White pine burned in a beautiful, clear blue flame, with no smoke; and in the center of the campfire left a golden heart. But Jones would not have any sitting up, and hustled us off to bed, saying we would be 'blamed' glad of it in about fifteen hours. I crawled into my sleeping-bag, made a hood of my Navajo blanket, and peeping from under it, watched the fire and the flickering shadows. The blaze burned down rapidly. Then the stars blinked. Arizona stars would be moons in any other State! How serene, peaceful, august, infinite and wonderfully bright! No breeze stirred the pines. The clear tinkle of the cowbells on the hobbled horses rang from near and distant parts of the forest. The prosaic bell of the meadow and the pasture brook, here, in this environment, jingled out different notes, as clear, sweet, musical as silver bells.

12
Old Tom

At daybreak our leader routed us out. The frost mantled the ground so heavily that it looked like snow, and the rare atmosphere bit like the breath of winter. The forest stood solemn and gray; the cañon lay wrapped in vapory slumber.

Hot biscuits and coffee, with a chop or two of the delicious Persian lamb meat, put a less Spartan tinge on the morning, and gave Wallace and me more strength— we needed not incentive—to leave the fire, hustle our saddles on the horses and get in line with our impatient leader. The hounds scampered over the frost, shoving their noses at the tufts of grass and bluebells. Lawson and Jim remained in camp; and the rest of us trooped southwest.

A mile or so in that direction, the forest of pine ended abruptly, and a wide belt of low, scrubby oak trees, breast high to a horse, fringed the rim of the cañon and appeared to broaden out and grow wavy southward. The edge of the forest was as dark and regular as if a band of woodchoppers had trimmed it. We threaded our way through this thicket, all peering into the bisecting deer trails for cougar tracks in the dust.

'Bring the dogs! Hurry!' suddenly called Jones from a thicket.

We lost no time complying, and found him standing in a trail, with his eyes on the sand. 'Take a look, boys. A good-sized male cougar passed here last night. Hyar, Sounder, Don, Moze, come on!'

It was a nervous, excited pack of hounds. Old Jude got to Jones first, and she sang out; then Sounder opened with his ringing bay, and before Jones could mount, a string of yelping dogs sailed straight for the forest.

'Ooze along boys!' yelled Frank, wheeling Spot.

With the cowboy leading, we strung into the pines, and I found myself behind. Presently even Wallace disappeared. I almost threw the reins at Satan, and yelled for him to go. The result enlightened me. Like an arrow from a bow, the black shot forward. Frank had told me of his speed, that when he found his stride it was like riding a flying feather to be on him. Jones, fearing he would kill me, had cautioned me always to hold him in, which I had done. Satan stretched out with long, graceful motions; he did not turn aside for logs, but cleared them with easy and powerful spring, and he swerved only slightly for the trees. This latter, I saw at once, made the danger for me. It became a matter of saving my legs, and dodging branches. The imperative need of this came to me with convincing force. I dodged a branch on one tree, only to be caught square in the middle by a snag on another. Crack! If the snag had not broken, Satan would have gone on riderless, and I would have been left hanging, a pathetic and drooping monition to the risks of the hunt. I kept ducking my head, now and then falling flat over the pommel to avoid a limb that would have brushed me off, and hugging the flanks of my horse with my knees. Soon I was at Wallace's heels, and had Jones in sight. Now and then glimpses of Frank's white horse gleamed through the trees.

We began to circle toward the south, to go up and down shallow hollows, to find the pines thinning out; then we shot out of the forest into the scrubby oak. Riding through this brush was the cruelest kind of work, but Satan kept on close to the sorrel. The hollows began to get deeper, and the ridges between them narrower. No longer could we keep a straight course.

On the crest of one of the ridges we found Jones awaiting us. Jude, Tige and Don lay panting at his feet. Plainly the Colonel appeared vexed.

'Listen,' he said, when we reined in.

We complied, but did not hear a sound.

'Frank's beyond there some place,' continued Jones, 'but I can't see him, nor hear the hounds any more. Don and Tige split again on deer trails. Old Jude hung on the lion track, but I stopped her here. There's something I can't figure. Moze held a beeline southwest, and he yelled seldom. Sounder gradually stopped baying. Maybe Frank can tell us something.'

Jones's long drawn-out signal was answered from the direction he expected, and after a little time, Frank's white horse shone out of the gray-green of a ridge a mile away.

This drew my attention to our position. We were on a high ridge out in the open, and I could see fifty miles of the shaggy slopes of Buckskin. Southward the gray, ragged line seemed to stop suddenly, and beyond it purple haze hung over a void I knew to be the cañon. And facing west, I came, at last, to understand perfectly the meaning of the breaks in the Siwash. They were nothing more than ravines that headed up on the slopes and ran down, getting deeper and steeper, though scarcely wider, to break into the cañon. Knife-crested ridges rolled westward, wave on wave, like the billows of a sea. I appreciated that these breaks were, at their sources, little washes easy to jump across, and at their mouths a mile deep and impassable. Huge pine trees shaded these gullies, to give way to the gray growth of stunted oak, which in turn merged into the dark green of piñon. A wonderful country for deer and lions, it seemed to me, but impassable, all but impossible for a hunter.

Frank soon appeared, brushing through the bending oaks, and Sounder trotted along behind him.

'Where's Moze?' inquired Jones.

'The last I heard of Moze he was out of the brush, goin' across the piñon flat, right for the cañon. He had a hot trail.'

'Well, we're certain of one thing; if it was a deer, he won't come back soon, and if it was a lion, he'll tree it, lose the scent, and come back. We've got to show the hounds a lion in a tree. They'd run a hot trail, bump into a tree, and then be at fault. What was wrong with Sounder?'

'I don't know. He came back to me.'

'We can't trust him, or any of them yet. Still, maybe they're doing better than we know.'

The outcome of the chase, so favorably started was a disappointment, which we all felt keenly. After some discussion, we turned south, intending to ride down to the rim wall and follow it back to camp. I happened to turn once, perhaps to look again at the far-distant pink cliffs of Utah, or the wave-like dome of Trumbull Mountain, when I saw Moze trailing close behind me. My yell halted the Colonel.

'Well, I'll be darned!' ejaculated he, as Moze hove in sight. 'Come hyar, you rascal!'

He was a tired dog, but had no sheepish air about him, such as he had worn when lagging in from deer chases. He wagged his tail, and flopped down to pant and pant, as if to say: 'What's wrong with you guys?'

'Boys, for two cents I'd go back and put Jude on that trail. It's just possible that Moze treed a lion. But—well, I expect there's more likelihood of his chasing the lion over the rim; so we may as well keep on. The strange thing is that Sounder wasn't with Moze. There may have been two lions. You see we are up a tree ourselves. I have known lions to run in pairs, and also a mother keep four two-year-olds with her. But such cases are rare. Here, in this country, though, maybe they run round and have parties.'

As we left the breaks behind we got out upon a level piñon flat. A few cedars grew with the piñons. Deer runways and trails were thick.

'Boys, look at that,' said Jones. 'This is great lion country, the best I ever saw.'

He pointed to the sunken, red, shapeless remains of two horses, and near them a ghastly scattering of bleached bones. 'A lion-lair right here on the flat. Those two horses were killed early this spring, and I see no signs of their carcasses having been covered with brush and dirt. I've got to learn lion lore over again, that's certain.'

As we paused at the head of a depression, which appeared to be a gap in the rim wall, filled with massed piñons and splintered piles of yellow stone, I caught Sounder going through some interesting moves. He stopped to smell a bush. Then he lifted his head, and electrified me with a great, deep-sounding bay.

'Hi! there, listen to that!' yelled Jones. 'What's Sounder got? Give him room— don't run him down. Easy now, old dog, easy, easy!'

Sounder suddenly broke down a trail. Moze howled, Don barked, and Tige let out his staccato yelp. They ran through the brush here, there, everywhere. Then all at once old Jude chimed in with her mellow voice, and Jones tumbled off his horse.

'By the Lord Harry! There's something there.'

'Here, Colonel, here's the bush Sounder smelt, and there's a sandy trail under it,' I called.

'There go Don an' Tige down into the break,' cried Frank. 'They've got a hot scent!'

Jones stooped over the place I designated, to jerk up with reddening face, and as he flung himself into the saddle roared out: 'After Sounder! Old Tom! Old Tom! Old Tom!'

We all heard Sounder, and at the moment of Jones's discovery, Moze got the scent and plunged ahead of us.

'Hi! Hi! Hi! Hi!' yelled the Colonel. Frank sent Spot forward like a white streak. Sounder called to us in irresistible bays, which Moze answered, and then crippled Jude bayed in baffled, impotent distress.

The atmosphere was charged with that lion. As if by magic, the excitation communicated itself to all, and men, horses and dogs acted in accord. The ride through the forest had been a jaunt. This was a steeplechase, a mad, heedless, perilous, glorious race. And we had for a pacemaker a cowboy mounted on a tireless mustang.

Always it seemed to me, while the wind rushed, the brush whipped, I saw Frank far ahead, sitting his saddle as if glued there, holding his reins loosely forward. To see him ride so was a beautiful sight. Jones let out his Comanche yell at every dozen jumps, and Wallace sent back a thrilling 'Waa-hoo-o!' In the excitement I had again checked my horse, and when I remembered, and loosed the bridle, how the noble animal responded! The pace he settled into dazed me; I could hardly distinguish the deer trail down which he was thundering. I lost my comrades ahead; the piñon blurred in my sight; I only faintly heard the hounds. It occurred to me we were making for the breaks, but I did not think of checking Satan. I thought only of flying on faster and faster.

'On! On! old fellow! Stretch out! Never lose this race! We've got to be there at the finish!' I called to Satan, and he seemed to understand and stretched lower, farther, quicker.

The brush pounded my legs and clutched and tore my clothes; the wind whistled; the piñon branches cut and whipped my face. Once I dodged to the left, as Satan swerved to the right, with the result that I flew out of the saddle, and crashed into a piñon tree, which marvelously brushed me back into the saddle. The wild yells and deep bays sounded nearer. Satan tripped and plunged down, throwing me as gracefully as an aërial tumbler wings his flight. I alighted in a bush, without feeling of scratch or pain. As Satan recovered and ran past, I did not seek to make him stop, but getting a good grip on the pommel, I vaulted up again. Once more he raced like a wild mustang. And from nearer and nearer in front pealed the alluring sounds of the chase.

Satan was creeping close to Wallace and Jones, with Frank looming white through the occasional piñons. Then all dropped out of sight, to appear again suddenly. They had reached the first break. Soon I was upon it. Two deer ran out of the ravine, almost brushing my horse in the haste. Satan went down and up in a few giant strides. Only the narrow ridge separated us from another break. It was up and down then for Satan, a work to which he manfully set himself. Occasionally I saw Wallace and Jones, but heard them oftener. All the time the breaks grew deeper, till finally Satan had to zigzag his way down and up. Discouragement fastened on me, when from the summit of the next ridge I saw Frank far down the break, with Jones and Wallace not a quarter of a mile away from him. I sent out a long, exultant yell as Satan crushed into the hard, dry wash in the bottom of the break.

I knew from the way he quickened under me that he intended to overhaul somebody. Perhaps because of the clear going, or because my frenzy had cooled to a thrilling excitement which permitted detail, I saw clearly and distinctly the speeding horsemen down the ravine. I picked out the smooth pieces of ground ahead, and with the slightest touch of the rein on his neck, guided Satan into them. How he ran! The light, quick beats of his hoofs were regular, pounding. Seeing Jones and Wallace sail high into the air, I knew they had jumped a ditch. Thus prepared, I managed to stick on when it yawned before me; and Satan, never slackening, leaped up and up, giving me a new swing.

Dust began to settle in little clouds before me; Frank, far ahead, had turned his mustang up the side of the break; Wallace, within hailing distance, now turned to wave me a hand. The rushing wind fairly sang in my ears; the walls of the break were confused blurs of yellow and green; at every stride Satan seemed to swallow a rod of the white trail.

Jones began to scale the ravine, heading up obliquely far on the side of where Frank had vanished, and as Wallace followed suit, I turned Satan. I caught Wallace at the summit, and we raced together out upon another flat of piñon. We heard Frank and Jones yelling in a way that caused us to spur our horses frantically. Spot, gleaming white near a clump of green piñons, was our guiding star. That last quarter of a mile was a ringing run, a ride to remember.

As our mounts crashed back with stiff forelegs and haunches, Wallace and I leaped off and darted into the clump of piñons, whence issued a hair-raising medley of yells and barks. I saw Jones, then Frank, both waving their arms, then Moze and Sounder running wildly, aimlessly about.

'Look there!' rang in my ear, and Jones smashed me on the back with a blow, which at any ordinary time would have laid me flat.

In a low, stubby piñon tree, scarce twenty feet from us, was a tawny form. An enormous mountain-lion, as large as an African lioness, stood planted with huge, round legs on two branches; and he faced us gloomily, neither frightened nor fierce. He watched the running dogs with pale, yellow eyes, waved his massive head and switched his long, black-tufted tail.

'It's Old Tom! sure as you're born! It's Old Tom!' yelled Jones. 'There's no two lions like that in one country. Hold still now. Jude is here, and she'll see him—she'll show him to the other hounds. Hold still!'

We heard Jude coming at a fast pace for a lame dog, and we saw her presently, running with her nose down for a moment, then up. She entered the clump of trees, and bumped her nose against the piñon Old Tom was in, and looked up like a dog that knew her business. The series of wild howls she broke into quickly brought Sounder and Moze to her side. They, too, saw the big lion, not fifteen feet over their heads.

We were all yelling and trying to talk at once, in some such state as the dogs.

'Hyar, Moze! Come down out of that!' hoarsely shouted Jones.

Moze had begun to climb the thick, many-branched, low piñon tree. He paid not the slightest attention to Jones, who screamed and raged at him.

'Cover the lion!' cried he to me. 'Don't shoot unless he crouches to jump on me.'

The little beaded front-sight wavered slightly as I held my rifle leveled at the grim, snarling face, and out of the corner of my eye, as it were, I saw Jones dash in under the lion and grasp Moze by the hind leg and haul him down. He broke from Jones and leaped again to the first low branch. His master then grasped his collar and carried him to where we stood and held him choking.

'Boys, we can't keep Tom up there. When he jumps, keep out of his way. Maybe we can chase him up a better tree.'

Old Tom suddenly left the branches, swinging violently; and hitting the ground like a huge cat on springs, he bounded off, tail up, in a most ludicrous manner. His running, however, did not lack speed, for he quickly outdistanced the bursting hounds.

A stampede for horses succeeded this move. I had difficulty in closing my camera, which I had forgotten until the last moment, and got behind the others. Satan sent the dust flying and the piñon branches crashing. Hardly had I time to bewail my ill-luck in being left, when I dashed out of a thick growth of trees to come upon my companions, all dismounted on the rim of the Grand Cañon.

'He's gone down! He's gone down!' raged Jones, stamping the ground. 'What luck! What miserable luck! But don't quit; spread along the rim, boys, and look for him. Cougars can't fly. There's a break in the rim somewhere.'

The rock wall, on which we dizzily stood, dropped straight down for a thousand feet, to meet a long, piñon-covered slope, which graded a mile to cut off into what must have been the second wall. We were far west of Clarke's trail now, and faced a point above where Kanab Cañon, a red gorge a mile deep, met the great cañon. As I ran along the rim, looking for a fissure or break, my gaze seemed impellingly drawn by the immensity of this thing I could not name, and for which I had as yet no intelligible emotion.

Two 'Waa-hoos' in the rear turned me back in double-quick time, and hastening by the horses, I found the three men grouped at the head of a narrow break.

'He went down here. Wallace saw him round the base of that tottering crag.'

The break was wedged-shaped, with the sharp end toward the rim, and it descended so rapidly as to appear almost perpendicular. It was a long, steep slide of small, weathered shale, and a place that no man in his right senses would ever have considered going down. But Jones, designating Frank and me, said in his cool, quick voice:

'You fellows go down. Take Jude and Sounder in leash. If you find his trail below along the wall, yell for us. Meanwhile, Wallace and I will hang over the rim and watch for him.'

Going down, in one sense, was much easier than had appeared, for the reason that once started we moved on sliding beds of weathered stone. Each of us now had an avalanche for a steed. Frank forged ahead with a roar, and then seeing danger below, tried to get out of the mass. But the stones were like quicksand; every step he took sank him in deeper. He grasped the smooth cliff, to find holding impossible. The slide poured over a fall like so much water. He reached and caught a branch of a piñon, and lifting his feet up, hung on till the treacherous area of moving stones had passed.

While I had been absorbed in his predicament, my avalanche augmented itself by slide on slide, perhaps loosened by his; and before I knew it, I was sailing down with ever-increasing momentum. The sensation was distinctly pleasant, and a certain spirit, before restrained in me, at last ran riot. The slide narrowed at the drop where Frank had jumped, and the stones poured over in a stream. I jumped also, but having a rifle in one hand, failed to hold, and plunged down into the slide again. My feet were held this time, as in a vise. I kept myself upright and waited. Fortunately, the jumble of loose stone slowed and stopped, enabling me to crawl over to one side where there was comparatively good footing. Below us, for fifty yards, was a sheet of rough stone, as bare as washed granite well could be. We slid down this in regular schoolboy fashion, and had reached another restricted neck in the fissure, when a sliding crash above warned us that the avalanches had decided to move of their own free will. Only a fraction of a moment had we to find footing along the yellow cliff, when, with a cracking roar, the mass struck the slippery granite. If we had been on that slope, our lives would not have been worth a grain of the dust flying in clouds above us. Huge stones, that had formed the bottom of the slides, shot ahead, and rolling, leaping, whizzed by us with frightful velocity, and the remainder groaned and growled its way down, to thunder over the second fall and die out in a distant rumble.

The hounds had hung back, and were not easily coaxed down to us. From there on, down to the base of the gigantic cliff, we descended with little difficulty.

'We might meet the old gray cat anywheres along here,' said Frank.

The wall of yellow limestone had shelves, ledges, fissures and cracks, any one of which might have concealed a lion. On these places I turned dark, uneasy glances. It seemed to me events succeeded one another so rapidly that I had no time to think, to examine, to prepare. We were rushed from one sensation to another.

'Gee! look here,' said Frank; 'here's his tracks. Did you ever see the like of that?'

Certainly I had never fixed my eyes on such enormous cat-tracks as appeared in the yellow dust at the base of the rim wall. The mere sight of them was sufficient to make a man tremble.

'Hold in the dogs, Frank,' I called. 'Listen. I think I heard a yell.'

From far above came a yell, which, though thinned out by distance, was easily recognized as Jones's. We returned to the opening of the break, and throwing our heads back, looked up the slide to see him coming down.

'Wait for me! Wait for me! I saw the lion go in a cave. Wait for me!'

With the same roar and crack and slide of rocks as had attended our descent, Jones bore down on us. For an old man it was a marvelous performance. He walked on the avalanches as though he wore seven-league boots, and presently, as we began to dodge whizzing bowlders, he stepped down to us, whirling his coiled lasso. His jaw bulged out; a flash made fire in his cold eyes.

'Boys, we've got Old Tom in a corner. I worked along the rim north and looked over every place I could. Now, maybe you won't believe it, but I heard him pant. Yes, sir, he panted like the tired lion he is. Well, presently I saw him lying along the base of the rim wall. His tongue was hanging out. You see, he's a heavy lion, and not used to running long distances. Come on, now. It's not far. Hold in the dogs. You there with the rifle, lead off, and keep your eyes peeled.'

Single file, we passed along in the shadow of the great cliff. A wide trail had been worn in the dust.

'A lion run-way,' said Jones. 'Don't you smell the cat?'

Indeed, the strong odor of cat was very pronounced; and that, without the big fresh tracks, made the skin on my face tighten and chill. As we turned a jutting point in the wall, a number of animals, which I did not recognize, plunged helter-skelter down the cañon slope.

'Rocky Mountain sheep!' exclaimed Jones. 'Look! Well, this is a discovery. I never heard of a bighorn in the cañon.'

It was indicative of the strong grip Old Tom had on us that we at once forgot the remarkable fact of coming upon those rare sheep in such a place.

Jones halted us presently before a deep curve described by the rim wall, the extreme end of which terminated across the slope in an impassable projecting corner.

'See across there, boys. See that black hole. Old Tom's in there.'

'What's your plan?' queried the cowboy sharply.

'Wait. We'll slip up to get better lay of the land.'

We worked our way noiselessly along the rim-wall curve for several hundred yards and came to a halt again, this time with a splendid command of the situation. The trail ended abruptly at the dark cave, so menacingly staring at us, and the corner of the cliff had curled back upon itself. It was a box-trap, with a drop at the end, too great for any beast, a narrow slide of weathered stone running down, and the rim wall trail. Old Tom would plainly be compelled to choose one of these directions if he left his cave.

'Frank, you and I will keep to the wall and stop near that scrub piñon, this side of the hole. If I rope him, I can use that tree.'

Then he turned to me:

'Are you to be depended on here?'

'I? What do you want me to do?' I demanded, and my whole breast seemed to sink in.

'You cut across the head of this slope and take up your position in the slide below the cave, say just by that big stone. From there you can command the cave, our position and your own. Now, if it is necessary to kill this lion to save me or Frank, or, of course, yourself, can you be depended upon to kill him?'

I felt a queer sensation around my heart and a strange tightening of the skin upon my face! What a position for me to be placed in! For one instant I shook like a quivering aspen leaf. Then because of the pride of a man, or perhaps inherited instincts cropping out at this perilous moment, I looked up and answered quietly:

'Yes. I will kill him!'

'Old Tom is cornered, and he'll come out. He can run only two ways: along this trail, or down that slide. I'll take my stand by the scrub piñon there so I can get a hitch if I rope him. Frank, when I give the word, let the dogs go. Grey, you block the slide. If he makes at us, even if I do get my rope on him, kill him! Most likely he'll jump down hill—then you'll *have* to kill him! Be quick. Now loose the hounds. Hi! Hi! Hi! Hi!'

I jumped into the narrow slide of weathered stone and looked up. Jones's stentorian yell rose high above the clamor of the hounds. He whirled his lasso.

A huge yellow form shot over the trail and hit the top of the slide with a crash. The lasso streaked out with arrowy swiftness, circled, and snapped viciously close to Old Tom's head. 'Kill him! Kill him!' roared Jones. Then the lion leaped, seemingly into the air above me. Instinctively I raised my little automatic rifle. I seemed to hear a million bellowing reports. The tawny body, with its grim, snarling face, blurred in my sight. I heard a roar of sliding stones at my feet. I felt a rush of wind. I caught a confused glimpse of a whirling wheel of fur, rolling down the slide.

Then Jones and Frank were pounding me, and yelling I know not what. From far above came floating down a long 'Waa-hoo!' I saw Wallace silhouetted against the blue sky. I felt the hot barrel of my rifle, and shuddered at the bloody stones below me—then, and then only, did I realize, with weakening legs, that Old Tom had jumped at me, and had jumped to his death.

13
Singing Cliffs

Old Tom had rolled two hundred yards down the cañon, leaving a red trail and bits of fur behind him. When I had clambered down to the steep slide where he had lodged, Sounder and Jude had just decided he was no longer worth biting, and were wagging their tails. Frank was shaking his head, and Jones, standing above the lion, lasso in hand, wore a disconsolate face.

'How I wish I had got the rope on him!'

'I reckon we'd be gatherin' up the pieces of you if you had,' said Frank, dryly.

We skinned the old king on the rocky slope of his mighty throne, and then, beginning to feel the effects of severe exertion, we cut across the slope for the foot of the break. Once there, we gazed up in dismay. That break resembled a walk of life—how easy to slip down, how hard to climb! Even Frank, inured as he was to strenuous toil, began to swear and wipe his sweaty brow before we had made one-tenth of the ascent. It was particularly exasperating, not to mention the danger of it, to work a few feet up a slide, and then feel it start to move. We had to climb in single file, which jeopardized the safety of those behind the leader. Sometimes we were all sliding at once, like boys on a pond, with the difference that we were in danger. Frank forged ahead, turning to yell now and then for us to dodge a cracking stone. Faithful old Jude could not get up in some places, so laying aside my rifle, I carried her, and returned for the weapon. It became necessary, presently, to hide behind cliff projections to escape the avalanches started by Frank, and to wait till he had surmounted the break. Jones gave out completely several times, saying the exertion affected his heart. What with my rifle, my camera and Jude, I could offer him no assistance, and was really in need of that myself. When it seemed as if one more step would kill us, we reached the rim, and fell panting with labored chests and dripping skins. We could not speak. Jones had worn a pair of ordinary shoes without thick soles and nails, and it seemed well to speak of them in the past tense. They were split into ribbons and hung on by the laces. His feet were cut and bruised.

On the way back to camp, we encountered Moze and Don coming out of the break where we had started Sounder on the trail. The paws of both hounds were

yellow with dust, which proved they had been down under the rim wall. Jones
doubted not in the least that they had chased a lion.

Upon examination, this break proved to be one of the two which Clarke used
for trails to his wild horse corral in the cañon. According to him, the distance
separating them was five miles by the rim wall, and less than half that in a straight
line. Therefore, we made for the point of the forest where it ended abruptly in
the scrub oak. We got into camp, a fatigued lot of men, horses and dogs. Jones
appeared particularly happy, and his first move, after dismounting, was to stretch
out the lion skin and measure it.

'Ten feet, three inches and a half!' he sang out.

'Shore it do beat hell!' exclaimed Jim in tones nearer to excitement than any I
had ever heard him use.

'Old Tom beats, by two inches, any cougar I ever saw,' continued Jones. 'He
must have weighed more than three hundred. We'll set about curing the hide. Jim,
stretch it well on a tree, and we'll take a hand in peeling of the fat.'

All of the party worked on the cougar skin that afternoon. The gristle at the
base of the neck, where it met the shoulders, was so tough and thick we could not
scrape it thin. Jones said this particular spot was so well protected because in
fighting, cougars were most likely to bite and claw there. For that matter, the whole
skin was tough, tougher than leather; and when it dried, it pulled all the horseshoe
nails out of the pine tree upon which we had it stretched.

About time for the sun to set, I strolled along the rim wall to look into the
cañon. I was beginning to feel something of its character and had growing
impressions. Dark purple smoke veiled the clefts deep down between the mesas.
I walked along to where points of cliff ran out like capes and peninsulas, all
seamed, cracked, wrinkled, scarred and yellow with age, with shattered, topping
ruins of rocks ready at a touch to go thundering down. I could not resist the
temptation to crawl out to the farthest point, even though I shuddered over the
yard-wide ridges; and when once seated on a bare promontory, two hundred feet
from the regular rim wall, I felt isolated, marooned.

The sun, a liquid red globe, had just touched its under side to the pink cliffs of
Utah, and fired a crimson flood of light over the wonderful mountains, plateaus,
escarpments, mesas, domes and turrets of the gorge. The rim wall of Powell's
Plateau was a thin streak of fire; the timber above like grass of gold; and the long
slopes below shaded from bright to dark. Point Sublime, bold and bare, ran out
toward the plateau, jealously reaching for the sun. Bass's Tomb peeped over the
Saddle. The Temple of Vishnu lay bathed in vapory shading clouds, and the
Shinumo Altar shone with rays of glory.

The beginning of the wondrous transformation, the dropping of the day's
curtain, was for me a rare and perfect moment. As the golden splendor of sunset

sought out a peak or mesa or escarpment, I gave it a name to suit my fancy; and as flushing, fading, its glory changed, sometimes I rechristened it. Jupiter's Chariot, brazen wheeled, stood ready to roll into the clouds. Semiramis's Bed, all gold, shone from a tower of Babylon. Castor and Pollux clasped hands over a Stygian river. The Spur of Doom, a mountain shaft as red as hell, and inaccessible, insurmountable, lured with strange light. Dusk, a bold, black dome, was shrouded by the shadow of a giant mesa. The Star of Bethlehem glittered from the brow of Point Sublime. The Wraith, fleecy, feathered curtain of mist, floated down among the ruins of castles and palaces, like the ghost of a goddess. Vales of Twilight, dim, dark ravines, mystic homes of specters, led into the awful Valley of the Shadow, clothed in purple night.

Suddenly, as the first puff of the night wind fanned my cheek, a strange, sweet, low moaning and sighing came to my ears. I almost thought I was in a dream. But the cañon, now blood-red, was there in overwhelming reality, a profound, solemn, gloomy thing, but real. The wind blew stronger, and then I was listening to a sad, sweet song, which lulled as the wind lulled. I realized at once that the sound was caused by the wind blowing into the peculiar formations of the cliffs. It changed, softened, shaded, mellowed, but it was always sad. It rose from low, tremulous, sweetly quavering sighs, to a sound like the last woeful, despairing wail of a woman. It was the song of the sea sirens and the music of the waves; it had the soft sough of the night wind in the trees, and the haunting moan of lost spirits.

With reluctance I turned my back to the gorgeously changing spectacle of the cañon and crawled in to the rim wall. At the narrow neck of stone I peered over to look down into misty blue nothingness.

That night Jones told stories of frightened hunters, and assuaged my mortification by saying 'buck-fever' was pardonable after the danger had passed, and especially so in my case, because of the great size and fame of Old Tom.

'The worst case of buck-fever I ever saw was on a buffalo hunt I had with a fellow named Williams,' went on Jones. 'I was one of the scouts leading a wagon-train west on the old Santa Fé trail. This fellow said he was a big hunter, and wanted to kill a buffalo, so I took him out. I saw a herd making over the prairie for a hollow where a brook ran, and by hard work, got in ahead of them. I picked out a position just below the edge of the bank, and we lay quiet, waiting. From the direction of the buffalo, I calculated we'd be just about right to get a shot at no very long range. As it was, I suddenly heard thumps on the ground, and cautiously raising my head, saw a huge buffalo just over us, not fifteen feet up the bank. I whispered to Williams:"For God's sake", don't shoot, don't move!' The bull's little fiery eyes snapped, and he reared. I thought we were goners, for when a bull comes down on anything with his forefeet, it's done for. But he slowly settled back, perhaps doubtful. Then, as another buffalo came to the edge of the bank, luckily a little way from us, the bull turned broadside, presenting a splendid target. Then I whispered to Williams: "Now's your chance. Shoot!" I waited for the shot, but none came. Looking at Williams, I saw he was white and trembling. Big drops of sweat stood out on his brow; his teeth chattered, and his hands shook. He had forgotten he carried a rifle.'

'That reminds me,' said Frank. 'They tell a story over at Kanab on a Dutchman named Schmitt. He was very fond of huntin', an' I guess had pretty good success after deer an' small game. One winter he was out in the Pink Cliffs with a Mormon named Shoonover, an' they run into a lammin' big grizzly track, fresh an' wet. They trailed him to a clump of chaparral, an' on goin' clear round it, found no tracks leadin' out. Shoonover said Schmitt commenced to sweat. They went back to the place where the trail led in, an' there they were, great big silver-tip tracks, bigger'n hoss-tracks, so fresh thet water was oozin' out of 'em. Schmitt said: "Zake, you go in und ged him. I hef took sick righdt now." '

Happy as we were over the chase of Old Tom, and our prospects—for Sounder, Jude and Moze had seen a lion in a tree—we sought our blankets early. I lay watching the bright stars, and listening to the roar of the wind in the pines. At intervals it lulled to a whisper, and then swelled to a roar, and then died away. Far off in the forest a coyote barked once. Time and time again, as I was gradually sinking into slumber, the sudden roar of the wind startled me. I imagined it was the crash of rolling, weathered stone, and I saw again that huge outspread flying lion above me.

I awoke sometime later to find Moze had sought the warmth of my side, and he lay so near my arm that I reached out and covered him with an end of the blanket I used to break the wind. It was very cold and the time must have been very late, for the wind had died down, and I heard not a tinkle from the hobbled horses. The absence of the cowbell music gave me a sense of loneliness, for without it the silence of the great forest was a thing to be felt.

This oppressiveness, however, was broken by a far-distant cry, unlike any sound I had ever heard. Not sure of myself, I freed my ears from the blanketed hood and listened. It came again, a wild cry, that made me think first of a lost child, and then of the mourning wolf of the north. It must have been a long distance off in the forest. An interval of some moments passed, then it pealed out again, nearer this time, and so human that it startled me. Moze raised his head and growled low in his throat and sniffed the keen air.

'Jones, Jones,' I called, reaching over to touch the old hunter.

He awoke at once, with the clear-headedness of the light sleeper.

'I heard the cry of some beast,' I said, 'and it was so weird, so strange. I want to know what it was.'

Such a long silence ensued that I began to despair of hearing the cry again, when, with a suddenness which straightened the hair on my head, a wailing shriek, exactly like a despairing woman might give in death agony, split the night silence. It seemed right on us.

'Cougar! Cougar! Cougar!' exclaimed Jones.

'What's up?' queried Frank, awakened by the dogs.

Their howling roused the rest of the party, and no doubt scared the cougar, for his womanish scream was not repeated. Then Jones got up and gathered his blankets in a roll.

'Where you oozin' for now?' asked Frank sleepily.

'I think that cougar just came up over the rim on a scouting hunt, and I'm going to go down to the head of the trail and stay there till morning. If he returns that way, I'll put him up a tree.'

With this, he unchained Sounder and Don, and stalked off under the trees, looking like an Indian. Once the deep bay of Sounder rang out; Jones's sharp command followed, and then the familiar silence encompassed the forest and was broken no more.

When I awoke all was gray, except toward the cañon, where the little bit of sky I saw through the pines glowed a delicate pink. I crawled out on the instant, got into my boots and coat, and kicked up the smoldering fire. Jim heard me, and said:

'Shore you're up early.'

'I'm going to see the sunrise from the north rim of the Grand Cañon,' I said, and knew when I spoke that very few men, out of all the millions of travelers, had ever seen this, probably the most surpassingly beautiful pageant in the world. At most, only a few geologists, scientists, perhaps an artist or two, and horse wranglers, hunters and prospectors have ever reached the rim on the north side; and these men, crossing from Bright Angel or Mystic Spring trails on the south rim, seldom or never get beyond Powell's Plateau.

The frost cracked under my boots like frail ice, and the bluebells peeped wanly from the white. When I reached the head of Clarke's trail it was just daylight; and there, under a pine, I found Jones rolled in his blankets, with Sounder and Moze asleep beside him. I turned without disturbing him, and went along the edge of the forest, but back a little distance from the rim wall.

I saw deer off in the woods, and tarrying, watched them throw up graceful heads, and look and listen. The soft pink glow through the pines deepened to rose, and suddenly I caught a point of red fire. Then I hurried to the place I had named Singing Cliffs, and keeping my eyes fast on the stone beneath me, crawled out to the very farthest point, drew a long, deep breath, and looked eastward.

The awfulness of sudden death and the glory of heaven stunned me! The thing that had been mystery at twilight, lay clear, pure, open in the rosy hue of dawn.

Out of the gates of the morning poured a light which glorified the palaces and pyramids, purged and purified the afternoon's inscrutable clefts, swept away the shadows of the mesas, and bathed that broad, deep world of mighty mountains, stately spars of rock, sculptured cathedrals and alabaster terraces in an artist's dream of color. A pearl from heaven had burst, flinging its heart of fire into this chasm. A stream of opal flowed out of the sun, to touch each peak, mesa, dome, parapet, temple and tower, cliff and cleft into the new-born life of another day.

I sat there for a long time and knew that every second the scene changed, yet I could not tell how. I knew I sat high over a hole of broken, splintered, barren mountains; I knew I could see a hundred miles of the length of it, and eighteen miles of the width of it, and a mile of the depth of it, and the shafts and rays of rose light on a million glancing, many-hued surfaces at once; but that knowledge was no help to me. I repeated a lot of meaningless superlatives to myself, and I found words inadequate and superfluous. The spectacle was too elusive and too great. It was life and death, heaven and hell.

I tried to call up former favorite views of mountain and sea, so as to compare them with this; but the memory pictures refused to come, even with my eyes closed. Then I returned to camp, with unsettled, troubled mind, and was silent, wondering at the strange feeling burning within me.

Jones talked about our visitor of the night before, and said the trail near where he had slept showed only one cougar track, and that led down into the cañon. It had surely been made, he thought, by the beast we had heard. Jones signified his intention of chaining several of the hounds for the next few nights at the head of this trail; so if the cougar came up, they would scent him and let us know. From which it was evident that to chase a lion bound into the cañon and one bound out were two different things.

The day passed lazily, with all of us resting on the warm, fragrant pine-needle beds, or mending a rent in a coat, or working on some camp task impossible of commission on exciting days.

About four o'clock, I took my little rifle and walked off through the woods in the direction of the carcass where I had seen the gray wolf. Thinking it best to make a wide detour, so as to face the wind, I circled till I felt the breeze was favorable to my enterprise, and then cautiously approached the hollow where the dead horse lay. Indian fashion, I slipped from tree to tree, a mode of forest travel not without its fascination and effectiveness, till I reached the height of a knoll beyond which I made sure was my objective point. On peeping out from behind the last pine, I found I had calculated pretty well, for there was the hollow, the big windfall, with its round, starfish-shaped roots exposed to the bright sun, and near that, the carcass. Sure enough, pulling hard at it, was the gray-white wolf I recognized as my 'lofer.'

But he presented an exceedingly difficult shot. Backing down the ridge, I ran a little way to come up behind another tree, from which I soon shifted to a fallen pine. Over this I peeped, to get a splendid view of the wolf. He had stopped tugging at the horse, and stood with his nose in the air. Surely he could not have scented me, for the wind was strong from him to me; neither could he have heard my soft footfalls on the pine needles; nevertheless, he was suspicious. Loth to spoil the picture he made, I risked a chance, and waited. Besides, though I prided myself on being able to take a fair aim, I had no great hope that I could hit him at such a distance. Presently he returned to his feeding, but not for long. Soon he raised his long, fine-pointed head, and trotted away a few yards, stopped to sniff again, then went back to his grewsome work.

At this juncture, I noiselessly projected my rifle barrel over the log. I had not, however, gotten the sights in line with him, when he trotted away reluctantly, and ascended the knoll on his side of the hollow. I lost him, and had just begun sourly to call myself a mollycoddle hunter, when he reappeared. He halted in an open glade, on the very crest of the knoll, and stood still as a statue wolf, a white, inspiriting target, against a dark green background. I could not stifle a rush of feeling, for I was a lover of the beautiful first, and a hunter secondly; but I steadied down as the front sight moved into the notch through which I saw the black and white of his shoulder.

Spang! How the little Remington sang! I watched closely, ready to send five more missiles after the gray beast. He jumped spasmodically, in a half-curve, high in the air, with loosely hanging head, then dropped in a heap. I yelled like a boy, ran down the hill, up the other side of the hollow, to find him stretched out dead, a small hole in his shoulder where the bullet had entered, a great one where it had come out.

The job I made of skinning him lacked some hundred degrees the perfection of my shot, but I accomplished it, and returned to camp in triumph.

'Shore I knowed you'd plunk him,' said Jim very much pleased. 'I shot one the other day same way, when he was feedin' off a dead horse. Now thet's a fine skin. Shore you cut through once or twice. But he's only half lofer, the other half is plain coyote. Thet accounts fer his feedin' on dead meat.'

My naturalist host and my scientific friend both remarked somewhat grumpily that I seemed to get the best of all the good things. I might have retaliated that I certainly had gotten the worst of all the bad jokes; but, being generously happy over my prize, merely remarked: 'If you want fame or wealth or wolves, go out and hunt for them.'

Five o'clock supper left a good margin of day, in which my thoughts reverted to the cañon. I watched the purple shadows stealing out of their caverns and rolling up about the base of the mesas. Jones came over to where I stood, and I persuaded him to walk with me along the rim wall. Twilight had stealthily advanced when we reached the Singing Cliffs, and we did not go out upon my promontory, but chose a more comfortable one nearer the wall.

The night breeze had not sprung up yet, so the music of the cliffs was hushed.

'You cannot accept the theory of erosion to account for this chasm?' I asked my companion, referring to a former conversation.

'I can for this part of it. But what stumps me is the mountain range three thousand feet high, crossing the desert and the cañon just above where we crossed the river. How did the river cut through that without the help of a split or earthquake?'

'I'll admit that is a poser to me as well as to you. But I suppose Wallace could explain it as erosion. He claims this whole western country was once under water, except the tips of the Sierra Nevada mountains. There came an uplift of the earth's crust, and the great inland sea began to run out, presumably by way of the Colorado. In so doing it cut out the upper cañon, this gorge eighteen miles wide. Then came a second uplift, giving the river a much greater impetus toward the sea, which cut out the second, or marble cañon. Now as to the mountain range crossing the cañon at right angles. It must have come with the second uplift. If so, did it dam the river back into another inland sea, and then wear down into that red perpendicular gorge we remember so well? Or was there a great break in the fold of granite, which let the river continue on its way? Or was there, at that particular point, a softer stone, like this limestone here, which erodes easily?'

'You must ask somebody wiser than I.'

'Well, let's not perplex our minds with its origin. It is, and that's enough for any mind. Ah! listen! Now you will hear my Singing Cliffs.'

From out of the darkening shadows murmurs rose on the softly rising wind. This strange music had a depressing influence; but it did not fill the heart with sorrow, only touched it lightly. And when, with the dying breeze, the song died away, it left the lonely crags lonelier for its death.

The last rosy gleam faded from the tip of Point Sublime; and as if that were a signal, in all clefts and cañons below, purple, shadowy clouds marshaled their forces and began to sweep upon the battlements, to swing colossal wings into amphitheaters where gods might have warred, slowly to enclose the magical sentinels. Night intervened, and a moving, changing, silent chaos pulsated under the bright stars.

'How infinite all this is! How impossible to understand!' I exclaimed.

'To me it is very simple,' replied my comrade. 'The world is strange. But this cañon—why, we can see it all! I can't make out why people fuss so over it. I only feel peace. It's only bold and beautiful, serene and silent.'

With the words of this quiet old plainsman, my sentimental passion shrank to the true appreciation of the scene. Self passed out to the recurring, soft strains of cliff song. I had been reveling in a species of indulgence, imagining I was a great lover of nature, building poetical illusions over storm-beaten peaks. The truth, told by one who had lived fifty years in the solitudes, among the rugged mountains, under the dark trees, and by the sides of the lonely streams, was the simple interpretation of a spirit in harmony with the bold, the beautiful, the serene, the silent.

He meant the Grand Cañon was only a mood of nature, a bold promise, a beautiful record. He meant that mountains had sifted away in its dust, yet the cañon was young. Man was nothing, so let him be humble. This cataclysm of the earth, this playground of a river was not inscrutable; it was only inevitable—as inevitable as nature herself. Millions of years in the bygone ages it had lain serene under a live moon; it would bask silent under a rayless sun, in the onward edge of time.

It taught simplicity, serenity, peace. The eye that saw only the strife, the war, the decay, the ruin, or only the glory and the tragedy, saw not all the truth. It spoke simply, though its words were grand: 'My spirit is the Spirit of Time, of Eternity, of God. Man is little, vain, vaunting. Listen. To-morrow he shall be gone. Peace! Peace!'

14
All Heroes But One

As we rode up the slope of Buckskin, the sunrise glinted red-gold through the aisles of frosted pines, giving us a hunter's glad greeting.

With all due respect to, and appreciation of, the breaks of the Siwash, we unanimously decided that if cougars inhabited any other section of cañon country, we preferred it, and were going to find it. We had often speculated on the appearance of the rim wall directly across the neck of the cañon upon which we were located. It showed a long stretch of breaks, fissures, caves, yellow crags, crumbled ruins and clefts green with piñon pine. As a crow flies, it was only a mile or two straight across from camp, but to reach it, we had to ascend the mountain and head the cañon which deeply indented the slope.

A thousand feet or more above the level bench, the character of the forest changed; the pines grew thicker, and interspersed among them were silver spruces and balsams. Here in the clumps of small trees and underbrush, we began to jump deer, and in a few moments a greater number than I had ever seen in all my hunting experiences loped within range of my eye. I could not look out into the forest where an aisle or lane or glade stretched to any distance, without seeing a big gray deer cross it. Jones said the herds had recently come up from the breaks, where they had wintered. These deer were twice the size of the Eastern species, and as fat as well-fed cattle. They were almost as tame, too. A big herd ran out of one glade, leaving behind several curious does, which watched us intently for a moment, then bounded off with the stiff, springy bounce that so amused me.

Sounder crossed fresh trails one after another; Jude, Tige and Ranger followed him, but hesitated often, barked and whined; Don started off once, to come sneaking back at Jones's stern call. But surly old Moze either would not or could not obey, and away he dashed. Bang! Jones sent a charge of fine shot after him. He yelped, doubled up as if stung, and returned as quickly as he had gone.

'Hyar, you white and black coon dog,' said Jones, 'get in behind, and stay there.'

We turned to the right after a while and got among shallow ravines. Gigantic pines grew on the ridges and in the hollows, and everywhere bluebells shone blue from the white frost. Why the frost did not kill these beautiful flowers was a mystery to me. The horses could not step without crushing them.

Before long, the ravines became so deep that we had to zigzag up and down their sides, and to force our horses through the aspen thickets in the hollows. Once from a ridge I saw a troop of deer, and stopped to watch them. Twenty-seven I counted outright, but there must have been three times that number. I saw the herd break across a glade, and watched them until they were lost in the forest. My companions having disappeared, I pushed on, and while working out of a wide, deep hollow, I noticed the sunny patches fade from the bright slopes, and the golden streaks vanish among the pines. The sky had become overcast, and the forest was darkening. The 'Waa-hoo' I cried out returned in echo only. The wind blew hard in my face, and the pines began to bend and roar. An immense black cloud enveloped Buckskin.

Satan had carried me no farther than the next ridge, when the forest frowned dark as twilight, and on the wind whirled flakes of snow. Over the next hollow, a white pall roared through the trees toward me. Hardly had I time to get the direction of the trail, and its relation to the trees nearby, when the storm enfolded me. Of his own accord Satan stopped in the lee of a bushy spruce. The roar in the pines equaled that of the cave under Niagara, and the bewildering, whirling mass of snow was as difficult to see through as the tumbling, seething waterfall.

I was confronted by the possibility of passing the night there, and calming my fears as best I could, hastily felt for my matches and knife. The prospect of being lost the next day in a white forest was also appalling, but I soon reassured myself that the storm was only a snow squall, and would not last long. Then I gave myself up to the pleasure and beauty of it. I could only faintly discern the dim trees; the limbs of the spruce, which partially protected me, sagged down to my head with their burden; I had but to reach out my hand for a snowball. Both the wind and snow seemed warm. The great flakes were like swan feathers on a summer breeze. There was something joyous in the whirl of snow and roar of wind. While I bent over to shake my holster, the storm passed as suddenly as it had come. When I looked up, there were the pines, like pillars of Pariar, marble, and a white shadow, a vanishing cloud fled, with receding roar, on the wings of the wind. Fast on this retreat burst the warm, bright sun.

I faced my course, and was delighted to see, through an opening where the ravine cut out of the forest, the red-tipped peaks of the cañon, and the vaulted dome I had named St Marks. As I started, a new and unexpected after-feature of the storm began to manifest itself. The sun being warm, even hot, began to melt the snow, and under the trees a heavy rain fell, and in the glades and hollows a fine mist blew. Exquisite rainbows hung from white-tipped branches and curved over the hollows. Glistening patches of snow fell from the pines, and broke the showers.

In a quarter of an hour, I rode out of the forest to the rim wall on dry ground. Against the green piñons Frank's white horse stood out conspicuously, and near him browsed the mounts of Jim and Wallace. The boys were not in evidence. Concluding they had gone down over the rim, I dismounted and kicked off my chaps, and taking my rifle and camera, hurried to look the place over.

To my surprise and interest, I found a long section of rim wall in ruins. It lay in a great curve between the two giant capes; and many short, sharp, projecting promontories, like the teeth of a saw, overhung the cañon. The slopes between these points of cliff were covered with a deep growth of piñon, and in these places descent would be easy. Everywhere in the corrugated wall were rents and rifts; cliffs stood detached like islands near a shore; yellow crags rose out of green clefts; jumble of rocks, and slides of rim wall, broken into blocks, massed under the promontories.

The singular raggedness and wildness of the scene took hold of me, and was not dispelled until the baying of Sounder and Don roused action in me. Apparently the hounds were widely separated. Then I heard Jim's yell. But it ceased when the wind lulled, and I heard it no more. Running back from the point, I began to go down. The way was steep, almost perpendicular; but because of the great stones and the absence of slides, was easy. I took long strides and jumps, and slid over rocks, and swung on piñon branches, and covered distance like a rolling stone. At the foot of the rim wall, or at a line where it would have reached had it extended regularly, the slope became less pronounced. I could stand up without holding on to a support. The largest piñons I had seen made a forest that almost stood on end. These trees grew up, down, and out, and twisted in curves, and many were two feet in thickness. During my descent, I halted at intervals to listen, and always heard one of the hounds, sometimes several. But as I descended for a long time, and did not get anywhere or approach the dogs, I began to grow impatient.

A large piñon, with a dead top, suggested a good outlook, so I climbed it, and saw I could sweep a large section of the slope. It was a strange thing to look down hill, over the tips of green trees. Below, perhaps four hundred yards, was a slide open for a long way; all the rest was green incline, with many dead branches sticking up like spars, and an occasional crag. From this perch I heard the hounds; then followed a yell I thought was Jim's, and after it the bellowing of Wallace's rifle. Then all was silent. The shots had effectually checked the yelping of the hounds. I let out a yell. Another cougar that Jones would not lasso! All at once I heard a familiar sliding of small rocks below me, and I watched the open slope with greedy eyes.

Not a bit surprised was I to see a cougar break out of the green, and go tearing down the slide. In less than six seconds, I had sent six steel-jacketed bullets after him. Puffs of dust rose closer and closer to him as each bullet went nearer the mark and the last showered him with gravel and turned him straight down the cañon slope.

I slid down the dead Piñon and jumped nearly twenty feet to the soft sand below, and after putting a loaded clip in my rifle, began kangaroo leaps down the slope. When I reached the point where the cougar had entered the slide, I called the hounds, but they did not come nor answer me. Notwithstanding my excitement, I appreciated the distance to the bottom of the slope before I reached it. In my haste, I ran upon the verge of a precipice twice as deep as the first rim wall, but one glance down sent me shudderingly backward.

With all the breath I had left I yelled: 'Waa-hoo! Waa-hoo!' From the echoes flung at me, I imagined at first that my friends were right on my ears. But no real answer came. The cougar had probably passed along this second rim wall to a break, and had gone down. His trail could easily be taken by any of the hounds. Vexed and anxious, I signaled again and again. Once, long after the echo had gone to sleep in some hollow cañon, I caught a faint 'Wa-a-ho-o-o!' But it might have come from the clouds. I did not hear a hound barking above me on the slope; but suddenly, to my amazement, Sounder's deep bay rose from the abyss below. I ran along the rim, called till I was hoarse, leaned over so far that the blood rushed to my head, and then sat down. I concluded this cañon hunting could bear some sustained attention and thought, as well as frenzied action.

Examination of my position showed how impossible it was to arrive at any clear idea of the depth or size, or condition of the cañon slopes from the main rim wall above. The second wall—a stupendous, yellow-faced cliff two thousand feet high—curved to my left round to a point in front of me. The intervening cañon might have been a half mile wide, and it might have been ten miles. I had become disgusted with judging distance. The slope above this second wall facing me ran up far above my head; it fairly towered, and this routed all my former judgments, because I remembered distinctly that from the rim this yellow and green mountain had appeared an insignificant little ridge. But it was when I turned to gaze up behind me that I fully grasped the immensity of the place. This wall and slope were the first two steps down the long stairway of the Grand Cañon, and they towered over me, straight up a half-mile in dizzy height. To think of climbing it took my breath away.

Then again Sounder's bay floated distinctly to me, but it seemed to come from a different point. I turned my ear to the wind, and in the succeeding moments I was more and more baffled. One bay sounded from below, and next from far to the right; another from the left. I could not distinguish voice from echo. The acoustic properties of the amphitheater beneath me were too wonderful for my comprehension.

As the bay grew sharper, and correspondingly more significant, I became distracted, and focused a strained vision on the cañon deeps. I looked along the slope to the notch where the wall curved and followed the base line of the yellow cliff. Quite suddenly I saw a very small black object moving with snail-like slowness. Although it seemed impossible for Sounder to be so small, I knew it was he. Having something now to judge distance from, I conceived it to be a mile, without the drop. If I could hear Sounder, he could hear me, so I yelled encouragement. The echoes clapped back at me like so many slaps in the face. I watched the hound until he disappeared among broken heaps of stone, and long after that his bay floated to me.

Having rested, I essayed the discovery of some of my lost companions or the hounds, and began to climb. Before I started, however, I was wise enough to study the rim wall above, to familiarize myself with the break so I would have a landmark. Like horns and spurs of gold the pinnacles loomed up. Massed closely together, they were not unlike an astounding pipe-organ. I had a feeling of my littleness, that I was lost, and should devote every moment and effort to the saving of my life. It did not seem possible I could be hunting. Though I climbed diagonally, and rested often, my heart pumped so hard I could hear it. A yellow crag, with a round head like an old man's cane, appealed to me as near the place where I last heard from Jim, and toward it I labored. Every time I glanced up, the distance seemed the same. A climb which I decided would not take more than fifteen minutes, required an hour.

While resting at the foot of the crag, I heard more baying of hounds, but for my life I could not tell whether the sound came from up or down, and I commenced to feel that I did not much care. Having signaled till I was hoarse, and receiving none but mock answers, I decided that if my companions had not toppled over a cliff, they were wisely withholding their breath.

Another stiff pull up the slope brought me under the rim wall, and there I groaned, because the wall was smooth and shiny, without a break. I plodded slowly along the base, with my rifle ready. Cougar tracks were so numerous I got tired of looking at them, but I did not forget that I might meet a tawny fellow or two among those narrow passes of shattered rock, and under the thick, dark piñons. Going on in this way, I ran point-blank into a pile of bleached bones before a cave. I had stumbled on the lair of a lion and from the looks of it one like that of Old Tom. I flinched twice before I threw a stone into the dark-mouthed cave. What impressed me as soon as I found I was in no danger of being pawed and clawed round the gloomy spot, was the fact of the bones being there. How did they come on a slope where a man could hardly walk? Only one answer seemed feasible. The lion had made his kill one thousand feet above, had pulled his quarry to the rim and pushed it over. In view of the theory that he might have had to drag his victim from the forest, and that very seldom two lions worked together, the fact of the location of the bones was startling. Skulls of wild horses and deer, antlers and countless bones, all crushed into shapelessness, furnished indubitable proof that the carcasses had fallen from a great height. Most remarkable of all was the skeleton of a cougar lying across that of a horse. I believed—I could not help but believe that the cougar had fallen with his last victim.

Not many rods beyond the lion den, the rim wall split into towers, crags and pinnacles. I thought I had found my pipe organ, and began to climb toward a narrow opening in the rim. But I lost it. The extraordinarily cut-up condition of the wall made holding to one direction impossible. Soon I realized I was lost in a labyrinth. I tried to find my way down again, but the best I could do was to reach the verge of a cliff, from which I could see the cañon. Then I knew where I was, yet I did not know, so I plodded wearily back. Many a blind cleft did I ascend in the maze of crags. I could hardly crawl along, still I kept at it, for the place was conducive to dire thoughts. A tower of Babel menaced me with tons of loose shale. A tower that leaned more frightfully than the Tower of Pisa threatened to build my tomb. Many a lighthouse-shaped crag sent down little scattering rocks in ominous notice.

After toiling in and out of passageways under the shadows of these strangely formed cliffs, and coming again and again to the same point, a blind pocket, I grew desperate. I named the baffling place Deception Pass, and then ran down a slide. I knew if I could keep my feet I could beat the avalanche. More by good luck than management I outran the roaring stones and landed safely. Then rounding the cliff below, I found myself on a narrow ledge, with a wall to my left, and to the right the tips of piñon trees level with my feet.

Innocently and wearily I passed round a pillar-like corner of wall, to come face to face with an old lioness and cubs. I heard the mother snarl, and at the same time her ears went back flat, and she crouched. The same fire of yellow eyes, the same grim snarling expression so familiar in my mind since Old Tom had leaped at me, faced me here.

My recent vow of extermination was entirely forgotten and one frantic spring carried me over the ledge.

Crash! I felt the brushing and scratching of branches, and saw a green blur. I went down straddling limbs and hit the ground with a thump. Fortunately, I landed mostly on my feet, in sand, and suffered no serious bruise. But I was stunned, and my right arm was numb for a moment. When I gathered myself together, instead of being grateful the ledge had not been on the face of Point Sublime—from which I would most assuredly have leaped—I was the angriest man ever let loose in the Grand Cañon.

Of course the cougars were far on their way by that time, and were telling neighbors about the brave hunter's leap for life; so I devoted myself to further efforts to find an outlet. The niche I had jumped into opened below, as did most of the breaks, and I worked out of it to the base of the rim wall, and tramped a long, long mile before I reached my own trail leading down. Resting every five steps, I climbed and climbed. My rifle grew to weigh a ton; my feet were lead; the camera strapped to my shoulder was the world. Soon climbing meant trapeze work—long reach of arm, and pull of weight, high step of foot, and spring of body. Where I had slid down with ease, I had to strain and raise myself by sheer muscle. I wore my left glove to tatters and threw it away to put the right one on my left hand. I thought many times I could not make another move; I thought my lungs would burst, but I kept on. When at last I surmounted the rim, I saw Jones, and flopped down beside him, and lay panting, dripping, boiling, with scorched feet, aching limbs and numb chest.

'I've been here two hours,' he said, 'and I knew things were happening below; but to climb up that slide would kill me. I am not young any more, and a steep climb like this takes a young heart. As it was I had enough work. Look!' He called my attention to his trousers. They had been cut to shreds, and the right trouser leg was missing from the knee down. His shin was bloody. 'Moze took a lion along the rim, and I went after him with all my horse could do. I yelled for the boys, but they didn't come. Right here it is easy to go down, but below, where Moze started this lion, it was impossible to get over the rim. The lion lit straight out of the piñons. I lost ground because of the thick brush and numerous trees.

Then Moze doesn't bark often enough. He treed the lion twice. I could tell by the way he opened up and bayed. The rascal coon-dog climbed the trees and chased the lion out. That's what Moze did! I got to an open space and saw him, and was coming up fine when he went down over a hollow which ran into the cañon. My horse tripped and fell, turning clear over with me before he threw me into the brush. I tore my clothes, and got this bruise, but wasn't much hurt. My horse is pretty lame.'

I began a recital of my experience, modestly omitting the incident where I bravely faced an old lioness. Upon consulting my watch, I found I had been almost four hours climbing out. At that moment, Frank poked a red face over the rim. He was in his shirt sleeves, sweating freely, and wore a frown I had never seen before. He puffed like a porpoise, and at first could hardly speak.

'Where—were—you—all?' he panted. 'Say! but mebbe this hasn't been a chase! Jim an' Wallace an' me went tumblin' down after the dogs, each one lookin' out for his perticular dog, an' darn me if I don't believe his lion, too. Don took one oozin' down the cañon, with me hot-footin' it after him. An' somewhere he treed that lion, right below me, in a box cañon, sort of an offshoot of the second rim, an' I couldn't locate him. I blamed near killed myself more'n once. Look at my knuckles! Barked 'em slidin' about a mile down a smooth wall. I thought once the lion had jumped Don, but soon I heard him barkin' again. All that time I heard Sounder, an' once I heard the pup. Jim yelled, an' somebody was shootin'. But I couldn't find nobody, or make nobody hear me. That cañon is a mighty deceivin' place. You'd never think so till you go down. I wouldn't climb up it again for all the lions in Buckskin. Hello, there comes Jim oozin' up.'

Jim appeared just over the rim, and when he got up to us, dusty, torn and fagged out, with Don, Tige and Ranger showing signs of collapse, we all blurted out questions. But Jim took his time.

'Shore thet cañon is one hell of a place,' he began finally. 'Where was everybody? Tige and the pup went down with me an' treed a cougar. Yes, they did, an' I set under a piñon holdin' the pup, while Tige kept the cougar treed. I yelled an' yelled. After about an hour or two, Wallace came poundin' down like a giant. It was a sure thing we'd get the cougar; an' Wallace was takin' his picture when the blamed cat jumped. It was embarrassin', because he wasn't polite about how he jumped. We scattered some, an' when Wallace got his gun, the cougar was humpin' down the slope, an' he was goin' so fast an' the piñons was so thick thet Wallace couldn't get a fair shot, an' missed. Tige an' the pup was so scared by the shots they wouldn't take the trail again. I heard some one shoot about a million times, an' shore thought the cougar was done for. Wallace went pluggin' down the slope an' I followed. I couldn't keep up with him—he shore takes long steps—an' I lost him. I'm reckonin' he went over the second wall. Then I made tracks for the top. Boys, the way you can see an' hear things down in thet cañon, an' the way you can't hear an' see things is pretty funny.'

'If Wallace went over the second rim wall, will he get back to-day?' we all asked.

'Shore, there's no tellin'.'

We waited, lounged, and slept for three hours, and were beginning to worry about our comrade when he hove in sight eastward, along the rim. He walked like a man whose next step would be his last. When he reached us, he fell flat, and lay breathing heavily for a while.

'Somebody once mentioned Israel Putnam's ascent of a hill,' he said slowly. 'With all respect to history and a patriot, I wish to say Putnam never saw a hill!'

'Ooze for camp,' called out Frank.

Five o'clock found us round a bright fire, all casting ravenous eyes at a smoking supper. The smell of the Persian meat would have made a wolf of a vegetarian. I devoured four chops, and could not have been counted in the running. Jim opened a can of maple sirup which he had been saving for a grand occasion, and Frank went him one better with two cans of peaches. How glorious to be hungry—to feel the craving for food, and to be grateful for it, to realize that the best of life lies in the daily needs of existence, and to battle for them!

Nothing could be stronger than the simple enumeration and statement of the facts of Wallace's experience after he left Jim. He chased the cougar, and kept it in sight, until it went over the second rim wall. Here he dropped over a precipice twenty feet high, to alight on a fan-shaped slide which spread toward the bottom. It began to slip and move by jerks, and then started off steadily, with an increasing roar. He rode an avalanche for one thousand feet. The jar loosened bowlders from the walls. When the slide stopped, Wallace extricated his feet and began to dodge the bowlders. He had only time to jump over the large ones or dart to one side out of their way. He dared not run. He had to watch them coming. One huge stone hurtled over his head and smashed a piñon tree below.

When these had ceased rolling, and he had passed down to the red shale, he heard Sounder baying near, and knew a cougar had been treed or cornered. Hurdling the stones and dead piñons, Wallace ran a mile down the slope, only to find he had been deceived in the direction. He sheered off to the left. Sounder's illusive bay came up from a deep cleft. Wallace plunged into a piñon, climbed to the ground, skidded down a solid slide, to come upon an impassable obstacle in the form of a solid wall of red granite. Sounder appeared and came to him, evidently having given up the chase.

Wallace consumed four hours in making the ascent. In the notch of the curve of the second rim wall, he climbed the slippery steps of a waterfall. At one point, if he had not been six feet five inches tall, he would have been compelled to attempt retracing his trail—an impossible task. But his height enabled him to reach a root, by which he pulled himself up. Sounder he lassoed *a la* Jones, and hauled up. At another spot, which Sounder climbed, he lassoed a piñon above, and walked up with his feet slipping from under him at every step. The knees of his corduroy trousers were holes, as were the elbows of his coat. The sole of his left boot—which he used most in climbing—was gone, and so was his hat.

15

Jones on Cougars

The mountain lion, or cougar, of our Rocky Mountain region, is nothing more nor less than the panther. He is a little different in shape, color and size, which vary according to his environment. The panther of the Rockies is usually light, taking the grayish hue of the rocks. He is stockier and heavier of build, and stronger of limb than the Eastern species, which difference comes from climbing mountains and springing down the cliffs after his prey.

In regions accessible to man, or where man is encountered even rarely, the cougar is exceedingly shy, seldom or never venturing from cover during the day. He spends the hours of daylight high on the most rugged cliffs, sleeping and basking in the sunshine, and watching with wonderfully keen sight the valleys below. His hearing equals his sight, and if danger threatens, he always hears it in time to skulk away unseen. At night he steals down the mountain side toward deer or elk he has located during the day. Keeping to the lowest ravines and thickets, he creeps upon his prey. His cunning and ferocity are keener and more savage in proportion to the length of time he has been without food. As he grows hungrier and thinner, his skill and fierce strategy correspondingly increase. A well-fed cougar will creep upon and secure only about one in seven of the deer, elk, antelope or mountain sheep that he stalks. But a starving cougar is another animal. He creeps like a snake, is as sure on the scent as a vulture, makes no more noise than a shadow, and he hides behind a stone or bush that would scarcely conceal a rabbit. Then he springs with terrific force, and intensity of purpose, and seldom fails to reach his victim, and once the claws of a starved lion touch flesh, they never let go.

A cougar seldom pursues his quarry after he has leaped and missed, either from disgust or failure, or knowledge that a second attempt would be futile. The animal making the easiest prey for the cougar is the elk. About every other elk attacked falls a victim. Deer are more fortunate, the ratio being one dead to five leaped at. The antelope, living on the lowlands or upland meadows, escapes nine times out of ten; and the mountain sheep, or bighorn, seldom falls to the onslaught of his enemy.

Once the lion gets a hold with the great forepaw, every movement of the struggling prey sinks the sharp, hooked claws deeper. Then as quickly as is possible, the lion fastens his teeth in the throat of his prey and grips till it is dead. In this way elk have carried lions for many rods. The lion seldom tears the skin of the neck, and never, as is generally supposed, sucks the blood of its victim; but he cuts into the side, just behind the foreshoulder, and eats the liver first. He rolls the skin back as neatly and tightly as a person could do it. When he has gorged himself, he drags the carcass into a ravine or dense thicket, and rakes leaves, sticks or dirt over it to hide it from other animals. Usually he returns to his cache on the second night, and after that the frequency of his visits depends on the supply of fresh prey. In remote regions, unfrequented by man, the lion will guard his cache from coyote and buzzards.

In sex there are about five female lions to one male. This is caused by the jealous and vicious disposition of the male. It is a fact that the old Toms kill every young lion they can catch. Both male and female of the litter suffer alike until after weaning time, and then only the males. In this matter wise animal logic is displayed by the Toms. The domestic cat, to some extent, possesses the same trait. If the litter is destroyed, the mating time is sure to come about regardless of the season. Thus this savage trait of the lions prevents overproduction, and breeds a hardy and intrepid race. If by chance or that cardinal feature of animal life—the survival of the fittest—a young male lion escapes to the weaning time, even after that he is persecuted. Young male lions have been killed and found to have had their flesh beaten until it was a mass of bruises and undoubtedly it had been the work of an old Tom. Moreover, old males and females have been killed, and found to be in the same bruised condition. A feature, and a conclusive one, is the fact that invariably the female is suckling her young at this period, and sustains the bruises in desperately defending her litter.

It is astonishing how cunning, wise and faithful an old lioness is. She seldom leaves her kittens. From the time they are six weeks old she takes them out to train them for the battles of life, and the struggle continues from birth to death. A lion hardly ever dies naturally. As soon as night descends, the lioness stealthily stalks forth, and because of her little ones, takes very short steps. The cubs follow, stepping in their mother's tracks. When she crouches for game, each little lion crouches also, and each one remains perfectly still until she springs, or signals them to come. If she secures the prey, they all gorge themselves. After the feast the mother takes her back trail, stepping in the tracks she made coming down the mountain. And the cubs are very careful to follow suit, and not to leave marks of their trail in the soft snow. No doubt this habit is practiced to keep their deadly enemies in ignorance of their existence. The old Toms and white hunters are their only foes. Indians never kill a lion. This trick of the lions has fooled many a hunter, concerning not only the direction, but particularly the number.

The only successful way to hunt lions is with trained dogs. A good hound can trail them for several hours after the tracks have been made, and on a cloudy or wet day can hold the scent much longer. In snow the hound can trail for three or four days after the track has been made.

When Jones was game warden of the Yellowstone National Park, he had unexampled opportunities to hunt cougars and learn their habits. All the cougars in that region of the Rockies made a rendezvous of the game preserve. Jones soon procured a pack of hounds, but as they had been trained to run deer, foxes and coyotes he had great trouble. They would break on the trail of these animals, and also on elk and antelope just when this was farthest from his wish. He soon realized that to train the hounds was a sore task. When they refused to come back at his call, he stung them with fine shot, and in this manner taught obedience. But obedience was not enough; the hounds must know how to follow and tree a lion. With this in mind, Jones decided to catch a lion alive and give his dogs practical lessons.

A few days after reaching this decision, he discovered the tracks of two lions in the neighborhood of Mt Everett. The hounds were put on the trail and followed it into an abandoned coal shaft. Jones recognized this as his opportunity, and taking his lasso and extra rope, he crawled into the hole. Not fifteen feet from the opening sat one of the cougars, snarling and spitting. Jones promptly lassoed it, passed his end of the lasso round a side prop of the shaft, and out to the soldiers who had followed him. Instructing them not to pull till he called, he cautiously began to crawl by the cougar, with the intention of getting farther back and roping its hind leg, so as to prevent disaster when the soldiers pulled it out. He accomplished this, not without some uneasiness in regard to the second lion, and giving the word to his companions, soon had his captive hauled from the shaft and tied so tightly it could not move.

Jones took the cougar and his hounds to an open place in the park, where there were trees, and prepared for a chase. Loosing the lion, he held his hounds back a moment, then let them go. Within one hundred yards the cougar climbed a tree, and the dogs saw the performance. Taking a forked stick, Jones mounted up to the cougar, caught it under the jaw with the stick, and pushed it out. There was a fight, a scramble, and the cougar dashed off to run up another tree. In this manner, he soon trained his hounds to the pink of perfection.

Jones discovered, while in the park, that the cougar is king of all the beasts of North America. Even a grizzly dashed away in great haste when a cougar made his appearance. At the road camp, near Mt Washburn, during the fall of 1904, the bears, grizzlies and others, were always hanging round the cook tent. There were cougars also, and almost every evening, about dusk, a big fellow would come parading past the tent. The bears would grunt furiously and scamper in every direction. It was easy to tell when a cougar was in the neighborhood, by the peculiar grunts and snorts of the bears, and the sharp, distinct, alarmed yelps of coyotes. A lion would just as lief kill a coyote as any other animal and he would devour it, too. As to the fighting of cougars and grizzlies, that was a mooted question, with the credit on the side of the former.

The story of the doings of cougars, as told in the snow, was intensely fascinating and tragical. How they stalked deer and elk, crept to within springing distance, then crouched flat to leap, was as easy to read as if it had been told in print. The leaps and bounds were beyond belief. The longest leap on a level measured eighteen and one-half feet. Jones trailed a half-grown cougar, which in turn was trailing a big elk. He found where the cougar had struck his game, had clung for many rods, to be dashed off by the low limb of a spruce tree. The imprint of the body of the cougar was a foot deep in the snow; blood and tufts of hair covered the place. But there was no sign of the cougar renewing the chase.

In rare cases cougars would refuse to run, or take to trees. One day Jones followed the hounds, eight in number, to come on a huge Tom holding the whole pack at bay. He walked to and fro, lashing his tail from side to side, and when Jones dashed up, he coolly climbed a tree. Jones shot the cougar, which, in falling, struck one of the hounds, crippling him. This hound would never approach a tree after this incident, believing probably that the cougar had sprung upon him.

Usually the hounds chased their quarry into a tree long before Jones rode up. It was always desirable to kill the animal with the first shot. If the cougar was wounded, and fell or jumped among the dogs, there was sure to be a terrible fight, and the best dogs always received serious injuries, if they were not killed outright. The lion would seize a hound, pull him close, and bite him in the brain.

Jones asserted that a cougar would usually run from a hunter, but that this feature was not to be relied upon. And a wounded cougar was as dangerous as a tiger. In his hunts Jones carried a shotgun, and shells loaded with ball for the cougar, and others loaded with fine shot for the hounds. One day, about ten miles from the camp, the hounds took a trail and ran rapidly, as there were only a few inches of snow. Jones found a large lion had taken refuge in a tree that had fallen against another, and aiming at the shoulder of the beast, he fired both barrels. The cougar made no sign he had been hit. Jones reloaded and fired at the head. The old fellow growled fiercely, turned in the tree and walked down head first, something he would not have been able to do had the tree been upright. The hounds were ready for him, but wisely attacked in the rear. Realizing he had been shooting fine shot at the animal, Jones began a hurried search for a shell loaded with ball. The lion made for him, compelling him to dodge behind trees. Even though the hounds kept nipping the cougar, the persistent fellow still pursued the hunter. At last Jones found the right shell, just as the cougar reached for him. Major, the leader of the hounds, darted bravely in, and grasped the leg of the beast just in the nick of time. This enabled Jones to take aim and fire at close range, which ended the fight. Upon examination, it was discovered the cougar had been half-blinded by the fine shot, which accounted for the ineffectual attempts he had made to catch Jones.

The mountain lion rarely attacks a human being for the purpose of eating. When hungry he will often follow the tracks of people, and under favorable circumstances may ambush them. In the park where game is plentiful, no one has ever known a cougar to follow the trail of a person; but outside the park lions have been known to follow hunters, and particularly stalk little children. The Davis family, living a few miles north of the park, have had children pursued to the very doors of their cabin. And other families relate similar experiences. Jones heard of only one fatality, but he believes that if the children were left alone in the woods, the cougars would creep closer and closer, and when assured there was no danger, would spring to kill.

Jones never heard the cry of a cougar in the National Park, which strange circumstance, considering the great number of the animals there, he believed to be on account of the abundance of game. But he had heard it when a boy in Illinois, and when a man all over the West, and the cry was always the same, weird and wild, like the scream of a terrified woman. He did not understand the significance of the cry, unless it meant hunger, or the wailing mourn of a lioness for her murdered cubs.

The destructiveness of this savage species was murderous. Jones came upon one old Tom's den, where there was a pile of nineteen elk, mostly yearlings. Only five or six had been eaten. Jones hunted this old fellow for months, and found that the lion killed on the average three animals a week. The hounds got him up at length, and chased him to the Yellowstone River, which he swam at a point impassable for man or horse. One of the dogs, a giant bloodhound named Jack, swam the swift channel, kept on after the lion, but never returned. All cougars have their peculiar traits and habits, the same as other creatures, and all old Toms have strongly marked characteristics, but this one was the most destructive cougar Jones ever knew.

During Jones's short sojourn as warden in the park, he captured numerous cougars alive, and killed seventy-two.

16
Kitty

It seemed my eyelids had scarcely touched when Jones's exasperating, yet stimulating, yell aroused me. Day was breaking. The moon and stars shone with wan luster. A white, snowy frost silvered the forest. Old Moze had curled close beside me, and now he gazed at me reproachfully and shivered. Lawson came hustling in with the horses. Jim busied himself around the campfire. My fingers nearly froze while I saddled my horse.

At five o'clock we were trotting up the slope of Buckskin, bound for the section of ruined rim wall where we had encountered the convention of cougars. Hoping to save time, we took a short cut, and were soon crossing deep ravines.

The sunrise coloring the purple curtain of cloud over the cañon was too much for me, and I lagged on a high ridge to watch it, thus falling behind my more practical companions. A far-off 'Waa-hoo!' brought me to a realization of the day's stern duty, and I hurried Satan forward on the trail.

I came suddenly upon our leader, leading his horse through the scrub piñon on the edge of the cañon, and I knew at once something had happened, for he was closely scrutinizing the ground.

'I declare this beats me all hollow!' began Jones. 'We might be hunting rabbits instead of the wildest animals on the continent. We jumped a bunch of lions in this clump of piñon. There must have been at least four. I thought first we'd run upon an old lioness with cubs, but all the trails were made by full-grown lions. Moze took one north along the rim, same as the other day, but the lion got away quick. Frank saw one lion. Wallace is following Sounder down into the first hollow. Jim has gone over the rim wall after Don. There you are! Four lions playing tag in broad daylight on top of this wall! I'm inclined to believe Clarke didn't exaggerate. But confound the luck! the hounds have split again. They're doing their best, of course, and it's up to us to stay with them. I'm afraid we'll lose some of them. Hello! I hear a signal. That's from Wallace. Waa-hoo! Waa-hoo! There he is, coming out of the hollow.'

The tall Californian reached us presently with Sounder beside him. He reported that the hound had chased a lion into an impassable break. We then joined Frank on a jutting crag of the cañon wall.

'Waa-hoo!' yelled Jones. There was no answer except the echo, and it rolled up out of the chasm with strange, hollow mockery.

'Don took a cougar down this slide,' said Frank. 'I saw the brute, an' Don was makin' him hump. A—ha! There! Listen to thet!'

From the green and yellow depths soared the faint yelp of a hound.

'That's Don! that's Don!' cried Jones. 'He's hot on something. Where's Sounder? Hyar, Sounder! By George! there he goes down the slide. Hear him! He's opened up! Hi! Hi! Hi!'

The deep, full mellow bay of the hound came ringing on the clear air.

'Wallace, you go down. Frank and I will climb out on the pointed crag. Grey, you stay here. Then we'll have the slide between us. Listen and watch!'

From my promontory I watched Wallace go down with his gigantic strides, sending the rocks rolling and cracking; and then I saw Jones and Frank crawl out to the end of a crumbling ruin of yellow wall which threatened to go splintering and thundering down into the abyss.

I thought, as I listened to the penetrating voice of the hound, that nowhere on earth could there be a grander scene for wild action, wild life. My position afforded a commanding view over a hundred miles of the noblest and most sublime work of nature. The rim wall where I stood sheered down a thousand feet, to meet a long wooded slope which cut abruptly off into another giant precipice; a second long slope descended, and jumped off into what seemed the grave of the world. Most striking in that vast void where the long, irregular points of rim wall, protruding into the Grand Cañon. From Point Sublime to the Pink Cliffs of Utah there were twelve of these colossal capes, miles apart, some sharp, some round, some blunt, all rugged and bold. The great chasm in the middle was full of purple smoke. It seemed a mighty sepulcher from which misty fumes rolled upward. The turrets, mesas, domes, parapets and escarpments of yellow and red rock gave the appearance of an architectural work of giant hands. The wonderful river of silt, the blood-red, mystic and sullen Rio Colorado, lay hidden except in one place far away, where it glimmered wanly. Thousands of colors were blended before my rapt gaze. Yellow predominated, as the walls and crags lorded it over the lower cliffs and tables; red glared in the sunlight; green softened these two, and then purple and violet, gray, blue and the darker hues shaded away into dim and distinct obscurity.

Excited yells from my companions on the other crag recalled me to the living aspect of the scene. Jones was leaning far down in a niche, at seeming great hazard of life, yelling with all the power of his strong lungs. Frank stood still farther out on a cracked point that made me tremble, and his yell reënforced Jones's. From far below rolled up a chorus of thrilling bays and yelps, and Jim's call, faint, but distinct on that wonderfully thin air, with its unmistakable note of warning.

Then on the slide I saw a lion headed for the rim wall and climbing fast. I added my exultant cry to the medley, and I stretched my arms wide to that illimitable void and gloried in a moment full to the brim of the tingling joy of existence. I did not consider how painful it must have been to the toiling lion. It was only the spell of wild environment, of perilous yellow crags, of thin, dry air, of voice of man and dog, of the stinging expectation of sharp action, of life.

I watched the lion growing bigger and bigger. I saw Don and Sounder run from the piñon into the open slide, and heard their impetuous burst of wild yelps as they saw their game. Then Jones's clarion yell made me bound for my horse. I reached him, was about to mount, when Moze came trotting toward me. I caught the old gladiator. When he heard the chorus from below, he plunged like a mad bull. With both arms round him I held on. I vowed never to let him get down that slide. He howled and tore, but I held on. My big black horse with ears laid back stood like a rock.

I heard the pattering of little sliding rocks below; stealthy padded footsteps and hard panting breaths, almost like coughs; then the lion passed out of the slide not twenty feet away. He saw us, and sprang into the piñon scrub with the leap of a scared deer.

Samson himself could no longer have held Moze. Away he darted with his sharp, angry bark. I flung myself upon Satan and rode out to see Jones ahead and Frank flashing through the green on the white horse.

At the end of the piñon thicket Satan overhauled Jones's bay, and we entered the open forest together. We saw Frank glinting across the dark pines.

'Hi! Hi!' yelled the Colonel.

No need was there to whip or spur those magnificent horses. They were fresh: the course was open, and smooth as a racetrack, and the impelling chorus of the hounds was in full blast. I gave Satan a loose rein, and he stayed neck and neck with the bay. There was not a log, nor a stone, nor a gully. The hollows grew wider and shallower as we raced along, and presently disappeared altogether. The lion was running straight from the cañon, and the certainty that he must sooner or later take to a tree, brought from me a yell of irresistible wild joy.

'Hi! Hi! Hi!' answered Jones.

The whipping wind with its pine-scented fragrance, warm as the breath of summer, was intoxicating as wine. The huge pines, too kingly for close communion with their kind, made wide arches under which the horses stretched out long and low, with supple, springy, powerful strides. Frank's yell rang clear as a bell. We saw him curve to the right, and took his yell as a signal for us to cut across. Then we began to close in on him, and to hear more distinctly the baying of the hounds.

'Hi! Hi! Hi! Hi!' bawled Jones, and his great trumpet voice rolled down the forest glades.

'Hi! Hi! Hi! Hi!' I screeched, in wild recognition of the spirit of the moment.

Fast as they were flying, the bay and the black responded to our cries, and quickened, strained and lengthened under us till the trees sped by in blurs.

There, plainly in sight ahead ran the hounds, Don leading, Sounder next, and Moze not fifty yards behind a desperately running lion.

There are all-satisfying moments of life. That chase through the open forest, under the stately pines, with the wild, tawny quarry in plain sight and the glad staccato yelps of the hound filling my ears and swelling my heart, with the splendid action of my horse carrying me on the wings of the wind, was glorious answer and fullness to the call and hunger of a hunter's blood.

But as such moments must be, they were brief. The lion leaped gracefully into the air, splintering the bark from a pine fifteen feet up, and crouched on a limb. The hounds tore madly round the tree.

'Full-grown female,' said Jones calmly, as we dismounted, 'and she's ours. We'll call her Kitty.'

Kitty was a beautiful creature, long, slender, glossy, with white belly and black-tipped ears and tail. She did not resemble the heavy, grimfaced brute that always hung in the air of my dreams. A low, brooding menacing murmur, that was not a snarl nor a growl, came from her. She watched the dogs with bright, steady eyes, and never so much as looked at us.

The dogs were worth attention, even from us, who certainly did not need to regard them from her personally hostile point of view. Don stood straight up, with his forepaws beating the air; he walked on his hind legs like the trained dog in the circus; he yelped continuously, as if it agonized him to see the lion safe out of his reach. Sounder had lost his identity. Joy had unhinged his mind and had made him a dog of double personality. He had always been unsociable with me, never responding to my attempts to caress him, but now he leaped into my arms and licked my face. He had always hated Jones till that moment, when he raised his paws to his master's breast. And perhaps more remarkable, time and time again he sprang up at Satan's nose, whether to bite him or kiss him, I could not tell. Then old Moze, he of Grand Cañon fame, made the delirious antics of his canine fellows look cheap. There was a small, dead pine that had fallen against a drooping branch of the tree Kitty had taken refuge in, and up this narrow ladder Moze began to climb. He was fifteen feet up, and Kitty had begun to shift uneasily, when Jones saw him.

'Hyar! you wild coon-chaser! Git out of that! Come down! Come down!'

But Jones might have been in the bottom of the cañon for all Moze heard or cared. Jones removed his coat, carefully coiled his lasso, and began to go hand and knee up the leaning pine.

'Hyar! dod-blast you, git down!' yelled Jones, and he kicked Moze off. The persistent hound returned, and followed Jones to a height of twenty feet, where again he was thrust off.

'Hold him, one of you!' called Jones.

'Not me,' said Frank, 'I'm lookin' out for myself.'

'Same here,' I cried, with a camera in one hand and a rifle in the other. 'Let Moze climb if he likes.'

Climb he did, to be kicked off again. But he went back. It was a way he had. Jones at last recognized either his own waste of time or Moze's greatness, for he desisted, allowing the hound to keep close after him.

The cougar, becoming uneasy, stood up, reached for another limb, climbed out upon it, and peering down, spat hissingly at Jones. But he kept steadily on with Moze close on his heels. I snapped my camera on them when Kitty was not more than fifteen feet above them. As Jones reached the snag which upheld the leaning tree, she ran out on her branch, and leaped into an adjoining pine. It was a good long jump, and the weight of the animal bent the limb alarmingly.

Jones backed down, and laboriously began to climb the other tree. As there were no branches low down, he had to hug the trunk with arms and legs as a boy climbs. His lasso hampered his progress. When the slow ascent was accomplished up to the first branch, Kitty leaped back into her first perch. Strange to say Jones did not grumble; none of his characteristic impatience manifested itself here. I supposed with him all the exasperating waits and vexatious obstacles were little things preliminary to the real work, to which he had now come. He was calm and deliberate, and slid down the pine, walked back to the leaning tree, and while resting a moment, shook his lasso at Kitty. This action fitted him, somehow; it was so compatible with his grim assurance.

To me, and to Frank, also, for that matter, it was all new and startling, and we were as excited as the dogs. We kept continually moving about, Frank mounted, and I afoot, to get good views of the cougar. When she crouched as if to leap, it was almost impossible to remain under the tree, and we kept moving.

Once more Jones crept up on hands and knees. Moze walked the slanting pine like a rope performer. Kitty began to grow restless. This time she showed both anger and impatience, but did not yet appear frightened. She growled low and deep, opened her mouth and hissed, and swung her tufted tail faster and faster.

'Look out, Jones! look out!' yelled Frank warningly.

Jones, who had reached the trunk of the tree, halted and slipped round it, placing it between him and Kitty. She had advanced on her limb, a few feet above Jones, and threateningly hung over. Jones backed down a little till she crossed to another branch, then he resumed his former position.

'Watch below,' called he.

Hardly any doubt was there as to how we watched. Frank and I were all eyes, except very high and throbbing hearts. When Jones thrashed the lasso at Kitty we both yelled. She ran out on the branch and jumped. This time she fell short of her point, clutched a dead snag, which broke, letting her through a bushy branch from where she hung head downward. For a second she swung free, then reaching toward the tree caught it with front paws, ran down like a squirrel, and leaped off when thirty feet from the ground. The action was as rapid as it was astonishing.

Like a yellow rubber ball she bounded up, and fled with the yelping hounds at her heels. The chase was short. At the end of a hundred yards Moze caught up with her and nipped her. She whirled with savage suddenness, and lunged at Moze, but he cunningly eluded the vicious paws. Then she sought safety in another pine.

Frank, who was as quick as the hounds, almost rode them down in his eagerness. While Jones descended from his perch, I led the two horses down the forest.

This time the cougar was well out on a low spreading branch. Jones conceived the idea of raising the loop of his lasso on a long pole, but as no pole of sufficient length could be found, he tried from the back of his horse. The bay walked forward well enough; when, however, he got under the beast and heard her growl, he reared and almost threw Jones. Frank's horse could not be persuaded to go near the tree. Satan evinced no fear of the cougar, and without flinching carried Jones directly beneath the limb and stood with ears back and forelegs stiff.

'Look at that! look at that!' cried Jones, as the wary cougar pawed the loop aside. Three successive times did Jones have the lasso just ready to drop over her neck, when she flashed a yellow paw and knocked the noose awry. Then she leaped far out over the waiting dogs, struck the ground with a light, sharp thud, and began to run with the speed of a deer. Frank's cowboy training now stood us in good stead. He was off like a shot and turned the cougar from the direction of the cañon. Jones lost not a moment in pursuit, and I, left with Jones's badly frightened bay, got going in time to see the race, but not to assist. For several hundred yards Kitty made the hounds appear slow. Don, being swiftest, gained on her steadily toward the close of the dash, and presently was running under her upraised tail. On the next jump he nipped her. She turned and sent him reeling. Sounder came flying up to bite her flank, and at the same moment fierce old Moze closed in on her. The next instant a struggling mass whirled on the ground. Jones and Frank, yelling like demons, almost rode over it. The cougar broke from her assailants, and dashing away leaped on the first tree. It was a half-dead pine with short snags low down and a big branch extending out over a ravine.

'I think we can hold her now,' said Jones. The tree proved to be a most difficult one to climb. Jones made several ineffectual attempts before he reached the first limb, which broke, giving him a hard fall. This calmed me enough to make me take notice of Jones's condition. He was wet with sweat and covered with the black pitch from the pines; his shirt was slit down the arm, and there was blood on his temple and his hand. The next attempt began by placing a good-sized log against the tree, and proved to be the necessary help. Jones got hold of the second limb and pulled himself up.

As he kept on, Kitty crouched low as if to spring upon him. Again Frank and I sent warning calls to him, but he paid no attention to us or to the cougar, and continued to climb. This worried Kitty as much as it did us. She began to move on the snags, stepping from one to the other, every moment snarling at Jones, and then she crawled up. The big branch evidently took her eye. She tried several times to climb up to it, but small snags close together made her distrustful. She walked uneasily out upon two limbs, and as they bent with her weight she hurried back. Twice she did this, each time looking up, showing her desire to leap to the big branch. Her distress became plainly evident; a child could have seen that she feared she would fall. At length, in desperation, she spat at Jones, then ran out and leaped. She all but missed the branch, but succeeded in holding to it and swinging to safety. Then she turned to her tormentor, and gave utterance to most savage sounds. As she did not intimidate her pursuer, she retreated out on the branch, which sloped down at a deep angle, and crouched on a network of small limbs.

When Jones had worked up a little farther, he commanded a splendid position for his operations. Kitty was somewhat below him in a desirable place, yet the branch she was on joined the tree considerably above his head. Jones cast his lasso. It caught on a snag. Throw after throw he made with like result. He recoiled and recast nineteen times, to my count, when Frank made a suggestion.

'Rope those dead snags an' break them off.'

This practical idea Jones soon carried out, which left him a clear path. The next fling of the lariat caused the cougar angrily to shake her head. Again Jones sent the noose flying. She pulled it off her back and bit it savagely.

Though very much excited, I tried hard to keep sharp, keen faculties alert so as not to miss a single detail of the thrilling scene. But I must have failed, for all of a sudden I saw how Jones was standing in the tree, something I had not before appreciated. He had one hand hold, which he could not use while recoiling the lasso, and his feet rested upon a precariously frail-appearing, dead snag. He made eleven casts of the lasso, all of which bothered Kitty, but did not catch her. The twelfth caught her front paw. Jones jerked so quickly and hard that he almost lost his balance, and he pulled the noose off. Patiently he recoiled the lasso.

'That's what I want. If I can get her front paw she's ours. My idea is to pull her off the limb, let her hang there, and then lasso her hind legs.'

Another cast, the unlucky thirteenth, settled the loop perfectly round her neck. She chewed on the rope with her front teeth and appeared to have difficulty in holding it.

'Easy! Easy! Ooze thet rope! Easy!' yelled the cowboy.

Cautiously Jones took up the slack and slowly tightened the nose, then a quick jerk, fastened it close round her neck.

We heralded this achievement with yells of triumph that made the forest ring.

Our triumph was short-lived. Jones had hardly moved when the cougar shot straight out into the air. The lasso caught on a branch, hauling her up short, and there she hung in mid air, writhing, struggling and giving utterance to sounds terribly human. For several seconds she swung, slowly descending, in which frenzied time I, with ruling passion uppermost, endeavored to snap a picture of her.

The unintelligible commands Jones was yelling to Frank and me ceased suddenly with a sharp crack of breaking wood. Then crash! Jones fell out of the tree. The lasso streaked up, ran over the limb, while the cougar dropped pell-mell into the bunch of waiting, howling dogs.

The next few moments it was impossible for me to distinguish what actually transpired. A great flutter of leaves whirled round a swiftly changing ball of brown and black and yellow, from which came a fiendish clamor.

Then I saw Jones plunge down the ravine and bounce here and there in mad efforts to catch the whipping lasso. He was roaring in a way that made all his former yells merely whispers. Starting to run, I tripped on a root, fell prone on my face into the ravine, and rolled over and over until I brought up with a bump against a rock.

What a tableau riveted my gaze! It staggered me so I did not think of my camera. I stood transfixed not fifteen feet from the cougar. She sat on her haunches with body well drawn back by the taut lasso to which Jones held tightly. Don was standing up with her, upheld by the hooked claws in his head. The cougar had her paws outstretched; her mouth open wide, showing long, cruel, white fangs; she was trying to pull the head of the dog to her. Don held back with all his power, and so did Jones. Moze and Sounder were tussling round her body. Suddenly both ears of the dog pulled out, slit into ribbons. Don had never uttered a sound, and once free, he made at her again with open jaws. One blow sent him reeling and stunned. Then began again that wrestling whirl.

'Beat off the dogs! Beat off the dogs!' roared Jones. 'She'll kill them! She'll kill them!'

Frank and I seized clubs and ran in upon the confused furry mass, forgetful of peril to ourselves. In the wild contagion of such a savage moment the minds of men revert wholly to primitive instincts. We swung our clubs and yelled; we fought all over the bottom of the ravine, crashing through the bushes, over logs and stones. I actually felt the soft fur of the cougar at one fleeting instant. The dogs had the strength born of insane fighting spirit. At last we pulled them to where Don lay, half-stunned, and with an arm tight round each, I held them while Frank turned to help Jones.

The disheveled Jones, bloody, grim as death, his heavy jaw locked, stood holding to the lasso. The cougar, her sides shaking with short, quick pants, crouched low on the ground with eyes of purple fire.

'For God's sake, get a half-hitch on the saplin'!' called the cowboy.

His quick grasp of the situation averted a tragedy. Jones was nearly exhausted, even as he was beyond thinking for himself or giving up. The cougar sprang, a yellow, frightful flash. Even as she was in the air, Jones took a quick step to one side and dodged as he threw his lasso round the sapling. She missed him, but one alarmingly outstretched paw grazed his shoulder. A twist of Jones's big hand fastened the lasso—and Kitty was a prisoner. While she fought, rolled, twisted, bounded, whirled, writhed with hissing, snarling fury, Jones sat mopping the sweat and blood from his face.

Kitty's efforts were futile; she began to weaken from the choking. Jones took another rope, and tightening a noose around her back paws, which he lassoed as she rolled over, he stretched her out. She began to contract her supple body, gave a savage, convulsive spring, which pulled Jones flat on the ground, then the terrible wrestling started again. The lasso slipped over her back paws. She leaped the whole length of the other lasso. Jones caught it and fastened it more securely; but this precaution proved unnecessary, for she suddenly sank down either exhausted or choked, and gasped with her tongue hanging out. Frank slipped the second noose over her back paws, and Jones did likewise with a third lasso over her right front paw. These lassoes Jones tied to different saplings.

'Now you are a good Kitty,' said Jones, kneeling by her. He took a pair of clippers from his hip pocket, and grasping a paw in his powerful fist he calmly clipped the points of the dangerous claws. This done, he called to me to get the collar and chain that were tied to his saddle. I procured them and hurried back. Then the old buffalo hunter loosened the lasso which was round her neck, and as soon as she could move her head, he teased her to bite a club. She broke two good sticks with her sharp teeth, but the third, being solid, did not break. While she was chewing it Jones forced her head back and placed his heavy knee on the club. In a twinkling he had strapped the collar round her neck. The chain he made fast to the sapling. After removing the club from her mouth he placed his knee on her neck, and while her head was in this helpless position he dexterously slipped a loop of thick copper wire over her nose, pushed it back and twisted it tight.

Following this, all done with speed and precision, he took from his pocket a piece of steel rod, perhaps one-quarter of an inch thick, and five inches long. He pushed this between Kitty's jaws, just back of her great white fangs, and in front of the copper wire. She had been shorn of her sharp weapons; she was muzzled, bound, helpless, an object to pity.

Lastly Jones removed the three lassoes. Kitty slowly gathered her lissom body in a ball and lay panting, with the same brave wildfire in her eyes. Jones stroked her black-tipped ears and ran his hand down her glossy fur. All the time he had kept up a low monotone, talking to her in the strange language he used toward animals. Then he rose to his feet.

'We'll go back to camp now, and get a pack-saddle and horse,' he said. 'She'll be safe here. We'll rope her again, tie her up, throw her over a pack-saddle, and take her to camp.'

To my utter bewilderment the hounds suddenly commenced fighting among themselves. Of all the vicious bloody dog-fights I ever saw that was the worst. I began to belabor them with a club, and Frank sprang to my assistance. Beating had no apparent effect. We broke a dozen sticks, and then Frank grappled with Moze and I with Sounder. Don kept on fighting either one till Jones secured him. Then we all took a rest, panting and weary.

'What's it mean?' I ejaculated, appealing to Jones.

'Jealous, that's all. Jealous over the lion.'

We all remained seated, men and hounds, a sweaty, dirty, bloody, ragged group. I discovered I was sorry for Kitty. I forgot all the carcasses of deer and horses, the brutality of this species of cat; and even forgot the grim, snarling yellow devil that had leaped at me. Kitty was beautiful and helpless. How brave she was, too! No sign of fear shone in her wonderful eyes, only hate, defiance, watchfulness.

On the ride back to camp Jones expressed himself thus: 'How happy I am that I can keep this lion and the others we are going to capture, for my own! When I was in the Yellowstone Park I did not get to keep one of the many I captured. The military officials took them from me.'

When we reached camp Lawson was absent, but fortunately Old Baldy browsed near at hand, and was easily caught. Frank said he would rather take Old Baldy for the cougar than any other horse we had. Leaving me in camp, he and Jones rode off to fetch Kitty.

About five o'clock they came trotting up through the forest with Jim, who had fallen in with them on the way. Old Baldy had remained true to his fame—nothing, not even a cougar bothered him. Kitty, evidently no worse for her experience, was chained to a pine tree about fifty feet from the campfire.

Wallace came riding wearily in, and when he saw the captive, he greeted us with an exultant yell. He got there just in time to see the first special features of Kitty's captivity. The hounds surrounded her, and could not be called off. We had to beat them. Whereupon the six jealous canines fell to fighting among themselves, and fought so savagely as to be deaf to our cries and insensible to blows. They had to be torn apart and chained.

About six o'clock Lawson loped in with the horses. Of course he did not know we had a cougar, and no one seemed interested enough to inform him. Perhaps only Frank and I thought of it; but I saw a merry snap in Frank's eyes, and kept silent. Kitty had hidden behind the pine tree. Lawson, astride Jim's pack horse, a crochety animal, reined in just abreast of the tree, and leisurely threw his leg over the saddle. Kitty leaped out to the extent of her chain, an fairly exploded in a frightful cat-spit.

Lawson had stated some time before that he was afraid of cougars, which was a weakness he need not have divulged in view of what happened. The horse plunged, throwing him ten feet, and snorting in terror, stampeded with the rest of the bunch and disappeared among the pines.

'Why the hell didn't you tell a feller?' reproachfully growled the Arizonian. Frank and Jim held each other upright, and the rest of us gave way to as hearty if not as violent mirth.

We had a gay supper, during which Kitty sat by her pine and watched our every movement.

'We'll rest up for a day or two,' said Jones. 'Things have commenced to come our way. If I'm not mistaken we'll bring an old Tom alive into camp. But it would never do for us to get a big Tom in the fix we had Kitty to-day. You see, I wanted to lasso her front paw, pull her off the limb, tie my end of the lasso to the tree, and while she hung I'd go down and rope her hind paws. It all went wrong to-day, and was as tough a job as I ever handled.'

Not until late next morning did Lawson corral all the horses. That day we lounged in camp mending broken bridles, saddles, stirrups, lassoes, boots, trousers, leggins, shirts and even broken skins.

During this time I found Kitty a most interesting study. She reminded me of an enormous yellow kitten. She did not appear wild or untamed until approached. Then she slowly sank down, laid back her ears, opened her mouth and hissed and spat, at the same time throwing both paws out viciously. Kitty may have rested, but did not sleep. At times she fought her chain, tugging and straining at it, and trying to bite it through. Everything in reach she clawed, particularly the bark of the tree. Once she tried to hang herself by leaping over a low limb. When any one walked by her she crouched low, evidently imagining herself unseen. If one of us walked toward her, or looked at her, she did not crouch. At other times, noticeably when no one was near, she would roll on her back and extend all four paws in the air. Her actions were beautiful, soft, noiseless, quick and subtle.

The day passed, as all days pass in camp, swiftly and pleasantly, and twilight stole down upon us round the ruddy fire. The wind roared in the pines and lulled to repose; the lonesome, friendly coyote barked; the bells on the hobbled horses jingled sweetly; the great watch stars blinked out of the blue.

The red glow of the burning logs lighted up Jones's calm, cold face. Tranquil, unalterable and peaceful it seemed; yet beneath the peace I thought I saw a suggestion of wild restraint, of mystery, of unslaked life.

Strangely enough, his next words confirmed my last thought.

'For forty years I've had an ambition. It's to get possession of an island in the Pacific, somewhere between Vancouver and Alaska, and then go to Siberia and capture a lot of Russian sables. I'd put them on the island and cross them with our silver foxes. I'm going to try it next year if I can find the time.'

The ruling passion and character determine our lives. Jones was sixty-three years old, yet the thing that had ruled and absorbed his mind was still as strong as the longing for freedom in Kitty's wild heart.

Hours after I had crawled into my sleeping-bag, in the silence of night I heard her working to get free. In darkness she was most active, restless, intense. I heard the clink of her chain, the crack of her teeth, the scrape of her claws. How tireless she was. I recalled the wistful light in her eyes that saw, no doubt, far beyond the campfire to the yellow crags, to the great downward slopes, to freedom. I slipped my elbow out of the bag and raised myself. Dark shadows were hovering under the pines. I saw Kitty's eyes gleam like sparks, and I seemed to see in them the hate, the fear, the terror she had of the clanking thing that bound her.

I shivered, perhaps from the cold night wind which moaned through the pines; I saw the stars glittering pale and far off, and under their wan light the still, set face of Jones, and blanketed forms of my other companions.

The last thing I remembered before dropping into dreamless slumber was hearing a bell tinkle in the forest, which I recognized as the one I had placed on Satan.

17
Conclusion

Kitty was not the only cougar brought into camp alive. The ensuing days were fruitful of cougars and adventure. There were more wild rides to the music of the baying hounds, and more heart-breaking cañon slopes to conquer, and more swinging, tufted tails and snarling savage faces in the piñons. Once again, I am sorry to relate, I had to glance down the sights of the little Remington, and I saw blood on the stones. Those eventful days sped by all too soon.

When the time for parting came it took no little discussion to decide on the quickest way of getting me to a railroad. I never fully appreciated the inaccessibility of the Siwash until the question arose of finding a way out. To return on our back trail would require two weeks, and to go out by the trail north to Utah meant half as much time over the same kind of desert. Lawson came to our help, however, with the information that an occasional prospector or horse hunter crossed the cañon from the Saddle, where a trail led down to the river.

'I've heard the trail is a bad one,' said Lawson, 'an' though I never seen it, I reckon it could be found. After we get to the Saddle we'll build two fires on one of the high points an' keep them burnin' well after dark. If Mr Bass, who lives on the other side, sees the fires he'll come down his trail next mornin' an' meet us at the river. He keeps a boat there. This is takin' a chance, but I reckon it's worth while.'

So it was decided that Lawson and Frank would try to get me out by way of the cañon; Wallace intended to go by the Utah route, and Jones was to return at once to his range and his buffalo.

That night round the campfire we talked over the many incidents of the hunt. Jones stated he had never in his life come so near getting his 'everlasting' as when the big bay horse tripped on a cañon slope and rolled over him. Notwithstanding the respect with which we regarded his statement we held different opinions. Then, with the unfailing optimism of hunters, we planned another hunt for the next year.

'I'll tell you what,' said Jones. 'Up in Utah there's a wild region called Pink Cliffs. A few poor sheep-herders try to raise sheep in the valleys. They wouldn't be so poor if it was not for the grizzly and black bears that live on the sheep. We'll go up there, find a place where grass and water can be had, and camp. We'll notify the sheep-herders we are there for business. They'll be only too glad to hustle in with news of a bear, and we can get the hounds on the trail by sun-up. I'll have a dozen hounds then, maybe twenty, and all trained. We'll put every black bear we chase up a tree, and we'll rope and tie him. As to grizzlies—well, I'm not saying so much. They can't climb trees, and they are not afraid of a pack of hounds. If we rounded up a grizzly, got him cornered, and threw a rope on him—there'd be some fun, eh, Jim?'

'Shore there would,' Jim replied.

On the strength of this I stored up food for future thought and thus reconciled myself to bidding farewell to the purple cañons and shaggy slopes of Buckskin Mountain.

At five o'clock next morning we were all stirring. Jones yelled at the hounds and untangled Kitty's chain. Jim was already busy with the biscuit dough. Frank shook the frost off the saddles. Wallace was packing. The merry jangle of bells came from the forest, and presently Lawson appeared driving in the horses. I caught my black and saddled him, then realizing we were soon to part I could not resist giving him a hug.

An hour later we all stood at the head of the trail leading down into the chasm. The east gleamed rosy red. Powell's Plateau loomed up in the distance, and under it showed the dark-fringed dip in the rim called the Saddle. Blue mist floated round the mesas and domes.

Lawson led the way down the trail. Frank started Old Baldy with the pack.

'Come,' he called, 'be oozin' along.'

I spoke the last good-by and turned Satan into the narrow trail. When I looked back Jones stood on the rim with the fresh glow of dawn shining on his face. The trail was steep, and claimed my attention and care, but time and time again I gazed back. Jones waved his hand till a huge jutting cliff walled him from view. Then I cast my eyes on the rough descent and the wonderful void beneath me. In my mind lingered a pleasing consciousness of my last sight of the old plainsman. He fitted the scene; he belonged there among the silent pines and the yellow crags.

LONE STAR RANGER

To
CAPTAIN JOHN HUGHES
and his Texas Rangers

It may seem strange to you that out of all the stories I heard on the Rio Grande I should choose as first that of Buck Duane—outlaw and gunman.

But, indeed, Ranger Coffee's story of the last of the Duanes has haunted me, and I have given full rein to imagination and have retold it in my own way. It deals with the old law—the old border days—therefore it is better first. Soon, perchance, I shall have the pleasure of writing of the border of to-day, which in Joe Sitter's laconic speech, 'Shore is 'most as bad an' wild as ever!'

In the North and East there is a popular idea that the frontier of the West is a thing long past, and remembered now only in stories. As I think of this I remember Ranger Sitter when he made that remark, while he grimly stroked an unhealed bullet wound. And I remember the giant Vaughn, that typical son of stalwart Texas, sitting there quietly with bandaged head, his thoughtful eye boding ill to the outlaw who had ambushed him. Only a few months have passed since then—when I had my memorable sojourn with you—and yet, in that short time, Russell and Moore have crossed the Divide, like Rangers.

Gentlemen,—I have the honor to dedicate this book to you, and the hope that it shall fall to my lot to tell the world the truth about a strange, unique, and misunderstood body of men—the Texas Rangers—who made the great Lone Star State habitable, who never know peaceful rest and sleep, who are passing, who surely will not be forgotten and will some day come into their own.

Zane Grey

BOOK I
THE OUTLAW

1

So it was in him, then—an inherited fighting instinct, a driving intensity to kill. He was the last of the Duanes, that old fighting stock of Texas. But not the memory of his dead father, nor the pleading of his soft-voiced mother, nor the warning of this uncle who stood before him now, had brought to Buck Duane so much realization of the dark passionate strain in his blood. It was the recurrence, a hundredfold increased in power, of a strange emotion that for the last three years had arisen in him.

'Yes, Cal Bain's in town, full of bad whisky an' huntin' for you,' repeated the elder man, gravely.

'It's the second time,' muttered Duane, as if to himself.

'Son, you can't avoid a meetin'. Leave town till Cal sobers up. He ain't got it in for you when he's not drinkin'.'

'But what's he want me for?' demanded Duane. 'To insult me again? I won't stand that twice.'

'He's got a fever that's rampant in Texas these days, my boy. He wants gun-play. If he meets you he'll try to kill you.'

Here it stirred in Duane again, that bursting gush of blood, like a wind of flame shaking all his inner being, and subsiding to leave him strangely chilled.

'Kill me! What for?' he asked.

'Lord knows there ain't any reason. But what's that to do with most of the shootin' these days? Didn't five cowboys over to Everall's kill one another dead all because they got to jerkin' at a quirt among themselves? An' Cal has no reason to love you. His girl was sweet on you.'

'I quit when I found out she was his girl.'

'I reckon she ain't quit. But never mind her or reasons. Cal's here, just drunk enough to be ugly. He's achin' to kill somebody. He's one of them four-flush gun-fighters. He'd like to be thought bad. There's a lot of wild cowboys who're ambitious for a reputation. They talk about how quick they are on the draw. They ape Bland an' King Fisher an' Hardin an' all the big outlaws. They make threats about joinin' the gangs along the Rio Grande. They laugh at the sheriffs an' brag about how they'd fix the rangers. Cal's sure not much for you to bother with, if you only keep out of his way.'

'You mean for me to run?' asked Duane, in scorn.

'I reckon I wouldn't put it that way. Just avoid him. Buck, I'm not afraid Cal would get you if you met down there in town. You've your father's eye an' his slick hand with a gun. What I'm most afraid of is that you'll kill Bain.'

Duane was silent, letting his uncle's earnest words sink in, trying to realize their significance.

'If Texas ever recovers from that fool war an' kills off these outlaws, why, a young man will have a lookout,' went on the uncle. 'You're twenty-three now, an' a powerful sight of a fine fellow, barrin' your temper. You've a chance in life. But if you go gun-fightin', if you kill a man, you're ruined. Then you'll kill another. It'll be the same old story. An' the rangers would make you an outlaw. The rangers mean law an' order for Texas. This even-break business doesn't work with them. If you resist arrest they'll kill you. If you submit to arrest, then you go to jail, an' mebbe you hang.'

'I'd never hang,' muttered Duane, darkly.

'I reckon you wouldn't,' replied the old man. 'You'd be like your father. He was ever ready to draw—too ready. In times like these, with the Texas rangers enforcin' the law, your Dad would have been driven to the river. An', son, I'm afraid you're a chip off the old block. Can't you hold in—keep your temper—run away from trouble? Because it'll only result in you gettin' the worst of it in the end. Your father was killed in a street-fight. An' it was told of him that he shot twice after a bullet had passed through his heart. Think of the terrible nature of a man to be able to do that. If you have any such blood in you, never give it a chance.'

'What you say is all very well, uncle,' returned Duane, 'but the only way out for me is to run, and I won't do it. Cal Bain and his outfit have already made me look like a coward. He says I'm afraid to come out and face him. A man simply can't stand that in this country. Besides, Cal would shoot me in the back some day if I didn't face him.'

'Well, then, what're you goin' to do?' inquired the elder man.

'I haven't decided—yet.'

'No, but you're comin' to it mighty fast. That damned spell is workin' in you. You're different today. I remember how you used to be moody an' lose your temper an' talk wild. Never was much afraid of you then. But now you're gettin' cool an' quiet, an' you think deep, an' I don't like the light in your eye. It reminds me of your father.'

'I wonder what Dad would say to me to-day if he were alive and here,' said Duane.

'What do you think? What could you expect of a man who never wore a glove on his right hand for twenty years?'

'Well, he'd hardly have said much. Dad never talked. But he would have done a lot. And I guess I'll go down-town and let Cal Bain find me.'

Then followed a long silence, during which Duane sat with downcast eyes, and the uncle appeared lost in sad thought of the future. Presently he turned to Duane with an expression that denoted resignation, and yet a spirit which showed wherein they were of the same blood.

'You've got a fast horse—the fastest I know of in this country. After you meet Bain hurry back home. I'll have a saddle-bag packed for you and the horse ready.'

With that he turned on his heel and went into the house, leaving Duane to revolve in his mind his singular speech. Buck wondered presently if he shared his uncle's opinion of the result of a meeting between himself and Bain. His thoughts were vague. But on the instant of final decision, when he had settled with himself that he would meet Bain, such a storm of passion assailed him that he felt as if he was being shaken with ague. Yet it was all internal, inside his breast, for his hand was like a rock and, for all he could see, not a muscle about him quivered. He had no fear of Bain or of any other man; but a vague fear of himself, of this strange force in him, made him ponder and shake his head. It was as if he had not all to say in this matter. There appeared to have been in him a reluctance to let himself go, and some voice, some spirit from a distance, something he was not accountable for, had compelled him. That hour of Duane's life was like years of actual living, and in it he became a thoughtful man.

He went into the house and buckled on his belt and gun. The gun was a Colt .45, six-shot, and heavy, with an ivory handle. He had packed it, on and off, for five years. Before that it had been used by his father. There were a number of notches filed in the bulge of the ivory handle. This gun was the one his father had fired twice after being shot through the heart, and his hand had stiffened so tightly upon it in the death-grip that his fingers had to be pried open. It had never been drawn upon any man since it had come into Duane's possession. But the cold, bright polish of the weapon showed how it had been used. Duane could draw it with inconceivable rapidity, and at twenty feet he could split a card pointing edgewise toward him.

Duane wished to avoid meeting his mother. Fortunately, as he thought, she was away from home. He went out and down the path toward the gate. The air was full of the fragrance of blossoms and the melody of birds. Outside in the road a neighbor woman stood talking to a countryman in a wagon; they spoke to him; and he heard, but did not reply. Then he began to stride down the road toward the town.

Wellston was a small town, but important in that unsettled part of the great state because it was the trading-center of several hundred miles of territory. On the main street there were perhaps fifty buildings, some brick, some frame, mostly adobe, and one-third of the lot, and by far the most prosperous, were saloons. From the road Duane turned into this street. It was a wide thoroughfare lined by hitching-rails and saddled horses and vehicles of various kinds. Duane's eye ranged down the street, taking in all at a glance, particularly persons moving leisurely up and down. Not a cowboy was in sight. Duane slackened his stride, and by the time he reached Sol White's place, which was the first saloon, he was walking slowly. Several people spoke to him and turned to look back after they had passed. He paused at the door of White's saloon, took a sharp survey of the interior, then stepped inside.

The saloon was large and cool, full of men and noise and smoke. The noise ceased upon his entrance, and the silence ensuing presently broke to the clink of Mexican silver dollars at a *monte* table. Sol White, who was behind the bar, straightened up when he saw Duane; then, without speaking, he bent over to rinse a glass. All eyes except those of the Mexican gamblers were turned upon Duane; and these glances were keen, speculative, questioning. These men knew Bain was looking for trouble; they probably had heard his boasts. But what did Duane intend to do? Several of the cowboys and ranchers present exchanged glances. Duane had been weighed by unerring Texas instinct, by men who all packed guns. The boy was the son of his father. Whereupon they greeted him and returned to their drinks and cards. Sol White stood with his big red hands out upon the bar; he was a tall, raw-boned Texan with a long mustache waxed to sharp points.

'Howdy, Buck,' was his greeting to Duane. He spoke carelessly and averted his dark gaze for an instant.

'Howdy, Sol,' replied Duane, slowly. 'Say, Sol, I hear there's a gent in town looking for me bad.'

'Reckon there is, Buck,' replied White. 'He came in heah aboot an hour ago. Shore he was some riled an' a-roarin' for gore. Told me confidential a certain party had given you a white silk scarf, an' he was hell-bent on wearin' it home spotted red.'

'Anybody with him?' queried Duane.

'Burt an' Sam Outcalt an' a little cowpuncher I never seen before. They-all was coaxin' him to leave town. But he's looked on the flowin' glass, Buck, an' he's heah for keeps.'

'Why doesn't Sheriff Oaks lock him up if he's that bad?'

'Oaks went away with the rangers. There's been another raid at Flesher's ranch. The King Fisher gang, likely. An' so the town's shore wide open.'

Duane stalked outdoors and faced down the street. He walked the whole length of the long block, meeting many people—farmers, ranchers, clerks, merchants, Mexicans, cowboys, and women. It was a singular fact that when he turned to retrace his steps the street was almost empty. He had not returned a hundred yards on his way when the street was wholly deserted. A few heads protruded from doors and around corners. That main street of Wellston saw some such situation every few days. If it was an instinct for Texans to fight, it was also instinctive for them to sense with remarkable quickness the signs of a coming gun-play. Rumor could not fly so swiftly. In less than ten minutes everybody who had been on the street or in the shops knew that Buck Duane had come forth to meet his enemy.

Duane walked on. When he came to within fifty paces of a saloon he swerved out into the middle of the street, stood there for a moment, then went ahead and back to the sidewalk. He passed on in this way the length of the block. Sol White was standing in the door of his saloon.

'Buck, I'm a-tippin' you off,' he said, quick and low-voiced. 'Cal Bain's over at Everall's. If he's a-huntin' you bad, as he brags, he'll show there.'

Duane crossed the street and started down. Notwithstanding White's statement Duane was wary and slow at every door. Nothing happened, and he traversed almost the whole length of the block without seeing a person. Everall's place was on the corner.

Duane knew himself to be cold, steady. He was conscious of a strange fury that made him want to leap ahead. He seemed to long for this encounter more than anything he had ever wanted. But, vivid as were his sensations, he felt as if in a dream.

Before he reached Everall's he heard loud voices, one of which was raised high. Then the short door swung outward as if impelled by a vigorous hand. A bow-legged cowboy wearing wooley chaps burst out upon the sidewalk. At sight of Duane he seemed to bound into the air, and he uttered a savage roar.

Duane stopped in his tracks at the outer edge of the sidewalk, perhaps a dozen rods from Everall's door.

If Bain was drunk he did not show it in his movement. He swaggered forward, rapidly closing up the gap. Red, sweaty, disheveled, and hatless, his face distorted and expressive of the most malignant intent, he was a wild and sinister figure. He had already killed a man, and this showed in his demeanor. His hands were extended before him, the right hand a little lower than the left. At every step he bellowed his rancor in speech, mostly curses. Gradually he slowed his walk, then halted. A good twenty-five paces separated the men.

'Won't nothin' make you draw, you—!' he shouted, fiercely.

'I'm waitin' on you, Cal,' replied Duane.

Bain's right hand stiffened—moved. Duane threw his gun as a boy throws a ball underhand—a draw his father had taught him. He pulled twice, his shots almost as one. Bain's big Colt boomed while it was pointed downward and he was falling. His bullet scattered dust and gravel at Duane's feet. He fell loosely, without contortion.

In a flash all was reality for Duane. He went forward and held his gun ready for the slightest movement on the part of Bain. But Bain lay upon his back, and all that moved were his breast and his eyes. How strangely the red had left his face—and also the distortion! The devil that had showed in Bain was gone. He was sober and conscious. He tried to speak, but failed. His eyes expressed something pitifully human. They changed—rolled—set blankly.

Duane drew a deep breath and sheathed his gun. He felt calm and cool, glad the fray was over. One violent expression burst from him. 'The fool!'

When he looked up there were men around him. 'Plumb center,' said one.

Another, a cowboy who evidently had just left the gaming-table, leaned down and pulled open Bain's shirt. He had the ace of spades in his hand. He laid it on Bain's breast, and the black figure on the card covered the two bullet-holes just over Bain's heart.

Duane wheeled and hurried away. He heard another man say:

'Reckon Cal got what he deserved. Buck Duane's first gun-play. Like father like son!'

2

A thought kept repeating itself to Duane, and it was that he might have spared himself concern through his imagining how awful it would be to kill a man. He had no such feeling now. He had rid the community of a drunken, bragging, quarrelsome cowboy.

When he came to the gate of his home and saw his uncle there with a mettlesome horse, saddled, with canteen, rope, and bags all in place, a subtle shock pervaded his spirit. It had slipped his mind—the consequence of his act. But sight of the horse and the look of his uncle recalled the fact that he must now become a fugitive. An unreasonable anger took hold of him.

'The d—d fool!' he exclaimed, hotly. 'Meeting Bain wasn't much, Uncle Jim. He dusted my boots, that's all. And for that I've got to go on the dodge.'

'Son, you killed him—then?' asked the uncle, huskily.

'Yes. I stood over him—watched him die. I did as I would have been done by.'

'I knew it. Long ago I saw it comin'. But now we can't stop to cry over spilt blood. You've got to leave town an' this part of the country.'

'Mother!' exclaimed Duane.

'She's away from home. You can't wait. I'll break it to her—what she always feared.'

Suddenly Duane sat down and covered his face with his hands.

'My God! Uncle, what have I done?' His broad shoulders shook.

'Listen, son, an' remember what I say,' replied the elder man, earnestly. 'Don't ever forget. You're not to blame. I'm glad to see you take it this way, because maybe you'll never grow hard an' callous. You're not to blame. This is Texas. You're your father's son. These are wild times. The law as the rangers are laying it down now can't change life all in a minute. Even your mother, who's a good, true woman, has had her share in making you what you are this moment. For she was one of the pioneers—the fightin' pioneers of this state. Those years of wild times, before you was born, developed in her instinct to fight, to save her life, her children, an' that instinct has cropped out in you. It will be many years before it dies out of the boys born in Texas.'

'I'm a murderer,' said Duane, shuddering.

'No, son, you're not. An' you never will be. But you've got to be an outlaw till time makes it safe for you to come home.'

'An outlaw?'

'I said it. If we had money an' influence we'd risk a trial but we've neither. An' I reckon the scaffold or jail is no place for Buckley Duane. Strike for the wild country, an' wherever you go an' whatever you do—be a man. Live honestly, if that's possible. If it isn't, be as honest as you can. If you have to herd with outlaws try not to become bad. There are outlaws who're not all bad—many who have been driven to the river by such a deal as this you had. When you get among these men avoid brawls. Don't drink; don't gamble. I needn't tell you what to do if it comes to gun-play, as likely it will. You can't come home. When this thing is lived down, if that time ever comes, I'll get word into the unsettled country. It'll reach you some day. That's all. Remember, be a man. Goodby.'

Duane, with blurred sight and contracting throat, gripped his uncle's hand and bade him a wordless farewell. Then he leaped astride the black and rode out of town.

As swiftly as was consistent with a care for his steed, Duane put a distance of fifteen or eighteen miles behind him. With that he slowed up, and the matter of riding did not require all his faculties. He passed several ranches and was seen by men. This did not suit him, and he took an old trail across country. It was a flat region with a poor growth of mesquite and prickly-pear cactus. Occasionally he caught a glimpse of low hills in the distance. He had hunted often in that section, and knew where to find grass and water. When he reached this higher ground he did not, however, halt at the first favorable camping-spot, but went on and on. Once he came out upon the brow of a hill and saw a considerable stretch of country beneath him. It had the gray sameness characterizing all that he had traversed. He seemed to want to see wide spaces—to get a glimpse of the great wilderness lying somewhere beyond to the southwest. It was sunset when he decided to camp at a likely spot he came across. He led the horse to water, and then began searching through the shallow valley for a suitable place to camp. He passed by old camp-sites that he well remembered. These, however, did not strike his fancy this time, and the significance of the change in him did not occur at the moment. At last he found a secluded spot, under cover of thick mesquites and oaks, at a goodly distance from the old trail. He took saddle and pack off the horse. He looked among his effects for a hobble, and, finding that his uncle had failed to put one in, he suddenly remembered that he seldom used a hobble, and never on this horse. He cut a few feet off the end of his lasso and used that. The horse, unused to such hampering of his free movements, had to be driven out upon the grass.

Duane made a small fire, prepared and ate his supper. This done, ending the work of that day, he sat down and filled his pipe. Twilight had waned into dusk. A few wan stars had just begun to show and brighten. Above the low continuous hum of insects sounded the evening carol of robins. Presently the birds ceased their singing, and then the quiet was more noticeable. When night set in and the place seemed all the more isolated and lonely for that Duane had a sense of relief.

It dawned upon him all at once that he was nervous, watchful, sleepless. The fact caused him surprise, and he began to think back, to take note of his late actions and their motives. The change one day had wrought amazed him. He who had always been free, easy, happy, especially when out alone in the open, had become in a few short hours bound, serious, preoccupied. The silence that had once been sweet now meant nothing to him except a medium whereby he might the better hear the sounds of pursuit. The loneliness, the night, the wild, that had always been beautiful to him, now only conveyed a sense of safety for the present. He watched, he listened, he thought. He felt tired, yet had no inclination to rest. He intended to be off by dawn, heading toward the southwest. Had he a destination? It was vague as his knowledge of that great waste of mesquite and rock bordering the Rio Grande. Somewhere out there was a refuge. For he was a fugitive from justice, an outlaw.

This being an outlaw then meant eternal vigilance. No home, no rest, no sleep, no content, no life worth the living! He must be a lone wolf or he must herd among men obnoxious to him. If he worked for an honest living he still must hide his identity and take risks of detection. If he did not work on some distant outlying ranch, how was he to live? The idea of stealing was repugnant to him. The future seemed gray and somber enough. And he was twenty-three years old.

Why had this hard life been imposed upon him?

The bitter question seemed to start a strange iciness that stole along his veins.

What was wrong with him? He stirred the few sticks of mesquite into a last flickering blaze. He was cold, and for some reason he wanted some light. The black circle of darkness weighed down upon him, closed in around him. Suddenly he sat bolt upright and then froze in that position. He had heard a step. It was behind him—no—on the side. Some one was there. He forced his hand down to his gun, and the touch of cold steel was another icy shock. Then he waited. But all was silent—silent as only a wilderness arroyo can be, with its low murmuring of wind in the mesquite. Had he heard a step? He began to breathe again.

But what was the matter with the light of his camp-fire? It had taken on a strange green luster and seemed to be waving off into the outer shadows. Duane heard no step, saw no movement; nevertheless, there was another present at that camp-fire vigil. Duane saw him. He lay there in the middle of the green brightness, prostrate, motionless, dying. Cal Bain! His features were wonderfully distinct, clearer than any cameo, more sharply outlined than those of any picture. It was a hard face softening at the threshold of eternity. The red tan of sun, the coarse signs of drunkenness, the ferocity and hate so characteristic of Bain were no longer there. This face represented a different Bain, showed all that was human in him fading, fading as swiftly as it blanched white. The lips wanted to speak, but had not the power. The eyes held an agony of thought. They revealed what might have been possible for this man if he lived—that he saw his mistake too late. Then they rolled, set blankly, and closed in death.

That haunting visitation left Duane sitting there in a cold sweat, a remorse gnawing at his vitals, realizing the curse that was on him. He divined that never would he be able to keep off that phantom. He remembered how his father had been eternally pursued by the furies of accusing guilt, how he had never been able to forget in work or in sleep those men he had killed.

The hour was late when Duane's mind let him sleep, and then dreams troubled him. In the morning he bestirred himself so early that in the gray gloom he had difficulty in finding his horse. Day had just broken when he struck the old trail again.

He rode hard all morning and halted in a shady spot to rest and graze his horse. In the afternoon he took to the trail at an easy trot. The country grew wilder. Bald, rugged mountains broke the level of the monotonous horizon. About three in the afternoon he came to a little river which marked the boundary line of his hunting territory.

The decision he made to travel up-stream for a while was owing to two facts: the river was high with quicksand bars on each side, and he felt reluctant to cross into that region where his presence alone meant that he was a marked man. The bottom-lands through which the river wound to the southwest were more inviting than the barrens he had traversed. The rest of that day he rode leisurely up-stream.

At sunset he penetrated the brakes of willow and cottonwood to spend the night. It seemed to him that in his lonely cover he would feel easy and content. But he did not. Every feeling, every imagining he had experienced the previous night returned somewhat more vividly and accentuated by newer ones of the same intensity and color.

In this kind of travel and camping he spent three more days, during which he crossed a number of trails, and one road where cattle—stolen cattle, probably— had recently passed. Thus time exhausted his supply of food, except salt, pepper, coffee, and sugar, of which he had a quantity. There were deer in the brakes; but, as he could not get close enough to kill them with a revolver, he had to satisfy himself with a rabbit. He knew he might as well content himself with the hard fare that assuredly would be his lot.

Somewhere up this river there was a village called Huntsville. It was distant about a hundred miles from Wellston, and had a reputation throughout south-western Texas. He had never been there. The fact was this reputation was such that honest travelers gave the town a wide berth. Duane had considerable money for him in his possession, and he concluded to visit Huntsville, if he could find it, and buy a stock of provisions.

The following day, toward evening, he happened upon a road which he believed might lead to the village. There were a good many fresh horse-tracks in the sand, and these made him thoughtful. Nevertheless, he followed the road, proceeding cautiously. He had not gone very far when the sound of rapid hoof-beats caught his ears. They came from his rear. In the darkening twilight he could not see any great distance back along the road. Voices, however, warned him that these riders, whoever they were, had approached closer than he liked. To go father down the road was not to be thought of, so he turned a little way in among the mesquites and halted, hoping to escape being seen or heard. As he was now a fugitive, it seemed every man was his enemy and pursuer.

The horsemen were fast approaching. Presently they were abreast of Duane's position, so near that he could hear the creak of saddles, the clink of spurs.

'Shore he crossed the river below,' said one man.

'I reckon you're right, Bill. He's slipped us,' replied another.

Rangers or a posse of ranchers in pursuit of a fugitive! The knowledge gave Duane a strange thrill. Certainly they could not have been hunting him. But the feeling their proximity gave him was identical to what it would have been had he been this particular hunted man. He held his breath; he clenched his teeth; he pressed a quieting hand upon his horse. Suddenly he became aware that these horsemen had halted. They were whispering. He could just make out a dark group closely massed. What had made them halt so suspiciously?

'You're wrong, Bill,' said a man, in a low but distinct voice. 'The idee of hearin' a hoss heave. You're wuss'n a ranger. An' you're hell-bent on killin' that rustler. Now I say let's go home an' eat.'

'Wal, I'll just take a look at the sand,' replied the man called Bill.

Duane heard the clink of spurs on steel stirrup and the thud of boots on the ground. There followed a short silence which was broken by a sharply breathed exclamation.

Duane waited for no more. They had found his trail. He spurred his horse straight into the brush. At the second crashing bound there came yells from the road, and then shots. Duane heard the hiss of a bullet close by his ear, and as it struck a branch it made a peculiar singing sound. These shots and the proximity of that lead missile roused in Duane a quick, hot resentment which mounted into a passion almost ungovernable. He must escape, yet it seemed that he did not care whether he did or not. Something grim kept urging him to halt and return the fire of these men. After running a couple of hundred yards he raised himself from over the pommel, where he had bent to avoid the stinging branches, and tried to guide his horse. In the dark shadows under mesquites and cottonwoods he was hard put to it to find open passage; however, he succeeded so well and made such little noise that gradually he drew away from his pursuers. The sound of their horses crashing through the thickets died away. Duane reined in and listened. He had distanced them. Probably they would go into camp till daylight, then follow his tracks. He started on again, walking his horse, and peered sharply at the ground, so that he might take advantage of the first trail he crossed. It seemed a long while until he came upon one. He followed it until a late hour, when, striking the willow brakes again and hence the neighborhood of the river, he picketed his horse and lay down to rest. But he did not sleep. His mind bitterly revolved the fate that had come upon him. He made efforts to think of other things, but in vain. Every moment he expected the chill, the sense of loneliness that yet was ominous of a strange visitation, the peculiarly imagined lights and shades of the night—these things that presaged the coming of Cal Bain. Doggedly Duane fought against the insidious phantom. He kept telling himself that it was just imagination, that it would wear off in time. Still in his heart he did not believe what he hoped. But he would not give up; he would not accept the ghost of his victim as a reality.

Gray dawn found him in the saddle again headed for the river. Half an hour of riding brought him to the dense chaparral and willow thickets. These he threaded to come at length to the ford. It was a gravel bottom, and therefore an easy crossing. Once upon the opposite shore he reined in his horse and looked darkly back. This action marked his acknowledgment of his situation: he had voluntarily sought the refuge of the outlaws; he was beyond the pale. A bitter and passionate curse passed his lips as he spurred his horse into the brakes on that alien shore.

He rode perhaps twenty miles, not sparing his horse nor caring whether or not he left a plain trail.

'Let them hunt me!' he muttered.

When the heat of the day began to be oppressive, and hunger and thirst made themselves manifest, Duane began to look about him for a place to halt for the noon-hours. The trail led into a road which was hard packed and smooth from the tracks of cattle. He doubted not that he had come across one of the roads used by border raiders. He headed into it, and had scarcely traveled a mile when, turning a curve, he came point-blank upon a single horseman riding toward him. Both riders wheeled their mounts sharply and were ready to run and shoot back. Not more than a hundred paces separated them. They stood then for a moment watching each other.

'Mawnin', stranger,' called the man, dropping his hand from his hip.

'Howdy,' replied Duane, shortly.

They rode toward each other, closing half the gap, then they halted again.

'I seen you ain't no ranger,' called the rider, 'an' shore I ain't none.'

He laughed loudly, as if he had made a joke.

'How'd you know I wasn't a ranger?' asked Duane, curiously. Somehow he had instantly divined that this horseman was no officer, or even a rancher trailing stolen stock.

'Wal,' said the fellow, starting his horse forward at a walk, 'a ranger'd never git ready to run the other way from one man.'

He laughed again. He was small and wiry, slouchy of attire, and armed to the teeth, and he bestrode a fine bay horse. He had quick, dancing brown eyes, at once frank and bold, and a coarse, bronzed face. Evidently he was a good-natured ruffian.

Duane acknowledged the truth of the assertion, and turned over in his mind how shrewdly the fellow had guessed him to be a hunted man.

'My name's Luke Stevens, an' I hail from the river. Who're you?' said this stranger.

Duane was silent.

'I reckon you're Buck Duane,' went on Stevens. 'I heerd you was a damn bad man with a gun.'

This time Duane laughed, not at the doubtful compliment, but at the idea that the first outlaw he met should know him. Here was proof of how swiftly facts about gun-play traveled on the Texas border.

'Wal, Buck,' said Stevens, in a friendly manner, 'I ain't presumin' on your time or company. I see you're headin' fer the river. But will you stop long enough to stake a feller to a bit of grub?'

'I'm out of grub, and pretty hungry myself,' admitted Duane.

'Been pushin' your hoss, I see. Wal, I reckon you'd better stock up before you hit thet stretch of country.'

He made a wide sweep of his right arm, indicating the southwest, and there was that in his action which seemed significant of a vast and barren region.

'Stock up?' queried Duane, thoughtfully.

'Shore. A feller has jest got to eat. I can rustle along without whisky, but not without grub. Thet's what makes it so embarrassin' travelin' these parts dodgin' your shadow. Now, I'm on my way to Mercer. It's a little two-bit town up the river a ways. I'm goin' to pack out some grub.'

Stevens's tone was inviting. Evidently he would welcome Duane's companionship, but he did not openly say so. Duane kept silence, however, and then Stevens went on.

'Stranger, in this here country two's a crowd. It's safer. I never was much on this lone-wolf dodgin', though I've done it of necessity. It takes a damn good man to travel alone any length of time. Why, I've been thet sick I was jest achin' fer some ranger to come along an' plug me. Give me a pardner any day. Now, mebbe you're not thet kind of a feller, an' I'm shore not presumin' to ask. But I just declares myself sufficient.'

'You mean you'd like me to go with you?' asked Duane.

Stevens grinned. 'Wal, I should smile. I'd be particular proud to be braced with a man of your reputation.'

'See here, my good fellow, that's all nonsense,' declared Duane, in some haste.

'Shore I think modesty becomin' to a youngster,' replied Stevens. 'I hate a brag. An' I've no use fer these four-flush cowboys thet 're always lookin' fer trouble an' talkin' gun-play. Buck, I don't know much about you. But every man who's lived along the Texas border remembers a lot about your Dad. It was expected of you, I reckon, an' much of your rep was established before you throwed your gun. I jest heerd thet you was lightnin' on the draw, an' when you cut loose with a gun, why the figger on the ace of spaces would cover your cluster of bullet-holes. Thet's the word thet's gone down the border. It's the kind of reputation most sure to fly far and swift ahead of a man in this country. An' the safest, too; I'll gamble on thet. It's the land of the draw. I see now you're only a boy, though you're shore a strappin' husky one. Now, Buck, I'm not a spring chicken, an' I've been long on the dodge. Mebbe a little of my society won't hurt you none. You'll need to learn the country.'

There was something sincere and likable about this outlaw.

'I dare say you're right,' replied Duane, quietly. 'And I'll go to Mercer with you.'

Next moment he was riding down the road with Stevens. Duane had never been much of a talker, and now he found speech difficult. But his companion did not seem to mind that. He was a jocose, voluble fellow, probably glad now to hear the sound of his own voice. Duane listened, and sometimes he thought with a pang of the distinction of name and heritage of blood his father had left to him.

3

Late that day, a couple of hours before sunset, Duane and Stevens, having rested their horses in the shade of some mesquites near the town of Mercer, saddled up and prepared to move.

'Buck, as we're lookin fer grub, an' not trouble, I reckon you'd better hang up out here,' Stevens was saying, as he mounted. 'You see, towns an' sheriffs an' rangers are always lookin' fer new fellers gone bad. They sort of forget most of the old boys, except those as are plumb bad. Now, nobody in Mercer will take notice of me. Reckon there's been a thousand men run into the river country to become outlaws since yours truly. You jest wait here an' be ready to ride hard. Mebbe my besettin' sin will go operatin' in spite of my good intentions. In which case there'll be—'

His pause was significant. He grinned, and his brown eyes danced with a kind of wild humor.

'Stevens, have you got any money?' asked Duane.

'Money!' exclaimed Luke, blankly. 'Say, I haven't owned a two-bit piece since—wal, fer some time.'

'I'll furnish money for grub,' returned Duane. 'And for whisky, too, providing you hurry back here—without making trouble.'

'Shore you're a downright good pard,' declared Stevens, in admiration, as he took the money. 'I give my word, Buck, an' I'm here to say I never broke it yet. Lay low, an' look fer me back quick.'

With that he spurred his horse and rode out of the mesquites toward the town. At that distance, about a quarter of a mile, Mercer appeared to be a cluster of low adobe houses set in a grove of cottonwoods. Pastures of alfalfa were dotted by horses and cattle. Duane saw a sheep-herder driving in a meager flock.

Presently Stevens rode out of sight into the town. Duane waited, hoping the outlaw would make good his word. Probably not a quarter of an hour had elapsed when Duane heard the clear reports of a Winchester rifle, the clatter of rapid hoof-beats, and yells unmistakably the kind to mean danger for a man like Stevens. Duane mounted and rode to the edge of the mesquites.

He saw a cloud of dust down the road and a bay horse running fast. Stevens apparently had not been wounded by any of the shots, for he had a steady seat in his saddle and his riding, even at the moment, struck Duane as admirable. He carried a large pack over the pommel, and he kept looking back. The shots had ceased, but the yells increased. Duane saw several men running and waving their arms. Then he spurred his horse and got into a swift stride, so Stevens would not pass him. Presently the outlaw caught up with him. Stevens was grinning, but there was now no fun in the dancing eyes. It was a devil that danced in them. His face seemed a shade paler.

'Was jest comin' out of the store,' yelled Stevens. 'Run plumb into a rancher—who knowed me. He opened up with a rifle. Think they'll chase us.'

They covered several miles before there were any signs of pursuit, and when horsemen did move into sight out of the cottonwoods Duane and his companion steadily drew farther away.

'No hosses in thet bunch to worry us,' called out Stevens.

Duane had the same conviction, and he did not look back again. He rode somewhat to the fore, and was constantly aware of the rapid thudding of hoofs behind, as Stevens kept close to him. At sunset they reached the willow brakes and the river. Duane's horse was winded and lashed with sweat and lather. It was not until the crossing had been accomplished that Duane halted to rest his animal. Stevens was riding up the low, sandy bank. He reeled in the saddle. With an exclamation of surprise Duane leaped off and ran to the outlaw's side.

Stevens was pale, and his face bore beads of sweat. The whole front of his shirt was soaked with blood.

'You're shot!' cried Duane.

'Wal, who'n hell said I wasn't? Would you mind givin' me a lift —on this here pack?'

Duane lifted the heavy pack down and then helped Stevens to dismount. The outlaw had a bloody foam on his lips, and he was spitting blood.

'Oh, why didn't you *say* so!' cried Duane. 'I never thought. You seemed all right.'

'Wal, Luke Stevens may be as gabby as an old woman, but sometimes he doesn't say anythin'. It wouldn't have done no good.'

Duane bade him sit down, removed his shirt, and washed the blood from his breast and back. Stevens had been shot in the breast, fairly low down, and the bullet had gone clear through him. His ride, holding himself and that heavy pack in the saddle, had been a feat little short of marvelous. Duane did not see how it had been possible, and he felt no hope for the outlaw. But he plugged the wounds and bound them tightly.

'Feller's name was Brown,' Stevens said. 'Me an' him fell out over a hoss I stole from him over in Huntsville. We had a shootin'-scrape then. Wal, as I was straddlin' my hoss back there in Mercer I seen this Brown, an' seen him before he seen me. Could have killed him, too. But I wasn't breakin' my word to you. I kind of hoped he wouldn't spot me. But he did—an' fust shot he got me here. What do you think of this hole?'

'It's pretty bad,' replied Duane; and he could not look the cheerful outlaw in the eyes.

'I reckon it is. Wal, I've had some bad wounds I lived over. Guess mebbe I can stand this one. Now, Buck, get me some place in the brakes, leave me some grub an' water at my hand, an' then you clear out.'

'Leave you here alone?' asked Duane, sharply.

'Shore. You see, I can't keep up with you. Brown an' his friends will foller us acrost the river a ways. You've got to think of number one in this game.'

'What would you do in my case?' asked Duane, curiously.

'Wal, I reckon I'd clear out an' save my hide,' replied Stevens.

Duane felt inclined to doubt the outlaw's assertion. For his own part he decided his conduct without further speech. First he watered the horses, filled canteens and water-bag, and then tied the pack upon his own horse. That done, he lifted Stevens upon his horse, and, holding him in the saddle, turned into the brakes, being careful to pick out hard or grassy ground that left little signs of tracks. Just about dark he ran across a trail that Stevens said was a good one to take into the wild country.

'Reckon we'd better keep right on in the dark—till I drop,' concluded Stevens, with a laugh.

All that night Duane, gloomy and thoughtful, attentive to the wounded outlaw, walked the trail and never halted till daybreak. He was tired then and very hungry. Stevens seemed in bad shape, although he was still spirited and cheerful. Duane made camp. The outlaw refused food, but asked for both whisky and water. Then he stretched out.

'Buck, will you take off my boots?' he asked, with a faint smile on his pallid face.

Duane removed them, wondering if the outlaw had the thought that he did not want to die with his boots on. Stevens seemed to read his mind.

'Buck, my old daddy used to say thet I was born to be hanged. But I wasn't—an' dyin' with your boots on is the next wust way to croak.'

'You've a chance to—to get over this,' said Duane.

'Shore. But I want to be correct about the boots—an' say, pard, if I do go over, jest you remember thet I was appreciatin' of your kindness.'

Then he closed his eyes and seemed to sleep.

Duane could not find water for the horses, but there was an abundance of dew-wet grass upon which he hobbled them. After that was done he prepared himself a much-needed meal. The sun was getting warm when he lay down to sleep, and when he awoke it was sinking in the west. Stevens was still alive, for he breathed heavily. The horses were in sight. All was quiet except the hum of insects in the brush. Duane listened awhile, then rose and went for the horses.

When he returned with them he found Stevens awake, bright-eyed, cheerful as usual, and apparently stronger.

'Wal, Buck, I'm still with you an' good fer another night's ride,' he said. 'Guess about all I need now is a big pull on thet bottle. Help me, will you? There! thet was bully. I ain't swallowin' my blood this evenin'. Mebbe I've bled all there was in me.'

While Duane got a hurried meal for himself, packed up the little outfit, and saddled the horses Stevens kept on talking. He seemed to be in a hurry to tell Duane all about the country. Another night ride would put them beyond fear of pursuit, within striking distance of the Rio Grande and the hiding-places of the outlaws.

When it came time for mounting the horses Stevens said, 'Reckon you can pull on my boots once more.' In spite of the laugh accompanying the words Duane detected a subtle change in the outlaw's spirit.

On this night travel was facilitated by the fact that the trail was broad enough for two horses abreast, enabling Duane to ride while upholding Stevens in the saddle.

The difficulty most persistent was in keeping the horses in a walk. They were used to a trot, and that kind of gait would not do for Stevens. The red died out of the west; a pale afterglow prevailed for a while; darkness set in; then the broad expanse of blue darkened and the stars brightened. After a while Stevens ceased talking and drooped in his saddle. Duane kept the horses going, however, and the slow hours wore away. Duane thought the quiet night would never break to dawn, that there was no end to the melancholy, brooding plain. But at length a grayness blotted out the stars and mantled the level of mesquite and cactus.

Dawn caught the fugitives at a green camping-site on the bank of a rocky little stream. Stevens fell a dead weight into Duane's arms, and one look at the haggard face showed Duane that the outlaw had taken his last ride. He knew it, too. Yet that cheerfulness prevailed.

'Buck, my feet are orful tired packin' them heavy boots,' he said, and seemed immensely relieved when Duane had removed them.

This matter of the outlaw's boots was strange, Duane thought. He made Stevens as comfortable as possible, then attended to his own needs. And the outlaw took up the thread of his conversation where he had left off the night before.

'This trail splits up a ways from here, an' every branch of it leads to a hole where you'll find men—a few, mebbe, like yourself—some like me—an' gangs of no-good hoss-thieves, rustlers, an' such. It's easy livin', Buck. I reckon, though, that you'll not find it easy. You'll never mix in. You'll be a lone wolf. I seen that right off. Wal, if a man can stand the loneliness, an' if he's quick on the draw, mebbe lone-wolfin' is the best. Shore I don't know. But these fellers in here will be suspicious of a man who goes it alone. If they get a chance they'll kill you.'

Stevens asked for water several times. He had forgotten or he did not want the whisky. His voice grew perceptibly weaker.

'Be quiet,' said Duane. 'Talking uses up your strength.'

'Aw, I'll talk till—I'm done,' he replied, doggedly. 'See here, pard, you can gamble on what I'm tellin' you. An' it'll be useful. From this camp we'll—you'll meet men right along. An' none of them will be honest men. All the same, some are better'n others. I've lived along the river for twelve years. There's three big gangs of outlaws. King Fisher—you know him, I reckon, fer he's half the time livin' among respectable folks. King is a pretty good feller. It'll do to tie up with him an' his gang. Now, there's Cheseldine, who hangs out in the Rim Rock way up the river. He's an outlaw chief. I never seen him, though I stayed once right in his camp. Late years he's got rich an' keeps back pretty well hid. But Bland—I knowed Bland fer years. An' I haven't any use fer him. Bland has the biggest gang. You ain't likely to miss strikin' his place sometime or other. He's got a regular town, I might say. Shore there's some gamblin' an' gun-fightin' goin' on at Bland's camp all the time. Bland has killed some twenty men, an' thet's not countin' greasers.'

Here Stevens took another drink and then rested for a while.

'You ain't likely to get on with Bland,' he resumed, presently. 'You're too strappin' big an' good-lookin' to please the chief. Fer he's got women in his camp. Then he'd be jealous of your possibilities with a gun. Shore I reckon he'd be careful, though. Bland's no fool, an' he loves his hide. I reckon any of the other gangs would be better fer you when you ain't goin' it alone.'

Apparently that exhausted the fund of information and advice Stevens had been eager to impart. He lapsed into silence and lay with closed eyes. Meanwhile the sun rose warm; the breeze waved the mesquites; the birds came down to splash in the shallow stream; Duane dozed in a comfortable seat. By and by something roused him. Stevens was once more talking, but with a changed tone.

'Feller's name—was Brown,' he rambled. 'We fell out—over a hoss I stole from him—in Huntsville. He stole it fust. Brown's one of them sneaks—afraid of the open—he steals an' pretends to be honest. Say, Buck, mebbe you'll meet Brown some day—You an' me are pards now.'

'I'll remember, if I ever meet him,' said Duane.

That seemed to satisfy the outlaw. Presently he tried to lift his head, but had not the strength. A strange shade was creeping across the bronzed rough face.

'My feet are pretty heavy. Shore you got my boots off?'

Duane held them up, but was not certain that Stevens could see them. The outlaw closed his eyes again and muttered incoherently. Then he fell asleep. Duane believed that sleep was final. The day passed, with Duane watching and waiting. Toward sundown Stevens awoke, and his eyes seemed clearer. Duane went to get some fresh water, thinking his comrade would surely want some. When he returned Stevens made no sign that he wanted anything. There was something bright about him, and suddenly Duane realized what it meant.

'Pard, you—stuck—to me!' the outlaw whispered.

Duane caught a hint of gladness in the voice; he traced a faint surprise in the haggard face. Stevens seemed like a little child.

To Duane the moment was sad, elemental, big, with a burden of mystery he could not understand.

Duane buried him in a shallow arroyo and heaped up a pile of stones to mark the grave. That done, he saddled his comrade's horse, hung the weapons over the pommel; and, mounting his own steed, he rode down the trail in the gathering twilight.

4

Two days later, about the middle of the forenoon, Duane dragged the two horses up the last ascent of an exceedingly rough trail and found himself on top of the Rim Rock, with a beautiful green valley at his feet, the yellow, sluggish Rio Grande shining in the sun, and the great, wild, mountainous barren of Mexico stretching to the south.

Duane had not fallen in with any travelers. He had taken the likeliest-looking trail he had come across. Where it had led him he had not the slightest idea, except that here was the river, and probably the inclosed valley was the retreat of some famous outlaw.

No wonder outlaws were safe in the wild refuge! Duane had spent the last two days climbing the roughest and most difficult trail he had ever seen. From the looks of the descent he imagined the worst part of his travel was yet to come. Not improbably it was two thousand feet down to the river. The wedge-shaped valley, green with alfalfa and cottonwood, and nestling down amid the bare walls of yellow rock was a delight and a relief to his tired eyes. Eager to get down to a level and to find a place to rest, Duane began the descent.

The trail proved to be the kind that could not be descended slowly. He kept dodging rocks which his horses loosed behind him. And in a short time he reached the valley, entering at the apex of the wedge. A stream of clear water tumbled out of the rocks here, and most of it ran into irrigation-ditches. His horses drank thirstily. And he drank with that fullness and gratefulness common to the desert traveler finding sweet water. Then he mounted and rode down the valley wondering what would be his reception.

The valley was much larger than it had appeared from the high elevation. Well watered, green with grass and tree, and farmed evidently by good hands, it gave Duane a considerable surprise. Horses and cattle were everywhere. Every clump of cottonwoods surrounded a small adobe house. Duane saw Mexicans working in the fields and horsemen going to and fro. Presently he passed a house bigger than the others with a porch attached. A woman, young and pretty he thought, watched him from a door. No one else appeared to notice.

Presently the trail widened into a road, and that into a kind of square lined by a number of adobe and log buildings of rudest structure. Within sight were horses, dogs, a couple of steers, Mexican women with children, and white men, all of whom appeared to be doing nothing. His advent created no interest until he rode up to the white men, who were lolling in the shade of a house. This place evidently was a store and saloon, and from the inside came a lazy hum of voices.

As Duane reined to a halt one of the loungers in the shade rose with a loud exclamation:

'Bust me if thet ain't Luke's hoss!'

The others accorded their interest, if not assent, by rising to advance toward Duane.

'How about it, Euchre? Ain't thet Luke's bay?' queried the first man.

'Plain as your nose,' replied the fellow called Euchre.

'There ain't no doubt about thet, then,' laughed another, 'fer Bosomer's nose is shore plain on the landscape.'

These men lined up before Duane, and as he coolly regarded them he thought they could have been recognized anywhere as desperadoes. The man called Bosomer, who had stepped forward, had a forbidding face which showed yellow eyes, an enormous nose, and a skin the color of dust, with a thatch of sandy hair.

'Stranger, who are you an' where in the hell did you git thet bay hoss?' he demanded. His yellow eyes took in Stevens's horse, then the weapons hung on the saddle, and finally turned their glinting, hard light upward to Duane.

Duane did not like the tone in which he had been addressed, and he remained silent. At least half his mind seemed busy with curious interest in regard to something that leaped inside him and made his breast feel tight. He recognized it as the strange emotion which had shot through him often of late, and which had decided him to go out to the meeting with Bain. Only now it was different, more powerful.

'Stranger, who are you?' asked another man, somewhat more civilly.

'My name's Duane,' replied Duane, curtly.

'An' how'd you come by the hoss?'

Duane answered briefly, and his words were followed by a short silence, during which the men looked at him. Bosomer began to twist the ends of his beard.

'Reckon he's dead, all right, or nobody'd hev his hoss an' guns,' presently said Euchre.

'Mister Duane,' began Bosomer, in low, stinging tones, 'I happen to be Luke Stevens's side-pardner.'

Duane looked him over, from dusty, worn-out boots to his slouchy sombrero. That look seemed to inflame Bosomer.

'An' I want the hoss an' them guns,' he shouted.

'You or anybody else can have them, for all I care. I just fetched them in. But the pack is mine,' replied Duane. 'And say, I befriended your pard. If you can't use a civil tongue you'd better cinch it.'

'Civil? Haw, haw!' rejoined the outlaw. 'I don't know you. How do we know you didn't plug Stevens, an' stole his hoss, an' jest happened to stumble down here?'

'You'll have to take my word, that's all,' replied Duane, sharply.

'———! I ain't takin' your word! Savvy thet? An' I was Luke's pard!'

With that Bosomer wheeled and, pushing his companions aside, he stamped into the saloon, where his voice broke out in a roar.

Duane dismounted and threw his bridle.

'Stranger, Bosomer is shore hot-headed,' said the man Euchre. He did not appear unfriendly, nor were the others hostile.

At this juncture several more outlaws crowded out of the door, and the one in the lead was a tall man of stalwart physique. His manner proclaimed him a leader. He had a long face, a flaming red beard, and clear, cold blue eyes that fixed in close scrutiny upon Duane. He was not a Texan; in truth, Duane did not recognize one of these outlaws as native to his state.

'I'm Bland,' said the tall man, authoritatively. 'Who're you and what're you doing here?'

Duane looked at Bland as he had at the others. This outlaw chief appeared to be reasonable, if he was not courteous. Duane told his story again, this time a little more in detail.

'I believe you,' replied Bland, at once. 'Think I know when a fellow is lying.'

'I reckon you're on the right trail,' put in Euchre. 'Thet about Luke wantin' his boots took off—thet satisfies me. Luke had a mortal dread of dyin' with his boots on.'

At this sally the chief and his men laughed.

'You said Duane—Buck Duane?' queried Bland. 'Are you a son of that Duane who was a gunfighter some years back?'

'Yes,' replied Duane.

'Never met him, and glad I didn't,' said Bland, with a grim humor. 'So you got in trouble and had to go on the dodge? What kind of trouble?'

'Had a fight.'

'Fight? Do you mean gun-play?' questioned Bland. He seemed eager, curious, speculative.

'Yes. It ended in gun-play, I'm sorry to say,' answered Duane.

'Guess I needn't ask the son of Duane if he killed his man,' went on Bland, ironically. 'Well, I'm sorry you bucked against trouble in my camp. But as it is, I guess you'd be wise to make yourself scarce.'

'Do you mean I'm politely told to move on?' asked Duane, quietly.

'Not exactly that,' said Bland, as if irritated. 'If this isn't a free place there isn't one on earth. Every man is equal here. Do you want to join my band?'

'No, I don't.'

'Well, even if you did I imagine that wouldn't stop Bosomer. He's an ugly fellow. He's one of the few gunmen I've met who wants to kill somebody all the time. Most men like that are four-flushes. But Bosomer is all one color, and that's red. Merely for your own sake I advise you to hit the trail.'

'Thanks. But if that's all I'll stay,' returned Duane. Even as he spoke he felt that he did not know himself.

Bosomer appeared at the door, pushing men who tried to detain him, and as he jumped clear of a last reaching hand he uttered a snarl like an angry dog. Manifestly the short while he had spent inside the saloon had been devoted to drinking and talking himself into a frenzy. Bland and the other outlaws quickly moved aside, letting Duane stand alone. When Bosomer saw Duane standing motionless and watchful a strange change passed quickly in him. He halted in his tracks, and as he did that the men who had followed him out piled over one another in their hurry to get to one side.

Duane saw all the swift action, felt intuitively the meaning of it, and in Bosomer's sudden change of front. The outlaw was keen, and he had expected a shrinking, or at least a frightened antagonist. Duane knew he was neither. He felt like iron, and yet thrill after thrill ran through him. It was almost as if this situation had been one long familiar to him. Somehow he understood this yellow- eyed

Bosomer. The outlaw had come out to kill him. And now, though somewhat checked by the stand of a stranger, he still meant to kill. Like so many desperadoes of his ilk, he was victim of a passion to kill for the sake of killing. Duane divined that no sudden animosity was driving Bosomer. It was just his chance. In that moment murder would have been joy to him. Very likely he had forgotten his pretext for a quarrel. Very probably his faculties were absorbed in conjecture as to Duane's possibilities.

But he did not speak a word. He remained motionless for a long moment, his eyes pale and steady, his right hand like a claw.

That instant gave Duane a power to read in his enemy's eyes the thought that preceded action. But Duane did not want to kill another man. Still he would have to fight, and he decided to cripple Bosomer. When Bosomer's hand moved Duane's gun was spouting fire. Two shots only—both from Duane's gun—and the outlaw fell with his right arm shattered. Bosomer cursed harshly and floundered in the dust, trying to reach the gun with his left hand. His comrades, however, seeing that Duane would not kill unless forced, closed in upon Bosomer and prevented any further madness on his part.

5

Of the outlaws present Euchre appeared to be the one most inclined to lend friendliness to curiosity; and he led Duane and the horses away to a small adobe shack. He tied the horses in an open shed and removed their saddles. Then, gathering up Stevens's weapons, he invited his visitor to enter the house.

It had two rooms—windows without coverings—bare floors. One room contained blankets, weapons, saddles, and bridles; the other a stone fireplace, rude table and bench, two bunks, a box cupboard, and various blackened utensils.

'Make yourself to home as long as you want to stay,' said Euchre. 'I ain't rich in this world's goods, but I own what's here, an' you're welcome.'

'Thanks. I'll stay awhile and rest. I'm pretty well played out,' replied Duane.

Euchre gave him a keen glance.

'Go ahead an' rest. I'll take your horses to grass.'

Euchre left Duane alone in the house. Duane relaxed then, and mechanically he wiped the sweat from his face. He was laboring under some kind of a spell or shock which did not pass off quickly. When it had worn away he took off his coat and belt and made himself comfortable on the blankets. And he had a thought that if he rested or slept what difference would it make on the morrow? No rest, no sleep could change the gray outlook of the future. He felt glad when Euchre came bustling in, and for the first time he took notice of the outlaw.

Euchre was old in years. What little hair he had was gray, his face clean-shaven and full of wrinkles; his eyes were half shut from long gazing through the sun and dust. He stooped. But his thin frame denoted strength and endurance still unimpaired.

'Hev a drink or a smoke?' he asked.

Duane shook his head. He had not been unfamiliar with whisky, and he had used tobacco moderately since he was sixteen. But now, strangely, he felt a disgust at the idea of stimulants. He did not understand clearly what he felt. There was that vague idea of something wild in his blood, something that made him fear himself.

Euchre wagged his head sympathetically. 'Reckon you feel a little sick. When it comes to shootin' I run. What's your age?'

'I'm twenty-three,' replied Duane.

Euchre showed surprise. 'You're only a boy! I thought you thirty anyways. Buck, I heard what you told Bland, an' puttin' thet with my own figurin', I reckon you're no criminal yet. Throwin' a gun in self-defense—thet ain't no crime!'

Duane finding relief in talking, told more about himself.

'Huh,' replied the old man. 'I've been on this river fer years, an' I've seen hundreds of boys come in on the dodge. Most of them, though, was no good. An' thet kind don't last long. This river country has been an' is the refuge fer criminals from all over the states. I've bunked with bank cashiers, forgers, plain thieves, an' out-an'-out murderers, all of which had no bizness on the Texas border. Fellers like Bland are exceptions. He's no Texan—you seen thet. The gang he rules here come from all over, an' they're tough cusses, you can bet on thet. They live fat an' easy. If it wasn't fer the fightin' among themselves they'd shore grow populous. The Rim Rock is no place for a peaceable, decent feller. I heard you tell Bland you wouldn't join his gang. Thet'll not make him take a likin' to you. Have you any money?'

'Not much,' replied Duane.

'Could you live by gamblin'? Are you any good at cards?'

'No.'

'You wouldn't steal hosses or rustle cattle?'

'No.'

'When your money's gone how'n hell will you live? There ain't any work a decent feller could do. You can't herd with greasers. Why, Bland's men would shoot at you in the fields. What'll you do, son?'

'God knows,' replied Duane, hopelessly. 'I'll make my money last as long as possible—then starve.'

'Wal, I'm pretty pore, but you'll never starve while I got anythin'.'

Here it struck Duane again—that something human and kind and eager which he had seen in Stevens. Duane's estimate of outlaws had lacked this quality. He had not accorded them any virtues. To him, as to the outside world, they had been merely vicious men without one redeeming feature.

'I'm much obliged to you, Euchre,' replied Duane. 'But of course I won't live with any one unless I can pay my share.'

'Have it any way you like, my son,' said Euchre, good-humoredly. 'You make a fire, an' I'll set about gettin' grub. I'm a sourdough, Buck. Thet man doesn't live who can beat my bread.'

'How do you ever pack supplies in here?' asked Duane, thinking of the almost inaccessible nature of the valley.

'Some comes across from Mexico, an' the rest down the river. Thet river trip is a bird. It's more'n five hundred miles to any supply point. Bland has *mozos*, greaser boatmen. Sometimes, too, he gets supplies in from down-river. You see, Bland sells thousands of cattle in Cuba. An' all this stock has to go down by boat to meet the ships.'

'Where on earth are the cattle driven down to the river?' asked Duane.

'Thet's not my secret,' replied Euchre, shortly. 'Fact is, I don't know. I've rustled cattle for Bland, but he never sent me through the Rim Rock with them.'

Duane experienced a sort of pleasure in the realization that interest had been stirred in him. He was curious about Bland and his gang, and glad to have something to think about. For every once in a while he had a sensation that was almost like a pang. He wanted to forget. In the next hour he did forget, and enjoyed helping in the preparation and eating of the meal. Euchre, after washing and hanging up the several utensils, put on his hat and turned to go out.

'Come along or stay here, as you want,' he said to Duane.

'I'll stay,' rejoined Duane, slowly.

The old outlaw left the room and trudged away, whistling cheerfully.

Duane looked around him for a book or paper, anything to read; but all the printed matter he could find consisted of a few words on cartridge-boxes and an advertisement on the back of a tobacco-pouch. There seemed to be nothing for him to do. He had rested; he did not want to lie down any more. He began to walk to and fro, from one end of the room to the other. And as he walked he fell into the lately acquired habit of brooding over his misfortune.

Suddenly he straightened up with a jerk. Unconsciously he had drawn his gun. Standing there with the bright cold weapon in his hand, he looked at it in consternation. How had he come to draw it? With difficulty he traced his thoughts backward, but could not find any that was accountable for his act. He discovered, however, that he had a remarkable tendency to drop his hand to his gun. That might have come from the habit long practice in drawing had given him. Likewise, it might have come from a subtle sense, scarcely thought of at all, of the late, close, and inevitable relation between that weapon and himself. He was amazed to find that, bitter as he had grown at fate, the desire to live burned strong in him. If he had been as unfortunately situated, but with the difference that no man wanted to put him in jail or take his life, he felt that this burning passion to be free, to save himself, might not have been so powerful. Life certainly held no bright prospects for him. Already he had begun to despair of ever getting back to his home. But to give up like a white-hearted coward, to let himself be hand-cuffed and jailed, to run from a drunken, bragging cowboy, or be shot in cold blood by some border brute who merely wanted to add another notch to his gun—these things were impossible for Duane because there was in him the temper to fight. In that hour he yielded only to fate and the spirit inborn in him. Hereafter this gun must be a living part of him. Right then and there he returned to a practice he had long discontinued—the draw. It was now a stern, bitter, deadly business with him. He did not need to fire the gun, for accuracy was a gift and had become assured. Swiftness on the draw, however, could be improved, and he set himself to acquire the limit of speed possible to any man. He stood still in his tracks; he paced the room; he sat down, lay down, put himself in awkward positions; and from every position he practised throwing his gun— practised it till he was hot and tired and his arm ached and his hand burned. That practice he determined to keep up every day. It was one thing, at least, that would help pass the weary hours.

Later he went outdoors to the cooler shade of the cottonwoods. From this point he could see a good deal of the valley. Under different circumstances Duane felt that he would have enjoyed such a beautiful spot. Euchre's shack sat against the first rise of the slope of the wall, and Duane, by climbing a few rods, got a view of the whole valley. Assuredly it was an outlaw settlement. He saw a good many Mexicans, who, of course, were hand and glove with Bland. Also he saw enormous flat-boats, crude of structure, moored along the banks of the river. The Rio Grande rolled away between high bluffs. A cable sagging deep in the middle, was stretched over the wide yellow stream, and an old scow, evidently used as a ferry, lay anchored on the far shore.

The valley was an ideal retreat for an outlaw band operating on a big scale. Pursuit scarcely need be feared over the broken trails of the Rim Rock. And the open end of the valley could be defended against almost any number of men coming down the river. Access to Mexico was easy and quick. What puzzled

Duane was how Bland got cattle down to the river, and he wondered if the rustler really did get rid of his stolen stock by use of boats.

Duane must have idled considerable time up on the hill, for when he returned to the shack Euchre was busily engaged around the camp-fire.

'Wal, glad to see you ain't so pale about the gills as you was,' he said, by way of greeting. 'Pitch in an' we'll soon have grub ready. There's shore one consolin' fact round this here camp.'

'What's that?' asked Duane.

'Plenty of good juicy beef to eat. An' it doesn't cost a short bit.'

'But it costs hard rides and trouble, bad conscience, and life, too, doesn't it?'

'I ain't shore about the bad conscience. Mine never bothered me none. An' as for life, why, thet's cheap in Texas.'

'Who is Bland?' asked Duane, quickly changing the subject. 'What do you know about him?'

'We don't know who he is or where he hails from,' replied Euchre. 'Thet's always been somethin' to interest the gang. He must have been a young man when he struck Texas. Now he's middle-aged. I remember how years ago he was softspoken an' not rough in talk or act like he is now. Bland ain't likely his right name. He knows a lot. He can doctor you, an' he's shore a knowin' feller with tools. He's the kind thet rules men. Outlaws are always ridin' in here to join his gang, an' if it hadn't been fer the gamblin' an' gun-play he'd have a thousand men around him.'

'How many in his gang now?'

'I reckon there's short of a hundred now. The number varies. Then Bland has several small camps up an' down the river. Also he has men back on the cattle-ranges.'

'How does he control such a big force?' asked Duane. 'Especially when his band's composed of bad men. Luke Stevens said he had no use for Bland. And I heard once somewhere that Bland was a devil.'

'Thet's it. He is a devil. He's as hard as flint, violent in temper, never made any friends except his right-hand men, Dave Rugg an' Chess Alloway. Bland'll shoot at a wink. He's killed a lot of fellers, an' some fer nothin'. The reason thet outlaws gather round him an' stick is because he's a safe refuge, an' then he's well heeled. Bland is rich. They say he has a hundred thousand *pesos* hid somewhere, an' lots of gold. But he's free with money. He gambles when he's not off with a shipment of cattle. He throws money around. An' the fact is there's always plenty of money where he is. Thet's what holds the gang. Dirty, bloody money!'

'It's a wonder he hasn't been killed. All these years on the border!' exclaimed Duane.

'Wal,' replied Euchre, dryly, 'he's been quicker on the draw than the other fellers who hankered to kill him, thet's all.'

Euchre's reply rather chilled Duane's interest for the moment. Such remarks always made his mind revolve round facts pertaining to himself.

'Speakin' of this here swift wrist game,' went on Euchre, 'there's been considerable talk in camp about your throwin' of a gun. You know, Buck, thet among us fellers—us hunted men—there ain't anythin' calculated to rouse respect like a slick hand with a gun. I heard Bland say this afternoon—an' he said it serious-like an' speculative—thet he'd never seen your equal. He was watchin' of you close, he said, an' just couldn't follow your hand when you drawed. All the fellers who seen you meet Bosomer had somethin' to say. Bo was about as handy with a gun as any man in this camp, barrin' Chess Alloway an' mebbe Bland himself. Chess is the captain with a Colt—or he was. An' he shore didn't like the references made about your speed. Bland was honest in acknowledgin' it, but he didn't like it, neither. Some of the fellers allowed your draw might have been just accident. But most of them figgered different. An' they all shut up when Bland told who an' what your Dad was. 'Pears to me I once seen your Dad in a gunscrape over at Santone, years ago. Wal, I put my oar in to-day among the fellers, an' I says: "What ails you locoed gents? Did young Duane budge an inch when Bo came roarin' out, blood in his eye? Wasn't he cool an' quiet, steady of lips, an' weren't his eyes readin' Bo's mind? An' thet lightnin' draw—can't you—all see thet's a family gift?" '

Euchre's narrow eyes twinkled, and he gave the dough he was rolling a slap with his flour-whitened hand. Manifestly he had proclaimed himself a champion and partner of Duane's, with all the pride an old man could feel in a young one whom he admired.

'Wal,' he resumed, presently, 'thet's your introduction to the border, Buck. An' your card was a high trump. You'll be let severely alone by real gunfighters an' men like Bland, Alloway, Rugg, an' the bosses of the other gangs. After all, these real men *are* men, you know, an' onless you cross them they're no more likely to interfere with you than you are with them. But there's a sight of fellers like Bosomer in the river country. They'll all want your game. An' every town you ride into will scare up some cowpuncher full of booze or a long-haired four-flush gunman or a sheriff—an' these men will be playin' to the crowd an' yellin' for your blood. Thet's the Texas of it. You'll have to hide fer ever in the brakes or you'll have to *kill* such men. Buck, I reckon this ain't cheerful news to a decent chap like you. I'm only tellin' you because I've taken a likin' to you, an' I seen right off thet you ain't border-wise. Let's eat now, an' afterward we'll go out so the gang can see you're not hidin'.'

*

When Duane went out with Euchre the sun was setting behind a blue range of mountains across the river in Mexico. The valley appeared to open to the southwest. It was a tranquil, beautiful scene. Somewhere in a house near at hand a woman was singing. And in the road Duane saw a little Mexican boy driving home some cows, one of which wore a bell. The sweet, happy voice of a woman and a whistling barefoot boy—these seemed utterly out of place here.

Euchre presently led to the square and the row of rough houses Duane remembered. He almost stepped on a wide imprint in the dust where Bosomer had confronted him. And a sudden fury beset him that he should be affected strangely by the sight of it.

'Let's have a look in here,' said Euchre.

Duane had to bend his head to enter the door. He found himself in a very large room inclosed by adobe walls and roofed with brush. It was full of rude benches, tables, seats. At one corner a number of kegs and barrels lay side by side in a rack. A Mexican boy was lighting lamps hung on posts that sustained the log rafters of the roof.

'The only feller who's goin' to put a close eye on you is Benson,' said Euchre. 'He runs the place an' sells drinks. The gang calls him Jackrabbit Benson, because he's always got his eye peeled an' his ear cocked. Don't notice him if he looks you over, Buck. Benson is scared to death of every new-comer who rustles into Bland's camp. An' the reason, I take it, is because he's done somebody dirt. He's hidin'. Not from a sheriff or ranger! Men who hide from them don't act like Jackrabbit Benson. He's hidin' from some guy who's huntin' him to kill him. Wal, I'm always expectin' to see some feller ride in here an' throw a gun on Benson. Can't say I'd be grieved.'

Duane casually glanced in the direction indicated, and he saw a spare, gaunt man with a face strikingly white beside the red and bronze and dark skins of the men around him. It was a cadaverous face. The black mustache hung down; a heavy lock of black hair dropped down over the brow; deepset, hollow, staring eyes looked out piercingly. The man had a restless, alert, nervous manner. He put his hands on the board that served as a bar and stared at Duane. But when he met Duane's glance he turned hurriedly to go on serving out liquor.

'What have you got against him?' inquired Duane, as he sat down beside Euchre. He asked more for something to say than from real interest. What did he care about a mean, haunted, craven-faced criminal?

'Wal, mebbe I'm cross-grained,' replied Euchre, apologetically. 'Shore an outlaw an' rustler such as me can't be touchy. But I never stole nothin' but cattle from some rancher who never missed 'em anyway. Thet sneak Benson—he was the means of puttin' a little girl in Bland's way.'

'Girl?' queried Duane, now with real attention.

'Shore. Bland's great on women. I'll tell you about this girl when we get out of here. Some of the gang are goin' to be sociable, an' I can't talk about the chief.'

During the ensuing half-hour a number of outlaws passed by Duane and Euchre, halted for a greeting or sat down for a moment. They were all gruff, loud-voiced, merry, and good-natured. Duane replied civilly and agreeably when he was personally addressed; but he refused all invitations to drink and gamble. Evidently he had been accepted, in a way, as one of their clan. No one made any hint of an allusion to his affair with Bosomer. Duane saw readily that Euchre was well liked. One outlaw borrowed from him: another asked for tobacco.

By the time it was dark the big room was full of outlaws and Mexicans, most of whom were engaged at *monte*. These gamblers, especially the Mexicans, were intense and quiet. The noise in the place came from the drinkers, the loungers. Duane had seen gambling-resorts—some of the famous ones in San Antonio and El Paso, a few in border towns where license went unchecked. But this place of Jackrabbit Benson's impressed him as one where guns and knives were accessories to the game. To his perhaps rather distinguishing eye the most prominent thing about the gamesters appeared to be their weapons. On several of the tables were piles of silver—Mexican *pesos*—as large and high as the crown of his hat. There were also piles of gold and silver in United States coin. Duane needed no experienced eyes to see that betting was heavy and that heavy sums exchanged hands. The Mexicans showed a sterner obsession, an intenser passion. Some of the Americans staked freely, nonchalantly, as befitted men to whom money was nothing. These latter were manifestly winning, for there were brother outlaws there who wagered coin with grudging, sullen, greedy eyes. Boisterous talk and laughter among the drinking men drowned, except at intervals, the low, brief talk of the gamblers. The clink of coin sounded incessantly; sometimes just low, steady musical rings; and again, when a pile was tumbled quickly, there was a silvery crash. Here an outlaw pounded on a table with the butt of his gun; there another noisily palmed a roll of dollars while he studied his opponent's face. The noises, however, in Benson's den did not contribute to any extent to the sinister aspect of the place. That seemed to come from the grim and reckless faces, from the bent, intent heads, from the dark lights and shades. There were bright lights, but these served only to make the shadows. And in the shadows lurked unrestrained lust of gain, a spirit ruthless and reckless, a something at once suggesting lawlessness, theft, murder, and hell.

'Bland's not here to-night,' Euchre was saying. 'He left today on one of his trips, takin' Alloway an' some others. But his other man, Rugg, he's here. See him standin' with them three fellers, all close to Benson. Rugg's the little bowlegged man with the half of his face shot off. He's one-eyed. But he can shore see out of the one he's got. An', darn me! there's Hardin. You know him? He's got an outlaw gang as big as Bland's. Hardin is standin' next to Benson. See how quiet an' unassumin' he looks. Yes, thet's Hardin. He comes here once in a while to see Bland. They're friends, which's shore strange. Do you see thet greaser there—the one with gold an' lace on his sombrero? Thet's Manuel, a Mexican bandit. He's a great gambler. Comes here often to drop his coin. Next to him is Bill Marr—the feller with the bandana round his head. Bill rode in the other day with some fresh bullet-holes. He's been shot more'n any feller I ever heard of. He's full of lead. Funny, because Bill's no trouble-hunter, an', like me, he'd rather run than shoot. But he's the best rustler Bland's got—a grand rider, an' a wonder with cattle. An' see the tow-headed youngster. Thet's Kid Fuller, the kid of Bland's gang. Fuller has hit the pace hard, an' he won't last the year out on the border. He killed his sweetheart's father, got run out of Staceytown, took to stealin' hosses. An' next he's here with Bland. Another boy gone wrong, an' now shore a hard nut.'

Euchre went on calling Duane's attention to other men, just as he happened to glance over them. Any one of them would have been a marked man in a respectable crowd. Here each took his place with more or less distinction, according to the record of his past wild prowess and his present possibilities. Duane, realizing that he was tolerated there, received in careless friendly spirit by this terrible class of outcasts, experienced a feeling of revulsion that amounted almost to horror. Was his being there not an ugly dream? What had he in common with such ruffians? Then in a flash of memory came the painful proof—he was a criminal in sight of Texas law; he, too, was an outcast.

For the moment Duane was wrapped up in painful reflections; but Euchre's heavy hand, clapping with a warning hold on his arm, brought him back to outside things.

The hum of voices, the clink of coin, the loud laughter had ceased. There was a silence that manifestly had followed some unusual word or action sufficient to still the room. It was broken by a harsh curse and the scrape of a bench on the floor. Some man had risen.

'You stacked the cards, you—!'

'Say that twice,' another voice replied, so different in its cool, ominous tone from the other.

'I'll say it three times. I'll whistle it. Are you deaf? You light-fingered gent! You stacked the cards!'

Silence ensued, deeper than before, pregnant with meaning. For all that Duane saw, not an outlaw moved for a full moment. Then suddenly the room was full of disorder as men rose and ran and dived everywhere.

'Run or duck!' yelled Euchre, close to Duane's ear. With that he dashed for the door. Duane leaped after him. They ran into a jostling mob. Heavy gunshots and hoarse yells hurried the crowd Duane was with pell-mell out into the darkness. There they all halted, and several peeped in at the door.

'Who was the Kid callin'?' asked one outlaw.

'Bud Marsh,' replied another.

'I reckon them fust shots was Bud's. *Adios* Kid. It was comin' to him,' went on yet another.

'How many shots?'

'Three or four, I counted.'

'Three heavy an' one light. The light one was the Kid's .38. Listen! There's the Kid hollerin' now. He ain't cashed, anyway.'

At this juncture most of the outlaws began to file back into the room. Duane thought he had seen and heard enough in Benson's den for one night and he started slowly down the walk. Presently Euchre caught up with him.

'Nobody hurt much, which's shore some strange,' he said. 'The Kid—young Fuller thet I was tellin' you about—he was drinkin' an' losin'. Lost his nut, too, callin' Bud Marsh thet way. Bud's as straight at cards as any of 'em. Somebody grabbed Bud, who shot into the roof. An' Fuller's arm was knocked up. He only hit a greaser.'

6

Next morning Duane found that a moody and despondent spell had fastened on him. Wishing to be alone, he went out and walked a trail leading round the river bluff. He thought and thought. After a while he made out that the trouble with him probably was that he could not resign himself to his fate. He abhorred the possibility chance seemed to hold in store for him. He could not believe there was no hope. But what to do appeared beyond his power to tell.

Duane had intelligence and keenness enough to see his peril—the danger threatening his character as a man, just as much as that which threatened his life. He cared vastly more, he discovered, for what he considered honor and integrity than he did for life. He saw that it was bad for him to be alone. But, it appeared, lonely months and perhaps years inevitably must be his. Another thing puzzled him. In the bright light of day he could not recall the state of mind that was his at twilight or dusk or in the dark night. By day these visitations became to him what they really were—phantoms of his conscience. He could dismiss the thought of them then. He could scarcely remember or believe that this strange feat of fancy or imagination had troubled him, pained him, made him sleepless and sick.

That morning Duane spent an unhappy hour wrestling decision out of the unstable condition of his mind. But at length he determined to create interest in all that he came across and so forget himself as much as possible. He had an opportunity now to see just what the outlaw's life really was. He meant to force himself to be curious, sympathetic, clearsighted. And he would stay there in the valley until its possibilities had been exhausted or until circumstances sent him out upon his uncertain way.

When he returned to the shack Euchre was cooking dinner.

'Say, Buck, I've news for you,' he said; and his tone conveyed either pride in his possession of such news or pride in Duane. 'Feller named Bradley rode in this mornin'. He's heard some about you. Told about the ace of spades they put over the bullet-holes in thet cowpuncher Bain you plugged. Then there was a rancher shot at a water-hole twenty miles south of Wellston. Reckon you didn't do it?'

'No, I certainly did not,' replied Duane.

'Wal, you get the blame. It ain't nothin' for a feller to be saddled with gun-plays he never made. An', Buck, if you ever get famous, as seems likely, you'll be blamed for many a crime. The border'll make an outlaw an' murderer out of you. Wal, thet's enough of thet. I've more news. You're goin' to be popular.'

'Popular? What do you mean?'

'I met Bland's wife this mornin'. She seen you the other day when you rode in. She shore wants to meet you, an' so do some of the other women in camp. They always want to meet the new fellers who've just come in. It's lonesome for women here, an' they like to hear news from the towns.'

'Well, Euchre, I don't want to be impolite, but I'd rather not meet any women,' rejoined Duane.

'I was afraid you wouldn't. Don't blame you much. Women are hell. I was hopin', though, you might talk a little to thet poor lonesome kid.'

'What kid?' inquired Duane, in surprise.

'Didn't I tell you about Jennie—the girl Bland's holden' here—the one Jackrabbit Benson had a hand in stealin'?'

'You mentioned a girl. That's all. Tell me now,' replied Duane, abruptly.

'Wal, I got it this way. Mebbe it's straight, an' mebbe it ain't. Some years ago Benson made a trip over the river to buy mescal an' other drinks. He'll sneak over there once in a while. An' as I get it he run across a gang of greasers with some gringo prisoners. I don't know, but I reckon there was some barterin', perhaps murderin'. Anyway, Benson fetched the girl back. She was more dead than alive. But it turned out she was only starved an' scared half to death. She hadn't been harmed. I reckon she was then about fourteen years old. Benson's idea, he said, was to use her in his den sellin' drinks an' the like. But I never went much on Jackrabbit's word. Bland seen the kid right off and took her—bought her from Benson. You can gamble Bland didn't do thet from notions of chivalry. I ain't gainsayin', however, but thet Jennie was better off with Kate Bland. She's been hard on Jennie, but she's kept Bland an' the other men from treatin' the kid shameful. Late Jennie has growed into a all-fired pretty girl, an' Kate is powerful jealous of her. I can see hell brewin' over there in Bland's cabin. Thet's why I wish you'd come with me. Bland's hardly ever home. His wife's invited you. Shore, if she gets sweet on you, as she has on—Wal, thet'd complicate matters. But you'd get to see Jennie, an' mebbe you could help her. Mind, I ain't hintin' nothin'. I'm just wantin' to put her in your way. You're a man an' can think fer yourself. I had a baby girl once, an' if she'd lived she be as big as Jennie now, an', by Gawd, I wouldn't want her here in Bland's camp.'

'I'll go, Euchre. Take me over,' replied Duane. He felt Euchre's eyes upon him. The old outlaw, however, had no more to say.

In the afternoon Euchre set off with Duane, and soon they reached Bland's cabin. Duane remembered it as the one where he had seen the pretty woman watching him ride by. He could not recall what she looked like. The cabin was the same as the other adobe structures in the valley, but it was larger and pleasantly located rather high up in a grove of cottonwoods. In the windows and upon the porch were evidences of a woman's hand. Through the open door Duane caught a glimpse of bright Mexican blankets and rugs.

Euchre knocked upon the side of the door.

'Is that you, Euchre?' asked a girl's voice, low, hesitatingly. The tone of it, rather deep and with a note of fear, struck Duane. He wondered what she would be like.

'Yes, it's me, Jennie. Where's Mrs Bland?' answered Euchre.

'She went over to Deger's. There's somebody sick,' replied the girl.

Euchre turned and whispered something about luck. The snap of the outlaw's eyes was added significance to Duane.

'Jennie, come out or let us come in. Here's the young man I was tellin' you about,' Euchre said.

'Oh, I can't! I look so—so—'

'Never mind how you look,' interrupted the outlaw, in a whisper. 'It ain't no time to care fer thet. Here's young Duane. Jennie, he's no rustler, no thief. He's different. Come out, Jennie, an' mebbe he'll—'

Euchre did not complete his sentence. He had spoken low, with his glance shifting from side to side.

But what he said was sufficient to bring the girl quickly. She appeared in the doorway with downcast eyes and a stain of red on her white cheek. She had a pretty, sad face and bright hair.

'Don't be bashful, Jennie,' said Euchre. 'You an' Duane have a chance to talk a little. Now I'll go fetch Mrs Bland, but I won't be hurryin'.'

With that Euchre went away through the cottonwoods.

'I'm glad to meet you, Miss—Miss Jennie,' said Duane. 'Euchre didn't mention your last name. He asked me to come over to—'

Duane's attempt at pleasantry halted short when Jennie lifted her lashes to look at him. Some kind of a shock went through Duane. Her gray eyes were beautiful, but it had not been beauty that cut short his speech. He seemed to see a tragic struggle between hope and doubt that shone in her piercing gaze. She kept looking, and Duane could not break the silence. It was no ordinary moment.

'What did you come here for?' she asked, at last.

'To see you,' replied Duane, glad to speak.

'Why?'

'Well—Euchre thought—he wanted me to talk to you, cheer you up a bit,' replied Duane, somewhat lamely. The earnest eyes embarrassed him.

'Euchre's good. He's the only person in this awful place who's been good to me. But he's afraid of Bland. He said you were different. Who are you?'

Duane told her.

'You're not a robber or rustler or murderer or some bad man come here to hide?'

'No I'm not,' replied Duane, trying to smile.

'Then why are you here?'

'I'm on the dodge. You know what that means. I got in a shooting-scrape at home and had to run off. When it blows over I hope to go back.'

'But you can't be honest here?'

'Yes, I can.'

'Oh, I know what these outlaws are. Yes, you're different.' She kept the strained gaze upon him, but hope was kindling, and the hard lines of her youthful face were softening.

Something sweet and warm stirred deep in Duane as he realized the unfortunate girl was experiencing a birth of trust in him.

'O God! Maybe you're the man to save me—to take me away before it's too late!'

Duane's spirit leaped.

'Maybe I am,' he replied, instantly.

She seemed to check a blind impulse to run into his arms. Her cheek flamed, her lips quivered, her bosom swelled under her ragged dress. Then the glow began to fade; doubt once more assailed her.

'It can't be. You're only—after me, too, like Bland—like all of them.'

Duane's long arms went out and his hands clasped her shoulders. He shook her.

'Look at me—straight in the eye. There are decent men. Haven't you a father—a brother?'

'They're dead—killed by raiders. We lived in Dimmit County. I was carried away,' Jennie replied, hurriedly. She put up an appealing hand to him. 'Forgive me. I believe—I know you're good. It was only—I live so much in fear—I'm half crazy—I've almost forgotten what good men are like, Mister Duane, you'll help me?'

'Yes, Jennie, I will. Tell me how. What must I do? Have you any plan?'

'Oh no. But take me away.'

'I'll try,' said Duane, simply. 'That won't be easy, though. I must have time to think. You must help me. There are many things to consider. Horses, food, trails, and then the best time to make the attempt. Are you watched—kept prisoner?'

'No. I could have run off lots of times. But I was afraid. I'd only have fallen into worse hands. Euchre has told me that. Mrs Bland beats me, half starves me, but she has kept me from her husband and these other dogs. She's been as good as that, and I'm grateful. She hasn't done it for love of me, though. She always hated me. And lately she's growing jealous. There was a man came here by the name of Spence—so he called himself. He tried to be kind to me. But she wouldn't let him. She was in love with him. She's a bad woman. Bland finally shot Spence, and that ended that. She's been jealous ever since. I hear her fighting with Bland about me. She swears she'll kill me before he gets me. And Bland laughs in her face. Then I've heard Chess Alloway try to persuade Bland to give me to him. But Bland doesn't laugh then. Just lately before Bland went away things almost came to a head. I couldn't sleep. I wished Mrs Bland would kill me. I'll certainly kill myself if they ruin me. Duane, you must be quick if you'd save me.'

'I realize that,' replied he, thoughtfully. 'I think my difficulty will be to fool Mrs Bland. If she suspected me she'd have the whole gang of outlaws on me at once.'

'She would that. You've got to be careful—and quick.'

'What kind of woman is she?' inquired Duane.

'She's—she's brazen. I've heard her with her lovers. They get drunk sometimes when Bland's away. She's got a terrible temper. She's vain. She likes flattery. Oh, you could fool her easy enough if you'd lower yourself to—to—'

'To make love to her?' interrupted Duane.

Jennie bravely turned shamed eyes to meet his.

'My girl, I'd do worse than that to get you away from here,' he said, bluntly.

'But—Duane,' she faltered, and again she put out the appealing hand. 'Bland will kill you.'

Duane made no reply to this. He was trying to still a rising strange tumult in his breast. The old emotions—the rush of an instinct to kill! He turned cold all over.

'Chess Alloway will kill you if Bland doesn't,' went on Jennie, with her tragic eyes on Duane's.

'Maybe he will,' replied Duane. It was difficult for him to force a smile. But he achieved one.

'Oh, better take me off at once,' she said. 'Save me without risking so much—without making love to Mrs Bland!'

'Surely, if I can. There! I see Euchre coming with a woman.'

'That's her. Oh, she mustn't see me with you.'

'Wait—a moment,' whispered Duane, as Jennie slipped indoors. 'We've settled it. Don't forget. I'll find some way to get word to you, perhaps through Euchre. Meanwhile keep up your courage. Remember I'll save you somehow. We'll try strategy first. Whatever you see or hear me do, don't think less of me—'

Jennie checked him with a gesture and a wonderful gray flash of eyes.

'I'll bless you with every drop of blood in my heart,' she whispered, passionately.

It was only as she turned away into the room that Duane saw she was lame and that she wore Mexican sandals over bare feet.

He sat down upon a bench on the porch and directed his attention to the approaching couple. The trees of the grove were thick enough for him to make reasonably sure that Mrs Bland had not seen him talking to Jennie. When the outlaw's wife drew near Duane saw that she was a tall, strong, fullbodied woman, rather good-looking with a fullblown, bold attractiveness. Duane was more concerned with her expression than with her good looks; and as she appeared unsuspicious he felt relieved. The situation then took on a singular zest.

Euchre came up on the porch and awkwardly introduced Duane to Mrs Bland. She was young, probably not over twenty-five, and not quite so prepossessing at close range. Her eyes were large, rather prominent, and brown in color. Her mouth, too, was large, with the lips full, and she had white teeth.

Duane took her proffered hand and remarked frankly that he was glad to meet her.

Mrs Bland appeared pleased; and her laugh, which followed, was loud and rather musical.

'Mr Duane—Buck Duane, Euchre said, didn't he?' she asked.

'Buckley,' corrected Duane. 'The nickname's not of my choosing.'

'I'm certainly glad to meet you, Buckley Duane,' she said, as she took the seat Duane offered her. 'Sorry to have been out. Kid Fuller's lying over at Deger's. You know he was shot last night. He's got fever to-day. When Bland's away I have to nurse all these shot-up boys, and it sure takes my time. Have you been waiting here alone? Didn't see that slattern girl of mine?'

She gave him a sharp glance. The woman had an extraordinary play of feature, Duane thought, and unless she was smiling was not pretty at all.

'I've been alone,' replied Duane. 'Haven't seen anybody but a sick-looking girl with a bucket. And she ran when she saw me.'

'That was Jen,' said Mrs Bland. 'She's the kid we keep here, and she sure hardly pays her keep. Did Euchre tell you about her?'

'Now that I think of it, he did say something or other.'

'What did he tell you about me?' bluntly asked Mrs Bland.

'Wal, Kate,' replied Euchre, speaking for himself, 'you needn't worry none, for I told Buck nothin' but compliments.'

Evidently the outlaw's wife liked Euchre, for her keen glance rested with amusement upon him.

'As for Jen, I'll tell you her story some day,' went on the woman. 'It's a common enough story along this river. Euchre here is a tender-hearted old fool, and Jen has taken him in.'

'Wal, seein' as you've got me figgered correct,' replied Euchre, dryly, 'I'll go in an' talk to Jennie if I may.'

'Certainly. Go ahead. Jen calls you her best friend,' said Mrs Bland, amiably. 'You're always fetching some Mexican stuff, and that's why, I guess.'

When Euchre had shuffled into the house Mrs Bland turned to Duane with curiosity and interest in her gaze.

'Bland told me about you.'

'What did he say?' queried Duane, in pretended alarm.

'Oh, you needn't think he's done you dirt. Bland's not that kind of a man. He said: 'Kate, there's a young fellow in camp—rode in here on the dodge. He's no criminal, and he refused to join my band. Wish he would. Slickest hand with a gun I've seen for many a day! I'd like to see him and Chess meet out there in the road.' Then Bland went on to tell how you and Bosomer came together.'

'What did you say?' inquired Duane, as she paused.

'Me? Why, I asked him what you looked like,' she replied, gayly.

'Well?' went on Duane.

'Magnificent chap, Bland said. Bigger than any man in the valley. Just a great blue-eyed sunburned boy!'

'Humph!' exclaimed Duane. 'I'm sorry he led you to expect somebody worth seeing.'

'But I'm not disappointed,' she returned, archly. 'Duane, are you going to stay long here in camp?'

'Yes, till I run out of money and have to move. Why?'

Mrs Bland's face underwent one of the singular changes. The smiles and flushes and glances, all that had been coquettish about her, had lent her a certain attractiveness, almost beauty and youth. But with some powerful emotion she changed and instantly became a woman of discontent, Duane imagined, of deep, violent nature.

'I'll tell you, Duane,' she said, earnestly. 'I'm sure glad if you mean to bide here awhile. I'm a miserable woman, Duane. I'm an outlaw's wife, and I hate him and the life I have to lead. I come of a good family in Brownsville. I never knew Bland was an outlaw till long after he married me. We were separated at times, and I imagined he was away on business. But the truth came out. Bland shot my own cousin, who told me. My family cast me off, and I had to flee with Bland. I was only eighteen then. I've lived here since. I never see a decent woman or man. I never hear anything about my old home or folks or friends. I'm buried here—buried alive with a lot of thieves and murderers. Can you blame me for being glad to see a young fellow—a gentleman—like the boys I used to go with? I tell you it makes me feel full—I want to cry. I'm sick for somebody to talk to. I have no children, thank God! If I had I'd not stay here. I'm sick of this hole. I'm lonely—'

There appeared to be no doubt about the truth of all this. Genuine emotion checked, then halted the hurried speech. She broke down and cried. It seemed strange to Duane that an outlaw's wife—and a woman who fitted her consort and the wild nature of their surroundings—should have weakness enough to weep. Duane believed and pitied her.

'I'm sorry for you,' he said.

'Don't be *sorry* for me,' she said. 'That only makes me see the—the difference between you and me. And don't pay any attention to what these outlaws say about me. They're ignorant. They couldn't understand me. You'll hear that Bland killed men who ran after me. But that's a lie. Bland, like all the other outlaws along this river, is always looking for somebody to kill. He *swears* not, but I don't believe him. He explains that gun-play gravitates to men who are the real thing—that it is provoked by the four-flushes, the bad men. I don't know. All I know is that somebody is being killed every other day. He hated Spence before Spence ever saw me.'

'Would Bland object if I called on you occasionally?' inquired Duane.

'No, he wouldn't. He likes me to have friends. Ask him yourself when he comes back. The trouble has been that two or three of his men fell in love with me, and when half drunk got to fighting. You're not going to do that.'

'I'm not going to get half drunk, that's certain,' replied Duane.

He was surprised to see her eyes dilate, then glow with fire. Before she could reply Euchre returned to the porch, and that put an end to the conversation.

Duane was content to let the matter rest there, and had little more to say. Euchre and Mrs Bland talked and joked, while Duane listened. He tried to form some estimate of her character. Manifestly she had suffered a wrong, if not worse, at Bland's hands. She was bitter, morbid, overemotional. If she was a liar, which seemed likely enough, she was a frank one, and believed herself. She had no cunning. The thing which struck Duane so forcibly was that she thirsted for respect. In that, better than in her weakness of vanity, he thought he had discovered a trait through which he could manage her.

Once, while he was revolving these thoughts, he happened to glance into the house, and deep in the shadow of a corner he caught a pale gleam of Jennie's face with great, staring eyes on him. She had been watching him, listening to what he said. He saw from her expression that she had realized what had been so hard for her to believe. Watching his chance, he flashed a look at her; and then it seemed to him the change in her face was wonderful.

Later, after he had left Mrs Bland with a meaningful '*Adios—mañana*,' and was walking along beside the old outlaw, he found himself thinking of the girl instead of the woman, and of how he had seen her face blaze with hope and gratitude.

7

That night Duane was not troubled by ghosts haunting his waking and sleeping hours. He awoke feeling bright and eager, and grateful to Euchre for having put something worth while into his mind. During breakfast, however, he was unusually thoughtful, working over the idea of how much or how little he would confide in the outlaw. He was aware of Euchre's scrutiny.

'Wal,' began the old man, at last, 'how'd you make out with the kid?'

'Kid?' inquired Duane, tentatively.

'Jennie, I mean. What'd you an' she talk about?'

'We had a little chat. You know you wanted me to cheer her up.'

Euchre sat with coffee-cup poised and narrow eyes studying Duane.

'Reckon you cheered her, all right. What I'm afeared of is mebbe you done the job too well.'

'How so?'

'Wal, when I went in to Jen last night I thought she was half crazy. She was burstin' with excitement, an' the look in her eyes hurt me. She wouldn't tell me a darn word you said. But she hung onto my hands, an' showed every way without speakin' how she wanted to thank me fer bringin' you over. Buck, it was plain to me thet you'd either gone the limit or else you'd been kinder prodigal of cheer an' hope. I'd hate to think you'd led Jennie to hope more'n ever would come true.'

Euchre paused, and, as there seemed no reply forthcoming, he went on:

'Buck, I've seen some outlaws whose word was good. Mine is. You can trust me. I trusted you, didn't I, takin' you over there an' puttin' you wise to my tryin' to help thet poor kid?'

Thus enjoined by Euchre, Duane began to tell the conversation with Jennie and Mrs Bland word for word. Long before he had reached an end Euchre set down the coffee-cup and began to stare, and at the conclusion of the story his face lost some of its red color and beads of sweat stood out thickly on his brow.

'Wal, if thet doesn't floor me!' he ejaculated, blinking at Duane. 'Young man, I figgered you was some swift, an' sure to make your mark on this river; but I reckon I missed your real caliber. So thet's what it means to be a man! I guess I'd forgot. Wal, I'm old, an' even if my heart was in the right place I never was built fer big stunts. Do you know what it'll take to do all you promised Jen?'

'I haven't any idea,' replied Duane, gravely.

'You'll have to pull the wool over Kate Bland's eyes, an' even if she falls in love with you, which's shore likely, thet won't be easy. An she'd kill you in a minnit, Buck, if she ever got wise. You ain't mistaken her none, are you?'

'Not me, Euchre. She's a woman. I'd fear her more than any man.'

'Wal, you'll have to kill Bland an' Chess Alloway an' Rugg, an' mebbe some others, before you can ride off into the hills with thet girl.'

'Why? Can't we plan to be nice to Mrs Bland and then at an opportune time sneak off without any gun-play?'

'Don't see how on earth,' returned Euchre, earnestly. 'When Bland's away he leaves all kinds of spies an' scouts watchin' the valley trails. They've all got rifles. You couldn't git by them. But when the boss is home there's a difference. Only, of course, him an' Chess keep their eyes peeled. They both stay to home pretty much, except when they're playin' *monte* or poker over at Benson's. So I say the best bet is to pick out a good time in the afternoon, drift over careless-like with a couple of hosses, choke Mrs Bland or knock her on the head, take Jennie with you, an' make a rush to git out of the valley. If you had luck you might pull thet stunt without throwin' a gun. But I reckon the best figgerin' would include dodgin' some lead an' leavin' at least Bland or Alloway dead behind you. I'm figgerin', of course, thet when they come home an' find out you're visitin' Kate frequent they'll jest naturally look fer results. Chess don't like you, fer no reason except you're swift on the draw—mebbe swifter 'n him. Thet's the hell of this gun-play business. No one can ever tell who's the swifter of two gunmen till they meet. Thet fact holds a fascination mebbe you'll learn some day. Bland would treat you civil onless there was reason not to, an' then I don't believe he'd invite himself to a meetin' with you. He'd set Chess or Rugg to put you out of the way. Still Bland's no coward, an' if you came across him at a bad moment you'd have to be quicker 'n you was with Bosomer.'

'All right. I'll meet what comes,' said Duane, quickly. 'The great point is to have horses ready and pick the right moment, then rush the trick through.'

'Thet's the *only* chance fer success. An' you can't do it alone.'

'I'll have to. I wouldn't ask you to help me. Leave you behind!'

'Wal, I'll take my chances,' replied Euchre, gruffly. 'I'm goin' to help Jennie, you can gamble your last peso on thet. There's only four men in this camp who would shoot me—Bland, an' his right-hand pards, an' thet rabbit-faced Benson. If you happened to put out Bland and Chess, I'd stand a good show with the other two. Anyway, I'm old an' tired—what's the difference if I do git plugged? I can risk as much as you, Buck, even if I am afraid of gun-play. You said correct, "Hosses ready, the right minnit, then rush the trick." Thet much 's settled. Now let's figger all the little details.'

They talked and planned, though in truth it was Euchre who planned, Duane who listened and agreed. While awaiting the return of Bland and his lieutenants it would be well for Duane to grow friendly with the other outlaws, to sit in a few games of *monte*, or show a willingness to spend a little money. The two schemers were to call upon Mrs Bland every day—Euchre to carry messages of cheer and warning to Jennie, Duane to blind the elder woman at any cost. These preliminaries decided upon, they proceeded to put them into action.

No hard task was it to win the friendship of the most of those good-natured outlaws. They were used to men of a better order than theirs coming to the hidden camps and sooner or later sinking to their lower level. Besides, with them everything was easy come, easy go. That was why life itself went on so carelessly and usually ended so cheaply. There were men among them, however, that made Duane feel that terrible inexplicable wrath rise in his breast. He could not bear to be near them. He could not trust himself. He felt that any instant a word, a deed, something might call too deeply to that instinct he could no longer control. Jackrabbit Benson was one of these men. Because of him and other outlaws of his ilk Duane could scarcely ever forget the reality of things. This was a hidden valley, a robbers' den, a rendezvous for murderers, a wild place stained red by deeds of wild men. And because of that there was always a charged atmosphere. The merriest, idlest, most careless moment might in the flash of an eye end in ruthless and tragic action. In an assemblage of desperate characters it could not be otherwise. The terrible thing that Duane sensed was this. The valley was beautiful, sunny, fragrant, a place to dream in: the mountain-tops were always blue or gold rimmed, the yellow river slid slowly and majestically by, the birds sang in the cottonwoods, the horses grazed and pranced, children played and women longed for love, freedom, happiness; the outlaws rode in and out, free with money and speech; they lived comfortably in their adobe homes, smoked, gambled, talked, laughed, whiled away the idle hours—and all the time life there was wrong, and the simplest moment might be precipitated by the evil into the most awful of contrasts. Duane felt rather than saw a dark, brooding shadow over the valley.

Then, without any solicitation or encouragement from Duane, the Bland woman fell passionately in love with him. His conscience was never troubled about the beginning of that affair. She launched herself. It took no great perspicuity on his part to see that. And the thing which evidently held her in check was the newness, the strangeness, and for the moment the all-satisfying fact of his respect for her. Duane exerted himself to please, to amuse, to interest, to fascinate her, and always with deference. That was his strong point, and it had made his part easy so far. He believed he could carry the whole scheme through without involving himself any deeper.

He was playing at a game of love—playing with life and death! Sometimes he trembled, not that he feared Bland or Alloway or any other man, but at the deeps of life he had come to see into. He was carried out of his old mood. Not once since this daring motive had stirred him had he been haunted by the phantom of Bain beside his bed. Rather had he been haunted by Jennie's sad face, her wistful smile, her eyes. He never was able to speak a word to her. What little communication he had with her was through Euchre, who carried short messages. But he caught glimpses of her every time he went to the Bland house. She contrived somehow to pass door or window, to give him a look when chance afforded. And Duane discovered with surprise that these moments were more thrilling to him than any with Mrs Bland. Often Duane knew Jennie was sitting just inside the window, and then he felt inspired in his talk, and it was all made for her. So at least she came to know him while as yet she was almost a stranger. Jennie had been instructed by Euchre to listen, to understand that this was Duane's only chance to help keep her mind from constant worry, to gather the import of every word which had a double meaning.

Euchre said that the girl had begun to wither under the strain, to burn up with intense hope which had flamed within her. But all the difference Duane could see was a paler face and darker, more wonderful eyes. The eyes seemed to be entreating him to hurry, that time was flying, that soon it might be too late. Then there was another meaning in them, a light, a strange fire wholly inexplicable to Duane. It was only a flash gone in an instant. But he remembered it because he had never seen it in any other woman's eyes. And all through those waiting days he knew that Jennie's face, and especially the warm, fleeting glance she gave him, was responsible for a subtle and gradual change in him. This change he fancied, was only that through remembrance of her he got rid of his pale, sickening ghosts.

One day a careless Mexican threw a lighted cigarette up into the brush matting that served as a ceiling for Benson's den, and there was a fire which left little more than the adobe walls standing. The result was that while repairs were being made there was no gambling and drinking. Time hung very heavily on the hands of some twoscore outlaws. Days passed by without a brawl, and Bland's valley saw more successive hours of peace than ever before. Duane, however, found the hours anything but empty. He spent more time at Mrs Bland's; he walked miles on all the trails leading out of the valley; he had a care for the condition of his two horses.

Upon his return from the latest of these tramps Euchre suggested that they go down to the river to the boat-landing.

'Ferry couldn't run ashore this mornin',' said Eucher. 'River gettin' low an' sand-bars makin' it hard fer hosses. There's a greaser freight-wagon stuck in the mud. I reckon we might hear news from the freighters. Bland's supposed to be in Mexico.'

Nearly all the outlaws in camp were assembled on the riverbank, lolling in the shade of the cottonwoods. The heat was oppressive. Not an outlaw offered to help the freighters, who were trying to dig a heavily freighted wagon out of the quicksand. Few outlaws would work for themselves, let alone for the despised Mexicans.

Duane and Euchre joined the lazy group and sat down with them. Euchre lighted a black pipe, and, drawing his hat over his eyes, lay back in comfort after the manner of the majority of the outlaws. But Duane was alert, observing, thoughtful. He never missed anything. It was his belief that any moment an idle word might be of benefit to him. Moreover, these rough men were always interesting.

'Bland's been chased acrost the river,' said one.

'Naw, he's deliverin' cattle to thet Cuban ship,' replied another.

'Big deal on, hey?'

'Some big, Rugg says the boss hed an order fer fifteen thousand.'

'Say, that order'll take a year to fill.'

'Naw. Hardin is in cahoots with Bland. Between 'em they'll fill orders bigger'n thet.'

'Wondered what Hardin was rustlin' in here fer.'

Duane could not possibly attend to all the conversation among the outlaws. He endeavored to get the drift of talk nearest to him.

'Kid Fuller's goin' to cash,' said a sandy-whiskered little outlaw.

'So Jim was tellin' me. Blood-poison, ain't it? Thet hole wasn't bad. But he took the fever,' rejoined a comrade.

'Deger says the Kid might pull through if he hed nursin'.'

'Wal, Kate Bland ain't nursin' any shot-up boys these days. She hasn't got time.'

A laugh followed this sally; then came a penetrating silence. Some of the outlaws glanced good-naturedly at Duane. They bore him no ill will. Manifestly they were aware of Mrs Bland's infatuation.

'Pete, 'pears to me you've said thet before.'

'Shore. Wal, it's happened before.'

This remark drew louder laughter and more significant glances at Duane. He did not choose to ignore them any longer.

'Boys, poke all the fun you like at me, but don't mention any lady's name again. My hand is nervous and itchy these days.'

He smiled as he spoke, and his speech was drawled; but the good humor in no wise weakened it. Then his latter remark was significant to a class of men who from inclination and necessity practised at gun-drawing until they wore callous and sore places on their thumbs and inculcated in the very deeps of their nervous organization a habit that made even the simplest and most innocent motion of the hand end at or near the hip. There was something remarkable about a gun-fighter's hand. It never seemed to be gloved, never to be injured, never out of sight or in an awkward position.

There were grizzled outlaws in that group, some of whom had many notches on their gun-handles, and they, with their comrades, accorded Duane silence that carried conviction of the regard in which he was held.

Duane could not recall any other instance where he had let fall a familiar speech to these men, and certainly he had never before hinted of his possibilities. He saw instantly that he could not have done better.

'Orful hot, ain't it?' remarked Bill Black, presently. Bill could not keep quiet for long. He was a typical Texas desperado, had never been anything else. He was stoop-shouldered and bow-legged from much riding; a wiry little man, all muscle, with a square head, a hard face partly black from scrubby beard and red from sun, and a bright, roving, cruel eye. His shirt was open at the neck, showing a grizzled breast.

'Is there any guy in this heah outfit sport enough to go swimmin'?' he asked.

'My Gawd, Bill, you ain't agoin' to wash!' exclaimed a comrade.

This raised a laugh in which Black joined. But no one seemed eager to join him in a bath.

'Laziest outfit I ever rustled with,' went on Bill, discontentedly. 'Nuthin' to do! Say, if nobody wants to swim maybe some of you'll gamble?'

He produced a dirty pack of cards and waved them at the motionless crowd.

'Bill, you're too good at cards,' replied a lanky outlaw.

'Now, Jasper, you say thet powerful sweet, an' you look sweet, er I might take it to heart,' replied Black, with a sudden change of tone.

Here it was again—that upflashing passion. What Jasper saw fit to reply would mollify the outlaw or it would not. There was an even balance.

'No offense, Bill,' said Jasper, placidly, without moving.

Bill grunted and forgot Jasper. But he seemed restless and dissatisfied. Duane knew him to be an inveterate gambler. And as Benson's place was out of running-order, Black was like a fish on dry land.

'Wal, if you-all are afraid of the cards, what will you bet on?' he asked, in disgust.

'Bill, I'll play you a game of mumbly peg fer two bits,' replied one.

Black eagerly accepted. Betting to him was a serious matter. The game obsessed him, not the stakes. He entered into the mumbly-peg contest with a thoughtful mien and a corded brow. He won. Other comrades tried their luck with him and lost. Finally, when Bill had exhausted their supply of two-bit pieces or their desire for that particular game, he offered to bet on anything.

'See thet turtle-dove there?' he said, pointing. 'I'll bet he'll scare at one stone or he won't. Five pesos he'll fly or he won't fly when some one chucks a stone. Who'll take me up?'

That appeared to be more than the gambling spirit of several outlaws could withstand.

'Take thet. Easy money,' said one.

'Who's goin' to chuck the stone?' asked another.

'Anybody,' replied Bill.

'Wal, I'll bet you I can scare him with one stone,' said the first outlaw.

'We're in on thet, Jim to fire the darnick,' chimed in the others.

The money was put up, the stone thrown. The turtle-dove took flight, to the great joy of all the outlaws except Bill.

'I'll bet you-all he'll come back to thet tree inside of five minnits,' he offered, imperturbably.

Hereupon the outlaws did not show any laziness in their alacrity to cover Bill's money as it lay on the grass. Somebody had a watch, and they all sat down, dividing attention between the timepiece and the tree. The minutes dragged by to the accompaniment of various jocular remarks anent a fool and his money. When four and three-quarter minutes had passed a turtle-dove alighted in the cottonwood. Then ensued an impressive silence while Bill calmly pocketed the fifty dollars.

'But it hain't the same dove!' exclaimed one outlaw, excitedly. 'This 'n' is smaller, dustier, not so purple.'

Bill eyed the speaker loftily.

'Wal, you'll have to ketch the other one to prove thet. *Sabe*, pard? Now I'll bet any gent heah the fifty I won thet I can scare thet dove with one stone.'

No one offered to take his wager.

'Wal, then, I'll bet any of you even money thet you *can't* scare him with one stone.'

Not proof against this chance, the outlaws made up a purse, in no wise disconcerted by Bill's contemptuous allusions to their banding together. The stone was thrown. The dove did not fly. Thereafter, in regard to that bird, Bill was unable to coax or scorn his comrades into any kind of wager.

He tried them with a multiplicity of offers, and in vain. Then he appeared at a loss for some unusual and seductive wager. Presently a little ragged Mexican boy came along the river trail, a particularly starved and poor-looking little fellow. Bill called to him and gave him a handful of silver coins. Speechless, dazed, he went his way hugging the money.

'I'll bet he drops some before he gits to the road,' declared Bill. 'I'll bet he runs. Hurry, you four-flush gamblers.'

Bill failed to interest any of his companions, and forthwith became sullen and silent. Strangely his good humor departed in spite of the fact that he had won considerable.

Duane, watching the disgruntled outlaw, marveled at him and wondered what was in his mind. These men were more variable than children, as unstable as water, as dangerous as dynamite.

'Bill, I'll bet you ten you can't spill whatever's in the bucket thet peon's packin',' said the outlaw called Jim.

Black's head came up with the action of a hawk about to swoop.

Duane glanced from Black to the road, where he saw a crippled peon carrying a tin bucket toward the river. This peon was a half-witted Indian who lived in a shack and did odd jobs for the Mexicans. Duane had met him often.

'Jim, I'll take you up,' replied Black.

Something, perhaps a harshness in his voice, caused Duane to whirl. He caught a leaping gleam in the outlaw's eye.

'Aw, Bill, thet's too fur a shot,' said Jasper, as Black rested an elbow on his knee and sighted over the long, heavy Colt. The distance to the peon was about fifty paces, too far for even the most expert shot to hit a moving object so small as a bucket.

Duane, marvelously keen in the alignment of sights, was positive that Black held too high. Another look at the hard face, now tense and dark with blood, confirmed Duane's suspicion that the outlaw was not aiming at the bucket at all. Duane leaped and struck the leveled gun out of his hand. Another outlaw picked it up.

Black fell back astounded. Deprived of his weapon, he did not seem the same man, or else he was cowed by Duane's significant and formidable front. Sullenly he turned away without even asking for his gun.

8

What a contrast, Duane thought, the evening of that day presented to the state of his soul!

The sunset lingered in golden glory over the distant Mexican mountains; twilight came slowly; a faint breeze blew from the river cool and sweet; the late cooing of a dove and the tinkle of a cowbell were the only sounds; a serene and tranquil peace lay over the valley.

Inside Duane's body there was strife. This third facing of a desperate man had thrown him off his balance. It had not been fatal, but it threatened so much. The better side of his nature seemed to urge him to die rather than to go on fighting or opposing ignorant, unfortunate, savage men. But the perversity of him was so great that it dwarfed reason, conscience. He could not resist it. He felt something dying in him. He suffered. Hope seemed far away. Despair had seized upon him and was driving him into a reckless mood when he thought of Jennie.

He had forgotten her. He had forgotten that he had promised to save her. He had forgotten that he meant to snuff out as many lives as might stand between her and freedom. The very remembrance sheered off his morbid introspection. She made a difference. How strange for him to realize that! He felt grateful to her. He had been forced into outlawry; she had been stolen from her people and carried into captivity. They had met in the river fastness, he to instill hope into her despairing life, she to be the means, perhaps, of keeping him from sinking to the level of her captors. He became conscious of a strong and beating desire to see her, talk with her.

These thoughts had run through his mind while on his way to Mrs Bland's house. He had let Euchre go on ahead because he wanted more time to compose himself. Darkness had about set in when he reached his destination. There was no light in the house. Mrs Bland was waiting for him on the porch.

She embraced him, and the sudden, violent, unfamiliar contact sent such a shock through him that he all but forgot the deep game he was playing. She, however, in her agitation did not notice his shrinking. From her embrace and the tender, incoherent words that flowed with it he gathered that Euchre had acquainted her of his action with Black.

'He might have killed you!' she whispered, more clearly; and if Duane had ever heard love in a voice he heard it then. It softened him. After all, she was a woman, weak, fated through her nature, unfortunate in her experience of life, doomed to unhappiness and tragedy. He met her advance so far that he returned the embrace and kissed her. Emotion such as she showed would have made any woman sweet, and she had a certain charm. It was easy, even pleasant, to kiss her; but Duane resolved that, whatever her abandonment might become, he would not go further than the lie she made him act.

'Buck, you love me?' she whispered.

'Yes—yes,' he burst out, eager to get it over, and even as he spoke he caught the pale gleam of Jennie's face through the window. He felt a shame he was glad she could not see. Did she remember that she had promised not to misunderstand any action of his? What did she think of him, seeing him out there in the dusk with this bold woman in his arms? Somehow that dim sight of Jennie's pale face, the big dark eyes, thrilled him, inspired him to his hard task of the present.

'Listen, dear,' he said to the woman, and he meant his words for the girl. 'I'm going to take you away from this outlaw den if I have to kill Bland, Alloway, Rugg—anybody who stands in my path. You were dragged here. You are good—I know it. There's happiness for you somewhere—a home among good people who will care for you. Just wait till—'

His voice trailed off and failed from excess of emotion. Kate Bland closed her eyes and leaned her head on his breast. Duane felt her heart beat against his, and conscience smote him a keen blow. If she loved him so much! But memory and understanding of her character hardened him again and he gave her such commiseration as was due her sex, and no more.

'Boy, that's good of you,' she whispered, 'but it's too late. I'm done for. I can't leave Bland. All I ask is that you love me a little and stop your gun-throwing.'

The moon had risen over the eastern bulge of dark mountain, and now the valley was flooded with mellow light, and shadows of cottonwoods wavered against the silver.

Suddenly the clip-clop, clip-clop of hoofs caused Duane to raise his head and listen. Horses were coming down the road from the head of the valley. The hour was unusual for riders to come in. Presently the narrow, moonlit lane was crossed at its far end by black moving objects. Two horses Duane discerned.

'It's Bland!' whispered the woman, grasping Duane with shaking hands. 'You must run! No, he'd see you. That'd be worse. It's Bland! I know his horse's trot.'

'But you said he wouldn't mind my calling here,' protested Duane. 'Euchre's with me. It'll be all right.'

'Maybe so,' she replied, with visible effort at self-control. Manifestly she had a great fear of Bland. 'If I could only think!'

Then she dragged Duane to the door, pushed him in.

'Euchre, come out with me! Duane, you stay with the girl! I'll tell Bland you're in love with her. Jen, if you give us away I'll wring your neck.'

The swift action and fierce whisper told Duane that Mrs. Bland was herself again. Duane stepped close to Jennie, who stood near the window. Neither spoke, but her hands were outstretched to meet his own. They were small, trembling hands, cold as ice. He held them close, trying to convey what he felt—that he would protect her. She leaned against him, and they looked out of the window. Duane felt calm and sure of himself. His most pronounced feeling besides that for the frightened girl was a curiosity as to how Mrs Bland would rise to the occasion. He saw the riders dismount down the lane and wearily come forward. A boy led away the horses. Euchre, the old fox, was talking loud and with remarkable ease, considering what he claimed was his natural cowardice.

'—that was way back in the sixties, about the time of the war,' he was saying. 'Rustlin' cattle wasn't nuthin' then to what it is now. An' times is rougher these days. This gun-throwin' has come to be a disease. Men have an itch for the draw same as they used to have fer poker. The only real gambler outside of greasers we ever had here was Bill an' I presume Bill is burnin' now.'

The approaching outlaws, hearing voices, halted a rod or so from the porch. Then Mrs Bland uttered an exclamation, ostensibly meant to express surprise, and hurried out to meet them. She greeted her husband warmly and gave welcome to the other man. Duane could not see well enough in the shadow to recognize Bland's companion, but he believed it was Alloway.

'Dog-tired we are and starved,' said Bland, heavily. 'Who's here with you?'

'That's Euchre on the porch. Duane is inside at the window with Jen,' replied Mrs Bland.

'Duane!' he exclaimed. Then he whispered low—something Duane could not catch.

'Why, I asked him to come,' said the chief's wife. She spoke easily and naturally and made no change in tone. 'Jen has been ailing. She gets thinner and whiter every day. Duane came here one day with Euchre, saw Jen, and went looney over her pretty face, same as all you men. So I let him come.'

Bland cursed low and deep under his breath. The other man made a violent action of some kind and apparently was quieted by a restraining hand.

'Kate, you let Duane make love to Jennie?' queried Bland, incredulously.

'Yes, I did,' replied the wife, stubbornly. 'Why not? Jen's in love with him. If he takes her away and marries her she can be a decent woman.'

Bland kept silent a moment, then his laugh pealed out loud and harsh.

'Chess, did you get that? Well, by God! what do you think of my wife?'

'She's lyin' or she's crazy,' replied Alloway, and his voice carried an unpleasant ring.

Mrs Bland promptly and indignantly told her husband's lieutenant to keep his mouth shut.

'Ho, ho, ho!' rolled out Bland's laugh.

Then he led the way to the porch, his spurs clinking, the weapons he was carrying rattling, and he flopped down on a bench.

'How are you, boss?' asked Euchre.

'Hello, old man. I'm well, but all in.'

Alloway slowly walked on to the porch and leaned against the rail. He answered Euchre's greeting with a nod. Then he stood there a dark, silent figure.

Mrs Bland's full voice in eager questioning had a tendency to ease the situation. Bland replied briefly to her, reporting a remarkably successful trip.

Duane thought it time to show himself. He had a feeling that Bland and Alloway would let him go for the moment. They were plainly non-plussed, and Alloway seemed sullen, brooding.

'Jennie,' whispered Duane, 'that was clever of Mrs Bland. We'll keep up the deception. Any day now be ready!'

She pressed close to him, and a barely audible 'Hurry!' came breathing into his ear.

'Good night, Jennie,' he said, aloud. 'Hope you feel better to-morrow.'

Then he stepped out into the moonlight and spoke. Bland returned the greeting, and, though he was not amiable, he did not show resentment.

'Met Jasper as I rode in,' said Bland, presently. 'He told me you made Bill Black mad, and there's liable to be a fight. What did you go off the handle about?'

Duane explained the incident. 'I'm sorry I happened to be there,' he went on. 'It wasn't my business.'

'Scurvy trick that'd been,' muttered Bland. 'You did right. All the same, Duane, I want you to stop quarreling with my men. If you were one of us—that'd be different. I can't keep my men from fighting. But I'm not called on to let an outsider hang around my camp and plug my rustlers.'

'I guess I'll have to be hitting the trail for somewhere,' said Duane.

'Why not join my band? You've got a bad start already, Duane, and if I know this border you'll never be a respectable citizen again. You're a born killer. I know every bad man on this frontier. More than one of them have told me that something exploded in their brain, and when sense came back there lay another dead man. It's not so with me. I've done a little shooting, too, but I never wanted to kill another man just to rid myself of the last one. My dead men don't sit on my chest at night. That's the gun-fighter's trouble. He's crazy. He has to kill a new man—he's driven to it to forget the last one.'

'But I'm no gun-fighter,' protested Duane. 'Circumstances made me—'

'No doubt,' interrupted Bland, with a laugh. 'Circumstances made me a rustler.

You don't know yourself. You're young; you've got a temper; your father was one of the most dangerous men Texas ever had. I don't see any other career for you. Instead of going it alone—a lone wolf, as the Texans say—why not make friends with other outlaws? You'll live longer.'

Euchre squirmed in his seat.

'Boss, I've been givin' the boy egzactly thet same line of talk. Thet's why I took him to bunk with me. If he makes pards among us there won't be any more trouble. An' he'd be a grand feller fer the gang. I've seen Wild Bill Hickok throw a gun, an' Billy the Kid, an' Hardin, an' Chess here—all the fastest men on the border. An' with apologies to present company, I'm here to say Duane has them all skinned. His draw is different. You can't see how he does it.'

Euchre's admiring praise served to create an effective little silence. Alloway shifted uneasily on his feet, his spurs jangling faintly, and did not lift his head. Bland seemed thoughtful.

'That's about the only qualification I have to make me eligible for your band,' said Duane, easily.

'It's good enough,' replied Bland, shortly. 'Will you consider the idea?'

'I'll think it over. Good night.'

He left the group, followed by Euchre. When they reached the end of the lane, and before they had exchanged a word, Bland called Euchre back. Duane proceeded slowly along the moonlit road to the cabin and sat down under the cottonwoods to wait for Euchre. The night was intense and quiet, a low hum of insects giving the effect of a congestion of life. The beauty of the soaring moon, the ebony cañons of shadow under the mountain, the melancholy serenity of the perfect night, made Duane shudder in the realization of how far aloof he now was from enjoyment of these things. Never again so long as he lived could he be natural. His mind was clouded. His eye and ear henceforth must register impressions of nature, but the joy of them had fled.

Still, as he sat there with a foreboding of more and darker work ahead of him there was yet a strange sweetness left to him, and it lay in thought of Jennie. The pressure of her cold little hands lingered in his. He did not think of her as a woman, and he did not analyze his feelings. He just had vague, dreamy thoughts and imaginations that were interspersed in the constant and stern revolving of plans to save her.

A shuffling step roused him. Euchre's dark figure came crossing the moonlit grass under the cottonwoods. The moment the outlaw reached him Duane saw that he was laboring under great excitement. It scarcely affected Duane. He seemed to be acquiring patience, calmness, strength.

'Bland kept you pretty long,' he said.

'Wait till I git my breath,' replied Euchre. He sat silent a little while, fanning himself with a sombrero, though the night was cool, and then he went into the cabin to return presently with a lighted pipe.

'Fine night,' he said; and his tone further acquainted Duane with Euchre's quaint humor. 'Fine night for love-affairs, by gum!'

'I'd noticed that,' rejoined Duane, dryly.

'Wal, I'm a son of a gun if I didn't stand an' watch Bland choke his wife till her tongue stuck out an' she got black in the face.'

'No!' ejaculated Duane.

'Hope to die if I didn't. Buck, listen to this here yarn. When I got back to the porch I seen Bland was wakin' up. He'd been too fagged out to figger much. Alloway an' Kate had gone in the house, where they lit up the lamps. I heard Kate's high voice, but Alloway never chirped. He's not the talkin' kind, an' he's damn dangerous when he's thet way. Bland asked me some questions right from the shoulder. I was ready for them, an' I swore the moon was green cheese. He was satisfied. Bland always trusted me, an' liked me, too, I reckon. I hated to lie black thet way. But he's a hard man with bad intentions toward Jennie, an' I'd double-cross him any day.

'Then we went into the house. Jennie had gone to her little room, an' Bland called her to come out. She said she was undressin'. An' he ordered her to put her clothes back on. Then, Buck, his next move was some surprisin'. He deliberately throwed a gun on Kate. Yes sir, he pointed his big blue Colt right at her, an' he says:

' "I've a mind to blow out your brains."

' "Go ahead," says Kate, cool as could be.

' "You lied to me," he roars.

'Kate laughed in his face. Bland slammed the gun down an' made a grab fer her. She fought him, but wasn't a match fer him, an' he got her by the throat. He choked her till I thought she was strangled. Alloway made him stop. She flopped down on the bed an' gasped fer a while. When she come to them hard-shelled cusses went after her, trying to make her give herself away. I think Bland was jealous. He suspected she'd got thick with you an' was foolin' him. I reckon thet's a sore feelin' fer a man to have—to guess pretty nice, but not to *be* sure. Bland gave it up after a while. An' then he cussed an' raved at her. One sayin' of his worth pinnin' in your sombrero: "It ain't nuthin' to kill a man. I don't need much fer thet. But I want to *know*, you hussy!"

'Then he went in an' dragged poor Jen out. She'd had time to dress. He was so mad he hurt her sore leg. You know Jen got thet injury fightin' off one of them devils in the dark. An' when I seen Bland twist her—hurt her—I had a queer hot feelin' deep down in me, an' fer the only time in my life I wished I was a gun-fighter.

'Wal, Jen amazed me. She was whiter'n a sheet, an' her eyes were big and stary, but she had nerve. Fust time I ever seen her show any.

' "Jennie," he said, "my wife said Duane came here to see you. I believe she's lyin'. I think she's been carryin' on with him, an' I want to *know*. If she's been an' you tell me the truth I'll let you go. I'll send you out to Huntsville, where you can communicate with your friends. I'll give you money."

'Thet must hev been a hell of a minnit fer Kate Bland. If ever I seen death in a man's eye I seen it in Bland's. He loves her. Thet's the strange part of it.

' "Has Duane been comin' here to see my wife?" Bland asked, fierce-like.

' "No," said Jennie.

' "He's been after you?"

' "Yes."

' "He has fallen in love with you? Kate said thet."

' "I—I'm not—I don't know—he hasn't told me."

' "But you're in love with him?"

' "Yes," she said; an', Buck, if you only could have *seen* her! She throwed up her head, an' her eyes were full of fire. Bland seemed dazed at sight of her. An' Alloway, why, thet little skunk of an outlaw cried right out. He was hit plumb center. He's in love with Jen. An' the look of her then was enough to make any feller quit. He jest slunk out of the room. I told you, mebbe, thet he'd been tryin' to git Bland to marry Jen to him. So even a tough like Alloway can love a woman!

'Bland stamped up an' down the room. He sure was dyin' hard.

' "Jennie," he said, once more turnin' to her. "You swear in fear of your life thet you're tellin' truth. Kate's not in love with Duane? She's let him come to see *you?* There's been nuthin' between them?"

' "No. I swear," answered Jennie: an' Bland sat down like a man licked.

' "Go to bed, you white-faced—" Bland choked on some word or other—a bad one, I reckon—an' he positively shook in his chair.

'Jennie went then, an' Kate began to have hysterics, an' your Uncle Euchre ducked his nut out of the door an' come home.'

Duane did not have a word to say at the end of Euchre's long harangue. He experienced relief. As a matter of fact, he had expected a good deal worse. He thrilled at the thought of Jennie perjuring herself to save that abandoned woman. What mysteries these feminine creatures were!

'Wal, there's where our little deal stands now,' resumed Euchre, meditatively. 'You know, Buck, as well as me thet if you'd been some feller who hadn't shown he was a wonder with a gun you'd now be full of lead. If you'd happen to kill Bland an' Alloway, I reckon you'd be as safe on this here border as you would in Santone. Such is gun fame in this land of the draw.'

9

Both men were awake early, silent with the premonition of trouble ahead, thoughtful of the fact that the time for the long-planned action was at hand. It was remarkable that a man as loquacious as Euchre could hold his tongue so long; and this was significant of the deadly nature of the intended deed. During breakfast he said a few words customary in the service of food. At the conclusion of the meal he seemed to come to an end of deliberation.

'Buck, the sooner the better now,' he declared, with a glint in his eye. 'The more time we use up now the less surprised Bland'll be.'

'I'm ready when you are,' replied Duane, quietly, and he rose from the table.

'Wal, saddle up, then,' went on Euchre, gruffly. 'Tie on them two packs I made, one fer each saddle. You can't tell—mebbe either hoss will be carryin' double. It's good they're both big, strong hosses. Guess thet wasn't a wise move of your Uncle Euchre's—bringin' in your hosses an' havin' them ready?'

'Euchre, I hope you're not going to get in bad here. I'm afraid you are. Let me do the rest now,' said Duane.

The old outlaw eyed him sarcastically.

'Thet'd be turrible now, wouldn't it? If you want to know, why, I'm in bad already. I didn't tell you thet Alloway called me last night. He's gettin' wise pretty quick.'

'Euchre, you're going with me?' queried Duane, suddenly divining the truth.

'Wal, I reckon. Either to hell or safe over the mountain! I wisht I was a gun-fighter. I hate to leave here without takin' a peg at Jackrabbit Benson. Now, Buck, you do some hard figgerin' while I go nosin' round. It's pretty early, which 's all the better.'

Euchre put on his sombrero, and as he went out Duane saw that he wore a gun-and-cartridge belt. It was the first time Duane had ever seen the outlaw armed.

Duane packed his few belongings into his saddle bags, and then carried the saddles out to the corral. An abundance of alfalfa in the corral showed that the horses had fared well. They had gotten almost fat during his stay in the valley. He watered them, put on the saddles loosely cinched, and then the bridles. His next move was to fill the two canvas waterbottles. That done, he returned to the cabin to wait.

At the moment he felt no excitement or agitation of any kind. There was no more thinking and planning to do. The hour had arrived, and he was ready. He understood perfectly the desperate chances he must take. His thoughts became confined to Euchre and the surprising loyalty and goodness in the hardened old outlaw. Time passed slowly. Duane kept glancing at his watch. He hoped to start the thing and get away before the outlaws were out of their beds. Finally he heard the shuffle of Euchre's boots on the hard path. The sound was quicker than usual.

When Euchre came around the corner of the cabin Duane was not so astounded as he was concerned to see the outlaw white and shaking. Sweat dripped from him. He had a wild look.

'Luck ours—so—fur, Buck!' he panted.

'You don't look it,' replied Duane.

'I'm turrible sick. Jest killed a man. Fust one I ever killed!'

'Who?' asked Duane, startled.

'Jackrabbit Benson. An' sick as I am, I'm gloryin' in it. I went nosin' round up the road. Saw Alloway goin' into Deger's. He's thick with the Degers. Reckon he's askin' questions. Anyway, I was sure glad to see him away from Bland's. An' he didn't see me. When I dropped into Benson's there wasn't nobody there but Jackrabbit an' some greasers he was startin' to work. Benson never had no use fer me. An' he up an' said he wouldn't give a two-bit piece fer my life. I asked him why.

' "You're double-crossin' the boss an' Chess," he said.

' "Jack, what'd you give fer your own life?" I asked him.

'He straightened up surprised an' mean-lookin'. An' I let him have it, plumb center! He wilted, an' the greasers run. I reckon I'll never sleep again. But I had to do it.'

Duane asked if the shot had attracted any attention outside.

'I didn't see anybody but the greasers, an' I sure looked sharp. Comin' back I cut across through the cottonwoods past Bland's cabin. I meant to keep out of sight, but somehow I had an idee I might find out if Bland was awake yet. Sure enough I run plumb into Beppo, the boy who tends Bland's hosses. Beppo likes me. An' when I inquired of his boss he said Bland had been up all night fightin' with the Señora. An', Buck, here's how I figger. Bland couldn't let up last night. He was sore, an' he went after Kate again, tryin' to wear her down. Jest as likely he might have went after Jennie, with wuss intentions. Anyway, he an' Kate must have had it hot an' heavy. We're pretty lucky.'

'It seems so. Well, I'm going,' said Duane, tersely.

'Lucky! I should smile! Bland's been up all night after a most draggin' ride home. He'll be fagged out this mornin', sleepy, sore, an' he won't be expectin' hell before breakfast. Now, you walk over to his house. Meet him how you like. Thet's your game. But I'm suggestin', if he comes out an' you want to parley, you can jest say you'd thought over his proposition an' was ready to join his band, or you ain't. You'll have to kill him, an' it'd save time to go fer your gun on sight. Might be wise, too, fer it's likely he'll do thet same.'

'How about the horses?'

'I'll fetch them an' come along about two minnits behind you. 'Pears to me you ought to have the job done an' Jennie outside by the time I git there. Once on them hosses, we can ride out of camp before Alloway or anybody else gits into action. Jennie ain't much heavier 'n a rabbit. Thet big black will carry you both.'

'All right. But once more let me persuade you to stay—not to mix any more in this,' said Duane, earnestly.

'Nope. I'm goin'. You heard what Benson told me. Alloway wouldn't give me the benefit of any doubts. Buck, a last word—look out fer thet Bland woman!'

Duane merely nodded, and then, saying that the horses were ready, he strode away through the grove. Accounting for the short cut across grove and field, it was about five minutes' walk up to Bland's house. To Duane it seemed long in time and distance, and he had difficulty in restraining his pace. As he walked there came a gradual and subtle change in his feelings. Again he was going out to meet a man in conflict. He could have avoided this meeting. But despite the fact of his courting the encounter he had not as yet felt that hot, inexplicable rush of blood. The motive of this deadly action was not personal, and somehow that made a difference.

No outlaws were in sight. He saw several Mexican herders with cattle. Blue columns of smoke curled up over some of the cabins. The fragrant smell of it reminded Duane of his home and cutting wood for the stove. He noted a cloud of creamy mist rising above the river, dissolving in the sunlight.

Then he entered Bland's lane.

While yet some distance from the cabin he heard loud, angry voices of man and woman. Bland and Kate still quarreling! He took a quick survey of the surroundings. There was now not even a Mexican in sight. Then he hurried a little. Halfway down the lane he turned his head to peer through the cottonwoods. This time he saw Euchre coming with the horses. There was no indication that the old outlaw might lose his nerve at the end. Duane had feared this.

Duane now changed his walk to a leisurely saunter. He reached the porch and then distinguished what was said inside the cabin.

'If you do, Bland, by Heaven I'll fix you and her!' That was panted out in Kate Bland's full voice.

'Let me loose! I'm going in there, I tell you!' replied Bland, hoarsely.

'What for?'

'I want to make a little love to her. Ha! ha! It'll be fun to have the laugh on her new lover.'

'You lie!' cried Kate Bland.

'I'm not saying what I'll do to her *afterward*.' His voice grew hoarser with passion. 'Let me go now!'

'No! no! I won't let you go. You'll choke the—the truth out of her—you'll kill her.'

'The *truth*!' hissed Bland.

'Yes. I lied. Jen lied. But she lied to save me. You needn't—murder her—for that.'

Bland cursed horribly. Then followed a wrestling sound of bodies in violent straining contact—the scrape of feet—the jangle of spurs—a crash of sliding table or chair, and then the cry of a woman in pain.

Duane stepped into the open door, inside the room. Kate Bland lay half across a table where she had been flung, and she was trying to get to her feet. Bland's back was turned. He had opened the door into Jennie's room and had one foot across the threshold. Duane caught the girl's low, shuddering cry. Then he called out loud and clear.

With cat-like swiftness Bland wheeled, then froze on the threshold. His sight, quick as his action, caught Duane's menacing unmistakable position.

Bland's big frame filled the door. He was in a bad place to reach for his gun. But he would not have time for a step. Duane read in his eyes the desperate calculation of chances. For a fleeting instant Bland shifted his glance to his wife. Then his whole body seemed to vibrate with the swing of his arm.

Duane shot him. He fell forward, his gun exploding as it hit into the floor, and dropped loose from stretching fingers. Duane stood over him, stooped to turn him on his back. Bland looked up with clouded gaze, then gasped his last.

'Duane, you've killed him!' cried Kate Bland, huskily. 'I knew you'd have to!'

She staggered against the wall, her eyes dilating, her strong hands clenching, her face slowly whitening. She appeared shocked, half stunned, but showed no grief.

'Jennie!' called Duane, sharply.

'Oh—Duane!' came a halting reply.

'Yes. Come out. Hurry!'

She came out with uneven steps, seeing only him, and she stumbled over Bland's body. Duane caught her arm, swung her behind him. He feared the woman when she realized how she had been duped. His action was protective, and his movement toward the door equally as significant.

'Duane!' cried Mrs Bland.

It was no time for talk. Duane edged on, keeping Jennie behind him. At that moment there was a pounding of iron-shod hoofs out in the lane. Kate Bland bounded to the door. When she turned back her amazement was changing to realization.

'Where're you taking Jen?' she cried, her voice like a man's.

'Get out of my way,' replied Duane. His look perhaps, without speech, was enough for her. In an instant she was transformed into a fury.

'You hound! All the time you were fooling me! You made love to me! You let me believe—you swore you loved me! Now I see what was queer about you. All for that girl! But you can't have her. You'll never leave here alive. Give me that girl! Let me—get at her! She'll never win any more men in this camp.'

She was a powerful woman, and it took all Duane's strength to ward off her onslaughts. She clawed at Jennie over his upheld arm. Every second her fury increased.

'*Help! help! help!*' she shrieked, in a voice that must have penetrated to the remotest cabin in the valley.

'Let go! Let go!' cried Duane, low and sharp. He still held his gun in his right hand, and it began to be hard for him to ward the woman off. His coolness had gone with her shriek for help. 'Let go!' he repeated, and he shoved her fiercely.

Suddenly she snatched a rifle off the wall and backed away, her strong hands fumbling at the lever. As she jerked it down, throwing a shell into the chamber and cocking the weapon, Duane leaped upon her. He struck up the rifle as it went off, the powder burning his face.

'Jennie, run out! Get on a horse!' he said.

Jennie flashed out of the door.

With an iron grasp Duane held the rifle-barrel. He had grasped it with his left hand, and he gave such a pull that he swung the crazed woman off the floor. But he could not loose her grip. She was as strong as he.

'Kate! Let go!'

He tried to intimidate her. She did not see his gun thrust in her face, or reason had given way to such an extent to passion that she did not care. She cursed. Her husband had used the same curses, and from her lips they seemed strange, unsexed, more deadly. Like a tigress she fought him; her face no longer resembled a woman's. The evil of that outlaw life, the wildness and rage, the meaning to kill, was even in such a moment terribly impressed upon Duane.

He heard a cry from outside—a man's cry, hoarse and alarming.

It made him think of loss of time. This demon of a woman might yet block his plan.

'Let go!' he whispered, and felt his lips stiff. In the grimness of that instant he relaxed his hold on the rifle-barrel.

With sudden, redoubled, irresistible strength she wrenched the rifle down and discharged it. Duane felt a blow—a shock—a burning agony tearing through his breast. Then in a frenzy he jerked so powerfully upon the rifle that he threw the woman against the wall. She fell and seemed stunned.

Duane leaped back, whirled, flew out of the door to the porch. The sharp cracking of a gun halted him. He saw Jennie holding to the bridle of his bay horse. Euchre was astride the other, and he had a Colt leveled, and he was firing down the lane. Then came a single shot, heavier, and Euchre's ceased. He fell from the horse.

A swift glance back showed to Duane a man coming down the lane. Chess Alloway! His gun was smoking. He broke into a run. Then in an instant he saw Duane, and tried to check his pace as he swung up his arm. But that slight pause was fatal. Duane shot, and Alloway was falling when his gun went off. His bullet whistled close to Duane and thudded into the cabin.

Duane bounded down to the horses. Jennie was trying to hold the plunging bay. Euchre lay flat on his back, dead, a bullet-hole in his shirt, his face set hard, and his hands twisted round gun and bridle.

'Jennie, you've nerve, all right!' cried Duane, as he dragged down the horse she was holding. 'Up with you now! There! Never mind—long stirrups! Hang on somehow!'

He caught his bridle out of Euchre's clutching grip and leaped astride. The frightened horses jumped into a run and thundered down the lane into the road. Duane saw men running from cabins. He heard shouts. But there were no shots fired. Jennie seemed able to stay on her horse, but without stirrups she was thrown about so much that Duane rode closer and reached out to grasp her arm.

Thus they rode through the valley to the trail that led up over the steep and broken Rim Rock. As they began to climb Duane looked back. No pursuers were in sight.

'Jennie, we're going to get away!' he cried, exultation for her in his voice.

She was gazing horror-stricken at his breast, as in turning to look back he faced her.

'Oh, Duane, your shirt's all bloody!' she faltered, pointing with trembling fingers.

With her words Duane became aware of two things—the hand he instinctively placed to his breast still held his gun, and he had sustained a terrible wound.

Duane had been shot through the breast far enough down to give him grave apprehension of his life. The clean-cut hole made by the bullet bled freely both at its entrance and where it had come out, but with no signs of hemorrhage. He did not bleed at the mouth; however, he began to cough up a reddish-tinged foam.

As they rode on, Jennie, with pale face and mute lips, looked at him.

'I'm badly hurt, Jennie,' he said, 'but I guess I'll stick it out.'

'The woman—did she shoot you?'

'Yes. She was a devil. Euchre told me to look out for her. I wasn't quick enough.'

'You didn't have to—to—' shivered the girl.

'No! no!' he replied.

They did not stop climbing while Duane tore a scarf and made compresses, which he bound tightly over his wounds. The fresh horses made fast time up the rough trail. From open places Duane looked down. When they surmounted the steep ascent and stood on top of the Rim Rock, with no signs of pursuit down in the valley, and with the wild, broken vastnesses before them, Duane turned to the girl and assured her that they now had every chance of escape.

'But—your—wound!' she faltered, with dark, troubled eyes. 'I see—the blood—dripping from your back!'

'Jennie, I'll take a lot of killing,' he said.

Then he became silent and attended to the uneven trail. He was aware presently that he had not come into Bland's camp by this route. But that did not matter; any trail leading out beyond the Rim Rock was safe enough. What he wanted was to get far away into some wild retreat where he could hide till he recovered from his wound. He seemed to feel a fire inside his breast, and his throat burned so that it was necessary for him to take a swallow of water every little while. He began to suffer considerable pain, which increased as the hours went by and then gave way to a numbness. Gradually he lost his steadiness and his keen sight; and he realized that if he were to meet foes, or if pursuing outlaws should come up with him, he could make only a poor stand. So he turned off on a trail that appeared seldom traveled.

Soon after this move he became conscious of a further thickening of his senses. He felt able to hold on to his saddle for a while longer, but he was failing. Then he thought he ought to advise Jennie, so in case she was left alone she would have some idea of what to do.

'Jennie, I'll give out soon,' he said. 'No—I don't mean—what you think. But I'll drop soon. My strength's going. If I die—you ride back to the main trail. Hide and rest by day. Ride at night. That trail goes to water. I believe you could get across the Nueces, where some rancher will take you in.'

Duane could not get the meaning of her incoherent reply. He rode on, and soon he could not see the trail or hear his horse. He did not know whether they traveled a mile or many times that far. But he was conscious when the horse stopped, and had a vague sense of falling and feeling Jennie's arms before all became dark to him.

When consciousness returned he found himself lying in a little hut of mesquite branches. It was well built and evidently some years old. There were two doors or openings, one in front and the other at the back. Duane imagined it had been built by a fugitive—one who meant to keep an eye both ways and not to be surprised. Duane felt weak and had no desire to move. Where was he, anyway? A strange, intangible sense of time, distance, of something far behind weighed upon him. Sight of the two packs Euchre had made brought his thought to Jennie. What had become of her? There was evidence of her work in a smoldering fire and a little blackened coffee-pot. Probably she was outside looking after the horses or getting water. He thought he heard a step and listened, but he felt tired, and presently his eyes closed and he fell into a doze.

Awakening from this, he saw Jennie sitting beside him. In some way she seemed to have changed. When he spoke she gave a start and turned eagerly to him.

'Duane!' she cried.

'Hello. How're you, Jennie, and how am I?' he said, finding it a little difficult to talk.

'Oh, I'm all right,' she replied. 'And you've come to—your wound's healed; but you've been sick. Fever, I guess. I did all I could.'

Duane saw now that the difference in her was a whiteness and tightness of skin, a hollowness of eye, a look of strain.

'Fever? How long have we been here?' he asked.

She took some pebbles from the crown of his sombrero and counted them.

'Nine. Nine days,' she answered.

'Nine days!' he exclaimed, incredulously. But another look at her assured him that she meant what she said. 'I've been sick all the time? You nursed me?'

'Yes.'

'Bland's men didn't come along here?'

'No.'

'Where are the horses?'

'I keep them grazing down in a gorge back of here. There's good grass and water.'

'Have you slept any?'

'A little. Lately I couldn't keep awake.'

'Good Lord! I should think not. You've had a time of it sitting here day and night nursing me, watching for the outlaws. Come, tell me all about it.'

'There's nothing much to tell.'

'I want to know, anyway, just what you did—how you felt.'

'I can't remember very well,' she replied, simply. 'We must have ridden forty miles that day we got away. You bled all the time. Toward evening you lay on your horse's neck. When we came to this place you fell out of the saddle. I dragged you in here and stopped your bleeding. I thought you'd die that night. But in the morning I had a little hope. I had forgotten the horses. But luckily they didn't stray far. I caught them and kept them down in the gorge. When your wounds closed and you began to breathe stronger I thought you'd get well quick. It was fever that put you back. You raved a lot, and that worried me, because I couldn't stop you. Anybody trailing us could have heard you a good ways. I don't know whether I was scared most then or when you were quiet, and it was so dark and lonely and still all around. Every day I put a stone in your hat.'

'Jennie, you saved my life,' said Duane.

'I don't know. Maybe. I did all I knew how to do,' she replied. 'You saved mine—more than my life.'

Their eyes met in a long gaze, and then their hands in a close clasp.

'Jennie, we're going to get away,' he said, with gladness. 'I'll be well in a few days. You don't know how strong I am. We'll hide by day and travel by night. I can get you across the river.'

'And then?' she asked.

'We'll find some honest rancher.'

'And then?' she persisted.

'Why,' he began, slowly, 'that's as far as my thoughts ever got. It was pretty hard, I tell you, to assure myself of so much. It means your safety. You'll tell your story. You'll be sent to some village or town and taken care of until a relative or friend is notified.'

'And you?' she inquired, in a strange voice.

Duane kept silence.

'What will you do?' she went on.

'Jennie, I'll go back to the brakes. I daren't show my face among respectable people. I'm an outlaw.'

'You're no criminal!' she declared, with deep passion.

'Jennie, on this border the little difference between an outlaw and a criminal doesn't count for much.'

'You won't go back among those terrible men? You, with your gentleness and sweetness—all that's good about you? Oh, Duane, don't—don't go!'

'I can't go back to the outlaws, at least not Bland's band. No, I'll go alone. I'll lone-wolf it, as they say on the border. What else can I do, Jennie?'

'Oh, I don't know. Couldn't you hide? Couldn't you slip out of Texas—go far away?'

'I could never get out of Texas without being arrested. I could hide, but a man must live. Never mind about me, Jennie.'

In three days Duane was able with great difficulty to mount his horse. During daylight, by short relays, he and Jennie rode back to the main trail, where they hid again till he had rested. Then in the dark they rode out of the cañons and gullies of the Rim Rock, and early in the morning halted at the first water to camp.

From that point they traveled after nightfall and went into hiding during the day. Once across the Nueces River, Duane was assured of safety for her and great danger for himself. They had crossed into a country he did not know. Somewhere east of the river there were scattered ranches. But he was as liable to find the rancher in touch with the outlaws as he was likely to find him honest. Duane hoped his good fortune would not desert him in this last service to Jennie. Next to the worry of that was realization of his condition. He had gotten up too soon; he had ridden too far and hard, and now he felt that any moment he might fall from his saddle. At last, far ahead over a barren mesquite-dotted stretch of dusty ground, he espied a patch of green and a little flat, red ranch-house. He headed his horse for it and turned a face he tried to make cheerful for Jennie's sake. She seemed both happy and sorry.

When near at hand he saw that the rancher was a thrifty farmer. And thrift spoke for honesty. There were fields of alfalfa, fruit-trees, corrals, windmill pumps, irrigation-ditches, all surrounding a neat little adobe house. Some children were playing in the yard. The way they ran at sight of Duane hinted of both the loneliness and the fear of their isolated lives. Duane saw a woman come to the door, then a man. The latter looked keenly, then stepped outside. He was a sandy-haired, freckled Texan.

'Howdy, stranger,' he called, as Duane halted. 'Get down, you an' your woman. Say, now, air you sick or shot or what? Let me—'

Duane, reeling in his saddle, bent searching eyes upon the rancher. He thought he saw good will, kindness, honesty. He risked all on that one sharp glance. Then he almost plunged from the saddle.

The rancher caught him, helped him to a bench.

'Martha, come out here!' he called. 'This man's sick. No; he's shot, or I don't know blood-stains.'

Jennie had slipped off her horse and to Duane's side. Duane appeared about to faint.

'Air you his wife?' asked the rancher.

'No. I'm only a girl he saved from outlaws. Oh, he's so pale! Duane, Duane!'

'Buck Duane!' exclaimed the rancher, excitedly. 'The man who killed Bland an' Alloway? Say, I owe him a good turn, an' I'll pay it, young woman.'

The rancher's wife came out, and with a manner at once kind and practical essayed to make Duane drink from a flask. He was not so far gone that he could not recognize its contents, which he refused, and weakly asked for water. When that was given him he found his voice.

'Yes, I'm Duane. I've only overdone myself—just all in. The wounds I got at

Bland's are healing. Will you take this girl in—hide her awhile till the excitement's over among the outlaws?'

'I shore will,' replied the Texan.

'Thanks. I'll remember you—I'll square it.'

'What're you goin' to do?'

'I'll rest a bit—then go back to the brakes.'

'Young man, you ain't in any shape to travel. See here—any rustlers on your trail?'

'I think we gave Bland's gang the slip.'

'Good. I'll tell you what. I'll take you in along with the girl, an' hide both of you till you get well. It'll be safe. My nearest neighbor is five miles off. We don't have much company.'

'You risk a great deal. Both outlaws and rangers are hunting me,' said Duane.

'Never seen a ranger yet in these parts. An' have always got along with outlaws, mebbe exceptin' Bland. I tell you I owe you a good turn.'

'My horses might betray you,' added Duane.

'I'll hide them in a place where there's water an' grass. Nobody goes to it. Come now, let me help you indoors.'

Duane's last fading sensations of that hard day were the strange feel of a bed, a relief at the removal of his heavy boots, and of Jennie's soft, cool hands on his hot face.

He lay ill for three weeks before he began to mend, and it was another week then before he could walk out a little in the dusk of the evenings. After that his strength returned rapidly. And it was only at the end of this long siege that he recovered his spirits. During most of his illness he had been silent, moody.

'Jennie, I'll be riding off soon,' he said, one evening. 'I can't impose on this good man Andrews much longer. I'll never forget his kindness. His wife, too—she's been so good to us. Yes, Jennie, you and I will have to say good-by very soon.'

'Don't hurry away,' she replied.

Lately Jennie had appeared strange to him. She had changed from the girl he used to see at Mrs Bland's house. He took her reluctance to say good-by as another indication of her regret that he must go back to the brakes. Yet somehow it made him observe her more closely. She wore a plain, white dress made from material Mrs Andrews had given her. Sleep and good food had improved her. If she had been pretty out there in the outlaw den now she was more than that. But she had the same paleness, the same strained look, the same dark eyes full of haunting shadows. After Duane's realization of the change in her he watched her more, with a growing certainty that he would be sorry not to see her again.

'It's likely we won't ever see each other again,' he said. 'That's strange to think of. We've been through some hard days, and I seem to have known you a long time.'

Jennie appeared shy, almost sad, so Duane changed the subject to something less personal.

Andrews returned one evening from a several days' trip to Huntsville.

'Duane, everybody's talkin' about how you cleaned up the Bland outfit,' he said, important and full of news. 'It's some exaggerated, accordin' to what you told me; but you've shore made friends on this side of the Nueces. I reckon there ain't a town where you wouldn't find people to welcome you. Huntsville, you know, is some divided in its ideas. Half the people are crooked. Likely enough, all them who was so loud in praise of you are the crookedest. For instance, I met King Fisher, the boss outlaw of these parts. Well, King thinks he's a decent citizen. He was tellin' me what a grand job yours was for the border an' honest cattlemen. Now that Bland and Alloway are done for, King Fisher will find rustlin' easier. There's talk of Hardin movin' his camp over to Bland's. But I don't know how true it is. I reckon there ain't much to it. In the past when a big outlaw chief went under, his band almost always broke up an' scattered. There's no one left who could run the outfit.'

'Did you hear of any outlaws hunting me?' asked Duane.

'Nobody from Bland's outfit is huntin' you, thet's shore,' replied Andrews. 'Fisher said there never was a hoss straddled to go on your trail. Nobody had any use for Bland. Anyhow, his men would be afraid to trail you. An' you could go right in to Huntsville, where you'd be some popular. Reckon you'd be safe, too, except when some of them fool saloon loafers or bad cowpunchers would try to shoot you for the glory in it. Them kind of men will bob up everywhere you go, Duane.'

'I'll be able to ride and take care of myself in a day or two,' went on Duane. 'Then I'll go—I'd like to talk to you about Jennie.'

'She's welcome to a home here with us.'

'Thank you, Andrews. You're a kind man. But I want Jennie to get farther away from the Rio Grande. She'd never be safe here. Besides, she may be able to find relatives. She has some, though she doesn't know where they are.'

'All right, Duane. Whatever you think best. I reckon now you'd better take her to some town. Go north an' strike for Shelbyville or Crockett. Them's both good towns. I'll tell Jennie the names of men who'll help her. You needn't ride into town at all.'

'Which place is nearer, and how far is it?'

'Shelbyville. I reckon about two days' ride. Poor stock country, so you ain't liable to meet rustlers. All the same, better hit the trail at night an' go careful.'

At sunset two days later Duane and Jennie mounted their horses and said good-by to the rancher and his wife. Andrews would not listen to Duane's thanks.

'I tell you I'm beholden to you yet,' he declared.

'Well, what can I do for you?' asked Duane. 'I may come along here again some day.'

'Get down an' come in, then, or you're no friend of mine. I reckon there ain't nothin' I can think of—I just happen to remember—' Here he led Duane out of earshot of the women and went on in a whisper. 'Buck, I used to be well-to-do. Got skinned by a man named Brown—Rodney Brown. He lives in Huntsville, an' he's my enemy. I never was much on fightin', or I'd fixed him. Brown ruined me—stole all I had. He's a hoss an' cattle thief, an' he has pull enough at home to protect him. I reckon I needn't say any more.'

'Is this Brown a man who shot an outlaw named Stevens?' queried Duane, curiously.

'Shore, he's the same. I heard the story. Brown swears he plugged Stevens through the middle. But the outlaw rode off, an' nobody ever knew for shore.'

'Luke Stevens died of that shot. I buried him,' said Duane.

Andrews made no further comment, and the two men returned to the woman.

'The main road for about three miles, then where it forks take the left-hand road and keep on straight. That what you said, Andrews?'

'Shore. An' good luck to you both!'

Duane and Jennie trotted away into the gathering twilight. At the moment an insistent thought bothered Duane. Both Luke Stevens and the rancher Andrews had hinted to Duane to kill a man named Brown. Duane wished with all his heart that they had not mentioned it, let alone taken for granted the execution of the deed. What a bloody place Texas was! Men who robbed and men who were robbed both wanted murder. It was in the spirit of the country. Duane certainly meant to avoid ever meeting this Rodney Brown. And that very determination showed Duane how dangerous he really was—to men and to himself. Sometimes he had a feeling of how little stood between his sane and better self and a self utterly wild and terrible. He reasoned that only intelligence could save him—only a thoughtful understanding of his danger and a hold upon some ideal.

Then he fell into low conversation with Jennie, holding out hopeful views of her future, and presently darkness set in. The sky was overcast with heavy clouds; there was no air moving; the heat and oppression threatened storm. By and by Duane could not see a rod in front of him, though his horse had no difficulty in keeping to the road. Duane was bothered by the blackness of the night. Traveling fast was impossible, and any moment he might miss the road that led off to the left. So he was compelled to give all his attention to peering into the thick shadows ahead. As good luck would have it, he came to higher ground where there was less mesquite, and therefore not such impenetrable darkness; and at this point he came to where the road split.

Once headed in the right direction, he felt easier in mind. To his annoyance, however, a fine, misty rain set in. Jennie was not well dressed for wet weather; and, for that matter, neither was he. His coat, which in that dry warm climate he seldom needed, was tied behind his saddle, and he put it on Jennie.

They traveled on. The rain fell steadily; if anything, growing thicker. Duane grew uncomfortably wet and chilly. Jennie, however, fared somewhat better by reason of the heavy coat. The night passed quickly despite the discomfort, and soon a gray, dismal, rainy dawn greeted the travelers.

Jennie insisted that he find some shelter where a fire could be built to dry his clothes. He was not in a fit condition to risk catching cold. In fact, Duane's teeth were chattering. To find a shelter in that barren waste seemed a futile task. Quite unexpectedly, however, they happened upon a deserted adobe cabin situated a little off the road. Not only did it prove to have a dry interior, but also there was firewood. Water was available in pools everywhere; however, there was no grass for the horses.

A good fire and hot food and drink changed the aspect of their condition as far as comfort went. And Jennie lay down to sleep. For Duane, however, there must be vigilance. This cabin was no hiding-place. The rain fell harder all the time, and the wind changed to the north. 'It's a norther, all right,' muttered Duane. 'Two or three days.' And he felt that his extraordinary luck had not held out. Still one point favored him, and it was that travelers were not likely to come along during the storm.

Jennie slept while Duane watched. The saving of this girl meant more to him than any task he had ever assumed. First it had been partly from a human feeling to succor an unfortunate woman, and partly a motive to establish clearly to himself that he was no outlaw. Lately, however, had come a different sense, a strange one, with something personal and warm and protective in it.

As he looked down upon her, a slight, slender girl with bedraggled dress and disheveled hair, her face, pale and quiet, a little stern in sleep, and her long, dark lashes lying on her cheek, he seemed to see her fragility, her prettiness, femininity as never before. But for him she might at the very moment have been a broken, ruined girl lying back in that cabin of the Bland's. The fact gave him a feeling of his importance in this shifting of her destiny. She was unharmed, still young; she would forget and be happy; she would live to be a good wife and mother. Somehow the thought swelled his heart. His act, death-dealing as it had been, was a noble one, and helped him to hold on to his drifting hopes. Hardly once since Jennie had entered into his thought had those ghosts returned to torment him.

To-morrow she would be gone among good, kind people with a possibility of finding her relatives. He thanked God for that; nevertheless, he felt a pang.

She slept more than half the day. Duane kept guard, always alert, whether he was sitting, standing, or walking. The rain pattered steadily on the roof and sometimes came in gusty flurries through the door. The horses were outside in a shed that afforded poor shelter, and they stamped restlessly. Duane kept them saddled and bridled.

About the middle of the afternoon Jennie awoke. They cooked a meal and afterward sat beside the little fire. She had never been, in his observation of her, anything but a tragic figure, an unhappy girl, the farthest removed from serenity and poise. That characteristic capacity for agitation struck him as stronger in her this day. He attributed it, however, to the long strain, the suspense nearing an end. Yet sometimes when her eyes were on him she did not seem to be thinking of her freedom, of her future.

'This time to-morrow you'll be in Shelbyville,' he said.

'Where will you be?' she asked, quickly.

'Me? Oh, I'll be making tracks for some lonesome place,' he replied.

The girl shuddered.

'I've been brought up in Texas. I remember what a hard lot the men of my family had. But poor as they were, they had a roof over their heads, a hearth with a fire, a warm bed—somebody to love them. And you, Duane—oh, my God! What must your life be? You must ride and hide and watch eternally. No decent food, no pillow, no friendly word, no clean clothes, no woman's hand! Horses, guns, trails, rocks, holes—these must be the important things in your life. You must go on riding, hiding, killing until you meet—'

She ended with a sob and dropped her head on her knees. Duane was amazed, deeply touched.

'My girl, thank you for that thought of me,' he said, with a tremor in his voice. 'You don't know how much that means to me.'

She raised her face, and it was tear-stained, eloquent, beautiful.

'I've heard tell—the best of men go to the bad out there. You won't. Promise me you won't. I never—knew any man—like you. I—I—we may never see each other again—after to-day. I'll never forget you. I'll pray for you, and I'll never give up trying to—to do something. Don't despair. It's never too late. It was my hope that kept me alive—out there at Bland's—before you came. I was only a poor weak girl. But if I could hope—so can you. Stay away from men. Be a lone wolf. Fight for your life. Stick out your exile—and maybe some day—'

Then she lost her voice. Duane clasped her hand and with feeling as deep as hers promised to remember her words. In her despair for him she had spoken wisdom—pointed out the only course.

Duane's vigilance, momentarily broken by emotion, had no sooner reasserted itself than he discovered the bay horse, the one Jennie rode, had broken his halter and gone off. The soft wet earth had deadened the sound of his hoofs. His tracks were plain in the mud. There were clumps of mesquite in sight, among which the horse might have strayed. It turned out, however, that he had not done so.

Duane did not want to leave Jennie alone in the cabin so near the road. So he put her up on his horse and bade her follow. The rain had ceased for the time being, though evidently the storm was not yet over. The tracks led up a wash to a wide flat where mesquite, prickly pear, and thorn-bush grew so thickly that Jennie could not ride into it. Duane was thoroughly concerned. He must have her horse. Time was flying. It would soon be night. He could not expect her to scramble quickly through that brake on foot. Therefore he decided to risk leaving her at the edge of the thicket and go in alone.

As he went in a sound startled him. Was it the breaking of a branch he had stepped on or thrust aside? He heard the impatient pound of his horse's hoofs. Then all was quiet. Still he listened, not wholly satisfied. He was never satisfied in regard to safety; he knew too well that there never could be safety for him in this country.

The bay horse had threaded the aisle of the thicket. Duane wondered what had drawn him there. Certainly it had not been grass, for there was none. Presently he heard the horse tramping along, and then he ran. The mud was deep, and the sharp thorns made going difficult. He came up with the horse, and at the same moment crossed a multitude of fresh horsetracks.

He bent lower to examine them, and was alarmed to find that they had been made very recently, even since it had ceased raining. They were tracks of well-shod horses. Duane straightened up with a cautious glance all around. His instant decision was to hurry back to Jennie. But he had come a goodly way through the thicket, and it was impossible to rush back. Once or twice he imagined he heard crashings in the brush, but did not halt to make sure. Certain he was now that some kind of danger threatened.

Suddenly there came an unmistakable thump of horses' hoofs off somewhere to the fore. Then a scream rent the air. It ended abruptly. Duane leaped forward, tore his way through the thorny brake. He heard Jennie cry again—an appealing call quickly hushed. It seemed more to his right, and he plunged that way. He burst into a glade where a smoldering fire and ground covered with footprints and tracks showed that campers had lately been. Rushing across this, he broke his passage out to the open. But he was too late. His horse had disappeared. Jennie was gone. There were no riders in sight. There was no sound. There was a heavy trail of horses going north. Jennie had been carried off—probably by outlaws. Duane realized that pursuit was out of the question—that Jennie was lost.

10

A hundred miles from the haunts most familiar with Duane's deeds, far up where the Nueces ran a trickling clear stream between yellow cliffs, stood a small deserted shack of covered mesquite poles. It had been made long ago, but was well preserved. A door faced the overgrown trail, and another faced down into a gorge of dense thickets. On the border fugitives from law and men who hid in fear of some one they had wronged never lived in houses with only one door.

It was a wild spot, lonely, not fit for human habitation except for the outcast. He, perhaps, might have found it hard to leave for most of the other wild nooks in that barren country. Down in the gorge there was never-failing sweet water, grass all the year round, cool, shady retreats, deer, rabbits, turkeys, fruit, and miles and miles of narrow-twisting, deep cañon full of broken rocks and impenetrable thickets. The scream of the panther was heard there, the squall of the wildcat, the cough of the jaguar. Innumerable bees buzzed in the spring blossoms, and, it seemed, scattered honey to the winds. All day there was continuous song of birds, that of the mocking-bird loud and sweet and mocking above the rest.

On clear days—and rare indeed were cloudy days—with the subsiding of the wind at sunset a hush seemed to fall around the little hut. Far-distant dim-blue mountains stood gold-rimmed gradually to fade with the shading of light.

At this quiet hour a man climbed up out of the gorge and sat in the westward door of the hut. This lonely watcher of the west and listener to the silence was Duane. And this hut was the one where, three years before, Jennie had nursed him back to life.

The killing of a man named Sellers, and the combination of circumstances that had made the tragedy a memorable regret, had marked, if not a change, at least a cessation in Duane's activities. He had trailed Sellers to kill him for the supposed abducting of Jennie. He had trailed him long after he had learned Sellers traveled alone. Duane wanted absolute assurance of Jennie's death. Vague rumors, a few words here and there, unauthenticated stories, were all Duane had gathered in years to substantiate his belief—that Jennie died shortly after the beginning of her second captivity. But Duane did not know surely. Sellers might have told him. Duane expected, if not to force it from him at the end, to read it in his eyes. But the bullet went too unerringly; it locked his lips and fixed his eyes.

After that meeting Duane lay long at the ranchhouse of a friend, and when he recovered from the wound Sellers had given him he started with horses and a pack for the lonely gorge on the Nueces. There he had been hidden for months, a prey to remorse, a dreamer, a victim of phantoms.

It took work for him to find subsistence in that rocky fastness. And work, action, helped to pass the hours. But he could not work all the time, even if he had found it to do. Then in his idle moments and at night his task was to live with the hell in his mind.

The sunset and the twilight hour made all the rest bearable. The little hut on the rim of the gorge seemed to hold Jennie's presence. It was not as if he felt her spirit. If it had been he would have been sure of her death. He hoped Jennie had not survived her second misfortune; and that intense hope had burned into belief, if not surety. Upon his return to that locality, on the occasion of his first visit to the hut, he had found things just as they had left them, and a poor, faded piece of ribbon Jennie had used to tie around her bright hair. No wandering outlaw or traveler had happened upon the lonely spot, which further endeared it to Duane.

A strange feature of this memory of Jennie was the freshness of it—the failure of years, toil, strife, death-dealing to dim it—to deaden the thought of what might have been. He had a marvelous gift of visualization. He could shut his eyes and see Jennie before him just as clearly as if she had stood there in the flesh. For hours he did that, dreaming, dreaming of life he had never tasted and now never would taste. He saw Jennie's slender, graceful figure, the old brown ragged dress in which he had seen her first at Bland's, her little feet in Mexican sandals, her fine hands coarsened by work, her round arms and swelling throat, and her pale, sad, beautiful face with its staring dark eyes. He remembered every look she had given him, every word she had spoken to him, every time she had touched him. He thought of her beauty and sweetness, of the few things which had come to mean to him that she must have loved him; and he trained himself to think of these in preference to her life at Bland's, the escape with him, and then her recapture, because such memories led to bitter, fruitless pain. He had to fight suffering because it was eating out his heart.

Sitting there, eyes wide open, he dreamed of the old homestead and his white-haired mother. He saw the old home life, sweetened and filled by dear new faces and added joys, go on before his eyes with him a part of it.

Then in the inevitable reaction, in the reflux of bitter reality, he would send out a voiceless cry no less poignant because it was silent: 'Poor fool! No, I shall never see mother again—never go home—never have a home. I am Duane, the Lone Wolf! Oh, God! I wish it were over! These dreams torture me! What have I to do with a mother, a home, a wife? No bright-haired boy, no dark-eyed girl will ever love me. I am an outlaw, an outcast, dead to the good and decent world. I am

alone—alone. Better be a callous brute or better dead! I shall go mad thinking!
Man, what is left to you? A hiding-place like a wolf's—lonely silent days, lonely
nights with phantoms! Or the trail and the road with their bloody tracks, and then
the hard ride, the sleepless, hungry ride to some hole in rocks or brakes. What
hellish thing drives me? Why can't I end it all? What is left? Only that damned
unquenchable spirit of the gun-fighter to live—to hang on to miserable life—to
have no fear of death, yet to cling like a leach—to die as gun-fighters seldom die,
with boots off! Bain, you were first, and you're long avenged, I'd change with you.
And Sellers, you were last, and you're avenged. And you others—you're avenged.
Lie quiet in your graves and give me peace!'

But they did not lie quiet in their graves and give him peace.

A group of specters trooped out of the shadows of dusk and, gathering around
him, escorted him to his bed.

When Duane had been riding the trails passion-bent to escape pursuers, or
passion-bent in his search, the constant action and toil and exhaustion made him
sleep. But when in hiding, as time passed, gradually he required less rest and sleep,
and his mind became more active. Little by little his phantoms gained hold on
him, and at length, but for the saving power of his dreams, they would have
claimed him utterly.

How many times he had said to himself: 'I am an intelligent man. I'm not crazy.
I'm in full possession of my faculties. All this is fancy—imagination—conscience.
I've no work, no duty, no ideal, no hope—and my mind is obsessed, thronged
with images. And these images naturally are of the men with whom I have dealt.
I can't forget them. They come back to me, hour after hour; and when my tortured
mind grows weak, then maybe I'm not just right till the mood wears out and lets
me sleep.'

So he reasoned as he lay down in his comfortable camp. The night was
star-bright above the cañon-walls, darkly shadowing down between them. The
insects hummed and chirped and thrummed a continuous thick song, low and
monotonous. Slow running water splashed softly over stones in the stream-bed.
From far down the cañon came the mournful hoot of an owl. The moment he
lay down, thereby giving up action for the day, all these things weighed upon
him like a great heavy mantle of loneliness. In truth, they did not constitute
loneliness.

And he could no more have dispelled thought than he could have reached out
to touch a cold, bright star.

He wondered how many outcasts like him lay under this star-studded, velvety
sky across the fifteen hundred miles of wild country between El Paso and the
mouth of the river. A vast wild territory—a refuge for outlaws! Somewhere he
had heard or read that the Texas Rangers kept a book with names and records of

outlaws—three thousand known outlaws! Yet these could scarcely be half of that unfortunate horde which had been recruited from all over the states. Duane had traveled from camp to camp, den to den, hiding-place to hiding-place, and he knew these men. Most of them were hopeless criminals; some were avengers; a few were wronged wanderers; and among them occasionally was a man, human in his way, honest as he could be, not yet lost to good.

But all of them were akin in one sense—their outlawry; and that starry night they lay with their dark faces up, some in packs like wolves, others alone like the gray wolf who knew no mate. It did not make much difference in Duane's thought of them that the majority were steeped in crime and brutality, more often than not stupid from rum, incapable of a fine feeling, just lost wild dogs.

Duane doubted that there was a man among them who did not realize his moral wreck and ruin. He had met poor, halfwitted wretches who knew it. He believed he could enter into their minds and feel the truth of all their lives—the hardened outlaw, coarse, ignorant, bestial, who murdered as Bill Black had murdered, who stole for the sake of stealing, who craved money to gamble and drink, defiantly ready for death, and, like that terrible outlaw, Helm, who cried out on the scaffold, 'Let her rip!'

The wild youngsters seeking notoriety and reckless adventure; the cowboys with a notch on their guns, with boastful pride in the knowledge that they were marked by rangers; the crooked men from the North, defaulters, forgers, murderers, all pale-faced, flat-chested men not fit for that wilderness and not surviving; the dishonest cattlemen, hand and glove with outlaws, driven from their homes; the old grizzled, bow-legged genuine rustlers—all these Duane had come in contact with, had watched and known, and as he felt with them he seemed to see that as their lives were bad, sooner or later to end dismally or tragically, so they must pay some kind of earthly penalty—if not of conscience, then of fear; if not of fear, then of that most terrible of all things to restless, active men—pain, the pang of flesh and bone.

Duane knew, for he had seen them pay. Best of all, moreover, he knew the internal life of the gun-fighter of that select but by no means small class of which he was representative. The world that judged him and his kind judged him as a machine, a killing-machine, with only mind enough to hunt, to meet, to slay another man. It had taken three endless years for Duane to understand his own father. Duane knew beyond all doubt that the gun-fighters like Bland, like Alloway, like Sellers, men who were evil and had no remorse, no spiritual accusing Nemesis, had something far more torturing to mind, more haunting, more murderous of rest and sleep and peace; and that something was abnormal fear of death. Duane knew this, for he had shot these men; he had seen the quick, dark shadow in eyes, the presentiment that the will could not control, and then the horrible certainty. These men must have been in agony at every meeting with a possible or certain foe—more agony than the hot rend of a bullet. They were haunted, too, haunted by this fear, by every victim calling from the grave that nothing was so inevitable as death, which lurked behind every corner, hid in every shadow, lay deep in the dark tube of every gun. These men could not have a friend; they could not love or trust a woman. They knew their one chance of holding on to life lay in their own distrust, watchfulness, dexterity, and that hope, by the very nature of their lives, could not be lasting. They had doomed themselves. What, then, could possibly have dwelt in the depths of their minds as they went to their beds on a starry night like this, with mystery in silence and shadow, with time passing surely, and the dark future and its secret approaching every hour—what, then, but hell?

The hell in Duane's mind was not fear of man or fear of death. He would have been glad to lay down the burden of life, providing death came naturally. Many times he had prayed for it. But that over-developed, superhuman spirit of defense in him precluded suicide or the inviting of an enemy's bullet. Sometimes he had a vague, scarcely analyzed idea that this spirit was what had made the Southwest habitable for the white man.

Every one of his victims, singly and collectively, returned to him for ever, it seemed, in cold, passionless, accusing domination of these haunted hours. They did not accuse him of dishonor or cowardice or brutality or murder; they only accused him of Death. It was as if they knew more than when they were alive, had learned that life was a divine mysterious gift not to be taken. They thronged about him with their voiceless clamoring, drifted around him with their fading eyes.

11

After nearly six months in the Nueces gorge the loneliness and inaction of his life drove Duane out upon the trails seeking anything rather than to hide longer alone, a prey to the scourge of his thoughts. The moment he rode into sight of men a remarkable transformation occurred in him. A strange warmth stirred in him—a longing to see the faces of people, to hear their voices—a pleasurable emotion sad and strange. But it was only a precursor of his old bitter, sleepless, and eternal vigilance. When he hid alone in the brakes he was safe from all except his deeper, better self; when he escaped from this into the haunts of men his force and will went to the preservation of his life.

Mercer was the first village he rode into. He had many friends there. Mercer claimed to owe Duane a debt. On the outskirts of the village there was a grave overgrown by brush so that the rude-lettered post which marked it was scarcely visible to Duane as he rode by. He had never read the inscription. But he thought now of Hardin, no other than the erstwhile ally of Bland. For many years Hardin had harassed the stockmen and ranchers in and around Mercer. On an evil day for him he or his outlaws had beaten and robbed a man who once succored Duane when sore in need. Duane met Hardin in the little plaza of the village, called him every name known to border men, taunted him to draw, and killed him in the act.

Duane went to the house of one Jones, a Texan who had known his father, and there he was warmly received. The feel of an honest hand, the voice of a friend, the prattle of children who were not afraid of him or his gun, good wholesome food, and change of clothes—these things for the time being made a changed man of Duane. To be sure, he did not often speak. The price of his head and the weight of his burden made him silent. But eagerly he drank in all the news that was told him. In the years of his absence from home he had never heard a word about his mother or uncle. Those who were his real friends on the border would have been the last to make inquiries, to write or receive letters that might give a clue to Duane's whereabouts.

Duane remained all day with this hospitable Jones, and as twilight fell was loath to go and yielded to a pressing invitation to remain overnight. It was seldom indeed that Duane slept under a roof. Early in the evening, while Duane sat on the porch with two awed and hero-worshiping sons of the house, Jones returned from a quick visit down to the postoffice. Summarily he sent the boys off. He labored under intense excitement.

'Duane, there's rangers in town,' he whispered. 'It's all over town, too, that you're here. You rode in long after sunup. Lots of people saw you. I don't believe there's a man or boy that'd squeal on you. But the women might. They gossip, and these rangers are handsome fellows—devils with the women.'

'What company of rangers?' asked Duane, quickly.

'Company A, under Captain MacNelly, the new ranger. He made a big name in the war. And since he's been in the ranger service he's done wonders. He's cleaned up some bad places south, and he's working north.'

'MacNelly. I've heard of him. Describe him to me.'

'Slight-built chap, but wiry and tough. Clean face, black mustache and hair. Sharp black eyes. He's got a look of authority. MacNelly's a fine man, Duane. Belongs to a good Southern family. I'd hate to have him look you up.'

Duane did not speak.

'MacNelly's got nerve, and his rangers are all experienced men. If they find out you're here they'll come after you. MacNelly's no gun-fighter, but he wouldn't hesitate to do his duty, even if he faced sure death. Which he would in this case. Duane, you mustn't meet Captain MacNelly. Your record is clean, if it is terrible. You never met a ranger or any officer except a rotten sheriff now and then, like Rod Brown.'

Still Duane kept silence. He was not thinking of danger, but of the fact of how fleeting must be his stay among friends.

'I've already fixed up a pack of grub,' went on Jones. 'I'll slip out to saddle your horse. You watch here.'

He had scarcely uttered the last word when soft, swift foot-steps sounded on the hard path. A man turned in at the gate. The light was dim, yet clean enough to disclose an unusually tall figure. When it appeared nearer he was seen to be walking with both arms raised, hands high. He slowed his stride.

'Does Burt Jones live here?' he asked, in a low, hurried voice.

'I reckon. I'm Burt. What can I do for you?' replied Jones.

The stranger peered around, stealthily came closer, still with his hands up.

'It is known that Buck Duane is here. Captain MacNelly's camping on the river just out of town. He sends word to Duane to come out there after dark.'

The stranger wheeled and departed as swiftly and strangely as he had come.

'Bust me! Duane, whatever do you make of that?' exclaimed Jones.

'A new one on me,' replied Duane, thoughtfully.

'First fool thing I ever heard of MacNelly doing. Can't make head nor tails of it. I'd have said off-hand that MacNelly wouldn't double-cross anybody. He struck me as a square man, sand all through. But, hell! he must mean treachery. I can't see anything else in that deal.'

'Maybe the Captain wants to give me a fair chance to surrender without bloodshed,' observed Duane. 'Pretty decent of him, if he meant that.'

'He *invites* you out to his camp *after dark*. Something strange about this, Duane. But MacNelly's a new man out here. He does some queer things. Perhaps he's getting a swelled head. Well, whatever his intentions, his presence around Mercer is enough for us. Duane, you hit the road and put some miles between you and the amiable Captain before daylight. To-morrow I'll go out there and ask him what in the devil he meant.'

'That messenger he sent—he was a ranger,' said Duane.

'Sure he was, and a nervy one! It must have taken sand to come bracing you that way. Duane, the fellow didn't pack a gun. I'll swear to that. Pretty odd, this trick. But you can't trust it. Hit the road, Duane.'

A little later a black horse with muffled hoofs, bearing a tall, dark rider who peered keenly into every shadow, trotted down a pasture lane back of Jones's house, turned into the road, and then, breaking into swifter gait, rapidly left Mercer behind.

Fifteen or twenty miles out Duane drew rein in a forest of mesquite, dismounted, and searched about for a glade with a little grass. Here he staked his horse on a long lariat; and, using his saddle for a pillow, his saddle-blanket for covering, he went to sleep.

Next morning he was off again, working south. During the next few days he paid brief visits to several villages that lay in his path. And in each some one particular friend had a piece of news to impart that made Duane profoundly thoughtful. A ranger had made a quiet, unobtrusive call upon these friends and left this message, 'Tell Buck Duane to ride into Captain MacNelly's camp some time after night.'

Duane concluded, and his friends all agreed with him, that the new ranger's main purpose in the Nueces country was to capture or kill Buck Duane, and that this message was simply an original and striking ruse, the daring of which might appeal to certain outlaws.

But it did not appeal to Duane. His curiosity was aroused; it did not, however, tempt him to any foolhardy act. He turned southwest and rode a hundred miles until he again reached the sparsely settled country. Here he heard no more of rangers. It was a barren region he had never but once ridden through, and that ride had cost him dear. He had been compelled to shoot his way out. Outlaws were not in accord with the few ranchers and their cowboys who ranged here. He learned that both outlaws and Mexican raiders had long been at bitter enmity with these ranchers. Being unfamiliar with roads and trails, Duane had pushed on into the heart of this district, when all the time he really believed he was traveling around it. A rifle-shot from a ranch-house, a deliberate attempt to kill him because he was an unknown rider in those parts, discovered to Duane his mistake; and a hard ride to get away persuaded him to return to his old methods of hiding by day and traveling by night.

He got into rough country, rode for three days without covering much ground, but believed that he was getting on safer territory. Twice he came to a wide bottom-land green with willow and cottonwood and thick as chaparral, somewhere through the middle of which ran a river he decided must be the lower Nueces.

One evening, as he stole out from a covert where he had camped, he saw the lights of a village. He tried to pass it on the left, but was unable to because the brakes of this bottom-land extended in almost to the outskirts of the village, and he had to retrace his steps and go round to the right. Wire fences and horses in pasture made this a task, so it was well after midnight before he accomplished it. He made ten miles or more then by daylight, and after that proceeded cautiously along a road which appeared to be well worn from travel. He passed several thickets where he would have halted to hide during the day but for the fact that he had to find water.

He was a long while in coming to it, and then there was no thicket or clump of mesquite near the waterhole that would afford him covert. So he kept on.

The country before him was ridgy and began to show cottonwoods here and there in the hollows and yucca and mesquite on the higher ground. As he mounted a ridge he noted that the road made a sharp turn, and he could not see what was beyond it. He slowed up and was making the turn, which was down-hill between high banks of yellow clay, when his mettlesome horse heard something to frighten him or shied at something and bolted.

The few bounds he took before Duane's iron arm checked him were enough to reach the curve. One flashing glance showed Duane the open once more, a little valley below with a wide, shallow, rocky stream, a clump of cottonwoods beyond, a somber group of men facing him, and two dark, limp, strangely grotesque figures hanging from branches.

The sight was common enough in southwest Texas, but Duane had never before found himself so unpleasantly close.

A hoarse voice pealed out: 'By hell! there's another one!'

'Stranger, ride down an' account fer yourself!' yelled another.

'Hands up!'

'Thet's right, Jack; don't take no chances. Plug him!'

These remarks were so swiftly uttered as almost to be continuous. Duane was wheeling his horse when a rifle cracked. The bullet struck his left forearm and he thought broke it, for he dropped the rein. The frightened horse leaped. Another bullet whistled past Duane. Then the bend in the road saved him probably from certain death. Like the wind his fleet steed went down the long hill.

Duane was in no hurry to look back. He knew what to expect. His chief concern of the moment was for his injured arm. He found that the bones were still intact; but the wound, having been made by a soft bullet, was an exceedingly bad one. Blood poured from it. Giving the horse his head, Duane wound his scarf tightly round the holes, and with teeth and hand tied it tightly. That done, he looked back over his shoulder.

Riders were making the dust fly on the hillside road. There were more coming round the cut where the road curved. The leader was perhaps a quarter of a mile back, and the others strung out behind him. Duane needed only one glance to tell him that they were fast and hard-riding cowboys in a land where all riders were good. They would not have owned any but strong, swift horses. Moreover, it was a district where ranchers had suffered beyond all endurance the greed and brutality of outlaws. Duane had simply been so unfortunate as to run right into a lynching party at a time of all times when any stranger would be in danger and any outlaw put to his limit to escape with his life.

Duane did not look back again till he had crossed the ridgy piece of ground and had gotten to the level road. He had gained upon his pursuers. When he ascertained this he tried to save his horse, to check a little that killing gait. This horse was a magnificent animal, big, strong, fast; but his endurance had never been put to a grueling test. And that worried Duane. His life had made it impossible to keep one horse very long at a time, and this one was an unknown quantity.

Duane had only one plan—the only plan possible in this case—and that was to make the river-bottoms, where he might elude his pursuers in the willow brakes. Fifteen miles or so would bring him to the river, and this was not a hopeless distance for any good horse if not too closely pressed. Duane concluded presently that the cowboys behind were losing a little in the chase because they were not extending their horses. It was decidedly unusual for such riders to save their mounts. Duane pondered over this, looking backward several times to see if their horses were stretched out. They were not, and the fact was disturbing. Only one reason presented itself to Duane's conjecturing, and it was that with him headed straight on that road his pursuers were satisfied not to force the running. He began to hope and look for a trail or a road turning off to right or left. There was none. A rough, mesquite-dotted and yucca-spired country extended away on either side. Duane believed that he would be compelled to take to this hard going. One thing was certain—he had to go round the village. The river, however, was on the outskirts of the village; and once in the willows, he would be safe.

Dust-clouds far ahead caused his alarm to grow. He watched with his eyes strained; he hoped to see a wagon, a few stray cattle. But no, he soon descried several horsemen. Shots and yells behind him attested to the fact that his pursuers likewise had seen these new-comers on the scene. More than a mile separated these two parties, yet that distance did not keep them from soon understanding each other. Duane waited only to see this new factor show signs of sudden quick action, and then, with a muttered curse, he spurred his horse off the road into the brush.

He chose the right side, because the river lay nearer that way. There were patches of open sandy ground between clumps of cactus and mesquite, and he found that despite a zigzag course he made better time. It was impossible for him to locate his pursuers. They would come together, he decided, and take to his tracks.

What, then, was his surprise and dismay to run out of a thicket right into a low ridge of rough, broken rock, impossible to get a horse over. He wheeled to the left along its base. The sandy ground gave place to a harder soil, where his horse did not labor so. Here the growths of mesquite and cactus became scanter, affording better travel but poor cover. He kept sharp eyes ahead, and, as he had expected, soon saw moving dust-clouds and the dark figures of horses. They were half a mile away, and swinging obliquely across the flat, which fact proved that they entertained a fair idea of the country and the fugitive's difficulty.

Without an instant's hesitation Duane put his horse to his best efforts, straight ahead. He had to pass those men. When this was seemingly made impossible by a deep wash from which he had to turn, Duane began to feel cold and sick. Was this the end? Always there had to be an end to an outlaw's career. He wanted then to ride straight at these pursuers. But reason outweighed instinct. He was fleeing for his life: nevertheless, the strongest instinct at the time was his desire to fight.

He knew when these three horsemen saw him, and a moment afterward he lost sight of them as he got into the mesquite again. He meant now to try to reach the road, and pushed his mount severely, though still saving him for a final burst. Rocks, thickets, bunches of cactus, washes—all operated against his following a straight line. Almost he lost his bearing, and finally would have ridden toward his enemies had not good fortune favored him in the matter of an open burned-over stretch of ground.

Here he saw both groups of pursuers, one on each side and almost within gunshot. Their sharp yells, as much as his cruel spurs, drove his horse into that pace which now meant life or death for him. And never had Duane bestrode a gamer, swifter, stancher beast. He seemed about to accomplish the impossible. In the dragging sand he was far superior to any horse in pursuit, and on this sandy open stretch he gained enough to spare a little in the brush beyond. Heated now and thoroughly terrorized, he kept the pace through thickets that almost tore Duane from his saddle. Something weighty and grim eased off Duane. He was going to get out in front! The horse had speed, fire, stamina.

Duane dashed out into another open place dotted by few trees, and here, right in his path, within pistol-range, stood horsemen waiting. They yelled, they spurred toward him, but did not fire at him. He turned his horse—faced to the right. Only one thing kept him from standing his ground to fight it out. He remembered those dangling limp figures hanging from the cottonwoods. These ranchers would rather hang an outlaw than do anything. They might draw all his fire and then capture him. His horror of hanging was so great as to be all out of proportion compared to his gun-fighter's instinct of self-preservation.

A race began then, a dusty, crashing drive through gray mesquite. Duane could scarcely see, he was so blinded by stinging branches across his eyes. The hollow wind roared in his ears. He lost his sense of the nearness of his pursuers. But they must have been close. Did they shoot at him? He imagined he heard shots. But that might have been the crackling of dead snags. His left arm hung limp, almost useless; he handled the rein with his right; and most of the time he hung low over the pommel. The gray walls flashing by him, the whip of twigs, the rush of wind, the heavy, rapid pound of hoofs, the violent motion of his horse—these vied in sensation with the smart of sweat in his eyes, the rack of his wound, the cold, sick cramp in his stomach. With these also was dull, raging fury. He had to run when he wanted to fight. It took all his mind to force back that bitter hate of himself, of his pursuers, of this race for his useless life.

Suddenly he burst out of a line of mesquite into the road. A long stretch of lonely road! How fiercely, with hot, strange joy, he wheeled his horse upon it! Then he was sweeping along, sure now that he was out in front. His horse still had strength and speed, but showed signs of breaking. Presently Duane looked back. Pursuers—he could not count how many—were loping along in his rear. He paid no more attention to them, and with teeth set he faced ahead, grimmer now in his determination to foil them.

He passed a few scattered ranch-houses where horses whistled from corrals, and men curiously watched him fly past. He saw one rancher running, and he felt intuitively that this fellow was going to join in the chase. Duane's steed pounded on, not noticeably slower, but with a lack of former smoothness, with a strained, convulsive, jerking stride which showed he was almost done.

Sight of the village ahead surprised Duane. He had reached it sooner than he expected. Then he made a discovery—he had entered the zone of wire fences. As he dared not turn back now, he kept on, intending to ride through the village. Looking backward, he saw that his pursuers were half a mile distant, too far to alarm any villagers in time to intercept him in his flight. As he rode by the first houses his horse broke and began to labor. Duane did not believe he would last long enough to go through the village.

Saddled horses in front of a store gave Duane an idea, not by any means new, and one he had carried out successfully before. As he pulled in his heaving mount and leaped off, a couple of ranchers came out of the place, and one of them stepped to a clean limbed, fiery bay. He was about to get into his saddle when he saw Duane, and then he halted, a foot in the stirrup.

Duane strode forward, grasped the bridle of this man's horse.

'Mine's done—but not killed,' he panted. 'Trade with me.'

'Wal, stranger, I'm shore always ready to trade,' drawled the man. 'But ain't you a little swift?'

Duane glanced back up the road. His pursuers were entering the village.

'I'm Duane—Buck Duane,' he cried, menacingly. 'Will you trade? Hurry!'

The rancher, turning white, dropped his foot from the stirrup and fell back.

'I reckon I'll trade,' he said.

Bounding up, Duane dug spurs into the bay's flanks. The horse snorted in fright, plunged into a run. He was fresh, swift, half wild. Duane flashed by the remaining houses on the street out into the open. But the road ended at the village or else led out from some other quarter, for he had ridden straight into the fields and from them into rough desert. When he reached the cover of mesquite once more he looked back to find six horsemen within rifle-shot of him, and more coming behind them.

His new horse had not had time to get warm before Duane reached a high sandy bluff below which lay the willow brakes. As far as he could see extended an immense flat strip of red-tinged willow. How welcome it was to his eye! He felt like a hunted wolf that, weary and lame, had reached his hole in the rocks. Zigzagging down the soft slope, he put the bay to the dense wall of leaf and branch. But the horse balked.

There was little time to lose. Dismounting, he dragged the stubborn beast into the thicket. This was harder and slower work than Duane cared to risk. If he had not been rushed he might have had better success. So he had to abandon the horse—a circumstance that only such sore straits could have driven him to. Then, he went slipping swiftly through the narrow aisles.

He had not gotten under cover any too soon. For he heard his pursuers piling over the bluff, loud-voiced, confident, brutal. They crashed into the willows.

'Hi, Sid! Heah's your hoss!' called one, evidently to the man Duane had forced into a trade.

'Say, if you locoed gents'll hold up a little I'll tell you somethin',' replied a voice from the bluff.

'Come on, Sid! We got him corralled,' said the first speaker.

'Wal, mebbe, an' if you hev it's liable to be damn hot. *Thet feller was Buck Duane!*'

Absolute silence followed that statement. Presently it was broken by a rattling of loose gravel and then low voices.

'He can't git acrost the river, I tell you,' came to Duane's ears. 'He's corralled in the brake. I know thet hole.'

Then Duane, gliding silently and swiftly through the willows, heard no more from his pursuers. He headed straight for the river. Threading a passage through a willow brake was an old task for him. Many days and nights had gone to the acquiring of a skill that might have been envied by an Indian.

The Rio Grande and its tributaries for the most of their length in Texas ran between wide, low, flat lands covered by a dense growth of willow. Cottonwood, mesquite, prickly pear, and other growths mingled with the willow, and altogether they made a matted, tangled copse, a thicket that an inexperienced man would have considered impenetrable. From above, these wild brakes looked green and red; from the inside they were gray and yellow—a striped wall. Trails and glades were scarce. There were a few deer-runways and sometimes little paths made by peccaries—the *jabali*, or wild pigs, of Mexico. The ground was clay and unusually dry, sometimes baked so hard that it left no imprint of a track. Where a growth of cottonwood had held back the encroachment of the willows there usually was thick grass and underbrush. The willows were short, slender poles with stems so close together that they almost touched, and with the leafy foliage forming a thick covering.

The depths of this brake Duane had penetrated was a silent, dreamy, strange place. In the middle of the day the light was weird and dim. When a breeze fluttered the foliage, then slender shafts and spears of sunshine pierced the green mantle and danced like gold on the ground.

Duane had always felt the strangeness of this kind of place, and likewise he had felt a protecting, harboring something which always seemed to him to be the sympathy of the brake for a hunted creature. Any unwounded creature, strong and resourceful, was safe when he had glided under the low, rustling green roof of this wild covert. It was not hard to conceal tracks; the springy soil gave forth no sound; and men could hunt each other for weeks, pass within a few yards of each other and never know it. The problem of sustaining life was difficult; but, then, hunted men and animals survived on very little.

Duane wanted to cross the river if that was possible, and, keeping in the brake, work his way up-stream till he had reached country more hospitable. Remembering what the man had said in regard to the river, Duane had his doubts about crossing. But he would take any chance to put the river between him and his hunters. He pushed on. His left arm had to be favored, as he could scarcely move it. Using his right to spread the willows, he slipped sideways between them and made fast time. There were narrow aisles and washes and holes low down and paths brushed by animals, all of which he took advantage of, running, walking, crawling, stooping any way to get along. To keep in a straight line was not easy—he did it by marking some bright sunlit stem or tree ahead, and when he reached it looked straight on to mark another. His progress necessarily grew slower, for as he advanced the brake became wilder, denser, darker. Mosquitoes began to whine about his head. He kept on without pause. Deepening shadows under the willows told him that the afternoon was far advanced. He began to fear he had wandered in a wrong direction. Finally a strip of light ahead relieved his anxiety, and after a toilsome penetration of still denser brush he broke through to the bank of the river.

He faced a wide, shallow, muddy stream with brakes on the opposite bank extending like a green and yellow wall. Duane perceived at a glance the futility of his trying to cross at this point. Everywhere the sluggish water laved quicksand bars. In fact, the bed of the river was all quicksand, and very likely there was not a foot of water anywhere. He could not swim; he could not crawl; he could not push a log across. Any solid thing touching that smooth yellow sand would be grasped and sucked down. To prove this he seized a long pole and, reaching down from the high bank, thrust it into the stream. Right there near shore there apparently was no bottom to the treacherous quicksand. He abandoned any hope of crossing the river. Probably for miles up and down it would be just the same as here. Before leaving the bank he tied his hat upon the pole and lifted enough water to quench his thirst. Then he worked his way back to where thinner growth made advancement easier, and kept on up-stream till the shadows were so deep he could not see. Feeling around for a place big enough to stretch out on, he lay down. For the time being he was as safe there as he would have been beyond in the Rim Rock. He was tired, though not exhausted, and in spite of the throbbing pain in his arm he dropped at once into sleep.

12

Some time during the night Duane awoke. A stillness seemingly so thick and heavy as to have substance blanketed the black willow brake. He could not see a star or a branch or tree-trunk or even his hand before his eyes. He lay there waiting, listening, sure that he had been awakened by an unusual sound. Ordinary noises of the night in the wilderness never disturbed his rest. His faculties, like those of old fugitives and hunted creatures, had become trained to a marvelous keenness. A long low breath of slow wind moaned through the willows, passed away; some stealthy, soft-footed beast trotted by him in the darkness; there was a rustling among dry leaves; a fox barked lonesomely in the distance. But none of these sounds had broken his slumber.

Suddenly, piercing the stillness, came a bay of a bloodhound. Quickly Duane sat up, chilled to his marrow. The action made him aware of his crippled arm. Then came other bays, lower, more distant. Silence enfolded him again, all the more oppressive and menacing in his suspense. Bloodhounds had been put on his trail, and the leader was not far away. All his life Duane had been familiar with bloodhounds; and he knew that if the pack surrounded him in this impenetrable darkness he would be held at bay or dragged down as wolves dragged a stag. Rising to his feet, prepared to flee as best he could, he waited to be sure of the direction he should take.

The leader of the hounds broke into cry again, a deep, full-toned, ringing bay, strange, ominous, terribly significant in its power. It caused a cold sweat to ooze out all over Duane's body. He turned from it, and with his uninjured arm outstretched to feel for the willows he groped his way along. As it was made impossible to pick out the narrow passages, he had to slip and squeeze and plunge between the yielding stems. He made such a crashing that he no longer heard the baying of the hounds. He had no hope to elude them. He meant to climb the first cottonwood that he stumbled upon in his blind flight. But it appeared he never was going to be lucky enough to run against one. Often he fell, sometimes flat, at others upheld by the willows. What made the work so hard was the fact that he had only one arm to open a clump of close-growing stems and his feet would catch or tangle in the narrow crotches, holding him fast. He had to struggle desperately. It was as if the willows were clutching hands, his enemies, fiendishly impeding his progress. He tore his clothes on sharp branches and his flesh suffered many a prick. But in a terrible earnestness he kept on until he brought up hard against a cottonwood tree.

There he leaned and rested. He found himself as nearly exhausted as he had ever been, wet with sweat, his hands torn and burning, his breast laboring, his legs stinging from innumerable bruises. While he leaned there to catch his breath he listened for the pursuing hounds. For a long time there was no sound from them. This, however, did not deceive him into any hopefulness. There were bloodhounds that bayed often on a trail, and others that ran mostly silent. The former were more valuable to their owner and the latter more dangerous to the fugitive. Presently Duane's ears were filled by a chorus of short ringing yelps. The pack had found where he had slept, and now the trail was hot. Satisfied that they would soon overtake him, Duane set about climbing the cottonwood, which in his condition was difficult of ascent.

It happened to be a fairly large tree with a fork about fifteen feet up, and branches thereafter in succession. Duane climbed until he got above the enshrouding belt of blackness. A pale gray mist hung above the brake, and through it shone a line of dim lights. Duane decided these were bonfires made along the bluff to render his escape more difficult on that side. Away round in the direction he thought was north he imagined he saw more fires, but, as the mist was thick, he could not be sure. While he sat there pondering the matter, listening for the hounds, the mist and the gloom on one side lightened; and this side he concluded was east and meant that dawn was near. Satisfying himself on this score, he descended to the first branch of the tree.

His situation now, though still critical, did not appear to be so hopeless as it had been. The hounds would soon close in on him, and he would kill them or drive them away. It was beyond the bounds of possibility that any men could have followed running hounds through that brake in the night. The thing that worried Duane was the fact of the bonfires. He had gathered from the words of one of his pursuers that the brake was a kind of trap, and he began to believe there was only one way out of it, and that was along the bank where he had entered, and where obviously all night long his pursuers had kept fires burning. Further conjecture on this point, however, was interrupted by a crashing in the willows and the rapid patter of feet.

Underneath Duane lay a gray, foggy obscurity. He could not see the ground, nor any object but the black trunk of the tree. Sight would not be needed to tell him when the pack arrived. With a pattering rush through the willows the hounds reached the tree; and then high above crash of brush and thud of heavy paws rose a hideous clamor. Duane's pursuers far off to the south would hear that and know what it meant. And at daybreak, perhaps before, they would take a short cut across the brake, guided by the baying of hounds that had treed their quarry.

It wanted only a few moments, however, till Duane could distinguish the vague forms of the hounds in the gray shadow below. Still he waited. He had no shots to spare. And he knew how to treat bloodhounds. Gradually the obscurity lightened, and at length Duane had good enough sight of the hounds for his purpose. His first shot killed the huge brute leader of the pack. Then, with unerring shots, he crippled several others. That stopped the baying. Piercing howls arose. The pack took fright and fled, its course easily marked by the howls of the crippled members. Duane reloaded his gun, and, making certain all the hounds had gone, he descended to the ground and set off at a rapid pace to the northward.

The mist had dissolved under a rising sun when Duane made his first halt some miles north of the scene where he had waited for the hounds. A barrier to further progress, in shape of a precipitous rocky bluff, rose sheer from the willow brake. He skirted the base of the cliff, where walking was comparatively easy, around in the direction of the river. He reached the end finally to see there was absolutely no chance to escape from the brake at that corner. It took extreme labor, attended by some hazard and considerable pain to his arm, to get down where he could fill his sombrero with water. After quenching his thirst he had a look at his wound. It was caked over with blood and dirt. When washed off the arm was seen to be inflamed and swollen around the bullet-hole. He bathed it, experiencing a soothing relief in the cool water. Then he bandaged it as best he could and arranged a sling round his neck. This mitigated the pain of the injured member and held it in a quiet and restful position, where it had a chance to begin mending.

As Duane turned away from the river he felt refreshed. His great strength and endurance had always made fatigue something almost unknown to him. However, tramping on foot day and night was as unusual to him as to any other riders of the Southwest, and it had begun to tell on him. Retracing his steps, he reached the point where he had abruptly come upon the bluff, and here he determined to follow along its base in the other direction until he found a way out or discovered the futility of such effort.

Duane covered ground rapidly. From time to time he paused to listen. But he was always listening, and his eyes were ever roving. This alertness had become second nature with him, so that except in extreme cases of caution he performed it while he pondered his gloomy and fateful situation. Such habit of alertness and thought made time fly swiftly.

By noon he had rounded the wide curve of the brake and was facing south. The bluff had petered out from a high, mountainous wall to a low abutment of rock, but it still held to its steep, rough nature and afforded no crack or slope where quick ascent could have been possible. He pushed on, growing warier as he approached the danger-zone, finding that as he neared the river on this side it was imperative to go deeper into the willows. In the afternoon he reached a point where he could see men pacing to and fro on the bluff. This assured him that whatever place was guarded was one by which he might escape. He headed toward these men and approached within a hundred paces of the bluff where they were. There were several men and several boys, all armed and, after the manner of Texans, taking their task leisurely. Farther down Duane made out black dots on the horizon of the bluff-line, and these he concluded were more guards stationed at another outlet. Probably all the available men in the district were on duty. Texans took a grim pleasure in such work. Duane remembered that upon several occasions he had served such duty himself.

Duane peered through the branches and studied the lay of the land. For several hundred yards the bluff could be climbed. He took stock of those careless guards. They had rifles, and that made vain any attempt to pass them in daylight. He believed an attempt by night might be successful; and he was swiftly coming to a determination to hide there till dark and then try it, when the sudden yelping of a dog betrayed him to the guards on the bluff.

The dog had likely been placed there to give an alarm, and he was lustily true to his trust. Duane saw the men run together and begin to talk excitedly and peer into the brake, which was a signal for him to slip away under the willows. He made no noise, and he assured himself he must be invisible. Nevertheless, he heard shouts, then the cracking of rifles, and bullets began to zip and swish through the leafy covert. The day was hot and windless, and Duane concluded that whenever he touched a willow stem, even ever so slightly, it vibrated to the top and sent a quiver among the leaves. Through this the guards had located his position. Once a bullet hissed by him; another thudded into the ground before him. This shooting loosed a rage in Duane. He had to fly from these men, and he hated them and himself because of it. Always in the fury of such moments he wanted to give back shot for shot. But he slipped on through the willows, and at length the rifles ceased to crack.

He sheered to the left again, in line with the rocky barrier, and kept on, wondering what the next mile would bring.

It brought worse, for he was seen by sharp-eyed scouts, and a hot fusillade drove him to run for his life, luckily to escape with no more than a bullet-creased shoulder.

Later that day, still undaunted, he sheered again toward the trap-wall, and found that the nearer he approached to the place where he had come down into the brake the greater his danger. To attempt to run the blockade of that trail by day would be fatal. He waited for night, and after the brightness of the fires had somewhat lessened he assayed to creep out of the brake. He succeeded in reaching the foot of the bluff, here only a bank, and had begun to crawl stealthily up under cover of a shadow when a hound again betrayed his position. Retreating to the willows was as perilous a task as had ever confronted Duane, and when he had accomplished it, right under what seemed a hundred blazing rifles, he felt that he had indeed been favored by Providence. This time men followed him a goodly ways into the brake, and the ripping of lead through the willows sounded on all sides of him.

When the noise of pursuit ceased Duane sat down in the darkness, his mind clamped between two things—whether to try again to escape or wait for possible opportunity. He seemed incapable of decision. His intelligence told him that every hour lessened his chances for escape. He had little enough chance in any case, and that was what made another attempt so desperately hard. Still it was not love of life that bound him. There would come an hour, sooner or later, when he would wrench decision out of this chaos of emotion and thought. But that time was not yet.

When he had remained quiet long enough to cool off and recover from his run he found that he was tired. He stretched out to rest. But the swarms of vicious mosquitoes prevented sleep. This corner of the brake was low and near the river, a breeding-ground for the blood-suckers. They sang and hummed and whined around him in an ever-increasing horde. He covered his head and hands with his coat and lay there patiently. That was a long and wretched night. Morning found him still strong physically, but in a dreadful state of mind.

First he hurried for the river. He could withstand the pangs of hunger, but it was imperative to quench thirst. His wound made him feverish, and therefore more than usually hot and thirsty. Again he was refreshed. That morning he was hard put to it to hold himself back from attempting to cross the river. If he could find a light log it was within the bounds of possibility that he might ford the shallow water and bars of quicksand. But not yet! Wearily, doggedly he faced about toward the bluff.

All that day and all that night, all the next day and all the next night, he stole like a hunted savage from river to bluff; and every hour forced upon him the bitter certainty that he was trapped.

Duane lost track of days, of events. He had come to an evil pass. There arrived an hour when, closely pressed by pursuers at the extreme southern corner of the brake, he took to a dense thicket of willows, driven to what he believed was his last stand.

If only these human bloodhounds would swiftly close in on him! Let him fight to the last bitter gasp and have it over! But these hunters, eager as they were to get him, had care of their own skins. They took few risks. They had him cornered.

It was the middle of the day, hot, dusty, oppressive, threatening storm. Like a snake Duane crawled into a little space in the darkest part of the thicket and lay still. Men had cut him off from the bluff, from the river, seemingly from all sides. But he heard voices only from in front and toward his left. Even if his passage to the river had not been blocked, it might just as well have been.

'Come on fellers—down hyar,' called one man from the bluff.

'Got him corralled at last,' shouted another.

'Reckon ye needn't be too shore. We thought thet more'n once,' taunted another.

'I seen him, I tell you.'

'Aw, thet was a deer.'

'But Bill found fresh tracks an' blood on the willows.'

'If he's winged we needn't hurry.'

'Hold on thar, you boys,' came a shout in authoritative tones from farther up the bluff. 'Go slow. You-all air gittin' foolish at the end of a long chase.'

'Thet's right, Colonel. Hold 'em back. There's nothin' shorer than somebody'll be stoppin' lead pretty quick. He'll be huntin' us soon!'

'Let's surround this corner an' starve him out.'

'Fire the brake.'

How clearly all this talk pierced Duane's ears! In it he seemed to hear his doom. This, then, was the end he had always expected, which had been close to him before, yet never like now.

'By God!' whispered Duane, 'the thing for me to do now—is go out—meet them!'

That was prompted by the fighting, the killing instinct in him. In that moment it had almost superhuman power. If he must die, that was the way for him to die. What else could be expected of Buck Duane? He got to his knees and drew his gun. With his swollen and almost useless hand he held what spare ammunition he had left. He ought to creep out noiselessly to the edge of the willows, suddenly face his pursuers, then, while there was a beat left in his heart, kill, kill, kill. These men all had rifles. The fight would be short. But the marksmen did not live on earth who could make such a fight go wholly against him. Confronting them suddenly he could kill a man for every shot in his gun.

Thus Duane reasoned. So he hoped to accept his fate—to meet this end. But when he tried to step forward something checked him. He forced himself; yet he could not go. The obstruction that opposed his will was as insurmountable as it had been physically impossible for him to climb the bluff.

Slowly he fell back, crouched low, and then lay flat. The grim and ghastly dignity that had been his a moment before fell away from him. He lay there stripped of his last shred of self-respect. He wondered was he afraid; had he, the last of the Duanes—had he come to feel fear? No! Never in all his wild life had he so longed to go out and meet men face to face. It was not fear that held him back. He hated this hiding, this eternal vigilance, this hopeless life. The damnable paradox of the situation was that if he went out to meet these men there was absolutely no doubt of his doom. If he clung to his covert there was a chance, a merest chance, for his life. These pursuers, dogged and unflagging as they had been, were mortally afraid of him. It was his fame that made them cowards. Duane's keenness told him that at the very darkest and most perilous moment there was still a chance for him. And the blood in him, the temper of his father, the years of his outlawry, the pride of his unsought and hated career, the nameless, inexplicable something in him made him accept that slim chance.

Waiting then became a physical and mental agony. He lay under the burning sun, parched by thirst, laboring to breathe, sweating and bleeding. His uncared-for wound was like a red-hot prong in his flesh. Blotched and swollen from the never-ending attack of flies and mosquitoes his face seemed twice its natural size, and it ached and stung.

On one side, then, was this physical torture; on the other the old hell, terribly augmented at this crisis, in his mind. It seemed that thought and imagination had never been so swift. If death found him presently, how would it come? Would he get decent burial or be left for the peccaries and the coyotes? Would his people ever know where he had fallen? How wretched, how miserable his state! It was cowardly, it was monstrous for him to cling longer to this doomed life. Then the hate in his heart, the hellish hate of these men on his trail—that was like a scourge. He felt no longer human. He had degenerated into an animal that could think. His heart pounded, his pulse beat, his breast heaved; and this internal strife seemed to thunder into his ears. He was now enacting the tragedy of all crippled, starved, hunted wolves at bay in their dens. Only his tragedy was infinitely more terrible because he had mind enough to see his plight, his resemblance to a lonely wolf, bloody-fanged, dripping, snarling, fire-eyed in a last instinctive defiance.

Mounted upon the horror of Duane's thought was a watching, listening intensity so supreme that it registered impressions which were creations of his imagination. He heard stealthy steps that were not there; he saw shadowy moving figures that were only leaves. A hundred times when he was about to pull trigger he discovered his error. Yet voices came from a distance, and steps and cracklings in the willows, and other sounds real enough. But Duane could not distinguish the real from the false. There were times when the wind which had arisen sent a hot, pattering breath down the willow aisles, and Duane heard it as an approaching army.

This straining of Duane's faculties brought on a reaction which in itself was a respite. He saw the sun darkened by thick slow spreading clouds. A storm appeared to be coming. How slowly it moved! The air was like steam. If there broke one of those dark, violent storms common though rare to the country, Duane believed he might slip away in the fury of wind and rain. Hope, that seemed unquenchable in him, resurged again. He hailed it with a bitterness that was sickening.

Then at a rustling step he froze into the old strained attention. He heard a slow patter of soft feet. A tawny shape crossed a little opening in the thicket. It was that of a dog. The moment while that beast came into full view was an age. The dog was not a bloodhound, and if he had a trail or a scent he seemed to be at fault on it. Duane waited for the inevitable discovery. Any kind of a hunting-dog could have found him in that thicket. Voices from outside could be heard urging on the dog. Rover they called him. Duane sat up at the moment the dog entered the little shaded covert. Duane expected a yelping, a baying, or at least a bark that would tell of his hiding-place. A strange relief swiftly swayed over Duane. The end was near now. He had no further choice. Let them come—a quick fierce exchange of shots—and then this torture past! He waited for the dog to give the alarm.

But the dog looked at him and trotted by into the thicket without a yelp. Duane could not believe the evidence of his senses. He thought he had suddenly gone deaf. He saw the dog disappear, heard him running to and fro among the willows, getting farther and farther away, till all sound from him ceased.

'Thar's Rover,' called a voice from the bluffside. 'He's been through thet black patch.'

'Nary a rabbit in there,' replied another.

'Bah! Thet pup's no good,' scornfully growled another man. 'Put a hound at thet clump of willows.'

'Fire's the game. Burn the brake before the rain comes.'

The voices droned off as their owners evidently walked up the ridge.

Then upon Duane fell the crushing burden of the old waiting, watching, listening spell. After all, it was not to end just now. His chance still persisted—looked a little brighter—led him on, perhaps, to forlorn hope.

All at once twilight settled quickly down upon the willow brake, or else Duane noted it suddenly. He imagined it to be caused by the approaching storm. But there was little movement of air or cloud, and thunder still muttered and rumbled at a distance. The fact was the sun had set, and at this time of overcast sky night was at hand.

Duane realized it with the awakening of all his old force. He would yet elude his pursuers. That was the moment when he seized the significance of all these fortunate circumstances which had aided him. Without haste and without sound he began to crawl in the direction of the river. It was not far, and he reached the bank before darkness set in. There were men up on the bluff carrying wood to build a bonfire. For a moment he half yielded to a temptation to try to slip along the river-shore, close in under the willows. But when he raised himself to peer out he saw that an attempt of this kind would be liable to failure. At the same moment he saw a rough-hewn plank lying beneath him, lodged against some willows. The end of the plank extended in almost to a point beneath him. Quick as a flash he saw where a desperate chance invited him. Then he tied his gun in an oilskin bag and put it in his pocket.

The bank was steep and crumbly. He must not break off any earth to splash into the water. There was a willow growing back some few feet from the edge of the bank. Cautiously he pulled it down, bent it over the water so that when he released it there would be no springing back. Then he trusted his weight to it, with his feet sliding carefully down the bank. He went into the water almost up to his knees, felt the quicksand grip his feet; then, leaning forward till he reached the plank, he pulled it toward him and lay upon it.

Without a sound one end went slowly under water and the farther end appeared lightly braced against the overhanging willows. Very carefully then Duane began to extricate his right foot from the sucking sand. It seemed as if his foot was incased in solid rock. But there was a movement upward, and he pulled with all the power he dared use. It came slowly and at length was free. The left one he released with less difficulty. The next few moments he put all his attention on the plank to ascertain if his weight would sink it into the sand. The far end slipped off the willows with a little splash and gradually settled to rest upon the bottom. But it sank no farther, and Duane's greatest concern was relieved. However, as it was manifestly impossible for him to keep his head up for long he carefully crawled out upon the plank until he could rest an arm and shoulder upon the willows.

When he looked up it was to find the night strangely luminous with fires. There was a bonfire on the extreme end of the bluff, another a hundred paces beyond. A great flare extended over the brake in that direction. Duane heard a roaring on the wind, and he knew his pursuers had fired the willows. He did not believe that would help them much. The brake was dry enough, but too green to burn readily. And as for the bonfires he discovered that the men, probably having run out of wood, were keeping up the light with oil and stuff from the village. A dozen men kept watch on the bluff scarcely fifty paces from where Duane lay concealed by the willows. They talked, cracked jokes, sang songs, and manifestly considered this outlaw-hunting a great lark. As long as the bright light lasted Duane dared not move. He had the patience and the endurance to wait for the breaking of the storm, and if that did not come, then the early hour before dawn when the gray fog and gloom were over the river.

Escape was now in his grasp. He felt it. And with that in his mind he waited, strong as steel in his conviction, capable of withstanding any strain endurable by the human frame.

The wind blew in puffs, grew wilder, and roared through the willows, carrying bright sparks upward. Thunder rolled down over the river, and lightning began to flash. Then the rain fell in heavy sheets, but not steadily. The flashes of lightning and the broad flares played so incessantly that Duane could not trust himself out on the open river. Certainly the storm rather increased the watchfulness of the men on the bluff. He knew how to wait, and he waited, grimly standing pain and cramp and chill. The storm wore away as desultorily as it had come, and the long night set in. There were times when Duane thought he was paralyzed, others when he grew sick, giddy, weak from the strained posture. The first paling of the stars quickened him with a kind of wild joy. He watched them grow paler, dimmer, disappear one by one. A shadow hovered down, rested upon the river, and gradually thickened. The bonfire on the bluff showed as through a foggy veil. The watchers were mere groping dark figures.

Duane, aware of how cramped he had become from long inaction, began to move his legs and uninjured arm and body, and at length overcame a paralyzing stiffness. Then, digging his hand in the sand and holding the plank with his knees, he edged it out into the river. Inch by inch he advanced until clear of the willows. Looking upward, he saw the shadowy figures of the men on the bluff. He realized they ought to see him, feared that they would. But he kept on, cautiously, noiselessly, with a heart numbing slowness. From time to time his elbow made a little gurgle and splash in the water. Try as he might, he could not prevent this. It got to be like the hollow roar of a rapid filling his ears with mocking sound. There was a perceptible current out in the river, and it hindered straight advancement. Inch by inch he crept on, expecting to hear the bang of rifles, the spattering of bullets. He tried not to look backward, but failed. The fire appeared a little dimmer, the moving shadows a little darker.

Once the plank stuck in the sand and felt as if it were settling. Bringing feet to aid his hand, he shoved it over the treacherous place. This way he made faster progress. The obscurity of the river seemed to be enveloping him. When he looked back again the figures of the men were coalescing with the surrounding gloom, the fires were streaky, blurred patches of light. But the sky above was brighter. Dawn was not far off.

To the west all was dark. With infinite care and implacable spirit and waning strength Duane shoved the plank along, and when at last he discerned the black border of bank it came in time, he thought, to save him. He crawled out, rested till the gray dawn broke, and then headed north through the willows.

13

How long Duane was traveling out of that region he never knew. But he reached familiar country and found a rancher who had before befriended him. Here his arm was attended to; he had food and sleep; and in a couple of weeks he was himself again.

When the time came for Duane to ride away on his endless trail his friend reluctantly imparted the information that some thirty miles south, near the village of Shirley, there was posted at a certain cross-road a reward for Buck Duane dead or alive. Duane had heard of such notices, but he had never seen one. His friend's reluctance and refusal to state for what particular deed this reward was offered roused Duane's curiosity. He had never been any closer to Shirley than this rancher's home. Doubtless some post-office burglary, some gun-shooting scrape had been attributed to him. And he had been accused of worse deeds. Abruptly Duane decided to ride over there and find out who wanted him dead or alive, and why.

As he started south on the road he reflected that this was the first time he had ever deliberately hunted trouble. Introspection awarded him this knowledge; during the last terrible flight on the lower Nueces and while he lay abed recuperating he had changed. A fixed, immutable, hopeless bitterness abided with him. He had reached the end of his rope. All the power of his mind and soul were unavailable to turn him back from his fate. That fate was to become an outlaw in every sense of the term, to be what he was credited with being—that is to say, to embrace evil. He had never committed a crime. He wondered now was crime close to him? He reasoned finally that the desperation of crime had been forced upon him, if not its motive; and that if driven, there was no limit to his possibilities. He understood now many of the hitherto inexplicable actions of certain noted outlaws—why they had returned to the scene of the crime that had outlawed them; why they took such strangely fatal chances; why life was no more to them than a breath of wind; why they rode straight into the jaws of death to confront wronged men or hunting rangers, vigilantes, to laugh in their very faces. It was such bitterness as this that drove these men.

Toward afternoon, from the top of a long hill, Duane saw the green fields and trees and shining roofs of a town he considered must be Shirley. And at the bottom of the hill he came upon an intersecting road. There was a placard nailed on the crossroad sign-post. Duane drew rein near it and leaned close to read the faded print. $1000 REWARD FOR BUCK DUANE DEAD OR ALIVE. Peering closer to read the finer, more faded print, Duane learned that he was wanted for the murder of Mrs Jeff Aiken at her ranch near Shirley. The month September was named, but the date was illegible. The reward was offered by the woman's husband, whose name appeared with that of a sheriff's at the bottom of the placard.

Duane read the thing twice. When he straightened he was sick with horror of his fate, wild with passion at those misguided fools who could believe that he had harmed a woman. Then he remembered Kate Bland, and, as always when she returned to him, he quaked inwardly. Years before word had gone abroad that he had killed her, and so it was easy for men wanting to fix a crime to name him. Perhaps it had been done often. Probably he bore on his shoulders a burden of numberless crimes.

A dark, passionate fury possessed him. It shook him like a storm shakes the oak. When it passed, leaving him cold, with clouded brow and piercing eye, his mind was set. Spurring his horse, he rode straight toward the village.

Shirley appeared to be a large, pretentious country town. A branch of some railroad terminated there. The main street was wide, bordered by trees and commodious houses, and many of the stores were of brick. A large plaza shaded by giant cottonwood trees occupied a central location.

Duane pulled his running horse and halted him, plunging and snorting, before a group of idle men who lounged on benches in the shade of a spreading cottonwood. How many times had Duane seen just that kind of lazy shirt-sleeved Texas group! Not often, however, had he seen such placid, lolling, good-natured men change their expression, their attitude so swiftly. His advent apparently was momentous. They evidently took him for an unusual visitor. So far as Duane could tell, not one of them recognized him, had a hint of his identity.

He slid off his horse and threw the bridle.

'I'm Buck Duane,' he said. 'I saw that placard—out there on a sign-post. It's a damn lie! Somebody find this man Jeff Aiken. I want to see him.'

His announcement was taken in absolute silence. That was the only effect he noted, for he avoided looking at these villagers. The reason was simple enough; Duane felt himself overcome with emotion. There were tears in his eyes. He sat down on a bench, put his elbows on his knees and his hands to his face. For once he had absolutely no concern for his fate. This ignominy was the last straw.

Presently, however, he became aware of some kind of commotion among these villagers. He heard whisperings, low, hoarse voices, then the shuffle of rapid feet moving away. All at once a violent hand jerked his gun from its holster. When

Duane rose a gaunt man, livid of face, shaking like a leaf, confronted him with his own gun.

'Hands up, thar, you Buck Duane!' he roared, waving the gun.

That appeared to be the cue for pandemonium to break loose. Duane opened his lips to speak, but if he had yelled at the top of his lungs he could not have made himself heard. In weary disgust he looked at the gaunt man, and then at the others, who were working themselves into a frenzy. He made no move, however, to hold up his hands. The villagers surrounded him, emboldened by finding him now unarmed. Then several men lay hold of his arms and pinioned them behind his back. Resistance was useless even if Duane had had the spirit. Some one of them fetched his halter from his saddle, and with this they bound him helpless.

People were running now from the street, the stores, the houses. Old men, cowboys, clerks, boys, ranchers came on the trot. The crowd grew. The increasing clamor began to attract women as well as men. A group of girls ran up, then hung back in fright and pity.

The presence of cowboys made a difference. They split up the crowd, got to Duane, and lay hold of him with rough, businesslike hands. One of them lifted his fists and roared at the frenzied mob to fall back, to stop the racket. He beat them back into a circle; but it was some little time before the hubbub quieted down so a voice could be heard.

'——shut up, will you-all?' he was yelling. 'Give us a chance to hear somethin'. Easy now—soho. There ain't nobody goin' to be hurt. Thet's right; everybody quiet now. Let's see what's come off.'

This cowboy, evidently one of authority, or at least one of strong personality, turned to the gaunt man, who still waved Duane's gun.

'Abe, put the gun down,' he said. 'It might go off. Here, give it to me. Now, what's wrong? Who's this roped gent, an' what's he done?'

The gaunt fellow, who appeared now about to collapse, lifted a shaking hand and pointed.

'Thet thar feller—he's Buck Duane!' he panted.

An angry murmur ran through the surrounding crowd.

'The rope! The rope! Throw it over a branch! String him up!' cried an excited villager.

'Buck Duane! Buck Duane!'

'Hang him!'

The cowboy silenced these cries.

'Abe, how do you know this fellow is Buck Duane?' he asked, sharply.

'Why—he said so,' replied the man called Abe.

'What!' came the exclamation, incredulously.

'It's a tarnal fact,' panted Abe, waving his hands importantly. He was an old man and appeared to be carried away with the significance of his deed. 'He like to rid' his hoss right over us all. Then he jumped off, says he was Buck Duane, an' he wanted to see Jeff Aiken bad.'

This speech caused a second commotion as noisy though not so enduring as the first. When the cowboy, assisted by a couple of his mates, had restored order again some one had slipped the noose-end of Duane's rope over his head.

'Up with him!' screeched a wild-eyed youth.

The mob surged closer but was shoved back by the cowboys.

'Abe, if you ain't drunk or crazy tell thet over,' ordered Abe's interlocutor.

With some show of resentment and more of dignity Abe reiterated his former statement.

'If he's Buck Duane how'n hell did you get hold of his gun?' bluntly queried the cowboy.

'Why—he set down thar—an' he kind of hid his face on his hand. An' I grabbed his gun an' got the drop on him.'

What the cowboy thought of this was expressed in a laugh. His mates likewise grinned broadly. Then the leader turned to Duane.

'Stranger, I reckon you'd better speak up for yourself,' he said.

That stilled the crowd as no command had done.

'I'm Buck Duane, all right,' said Duane, quietly. 'It was this way—'

The big cowboy seemed to vibrate with a shock. All the ruddy warmth left his face; his jaw began to bulge; the corded veins in his neck stood out in knots. In an instant he had a hard, stern, strange look. He shot out a powerful hand that fastened in the front of Duane's blouse.

'Somethin' queer here. But if you're Duane you're sure in bad. Any fool ought to know that. You mean it, then?'

'Yes.'

'Rode in to shoot up the town, eh? Same old stunt of you gun-fighters? Meant to kill the man who offered a reward? Wanted to see Jeff Aiken bad, huh?'

'No,' replied Duane. 'Your citizen here misrepresented things. He seems a little off his head.'

'Reckon he is. Somebody is, that's sure. You claim Buck Duane, then, an' all his doings?'

'I'm Duane; yes. But I won't stand for the blame of things I never did. That's why I'm here. I saw that placard out there offering the reward. Until now I never was within half a day's ride of this town. I'm blamed for what I never did. I rode in here, told who I was, asked somebody to send for Jeff Aiken.'

'An' then you set down an' let this old guy throw your own gun on you?' queried the cowboy in amazement.

'I guess that's it,' replied Duane.

'Well, it's powerful strange, if you're really Buck Duane.'

A man elbowed his way into the circle.

'It's Duane. I recognize him. I seen him in more'n one place,' he said. 'Sibert, you can rely on what I tell you. I don't know if he's locoed or what. But I do know he's the genuine Buck Duane. Any one who'd ever seen him once would never forget him.'

'What do you want to see Aiken for?' asked the cowboy Sibert.

'I want to face him, and tell him I never harmed his wife.'

'Why?'

'Because I'm innocent, that's all.'

'Suppose we send for Aiken an' he hears you an' doesn't believe you; what then?'

'If he won't believe me—why, then my case's so bad—I'd be better off dead.'

A momentary silence was broken by Sibert.

'If this isn't a queer deal! Boys, reckon we'd better send for Jeff.'

'Somebody went fer him. He'll be comin' soon,' replied a man.

Duane stood a head taller than that circle of curious faces. He gazed out above and beyond them. It was in this way that he chanced to see a number of women on the outskirts of the crowd. Some were old, with hard faces, like the men. Some were young and comely, and most of these seemed agitated by excitement or distress. They cast fearful, pitying glances upon Duane as he stood there with that noose round his neck. Women were more human than men, Duane thought. He met eyes that dilated, seemed fascinated at his gaze, but were not averted. It was the old women who were voluble, loud in expression of their feelings.

Near the trunk of the cottonwood stood a slender woman in white. Duane's wandering glance rested upon her. Her eyes were riveted upon him. A soft-hearted woman, probably, who did not want to see him hanged!

'Thar comes Jeff Aiken now,' called a man, loudly.

The crowd shifted and trampled in eagerness.

Duane saw two men coming fast, one of whom, in the lead, was of stalwart build. He had a gun in his hand, and his manner was that of fierce energy.

The cowboy Sibert thrust open the jostling circle of men.

'Hold on, Jeff,' he called, and he blocked the man with the gun. He spoke so low Duane could not hear what he said, and his form hid Aiken's face. At that juncture the crowd spread out, closed in, and Aiken and Sibert were caught in the circle. There was a pushing forward, a pressing of many bodies, hoarse cries and flinging hands—again the insane tumult was about to break out—the demand for an outlaw's blood, the call for a wild justice executed a thousand times before on Texas's bloody soil.

Sibert bellowed at the dark encroaching mass. The cowboys with him beat and cuffed in vain.

'Jeff, will you listen?' broke in Sibert, hurriedly, his hand on the other man's arm.

Aiken nodded coolly. Duane, who had seen many men in perfect control of themselves under circumstances like these, recognized the spirit that dominated Aiken. He was white, cold, passionless. There were lines of bitter grief deep round his lips. If Duane ever felt the meaning of death he felt it then.

'Sure this's your game, Aiken,' said Sibert. 'But hear me a minute. Reckon there's no doubt about this man bein' Buck Duane. He seen the placard out at the cross-roads. He rides in to Shirley. He says he's Buck Duane an' he's lookin' for Jeff Aiken. That's all clear enough. You know how these gun-fighters go lookin' for trouble. But here's what stumps me. Duane sits down there on the bench and lets old Abe Strickland grab his gun an' get the drop on him. More'n that, he gives me some strange talk about how, if he couldn't make you believe he's innocent, he'd better be dead. You see for yourself Duane ain't drunk or crazy or locoed. He doesn't strike me as a man who rode in here huntin' blood. So I reckon you'd better hold on till you hear what he has to say.'

Then for the first time the drawn-faced, hungry-eyed giant turned his gaze upon Duane. He had intelligence which was not yet subservient to passion. Moreover, he seemed the kind of man Duane would care to have judge him in a critical moment like this.

'Listen,' said Duane, gravely, with his eyes steady on Aiken's, 'I'm Buck Duane. I never lied to any man in my life. I was forced into outlawry. I've never had a chance to leave the country. I've killed men to save my own life. I never intentionally harmed any woman. I rode thirty miles to-day—deliberately to see what this reward was, who made it, what for. When I read the placard I went sick to the bottom of my soul. So I rode in here to find you—to tell you this: I never saw Shirley before today. It was impossible for me to have—killed your wife. Last September I was two hundred miles north of here on the upper Nueces. I can prove that. Men who know me will tell you I couldn't murder a woman. I haven't any idea why such a deed should be laid at my hands. It's just that wild border gossip. I have no idea what reasons you have for holding me responsible. I only know—you're wrong. You've been deceived. And see here, Aiken. You understand I'm a miserable man. I'm about broken, I guess. I don't care any more for life, for anything. If you can't look me in the eyes, man to man, believe what I say—why, by God! you can kill me!'

Aiken heaved a great breath.

'Buck Duane, whether I'm impressed or not by what you say needn't matter. You've had accusers, justly or unjustly, as will soon appear. The thing is we can prove you innocent or guilty. My girl Lucy saw my wife's assailant.'

He motioned for the crowd of men to open up.

'Somebody—you, Sibert—go for Lucy. That'll settle this thing.'

Duane heard as a man in an ugly dream. The faces around him, the hum of voices, all seemed far off. His life hung by the merest thread. Yet he did not think of that so much as of the brand of a woman-murderer which might be soon sealed upon him by a frightened, imaginative child.

The crowd trooped apart and closed again. Duane caught a blurred image of a slight girl clinging to Sibert's hand. He could not see distinctly. Aiken lifted the child, whispered soothingly to her not to be afraid. Then he fetched her closer to Duane.

'Lucy, tell me. Did you ever see this man before?' asked Aiken, huskily and low. 'Is he the one—who came in the house that day—struck you down—and dragged mama—?'

Aiken's voice failed.

A lightning flash seemed to clear Duane's blurred sight. He saw a pale, sad face and violet eyes fixed in gloom and horror upon his. No terrible moment in Duane's life ever equaled this one of silence—of suspense.

'It's ain't him!' cried the child.

Then Sibert was flinging the noose off Duane's neck and unwinding the bonds round his arms. The spellbound crowd awoke to hoarse exclamations.

'See there, my locoed gents, how easy you'd hang the wrong man,' burst out the cowboy, as he made the rope-end hiss. 'You-all are a lot of wise rangers. Haw! haw!'

He freed Duane and thrust the bone-handled gun back in Duane's holster.

'You Abe, there. Reckon you pulled a stunt! But don't try the like again. And, men, I'll gamble there's a hell of a lot of bad work Buck Duane's named for—which all he never done. Clear away there. Where's his hoss? Duane, the road's open out of Shirley.'

Sibert swept the gaping watchers aside and pressed Duane toward the horse, which another cowboy held. Mechanically Duane mounted, felt a lift as he went up. Then the cowboy's hard face softened in a smile.

'I reckon it ain't uncivil of me to say—hit that road quick!' he said, frankly.

He led the horse out of the crowd. Aiken joined him, and between them they escorted Duane across the plaza. The crowd appeared irresistibly drawn to follow.

Aiken paused with his big hand on Duane's knee. In it, unconsciously probably, he still held the gun.

'Duane, a word with you,' he said. 'I believe you're not so black as you've been painted. I wish there was time to say more. Tell me this, anyway. Do you know the Ranger Captain MacNelly?'

'I do not,' replied Duane, in surprise.

'I met him only a week ago over in Fairfield,' went on Aiken, hurriedly. 'He declared you never killed my wife. I didn't believe him—argued with him. We almost had hard words over it. Now—I'm sorry. The last thing he said was: "If you ever see Duane don't kill him. Send him into my camp after dark!" He meant something strange. What—I can't say. But he was right, and I was wrong. If Lucy had batted an eye I'd have killed you. Still, I wouldn't advise you to hunt up MacNelly's camp. He's clever. Maybe he believes there's no treachery in his new ideas of ranger tactics. I tell you for all it's worth. Good-by. May God help you further as he did this day!'

Duane said good-by and touched the horse with his spurs.

'So long, Buck!' called Sibert, with that frank smile breaking warm over his brown face; and he held his sombrero high.

14

When Duane reached the crossing of the roads the name Fairfield on the sign-post seemed to be the thing that tipped the oscillating balance of decision in favor of that direction.

He answered here to unfathomable impulse. If he had been driven to hunt up Jeff Aiken, now he was called to find this unknown ranger captain. In Duane's state of mind clear reasoning, common sense, or keenness were out of the question. He went because he felt he was compelled.

Dusk had fallen when he rode into a town which inquiry discovered to be Fairfield. Captain MacNelly's camp was stationed just out of the village limits on the other side.

No one except the boy Duane questioned appeared to notice his arrival. Like Shirley, the town of Fairfield was large and prosperous, compared to the innumerable hamlets dotting the vast extent of southwestern Texas. As Duane rode through, being careful to get off the main street, he heard the tolling of a church-bell that was a melancholy reminder of his old home.

There did not appear to be any camp on the outskirts of the town. But as Duane sat his horse, peering around and undecided what further move to make, he caught the glint of flickering lights through the darkness. Heading toward them, he rode perhaps a quarter of a mile to come upon a grove of mesquite. The brightness of several fires made the surrounding darkness all the blacker. Duane saw the moving forms of men and heard horses. He advanced naturally, expecting any moment to be halted.

'Who goes there?' came the sharp call out of the gloom.

Duane pulled his horse. The gloom was impenetrable.

'One man—alone,' replied Duane.

'A stranger?'

'Yes.'

'What do you want?'

'I'm trying to find the ranger camp.'

'You've struck it. What's your errand?'

'I want to see Captain MacNelly.'

'Get down and advance. Slow. Don't move your hands. It's dark, but I can see.'

Duane dismounted, and, leading his horse, slowly advanced a few paces. He saw a dully bright object—a gun—before he discovered the man who held it. A few more steps showed a dark figure blocking the trail. Here Duane halted.

'Come closer, stranger. Let's have a look at you,' the guard ordered, curtly.

Duane advanced again until he stood before the man. Here the rays of light from the fires flickered upon Duane's face.

'Reckon you're a stranger, all right. What's your name and your business with the Captain?'

Duane hesitated, pondering what best to say.

'Tell Captain MacNelly I'm the man he's been asking to ride into his camp—after dark,' finally said Duane.

The ranger bent forward to peer hard at this night visitor. His manner had been alert, and now it became tense.

'Come here, one of you men, quick,' he called, without turning in the least toward the camp-fire.

'Hello! What's up, Pickens?' came the swift reply. It was followed by a rapid thud of boots on soft ground. A dark form crossed the gleams from the fire-light. Then a ranger loomed up to reach the side of the guard. Duane heard whispering, the purport of which he could not catch. The second ranger swore under his breath. Then he turned away and started back.

'Here, ranger, before you go, understand this. My visit is peaceful—friendly if you'll let it be. Mind, I was asked to come here—after dark.'

Duane's clear, penetrating voice carried far. The listening rangers at the camp-fire heard what he said.

'Ho, Pickens! Tell that fellow to wait,' replied an authoritative voice. Then a slim figure detached itself from the dark, moving group at the camp-fire and hurried out.

'Better be foxy, Cap,' shouted a ranger, in warning.

'Shut up—all of you,' was the reply.

This officer, obviously Captain MacNelly, soon joined the two rangers who were confronting Duane. He had no fear. He strode straight up to Duane.

'I'm MacNelly,' he said. 'If you're my man, don't mention your name—yet.'

All this seemed so strange to Duane, in keeping with much that had happened lately.

'I met Jeff Aiken to-day,' said Duane. 'He sent me—'

'You've met Aiken!' exclaimed MacNelly, sharp, eager, low. 'By all that's bully!' Then he appeared to catch himself, to grow restrained.

'Men, fall back, leave us alone a moment.'

The rangers slowly withdrew.

'Buck Duane! It's you?' he whispered, eagerly.

'Yes.'

'If I give my word you'll not be arrested—you'll be treated fairly—will you come into camp and consult with me?'

'Certainly.'

'Duane, I'm sure glad to meet you,' went on MacNelly; and he extended his hand.

Amazed and touched, scarcely realizing this actuality, Duane gave his hand and felt no unmistakable grip of warmth.

'It doesn't seem natural, Captain MacNelly, but I believe I'm glad to meet you,' said Duane, soberly.

'You will be. Now we'll go back to camp. Keep your identity mum for the present.'

He led Duane in the direction of the camp-fire.

'Pickens, go back on duty,' he ordered, 'and, Beeson, you look after this horse.'

When Duane got beyond the line of mesquite, which had hid a good view of the camp-site, he saw a group of perhaps fifteen rangers sitting around the fires, near a long low shed where horses were feeding, and a small adobe house at one side.

'We've just had grub, but I'll see you get some. Then we'll talk,' said MacNelly. 'I've taken up temporary quarters here. Have a rustler job on hand. Now, when you've eaten, come right into the house.'

Duane was hungry, but he hurried through the ample supper that was set before him, urged on by curiosity and astonishment. The only way he could account for his presence there in a ranger's camp was that MacNelly hoped to get useful information out of him. Still that would hardly have made this captain so eager. There was a mystery here, and Duane could scarcely wait for it to be solved. While eating he had bent keen eyes around him. After a first quiet scrutiny the rangers apparently paid no more attention to him. They were all veterans in service—Duane saw that—and rugged, powerful men of iron constitution. Despite the occasional joke and sally of the more youthful members, and a general conversation of camp-fire nature, Duane was not deceived about the fact that his advent had been an unusual and striking one, which had caused an undercurrent of conjecture and even consternation among them. These rangers were too well trained to appear openly curious about their captain's guest. If they had not deliberately attempted to be oblivious of his presence Duane would have concluded they thought him an ordinary visitor, somehow of use to MacNelly. As it was, Duane felt a suspense that must have been due to a hint of his identity.

He was not long in presenting himself at the door of the house.

'Come in and have a chair,' said MacNelly, motioning for the one other occupant of the room to rise. 'Leave us, Russell, and close the door. I'll be through these reports right off.'

MacNelly sat at a table upon which was a lamp and various papers. Seen in the light he was a fine-looking, soldierly man of about forty years, dark-haired and dark-eyed, with a bronzed face, shrewd, stern, strong, yet not wanting in kindliness. He scanned hastily over some papers, fussed with them, and finally put them in envelopes. Without looking up he pushed a cigarcase toward Duane, and upon Duane's refusal to smoke he took a cigar, rose to light it at the lamp-chimney, and then, settling back in his chair, he faced Duane, making a vain attempt to hide what must have been the fulfilment of a long-nourished curiosity.

'Duane, I've been hoping for this for two years,' he began.

Duane smiled a little—a smile that felt strange on his face. He had never been much of a talker. And speech here seemed more than ordinarily difficult.

MacNelly must have felt that.

He looked long and earnestly at Duane, and his quick, nervous manner changed to grave thoughtfulness.

'I've lots to say, but where to begin,' he mused. 'Duane, you've had a hard life since you went on the dodge. I never met you before, don't know what you looked like as a boy. But I can see what—well, even ranger life isn't all roses.'

He rolled his cigar between his lips and puffed clouds of smoke.

'Ever hear from home since you left Wellston?' he asked, abruptly.

'No.'

'Never a word?'

'Not one,' replied Duane, sadly.

'That's tough. I'm glad to be able to tell you that up to just lately your mother, sister, uncle—all your folks, I believe—were well. I've kept posted. But haven't heard lately.'

Duane averted his face a moment, hesitated till the swelling left his throat, and then said, 'It's worth what I went through to-day to hear that.'

'I can imagine how you feel about it. When I was in the war—but let's get down to the business of this meeting.'

He pulled his chair close to Duane's.

'You've had word more than once in the last two years that I wanted to see you?'

'Three times, I remember,' replied Duane.

'Why didn't you hunt me up?'

'I supposed you imagined me one of those gunfighters who couldn't take a dare and expected me to ride up to your camp and be arrested.'

'That was natural, I suppose,' went on MacNelly. 'You didn't know me, otherwise you would have come. I've been a long time getting to you. But the nature of my job, as far as you're concerned, made me cautious. Duane, you're aware of the hard name you bear all over the Southwest?'

'Once in a while I'm jarred into realizing,' replied Duane.

'It's the hardest, barring Murrell and Cheseldine, on the Texas border. But there's this difference. Murrell in his day was known to deserve his infamous name. Cheseldine in his day also. But I've found hundreds of men in southwest Texas who're your friends, who swear you never committed a crime. The farther south I get the clearer this becomes. What I want to know is the truth. Have you ever done anything criminal? Tell me the truth, Duane. It won't make any difference in my plan. And when I say crime I mean what *I* would call crime, or any reasonable Texan.'

'That way my hands are clean,' replied Duane.

'You never held up a man, robbed a store for grub, stole a horse when you needed him bad—never anything like that?'

'Somehow I always kept out of that, just when pressed the hardest.'

'Duane, I'm damn glad!' MacNelly exclaimed, gripping Duane's hand. 'Glad for your mother's sake! But, all the same, in spite of this, you are a Texas outlaw accountable to the state. You're perfectly aware that under existing circumstances, if you fell into the hands of the law, you'd probably hang, at least go to jail for a long term.'

'That's what kept me on the dodge all these years,' replied Duane.

'Certainly.' MacNelly removed his cigar. His eyes narrowed and glittered. The muscles along his brown cheeks set hard and tense. He leaned closer to Duane, laid sinewy, pressing fingers upon Duane's knee.

'Listen to this,' he whispered, hoarsely. 'If I place a pardon in your hand—make you a free, honest citizen once more, clear your name of infamy, make your mother, your sister proud of you—will you swear yourself to a service, *any* service I demand of you?'

Duane sat stock still, stunned.

Slowly, more persuasively, with show of earnest agitation, Captain MacNelly reiterated his startling query.

'My God!' burst from Duane. 'What's this? MacNelly, you *can't* be in earnest!'

'Never more so in my life. I've a deep game. I'm playing it square. What do you say?'

He rose to his feet. Duane, as if impelled, rose with him. Ranger and outlaw then locked eyes that searched each other's souls. In MacNelly's Duane read truth, strong, fiery purpose, hope, even gladness, and a fugitive mounting assurance of victory.

Twice Duane endeavored to speak, failed of all save a hoarse, incoherent sound, until, forcing back a flood of speech, found a voice.

'Any service? Every service! MacNelly, I give my word,' said Duane.

A light played over MacNelly's face, warming out all the grim darkness. He held out his hand. Duane met it with his in a clasp that men unconsciously give in moments of stress.

When they unclasped and Duane stepped back to drop into a chair MacNelly fumbled for another cigar—he had bitten his other into shreds—and, lighting it as before, he turned to his visitor, now calm and cool. He had the look of a man who had justly won something at considerable cost. His next move was to take a long leather case from his pocket and extract from it several folded papers.

'Here's your pardon from the Governor,' he said, quietly. 'You'll see, when you look it over, that it's conditional. When you sign this paper I have here the condition will be met.'

He smoothed out the paper, handed Duane a pen, ran his forefinger along a dotted line.

Duane's hand was shaky. Years had passed since he had held a pen. It was with difficulty that he achieved his signature. Buckley Duane—how strange the name looked!

'Right here ends the career of Buck Duane, outlaw and gun-fighter,' said MacNelly; and, seating himself, he took the pen from Duane's fingers and wrote several lines in several places upon the paper. Then with a smile he handed it to Duane.

'That makes you a member of Company A, Texas Rangers.'

'So that's it!' burst out Duane, a light breaking in upon his bewilderment. 'You want me for ranger service?'

'Sure. That's it,' replied the Captain, dryly. 'Now to hear what service is to be. I've been a busy man since I took this job, and, as you may have heard, I've done a few things. I don't mind telling you that political influence put me in here and that up Austin way there's a good deal of friction in the Department of State in regard to whether or not the ranger service is any good—whether it should be discontinued or not. I'm on the party side who's defending the ranger service. I contend that it's made Texas habitable. Well, it's been up to me to produce results. So far I have been successful. My great ambition is to break up the outlaw gangs along the river. I have never ventured in there yet because I've been waiting to get the lieutenant I needed. You, of course, are the man I had in mind. It's my idea to start up the Rio Grande and begin with Cheseldine. He's the strongest, the worst outlaw of the times. He's more than rustler. It's Cheseldine and his gang who are operating on the banks. They're doing bank-robbing. That's my private opinion, but it's not been backed up by any evidence. Cheseldine doesn't leave evidences. He's intelligent, cunning. No one seems to have seen him—to know what he looks like. I assume, of course, that you are a stranger to the country he dominates. It's five hundred miles west of your ground. There's a little town over there called Fairdale. It's the nest of a rustler gang. They rustle and murder at will. Nobody knows who the leader is. I want you to find out. Well, whatever way you decide is best you will proceed to act upon. You are your own boss. You know such men and how they can be approached. You will take all the time needed, if it's months. It will be necessary for you to communicate with me, and that will be a difficult matter. For Cheseldine dominates several whole counties. You must find some way to let me know when I and my rangers are needed. The plan is to break up Cheseldine's gang. It's the toughest job on the border. Arresting him alone isn't to be heard of. He couldn't be brought out. Killing him isn't much better, for his select men, the ones he operates with, are as dangerous to the community as he is. We want to kill or jail this choice selection of robbers and break up the rest of the gang. To find them, to get among them somehow, to learn their movements, to lay your trap for us rangers to spring—that, Duane, is your service to me, and God knows it's a great one!'

'I have accepted it,' replied Duane.

'Your work will be secret. You are now a ranger in my service. But no one except the few I choose to tell will know of it until we pull off the job. You will simply be Buck Duane till it suits our purpose to acquaint Texas with the fact that you're a ranger. You'll see there's no date on that paper. No one will ever know just when you entered the service. Perhaps we can make it appear that all or most of your outlawry has really been good service to the state. At that, I'll believe it'll turn out so.'

MacNelly paused a moment in his rapid talk, chewed his cigar, drew his brows together in a dark frown, and went on. 'No man on the border knows so well as you the deadly nature of this service. It's a thousand to one that you'll be killed. I'd say there was no chance at all for any other man beside you. Your reputation will go far among the outlaws. Maybe that and your nerve and your gun-play will pull you through. I'm hoping so. But it's a long, long chance against your ever coming back.'

'That's not the point,' said Duane. 'But in case I get killed out there—what—'

'Leave that to me,' interrupted Captain MacNelly. 'Your folks will know at once of your pardon and your ranger duty. If you lose your life out there I'll see your name cleared—the service you render known. You can rest assured of that.'

'I am satisfied,' replied Duane. 'That's so much more than I've dared to hope.'

'Well, it's settled, then. I'll give you money for expenses. You'll start as soon as you like—the sooner the better. I hope to think of other suggestions, especially about communicating with me.'

Long after the lights were out and the low hum of voices had ceased round the camp-fire Duane lay wide awake, eyes staring into the blackness, marveling over the strange events of the day. He was humble, grateful to the depths of his soul. A huge and crushing burden had been lifted from his heart. He welcomed this hazardous service to the man who had saved him. Thought of his mother and sister and Uncle Jim, of his home, of old friends came rushing over him the first time in years that he had happiness in the memory. The disgrace he had put upon them would now be removed; and in the light of that, his wasted life of the past, and its probable tragic end in future service as atonement changed their aspects. And as he lay there, with the approach of sleep finally dimming the vividness of his thought, so full of mystery, shadowy faces floated in the blackness around him, haunting him as he had always been haunted.

It was broad daylight when he awakened. MacNelly was calling him to breakfast. Outside sounded voices of men, crackling of fires, snorting and stamping of horses, the barking of dogs. Duane rolled out of his blankets and made good use of the soap and towel and razor and brush near by on a bench—things of rare luxury to an outlaw on the ride. The face he saw in the mirror was as strange as the past he had tried so hard to recall. Then he stepped to the door and went out.

The rangers were eating in a circle round a tarpaulin spread upon the ground.

'Fellows,' said MacNelly, 'shake hands with Buck Duane. He's on secret ranger service for me. Service that'll likely make you all hump soon! Mind you, keep mum about it.'

The rangers surprised Duane with a roaring greeting, the warmth of which he soon divined was divided between pride of his acquisition to their ranks and eagerness to meet that violent service of which their captain hinted. They were jolly wild fellows, with just enough gravity in their welcome to show Duane their respect and appreciation, while not forgetting his lone-wolf record. When he had seated himself in that circle, now one of them, a feeling subtle and uplifting pervaded him.

After the meal Captain MacNelly drew Duane aside.

'Here's the money. Make it go as far as you can. Better strike straight for El Paso, snook around there and hear things. Then go to Valentine. That's near the river and within fifty miles or so of the edge of the Rim Rock. Somewhere up there Cheseldine holds fort. Somewhere to the north is the town Fairdale. But he doesn't hide all the time in the rocks. Only after some daring raid or hold-up. Cheseldine's got border towns on his staff, or scared of him, and these places we want to know about, especially Fairdale. Write me care of the adjutant at Austin. I don't have to warn you to be careful where you mail letters. Ride a hundred, two hundred miles, if necessary, or go clear to El Paso.'

MacNelly stopped with an air of finality, and then Duane slowly rose.

'I'll start at once,' he said, extending his hand to the Captain. 'I wish—I'd like to thank you!'

'Hell, man! Don't thank me!' replied MacNelly, crushing the proffered hand. 'I've sent a lot of good men to their deaths, and maybe you're another. But, as I've said, you've one chance in a thousand. And, by Heaven! I'd hate to be Cheseldine or any other man you were trailing. No, not good-by—*Adios*, Duane! May we meet again!'

BOOK II
THE RANGER

15

West of the Pecos River Texas extended a vast wild region, barren in the north where the Llano Estacado spread its shifting sands, fertile in the south along the Rio Grande. A railroad marked an undeviating course across five hundred miles of this country, and the only villages and towns lay on or near this line of steel. Unsettled as was this western Texas, and despite the acknowledged dominance of the outlaw bands, the pioneers pushed steadily into it. First had come the lone rancher; then his neighbors in near and far valleys; then the hamlets; at last the railroad and the towns. And still the pioneers came, spreading deeper into the valleys, farther and wider over the plains. It was mesquite-dotted, cactus-covered desert, but rich soil upon which water acted like magic. There was little grass to an acre, but there were millions of acres. The climate was wonderful. Cattle flourished and ranchers prospered.

The Rio Grande flowed almost due south along the western boundary for a thousand miles, and then, weary of its course, turned abruptly north, to make what was called the Big Bend. The railroad, running west, cut across this bend, and all that country bounded on the north by the railroad and on the south by the river was as wild as the Staked Plains. It contained not one settlement. Across the face of this Big Bend, as if to isolate it, stretched the Ord mountain range, of which Mount Ord, Cathedral Mount, and Elephant Mount raised bleak peaks above their fellows. In the valleys of the foothills and out across the plains were ranches, and farther north villages, and the towns of Alpine and Marfa.

Like other parts of the great Lone Star State, this section of Texas was a world in itself—a world where the riches of the rancher were ever enriching the outlaw. The village closest to the gateway of this outlaw-infested region was a little place called Ord, named after the dark peak that loomed some miles to the south. It had been settled originally by Mexicans—there were still the ruins of adobe missions—but with the advent of the rustler and outlaw many inhabitants were shot or driven away, so that at the height of Ord's prosperity and evil sway there were but few Mexicans living there, and these had their choice between holding hand-and-glove with the outlaws or furnishing target practice for that wild element.

Toward the close of a day in September a stranger rode into Ord, and in a community where all men were remarkable for one reason or another he excited interest. His horse, perhaps, received the first and most engaging attention—horses in that region being apparently more important than men. This particular horse did not attract with beauty. At first glance he seemed ugly. But he was a giant, black as coal, rough despite the care manifestly bestowed upon him, long of body, ponderous of limb, huge in every way. A bystander remarked that he had a grand head. True, if only his head had been seen he would have been a beautiful horse. Like men, horses show what they are in the shape, the size, the line, the character of the head. This one denoted fire, speed, blood, loyalty, and his eyes were as soft and dark as a woman's. His face was solid black, except in the middle of his forehead, where there was a round spot of white.

'Say mister, mind tellin' me his name?' asked a ragged urchin, with born love of a horse in his eyes.

'Bullet,' replied the rider.

'Thet there's fer the white mark, ain't it?' whispered the youngster to another. 'Say, ain't he a whopper? Biggest hoss I ever seen.'

Bullet carried a huge black silver-ornamented saddle of Mexican make, a lariat and canteen, and a small pack rolled into a tarpaulin.

This rider apparently put all care of appearances upon his horse. His apparel was the ordinary jeans of the cowboy without vanity, and it was torn and travel-stained. His boots showed evidence of an intimate acquaintance with cactus. Like his horse, this man was a giant in stature, but rangier, not so heavily built. Otherwise the only striking thing about him was his somber face with its piercing eyes, and hair white over the temples. He packed two guns, both low down—but that was too common a thing to attract notice in the Big Bend. A close observer, however, would have noted a singular fact—this rider's right hand was more bronzed, more weather-beaten than his left. He never wore a glove on that right hand!

He had dismounted before a ramshackle structure that bore upon its wide, high-boarded front the sign, 'Hotel.' There were horsemen coming and going down the wide street between its rows of old stores, saloons, and houses. Ord certainly did not look enterprising. Americans had manifestly assimilated much of the leisure of the Mexicans. The hotel had a wide platform in front, and this did duty as porch and sidewalk. Upon it, and leaning against a hitching-rail, were men of varying ages, most of them slovenly in old jeans and slouched sombreros. Some were booted, belted, and spurred. No man there wore a coat, but all wore vests. The guns in that group would have outnumbered the men.

It was a crowd seemingly too lazy to be curious. Good nature did not appear to be wanting, but it was not the frank and boisterous kind natural to the cowboy or rancher in town for a day. These men were idlers; what else, perhaps, was easy to conjecture. Certainly to this arriving stranger, who flashed a keen eye over them, they wore an atmosphere never associated with work.

Presently a tall man, with a drooping, sandy mustache, leisurely detached himself from the crowd.

'Howdy, stranger,' he said.

The stranger had bent over to loosen the cinches; he straightened up and nodded. Then: 'I'm thirsty!'

That brought a broad smile to faces. It was characteristic greeting. One and all trooped after the stranger into the hotel. It was a dark, ill-smelling barn of a place, with a bar as high as a short man's head. A bartender with a scarred face was serving drinks.

'Line up, gents,' said the stranger.

They piled over one another to get to the bar, with coarse jests and oaths and laughter. None of them noted that the stranger did not appear so thirsty as he had claimed to be. In fact, though he went through the motions, he did not drink at all.

'My name's Jim Fletcher,' said the tall man with the drooping, sandy mustache. He spoke laconically, nevertheless there was a tone that showed he expected to be known. Something went with that name. The stranger did not appear to be impressed.

'My name might be Blazes, but it ain't,' he replied. 'What do you call this burg?'

'Stranger, this heah me-tropoles bears the handle Ord. Is thet new to you?'

He leaned back against the bar, and now his little yellow eyes, clear as crystal, flawless as a hawk's, fixed on the stranger. Other men crowded close, forming a circle, curious, ready to be friendly or otherwise, according to how the tall interrogator marked the new-comer.

'Sure, Ord's a little strange to me. Off the rail-road some, ain't it? Funny trails hereabouts.'

'How fur was you goin'?'

'I reckon I was goin' as far as I could,' replied the stranger, with a hard laugh.

His reply had subtle reaction on that listening circle. Some of the men exchanged glances. Fletcher stroked his drooping mustache, seemed thoughtful, but lost something of that piercing scrutiny.

'Wal, Ord's the jumpin'-off place,' he said, presently. 'Sure you've heerd of the Big Bend country?'

'I sure have, an' was makin' tracks fer it,' replied the stranger.

Fletcher turned toward a man in the outer edge of the group. 'Knell, come in heah.'

This individual elbowed his way in and was seen to be scarcely more than a boy, almost pale beside those bronzed men, with a long, expressionless face, thin and sharp.

'Knell, this heah's—' Fletcher wheeled to the stranger. 'What'd you call yourself?'

'I'd hate to mention what I've been callin' myself lately.'

This sally fetched another laugh. The stranger appeared cool, careless, indifferent. Perhaps he knew, as the others present knew, that this show of Fletcher's, this pretense of introduction, was merely talk while he was looked over.

Knell stepped up, and it was easy to see, from the way Fletcher relinquished his part in the situation, that a man greater than he had appeared upon the scene.

'Any business here?' he queried, curtly. When he spoke his expressionless face was in strange contrast with the ring, the quality, the cruelty of his voice. This voice betrayed an absence of humor, of friendliness, of heart.

'Nope,' replied the stranger.

'Know anybody hereabouts?'

'Nary one.'

'Jest ridin' through?'

'Yep.'

'Slopin' fer back country, eh?'

There came a pause. The stranger appeared to grow a little resentful and drew himself up disdainfully.

'Wal, considerin' you-all seem so damn friendly an' oncurious down here in this Big Bend country, I don't mind sayin' yes—I am in on the dodge,' he replied, with deliberate sarcasm.

'From west of Ord—out El Paso way, mebbe?'

'Sure.'

'A-huh! Thet so?' Knell's words cut the air, stilled the room. 'You're from way down the river. Thet's what they say down there—'on the dodge.' … Stranger, you're a liar!'

With swift clink of spur and thump of boot the crowd split, leaving Knell and the stranger in the center.

Wild breed of that ilk never made a mistake in judging a man's nerve. Knell had cut out with the trenchant call, and stood ready. The stranger suddenly lost his every semblance to the rough and easy character before manifest in him. He became bronze. That situation seemed familiar to him. His eyes held a singular piercing light that danced like a compass-needle.

'Sure I lied,' he said; 'so I ain't takin' offense at the way you called me. I'm lookin' to make friends, not enemies. You don't strike me as one of the four-flushes, achin' to kill somebody. But if you are—go ahead an' open the ball. … You see, I never throw a gun on them fellers till they go fer theirs.'

Knell coolly eyed his antagonist, his strange face not changing in the least. Yet somehow it was evident in his look that here was metal which rang differently from what he had expected. Invited to start a fight or withdraw, as he chose, Knell proved himself big in the manner characteristic of only the genuine gunman.

'Stranger, I pass,' he said, and, turning to the bar, he ordered liquor.

The tension relaxed, the silence broke, the men filled up the gap; the incident seemed closed. Jim Fletcher attached himself to the stranger, and now both respect and friendliness tempered his asperity.

'Wal, fer want of a better handle I'll call you Dodge,' he said.

'Dodge's as good as any. ... Gents, line up again—an' if you can't be friendly, be careful!'

Such was Buck Duane's debut in the little outlaw hamlet of Ord.

Duane had been three months out of the Nueces country. At El Paso he bought the finest horse he could find, and, armed and otherwise outfitted to suit him, he had taken to unknown trails. Leisurely he rode from town to town, village to village, ranch to ranch, fitting his talk and his occupation to the impression he wanted to make upon different people whom he met. He was in turn a cowboy, a rancher, a cattleman, a stockbuyer, a boomer, a land-hunter; and long before he reached the wild and inhospitable Ord he had acted the part of an outlaw, drifting into new territory. He passed on leisurely because he wanted to learn the lay of the country, the location of villages and ranches, the work, habit, gossip, pleasures, and fears of the people with whom he came in contact. The one subject most impelling to him—outlaws—he never mentioned; but by talking all around it, sifting the old ranch and cattle story, he acquired a knowledge calculated to aid his plot. In this game time was of no moment; if necessary he would take years to accomplish his task. The stupendous and perilous nature of it showed in the slow, wary preparation. When he heard Fletcher's name and faced Knell he knew he had reached the place he sought. Ord was a hamlet on the fringe of the grazing country, of doubtful honesty, from which, surely, winding trails led down into that free and never-disturbed paradise of outlaws—the Big Bend.

Duane made himself agreeable, yet not too much so, to Fletcher and several other men disposed to talk and drink and eat; and then, after having a care for his horse, he rode out of town a couple of miles to a grove he had marked, and there, well hidden, he prepared to spend the night. This proceeding served a double purpose—he was safer, and the habit would look well in the eyes of outlaws, who would be more inclined to see in him the lone-wolf fugitive.

Long since Duane had fought out a battle with himself, won a hard-earned victory. His outer life, the action, was much the same as it had been; but the inner life had tremendously changed. He could never become a happy man, he could never shake utterly those haunting phantoms that had once been his despair and madness; but he had assumed a task impossible for any man save one like him, he had felt the meaning of it grow strangely and wonderfully, and through that flourished up consciousness of how passionately he now clung to this thing which would blot out his former infamy. The iron fetters no more threatened his hands; the iron door no more haunted his dreams. He never forgot that he was free. Strangely, too, along with this feeling of new manhood there gathered the force of imperious desire to run these chief outlaws to their dooms. He never called them outlaws—but rustlers, thieves, robbers, murderers, criminals. He sensed the growth of a relentless driving passion, and sometimes he feared that, more than the newly acquired zeal and pride in this ranger service, it was the old, terrible inherited killing instinct lifting its hydra-head in new guise. But of that he could not be sure. He dreaded the thought. He could only wait.

Another aspect of the change in Duane, neither passionate nor driving, yet not improbably even more potent of new significance to life, was the imperceptible return of an old love of nature dead during his outlaw days.

For years a horse had been only a machine of locomotion, to carry him from place to place, to beat and spur and goad mercilessly in flight; now this giant black, with his splendid head, was a companion, a friend, a brother, a loved thing, guarded jealously, fed and trained and ridden with an intense appreciation of his great speed and endurance. For years the daytime, with its birth of sunrise on through long hours to the ruddy close, had been used for sleep or rest in some rocky hole or willow brake or deserted hut, had been hated because it augmented danger of pursuit, because it drove the fugitive to lonely, wretched hiding; now the dawn was a greeting, a promise of another day to ride, to plan, to remember, and sun, wind, cloud, rain, sky—all were joys to him, somehow speaking his freedom. For years the night had been a black space, during which he had to ride unseen along the endless trails, to peer with cat-eyes through gloom for the moving shape that ever pursued him; now the twilight and the dusk and the shadows of grove and cañon darkened into night with its train of stars, and brought him calm reflection of the day's happenings, of the morrow's possibilities, perhaps a sad, brief procession of the old phantoms, then sleep. For years cañons and valleys and mountains had been looked at as retreats that might be dark and wild enough to hide even an outlaw; now he saw these features of the great desert with something of the eyes of the boy who had once burned for adventure and life among them.

This night a wonderful afterglow lingered long in the west, and against the golden-red of clear sky the bold, black head of Mount Ord reared itself aloft, beautiful but aloof, sinister yet calling. Small wonder that Duane gazed in fascination upon the peak! Somewhere deep in its corrugated sides or lost in a rugged cañon was hidden the secret stronghold of the master outlaw Cheseldine. All down along the ride from El Paso Duane had heard of Cheseldine, of his band, his fearful deeds, his cunning, his widely separated raids, of his flitting here and there like a Jack-o'-lantern; but never a word of his den, never a word of his appearance.

Next morning Duane did not return to Ord. He struck off to the north, riding down a rough, slow-descending road that appeared to have been used occasionally for cattle-driving. As he had ridden in from the west, this northern direction led him into totally unfamiliar country. While he passed on, however, he exercised such keen observation that in the future he would know whatever might be of service to him if he chanced that way again.

The rough, wild, brush-covered slope down from the foothills gradually leveled out into plain, a magnificent grazing country, upon which till noon of that day Duane did not see a herd of cattle or a ranch. About that time he made out smoke from the railroad, and after a couple of hours' riding he entered a town which inquiry discovered to be Bradford. It was the largest town he had visited since Marfa, and he calculated must have a thousand or fifteen hundred inhabitants, not including Mexicans. He decided this would be a good place for him to hold up for a while, being the nearest town to Ord, only forty miles away. So he hitched his horse in front of a store and leisurely set about studying Bradford.

It was after dark, however, that Duane verified his suspicions concerning Bradford. The town was awake after dark, and there was one long row of saloons, dance-halls, gambling-resorts in full blast. Duane visited them all, and was surprised to see wildness and license equal to that of the old river camp of Bland's in its palmiest days. Here it was forced upon him that the farther west one traveled along the river the sparser the respectable settlements, the more numerous the hard characters, and in consequence the greater the element of lawlessness. Duane returned to his lodging-house with the conviction that MacNelly's task of cleaning up the Big Bend country was a stupendous one. Yet, he reflected, a company of intrepid and quick-shooting rangers could have soon cleaned up this Bradford.

The innkeeper had one other guest that night, a long black-coated and wide-sombreroed Texan who reminded Duane of his grandfather. This man had penetrating eyes, a courtly manner, and an unmistakable leaning toward companionship and mintjuleps. The gentleman introduced himself as Colonel Webb, of Marfa, and took it as a matter of course that Duane made no comment about himself.

'Sir, it's all one to me,' he said, blandly, waving his hand. 'I have traveled. Texas is free, and this frontier is one where it's healthier and just as friendly for a man to have no curiosity about his companion. You might be Cheseldine, of the Big Bend, or you might be Judge Little, of El Paso—it's all one to me. I enjoy drinking with you anyway.'

Duane thanked him, conscious of a reserve and dignity that he could not have felt or pretended three months before. And then, as always, he was a good listener. Colonel Webb told, among other things, that he had come out to the Big Bend to look over the affairs of a deceased brother who had been a rancher and a sheriff of one of the towns. Fairdale by name.

'Found no affairs, no ranch, not even his grave,' said Colonel Webb. 'And I tell you, sir, if hell's any tougher than this Fairdale I don't want to expiate my sins there.'

'Fairdale. ... I imagine sheriffs have a hard row to hoe out here,' replied Duane, trying not to appear curious.

The Colonel swore lustily.

'My brother was the only honest sheriff Fairdale ever had. It was wonderful how long he lasted. But he had nerve, he could throw a gun, and he was on the square. Then he was wise enough to confine his work to offenders of his own town and neighborhood. He let the riding outlaws alone, else he wouldn't have lasted at all. ... What this frontier needs, sir, is about six companies of Texas Rangers.'

Duane was aware of the Colonel's close scrutiny.

'Do you know anything about the service?' he asked.

'I used to. Ten years ago when I lived in San Antonio. A fine body of men, sir, and the salvation of Texas.'

'Governor Stone doesn't entertain that opinion,' said Duane.

Here Colonel Webb exploded. Manifestly the governor was not his choice for a chief executive of the great state. He talked politics for a while, and of the vast territory west of the Pecos that seemed never to get a benefit from Austin. He talked enough for Duane to realize that here was just the kind of intelligent, well-informed, honest citizen that he had been trying to meet. He exerted himself thereafter to be agreeable and interesting; and he saw presently that here was an opportunity to make a valuable acquaintance, if not a friend.

'I'm a stranger in these parts,' said Duane, finally. 'What is this outlaw situation you speak of?'

'It's damnable, sir, and unbelievable. Not rustling any more, but just wholesale herd-stealing, in which some big cattlemen, supposed to be honest, are equally guilty with the outlaws. On this border, you know, the rustler has always been able to steal cattle in any numbers. But to get rid of big bunches—that's the hard job. The gang operating between here and Valentine evidently have not this trouble. Nobody knows where the stolen stock goes. But I'm not alone in my opinion that most of it goes to several big stockmen. They ship to San Antonio, Austin, New Orleans, also to El Paso. If you travel the stock-road between here and Marfa and Valentine you'll see dead cattle all along the line and stray cattle out in the scrub.

The herds have been driven fast and far, and stragglers are not rounded up.'

'Wholesale business, eh?' remarked Duane. 'Who are these—er—big stock-buyers?'

Colonel Webb seemed a little startled at the abrupt query. He bent his penetrating gaze upon Duane and thoughtfully stroked his pointed beard.

'Names, of course, I'll not mention. Opinions are one thing, direct accusation another. This is not a healthy country for the informer.'

When it came to the outlaws themselves Colonel Webb was disposed to talk freely. Duane could not judge whether the Colonel had a hobby of that subject or the outlaws were so striking in personality and deed that any man would know all about them. The great name along the river was Cheseldine, but it seemed to be a name detached from an individual. No person of veracity known to Colonel Webb had ever seen Cheseldine, and those who claimed that doubtful honor varied so diversely in descriptions of the chief that they confused the reality and lent to the outlaw only further mystery. Strange to say of an outlaw leader, as there was no one who could identify him, so there was no one who could prove he had actually killed a man. Blood flowed like water over the Big Bend country, and it was Cheseldine who spilled it. Yet the fact remained there were no eye-witnesses to connect any individual called Cheseldine with these deeds of violence. But in striking contrast to this mystery was the person, character, and cold-blooded action of Poggin and Knell, the chief's lieutenants. They were familiar figures in all the towns within two hundred miles of Bradford. Knell had a record, but as gunman with an incredible list of victims Poggin was supreme. If Poggin had a friend no one ever heard of him. There were a hundred stories of his nerve, his wonderful speed with a gun, his passion for gambling, his love of a horse—his cold, implacable, inhuman wiping out of his path any man that crossed it.

'Cheseldine is a name, a terrible name,' said Colonel Webb. 'Sometimes I wonder if he's not only a name. In that case where does the brains of this gang come from? No; there must be a master craftsman behind this border pillage; a master capable of handling those terrors Poggin and Knell. Of all the thousands of outlaws developed by western Texas in the last twenty years these three are the greatest. In southern Texas, down between the Pecos and the Nueces, there have been and are still many bad men. But I doubt if any outlaw there, possibly excepting Buck Duane, ever equaled Poggin. You've heard of this Duane?'

'Yes, a little,' replied Duane, quietly. 'I'm from southern Texas. Buck Duane then is known out here?'

'Why, man, where isn't his name known?' returned Colonel Webb. 'I've kept track of his record as I have all the others. Of course, Duane, being a lone outlaw, is somewhat of a mystery also, but not like Cheseldine. Out here there have drifted many stories of Duane, horrible some of them. But despite them a sort of romance

clings to that Nueces outlaw. He's killed three great outlaw leaders, I believe—
Bland, Hardin, and the other I forgot. Hardin was known in the Big Bend, had
friends there. Bland had a hard name at Del Rio.'

'Then this man Duane enjoys rather an unusual repute west of the Pecos?'
inquired Duane.

'He's considered more of an enemy to his kind than to honest men. I
understand Duane had many friends, that whole counties swear by him—secretly,
of course, for he's a hunted outlaw with rewards on his head. His fame in this
country appears to hang on his matchless gun-play and his enmity toward outlaw
chiefs. I've heard many a rancher say: "I wish to God that Buck Duane would
drift out here! I'd give a hundred pesos to see him and Poggin' meet." It's a singular
thing, stranger, how jealous these great outlaws are of each other.'

'Yes, indeed, all about them is singular,' replied Duane. 'Has Cheseldine's gang
been busy lately?'

'No. This section has been free of rustling for months, though there's unex-
plained movements of stock. Probably all the stock that's being shipped now was
rustled long ago. Cheseldine works over a wide section, too wide for news to travel
inside of weeks. Then sometimes he's not heard of at all for a spell. These lulls
are pretty surely indicative of a big storm sooner or later. And Cheseldine's deals,
as they grow fewer and father between, certainly get bigger, more daring. There
are some people who think Cheseldine had nothing to do with the bank-robberies
and train-holdups during the last few years in this country. But that's poor
reasoning. The jobs have been too well done, too surely covered, to be the work
of greasers or ordinary outlaws.'

'What's your view of the outlook? How's all this gang to wind up? Will the
outlaw ever be driven out?' asked Duane.

'Never. There will always be outlaws along the Rio Grande. All the armies in
the world couldn't comb the wild brakes of that fifteen hundred miles of river.
But the sway of the outlaw, such as is enjoyed by these leaders, will sooner or later
be past. The criminal element flock to the Southwest. But not so thick and fast as
the pioneers. Besides, the outlaws kill themselves, and the ranchers are slowly
rising in wrath, if not in action. That will come soon. If they only had a leader to
start the fight! But that will come. There's talk of Vigilantes, the same that were
organized in California and are now in force in Idaho. So far it's only talk. But the
time will come. And the days of Cheseldine and Poggin are numbered.'

Duane went to bed that night exceedingly thoughtful. The long trail was growing
hot. This voluble colonel had given him new ideas. It came to Duane in surprise
that he was famous along the upper Rio Grande. Assuredly he would not long be

able to conceal his identity. He had no doubt that he would soon meet the chiefs of this clever and bold rustling gang. He could not decide whether he would be safer unknown or known. In the latter case his one chance lay in the fatality connected with his name, in his power to look it and act it. Duane had never dreamed of any sleuth-hound tendency in his nature, but now he felt something like one. Above all others his mind fixed on Poggin—Poggin the brute, the executor of Cheseldine's will, but mostly upon Poggin the gunman. This in itself was a warning to Duane. He felt terrible forces at work within him. There was the stern and indomitable resolve to make MacNelly's boast good to the governor of the state—to break up Cheseldine's gang. Yet this was not in Duane's mind before a strange grim and deadly instinct—which he had to drive away for fear he would find in it a passion to kill Poggin, not for the state, nor for his word to MacNelly, but for himself. Had his father's blood and the hard years made Duane the kind of man who instinctively wanted to meet Poggin? He was sworn to MacNelly's service, and he fought himself to keep that, and that only, in his mind.

Duane ascertained that Fairdale was situated two days' ride from Bradford toward the north. There was a stage which made the journey twice a week.

Next morning Duane mounted his horse and headed for Fairdale. He rode leisurely, as he wanted to learn all he could about the country. There were few ranches. The farther he traveled the better grazing he encountered, and, strange to note, the fewer herds of cattle.

It was just sunset when he made out a cluster of adobe houses that marked the half-way point between Bradford and Fairdale. Here, Duane had learned, was stationed a comfortable inn for wayfarers.

When he drew up before the inn the landlord and his family and a number of loungers greeted him laconically.

'Beat the stage in, hey?' remarked one.

'There she comes now,' said another. 'Joel shore is drivin' to-night.'

Far down the road Duane saw a cloud of dust and horses and a lumbering coach. When he had looked after the needs of his horse he returned to the group before the inn. They awaited the stage with that interest common to isolated people. Presently it rolled up, a large mud-bespattered and dusty vehicle, littered with baggage on top and tied on behind. A number of passengers alighted, three of whom excited Duane's interest. One was a tall, dark, striking-looking man, and the other two were ladies, wearing long gray ulsters and veils. Duane heard the proprietor of the inn address the man as Colonel Longstreth, and as the party entered the inn Duane's quick ears caught a few words which acquainted him with the fact that Longstreth was the Mayor of Fairdale.

Duane passed inside himself to learn that supper would soon be ready. At table he found himself opposite the three who had attracted his attention.

'Ruth, I envy the lucky cowboys,' Longstreth was saying.

Ruth was a curly-headed girl with gray or hazel eyes.

'I'm crazy to ride bronchos,' she said.

Duane gathered she was on a visit to western Texas. The other girl's deep voice, sweet like a bell, made Duane regard her closer. She had beauty as he had never seen it in another woman. She was slender, but the development of her figure gave Duane the impression she was twenty years old or more. She had the most exquisite hands Duane had ever seen. She did not resemble the Colonel, who was evidently her father. She looked tired, quiet, even melancholy. A finely chiseled oval face; clear, olive-tinted skin, long eyes set wide apart and black as coal, beautiful to look into; a slender, straight nose that had something nervous and delicate about it which made Duane think of a thoroughbred; and a mouth by no means small, but perfectly curved; and hair like jet—all these features proclaimed her beauty to Duane. Duane believed her a descendant of one of the old French families of eastern Texas. He was sure of it when she looked at him, drawn by his rather persistent gaze. There were pride, fire, and passion in her eyes. Duane felt himself blushing in confusion. His stare at her had been rude, perhaps, but unconscious. How many years had passed since he had seen a girl like her! Thereafter he kept his eyes upon his plate, yet he seemed to be aware that he had aroused the interest of both girls.

After supper the guests assembled in a big sitting-room where an open fire place with blazing mesquite sticks gave out warmth and cheery glow. Duane took a seat by a table in the corner, and, finding a paper, began to read. Presently when he glanced up he saw two dark-faced men, strangers who had not appeared before, and were peering in from a doorway. When they saw Duane had observed them they stepped back out of sight.

It flashed over Duane that the strangers acted suspiciously. In Texas in the seventies it was always bad policy to let strangers go unheeded. Duane pondered a moment. Then he went out to look over these two men. The doorway opened into a patio, and across that was a little dingy, dim-lighted bar-room. Here Duane found the innkeeper dispensing drinks to the two strangers. They glanced up when he entered, and one of them whispered. He imagined he had seen one of them before. In Texas, where outdoor men were so rough, bronzed, bold, and some-times grim of aspect, it was no easy task to pick out the crooked ones. But Duane's years on the border had augmented a natural instinct or gift to read character, or at least to sense the evil in men; and he knew at once that these strangers were dishonest.

'Hev somethin?' one of them asked, leering. Both looked Duane up and down.

'No thanks, I don't drink,' Duane replied, and returned their scrutiny with interest. 'How's tricks in the Big Bend?'

Both men stared. It had taken only a close glance for Duane to recognize a type of ruffian most frequently met along the river. These strangers had that stamp, and their surprise proved he was right. Here the innkeeper showed signs of uneasiness, and seconded the surprise of his customers. No more was said at the instant, and the two rather hurriedly went out.

'Say, boss, do you know those fellows?' Duane asked the innkeeper.

'Nope.'

'Which way did they come?'

'Now I think of it, them fellers rid in from both corners today,' he replied, and he put both hands on the bar and looked at Duane. 'They nooned heah, comin' from Bradford, they said, an' trailed in after the stage.'

When Duane returned to the sitting-room Colonel Longstreth was absent, also several of the other passengers. Miss Ruth sat in the chair he had vacated, and across the table from her sat Miss Longstreth. Duane went directly to them.

'Excuse me,' said Duane, addressing them. 'I want to tell you there are a couple of rough-looking men here. I've just seen them. They mean evil. Tell your father to be careful. Lock your doors—bar your windows to-night.'

'Oh!' cried Ruth, very low. 'Ray, do you hear?'

'Thank you; we'll be careful,' said Miss Longstreth, gracefully. The rich color had faded in her cheek. 'I saw those men watching you from that door. They had such bright black eyes. Is there really danger—here?'

'I think so,' was Duane's reply.

Soft swift steps behind him preceded a harsh voice: 'Hands up!'

No man quicker than Duane to recognize the intent in those words! His hands shot up. Miss Ruth uttered a little frightened cry and sank into her chair. Miss Longstreth turned white, her eyes dilated. Both girls were staring at some one behind Duane.

'Turn around!' ordered the harsh voice.

The big, dark stranger, the bearded one who had whispered to his comrade in the bar-room and asked Duane to drink, had him covered with a cocked gun. He strode forward, his eyes gleaming, pressed the gun against him, and with his other hand dove into his inside coat pocket and tore out his roll of bills. Then he reached low at Duane's hip, felt his gun, and took it. Then he slapped the other hip, evidently in search of another weapon. That done, he backed away, wearing an expression of fiendish satisfaction that made Duane think he was only a common thief, a novice at this kind of game.

His comrade stood in the door with a gun leveled at two other men, who stood there frightened, speechless.

'Git a move on, Bill,' called this fellow; and he took a hasty glance backward. A stamp of hoofs came from outside. Of course the robbers had horses waiting.

The one called Bill strode across the room, and with brutal, careless haste began to prod the two men with his weapon and to search them. The robber in the doorway called 'Rustle!' and disappeared.

Duane wondered where the innkeeper was, and Colonel Longstreth and the other two passengers. The bearded robber quickly got through with his searching, and from his growls Duane gathered he had not been well remunerated. Then he wheeled once more. Duane had not moved a muscle, stood perfectly calm with his arms high. The robber strode back with his bloodshot eyes fastened upon the girls. Miss Longstreth never flinched, but the little girl appeared about to faint.

'Don't yap, there!' he said, low and hard. He thrust the gun close to Ruth. Then Duane knew for sure that he was no knight of the road, but a plain cutthroat robber. Danger always made Duane exult in a kind of cold glow. But now something hot worked within him. He had a little gun in his pocket. The robber had missed it. And he began to calculate chances.

'Any money, jewelry, diamonds!' ordered the ruffian, fiercely.

Miss Ruth collapsed. Then he made at Miss Longstreth. She stood with her hands at her breast. Evidently the robber took this position to mean that she had valuables concealed there. But Duane fancied she had instinctively pressed her hands against a throbbing heart.

'Come out with it!' he said, harshly, reaching for her.

'Don't dare touch me!' she cried, her eyes ablaze. She did not move. She had nerve.

It made Duane thrill. He saw he was going to get a chance. Waiting had been a science with him. But here it was hard. Miss Ruth had fainted, and that was well. Miss Longstreth had fight in her, which fact helped Duane, yet made injury possible to her. She eluded two lunges the man made at her. Then his rough hand caught her waist, and with one pull ripped it asunder, exposing her beautiful shoulder, white as snow.

She cried out. The prospect of being robbed or even killed had not shaken Miss Longstreth's nerve as had this brutal tearing off of half her waist.

The ruffian was only turned partially away from Duane. For himself he could have waited no longer. But for her! That gun was still held dangerously upward close to her. Duane watched only that. Then a bellow made him jerk his head. Colonel Longstreth stood in the doorway in a magnificent rage. He had no weapon. Strange how he showed no fear! He bellowed something again.

Duane's shifting glance caught the robber's sudden movement. It was a kind of start. He seemed stricken. Duane expected him to shoot Longstreth. Instead the hand that clutched Miss Longstreth's torn waist loosened its hold. The other hand with its cocked weapon slowly dropped till it pointed to the floor. That was Duane's chance.

Swift as a flash he drew his gun and fired. Thud! went his bullet, and he could not tell on the instant whether it hit the robber or went into the ceiling. Then the robber's gun boomed harmlessly. He fell with blood spurting over his face. Duane realized he had hit him, but the small bullet had glanced.

Miss Longstreth reeled and might have fallen had Duane not supported her. It was only a few steps to a couch, to which he half led, half carried her. Then he rushed out of the room, across the patio, through the bar to the yard. Nevertheless, he was cautious. In the gloom stood a saddled horse, probably the one belonging to the fellow he had shot. His comrade had escaped. Returning to the sitting-room, Duane found a condition approaching pandemonium.

The innkeeper rushed in, pitchfork in hands. Evidently he had been out at the barn. He was now shouting to find out what had happened. Joel, the stage-driver, was trying to quiet the men who had been robbed. The woman, wife of one of the men, had come in, and she had hysterics. The girls were still and white. The robber Bill lay where he had fallen, and Duane guessed he had made a fair shot, after all. And, lastly, the thing that struck Duane most of all was Longstreth's rage. He never saw such passion. Like a caged lion Longstreth stalked and roared. There came a quieter moment in which the innkeeper shrilly protested:

'Man, what're you ravin' aboot? Nobody's hurt, an' thet's lucky. I swear to God I hadn't nothin' to do with them fellers!'

'I ought to kill you anyhow!' replied Longstreth. And his voice now astounded Duane, it was so full of power.

Upon examination Duane found that his bullet had furrowed the robber's temple, torn a great piece out of his scalp, and, as Duane had guessed, had glanced. He was not seriously injured, and already showed signs of returning consciousness.

'Drag him out of here!' ordered Longstreth; and he turned to his daughter.

Before the innkeeper reached the robber Duane had secured the money and gun taken from him; and presently recovered the property of the other men. Joel helped the innkeeper carry the injured man somewhere outside.

Miss Longstreth was sitting white but composed upon the couch, where lay Miss Ruth, who evidently had been carried there by the Colonel. Duane did not think she had wholly lost consciousness, and now she lay very still, with eyes dark and shadowy, her face pallid and wet. The Colonel, now that he finally remembered his women-folk, seemed to be gentle and kind. He talked soothingly to Miss Ruth, made light of the adventure, said she must learn to have nerve out here where things happened.

'Can I be of any service?' asked Duane, solicitously.

'Thanks; I guess there's nothing you can do. Talk to these frightened girls while I go see what's to be done with that thick-skulled robber,' he replied, and, telling the girls that there was no more danger, he went out.

Miss Longstreth sat with one hand holding her torn waist in place; the other she extended to Duane. He took it awkwardly, and he felt a strange thrill.

'You saved my life,' she said, in grave, sweet seriousness.

'No, no!' Duane exclaimed. 'He might have struck you, hurt you, but no more.'

'I saw murder in his eyes. He thought I had jewels under my dress. I couldn't bear his touch. The beast! I'd have fought. Surely my life was in peril.'

'Did you kill him?' asked Miss Ruth, who lay listening.

'Oh no. He's not badly hurt.'

'I'm very glad he's alive,' said Miss Longstreth, shuddering.

'My intention was bad enough,' Duane went on. 'It was a ticklish place for me. You see, he was half drunk, and I was afraid his gun might go off. Fool careless he was!'

'Yet you say you didn't save me,' Miss Longstreth returned, quickly.

'Well, let it go at that,' Duane responded. 'I saved you something.'

'Tell me all about it?' asked Miss Ruth, who was fast recovering.

Rather embarrassed, Duane briefly told the incident from his point of view.

'Then you stood there all the time with your hands up thinking of nothing— watching for nothing except a little moment when you might draw your gun?' asked Miss Ruth.

'I guess that's about it,' he replied.

'Cousin,' said Miss Longstreth, thoughtfully, 'it was fortunate for us that this gentleman happened to be here. Papa scouts—laughs at danger. He seemed to think there was no danger. Yet he raved after it came.'

'Go with us all the way to Fairdale—please?' asked Miss Ruth, sweetly offering her hand. 'I am Ruth Herbert. And this is my cousin, Ray Longstreth.'

'I'm traveling that way,' replied Duane, in great confusion. He did not know how to meet the situation.

Colonel Longstreth returned then, and after bidding Duane a good night, which seemed rather curt by contrast to the graciousness of the girls, he led them away.

Before going to bed Duane went outside to take a look at the injured robber and perhaps to ask him a few questions. To Duane's surprise, he was gone, and so was his horse. The innkeeper was dumbfounded. He said that he left the fellow on the floor in the bar-room.

'Had he come to?' inquired Duane.

'Sure. He asked for whisky.'

'Did he say anything else?'

'Not to me. I heard him talkin' to the father of them girls.'

'You mean Colonel Longstreth?'

'I reckon. He sure was some riled, wasn't he? Jest as if I was to blame fer that two-bit of a hold-up!'

'What did you make of the old gent's rage?' asked Duane, watching the innkeeper. He scratched his head dubiously. He was sincere, and Duane believed in his honesty.

'Wal, I'm doggoned if I know what to make of it. But I reckon he's either crazy or got more nerve than most Texans.'

'More nerve, maybe,' Duane replied. 'Show me a bed now, innkeeper.'

Once in bed in the dark, Duane composed himself to think over the several events of the evening. He called up the details of the holdup and carefully revolved them in mind. The Colonel's wrath, under circumstances where almost any Texan would have been cool, nonplussed Duane, and he put it down to a choleric temperament. He pondered long on the action of the robber when Longstreth's bellow of rage burst in upon him. This ruffian, as bold and mean a type as Duane had ever encountered, had, from some cause or other, been startled. From whatever point Duane viewed the man's strange indecision he could come to only one conclusion—his start, his check, his fear had been that of recognition. Duane compared this effect with the suddenly acquired sense he had gotten of Colonel Longstreth's powerful personality. Why had that desperate robber lowered his gun and stood paralyzed at sight and sound of the Mayor of Fairdale? This was not answerable. There might have been a number of reasons, all to Colonel Longstreth's credit, but Duane could not understand. Longstreth had not appeared to see danger for his daughter, even though she had been roughly handled, and had advanced in front of a cocked gun. Duane probed deep into this singular fact, and he brought to bear on the thing all his knowledge and experience of violent Texas life. And he found that the instant Colonel Longstreth had appeared on the scene there *was* no further danger threatening his daughter. Why? That likewise Duane could not answer. Then his rage, Duane concluded, had been solely at the idea of *his* daughter being assaulted by a robber. This deduction was indeed a thought-disturber, but Duane put it aside to crystallize and for more careful consideration.

Next morning Duane found that the little town was called Sanderson. It was larger than he had at first supposed. He walked up the main street and back again. Just as he arrived some horsemen rode up to the inn and dismounted. And at this juncture the Longstreth party came out. Duane heard Colonel Longstreth utter an exclamation. Then he saw him shake hands with a tall man. Longstreth looked surprised and angry, and he spoke with force; but Duane could not hear what it was he said. The fellow laughed, yet somehow he struck Duane as sullen, until suddenly he espied Miss Longstreth. Then his face changed, and he removed his sombrero. Duane went closer.

'Floyd, did you come with the teams?' asked Longstreth, sharply.

'Not me. I rode a horse, good and hard,' was the reply.

'Humph! I'll have a word to say to you later.' Then Longstreth turned to his daughter. 'Ray, here's the cousin I've told you about. You used to play with him ten years ago—Floyd Lawson. Floyd, my daughter—and my niece, Ruth Herbert.'

Duane always scrutinized every one he met, and now with a dangerous game to play, with a consciousness of Longstreth's unusual and significant personality, he bent a keen and searching glance upon this Floyd Lawson.

He was under thirty, yet gray at his temples—dark, smooth-shaven, with lines left by wildness, dissipation, shadows under dark eyes, a mouth strong and bitter, and a square chin—a reckless, careless, handsome, sinister face strangely losing the hardness when he smiled. The grace of a gentleman clung round him, seemed like an echo in his mellow voice. Duane doubted not that he, like many a young man, had drifted out to the frontier, where rough and wild life had wrought sternly but had not quite effaced the mark of good family.

Colonel Longstreth apparently did not share the pleasure of his daughter and his niece in the advent of this cousin. Something hinged on this meeting. Duane grew intensely curious, but, as the stage appeared ready for the journey, he had no further opportunity to gratify it.

16

Duane followed the stage through the town, out into the open, on to a wide, hard-packed road showing years of travel. It headed northwest. To the left rose a range of low, bleak mountains he had noted yesterday, and to the right sloped the mesquite-patched sweep of ridge and flat. The driver pushed his team to a fast trot, which gait surely covered ground rapidly.

The stage made three stops in the forenoon, one at a place where the horses could be watered, the second at a chuckwagon belonging to cowboys who were riding after stock, and the third at a small cluster of adobe and stone houses constituting a hamlet the driver called Longstreth, named after the Colonel. From that point on to Fairdale there were only a few ranches, each one controlling great acreage.

Early in the afternoon from a ridge-top Duane sighted Fairdale, a green patch in the mass of gray. For the barrens of Texas it was indeed a fair sight. But he was more concerned with its remoteness from civilization than its beauty. At that time, in the early seventies, when the vast western third of Texas was a wilderness, the pioneer had done wonders to settle there and establish places like Fairdale.

It needed only a glance for Duane to pick out Colonel Longstreth's ranch. The house was situated on the only elevation around Fairdale, and it was not high, nor more than a few minutes' walk from the edge of the town. It was a low, flat-roofed structure made of red adobe bricks, and covered what appeared to be fully an acre of ground. All was green about it, except where the fenced corrals and numerous barns or sheds showed gray and red.

Duane soon reached the shady outskirts of Fairdale, and entered the town with mingled feelings of curiosity, eagerness, and expectation. The street he rode down was a main one, and on both sides of the street was a solid row of saloons, resorts, hotels. Saddled horses stood hitched all along the sidewalk in two long lines, with a buckboard and team here and there breaking the continuity. This block was busy and noisy.

From all outside appearances Fairdale was no different from other frontier towns, and Duane's expectations were scarcely realized. As the afternoon was waning he halted at a little inn. A boy took charge of his horse. Duane questioned the lad about Fairdale and gradually drew to the subject most in mind.

'Colonel Longstreth has a big outfit, eh?'

'Reckon he has,' replied the lad, 'Doan know how many cowboys. They're always comin' and goin'. I ain't acquainted with half of them.'

'Much movement of stock these days?'

'Stock's always movin',' he replied, with a queer look.

'Rustlers?'

But he did not follow up that look with the affirmative Duane expected.

'Lively place, I hear—Fairdale is?'

'Ain't so lively as Sanderson, but it's bigger.'

'Yes, I heard it was. Fellow down there was talking about two cowboys who were arrested.'

'Sure. I heered all about that. Joe Bean an' Brick Higgins—they belong heah, but they ain't heah much. Longstreth's boys.'

Duane did not want to appear over-inquisitive, so he turned the talk into other channels.

After getting supper Duane strolled up and down the main street. When darkness set in he went into a hotel, bought cigars, sat around, and watched. Then he passed out and went into the next place. This was of rough crude exterior, but the inside was comparatively pretentious and ablaze with lights. It was full of men coming and going—a dusty-booted crowd that smelled of horses and smoke. Duane sat down for a while, with wide eyes and open ears. Then he hunted up the bar, where most of the guests had been or were going. He found a great square room lighted by six huge lamps, a bar at one side, and all the floorspace taken up by tables and chairs. This was the only gambling-place of any size in southern Texas in which he had noted the absence of Mexicans. There was some card-playing going on at this moment. Duane stayed in there for a while, and knew that strangers were too common in Fairdale to be conspicuous. Then he returned to the inn where he had engaged a room.

Duane sat down on the steps of the dingy little restaurant. Two men were conversing inside, and they had not noticed Duane.

'Laramie, what's the stranger's name?' asked one.

'He didn't say,' replied the other.

'Sure was a strappin' big man. Struck me a little odd, he did. No cattleman, him. How'd you size him?'

'Well, like one of them cool, easy, quiet Texans who's been lookin' for a man for years—to kill him when he found him.'

'Right you are, Laramie; and, between you an' me, I hope he's lookin' for Long—'

' 'S-sh!' interrupted Laramie. 'You must be half drunk, to go talkin' that way.'

Thereafter they conversed in too low a tone for Duane to hear, and presently Laramie's visitor left. Duane went inside, and, making himself agreeable, began to ask casual questions about Fairdale. Laramie was not communicative.

Duane went to his room in a thoughtful frame of mind. Had Laramie's visitor meant he hoped some one had come to kill Longstreth? Duane inferred just that from the interrupted remark. There was something wrong about the Mayor of Fairdale. Duane felt it. And he felt also, if there was a crooked and dangerous man, it was this Floyd Lawson. The innkeeper Laramie would be worth cultivating. And last in Duane's thoughts that night was Miss Longstreth. He could not help thinking of her—how strangely the meeting with her had affected him. It made him remember that long-past time when girls had been a part of his life. What a sad and dark and endless void lay between that past and the present! He had no right even to dream of a beautiful woman like Ray Longstreth. That conviction, however, did not dispel her; indeed, it seemed perversely to make her grow more fascinating. Duane grew conscious of a strange, unaccountable hunger, a something that was like a pang in his breast.

Next day he lounged about the inn. He did not make any overtures to the taciturn proprietor. Duane had no need of hurry now. He contented himself with watching and listening. And at the close of that day he decided Fairdale was what MacNelly had claimed it to be, and that he was on the track of an unusual adventure. The following day he spent in much the same way, though on one occasion he told Laramie he was looking for a man. The innkeeper grew a little less furtive and reticent after that. He would answer casual queries, and it did not take Duane long to learn that Laramie had seen better days—that he was now broken, bitter, and hard. Some one had wronged him.

Several days passed. Duane did not succeed in getting any closer to Laramie, but he found the idlers on the corners and in front of the stores unsuspicious and willing to talk. It did not take him long to find out that Fairdale stood parallel with Huntsville for gambling, drinking, and fighting. The street was always lined with dusty, saddled horses, the town full of strangers. Money appeared more abundant than in any place Duane had ever visited; and it was spent with the abandon that spoke forcibly of easy and crooked acquirement. Duane decided that Sanderson, Bradford, and Ord were but notorious outposts to this Fairdale, which was a secret center of rustlers and outlaws. And what struck Duane strangest of all was the fact that Longstreth was mayor here and held court daily. Duane knew intuitively, before a chance remark gave him proof, that this court was a sham, a farce. And he wondered if it were not a blind. This wonder of his was equivalent to suspicion of Colonel Longstreth, and Duane reproached himself. Then he realized that the reproach was because of the daughter. Inquiry had brought him the fact that Ray Longstreth had just come to live with her father. Longstreth had originally been a planter in Louisiana, where his family had remained after his advent in the West. He was a rich rancher; he owned half of Fairdale; he was a cattle-buyer on a large scale. Floyd Lawson was his lieutenant and associate in deals.

On the afternoon of the fifth day of Duane's stay in Fairdale he returned to the inn from his usual stroll, and upon entering was amazed to have a rough-looking young fellow rush by him out of the door. Inside Laramie was lying on the floor, with a bloody bruise on his face. He did not appear to be dangerously hurt.

'Bo Snecker! He hit me and went after the cash-drawer,' said Laramie, laboring to his feet.

'Are you hurt much?' queried Duane.

'I guess not. But Bo needn't to have soaked me. I've been robbed before without that.'

'Well, I'll take a look after Bo,' replied Duane.

He went out and glanced down the street toward the center of the town. He did not see any one he could take for the innkeeper's assailant. Then he looked up the street, and he saw the young fellow about a block away, hurrying along and gazing back.

Duane yelled for him to stop and started to go after him. Snecker broke into a run. Then Duane set out to overhaul him. There were two motives in Duane's action—one of anger, and the other a desire to make a friend of this man Laramie, whom Duane believed could tell him much.

Duane was light on his feet, and he had a giant stride. He gained rapidly upon Snecker, who, turning this way and that, could not get out of sight. Then he took to the open country and ran straight for the green hill where Longstreth's house stood. Duane had almost caught Snecker when he reached the shrubbery and trees and there eluded him. But Duane kept him in sight, in the shade, on the paths, and up the road into the courtyard, and he saw Snecker go straight for Longstreth's house.

Duane was not to be turned back by that, singular as it was. He did not stop to consider. It seemed enough to know that fate had directed him to the path of this rancher Longstreth. Duane entered the first open door on that side of the court. It opened into a corridor which led into a plaza. It had wide, smooth stone porches, and flowers and shrubbery in the center. Duane hurried through to burst into the presence of Miss Longstreth and a number of young people. Evidently she was giving a little party.

Lawson stood leaning against one of the pillars that supported the porch roof; at sight of Duane his face changed remarkably, expressing amazement, consternation, then fear.

In the quick ensuing silence Miss Longstreth rose white as her dress. The young women present stared in astonishment, if they were not equally perturbed. There were cowboys present who suddenly grew intent and still. By these things Duane gathered that his appearance must be disconcerting. He was panting. He wore no hat or coat. His big gun-sheath showed plainly at his hip.

Sight of Miss Longstreth had an unaccountable effect upon Duane. He was plunged into confusion. For the moment he saw no one but her.

'Miss Longstreth—I came—to search—your house,' panted Duane.

He hardly knew what he was saying, yet the instant he spoke he realized that that should have been the last thing for him to say. He had blundered. But he was not used to women, and this dark-eyed girl made him thrill and his heart beat thickly and his wits go scattering.

'Search my house!' exclaimed Miss Longstreth; and red succeeded the white in her cheeks. She appeared astonished and angry. 'What for? Why, how dare you! This is unwarrantable!'

'A man—Bo Snecker—assaulted and robbed Jim Laramie,' replied Duane, hurriedly. 'I chased Snecker here—saw him run into the house.'

'Here? Oh, sir, you must be mistaken. We have seen no one. In the absence of my father I'm mistress here. I'll not permit you to search.'

Lawson appeared to come out of his astonishment. He stepped forward.

'Ray, don't be bothered now,' he said, to his cousin. 'This fellow's making a bluff. I'll settle him. See here, Mister, you clear out!'

'I want Snecker. He's here, and I'm going to get him,' replied Duane, quietly.

'Bah! That's all a bluff,' sneered Lawson. 'I'm on to your game. You just wanted an excuse to break in here—to see my cousin again. When you saw the company you invented that excuse. Now, be off, or it'll be the worse for you.'

Duane felt his face burn with a tide of hot blood. Almost he felt that he was guilty of such motive. Had he not been unable to put this Ray Longstreth out of his mind? There seemed to be scorn in her eyes now. And somehow that checked his embarrassment.

'Miss Longstreth, will you let me search the house?' he asked.

'No.'

'Then—I regret to say—I'll do so without your permission.'

'You'll not dare!' she flashed. She stood erect, her bosom swelling.

'Pardon me—yes, I will.'

'Who are you?' she demanded, suddenly.

'I'm a Texas Ranger,' replied Duane.

'*A Texas Ranger!*' she echoed.

Floyd Lawson's dark face turned pale.

'Miss Longstreth, I don't need warrants to search houses,' said Duane. 'I'm sorry to annoy you. I'd prefer to have your permission. A ruffian has taken refuge here—in your father's house. He's hidden somewhere. May I look for him?'

'If you are indeed a ranger.'

Duane produced his papers. Miss Longstreth haughtily refused to look at them.

'Miss Longstreth, I've come to make Fairdale a safer, cleaner, better place for women and children. I don't wonder at your resentment. But to doubt me—insult me. Some day you may be sorry.'

Floyd Lawson made a violent motion with his hands.

'All stuff! Cousin, go on with your party. I'll take a couple of cowboys and go with this—this Texas Ranger.'

'Thanks,' said Duane, coolly, as he eyed Lawson. 'Perhaps you'll be able to find Snecker quicker than I could.'

'What do you mean?' demanded Lawson, and now he grew livid. Evidently he was a man of fierce quick passions.

'Don't quarrel,' said Miss Longstreth. 'Floyd, you go with him. Please hurry. I'll be nervous till—the man's found or you're sure there's not one.'

They started with several cowboys to search the house. They went through the rooms searching, calling out, peering into dark places. It struck Duane more than forcibly that Lawson did all the calling. He was hurried, too, tried to keep in the lead. Duane wondered if he knew his voice would be recognized by the hiding man. Be that as it might, it was Duane who peered into a dark corner and then, with gun leveled, said 'Come out!'

He came forth into the flare—a tall, slim, dark-faced youth, wearing sombrero, blouse and trousers. Duane collared him before any of the others could move and held the gun close enough to make him shrink. But he did not impress Duane as being frightened just then; nevertheless, he had a clammy face, the pallid look of a man who had just gotten over a shock. He peered into Duane's face, then into that of the cowboy next to him, then into Lawson's, and if ever in Duane's life he beheld relief it was then. That was all Duane needed to know, but he meant to find out more if he could.

'Who're you?' asked Duane, quietly.

'Bo Snecker,' he said.

'What'd you hide here for?'

He appeared to grow sullen.

'Reckoned I'd be as safe in Longstreth's as anywheres.'

'Ranger, what'll you do with him?' Lawson queried, as if uncertain, now the capture was made.

'I'll see to that,' replied Duane, and he pushed Snecker in front of him out into the court.

Duane had suddenly conceived the idea of taking Snecker before Mayor Longstreth in the court.

When Duane arrived at the hall where court was held there were other men there, a dozen or more, and all seemed excited; evidently, news of Duane had preceded him. Longstreth sat at a table up on a platform. Near him sat a thick-set grizzled man, with deep eyes, and this was Hanford Owens, county judge. To the right stood a tall, angular, yellowed-faced fellow with a drooping sandy mustache. Conspicuous on his vest was a huge silver shield. This was Gorsech, one of Longstreth's sheriffs. There were four other men whom Duane knew by sight, several whose faces were familiar, and half a dozen strangers, all dusty horsemen.

Longstreth pounded hard on the table to be heard. Mayor or not, he was unable at once to quell the excitement. Gradually, however, it subsided, and from the last few utterances before quiet was restored Duane gathered that he had intruded upon some kind of a meeting in the hall.

'What'd you break in here for?' demanded Longstreth.

'Isn't this the court? Aren't you the Mayor of Fairdale?' interrogated Duane. His voice was clear and loud, almost piercing.

'Yes,' replied Longstreth. Like flint he seemed, yet Duane felt his intense interest.

'I've arrested a criminal,' said Duane.

'Arrested a criminal!' ejaculated Longstreth. '*You*? Who're you?'

'I'm a ranger,' replied Duane.

A significant silence ensued.

'I charge Snecker with assault on Laramie and attempted robbery—if not murder. He's had a shady past here, as this court will know if it keeps a record.'

'What's this I hear about you, Bo? Get up and speak for yourself,' said Longstreth, gruffly.

Snecker got up, not without a furtive glance at Duane, and he had shuffled forward a few steps toward the Mayor. He had an evil front, but not the boldness even of a rustler.

'It ain't so, Longstreth,' he began, loudly. 'I went in Laramie's place fer grub. Some feller I never seen before come in from the hall an' hit Laramie an' wrastled him on the floor. I went out. Then this big ranger chased me an' fetched me here. I didn't do nothin'. This ranger's hankerin' to arrest somebody. Thet's my hunch, Longstreth.'

Longstreth said something in an undertone to Judge Owens, and that worthy nodded his great bushy head.

'Bo, you're discharged,' said Longstreth, bluntly. 'Now the rest of you clear out of here.'

He absolutely ignored the ranger. That was his rebuff to Duane—his slap in the face to an interfering ranger service. If Longstreth was crooked he certainly had magnificent nerve. Duane almost decided he was above suspicion. But his nonchalance, his air of finality, his authoritative assurance—these to Duane's keen and practised eyes were in significant contrast to a certain tenseness of line about his mouth and a slow paling of his olive skin. In that momentary lull Duane's scrutiny of Longstreth gathered an impression of the man's intense curiosity.

Then the prisoner, Snecker, with a cough that broke the spell of silence, shuffled a couple of steps toward the door.

'Hold on!' called Duane. The call halted Snecker, as if it had been a bullet.

'Longstreth, I saw Snecker attack Laramie,' said Duane, his voice still ringing. 'What has the court to say to that?'

'The court has this to say. West of the Pecos we'll not aid any ranger service. We don't want you out here. Fairdale doesn't need you.'

'That's a lie, Longstreth,' retorted Duane. 'I've letters from Fairdale citizens all begging for ranger service.'

Longstreth turned white. The veins corded at his temples. He appeared about to burst into rage. He was at a loss for quick reply.

Floyd Lawson rushed in and up to the table. The blood showed black and thick in his face; his utterance was incoherent, his uncontrollable outbreak of temper seemed out of all proportion to any cause he should reasonably have had for anger. Longstreth shoved him back with a curse and a warning glare.

'Where's your warrant to arrest Snecker?' shouted Longstreth.

'I don't need warrants to make arrests. Longstreth, you're ignorant of the power of Texas Rangers.'

'You'll come none of your damned ranger stunts out here. I'll block you.'

That passionate reply of Longstreth's was the signal Duane had been waiting for. He had helped on the crisis. He wanted to force Longstreth's hand and show the town his stand.

Duane backed clear of everybody.

'Men! I call on you all!' cried Duane, piercingly. 'I call on you to witness the arrest of a criminal prevented by Longstreth, Mayor of Fairdale. It will be recorded in the report to the Adjutant-General at Austin. Longstreth, you'll never prevent another arrest.'

Longstreth sat white with working jaw.

'Longstreth, you've shown your hand,' said Duane, in a voice that carried far and held those who heard. 'Any honest citizen of Fairdale can now see what's plain—yours is a damn poor hand! You're going to hear me call a spade a spade. In the two years you've been Mayor you've never arrested one rustler. Strange, when Fairdale's a nest for rustlers! You've never sent a prisoner to Del Rio, let alone to Austin. You have no jail. There have been nine murders during your office—innumerable street-fights and holdups. Not one arrest! But you have ordered arrests for trivial offenses, and have punished these out of all proportion. There have been lawsuits in your courts—suits over water-rights, cattle deals, property lines. Strange how in these lawsuits you or Lawson or other men close to you were always involved! Strange how it seems the law was stretched to favor your interest!'

Duane paused in his cold, ringing speech. In the silence, both outside and inside the hall, could be heard the deep breathing of agitated men. Longstreth was indeed a study. Yet did he betray anything but rage at this interloper?

'Longstreth, here's plain talk for you and Fairdale,' went on Duane. 'I don't accuse you and your court of dishonesty. I say *strange*! Law here has been a farce. The motive behind all this laxity isn't plain to me—yet. But I call your hand!'

17

Duane left the hall, elbowed his way through the crowd, and went down the street. He was certain that on the faces of some men he had seen ill-concealed wonder and satisfaction. He had struck some kind of a hot trail, and he meant to see where it led. It was by no means unlikely that Cheseldine might be at the other end. Duane controlled a mounting eagerness. But ever and anon it was shot through with a remembrance of Ray Longstreth. He suspected her father of being not what he pretended. He might, very probably would, bring sorrow and shame to this young woman. The thought made him smart with pain. She began to haunt him, and then he was thinking more of her beauty and sweetness than of the disgrace he might bring upon her. Some strange emotion, long locked inside Duane's heart, knocked to be heard, to be let out. He was troubled.

Upon returning to the inn he found Laramie there, apparently none the worse for his injury.

'How are you, Laramie?' he asked.

'Reckon I'm feelin' as well as could be expected,' replied Laramie. His head was circled by a bandage that did not conceal the lump where he had been struck. He looked pale, but was bright enough.

'That was a good crack Snecker gave you,' remarked Duane.

'I ain't accusin' Bo,' remonstrated Laramie, with eyes that made Duane thoughtful.

'Well, I accuse him. I caught him—took him to Longstreth's court. But they let him go.'

Laramie appeared to be agitated by this intimation of friendship.

'See here, Laramie,' went on Duane, 'in some parts of Texas it's policy to be close-mouthed. Policy and health-preserving! Between ourselves, I want you to know I lean on your side of the fence.'

Laramie gave a quick start. Presently Duane turned and frankly met his gaze. He had startled Laramie out of his habitual set taciturnity; but even as he looked the light that might have been amaze and joy faded out of his face, leaving it the same old mask. Still Duane had seen enough. Like a blood hound he had a scent.

'Talking about work, Laramie, who'd you say Snecker worked for?'

'I didn't say.'

'Well, say now, can't you? Laramie, you're powerful peevish to-day. It's that bump on your head. Who does Snecker work for?'

'When he works at all, which sure ain't often, he rides for Longstreth.'

'Humph! Seems to me that Longstreth's the whole circus round Fairdale. I was some sore the other day to find I was losing good money at Longstreth's faro game. Sure if I'd won I wouldn't have been sore—ha, ha! But I was surprised to hear some one say Longstreth owned the Hope So joint.'

'He owns considerable property hereabouts,' replied Laramie, constrainedly.

'Humph again! Laramie, like every other fellow I meet in this town, you're afraid to open your trap about Longstreth. Get me straight, Laramie. I don't care a damn for Colonel Mayor Longstreth. And for cause I'd throw a gun on him just as quick as on any rustler in Pecos.'

'Talk's cheap,' replied Laramie, making light of his bluster, but the red was deeper in his face.

'Sure. I know that,' Duane said. 'And usually I don't talk. Then it's not well known that Longstreth owns the Hope So?'

'Reckon it's known in Pecos, all right. But Longstreth's name isn't connected with the Hope So. Blandy runs the place.'

'That Blandy. His faro game's crooked, or I'm a locoed bronch. Not that we don't have lots of crooked faro-dealers. A fellow can stand for them. But Blandy's mean, back-handed, never looks you in the eyes. That Hope So place ought to be run by a good fellow like you, Laramie.'

'Thanks,' replied he; and Duane imagined his voice a little husky. 'Didn't you hear I used to—run it?'

'No. Did you?' Duane said, quickly.

'I reckon. I built the place, made additions twice, owned it for eleven years.'

'Well, I'll be doggoned.' It was indeed Duane's turn to be surprised, and with the surprise came a glimmering. 'I'm sorry you're not there now. Did you sell out?'

'No. Just lost the place.'

Laramie was bursting for relief now—to talk, to tell. Sympathy had made him soft.

'It was two years ago—two years last March,' he went on. 'I was in a big cattle deal with Longstreth. We got the stock—an' my share, eighteen hundred head, was rustled off. I owed Longstreth. He pressed me. It come to a lawsuit—an' I was ruined.'

It hurt Duane to look at Laramie. He was white, and tears rolled down his cheeks. Duane saw the bitterness, the defeat, the agony of the man. He had failed to meet his obligations; nevertheless, he had been swindled. All that he suppressed, all that would have been passion had the man's spirit not been broken, lay bare for Duane to see. He had now the secret of his bitterness. But the reason he did not openly accuse Longstreth, the secret of his reticence and fear—these Duane thought best to try to learn at some later time.

'Hard luck! It certainly was tough,' Duane said. 'But you're a good loser. And the wheel turns! Now, Laramie, here's what. I need your advice. I've got a little money. But before I lose it I want to invest some. Buy some stock, or buy an interest in some rancher's herd. What I want you to steer me on is a good square rancher. Or maybe a couple of ranchers, if there happen to be two honest ones. Ha, ha! No deals with ranchers who ride in the dark with rustlers! I've a hunch Fairdale is full of them. Now, Laramie, you've been here for years. Sure you must know a couple of men above suspicion.'

'Thank God I do,' he replied, feelingly. 'Frank Morton an' Si Zimmer, my friends an' neighbors all my prosperous days, an' friends still. You can gamble on Frank and Si. But if you want advice from me—don't invest money in stock now.'

'Why?'

'Because any new feller buyin' stock these days will be rustled quicker'n he can say Jack Robinson. The pioneers, the new cattlemen—these are easy pickin' for the rustlers. Lord knows all the ranchers are easy enough pickin'. But the new fellers have to learn the ropes. They don't know anythin' or anybody. An' the old ranchers are wise an' sore. They'd fight if they—'

'What?' Duane put in, as he paused. 'If they knew who was rustling the stock?'

'Nope.'

'If they had the nerve?'

'Not thet so much.'

'What then? What'd make them fight?'

'A leader!'

'Howdy thar, Jim,' boomed a big voice.

A man of great bulk, with a ruddy, merry face, entered the room.

'Hello, Morton,' replied Laramie. 'I'd introduce you to my guest here, but I don't know his name.'

'Haw! Haw! Thet's all right. Few men out hyar go by their right names.'

'Say, Morton,' put in Duane, 'Laramie gave me a hunch you'd be a good man to tie to. Now, I've a little money and before I lose it I'd like to invest it in stock.'

Morton smiled broadly.

'I'm on the square,' Duane said, bluntly. 'If you fellows never size up your neighbors any better than you have sized me—well, you won't get any richer.'

It was enjoyment for Duane to make his remarks to these men pregnant with meaning. Morton showed his pleasure, his interest, but his faith held aloof.

'I've got some money. Will you let me in on some kind of deal? Will you start me up as a stockman with a little herd all my own?'

'Wal, stranger, to come out flat-footed, you'd be foolish to buy cattle now. I don't want to take your money an' see you lose out. Better go back across the Pecos where the rustlers ain't so strong. I haven't had more'n twenty-five hundred herd of stock for ten years. The rustlers let me hang on to a breedin' herd. Kind of them, ain't it?'

'Sort of kind. All I hear is rustlers, Morton,' replied Duane, with impatience. 'You see, I haven't ever lived long in a rustler-run county. Who heads the gang, anyway?'

Morton looked at Duane with a curiously amused smile, then snapped his big jaw as if to shut in impulsive words.

'Look here, Morton. It stands to reason, no matter how strong these rustlers are, how hidden their work, however involved with supposedly honest men—they *can't* last.'

'They come with the pioneers, an' they'll last till thar's a single steer left,' he declared.

'Well, if you take that view of circumstances I just figure you as one of the rustlers!'

Morton looked as if he were about to brain Duane with the butt of his whip. His anger flashed by then, evidently as unworthy of him, and, something striking him as funny, he boomed out a laugh.

'It's not so funny,' Duane went on. 'If you're going to pretend a yellow streak, what else will I think?'

'Pretend?' he repeated.

'Sure. I know men of nerve. And here they're not any different from those in other places. I say if you show anything like a lack of sand it's all bluff. By nature you've got nerve. There are a lot of men around Fairdale who're afraid of their shadows—afraid to be out after dark—afraid to open their mouths. But you're not one. So I say if you claim these rustlers will last you're pretending lack of nerve just to help the popular idea along. For they *can't* last. What you need out here is some new blood. Savvy what I mean?'

'Wal, I reckon I do,' he replied, looking as if a storm had blown over him. 'Stranger, I'll look you up the next time I come to town.'

Then he went out.

Laramie had eyes like flint striking fire.

He breathed a deep breath and looked around the room before his gaze fixed again on Duane.

'Wal,' he replied, speaking low. 'You've picked the right men. Now, who in the hell are you?'

Reaching into the inside pocket of his buckskin vest, Duane turned the lining out. A star-shaped bright silver object flashed as he shoved it, pocket and all, under Jim's hard eyes.

'*Ranger!*' he whispered cracking the table with his fist. 'You sure rung true to me.'

'Laramie, do you know who's boss of this secret gang of rustlers hereabouts?' asked Duane, bluntly. It was characteristic of him to come sharp to the point. His voice—something deep, easy, cool about him—seemed to steady Laramie.

'No,' replied Laramie.

'Does anybody know?' went on Duane.

'Wal, I reckon there's not one honest native who *knows.*'

'But you have your suspicions?'

'We have.'

'Give me your idea about this crowd that hangs round the saloons—the regulars.'

'Jest a bad lot,' replied Laramie, with the quick assurance of knowledge. 'Most of them have been here years. Others have drifted in. Some of them work, odd times. They rustle a few steers, steal, rob, anythin' for a little money to drink an' gamble. Jest a bad lot!'

'Have you any idea whether Cheseldine and his gang are associated with this gang here?'

'Lord knows. I've always suspected them the same gang. None of us ever seen Cheseldine—an' thet's strange, when Knell, Poggin, Panhandle Smith, Blossom Kane, and Fletcher, they all ride here often. No, Poggin doesn't come often. But the others do. For thet matter, they're around all over west of the Pecos.'

'Now I'm puzzled over this,' said Duane. 'Why do men—apparently honest men—seem to be closemouthed here? Is that a fact, or only my impression?'

'It's a sure fact,' replied Laramie, darkly. 'Men have lost cattle an' property in Fairdale—lost them honestly or otherwise, as hasn't been proved. An' in some cases when they talked—hinted a little—they was found dead. Apparently held up an' robbed. But dead. Dead men don't talk! Thet's why we're close-mouthed.'

Duane felt a dark, somber sternness. Rustling cattle was not intolerable. Western Texas had gone on prospering, growing in spite of the hordes of rustlers ranging its vast stretches; but a cold, secret, murderous hold on a little struggling community was something too strange, too terrible for men to stand long.

The ranger was about to speak again when the clatter of hoofs interrupted him. Horses halted out in front, and one rider got down. Floyd Lawson entered. He called for tobacco.

If his visit surprised Laramie he did not show any evidence. But Lawson showed rage as he saw the ranger, and then a dark glint flitted from the eyes that shifted from Duane to Laramie and back again. Duane leaned easily against the counter.

'Say, that was a bad break of yours,' Lawson said. 'If you come fooling round the ranch again there'll be hell.'

It seemed strange that a man who had lived west of the Pecos for ten years could not see in Duane something which forbade that kind of talk. It certainly was not nerve Lawson showed; men of courage were seldom intolerant. With the matchless nerve that characterized the great gunmen of the day there was a cool, unobtrusive manner, a speech brief, almost gentle, certainly courteous. Lawson was a hot-headed Louisianian of French extraction; a man, evidently, who had never been crossed in anything, and who was strong, brutal, passionate, which qualities in the face of a situation like this made him simply a fool.

'I'm saying again, you used your ranger bluff just to get near Ray Longstreth,' Lawson sneered. 'Mind you, if you come up there again there'll be hell.'

'You're right. But not the kind you think,' Duane retorted, his voice sharp and cold.

'Ray Longstreth wouldn't stoop to know a dirty blood-tracker like you,' said Lawson, hotly. He did not seem to have a deliberate intention to rouse Duane; the man was simply rancorous, jealous. 'I'll call you right. You cheap bluffer! You four-flusher! You damned interfering, conceited ranger!'

'Lawson, I'll not take offense, because you seem to be championing your beautiful cousin,' replied Duane, in slow speech. 'But let me return your compliment. You're a fine Southerner! Why, you're only a cheap four-flush—damned, bull-headed *rustler!*'

Duane hissed the last word. Then for him there was the truth in Lawson's working passion-blackened face.

Lawson jerked, moved, meant to draw. But how slow! Duane lunged forward. His long arm swept up. And Lawson staggered backward, knocking table and chairs, to fall hard, in a half-sitting posture against the wall.

'Don't draw!' warned Duane.

'Lawson, git away from your gun!' yelled Laramie.

But Lawson was crazed with fury. He tugged at his hip, his face corded with purple welts, malignant, murderous. Duane kicked the gun out of his hand. Lawson got up, raging, and rushed out.

Laramie lifted his shaking hands.

'What'd you wing him for?' he wailed. 'He was drawin' on you. Kickin' men like him won't do out here.'

'That bull-headed fool will roar and butt himself with all his gang right into our hands. He's just the man I've needed to meet. Besides, shooting him would have been murder.'

'Murder!' exclaimed Laramie.

'Yes, for me,' replied Duane.

'That may be true—whoever you are—but if Lawson's the man you think he is he'll begin thet secret underground bizness. Why, Lawson won't sleep of nights now. He an' Longstreth have always been after me.'

'Laramie, what are your eyes for?' demanded Duane. 'Watch out. And now here. See your friend Morton. Tell him this game grows hot. Together you approach four or five men you know well and can absolutely trust. I may need your help.'

Then Duane went from place to place, corner to corner, bar to bar, watching, listening, recording. The excitement had preceded him, and speculation was rife. He thought best to keep out of it. After dark he stole up to Longstreth's ranch. The evening was warm; the doors were open; and in the twilight the only lamps that had been lit were in Longstreth's big sitting-room, at the far end of the house. When a buckboard drove up and Longstreth and Lawson alighted, Duane was well hidden in the bushes, so well screened that he could get out a fleeting glimpse of Longstreth as he went in. For all Duane could see, he appeared to be a calm and quiet man, intense beneath the surface, with an air of dignity under insult. Duane's chance to observe Lawson was lost. They went into the house without speaking and closed the door.

At the other end of the porch, close under a window, was an offset between step and wall, and there in the shadow Duane hid. So Duane waited there in the darkness with patience born of many hours of hiding.

Presently a lamp was lit; and Duane heard the swish of skirts.

'Something's happened surely, Ruth,' he heard Miss Longstreth say, anxiously. 'Papa just met me in the hall and didn't speak. He seemed pale, worried.'

'Cousin Floyd looked like a thunder-cloud,' said Ruth. 'For once he didn't try to kiss me. Something's happened. Well, Ray, this has been a bad day.'

'Oh, dear! Ruth, what can we do? These are wild men. Floyd makes life miserable for me. And he teases you unmer—'

'I don't call it teasing. Floyd wants to spoon,' declared Ruth, emphatically. 'He'd run after any woman.'

'A fine compliment to me, Cousin Ruth,' laughed Ray.

'I don't care,' replied Ruth, stubbornly. 'It's so. He's mushy. And when he's been drinking and tries to kiss me—I hate him!'

There were steps on the hall floor.

'Hello, girls!' sounded out Lawson's voice, minus its usual gaiety.

'Floyd, what's the matter?' asked Ray, presently. 'I never saw papa as he is to-night, nor you so—so worried. Tell me, what has happened?'

'Well, Ray, we had a jar to-day,' replied Lawson, with a blunt, expressive laugh.

'Jar?' echoed both the girls, curiously.

'We had to submit to a damnable outrage,' added Lawson, passionately, as if the sound of his voice augmented his feeling. 'Listen, girls; I'll tell you all about it.' He coughed, cleared his throat in a way that betrayed he had been drinking.

Duane sunk deeper into the shadow of his covert, and, stiffening his muscles for a protracted spell of rigidity, prepared to listen with all acuteness and intensity. Just one word from this Lawson, inadvertently uttered in a moment of passion might be the word Duane needed for his clue.

'It happened at the town hall,' began Lawson, rapidly. 'Your father and Judge Owens and I were there in consultation with three ranchers from out of town. Then that damned ranger stalked in dragging Snecker, the fellow who hid here in the house. He had arrested Snecker for alleged assault on a restaurant-keeper named Laramie. Snecker being obviously innocent, he was discharged. Then this ranger began shouting his insults. Law was a farce in Fairdale. The court was a farce. There was no law. Your father's office as mayor should be impeached. He made arrests only for petty offenses. He was afraid of the rustlers, highwaymen, murderers. He was afraid or—he just let them alone. He used his office to cheat ranchers and cattlemen in lawsuits. All this the ranger yelled for every one to hear. A damnable outrage. Your father, Ray, insulted in his own court by a rowdy ranger!'

'Oh!' cried Ray Longstreth, in mingled distress and anger.

'The ranger service wants to rule western Texas,' went on Lawson. 'These rangers are all a low set, many of them worse than the outlaws they hunt. Some of them were outlaws and gun-fighters before they became rangers. This is one of the worst of the lot. He's keen, intelligent, smooth, and that makes him more to be feared. For he is to be feared. He wanted to kill. He would kill. If your father had made the least move he would have shot him. He's a cold-nerved devil—the born gunman. My God, any instant I expected to see your father fall dead at my feet!'

'Oh, Floyd! The unspeakable ruffian!' cried Ray Longstreth, passionately.

'You see, Ray, this fellow, like all rangers, seeks notoriety. He made that play with Snecker just for a chance to rant against your father. He tried to inflame all Fairdale against him. That about the lawsuits was the worst! Damn him! He'll make us enemies.'

'What do you care for the insinuations of such a man?' said Ray Longstreth, her voice now deep and rich with feeling. 'After a moment's thought no one will be influenced by them. Do not worry, Floyd. Tell papa not to worry. Surely after all these years he can't be injured in reputation by—by an adventurer.'

'Yes, he can be injured,' replied Floyd, quickly. 'The frontier is a queer place. There are many bitter men here—men who have failed at ranching. And your father has been wonderfully successful. The ranger has dropped poison, and it'll spread.'

18

Strangers rode into Fairdale; and other hard-looking customers, new to Duane if not to Fairdale, helped to create a charged and waiting atmosphere. The saloons did unusual business and were never closed. Respectable citizens of the town were awakened in the early dawn by rowdies carousing in the streets.

Duane kept pretty close under cover during the day. He did not entertain the opinion that the first time he walked down-street he would be a target for guns. Things seldom happened that way; and when they did happen so, it was more accident than design. But at night he was not idle. He met Laramie, Morton, Zimmer, and others of like character; a secret club had been formed; and all the members were ready for action. Duane spent hours at night watching the house where Floyd Lawson stayed when he was not up at Longstreth's. At night he was visited, or at least the house was, by strange men who were swift, stealthy, mysterious—all that kindly disposed friends or neighbors would not have been. Duane had not been able to recognize any of these night visitors; and he did not think the time was ripe for a bold holding-up of one of them. Nevertheless, he was sure such an event would discover Lawson, or some one in that house, to be in touch with crooked men.

Laramie was right. Not twenty-four hours after his last talk with Duane, in which he advised quick action, he was found behind the little bar of his restaurant with a bullet-hole in his breast, dead. No one could be found who had heard a shot. It had been deliberate murder, for upon the bar had been left a piece of paper rudely scrawled with a pencil: 'All friends of rangers look for the same.'

This roused Duane. His first move, however, was to bury Laramie. None of Laramie's neighbors evinced any interest in the dead man or the unfortunate family he had left. Duane saw that these neighbors were held in check by fear. Mrs Laramie was ill; the shock of her husband's death was hard on her; and she had been left almost destitute with five children. Duane rented a small adobe house on the outskirts of town and moved the family into it. Then he played the part of provider and nurse and friend.

After several days Duane went boldly into town and showed that he meant business. It was his opinion that there were men in Fairdale secretly glad of

a ranger's presence. What he intended to do was food for great speculation.
A company of militia could not have had the effect upon the wild element of
Fairdale that Duane's presence had. It got out that he was a gunman lightning
swift on the draw. It was death to face him. He had killed thirty men—wildest
rumor of all. It was actually said of him he had the gun-skill of Buck Duane or of
Poggin.

At first there had not only been great conjecture among the vicious element,
but also a very decided checking of all kinds of action calculated to be conspicuous
to a keen-eyed ranger. At the tables, at the bars and lounging-places Duane heard
the remarks: 'Who's thet ranger after? What'll he do fust off? Is he waitin' fer
somebody? Who's goin' to draw on him fust—an' go to hell? Jest about how soon
will he be found somewheres full of lead?'

When it came out somewhere that Duane was openly cultivating the honest
stay-at-home citizens to array them in time against the other element, then Fairdale
showed its wolf teeth. Several times Duane was shot at in the dark and once slightly
injured. Rumor had it that Poggin, the gunman, was coming to meet him. But the
lawless element did not rise up in mass to slay Duane on sight. It was not so much
that the enemies of the law awaited his next move, but just a slowness peculiar to
the frontier. The ranger was in their midst. He was interesting, if formidable. He
would have been welcomed at card-tables, at the bars, to play and drink with the
men who knew they were under suspicion. There was a rude kind of good humor
even in their open hostility.

Besides, one ranger or a company of rangers could not have held the undivided
attention of these men from their games and drinks and quarrels except by some
decided move. Excitement, greed, appetite were rife in them. Duane marked,
however, a striking exception to the usual run of strangers he had been in the habit
of seeing. Snecker had gone or was under cover. Again Duane caught a vague
rumor of the coming of Poggin, yet he never seemed to arrive. Moreover, the
goings-on among the habitués of the resorts and the cowboys who came in to
drink and gamble were unusually mild in comparison with former conduct. This
lull, however, did not deceive Duane. It could not last. The wonder was that it
had lasted so long.

Duane went often to see Mrs Laramie and her children. One afternoon while
he was there he saw Miss Longstreth and Ruth ride up to the door. They carried
a basket. Evidently they had heard of Mrs Laramie's trouble. Duane felt strangely
glad, but he went into an adjoining room rather than meet them.

'Mrs Laramie, I've come to see you,' said Miss Longstreth, cheerfully.

The little room was not very light, there being only one window and the doors,
but Duane could see plainly enough. Mrs Laramie lay, hollow-cheeked
and haggard, on a bed. Once she had evidently been a woman of some comeliness.

The ravages of trouble and grief were there to read in her worn face; it had not, however, any of the hard and bitter lines that had characterized her husband's.

Duane wondered, considering that Longstreth had ruined Laramie, how Mrs Laramie was going to regard the daughter of an enemy.

'So you're Granger Longstreth's girl?' queried the woman, with her bright, black eyes fixed on her visitor.

'Yes,' replied Miss Longstreth, simply. 'This is my cousin, Ruth Herbert. We've come to nurse you, take care of the children, help you in any way you'll let us.'

There was a long silence.

'Well, you look a little like Longstreth,' finally said Mrs Laramie, 'but you're not *at all* like him. You must take after your mother. Miss Longstreth, I don't know if I can—if I ought accept anything from you. Your father ruined my husband.'

'Yes, I know,' replied the girl, sadly. 'That's all the more reason you should let me help you. Pray don't refuse. It will—mean so much to me.'

If this poor, stricken woman had any resentment it speedily melted in the warmth and sweetness of Miss Longstreth's manner. Duane's idea was that the impression of Ray Longstreth's beauty was always swiftly succeeded by that of her generosity and nobility. At any rate, she had started well with Mrs Laramie, and no sooner had she begun to talk to the children than both they and the mother were won. The opening of that big basket was an event. Poor, starved little beggars! Duane's feelings seemed too easily roused. Hard indeed would it have gone with Jim Laramie's slayer if he could have laid eyes on him then. However, Miss Longstreth and Ruth, after the nature of tender and practical girls, did not appear to take the sad situation to heart. The havoc was wrought in that household. The needs now were cheerfulness, kindness, help, action—and these the girls furnished with a spirit that did Duane good.

'Mrs Laramie, who dressed this baby?' presently asked Miss Longstreth. Duane peeped in to see a dilapidated youngster on her knee. That sight, if any other was needed, completed his full and splendid estimate of Ray Longstreth and wrought strangely upon his heart.

'The ranger,' replied Mrs Laramie.

'The ranger!' exclaimed Miss Longstreth.

'Yes, he's taken care of us all since—since—' Mrs Laramie choked.

'Oh! So you've had no help but his,' replied Miss Longstreth, hastily. 'No women. Too bad! I'll send some one, Mrs Laramie, and I'll come myself.'

'It'll be good of you,' went on the older woman. 'You see, Jim had few friends—that is, right in town. And they've been afraid to help us—afraid they'd get what poor Jim—'

'That's awful!' burst out Miss Longstreth, passionately. 'A brave lot of friends!

Mrs Laramie, don't you worry any more. We'll take care of you. Here, Ruth, help me. Whatever is the matter with baby's dress?'

Manifestly Miss Longstreth had some difficulty in subduing her emotion.

'Why, it's on hind side before,' declared Ruth. 'I guess Mr Ranger hasn't dressed many babies.'

'He did the best he could,' said Mrs Laramie. 'Lord only knows what would have become of us!'

'Then he is—is something more than a ranger?' queried Miss Longstreth, with a little break in her voice.

'He's more than I can tell,' replied Mrs Laramie. 'He buried Jim. He paid our debts. He fetched us here. He bought food for us. He cooked for us and fed us. He washed and dressed the baby. He sat with me the first two nights after Jim's death, when I thought I'd die myself. He's so kind, so gentle, so patient. He has kept me up just by being near. Sometimes I'd wake from a doze, an', seeing him there, I'd know how false were all these tales Jim heard about him and believed at first. Why, he plays with the children just—just like any good man might. When he has the baby up I can't believe he's a bloody gunman, as they say. He's good, but he isn't happy. He has such sad eyes. He looks far off sometimes when the children climb round him. They love him. His life is sad. Nobody need tell me—he sees the good in things. Once he said somebody had to be a ranger. Well, I say, "Thank God for a ranger like him!" '

Duane did not want to hear more, so he walked into the room.

'It was thoughtful of you,' Duane said. 'Womankind are needed here. I could do so little. Mrs Laramie, you look better already. I'm glad. And here's baby, all clean and white. Baby, what a time I had trying to puzzle out the way your clothes went on! Well, Mrs Laramie, didn't I tell you—friends would come? So will the brighter side.'

'Yes, I've more faith than I had,' replied Mrs Laramie. 'Granger Longstreth's daughter has come to me. There for a while after Jim's death I thought I'd sink. We have nothing. How could I ever take care of my little ones? But I'm gaining courage to—'

'Mrs Laramie, do not distress yourself any more,' said Miss Longstreth. 'I shall see you are well cared for. I promise you.'

'Miss Longstreth, that's fine!' exclaimed Duane. 'It's what I'd have—expected of you.'

It must have been sweet praise to her, for the whiteness of her face burned out in a beautiful blush.

'And it's good of you, too, Miss Herbert, to come,' added Duane. 'Let me thank you both. I'm glad I have you girls as allies in part of my lonely task here. More than glad for the sake of this good woman and the little ones. But both of you be careful about coming here alone. There's risk. And now I'll be going. Good-by, Mrs Laramie. I'll drop in again to-night. Good-by.'

'Mr Ranger, wait!' called Miss Longstreth, as he went out. She was white and wonderful. She stepped out of the door close to him.

'I have wronged you!' she said, impulsively.

'Miss Longstreth! How can you say that?' he returned.

'I believed what my father and Floyd Lawson said about you. Now I see—I wronged you.'

'You make me very glad. But, Miss Longstreth, please don't speak of wronging me. I have been a—a gunman, I *am* a ranger—and much said of me is true. My duty is hard on others—sometimes on those who are innocent, alas! But God knows that duty is hard, too, on me.'

'I did wrong you. If you entered my home again I would think it an honor. I—'

'Please—please don't, Miss Longstreth,' interrupted Duane.

'But, sir, my conscience flays me,' she went on. There was no other sound like her voice. 'Will you take my hand? Will you forgive me?'

She gave it royally, while the other was there pressing at her breast. Duane took the proffered hand. He did not know what else to do.

Then it seemed to dawn upon him that there was more behind this white, sweet, noble intensity of her than just the making amends for a fancied or real wrong. Duane thought the man did not live on earth who could have resisted her then.

'I honor you for your goodness to this unfortunate woman,' she said, and now her speech came swiftly. 'When she was all alone and helpless you were her friend. It was the deed of a man. But Mrs Laramie isn't the only unfortunate woman in the world. I, too, am unfortunate. Ah, how *I* may soon need a friend! Will *you* be my friend? I'm so alone. I'm terribly worried. I fear—I fear—Oh, surely I'll need a friend soon—soon. Oh, I'm afraid of what you'll find out sooner or later. I want to help you. Let us save life if not honor. Must I stand alone—all alone? Will you—will you be—' Her voice failed.

It seemed to Duane that she must have discovered what he had begun to suspect—that her father and Lawson were not the honest ranchers they pretended to be. Perhaps she knew more! Her appeal to Duane shook him deeply. He wanted to help her more than he had ever wanted anything. And with the meaning of the tumultuous sweetness she stirred in him there came realization of a dangerous situation.

'I must be true to my duty,' he said, hoarsely.

'If you knew me you'd know I could never ask you to be false to it.'

'Well, then—I'll do anything for you.'

'Oh, thank you! I'm ashamed that I believed my cousin Floyd! He lied—he lied. I'm all in the dark, strangely distressed. My father wants me to go back home. Floyd is trying to keep me here. They've quarreled. Oh, I know something dreadful will happen. I know I'll need you if—if—Will you help me?'

'Yes,' replied Duane, and his look brought the blood to her face.

19

After supper Duane stole out for his usual evening's spying. The night was dark, without starlight, and a still wind rustled the leaves. Duane bent his steps toward Longstreth's ranchhouse. He had so much to think about that he never knew where the time went. This night when he reached the edge of the shrubbery he heard Lawson's well-known footsteps and saw Longstreth's door open, flashing a broad bar of light in the darkness. Lawson crossed the threshold, the door closed, and all was dark again outside. Not a ray of light escaped from the window.

Little doubt there was that his talk with Longstreth would be interesting to Duane. He tiptoed to the door and listened, but could hear only a murmur of voices. Besides, that position was too risky. He went round the corner of the house.

This side of the big adobe house was of much older construction than the back and larger part. There was a narrow passage between the houses, leading from the outside through to the patio.

This passage now afforded Duane an opportunity, and he decided to avail himself of it in spite of the very great danger. Crawling on very stealthily, he got under the shrubbery to the entrance of the passage. In the blackness a faint streak of light showed the location of a crack in the wall. He had to slip in sidewise. It was a tight squeeze, but he entered without the slightest noise. As he progressed the passage grew a very little wider in that direction, and that fact gave rise to the thought that in case of a necessary and hurried exit he would do best by working toward the patio. It seemed a good deal of time was consumed in reaching a vantage-point. When he did get there the crack he had marked was a foot over his head. There was nothing to do but find toe-holes in the crumbling walls, and by bracing knees on one side, back against the other, hold himself up. Once with his eye there he did not care what risk he ran. Longstreth appeared disturbed; he sat stroking his mustache; his brow was clouded. Lawson's face seemed darker, more sullen, yet lighted by some indomitable resolve.

'We'll settle both deals to-night,' Lawson was saying. 'That's what I came for.'

'But suppose I don't choose to talk here?' protested Longstreth, impatiently. 'I never before made my house a place to—'

'We've waited long enough. This place's as good as any. You've lost your nerve since that ranger hit the town. First now, will you give Ray to me?'

'Floyd, you talk like a spoiled boy. Give Ray to you! Why, she's a woman, and I'm finding out that she's got a mind of her own. I told you I was willing for her to marry you. I tried to persuade her. But Ray hasn't any use for you now. She liked you at first. But now she doesn't. So what can I do?'

'You can make her marry me,' replied Lawson.

'Make that girl do what she doesn't want to? It couldn't be done even if I tried. And I don't believe I'll try. I haven't the highest opinion of you as a prospective son-in-law, Floyd. But if Ray loved you I would consent. We'd all go away together before this damned miserable business is out. Then she'd never know. And maybe you might be more like you used to be before the West ruined you. But as matters stand, you fight your own game with her. And I'll tell you now you'll lose.'

'What'd you want to let her come out here for?' demanded Lawson, hotly. 'It was a dead mistake. I've lost my head over her. I'll have her or die. Don't you think if she was my wife I'd soon pull myself together? Since she came we've none of us been right. And the gang has put up a holler. No, Longstreth, we've got to settle things to-night.'

'Well, we can settle what Ray's concerned in, right now,' replied Longstreth, rising. 'Come on; we'll ask her. See where you stand.'

They went out, leaving the door open. Duane dropped down to rest himself and to wait. He would have liked to hear Miss Longstreth's answer. But he could guess what it would be. Lawson appeared to be all Duane had thought him, and he believed he was going to find out presently that he was worse.

The men seemed to be absent a good while, though that feeling might have been occasioned by Duane's thrilling interest and anxiety. Finally he heard heavy steps. Lawson came in alone. He was leaden–faced, humiliated. Then something abject in him gave place to rage. He strode the room; he cursed. Then Longstreth returned, now appreciably calmer. Duane could not but decide that he felt relief at the evident rejection of Lawson's proposal.

'Don't fuss about it, Floyd,' he said. 'You see I can't help it. We're pretty wild out here, but I can't rope my daughter and give her to you as I would an unruly steer.'

'Longstreth, I can *make* her marry me,' declared Lawson, thickly.

'How?'

'You know the hold I got on you—the deal that made you boss of this rustler gang?'

'It isn't likely I'd forget,' replied Longstreth, grimly.

'I can go to Ray, tell her that, make her believe I'd tell it broadcast—tell this ranger—unless she'd marry me.'

Lawson spoke breathlessly, with haggard face and shadowed eyes. He had no shame. He was simply in the grip of passion.

Longstreth gazed with dark, controlled fury at this relative. In that look, Duane saw a strong, unscrupulous man fallen into evil ways, but still a man. It betrayed Lawson to be the wild and passionate weakling. Duane seemed to see also how during all the years of association this strong man had upheld the weak one. But that time had gone for ever, both in intent on Longstreth's part and in possibility. Lawson, like the great majority of evil and unrestrained men on the border, had reached a point where influence was futile. Reason had degenerated. He saw only himself.

'But, Floyd, Ray's the one person on earth who must never know I'm a rustler, a thief, a red-handed ruler of the worst gang on the border,' replied Longstreth, impressively.

Floyd bowed his head at that, as if the significance had just occurred to him. But he was not long at a loss.

'She's going to find it out sooner or later. I tell you she knows now there's something wrong out here. She's got eyes. Mark what I say.'

'Ray has changed, I know. But she hasn't any idea yet that her daddy's a boss rustler. Ray's concerned about what she calls my duty as mayor. Also I think she's not satisfied with my explanations in regard to certain property.'

Lawson halted in his restless walk and leaned against the stone mantelpiece. He had his hands in his pockets. He squared himself as if this was his last stand. He looked desperate, but on the moment showed an absence of his usual nervous excitement.

'Longstreth, that may well be true,' he said. 'No doubt all you say is true. But it doesn't help me. I want the girl. If I don't get her—I reckon we'll all go to hell!'

He might have meant anything, probably meant the worst. He certainly had something more in mind. Longstreth gave a slight start, barely perceptible, like the switch of an awakening tiger. He sat there, head down, stroking his mustache. Almost Duane saw his thought. He had long experience in reading men under stress of such emotion. He had no means to vindicate his judgment, but his conviction was that Longstreth right then and there decided that the thing to do was to kill Lawson. For Duane's part he wondered that Longstreth had not come to such a conclusion before. Not improbably the advent of his daughter had put Longstreth in conflict with himself.

Suddenly he threw off a somber cast of countenance, and he began to talk. He talked swiftly, persuasively, yet Duane imagined he was talking to smooth Lawson's passion for the moment. Lawson no more caught the fateful significance of a line crossed, a limit reached, a decree decided than if he had not been present. He was obsessed with himself. How, Duane wondered, had a man of his mind ever lived so long and gone so far among the exacting conditions of the Southwest? The answer was, perhaps, that Longstreth had guided him, upheld him, protected him. The coming of Ray Longstreth had been the entering-wedge of dissension.

'You're too impatient,' concluded Longstreth. 'You'll ruin any chance of happiness if you rush Ray. She might be won. If you told her who I am she'd hate you for ever. She might marry you to save me, but she'd hate you. That isn't the way. Wait. Play for time. Be different with her. Cut out your drinking. She despises that. Let's plan to sell out here—stock, ranch, property—and leave the country. Then you'd have a show with her.'

'I told you we've got to stick,' growled Lawson. 'The gang won't stand for our going. It can't be done unless you want to sacrifice everything.'

'You mean double-cross the men? Go without their knowing? Leave them here to face whatever comes?'

'I mean just that.'

'I'm bad enough, but not that bad,' returned Longstreth. 'If I can't get the gang to let me off, I'll stay and face the music. All the same, Lawson, did it ever strike you that most of the deals the last few years have been *yours*?'

'Yes. If I hadn't rung them in there wouldn't have been any. You've had cold feet, and especially since this ranger has been here.'

'Well, call it cold feet if you like. But I call it sense. We reached our limit long ago. We began by rustling a few cattle—at a time when rustling was laughed at. But as our greed grew so did our boldness. Then came the gang, the regular trips, the one thing and another till, before we knew it—before *I* knew it—we had shady deals, holdups, and *murders* on our record. Then we *had* to go on. Too late to turn back!'

'I reckon we've all said that. None of the gang wants to quit. They all think, and I think, we can't be touched. We may be blamed, but nothing can be proved. We're too strong.'

'There's where you're dead wrong,' rejoined Longstreth, emphatically. 'I imagined that once, not long ago. I was bullheaded. Who would ever connect Granger Longstreth with a rustler gang? I've changed my mind. I've begun to think. I've reasoned out things. We're crooked, and we can't last. It's the nature of life, even here, for conditions to grow better. The wise deal for us would be to divide equally and leave the country, all of us.'

'But you and I have all the stock—all the gain,' protested Lawson.

'I'll split mine.'

'I won't—that settles that,' added Lawson, instantly.

Longstreth spread wide his hands as if it was useless to try to convince this man. Talking had not increased his calmness, and he now showed more than impatience. A dull glint gleamed deep in his eyes.

'Your stock and property will last a long time—do you lots of good when this ranger—'

'Bah!' hoarsely croaked Lawson. The ranger's name was a match applied to powder. 'Haven't told you he'd be dead soon—any time—same as Laramie is?'

'Yes, you mentioned the—the supposition,' replied Longstreth, sarcastically. 'I inquired, too, just how that very desired event was to be brought about.'

'The gang will lay him out.'

'Bah!' retorted Longstreth, in turn. He laughed contemptuously.

'Floyd, don't be a fool. You've been on the border for ten years. You've packed a gun and you've used it. You've been with rustlers when they killed their men. You've been present at many fights. But you never in all that time saw a man like this ranger. You haven't got sense enough to see him right if you had a chance. Neither have any of you. The only way to get rid of him is for the gang to draw on him, all at once. Then he's going to drop some of them.'

'Longstreth, you say that like a man who wouldn't care much if he did drop some of them,' declared Lawson; and now he was sarcastic.

'To tell you the truth, I wouldn't,' returned the other, bluntly. 'I'm pretty sick of this mess.'

Lawson cursed in amazement. His emotions were all out of proportion to his intelligence. He was not at all quick-witted. Duane had never seen a vainer or more arrogant man.

'Longstreth, I don't like your talk,' he said.

'If you don't like the way I talk you know what you can do,' replied Longstreth, quickly. He stood up then, cool and quiet, with flash of eyes and set of lips that told Duane he was dangerous.

'Well, after all, that's neither here nor there,' went on Lawson, unconsciously cowed by the other. 'The thing is, do I get the girl?'

'Not by any means except her consent.'

'You'll not make her marry me?'

'No. No,' replied Longstreth, his voice still cold, low-pitched.

'All right. Then I'll make her.'

Evidently Longstreth understood the man before him so well that he wasted no more words. Duane knew what Lawson never dreamed of, and that was that Longstreth had a gun somewhere within reach and meant to use it. Then heavy footsteps sounded outside tramping upon the porch. Duane might have been mistaken, but he believed those footsteps saved Lawson's life.

'There they are,' said Lawson, and he opened the door.

Five masked men entered. They all wore coats hiding any weapons. A big man with burly shoulders shook hands with Longstreth, and the others stood back.

The atmosphere of that room had changed. Lawson might have been a nonentity for all he counted. Longstreth was another man—a stranger to Duane. If he had entertained a hope of freeing himself from this band, of getting away to a safer country, he abandoned it at the very sight of these men. There was power here, and he was bound.

The big man spoke in low, hoarse whispers, and at this all the others gathered around him close to the table. There were evidently some signs of membership not plain to Duane. Then all the heads bent over the table. Low voices spoke, queried, answered, argued. By straining his ears Duane caught a word here and there. They were planning, and they were brief. Duane gathered they were to have a rendezvous at or near Ord.

Then the big man, who evidently was the leader of the present convention, got up to depart. He went as swiftly as he had come, and was followed by his comrades. Longstreth prepared for a quiet smoke. Lawson seemed uncommunicative and unsociable. He smoked fiercely and drank continually. All at once he straightened up as if listening.

'What's that?' he called, suddenly.

Duane's strained ears were pervaded by a slight rustling sound.

'Must be a rat,' replied Longstreth.

The rustle became a rattle.

'Sounds like a rattlesnake to me,' said Lawson.

Longstreth got up from the table and peered round the room.

Just at that instant Duane felt an almost inappreciable movement of the adobe wall which supported him. He could scarcely credit his senses. But the rattle inside Longstreth's room was mingling with little dull thuds of falling dirt. The adobe wall, merely dried mud, was crumbling. Duane distinctly felt a tremor pass through it. Then the blood gushed back to his heart.

'What in the hell!' exclaimed Longstreth.

'I smell dust,' said Lawson, sharply.

That was the signal for Duane to drop down from his perch, yet despite his care he made a noise.

'Did you hear a step?' queried Longstreth.

No one answered. But a heavy piece of the adobe wall fell with a thud. Duane heard it crack, felt it shake.

'There's somebody between the walls!' thundered Longstreth.

Then a section of the wall fell inward with a crash. Duane began to squeeze his body through the narrow passage toward the patio.

'Hear him!' yelled Lawson. 'This side!'

'No, he's going that way,' yelled Longstreth.

The tramp of heavy boots lent Duane the strength of desperation. He was not shirking a fight, but to be cornered like a trapped coyote was another matter. He almost tore his clothes off in that passage. The dust nearly stifled him. When he burst into the patio it was not a single instant too soon. But one deep gap of breath revived him and he was up, gun in hand, running for the outlet into the court. Thumping footsteps turned him back. While there was a chance to get away he did not want to fight. He thought he heard some one running into the patio from the other end. He stole along, and coming to a door, without any idea of where it might lead, he softly pushed it open a little way and slipped in.

20

A low cry greeted Duane. The room was light. He saw Ray Longstreth sitting on her bed in her dressing-gown. With a warning gesture to her to be silent he turned to close the door. It was a heavy door without bolt or bar, and when Duane had shut it he felt safe only for the moment. Then he gazed around the room. There was one window with blind closely drawn. He listened and seemed to hear footsteps retreating, dying away.

Then Duane turned to Miss Longstreth. She had slipped off the bed, half to her knees, and was holding out trembling hands. She was as white as the pillow on her bed. She was terribly frightened. Again with warning hand commanding silence, Duane stepped softly forward, meaning to reassure her.

'Oh!' she whispered, wildly; and Duane thought she was going to faint. When he got close and looked into her eyes he understood the strange, dark expression in them. She was terrified because she believed he meant to kill her, or do worse, probably worse. Duane realized he must have looked pretty hard and fierce bursting into her room with that big gun in hand.

The way she searched Duane's face with doubtful, fearful eyes hurt him.

'Listen. I didn't know this was your room. I came here to get away—to save my life. I was pursued. I was spying on—on your father and his men. They heard me, but did not see me. They don't know who was listening. They're after me now.'

Her eyes changed from blank gulfs to dilating, shadowing, quickening windows of thoughts.

Then she stood up and faced Duane with the fire and intelligence of a woman in her eyes.

'Tell me now. You were spying on my father?'

Briefly Duane told her what had happened before he entered her room, not omitting a terse word as to the character of the men he had watched.

'My God! So it's that? I knew something was terribly wrong here—with him—with the place—the people. And right off I hated Floyd Lawson. Oh, it'll kill me if—if—It's so much worse than I dreamed. What shall I do?'

The sound of soft steps somewhere near distracted Duane's attention, reminded him of her peril, and now, what counted more with him, made clear the probability of being discovered in her room.

'I'll have to get out of here,' whispered Duane.

'Wait,' she replied. 'Didn't you say they were hunting for you?'

'They sure are,' he returned, grimly.

'Oh, then you mustn't go. They might shoot you before you got away. Stay. If we hear them you can hide. I'll turn out the light. I'll meet them at the door. You can trust me. Wait till all quiets down, if we have to wait till morning. Then you can slip out.'

'I oughn't to stay. I don't want to—I won't,' Duane replied, perplexed and stubborn.

'But you must. It's the only safe way. They won't come here.'

'Suppose they should? It's an even chance Longstreth'll search every room and corner in this old house. If they found me here I couldn't start a fight. You might be hurt. Then—the fact of my being here—'

Duane did not finish what he meant, but instead made a step toward the door. White of face and dark of eye, she took hold of him to detain him. She was as strong and supple as a panther. But she need not have been either resolute or strong, for the clasp of her hand was enough to make Duane weak.

'Up yet, Ray?' came Longstreth's clear voice, too strained, too eager to be natural.

'No. I'm in bed reading. Good night,' instantly replied Miss Longstreth, so calmly and naturally that Duane marveled at the difference between man and woman. Then she motioned for Duane to hide in the closet. He slipped in, but the door would not close altogether.

'Are you alone?' went on Longstreth's penetrating voice.

'Yes,' she replied. 'Ruth went to bed.'

The door swung inward with a swift scrape and jar. Longstreth half entered, haggard, flaming-eyed. Behind him Duane saw Lawson, and indistinctly another man.

Longstreth barred Lawson from entering, which action showed control as well as distrust. He wanted to see into the room. When he had glanced around he went out and closed the door.

Then what seemed a long interval ensued. The house grew silent once more. Duane could not see Miss Longstreth, but he heard her quick breathing. How long did she mean to let him stay hidden there? Hard and perilous as his life had been, this was a new kind of adventure. He had divined the strange softness of his feeling as something due to the magnetism of this beautiful woman. It hardly seemed possible that he, who had been outside the pale for so many years, could have fallen in love. Yet that must be the secret of his agitation.

Presently he pushed open the closet door and stepped forth. Miss Longstreth had her head lowered upon her arms and appeared to be in distress. At his touch she raised a quivering face.

'I think I can go now—safely,' he whispered.

'Go then, if you must, but you may stay till you're safe,' she replied.

'I—I couldn't thank you enough. It's been hard on me—this finding out—and you his daughter. I feel strange. I don't understand myself well. But I want you to know—if I were not an outlaw—a ranger—I'd lay my life at your feet.'

'Oh! You have seen so—so little of me,' she faltered.

'All the same it's true. And that makes me feel more the trouble my coming caused you.'

'You will not fight my father?'

'Not if I can help it. I'm trying to get out of his way.'

'But you spied upon him.'

'I am a ranger, Miss Longstreth.'

'And oh! I am a rustler's daughter,' she cried. 'That's so much more terrible than I'd suspected. It was tricky cattle deals I imagined he was engaged in. But only to-night I had strong suspicions aroused.'

'How? Tell me.'

'I overheard Floyd say that men were coming tonight to arrange a meeting for my father at a rendezvous near Ord. Father did not want to go. Floyd taunted him with a name.'

'What name?' queried Duane.

'It was Cheseldine.'

'*Cheseldine!* My God! Miss Longstreth, why did *you* tell me that?'

'What difference does that make?'

'Your father and Cheseldine are one and the same,' whispered Duane, hoarsely.

'I gathered so much myself,' she replied, miserably. 'But Longstreth is father's real name.'

Duane felt so stunned he could not speak at once. It was the girl's part in this tragedy that weakened him. The instant she betrayed the secret Duane realized perfectly that he did love her. The emotion was like a great flood.

'Miss Longstreth, all this seems so unbelievable,' he whispered. 'Cheseldine is the rustler chief I've come out here to get. He's only a name. Your father is the real man. I've sworn to get him. I'm bound by more than law or oaths. I can't break what binds me. And I must disgrace you—wreck your life! Why, Miss Longstreth, I believe I—I love you. It's all come in a rush. I'd die for you if I could. How fatal—terrible—this is! How things work out!'

She slipped to her knees, with her hands on his.

'You won't kill him?' she implored. 'If you care for me—you won't kill him?'

'No. That I promise you.'

With a low moan she dropped her head upon the bed.

Duane opened the door and stealthily stole out through the corridor to the court.

When Duane got out into the dark, where his hot face cooled in the wind, his relief equaled his other feelings.

The night was dark, windy, stormy, yet there was no rain. Duane hoped as soon as he got clear of the ranch to lose something of the pain he felt. But long after he had tramped out into the open there was a lump in his throat and an ache in his breast. All his thought centered around Ray Longstreth. What a woman she had turned out to be! He seemed to have a vague, hopeless hope that there might be, there must be, some way he could save her.

21

Before going to sleep that night Duane had decided to go to Ord and try to find the rendezvous where Longstreth was to meet his men. These men Duane wanted even more than their leader. If Longstreth, or Cheseldine, was the brains of that gang, Poggin was the executor. It was Poggin who needed to be found and stopped. Poggin and his right-hand men! Duane experienced a strange, tigerish thrill. It was thought of Poggin more than thought of success for MacNelly's plan. Duane felt dubious over this emotion.

Next day he set out for Bradford. He was glad to get away from Fairdale for a while. But the hours and miles in no wise changed the new pain in his heart. The only way he could forget Miss Longstreth was to let his mind dwell upon Poggin, and even this was not always effective.

He avoided Sanderson, and at the end of the day and a half he arrived at Bradford.

The night of the day before he reached Bradford, No. 6, the mail and express train going east, was held up by train-robbers, the Wells-Fargo messenger killed over his safe, the mail-clerk wounded, the bags carried away. The engine of No. 6 came into town minus even a tender, and engineer and fireman told conflicting stories. A posse of railroad men and citizens, led by a sheriff Duane suspected was crooked, was made up before the engine steamed back to pick up the rest of the train. Duane had the sudden inspiration that he had been cudgeling his mind to find; and, acting upon it, he mounted his horse again and left Bradford unobserved. As he rode out into the night, over a dark trail in the direction of Ord, he uttered a short, grim, sardonic laugh at the hope that he might be taken for a train-robber.

He rode at an easy trot most of the night, and when the black peak of Ord Mountain loomed up against the stars he halted, tied his horse, and slept until dawn. He had brought a small pack, and now he took his time cooking breakfast. When the sun was well up he saddled Bullet, and, leaving the trail where his tracks showed plain in the ground, he put his horse to the rocks and brush. He selected an exceedingly rough, roundabout, and difficult course to Ord, hid his tracks with the skill of a long-hunted fugitive, and arrived there with his horse winded and covered with lather. It added considerably to his arrival that the man Duane remembered as Fletcher and several others saw him come in the back way through the lots and jump a fence into the road.

Duane led Bullet up to the porch where Fletcher stood wiping his beard. He was hatless, restless, and evidently had just enjoyed a morning drink.

'Howdy, Dodge,' said Fletcher, laconically.

Duane replied, and the other man returned the greeting with interest.

'Jim, my hoss's done up. I want to hide him from any chance tourists as might happen to ride up curious-like.'

'Haw! haw! haw!'

Duane gathered encouragement from that chorus of coarse laughter.

'Wal, if them tourists ain't too durned snooky the hoss'll be safe in the 'dobe shack back of Bill's here. Feed thar, too, but you'll hev to rustle water.'

Duane led Bullet to the place indicated, had care of his welfare, and left him there. Upon returning to the tavern porch Duane saw the group of men had been added to by others, some of whom he had seen before. Without comment Duane walked along the edge of the road, and wherever one of the tracks of his horse showed he carefully obliterated it. This procedure was attentively watched by Fletcher and his companions.

'Wal, Dodge,' remarked Fletcher, as Duane returned, 'thet's safer 'n prayin' fer rain.'

Duane's reply was a remark as loquacious as Fletcher's, to the effect that a long, slow, monotonous ride was conducive to thirst. They all joined him, unmistakably friendly. But Knell was not there, and most assuredly not Poggin. Fletcher was no common outlaw, but, whatever his ability, it probably lay in execution of orders. Apparently at that time these men had nothing to do but drink and lounge around the tavern. Evidently they were poorly supplied with money, though Duane observed they could borrow a peso occasionally from the bartender. Duane set out to make himself agreeable and succeeded. There was card-playing for small stakes, idle jests of coarse nature, much bantering among the younger fellows, and occasionally a mild quarrel. All morning men came and went, until, all told, Duane calculated he had seen at least fifty. Toward the middle of the afternoon a young fellow burst into the saloon and yelled one word:

'Posse!'

From the scramble to get outdoors Duane judged that word and the ensuing action was rare in Ord.

'What the hell!' muttered Fletcher, as he gazed down the road at a dark, compact bunch of horses and riders. 'Fust time I ever seen thet in Ord! We're gettin' popular like them camps out of Valentine. Wish Phil was here or Poggy. Now all you gents keep quiet. I'll do the talkin'.'

The posse entered the town, trotted up on dusty horses, and halted in a bunch before the tavern. The party consisted of about twenty men, all heavily armed, and evidently in charge of a clean-cut, lean-limbed cowboy. Duane experienced considerable satisfaction at the absence of the sheriff who he had understood was to lead the posse. Perhaps he was out in another direction with a different force.

'Hello, Jim Fletcher,' called the cowboy.

'Howdy,' replied Fletcher.

At his short, dry response and the way he strode leisurely out before the posse Duane found himself modifying his contempt for Fletcher. The outlaw was different now.

'Fletcher, we've tracked a man to all but three miles of this place. Tracks as plain as the nose on your face. Found his camp. Then he hit into the brush, an' we lost the trail. Didn't have no tracker with us. Think he went into the mountains. But we took a chance an' rid over the rest of the way, seein' Ord was so close. Anybody come in here late last night or early this mornin'?'

'Nope,' replied Fletcher.

His response was what Duane had expected from his manner, and evidently the cowboy took it as a matter of course. He turned to the others of the posse, entering into a low consultation. Evidently there was difference of opinion, if not real dissension, in that posse.

'Didn't I tell ye this was a wild-goose chase, comin' way out here?' protested an old hawk-faced rancher. 'Them hoss tracks we follored ain't like any of them we seen at the water-tank where the train was held up.'

'I'm not sure of that,' replied the leader.

'Wal, Guthrie, I've follored tracks all my life—'

'But you couldn't keep to the trail this feller made in the brush.'

'Gimme time, an' I could. Thet takes time. An' heah you go hell-bent fer election! But it's a wrong lead out this way. If you're right this road-agent, after he killed his pals, would hev rid back right through town. An' with them mail-bags! Supposin' they was greasers? Some greasers has sense, an' when it comes to thievin' they're shore cute.'

'But we ain't got any reason to believe this robber who murdered the greasers is a greaser himself. I tell you it was a slick job done by no ordinary sneak. Didn't you hear the facts? One greaser hopped the engine an' covered the engineer an' fireman. Another greaser kept flashin' his gun outside the train. The big man who shoved back the car-door an' did the killin'—he was the real gent, an' don't you forget it.'

Some of the posse sided with the cowboy leader and some with the old cattleman. Finally the young leader disgustedly gathered up his bridle.

'Aw, hell! Thet sheriff shoved you off this trail. Mebbe he hed reason! Savvy thet? If I hed a bunch of cowboys with me—I tell you what—I'd take a chance an' clean up this hole!'

All the while Jim Fletcher stood quietly with his hands in his pockets.

'Guthrie, I'm shore treasurin' up your friendly talk,' he said. The menace was in the tone, not the content of his speech.

'You can—an' be damned to you, Fletcher!' called Guthrie, as the horses started.

Fletcher, standing out alone before the others of his clan, watched the posse out of sight.

'Luck fer you-all thet Poggy wasn't here,' he said, as they disappeared. Then with a thoughtful mien he strode up on the porch and led Duane away from the others into the barroom. When he looked into Duane's face it was somehow an entirely changed scrutiny.

'Dodge, where'd you hide the stuff? I reckon I git in on this deal, seein' I staved off Guthrie.'

Duane played his part. Here was his opportunity, and like a tiger after prey he seized it. First he coolly eyed the outlaw and then disclaimed any knowledge whatever of the train-robbery other than Fletcher had heard himself. Then at Fletcher's persistence and admiration and increasing show of friendliness he laughed occasionally and allowed himself to swell with pride, though still denying. Next he feigned a lack of consistent will-power and seemed to be wavering under Fletcher's persuasion and grew silent, then surly. Fletcher, evidently sure of ultimate victory, desisted for the time being; however, in his solicitous regard and close companionship for the rest of that day he betrayed the bent of his mind.

Later, when Duane started up announcing his intention to get his horse and make for camp out in the brush, Fletcher seemed grievously offended.

'Why don't you stay with me? I've got a comfortable 'dobe over here. Didn't I stick by you when Guthrie an' his bunch come up? Supposin' I hedn't showed down a cold hand to him? You'd be swingin' somewheres now. I tell you, Dodge, it ain't square.'

'I'll square it. I pay my debts,' replied Duane. 'But I can't put up here all night. If I belonged to the gang it'd be different.'

'What gang?' asked Fletcher, bluntly.

'Why, Cheseldine's.'

Fletcher's beard nodded as his jaw dropped.

Duane laughed. 'I run into him the other day. Knowed him on sight. Sure, he's the king-pin rustler. When he seen me an' asked me what reason I had for bein' on earth or some such like—why, I up an' told him.'

Fletcher appeared staggered.

'Who in all-fired hell air you talkin' about?'

'Didn't I tell you once? Cheseldine. He calls himself Longstreth over there.'

All of Fletcher's face not covered by hair turned a dirty white.

'Cheseldine—Longstreth!' he whispered, hoarsely. 'Gord Almighty! You braced the—' Then a remarkable transformation came over the outlaw. He gulped; he straightened his face; he controlled his agitation. But he could not send the healthy brown back to his face. Duane, watching this rude man, marveled at the change in him, the sudden checking movement, the proof of a wonderful fear and loyalty. It all meant Cheseldine, a master of men!

'*Who air you?*' queried Fletcher, in a queer, strained voice.

'You gave me a handle, didn't you? Dodge. Thet's as good as any. Shore it hits me hard. Jim, I've been pretty lonely for years, an' I'm gettin' in need of pals. Think it over, will you? See you *mañana*.'

The outlaw watched Duane go off after his horse, watched him as he returned to the tavern, watched him ride out into the darkness—all without a word.

Duane left the town, threaded a quiet passage through cactus and mesquite to a spot he had marked before, and made ready for the night. His mind was so full that he found sleep aloof. Luck at last was playing his game. He sensed the first slow heave of a mighty crisis. The end, always haunting, had to be sternly blotted from thought. It was the approach that needed all his mind.

He passed the night there, and late in the morning, after watching trail and road from a ridge, he returned to Ord. If Jim Fletcher tried to disguise his surprise the effort was a failure. Certainly he had not expected to see Duane again. Duane allowed himself a little freedom with Fletcher, an attitude hitherto lacking.

That afternoon a horseman rode in from Bradford, an outlaw evidently well known and liked by his fellows, and Duane heard him say, before he could possibly have been told the train-robber was in Ord, that the loss of money in the holdup was slight. Like a flash Duane saw the luck of this report. He pretended not to have heard.

In the early twilight at an opportune moment he called Fletcher to him, and, linking his arm within the outlaw's, he drew him off in a stroll to a log bridge spanning a little gully. Here after gazing around, he took out a roll of bills, spread it out, split it equally, and without a word handed one half to Fletcher. With clumsy fingers Fletcher ran through the roll.

'Five hundred!' he exclaimed. 'Dodge, thet's damn handsome of you, considerin' the job wasn't—'

'Considerin' nothin',' interrupted Duane. 'I'm makin' no reference to a job here or there. You did me a good turn. I split my pile. If thet doesn't make us pards, good turns an' money ain't no use in this country.'

Fletcher was won.

The two men spent much time together. Duane made up a short fictitious history about himself that satisfied the outlaw, only it drew forth a laughing jest upon Duane's modesty. For Fletcher did not hide his belief that his new partner was a man of achievements. Knell and Poggin, and then Cheseldine himself, would be persuaded of this fact, so Fletcher boasted. He had influence. He would use it. He thought he pulled a stroke with Knell. But nobody on earth, not even the boss, had any influence on Poggin. Poggin was concentrated ice part of the time; all the rest he was bursting hell. But Poggin loved a horse. He never loved anything else. He could be won with that black horse Bullet. Cheseldine was already won by Duane's monumental nerve; otherwise he would have killed Duane.

Little by little the next few days Duane learned the points he longed to know; and how indelibly they etched themselves in his memory! Cheseldine's hiding-place was on the far slope of Mount Ord, in a deep, high-walled valley. He always went there just before a contemplated job, where he met and planned with his lieutenants. Then while they executed he basked in the sunshine before one or another of the public places he owned. He was there in the Ord den now, getting ready to plan the biggest job yet. It was a bank-robbery; but where, Fletcher had not as yet been advised.

Then when Duane had pumped the now amenable outlaw of all details pertaining to the present he gathered data and facts and places covering a period of ten years Fletcher had been with Cheseldine. And herewith was unfolded a history so dark in its bloody regime, so incredible in its brazen daring, so appalling in its proof of the outlaw's sweep and grasp of the country from Pecos to Rio Grande, that Duane was stunned. Compared to this Cheseldine of the Big Bend, to this rancher, stock-buyer, cattle speculator, property-holder, all the outlaws Duane had ever known sank into insignificance. The power of the man stunned Duane; the strange fidelity given him stunned Duane; the intricate inside working of his great system was equally stunning. But when Duane recovered from that fact the old terrible passion to kill consumed him, and it raged fiercely and it could not be checked. If that red-handed Poggin, if that cold-eyed, dead-faced Knell had only been at Ord! But they were not, and Duane with help of time got what he hoped was the upper hand of himself.

22

Again inaction and suspense dragged at Duane's spirit. Like a leashed hound with a keen scent in his face Duane wanted to leap forth when he was bound. He almost fretted. Something called to him over the bold, wild brow of Mount Ord. But while Fletcher stayed in Ord waiting for Knell and Poggin, or for orders, Duane knew his game was again a waiting one.

But one day there were signs of the long quiet of Ord being broken. A messenger strange to Duane rode in on a secret mission that had to do with Fletcher. When he went away Fletcher became addicted to thoughtful moods and lonely walks. He seldom drank, and this in itself was a striking contrast to former behavior. The messenger came again. Whatever communication he brought, it had a remarkable effect upon the outlaw. Duane was present in the tavern when the fellow arrived, saw the few words whispered, but did not hear them. Fletcher turned white with anger or fear, perhaps both, and he cursed like a madman. The messenger, a lean, dark-faced, hard-riding fellow reminding Duane of the cowboy Guthrie, left the tavern without even a drink and rode away off to the west. This west mystified and fascinated Duane as much as the south beyond Mount Ord. Where were Knell and Poggin? Apparently they were not at present with the leader on the mountain. After the messenger left Fletcher grew silent and surly. He had presented a variety of moods to Duane's observation, and this latest one was provocative of thought. Fletcher was dangerous. It became clear now that the other outlaws of the camp feared him, kept out of his way. Duane let him alone, yet closely watched him.

Perhaps an hour after the messenger had left, not longer, Fletcher manifestly arrived at some decision, and he called for his horse. Then he went to his shack and returned. To Duane the outlaw looked in shape both to ride and to fight. He gave orders for the men in camp to keep close until he returned. Then he mounted.

'Come here, Dodge,' he called.

Duane went up and laid a hand on the pommel of the saddle. Fletcher walked his horse, with Duane beside him, till they reached the log bridge, when he halted.

'Dodge, I'm in bad with Knell,' he said. 'An' it 'pears I'm the cause of friction between Knell an' Poggy. Knell never had any use fer me, but Poggy's been square, if not friendly. The boss has a big deal on, an' here it's been held up because of this scrap. He's waitin' over there on the mountain to give orders to Knell or Poggy, an' neither one's showin' up. I've got to stand in the breach, an' I ain't enjoyin' the prospects.'

'What's the trouble about, Jim?' asked Duane.

'Reckon it's a little about you, Dodge,' said Fletcher, dryly. 'Knell hadn't any use fer you thet day. He ain't got no use fer a man unless he can rule him. Some of the boys here hev blabbed before I edged in with my say, an' there's hell to pay. Knell claims to know somethin' about you that'll make both the boss an' Poggy sick when he springs it. But he's keepin' quiet. Hard man to figger, thet Knell. Reckon you'd better go back to Bradford fer a day or so, then camp out near here till I come back.'

'Why?'

'Wal, because there ain't any use fer you to git in bad, too. The gang will ride over here any day. If they're friendly I'll light a fire on the hill there, say three nights from tonight. If you don't see it thet night you hit the trail. I'll do what I can. Jim Fletcher sticks to his pals. So long, Dodge.'

Then he rode away.

He left Duane in a quandary. This news was black. Things had been working out so well. Here was a setback. At the moment Duane did not know which way to turn, but certainly he had no idea of going back to Bradford. Friction between the two great lieutenants of Cheseldine! Open hostility between one of them and another of the chief's right-hand men! Among outlaws that sort of thing was deadly serious. Generally such matters were settled with guns. Duane gathered encouragement even from disaster. Perhaps the disintegration of Cheseldine's great band had already begun. But what did Knell know? Duane did not circle around the idea with doubts and hopes; if Knell knew anything it was that this stranger in Ord, this new partner of Fletcher's, was no less than Buck Duane. Well, it was about time, thought Duane, that he made use of his name if it were to help him at all. That name had been MacNelly's hope. He had anchored all his scheme to Duane's fame. Duane was tempted to ride off after Fletcher and stay with him. This, however, would hardly be fair to an outlaw who had been fair to him. Duane concluded to await developments and when the gang rode in to Ord, probably from their various hiding-places, he would be there ready to be denounced by Knell. Duane could not see any other culmination of this series of events than a meeting between Knell and himself. If that terminated fatally for Knell there was all probability of Duane's being in no worse situation than he was now. If Poggin took up the quarrel! Here Duane accused himself again—tried in vain to revolt from a judgment that he was only reasoning out excuses to meet these outlaws.

Meanwhile, instead of waiting, why not hunt up Cheseldine in his mountain retreat? The thought no sooner struck Duane than he was hurrying for his horse.

He left Ord, ostensibly toward Bradford, but, once out of sight, he turned off the road, circled through the brush, and several miles south of town he struck a narrow grass-grown trail that Fletcher had told him led to Cheseldine's camp. The horse tracks along this trail were not less than a week old, and very likely much more. It wound between low, brush-covered foothills, through arroyos and gullies lined with mesquite, cottonwood, and scrub-oak.

In an hour Duane struck the slope of Mount Ord, and as he climbed he got a view of the rolling, black-spotted country, partly desert, partly fertile, with long, bright lines of dry streambeds winding away to grow dim in the distance. He got among broken rocks and cliffs, and here the open, downward-rolling land disappeared, and he was hard put to it to find the trail. He lost it repeatedly and made slow progress. Finally he climbed into a region of all rock benches, rough here, smooth there, with only an occasional scratch of iron horseshoe to guide him. Many times he had to go ahead and then work to right or left till he found his way again. It was slow work; it took all day; and night found him half-way up the mountain. He halted at a little side-cañon with grass and water, and here he made camp. The night was clear and cool at that height, with a dark-blue sky and a streak of stars blinking across. With this day of action behind him he felt better satisfied than he had been for some time. Here, on this venture, he was answering to a call that had so often directed his movements, perhaps his life, and it was one that logic or intelligence could take little stock of. And on this night, lonely like the ones he used to spend in the Nueces gorge, and memorable of them because of a likeness to that old hiding-place, he felt the pressing return of old haunting things—the past so long ago, wild fights, dead faces—and the places of these were taken by one quiveringly alive, white, tragic, with its dark, intent, speaking eyes—Ray Longstreth's.

That last memory he yielded to until he slept.

In the morning, satisfied that he had left still fewer tracks than he had followed up this trail, he led his horse up to the head of the cañon, there a narrow crack in low cliffs, and with branches of cedar fenced him in. Then he went back and took up the trail on foot.

Without the horse he made better time and climbed through deep clefts, wide cañons, over ridges, up shelving slopes, along precipices—a long, hard climb—till he reached what he concluded was a divide. Going down was easier, though the farther he followed this dim and winding trail the wider the broken battlements of rock. Above him he saw the black fringe of piñon and pine, and above that the bold peak, bare, yellow, like a desert butte. Once, through a wide gateway between great escarpments, he saw the lower country beyond the range, and beyond this, vast and clear as it lay in his sight, was the great river that made the Big Bend. He went down and down, wondering how a horse could follow that broken trail, believing there must be another better one somewhere into Cheseldine's hiding-place.

He rounded a jutting corner, where view had been shut off, and presently came out upon the rim of a high wall. Beneath, like a green gulf seen through blue haze, lay an amphitheater walled in on the two sides he could see. It lay perhaps a thousand feet below him; and, plain as all the other features of that wild environ-ment, there shone out a big red stone or adobe cabin, white water shining away between great borders, and horses and cattle dotting the levels. It was a peaceful, beautiful scene. Duane could not help grinding his teeth at the thought of rustlers living there in quiet and ease.

Duane worked half-way down to the level, and, well hidden in a niche, he settled himself to watch both trail and valley. He made note of the position of the sun and saw that if anything developed or if he decided to descend any farther there was small likelihood of his getting back to his camp before dark. To try that after nightfall he imagined would be vain effort.

Then he bent his keen eyes downward. The cabin appeared to be a crude structure. Though large in size, it had, of course, been built by outlaws.

There was no garden, no cultivated field, no corral. Excepting for the rude pile of stones and logs plastered together with mud, the valley was as wild, probably, as on the day of discovery. Duane seemed to have been watching for a long time before he saw any sign of man, and this one apparently went to the stream for water and returned to the cabin.

The sun went down behind the wall, and shadows were born in the darker places of the valley. Duane began to want to get closer to that cabin. What had he taken this arduous climb for? He held back, however, trying to evolve further plans.

While he was pondering the shadows quickly gathered and darkened. If he was to go back to camp he must set out at once. Still he lingered. And suddenly his wide-roving eye caught sight of two horsemen riding up the valley. They must have entered at a point below, round the huge abutment of rock, beyond Duane's range of sight. Their horses were tired and stopped at the stream for a long drink.

Duane left his perch, took to the steep trail, and descended as fast as he could without making noise. It did not take him long to reach the valley floor. It was almost level, with deep grass, and here and there clumps of bushes. Twilight was already thick down there. Duane marked the location of the trail, and then began to slip like a shadow through the grass and from bush to bush. He saw a bright light before he made out the dark outline of the cabin. Then he heard voices, a merry whistle, a coarse song, and the clink of iron cooking-utensils. He smelled fragrant wood-smoke. He saw moving dark figures cross the light. Evidently there was a wide door, or else the fire was out in the open.

Duane swerved to the left, out of direct line with the light, and thus was able to see better. Then he advanced noiselessly but swiftly toward the back of the house. There were trees close to the wall. He would make no noise, and he could scarcely be seen—if only there was no watch-dog! But all his outlaw days he had taken risks with only his useless life at stake; now, with that changed, he advanced stealthy and bold as an Indian. He reached the cover of the trees, knew he was hidden in their shadows, for at few paces' distance he had been able to see only their tops. From there he slipped up to the house and felt along the wall with his hands.

He came to a little window where light shone through. He peeped in. He saw a room shrouded in shadows, a lamp turned low, a table, chairs. He saw an open door, with bright flare beyond, but could not see the fire. Voices came indistinctly. Without hesitation Duane stole farther along—all the way to the end of the cabin. Peeping round, he saw only the flare of light on bare ground. Retracing his cautious steps, he paused at the crack again, saw that no man was in the room, and then he went on round that end of the cabin. Fortune favored him. There were bushes, an old shed, a wood-pile, all the cover he needed at that corner. He did not even need to crawl.

Before he peered between the rough corner of the wall and the bush growing close to it Duane paused a moment. This excitement was different from that he had always felt when pursued. It had no bitterness, no pain, no dread. There was as much danger here, perhaps more, yet it was not the same. Then he looked.

He saw a bright fire, a red-faced man bending over it, whistling, while he handled a steaming pot. Over him was a roofed shed built against the wall, with two open sides and two supporting posts. Duane's second glance, not so blinded by the sudden bright light, made out other men, three in the shadow, two in the flare, but with backs to him.

'It's a smoother trail by long odds, but ain't so short as this one right over the mountain,' one outlaw was saying.

'What's eatin' you, Panhandle?' ejaculated another. 'Blossom an' me rode from Faraway Springs, where Poggin is with some of the gang.'

'Excuse me, Phil. Shore I didn't see you come in, an' Boldt never said nothin'.'

'It took you a long time to get here, but I guess that's just as well,' spoke up a smooth, suave voice with a ring in it.

Longstreth's voice—Cheseldine's voice!

Here they were—Cheseldine, Phil Knell, Blossom Kane, Panhandle Smith, Boldt—how well Duane remembered the names!—all here, the big men of Cheseldine's gang, except the biggest—Poggin. Duane had holed them, and his sensations of the moment deadened sight and sound of what was before him. He sank down, controlled himself, silenced a mounting exultation, then from a less-strained position he peered forth again.

The outlaws were waiting for supper. Their conversation might have been that of cowboys in camp, ranchers at a roundup. Duane listened with eager ears, waiting for the business talk that he felt would come. All the time he watched with the eyes of a wolf upon its quarry. Blossom Kane was the lean-limbed messenger who had so angered Fletcher. Boldt was a giant in stature, dark, bearded, silent. Panhandle Smith was the red-faced cook, merry, profane, a short, bow-legged man resembling many rustlers Duane had known, particularly Luke Stevens. And Knell, who sat there, tall, slim, like a boy in build, like a boy in years, with his pale, smooth, expressionless face and his cold, gray eyes. And Longstreth, who leaned against the wall, handsome, with his dark face and beard like an aristocrat, resembled many a rich Louisiana planter Duane had met. The sixth man sat so much in the shadow that he could not be plainly discerned, and, though addressed, his name was not mentioned.

Panhandle Smith carried pots and pans into the cabin, and cheerfully called out: 'If you gents air hungry fer grub, don't look fer me to feed you with a spoon.'

The outlaws piled inside, made a great bustle and clatter as they sat to their meal. Like hungry men, they talked little.

Duane waited there awhile, then guardedly got up and crept round to the other side of the cabin. After he became used to the dark again he ventured to steal along the wall to the window and peeped in. The outlaws were in the first room and could not be seen.

Duane waited. The moments dragged endlessly. His heart pounded. Longstreth entered, turned up the light, and, taking a box of cigars from the table, he carried it out.

'Here, you fellows, go outside and smoke,' he said. 'Knell, come on in now. Let's get it over.'

He returned, sat down, and lighted a cigar for himself. He put his booted feet on the table.

Duane saw that the room was comfortably, even luxuriously furnished. There must have been a good trail, he thought, else how could all that stuff have been packed in there. Most assuredly it could not have come over the trail he had traveled. Presently he heard the men go outside, and their voices became indistinct. Then Knell came in and seated himself without any of his chief's ease. He seemed preoccupied and, as always, cold.

'What's wrong, Knell? Why didn't you get here sooner?' queried Longstreth.

'Poggin, damn him! We're on the outs again.'

'What for?'

'Aw, he needn't have got sore. He's breakin' a new hoss over there at Faraway, an' you know him where a hoss's concerned. That kept him, I reckon, more than anythin'.'

'What else? Get it out of your system so we can go on to the new job.'

'Well, it begins back a ways. I don't know how long ago—weeks—a stranger rode into Ord an' got down easy-like as if he owned the place. He seemed familiar to me. But I wasn't sure. We looked him over, an' I left, tryin' to place him in my mind.'

'What'd he look like?'

'Rangy, powerful man, white hair over his temples, still, hard face, eyes like knives. The way he packed his guns, the way he walked an' stood an' swung his right hand showed me what he was. You can't fool me on the gun-sharp. An' he had a grand horse, a big black.'

'I've met your man,' said Longstreth.

'No!' exclaimed Knell. It was wonderful to hear surprise expressed by this man that did not in the least show it in his strange physiognomy. Knell laughed a short, grim, hollow laugh. 'Boss, this here big gent drifts into Ord again an' makes up to Jim Fletcher. Jim, you know, is easy led. He likes men. An' when a posse come along trailin' a blind lead, huntin' the wrong way for the man who held up No. 6, why, Jim—he up an' takes this stranger to be the fly road-agent an' cottons to him. Got money out of him sure. An' that's what stumps me more. What's this man's game? I happen to know, boss, that he couldn't have held up No. 6.'

'How do you know?' demanded Longstreth.

'Because I did the job myself.'

A dark and stormy passion clouded the chief's face.

'Damn you, Knell! You're incorrigible. You're unreliable. Another break like that queers you with me. Did you tell Poggin?'

'Yes. That's one reason we fell out. He raved. I thought he was goin' to kill me.'

'Why did you tackle such a risky job without help or plan?'

'It offered, that's all. An' it was easy. But it was a mistake. I got the country an' the railroad hollerin' for nothin'. I just couldn't help it. You know what idleness means to one of us. You know also that this very life breeds fatality. It's wrong—that's why. I was born of good parents, an' I know what's right. We're wrong, an' we can't beat the end, that's all. An' for my part I don't care a damn when that comes.'

'Fine wise talk from you, Knell,' said Longstreth, scornfully. 'Go on with your story.'

'As I said, Jim cottons to the pretender, an' they get chummy. They're together all the time. You can gamble Jim told all he knew an' then some. A little liquor loosens his tongue. Several of the boys rode over from Ord, an' one of them went to Poggin an' says Jim Fletcher has a new man for the gang. Poggin, you know, is always ready for any new man. He says if one doesn't turn out good he can be shut off easy. He rather liked the way this new pard of Jim's was boosted. Jim an' Poggin always hit it up together. So until I got on the deal Jim's pard was already in the gang, without Poggin or you ever seein' him. Then I got to figurin' hard. Just where had I ever seen that chap? As it turned out, I never had seen him, which accounts for my bein' doubtful. I'd never forget any man I'd seen. I dug up a lot of old papers from my kit an' went over them. Letters, pictures, clippin's, an' all that. I guess I had a pretty good notion what I was lookin' for an' who I wanted to make sure of. At last I found it. An' I knew my man. But I didn't spring it on Poggin. Oh no! I want to have some fun with him when the time comes. He'll be wilder than a trapped wolf. I sent Blossom over to Ord to get word from Jim, an' when he verified all this talk I sent Blossom again with a message calculated to make Jim hump. Poggin got sore, said he'd wait for Jim, an' I could come over here to see you about the new job. He'd meet me in Ord.'

Knell had spoken hurriedly and low, now and then with passion. His pale eyes glinted like fire in ice, and now his voice fell to a whisper.

'Who do you think Fletcher's new man is?'

'Who?' demanded Longstreth.

'*Buck Duane!*'

Down came Longstreth's boots with a crash, then his body grew rigid.

'That Nueces outlaw? That two-shot ace-of-spades gunthrower who killed Bland, Alloway—?'

'An' Hardin.' Knell whispered this last name with more feeling that the apparent circumstance demanded.

'Yes; and Hardin, the best one of the Rim Rock fellows—Buck Duane!'

Longstreth was so ghastly white now that his black mustache seemed outlined against chalk. He eyed his grim lieutenant. They understood each other without more words. It was enough that Buck Duane was there in the Big Bend. Longstreth rose presently and reached for a flask, from which he drank, then offered it to Knell. He waved it aside.

'Knell,' began the chief, slowly, as he wiped his lips, 'I gathered you have some grudge against this Buck Duane.'

'Yes.'

'Well, don't be a— fool now and do what Poggin or almost any of you men would —don't meet this Buck Duane. I've reason to believe he's a Texas Ranger now.'

'The hell you say!' exclaimed Knell.

'Yes. Go to Ord and give Jim Fletcher a hunch. He'll get Poggin, and they'll fix even Buck Duane.'

'All right. I'll do my best. But if I run into Duane—'

'Don't run into him!' Longstreth's voice fairly rang with the force of its passion and command. He wiped his face, drank again from the flask, sat down, resumed his smoking, and, drawing a paper from his vest pocket he began to study it.

'Well, I'm glad that's settled,' he said, evidently referring to the Duane matter. 'Now for the new job. This is October the eighteenth. On or before the twenty-fifth there will be a shipment of gold reach the Rancher's Bank of Val Verde. After you return to Ord give Poggin these orders. Keep the gang quiet. You, Poggin, Kane, Fletcher, Panhandle Smith, and Boldt to be in on the secret and the job. Nobody else. You'll leave Ord on the twenty-third, ride across country by the trail till you get within sight of Mercer. It's a hundred miles from Bradford to Val Verde—about the same from Ord. Time your travel to get you near Val Verde on the morning of the twenty-sixth. You won't have to more than trot your horses. At two o'clock in the afternoon, sharp, ride into town and up to the Rancher's Bank. Val Verde's a pretty big town. Never been any holdups there. Town feels safe. Make it a clean, fast, daylight job. That's all. Have you got the details?'

Knell did not even ask for the dates again.

'Suppose Poggin or me might be detained?' he asked.

Longstreth bent a dark glance upon his lieutenant.

'You never can tell what'll come off,' continued Knell. 'I'll do my best.'

'The minute you see Poggin tell him. A job on hand steadies him. And I say again—look to it that nothing happens. Either you or Poggin carry the job through. But I want both of you in it. Break for the hills, and when you get up in the rocks where you can hide your tracks head for Mount Ord. When all's quiet again I'll join you here. That's all. Call in the boys.'

Like a swift shadow and as noiseless Duane stole across the level toward the dark wall of rock. Every nerve was a strung wire. For a little while his mind was cluttered and clogged with whirling thoughts, from which, like a flashing scroll, unrolled the long, baffling order of action. The game was now in his hands. He must cross Mount Ord at night. The feat was improbable, but it might be done. He must ride into Bradford, forty miles from the foothills before eight o'clock next morning. He must telegraph MacNelly to be in Val Verde on the twenty-fifth. He must ride back to Ord, to intercept Knell, face him, be denounced, kill him, and while the iron was hot strike hard to win Poggin's half-won interest as he had wholly won Fletcher's. Failing that last, he must let the outlaws alone to bide their time in Ord, to be free to ride on their new job in Val Verde. In the meantime he must plan to arrest Longstreth. It was a magnificent outline, incredible, alluring, unfathomable in its nameless certainty. He felt like fate. He seemed to be the iron consequences falling upon these doomed outlaws.

Under the wall the shadows were black, only the tips of trees and crags showing, yet he went straight to the trail. It was merely a grayness between borders of black. He climbed and never stopped. It did not seem steep. His feet might have had eyes. He surmounted the wall, and, looking down into the ebony gulf pierced by one point of light, he lifted a menacing arm and shook it. Then he strode on and did not falter till he reached the huge shelving cliffs. Here he lost the trail; there was none; but he remembered the shapes, the points, the notches of rock above. Before he reached the ruins of splintered ramparts and jumbles of broken walls the moon topped the eastern slope of the mountain, and the mystifying blackness he had dreaded changed to magic silver light. It seemed as light as day, only soft, mellow, and the air held a transparent sheen. He ran up the bare ridges and down the smooth slopes, and, like a goat, jumped from rock to rock. In this light he knew his way and lost no time looking for a trail. He crossed the divide and then had all downhill before him. Swiftly he descended, almost always sure of his memory of the landmarks. He did not remember having studied them in the ascent, yet here they were, even in changed light, familiar to his sight. What he had once seen was pictured on his mind. And, true as a deer striking for home, he reached the cañon where he had left his horse.

Bullet was quickly and easily found. Duane threw on the saddle and pack, cinched them tight, and resumed his descent. The worst was now to come. Bare downward steps in rock, sliding, weathered slopes, narrow black gullies, a thousand openings in a maze of broken stone—these Duane had to descend in fast time, leading a giant of a horse. Bullet cracked the loose fragments, sent them rolling, slid on the scaly slopes, plunged down the steps, followed like a faithful dog at Duane's heels.

Hours passed as moments. Duane was equal to his great opportunity. But he could not quell that self in him which reached back over the lapse of lonely, searing years and found the boy in him. He who had been worse than dead was now grasping at the skirts of life—which meant victory, honor, happiness. Duane knew he was not just right in part of his mind. Small wonder that he was not insane, he thought! He tramped on downward, his marvelous faculty for covering rough ground and holding to the true course never before even in flight so keen and acute. Yet all the time a spirit was keeping step with him. Thought of Ray Longstreth as he had left her made him weak. But now, with the game clear to its end, with the trap to spring, with success strangely haunting him, Duane could not dispel memory of her. He saw her white face, with its sweet sad lips and the dark eyes so tender and tragic. And time and distance and risk and toil were nothing.

The moon sloped to the west. Shadows of trees and crags now crossed to the other side of him. The stars dimmed. Then he was out of the rocks, with the dim trail pale at his feet. Mounting Bullet, he made short work of the long slope and the foothills and the rolling land leading down to Ord. The little outlaw camp, with its shacks and cabins and row of houses, lay silent and dark under the paling moon. Duane passed by on the lower trail, headed into the road, and put Bullet to a gallop. He watched the dying moon, the waning stars, and the east. He had time to spare, so he saved the horse. Knell would be leaving the rendezvous about the time Duane turned back toward Ord. Between noon and sunset they would meet.

The night wore on. The moon sank behind low mountains in the west. The stars brightened for a while, then faded. Gray gloom enveloped the world, thickened, lay like smoke over the road. Then shade by shade it lightened, until through the transparent obscurity shone a dim light.

Duane reached Bradford before dawn. He dismounted some distance from the tracks, tied his horse, and then crossed over to the station. He heard the clicking of the telegraph instrument, and it thrilled him. An operator sat inside reading. When Duane tapped on the window he looked up with startled glance, then went swiftly to unlock the door.

'Hello. Give me paper and pencil. Quick,' whispered Duane.

With trembling hands the operator complied. Duane wrote out the message he had carefully composed.

'Send this—repeat it to make sure—then keep mum. I'll see you again. Good-by.'

The operator stared, but did not speak a word.

Duane left as stealthily and swiftly as he had come. He walked his horse a couple of miles back on the road and then rested him till break of day. The east began to redden, Duane turned grimly in the direction of Ord.

When Duane swung into the wide, grassy square on the outskirts of Ord he saw a bunch of saddled horses hitched in front of the tavern. He knew what that meant. Luck still favored him. If it would only hold! But he could ask no more. The rest was a matter of how greatly he could make his power felt. An open conflict against odds lay in the balance. That would be fatal to him, and to avoid it he had to trust to his name and a presence he must make terrible. He knew outlaws. He knew what qualities held them. He knew what to exaggerate.

There was not an outlaw in sight. The dusty horses had covered distance that morning. As Duane dismounted he heard loud, angry voices inside the tavern. He removed coat and vest, hung them over the pommel. He packed two guns, one belted high on the left hip, the other swinging low on the right side. He neither looked nor listened, but boldly pushed the door and stepped inside.

The big room was full of men, and every face pivoted toward him. Knell's pale face flashed into Duane's swift sight; then Boldt's, then Blossom Kane's, then Panhandle Smith's, then Fletcher's, then others that were familiar, and last that of Poggin. Though Duane had never seen Poggin or heard him described, he knew him. For he saw a face that was a record of great and evil deeds.

There was absolute silence. The outlaws were lined back of a long table upon which were papers, stacks of silver coin, a bundle of bills, and a huge gold-mounted gun.

'Are you gents lookin' for me?' asked Duane. He gave his voice all the ringing force and power of which he was capable. And he stepped back, free of anything, with the outlaws all before him.

Knell stood, quivering, but his face might have been a mask. The other outlaws looked from him to Duane. Jim Fletcher flung up his hands.

'My Gawd, Dodge, what'd you bust in here fer?' he said, plaintively, and slowly stepped forward. His action was that of a man true to himself. He meant he had been sponsor for Duane and now he would stand by him.

'Back, Fletcher!' called Duane, and his voice made the outlaw jump.

'Hold on, Dodge, an' you-all, everybody,' said Fletcher. 'Let me talk, seein' I'm in wrong here.'

His persuasions did not ease the strain.

'Go ahead. Talk,' said Poggin.

Fletcher turned to Duane. 'Pard, I'm takin' it on myself thet you meet enemies here when I swore you'd meet friends. It's my fault. I'll stand by you if you let me.'

'No, Jim,' replied Duane.

'But what'd you come fer without the signal?' burst out Fletcher, in distress. He saw nothing but catastrophe in this meeting.

'Jim, I ain't pressin' my company none. But when I'm wanted bad—'

Fletcher stopped him with a raised hand. Then he turned to Poggin with a rude dignity.

'Poggy, he's my pard, an' he's riled. I never told him a word thet'd make him sore. I only said Knell hadn't no more use fer him than fer me. Now, what you say goes in this gang. I never failed you in my life. Here's my pard. I vouch fer him. Will you stand fer me? There's goin' to be hell if you don't. An' us with a big job on hand!'

While Fletcher toiled over his slow, earnest persuasion Duane had his gaze riveted upon Poggin. There was something leonine about Poggin. He was tawny. He blazed. He seemed beautiful as fire was beautiful. But looked at closer, with glance seeing the physical man, instead of that thing which shone from him, he was of perfect build, with muscles that swelled and rippled, bulging his clothes, with the magnificent head and face of the cruel, fierce, tawny-eyed jaguar.

Looking at this strange Poggin, instinctively divining his abnormal and hideous power, Duane had for the first time in his life the inward quaking fear of a man. It was like a cold-tongued bell ringing within him and numbing his heart. The old instinctive firing of blood followed, but did not drive away that fear. He knew. He felt something here deeper than thought could go. And he hated Poggin.

That individual had been considering Fletcher's appeal.

'Jim, I ante up,' he said, 'an' if Phil doesn't raise us out with a big hand—why, he'll get called, an' your pard can set in the game.'

Every eye shifted to Knell. He was dead white. He laughed, and any one hearing that laugh would have realized his intense anger equally with an assurance which made him master of the situation.

'Poggin, you're a gambler, you are—the ace-high, straight-flush hand of the Big Bend,' he said, with stinging scorn. 'I'll bet you my roll to a greaser peso that I can deal you a hand you'll be afraid to play.'

'Phil, you're talkin' wild,' growled Poggin, with both advice and menace in his tone.

'If there's anything' you hate it's a man who pretends to be somebody else when he's not. Thet so?'

Poggin nodded in slow-gathering wrath.

'Well, Jim's new pard—this man Dodge—he's not who he seems. Oh-ho! He's a hell of a lot different. But *I* know him. An' when I spring his name on you, Poggin, you'll freeze to your gizzard. Do you get me? You'll freeze, an' your hand'll be stiff when it ought to be lightnin'—All because you'll realize you've been standin' there five minutes—five minutes *alive* before him!'

If not hate, then assuredly great passion toward Poggin manifested itself in Knell's scornful, fiery address, in the shaking hand he thrust before Poggin's face. In the ensuing silent pause Knell's panting could be plainly heard. The other men were pale, watchful, cautiously edging either way to the wall, leaving the principals and Duane in the center of the room.

'Spring his name, then, you—' said Poggin, violently, with a curse.

Strangely Knell did not even look at the man he was about to denounce. He leaned toward Poggin, his hands, his body, his long head all somewhat expressive of what his face disguised.

'*Buck Duane!*' he yelled, suddenly.

The name did not make any great difference in Poggin. But Knell's passionate, swift utterance carried the suggestion that the name ought to bring Poggin to quick action. It was possible, too, that Knell's manner, the import of his denunciation, the meaning back of all his passion held Poggin bound more than the surprise. For the outlaw certainly was surprised, perhaps staggered at the idea that he, Poggin, had been about to stand sponsor with Fletcher for a famous outlaw hated and feared by all outlaws.

Knell waited a long moment, and then his face broke to its cold immobility in an extraordinary expression of devilish glee. He had hounded the great Poggin into something that gave him vicious, monstrous joy.

'BUCK DUANE! Yes,' he broke out, hotly. 'The Nueces gunman! That two-shot, ace-of-spades lone wolf! You an' I—we've heard a thousand times of him—talked about him often. An' here he is *in front* of you! Poggin, you were backin' Fletcher's new pard, Buck Duane. An' he'd fooled you both but for me. But *I* know him. An' I know why he drifted in here. To flash a gun on Cheseldine—on you—on me! Bah! Don't tell me he wanted to join the gang. You know a gunman, for you're one yourself. Don't you always want to kill another man? An' don't you always want to meet a real man, not a four-flush? It's the madness of the gunman, an' I know it. Well, Duane faced you—called you! An' when I sprung his name, what ought you have done? What would the boss—anybody—have expected of Poggin? Did you throw your gun, swift, like you have so often? Naw: you froze. An' why? Because here's a man with the kind of nerve you'd love to have. Because he's great—meetin' us here alone. Because you know he's a wonder with a gun an' you love life. Because you an' I an' every damned man here had to take his front, each to himself. If we all drew we'd kill him. Sure! But who's goin' to lead? Who was goin' to be first? Who was goin' to make him draw? Not you, Poggin! You leave that for a lesser man—me—who've lived to see you a coward. It comes once to every gunman. You've met your match in Buck Duane. An', by God, I'm glad! Here's once I show you up!'

The hoarse, taunting voice failed. Knell stepped back from the comrade he hated. He was wet, shaking, haggard, but magnificent.

'Buck Duane, do you remember Hardin?' he asked, in scarcely audible voice.

'Yes,' replied Duane, and a flash of insight made clear Knell's attitude.

'You met him—forced him to draw—killed him?'

'Yes.'

'Hardin was the best pard I ever had.'

His teeth clicked together tight, and his lips set in a thin line.

The room grew still. Even breathing ceased. The time for words had passed. In that long moment of suspense Knell's body gradually stiffened, and at last the quivering ceased. He crouched. His eyes had a soul-piercing fire.

Duane watched them. He waited. He caught the thought—the breaking of Knell's muscle-bound rigidity. Then he drew.

Through the smoke of his gun he saw two red spurts of flame. Knell's bullets thudded into the ceiling. He fell with a scream like a wild thing in agony.

Duane did not see Knell die. He watched Poggin. And Poggin, like a stricken and astounded man, looked down upon his prostrate comrade.

Fletcher ran at Duane with hands aloft.

'Hit the trail, you liar, or you'll hev to kill me!' he yelled.

With hands still up, he shouldered and bodied Duane out of the room.

Duane leaped on his horse, spurred, and plunged away.

23

Duane returned to Fairdale and camped in the mesquite till the twenty-third of the month. The few days seemed endless. All he could think of was that the hour in which he must disgrace Ray Longstreth was slowly but inexorably coming. In that waiting time he learned what love was and also duty. When the day at last dawned he rode like one possessed down the rough slope, hurdling the stones and crashing through the brush, with a sound in his ears that was not all the rush of the wind. Something dragged at him.

Apparently one side of his mind was unalterably fixed, while the other was a hurrying conglomeration of flashes of thought, reception of sensation. He could not get calmness. By and by, almost involuntarily, he hurried faster on. Action seemed to make his state less oppressive; it eased the weight. But the farther he went on the harder it was to continue. Had he turned his back upon love, happiness, perhaps on life itself?

There seemed no use to go on farther until he was absolutely sure of himself. Duane received a clear warning thought that such work as seemed haunting and driving him could never be carried out in the mood under which he labored. He hung on to that thought. Several times he slowed up, then stopped, only to go on again. At length, as he mounted a low ridge, Fairdale lay bright and green before him not far away, and the sight was a conclusive check. There were mesquites on the ridge, and Duane sought the shade beneath them. It was the noon-hour, with hot, glary sun and no wind. Here Duane had to have out his fight. Duane was utterly unlike himself; he could not bring the old self back; he was not the same man he once had been. But he could understand why. It was because of Ray Longstreth. Temptation assailed him. To have her his wife! It was impossible. The thought was insidiously alluring. Duane pictured a home. He saw himself riding through the cotton and rice and cane, home to a stately old mansion, where long-eared hounds bayed him welcome, and a woman looked for him and met him with happy and beautiful smile. There might—there would be children. And something new, strange, confounding with its emotion, came to life deep in Duane's heart. There would be children! Ray their mother! The kind of life a lonely outcast always yearned for and never had! He saw it all, felt it all.

But beyond and above all other claims came Captain MacNelly's. It was then there was something cold and death-like in Duane's soul. For he knew, whatever happened, of one thing he was sure—he would have to kill either Longstreth or Lawson. Longstreth might be trapped into arrest; but Lawson had no sense, no control, no fear. He would snarl like a panther and go for his gun, and he would have to be killed. This, of all consummations, was the one to be calculated upon.

Duane came out of it all bitter and callous and sore—in the most fitting of moods to undertake a difficult and deadly enterprise. He had fallen upon his old strange, futile dreams, now rendered poignant by reason of love. He drove away those dreams. In their places came the images of the olive–skinned Longstreth with his sharp eyes, and the dark, evil-faced Lawson, and then returned tenfold more thrilling and sinister the old strange passion to meet Poggin.

It was about one o'clock when Duane rode into Fairdale. The streets for the most part were deserted. He went directly to find Morton and Zimmer. He found them at length, restless, somber, anxious, but unaware of the part he had played at Ord. They said Longstreth was home, too. It was possible that Longstreth had arrived home in ignorance.

Duane told them to be on hand in town with their men in case he might need them, and then with teeth locked he set off for Longstreth's ranch.

Duane stole through the bushes and trees, and when nearing the porch he heard loud, angry, familiar voices. Longstreth and Lawson were quarreling again. How Duane's lucky star guided him! He had no plan of action, but his brain was equal to a hundred lightning-swift evolutions. He meant to take any risk rather than kill Longstreth. Both of the men were out on the porch. Duane wormed his way to the edge of the shrubbery and crouched low to watch for his opportunity.

Longstreth looked haggard and thin. He was in his shirtsleeves, and he had come out with a gun in his hand. This he laid on a table near the wall. He wore no belt.

Lawson was red, bloated, thick-lipped, all fiery and sweaty from drink, though sober on the moment, and he had the expression of a desperate man in his last stand. It was his last stand, though he was ignorant of that.

'What's your news? You needn't be afraid of my feelings,' said Lawson.

'Ray confessed to an interest in this ranger,' replied Longstreth.

Duane thought Lawson would choke. He was thick-necked anyway, and the rush of blood made him tear at the soft collar of his shirt. Duane awaited his chance, patient, cold, all his feelings shut in a vise.

'But *why* should your daughter meet this ranger?' demanded Lawson, harshly. 'She's in love with him, and he's in love with her.'

Duane reveled in Lawson's condition. The statement might have had the force of a juggernaut. Was Longstreth sincere? What was his game?

Lawson, finding his voice, cursed Ray, cursed the ranger, then Longstreth.

'You damned selfish fool!' cried Longstreth, in deep bitter scorn. 'All you think of is yourself—your loss of the girl. Think once of *me*—my home—my life!'

Then the connection subtly put out by Longstreth apparently dawned upon the other. Somehow through this girl her father and cousin were to be betrayed. Duane got that impression, though he could not tell how true it was. Certainly Lawson's jealousy was his paramount emotion.

'To hell with you!' burst Lawson, incoherently. He was frenzied. 'I'll have her, or nobody else will!'

'You never will,' returned Longstreth, stridently. 'So help me God I'd rather see her the ranger's wife than yours!'

While Lawson absorbed that shock Longstreth leaned toward him, all of hate and menace in his mien.

'Lawson, you made me what I am,' continued Longstreth. 'I backed you— shielded you. *You're* Cheseldine—if the truth is told! Now it's ended. I quit you. I'm done!'

Their gray passion-corded faces were still as stones.

'*Gentlemen*!' Duane called in far-reaching voice as he stepped out. '*You're both done*!'

They wheeled to confront Duane.

'Don't move! Not a muscle! Not a finger!' he warned.

Longstreth read what Lawson had not the mind to read. His face turned from gray to ashen.

'What d'ye mean?' yelled Lawson, fiercely, shrilly. It was not in him to obey a command, to see impending death.

All quivering and strung, yet with perfect control, Duane raised his left hand to turn back a lapel of his open vest. The silver star flashed brightly.

Lawson howled like a dog. With barbarous and insane fury, with sheer impotent folly, he swept a clawing hand for his gun. Duane's shot broke his action.

Before Lawson ever tottered, before he loosed the gun, Longstreth leaped behind him, clasped him with left arm, quick as lightning jerked the gun from both clutching fingers and sheath. Longstreth protected himself with the body of the dead man. Duane saw red flashes, puffs of smoke; he heard quick reports.

Something stung his left arm. Then a blow like wind, light of sound yet shocking in impact, struck him, staggered him. The hot rend of lead followed the blow. Duane's heart seemed to explode, yet his mind kept extraordinarily clear and rapid.

Duane heard Longstreth work the action of Lawson's gun. He heard the hammer click, fall upon empty shells. Longstreth had used up all the loads in Lawson's gun. He cursed as a man cursed at defeat. Duane waited, cool and sure now. Longstreth tried to lift the dead man, to edge him closer toward the table where his own gun lay. But, considering the peril of exposing himself, he found the task beyond him. He bent peering at Duane under Lawson's arm, which flopped out from his side. Longstreth's eyes were the eyes of a man who meant to kill. There was never any mistaking the strange and terrible light of eyes like those. More than once Duane had a chance to aim at them, at the top of Longstreth's head, at a strip of his side.

Longstreth flung Lawson's body off. But even as it dropped, before Longstreth could leap, as he surely intended, for the gun, Duane covered him, called piercingly to him:

'Don't jump for the gun! Don't! I'll kill you! Sure as God I'll kill you!'

Longstreth stood perhaps ten feet from the table where his gun lay. Duane saw him calculating chances. He was game. He had the courage that forced Duane to respect him. Duane just saw him measure the distance to that gun. He was magnificent. He meant to do it. Duane would have to kill him.

'Longstreth, listen,' cried Duane, swiftly. 'The game's up. You're done. But think of your daughter! I'll spare your life—I'll try to get you freedom on one condition. For her sake! I've got you nailed—all the proofs. There lies Lawson. You're alone. I've Morton and men to my aid. Give up. Surrender. Consent to demands, and I'll spare you. Maybe I can persuade MacNelly to let you go free back to your old country. It's for Ray's sake! Her life, perhaps her happiness, can be saved! Hurry, man! Your answer!'

'Suppose I refuse?' he queried, with a dark and terrible earnestness.

'Then I'll kill you in your tracks! You can't move a hand! Your word or death! Hurry, Longstreth! Be a man! For her sake! Quick! Another second now—I'll kill you!'

'All right, Buck Duane, I give my word,' he said, and deliberately walked to the chair and fell into it.

Longstreth looked strangely at the bloody blot on Duane's shoulder.

'There come the girls!' he suddenly exclaimed. 'Can you help me drag Lawson inside? They mustn't see him.'

Duane was facing down the porch toward the court and corrals. Miss Longstreth and Ruth had come in sight, were swiftly approaching, evidently alarmed. The two men succeeded in drawing Lawson into the house before the girls saw him.

'Duane, you're not hard hit?' said Longstreth.

'Reckon not,' replied Duane.

'I'm sorry. If only you could have told me sooner! Lawson damn him! Always I've split over him!'

'But the last time, Longstreth.'

'Yes, and I came near driving you to kill me, too. Duane, you talked me out of it. For Ray's sake! She'll be in here in a minute. This'll be harder than facing a gun.'

'Hard now. But I hope it'll turn out all right.'

'Duane, will you do me a favor?' he asked, and he seemed shamefaced.

'Sure.'

'Let Ray and Ruth think Lawson shot you. He's dead. It can't matter. Duane, the old side of my life is coming back. It's been coming. It'll be here just about when she enters this room. And, by God, I'd change places with Lawson if I could!'

'Glad you—said that, Longstreth,' replied Duane. 'And sure—Lawson plugged me. It's our secret.'

Just then Ray and Ruth entered the room. Duane heard two low cries, so different in tone, and he saw two white faces. Ray came to his side. She lifted a shaking hand to point at the blood upon his breast. White and mute, she gazed from that to her father.

'Papa!' cried Ray, wringing her hands.

'Don't give way,' he replied, huskily. 'Both you girls will need your nerve. Duane isn't badly hurt. But Floyd is—is dead. Listen. Let me tell it quick. There's been a fight. It—it was Lawson—it was Lawson's gun that shot Duane. Duane let me off. In fact, Ray, he saved me. I'm to divide my property—return so far as possible what I've stolen—leave Texas at once with Duane, under arrest. He says maybe he can get MacNelly, the ranger captain, to let me go. For your sake!'

She stood there, realizing her deliverance, with the dark and tragic glory of her eyes passing from her father to Duane.

'You must rise above this,' said Duane to her. 'I expected this to ruin you. But your father is alive. He will live it down. I'm sure I can promise you he'll be free. Perhaps back there in Louisiana the dishonor will never be known. This country is far from your old home. And even in San Antonio and Austin a man's evil repute means little. Then the line between a rustler and a rancher is hard to draw in these wild border days. Rustling is stealing cattle, and I once heard a well-known rancher say that all rich cattlemen had done a little stealing. Your father drifted out here, and, like a good many others, he succeeded. It's perhaps just as well not to split hairs, to judge by the law and morality of a civilized country. Some way or other he drifted in with bad men. Maybe a deal that was honest somehow tied his hands. This matter of land, water, a few stray head of stock had to be decided out of court. I'm sure in his case he never realized where he was drifting. Then one thing led to another, until he was face to face with dealing that took on a crooked form. To protect himself he bound men to him. And so the gang developed. Many powerful gangs have developed that way out here. He could not control them. He became involved with them. And eventually their dealings became deliberately and boldly dishonest. That meant the inevitable spilling of blood sooner or later, and so he grew into the leader because he was the strongest. Whatever he is to be judged for, I think he could have been infinitely worse.'

24

On the morning of the twenty-sixth Duane rode into Bradford in time to catch the early train. His wounds did not seriously incapacitate him. Longstreth was with him. And Miss Longstreth and Ruth Herbert would not be left behind. They were all leaving Fairdale for ever. Longstreth had turned over the whole of his property to Morton, who was to divide it as he and his comrades believed just. Duane had left Fairdale with his party by night, passed through Sanderson in the early hours of dawn, and reached Bradford as he had planned.

That fateful morning found Duane outwardly calm, but inwardly he was in a tumult. He wanted to rush to Val Verde. Would Captain MacNelly be there with his rangers, as Duane had planned for them to be? Memory of that tawny Poggin returned with strange passion. Duane had borne hours and weeks and months of waiting, had endured the long hours of the outlaw, but now he had no patience. The whistle of the train made him leap.

It was a fast train, yet the ride seemed slow.

Duane, disliking to face Longstreth and the passengers in the car, changed his seat to one behind his prisoner. They had seldom spoken. Longstreth sat with bowed head, deep in thought. The girls sat in a seat near by and were pale but composed. Occasionally the train halted briefly at a station. The latter half of that ride Duane had observed a wagon-road running parallel with the railroad, sometimes right alongside, at others near or far away. When the train was about twenty miles from Val Verde Duane espied a dark group of horsemen trotting eastward.

His blood beat like a hammer at his temples. The gang! He thought he recognized the tawny Poggin and felt a strange inward contraction.

He thought he recognized the clean-cut Blossom Kane, the black-bearded giant Boldt, the red-faced Panhandle Smith, and Fletcher. There was another man strange to him. Was that Knell? No! it could not have been Knell.

Duane leaned over the seat and touched Longstreth on the shoulder.

'Look!' he whispered. Cheseldine was stiff. He had already seen.

The train flashed by; the outlaw gang receded out of range of sight.

'Did you notice Knell wasn't with them?' whispered Duane.

Duane did not speak to Longstreth again till the train stopped at Val Verde.

They got off the car, and the girls followed as naturally as ordinary travelers. The station was a good deal larger than that at Bradford, and there was considerable action and bustle incident to the arrival of the train.

Duane's sweeping gaze searched faces, rested upon a man who seemed familiar. This fellow's look, too, was that of one who knew Duane, but was waiting for a sign, a cue. Then Duane recognized him—MacNelly, clean-shaven. Without mustache he appeared different, younger.

When MacNelly saw that Duane intended to greet him, to meet him, he hurried forward. A keen light flashed from his eyes. He was glad, eager, yet suppressing himself, and the glances he sent back and forth from Duane to Longstreth were questioning, doubtful. Certainly Longstreth did not look the part of an outlaw.

'Duane! Lord, I'm glad to see you,' was the Captain's greeting. Then at closer look into Duane's face his warmth fled—something he saw there checked his enthusiasm, or at least its utterance.

'MacNelly, shake hand with Cheseldine,' said Duane, low-voiced.

The ranger captain stood dumb, motionless. But he saw Longstreth's instant action, and awkwardly he reached for the outstretched hand.

'Any of your men down here?' queried Duane, sharply.

'No. They're up-town.'

'Come. MacNelly, you walk with him. We've ladies in the party. I'll come behind with them.'

They set off up-town. Longstreth walked as if he were with friends on the way to dinner. The girls were mute. MacNelly walked like a man in a trance. There was not a word spoken in four blocks.

Presently Duane espied a stone building on a corner of the broad street. There was a big sign, 'Rancher's Bank.'

'There's the hotel,' said MacNelly. 'Some of my men are there. We've scattered around.'

They crossed the street, went through office and lobby, and then Duane asked MacNelly to take them to a private room. Without a word the Captain complied.

When they were all inside Duane closed the door, and, drawing a deep breath as if of relief, he faced them calmly.

'Miss Longstreth, you and Miss Ruth try to make yourselves comfortable now,' he said. 'And don't be distressed.' Then he turned to his captain. 'MacNelly, this girl is the daughter of the man I've brought to you, and this one is his niece.'

Then Duane briefly related Longstreth's story, and, though he did not spare the rustler chief, he was generous.

'When I went after Longstreth,' concluded Duane, 'it was either to kill him or offer him freedom on conditions. So I chose the latter for his daughter's sake. He has already disposed of all his property. I believe he'll live up to the conditions. He's to leave Texas never to return. The name Cheseldine has been a mystery, and now it'll fade.'

A few moments later Duane followed MacNelly to a large room, like a hall, and here were men reading and smoking. Duane knew them—rangers!

MacNelly beckoned to his men.

'Boys, here he is.'

'How many men have you?' asked Duane.

'Fifteen.'

MacNelly almost embraced Duane, would probably have done so but for the dark grimness that seemed to be coming over the man. Instead he glowed, he sputtered, he tried to talk, to wave his hands. He was beside himself. And his rangers crowded closer, eager, like hounds ready to run. They all talked at once, and the word most significant and frequent in their speech was 'outlaws.'

MacNelly clapped his fist in his hand.

'This'll make the adjutant sick with joy. Maybe we won't have it on the Governor! We'll show them about the ranger service. Duane! how'd you ever do it?'

'Now, Captain, not the half nor the quarter of this job's done. The gang's coming down the road. I saw them from the train. They'll ride into town on the dot—two-thirty.'

'How many?' asked MacNelly.

'Poggin, Blossom Kane, Panhandle Smith, Boldt, Jim Fletcher, and another man I don't know. These are the picked men of Cheseldine's gang. I'll bet they'll be the fastest, hardest bunch you rangers ever faced.'

'Poggin—that's the hard nut to crack! I've heard their records since I've been in Val Verde. Where's Knell? They say he's a boy, but hell and blazes!'

'Knell's dead.'

'Ah!' exclaimed MacNelly, softly. Then he grew businesslike, cool, and of harder aspect. 'Duane, it's your game today. I'm only a ranger under orders. We're all under your orders. We've absolute faith in you. Make your plan quick, so I can go around and post the boys who're not here.'

'You understand there's no sense in trying to arrest Poggin, Kane, and that lot?' queried Duane.

'No, I don't understand that,' replied MacNelly, bluntly.

'It can't be done. The drop can't be got on such men. If you meet them they shoot, and mighty quick and straight. Poggin! That outlaw has no equal with a gun—unless—He's got to be killed quick. They'll all have to be killed. They're all bad, desperate, know no fear, are lightning in action.'

'Very well, Duane; then it's a fight. That'll be easier, perhaps. The boys are spoiling for a fight. Out with your plan, now.'

'Put one man at each end of this street, just at the edge of town. Let him hide there with a rifle to block the escape of any outlaw that we might fail to get. I had a good look at the bank building. It's well situated for our purpose. Put four men up in that room over the bank—four men, two at each open window. Let them hide till the game begins. They want to be there so in case these foxy outlaws get wise before they're down on the ground or inside the bank. The rest of your men put inside behind the counters, where they'll hide. Now go over to the bank, spring the thing on the bank officials and don't let them shut up the bank. You want their aid. Let them make sure of their gold. But the clerks and cashier ought to be at their desks or window when Poggin rides up. He'll glance in before he gets down. They make no mistakes, these fellows. We must be slicker than they are, or lose. When you get the bank people wise, send your men over one by one. No hurry, no excitement, no unusual thing to attract notice in the bank.'

'All right. That's great. Tell me, where do you intend to wait?'

Duane heard MacNelly's question, and it struck him peculiarly. He had seemed to be planning and speaking mechanically. As he was confronted by the fact it nonplussed him somewhat, and he became thoughtful, with lowered head.

'Where'll you wait, Duane?' insisted MacNelly, with keen eyes speculating.

'I'll wait in front—just inside the door,' replied Duane, with an effort.

'Why?' demanded the Captain.

'Well,' began Duane, slowly, 'Poggin will get down first and start in. But the others won't be far behind. They'll not get swift till inside. The thing is—they *mustn't* get clear inside, because the instant they do they'll pull guns. That means death to somebody. If we can we want to stop them just at the door.'

'But will you hide?' asked MacNelly.

'Hide!' The idea had not occurred to Duane.

'There's a wide-open doorway, a sort of round hall, a vestibule, with steps leading up to the bank. There's a door in the vestibule, too. It leads somewhere. We can put men in there. You can be there.'

Duane was silent.

'See here, Duane,' began MacNelly, nervously. 'You sha'n't take any undue risk here. You'll hide with the rest of us?'

'No!' The word was wrenched from Duane.

MacNelly stared, and then a strange, comprehending light seemed to flit over his face.

'Duane, I can give you no orders to-day,' he said, distinctly. 'I'm only offering advice. Need you take any more risks? You've done a grand job for the service—already. You've paid me a thousand times for that pardon. You've redeemed yourself. The Governor, the adjutant-general—the whole state will rise up and honor you. The game's almost up. We'll kill these outlaws, or enough of them to break for ever their power. I say, as a ranger, need you take more risk than your captain?'

Still Duane remained silent. He was locked between two forces. And one, a tide that was bursting at its bounds, seemed about to overwhelm him. Finally that side of him, the retreating self, the weaker, found a voice.

'Captain, you want this job to be sure?' he asked.

'Certainly.'

'I've told you the way. I alone know the kind of men to be met. Just *what* I'll do or *where* I'll be I can't say yet. In meetings like this the moment decides. But I'll be there!'

MacNelly spread wide his hands, looked helplessly at his curious and sympathetic rangers, and shook his head.

'Now, you've done your work—laid the trap—is this strange move of yours going to be fair to Miss Longstreth?' asked MacNelly, in significant low voice.

Like a great tree chopped at the roots Duane vibrated to that. He looked up as if he had seen a ghost.

Mercilessly the ranger captain went on: 'You can win her, Duane! Oh, you can't fool me. I was wise in a minute. Fight with us from cover—then go back to her. You will have served the Texas Rangers as no other man has. I'll accept your resignation. You'll be free, honored, happy. That girl loves you! I saw it in her eyes. She's—'

But Duane cut him short with a fierce gesture. He lunged up to his feet, and the rangers fell back. Dark, silent, grim as he had been, still there was a transformation singularly more sinister, stranger.

'Enough. I'm done,' he said, somberly. 'I've planned. Do we agree—or shall I meet Poggin and his gang alone?'

MacNelly cursed and again threw up his hands, this time in baffled chagrin. There was deep regret in his dark eyes as they rested upon Duane.

Duane was left alone.

Never had his mind been so quick, so clear, so wonderful in its understanding of what had heretofore been intricate and elusive impulses of his strange nature. His determination was to meet Poggin; meet him before any one else had a chance—Poggin first—and then the others! He was as unalterable in that decision as if on the instant of its acceptance he had become stone.

Why? Then came realization. He was not a ranger now. He cared nothing for the state. He had no thought of freeing the community of a dangerous outlaw, of ridding the country of an obstacle to its progress and prosperity. He wanted to kill Poggin. It was significant now that he forgot the other outlaws. He was the gunman, the gun-thrower, the gun-fighter, passionate and terrible. His father's blood, that dark and fierce strain, his mother's spirit, that strong and unquenchable spirit of the surviving pioneer—these had been in him; and the killings, one after another, the wild and haunted years had made him, absolutely in spite of his will, the gunman. He realized it now, bitterly, hopelessly. The thing he had intelligence enough to hate he had become. At last he shuddered under the driving, ruthless, inhuman blood-lust of the gunman. Long ago he had seemed to seal in a tomb that horror of his kind—the need, in order to forget the haunting, sleepless presence of his last victim, to go out and kill another. But it was still there in his mind, and now it stalked out, worse, more powerful, magnified by its rest, augmented by the violent passions peculiar and inevitable to that strange, wild product of the Texas frontier—the gun-fighter. And those passions were so violent, so raw, so base, so much lower than what ought to have existed in a thinking man. Actual pride of his record! Actual vanity in his speed with a gun! Actual jealousy of any rival!

Duane could not believe it. But there he was, without a choice. What he had feared for years had become a monstrous reality. Respect for himself, blindness, a certain honor that he had clung to while in outlawry—all, like scales, seemed to fall away from him. He stood stripped bare, his soul naked—the soul of Cain. Always since the first brand had been forced and burned upon him he had been ruined. But now with conscience flayed to the quick, yet utterly powerless over this tiger instinct, he was lost. He said it. He admitted it. And at the utter abasement the soul he despised suddenly leaped and quivered with the thought of Ray Longstreth.

Then came agony. As he could not govern all the chances of this fatal meeting—as all his swift and deadly genius must be occupied with Poggin, perhaps in vain—as hard-shooting men whom he could not watch would be close behind, this almost certainly must be the end of Buck Duane. That did not matter. But he loved the girl. He wanted her. All her sweetness, her fire, and pleading returned to torture him.

At that moment the door opened, and Ray Longstreth entered.

'Duane,' she said, softly. 'Captain MacNelly sent me to you.'

'But you shouldn't have come,' replied Duane.

'As soon as he told me I would have come whether he wished it or not. You left me—all of us—stunned. I had no time to thank you. Oh, I do—with all my soul. It was noble of you. Father is overcome. He didn't expect so much. And he'll be true. But, Duane, I was told to hurry, and here I'm selfishly using time.'

'Go, then—and leave me. You mustn't unnerve me now, when there's a desperate game to finish.'

'Need it be desperate?' she whispered, coming close to him.

'Yes; it can't be else.'

MacNelly had sent her to weaken him; of that Duane was sure. And he felt that she had wanted to come. Her eyes were dark, strained, beautiful, and they shed a light upon Duane he had never seen before.

'You're going to take some mad risk,' she said. 'Let me persuade you not to. You said—you cared for me—and I—oh, Duane—don't you—know—?'

The low voice, deep, sweet as an old chord, faltered and broke and failed.

Duane sustained a sudden shock and an instant of paralyzed confusion of thought.

She moved, she swept out her hands, and the wonder of her eyes dimmed in a flood of tears.

'My God! You can't care for me?' he cried, hoarsely.

Then she met him, hands outstretched.

'But I do—I do!'

Swift as light Duane caught her and held her to his breast. He stood holding her tight, with the feel of her warm, throbbing breast and the clasp of her arms as flesh and blood realities to fight a terrible fear. He felt her, and for the moment the might of it was stronger than all the demons that possessed him. And he held her as if she had been his soul, his strength on earth, his hope of Heaven, against his lips.

The strife of doubt all passed. He found his sight again. And there rushed over him a tide of emotion unutterably sweet and full, strong like an intoxicating wine, deep as his nature, something glorious and terrible as the blaze of the sun to one long in darkness. He had become an outcast, a wanderer, a gunman, a victim of circumstances; he had lost and suffered worse than death in that loss; he had gone down the endless bloody trail, a killer of men, a fugitive whose mind slowly and inevitably closed to all except the instinct to survive and a black despair; and now, with this woman in his arms, her swelling breast against his, in this moment almost of resurrection, he bent under the storm of passion and joy possible only to him who had endured so much.

'Do you care—a little?' he whispered, unsteadily.

He bent over her, looking deep into the dark wet eyes.

She uttered a low laugh that was half sob, and her arms slipped up to his neck.

'A little! Oh, Duane—Duane—a great deal!'

Their lips met in their first kiss. The sweetness, the fire of her mouth seemed so new, so strange, so irresistible to Duane. His sore and hungry heart throbbed with thick and heavy beats. He felt the outcast's need of love. And he gave up to the enthralling moment. She met him half-way, returned kiss for kiss, clasp for clasp, her face scarlet, her eyes closed, till, her passion and strength spent, she fell back upon his shoulder.

Duane suddenly thought she was going to faint. He divined then that she had understood him, would have denied him nothing, not even her life, in that moment. But she was overcome, and he suffered a pang of regret at his unrestraint.

Presently she recovered, and she drew only the closer, and leaned upon him with her face upturned. He felt her hands on his, and they were soft, clinging, strong, like steel under velvet. He felt the rise and fall, the warmth of her breast. A tremor ran over him. He tried to draw back, and if he succeeded a little her form swayed with him, pressing closer. She held her face up, and he was compelled to look. It was wonderful now: white, yet glowing, with the red lips parted, and dark eyes alluring. But that was not all. There was passion, unquenchable spirit, woman's resolve deep and mighty.

'I love you, Duane!' she said. 'For my sake don't go out to meet this outlaw face to face. It's something wild in you. Conquer it if you love me.'

Duane became suddenly weak, and when he did take her into his arms again he scarcely had strength to lift her to a seat beside him. She seemed more than a dead weight. Her calmness had fled. She was throbbing, palpitating, quivering, with hot wet cheeks and arms that clung to him like vines. She lifted her mouth to his, whispering, 'Kiss me!' She meant to change him, hold him.

Duane bent down, and her arms went round his neck and drew him close. With his lips on hers he seemed to float away. That kiss closed his eyes, and he could not lift his head. He sat motionless holding her, blind and helpless, wrapped in a sweet dark glory. She kissed him—one long endless kiss—or else a thousand times. Her lips, her wet cheeks, her hair, the softness, the fragrance of her, the tender clasp of her arms, the swell of her breast—all these seemed to inclose him.

Duane could not put her from him. He yielded to her lips and arms, watching her, involuntarily returning her caresses, sure now of her intent, fascinated by the sweetness of her, bewildered, almost lost. This was what it was to be loved by a woman. His years of outlawry had blotted out any boyish love he might have known. This was what he had to give up—all this wonder of her sweet person, this strange fire he feared yet loved, this mate his deep and tortured soul recognized. Never until that moment had he divined the meaning of a woman to a man. That meaning was physical inasmuch that he learned what beauty was, what marvel in the touch of quickening flesh; and it was spiritual in that what he saw there might have been for him, under happier circumstances, a life of noble deeds lived for such a woman.

'Don't go! Don't go!' she cried, as he started violently.

'I must. Dear, good-by! Remember I loved you!'

He pulled her hands loose from his, stepped back.

'Ray, dearest—I believe—I'll come back!' he whispered.

These last words were falsehood.

He reached the door, gave her one last piercing glance, to fix for ever in memory that white face with its dark, staring, tragic eyes.

'*Duane!*'

He fled with that moan like thunder, death, hell in his ears.

To forget her, to get back his nerve, he forced into mind the image of Poggin—Poggin, the tawny-haired, the yellow-eyed, like a jaguar, with his rippling muscles. He brought back his sense of the outlaw's wonderful presence, his own unaccountable fear and hate. Yes, Poggin had sent the cold sickness of fear to his marrow. Why, since he hated life so? Poggin was his supreme test. And this abnormal and stupendous instinct, now deep as the very foundation of his life, demanded its wild and fatal issue. There was a horrible thrill in his sudden remembrance that Poggin likewise had been taunted in fear of him.

So the dark tide overwhelmed Duane, and when he left the room he was fierce, implacable, steeled to any outcome, quick like a panther, somber as death, in the thrall of his strange passion.

There was no excitement in the street. He crossed to the bank corner. A clock inside pointed the hour of two. He went through the door into the vestibule, looked around, passed up the steps into the bank. The clerks were at their desks, apparently busy. But they showed nervousness. The cashier paled at sight of Duane. There were men—the rangers—crouching down behind the low partition. All the windows had been removed from the iron grating before the desks. The safe was closed. There was no money in sight. A customer came in, spoke to the cashier, and was told to come to-morrow.

Duane returned to the door. He could see far down the street, out into the country. There he waited, and minutes were eternities. He saw no person near him; he heard no sound. He was insulated in his unnatural strain.

At a few minutes before half past two a dark, compact body of horsemen appeared far down, turning into the road. They came at a sharp trot—a group that would have attracted attention anywhere at any time. They came a little faster as they entered town; then faster still; now they were four blocks away, now three, now two. Duane backed down the middle of the vestibule, up the steps, and halted in the center of the wide doorway.

There seemed to be a rushing in his ears through which pierced sharp, ringing clip-clop of iron hoofs. He could see only the corner of the street. But suddenly into that shot lean-limbed dusty bay horses. There was a clattering of nervous hoofs pulled to a halt.

Duane saw the tawny Poggin speak to his companions. He dismounted quickly. They followed suit. They had the manner of ranchers about to conduct some business. No guns showed. Poggin started leisurely for the bank door, quickening step a little. The others, close together, came behind him. Blossom Kane had a bag in his left hand. Jim Fletcher was left at the curb, and he had already gathered up the bridles.

Poggin entered the vestibule first, with Kane on one side, Boldt on the other, a little in his rear.

As he strode in he saw Duane.

'*Hell's Fire!*' he cried.

Something inside Duane burst, piercing all of him with cold. Was it that fear? 'BUCK DUANE!' echoed Kane.

One instant Poggin looked up and Duane looked down.

Like a striking jaguar Poggin moved. Almost as quickly Duane threw his arm. The guns boomed almost together.

Duane felt a blow just before he pulled trigger. His thoughts came fast, like the strange dots before his eyes. His rising gun had loosened in his hand. Poggin had drawn quicker! A tearing agony encompassed his breast. He pulled—pulled—at random. Thunder of booming shots all about him! Red flashes, jets of smoke, shrill yells! He was sinking. The end; yes, the end! With fading sight he saw Kane go down, then Boldt. But supreme torture, bitterer than death, Poggin stood, mane like a lion's, back to the wall, bloody-faced, grand, with his guns spouting red!

All faded, darkened. The thunder deadened. Duane fell, seemed floating. There it drifted—Ray Longstreth's sweet face, white, with dark, tragic eyes, fading from his sight … fading … fading …

25

Light shone before Duane's eyes—thick, strange light that came and went. For a long time dull and booming sounds rushed by, filling all. It was a dream in which there was nothing; a drifting under a burden; darkness, light, sound, movement; and vague, obscure sense of time—time that was very long. There was fire-creeping, consuming fire. A dark cloud of flame enveloped him, rolled him away.

He saw then, dimly, a room that was strange, strange people moving about over him, with faint voices, far away, things in a dream. He saw again, clearly, and consciousness returned, still unreal, still strange, full of those vague and faraway things. Then he was not dead. He lay stiff, like a stone, with a weight ponderous as a mountain upon him and all his bound body racked in slow, dull-beating agony.

A woman's face hovered over him, white and tragic-eyed, like one of his old haunting phantoms, yet sweet and eloquent. Then a man's face bent over him, looked deep into his eyes, and seemed to whisper from a distance: 'Duane—Duane! Ah, he knew me!'

After that there was another long interval of darkness. When the light came again, clearer this time, the same earnest-faced man bent over him. It was MacNelly. And with recognition the past flooded back.

Duane tried to speak. His lips were weak, and he could scarcely move them.

'Poggin!' he whispered. His first real conscious thought was for Poggin. Ruling passion—eternal instinct!

'Poggin is dead, Duane; shot to pieces,' replied MacNelly, solemnly. 'What a fight he made! He killed two of my men, wounded others. God! he was a tiger. He used up three guns before we downed him.'

'Who—got—away?'

'Fletcher, the man with the horses. We downed all the others. Duane, the job's done—it's done! Why, man, you're—'

'What of—of—*her?*'

'Miss Longstreth has been almost constantly at your bedside. She helped the doctor. She watched your wounds. And, Duane, the other night, when you sank low—so low—I think it was her spirit that held yours back. Oh, she's a wonderful girl. Duane, she never gave up, never lost her nerve for a moment. Well, we're going to take you home, and she'll go with us. Colonel Longstreth left for

Louisiana right after the fight. I advised it. There was great excitement. It was best for him to leave.'

'Have I—a—chance—to recover?'

'Chance? Why, man,' exclaimed the Captain, 'you'll get well! You'll pack a sight of lead all your life. But you can stand that. Duane, the whole Southwest knows your story. You need never again be ashamed of the name Buck Duane. The brand outlaw is washed out. Texas believes you've been a secret ranger all the time. You're a hero. And now think of home, your mother, of this noble girl—of your future.'

The rangers took Duane home to Wellston.

A railroad had been built since Duane had gone into exile. Wellston had grown. A noisy crowd surrounded the station, but it stilled as Duane was carried from the train.

A sea of faces pressed close. Some were faces he remembered—schoolmates, friends, old neighbors. There was an upflinging of many hands. Duane was being welcomed home to the town from which he had fled. A deadness within him broke. This welcome hurt him somehow, quickened him; and through his cold being, his weary mind, passed a change. His sight dimmed.

Then there was a white house, his old home. How strange, yet how real! His heart beat fast. Had so many, many years passed? Familiar yet strange it was, and all seemed magnified.

They carried him in, these ranger comrades, and laid him down, and lifted his head upon pillows. The house was still, though full of people. Duane's gaze sought the open door.

Some one entered—a tall girl in white, with dark, wet eyes and a light upon her face. She was leading an old lady, gray-haired, austere-faced, somber and sad. His mother! She was feeble, but she walked erect. She was pale, shaking, yet maintained her dignity.

The some one in white uttered a low cry and knelt by Duane's bed. His mother flung wide her arms with a strange gesture.

'This man! They've not brought back my boy. This man's his father! Where is my son? My son—oh, my son!'

When Duane grew stronger it was a pleasure to lie by the west window and watch Uncle Jim whittle his stick and listen to his talk. The old man was broken now. He told many interesting things about people Duane had known—people who had grown up and married, failed, succeeded, gone away, and died. But it was hard to keep Uncle Jim off the subject of guns, outlaws, fights. He could not seem to divine how mention of these things hurt Duane. Uncle Jim was childish now, and he had a great pride in his nephew. He wanted to hear of all of Duane's exile. And if there was one thing more than another that pleased him it was to talk about the bullets which Duane carried in his body.

'Five bullets, ain't it?' he asked, for the hundredth time. 'Five in that last scrap! By gum! And you had six before?'

'Yes, uncle,' replied Duane.

'Five and six. That makes eleven. By gum! A man's a man, to carry all that lead. But, Buck, you could carry more. There's that nigger Edwards, right here in Wellston. He's got a ton of bullets in him. Doesn't seem to mind them none. And there's Cole Miller. I've seen him. Been a bad man in his day. They say he packs twenty-three bullets. But he's bigger than you—got more flesh. … Funny, wasn't it, Buck, about the doctor only bein' able to cut one bullet out of you—that one in your breast-bone? It was a forty-one caliber, an unusual cartridge. I saw it, and I wanted it, but Miss Longstreth wouldn't part with it. Buck, there was a bullet left in one of Poggin's guns, and that bullet was the same kind as the one cut out of you. By gum! Boy, it'd have killed you if it'd stayed there.'

'It would indeed, uncle,' replied Duane, and the old, haunting, somber mood returned.

But Duane was not often at the mercy of childish old hero-worshiping Uncle Jim. Miss Longstreth was the only person who seemed to divine Duane's gloomy mood, and when she was with him she warded off all suggestion.

One afternoon, while she was there at the west window, a message came for him. They read it together.

> You have saved the ranger service to the Lone Star State
>
> MacNelly.

Ray knelt beside him at the window, and he believed she meant to speak then of the thing they had shunned. Her face was still white, but sweeter now, warm with rich life beneath the marble; and her dark eyes were still intent, still haunted by shadows, but no longer tragic.

'I'm glad for MacNelly's sake as well as the state's,' said Duane.

She made no reply to that and seemed to be thinking deeply. Duane shrank a little.

'The pain—Is it any worse to-day?' she asked, instantly.

'No; it's the same. It will always be the same. I'm full of lead, you know. But I don't mind a little pain.'

'Then—it's the old mood—the fear?' she whispered. 'Tell me.'

'Yes. It haunts me. I'll be well soon—able to go out. Then that—that hell will come back!'

'No, no!' she said, with emotion.

'Some drunken cowboy, some fool with a gun, will hunt me out in every town, wherever I go,' he went on, miserably. 'Buck Duane! To kill Buck Duane!'

'Hush! Don't speak so. Listen. You remember that day in Val Verde, when I came to you—pleaded with you not to meet Poggin? Oh, that was a terrible hour for me. But it showed me the truth. I saw the struggle between your passion to kill and your love for me. I could have saved you then had I known what I know now. Now I understand that—that thing which haunts you. But you'll never have to draw again. You'll never have to kill another man, thank God!'

Like a drowning man he would have grasped at straws, but he could not voice his passionate query.

She put tender arms round his neck. 'Because you'll have me with you always,' she replied. 'Because always I shall be between you and that—that terrible thing.'

It seemed with the spoken thought absolute assurance of her power came to her. Duane realized instantly that he was in the arms of a stronger woman than she who had pleaded with him that fatal day.

'We'll—we'll be married and leave Texas,' she said, softly, with the red blood rising rich and dark in her cheeks.

'Ray!'

'Yes we will, though you're laggard in asking me, sir.'

'But, dear—suppose,' he replied, huskily, 'suppose there might be—be children—a boy. A boy with his father's blood!'

'I pray God there will be. I do not fear what you fear. But even so—he'll be half my blood.'

Duane felt the storm rise and break in him. And his terror was that of joy quelling fear. The shining glory of love in this woman's eyes made him weak as a child. How could she love him—how could she bravely face a future with him? Yet she held him in her arms, twining her hands round his neck, and pressing close to him. Her faith and love and beauty—these she meant to throw between him and all that terrible past. They were her power, and she meant to use them all. He dared not think of accepting her sacrifice.

'But Ray—you dear, noble girl—I'm poor. I have nothing. And I'm a cripple.'

'Oh, you'll be well some day,' she replied. 'And listen. I have money. My mother left me well off. All she had was her father's—Do you understand? We'll take Uncle Jim and your mother. We'll go to Louisiana—to my old home. It's far from here. There's a plantation to work. There are horses and cattle—a great cypress forest to cut. Oh, you'll have much to do. You'll forget there. You'll learn to love my home. It's a beautiful old place. There are groves where the gray moss blows all day and the nightingales sing all night.'

'My darling!' cried Duane, brokenly. 'No, no, no!'

Yet he knew in his heart that he was yielding to her, that he could not resist her a moment longer. What was this madness of love?

'We'll be happy,' she whispered. 'Oh, I know. Come!—come!—come!'

Her eyes were closing, heavy-lidded, and she lifted sweet, tremulous, waiting lips.

With bursting heart Duane bent to them. Then he held her, close pressed to him, while with dim eyes he looked out over the line of low hills in the west, down where the sun was setting gold and red, down over the Nueces and the wild brakes of the Rio Grande which he was never to see again.

It was in this solemn and exalted moment that Duane accepted happiness and faced a new life, trusting this brave and tender woman to be stronger than the dark and fateful passion that had shadowed his past.

It would come back—that wind of flame, that madness to forget, that driving, relentless instinct for blood. It would come back with those pale, drifting, haunting faces and the accusing fading eyes, but all his life, always between them and him, rendering them powerless, would be the faith and love and beauty of this noble woman.